THE PENGUIN ANTHOLOGY OF AUSTRALIAN WOMEN'S WRITING

Edited by Dale Spender

PENGUIN BOOKS

Penguin Books Australia Ltd
487 Maroondah Highway, PO Box 257
Ringwood, Victoria, 3134, Australia
Penguin Books Ltd
Harmondsworth, Middlesex, England
Viking Penguin Inc.
40 West 23rd Street, New York, NY 10010, USA
Penguin Books Canada Limited
2801 John Street, Markham, Ontario, Canada, L3R 1B4
Penguin Books (N.Z.) Ltd
182-190 Wairau Road, Auckland 10, New Zealand

First published by Penguin Books Australia, 1988
© Introduction Dale Spender
Copyright © this collection Penguin Books Australia 1988
Copyright © of individual pieces remains with the writers

Typeset in Australia by Midland Typesetters
Made and printed in Australia by The Book Printer

The Penguin anthology of Australian women's writing.

ISBN 0 14 011237 5.

1. Australian literature – Women authors. I. Spender,
Dale. (Series: Penguin Australian women's library).

A820.8'09287

For my mother and father, Ivy and Harry Spender . . .
a promised good read

CONTENTS

ACKNOWLEDGEMENTS

The initial research of Debra Adelaide provided both the background and much of the impetus for this anthology and I am extremely grateful to her for her goodwill as well as her competence. And to Kirsten Lees, I am indebted for her perseverance, proficiency and personality; in the course of checking references, finding lost authors (and manipulating the mechanical means for obtaining material) she has become a valued friend as well as working companion. Susan Martin is another young woman whose research skills and generosity inspire warm appreciation and affection; she has so willingly and efficiently done so much of the tedious checking as well as providing new and exciting information; to Susan Martin I owe my introduction to the work of Mary Gaunt.

Without undue complaint, Frances McHarg has carefully transformed almost illegible manuscripts into clear copy — hopefully without permanent damage to her back or her eye sight. And if I had gold medals to hand out I would gladly give them to Carolyn Knowles of Kwik Kopy and Isis Moses of the Mitchell Library for their efforts way and above the call of duty in photocopying reams of manuscripts.

Florence James has been an invaluable (and delightful) source of information and Elizabeth Webby has been a constant source of support. I am extremely grateful to Elizabeth Morrison for providing me with a copy of Ada Cambridge's novel; to Lucy Sussex for stories by Mrs Fortune; to Barbara Ross for material on Dorothy Cottrell; and to Helen Thomson, Margaret Allen and Sneja Gunew for their cooperation and expertise.

The anthology could not have been compiled without the assistance of the Mitchell Library – and the librarian, Shirley Humphries, nor without the efforts of Trevor Mills and James

Rigney at the Rare Books Department, Fisher Library, University of Sydney. I am grateful to them – and to many of their colleagues – who have played a part in the production of this volume.

Janine Burke and Peter Pinson graciously enlightened me about many Australian women artists; and the patience, skill and support of Susan Hawthorne and Peg McColl at Penguin cannot pass without acknowledgement.

I find it difficult to express my gratitude to my 'extended family' who have continued to provide me with every form of support over the last few difficult years as I have been transformed into a non-smoker who resides primarily in Australia. To Renate Klein who is such a constant friend, I have debts I cannot repay; to Ted Brown who always believed in me and in a literary life after smoking, I am healthily grateful; to my parents who continue to subsidise my political, emotional and financial existence, I can only give my thanks.

And to my sister Lynne there is little that I can say which adequately conveys my appreciation; anyone who reads every word I write, who corrects my typos and my excesses, who continues to make positive suggestions – and still maintain a sense of humour while becoming a non-smoker herself – deserves greater repayment than could ever be available.

INTRODUCTION

1. Literary Tradition and the Women Writers of Australia

Only when all the women writers of Australia are brought together is it possible to identify common patterns and themes, and to speak of a distinctive female literary tradition. Yet surprisingly, this simple exercise of gathering the women together and of constructing their tradition, has not been undertaken before.

It cannot be because there are not enough of them, or because they have not produced sufficient work to form the substance of a literary heritage, that the women writers of Australia have been overlooked. Debra Adelaide lists the astonishing number of four hundred and fifty women in her compendium of Australian women authors (*Australian Women Writers: A Bibliographic Guide*, 1988) and their publications can be counted in thousands. If the women do not feature in the mainstream literary records, it cannot be because they have not written or because what they have written does not warrant inclusion. Rather, there have been so many women writers whose work has been so good, so many like the nineteenth-century novelists Rosa Praed, 'Tasma' and Ada Cambridge who achieved international fame and acclaim, that their omission is more a reflection of their refusal to conform to the masculine image of the mainstream than it is an indication of the force and fascination of their work.

Too frequently the characteristics of Australian literature are held to be exclusively those of the 'outback'; of the contest and the conquest of land and life that was carried out by brave men; yet even as this particular image of people and place was being pieced together, there were women writers who were giving expression to very different concerns. They were writing about different issues and in different ways from the men; they were even writing about the men in a way that men rarely wrote about themselves. What women writers saw and made of the continent and its inhabitants was a long way from the world of 'mateship' and marks a decidedly different body of literature with distinctively different traditions.

This is why it is so stimulating and so satisfying to find some of these women writers of the past and to trace the growth and development of their common consciousness. Not only is it exciting to realise just how many women there have been who have written, it is enriching to become familiar with their alternative view of the country, the customs and the culture. It is affirming to find women's views and values at the centre of the literary stage shaping the issues and the form of expression.

The literary traditions of white women in Australia can be traced to an identifiable source; letter writing was the formative activity. Apart from the fact that it was a type of writing permitted – even encouraged – among women (who were invariably denied access to more professional literary pursuits) letter writing was in keeping with women's responsibility for maintaining family ties. So the first white women who settled in Australia soon turned to letter writing, even if they had not always cultivated the habit before. From convict woman Margaret Catchpole (1762-1819) to Elizabeth Macarthur, (1769-1850), officer's wife, they wrote and they wrote, and they wrote – to friends and family back home, whenever the opportunity was available. The limits placed on their letter writing were those of literacy, paper, ships and time.

This need to write, however, was not prompted solely by the desire to discover what was going on 'back home': it was also to recount what was happening in the new world. It was a strange country the women had journeyed to; it often did strange things to them. So many women were changed by their Australian experience that they used their letters to describe and define their new identities, to make sense of their new selves and their new lives, which is why self-analysis and self-development feature so prominently in the literary traditions of Australian women.

But this is not the end of the influence that the penchant for letter writing exerted. In the first few decades of settlement in Australia the post was – to say the least – erratic. There was no 'system' for conveying precious letters from one side of the world to the other. Rather, 'personal arrangements' generally had to be made: the services of obliging sea captains and passengers of good will had to be enlisted if letters were to make their way from the colony of New South Wales to the counties and provinces of Great Britain. And add to this the possibility that the person carrying the post could fall ill or die, that the few ships which did make the dangerous voyage could be diverted from their course or sink, and it is no wonder that the writers often revealed themselves to be preoccupied with plans for ensuring that the post got through.

No wonder, either, that the letter-writers did not necessarily seek to hear from family and friends before replying: in contrast to contemporary times when letters may be regularly received – and responded to – the letter writers in the early years of settlement could not assume such an *exchange* of epistles.

So they wrote 'monologues': many of their letters were written over long periods, a 'chapter' at a time in serial form. Day by day, week by week, even month by month, women added to their narratives, reported on themselves and their lives, although they did not know how family and friends fared far away, even whether loved ones were still alive. But they went on keeping the records as they waited for a ship to bring the news, and to take away their stories to the old world.

In many respects this was a migrant literature; letters sent from those who willingly or unwillingly had left their home and whose security was linked with people, places, pressures, in another land. The voice of 'the exile' continues to resonate through Australian women's writing.

The women who wrote these important letters were often acutely conscious of their audiences, and the manner in which their letters would be treated. They knew it was likely that the long letter from Australia would be read aloud to the assembled family, that it would provide drama, entertainment, fascination, before being passed on to scattered relatives and preserved as a record of exciting events in exotic places. The letter writers knew that they could be the heroines in these thrilling tales. So the letters of Rachel Henning (1826-1914) (which have recently been reprinted and are now widely available) were written with a strong sense of story-telling, with an awareness of the interest they would arouse in the listener, and an appreciation of the letter writer's role, centre-stage.

On reading the letters of Rachel Henning – and many other women as well (some of whom are included here) – the links between the letter and the novel become readily apparent. While Fanny Burney (1752-1840), that outstanding epistolary novelist of the eighteenth century, may have drawn more on 'fantasy' and Rachel Henning more on 'fact' for the substance of their accounts, few other distinctions can be made about the form of their work. The published letters of Rachel Henning tell such an exciting, and such a romantic tale.

Another reason these letters contained such wonderful stories was that the writers did not want to cause their relations undue concern. Although some of the events the women recounted were truly terrible, they were often transformed by the pen into amusing and entertaining yarns. After all, the letter-writer had obviously survived the danger, the drama, the disaster, the disappointment, and lived to tell the tale. So best to make light of the flood, the drought, the fire, the accident, the snake bite, the childbirth. This typical facility for transforming some of the trials and the tragedies of life into funny stories, has some of its foundations in women's desire to write reassuring and soothing letters to those 'back home'.

Such a consideration, however, is not to be found in much of the journal writing undertaken by women in Australia. Like the letter, the diary or the journal is part of the traditional literature of women and has for centuries served numerous personal needs, although not always the same ones as those that have found expression in letters. For whereas Elizabeth Macarthur and Rachel Henning wrote to their families to let them know all was well, Georgiana McCrae (1804-1890), for example, wrote in her journal to dispel some of her darkest doubts. White women in the early days of settlement and from all walks of life, who were cut off from familiar sources of replenishment, who were deprived of so many of their cultural forms and the comforts of home, often took up their pens as a form of therapy, to make sense of self and the world. Through writing they were able to break their silence, to create an audience, to keep their sanity.

Even in the traditional writing of women it is possible to see the two strands coming together in the cultural heritage. There are the good yarns and outgoing reassurances, as well as the bitter reflections, the personal fears, failures and recriminations. Both frames of reference have helped to shape the women's world of letters. And just as specific conditions and specific activities have contributed to the development of particular literary styles, so too has the specific experience of women led to the evolution of some identifiable common themes.

One of the most striking patterns to emerge when the women writers are placed together is the extent to which white women have expressed concern at the plight of the Aborigines. It is no exaggeration to state that most white women writers have made reference to black experiences and not always as something that is alien.

Again and again women's literature exposes the cruel exploitation of black women by white men; sometimes, when women writers raise the issue of the exploitation of white women by white men, connections are made about the common experience of women. There are numerous stories within women's literary heritage which depict black women subjected to the same master, and experiencing an inextricably linked fate.

Stories too about childbirth; about black and white women in remote regions, each offering the other assistance and support. And while there are references to disasters and difficulties, while there may be accounts of anger, antagonism, antipathy, there is nothing in the literature of white women which symbolises black women as the 'enemy'. White women did not live in fear of black women, they did not see them as a physical threat, a force to be subdued. Not only does this make their literature about the dispossessed Aborigines crucially different from that of their male counterparts, but women's writing provides another, often subversive perspective, on the attitudes and values of the country and its development.

By contemporary standards some of the expressions of empathy and understanding of nineteenth and early twentieth century women writers are racist. While not wanting to exonerate them it is as well to remember that they were – as we are – products of the time. Sentiments which may now give offence could well have branded the writer as a radical in her own day, and brought censure. But in the compilation of this anthology, the racism of some of the women of the past certainly poses a problem which it would be irresponsible to ignore.

On the one hand, one of the purposes of this volume is to reclaim some of the lost women writers of the past and to present them to a contemporary audience in a positive light; in this context it would be counterproductive – and could well amount to a distortion – to select material which accentuates their racist attitudes and which at the expense of their other attributes, could quickly become the focus for discussion. On the other hand, it would be racist to ignore their racism.

So much of the literature reprinted here reflects the views and values of women in Australia; it is predominantly by white women about black women, and some of it is racist. But an attempt has been made to contextualise the contributions and to show the strengths as well as the limitations of white women's challenge to racism.

It is co-existence rather than conflict which often characterises the literature of women and it extends to many aspects of their environment. Search as one might through the reams that Australian women have written over the centuries, there is little to be found which would support a theme of conquest, little which shows women trying to subdue a people, or a place: there is much, however, which shows women being subdued.

Far from finding friendship and fulfilment in the bush, the drover's wife was more likely to go mad[1], or to become a victim of the harrowing conditions of outback life. Many women persevered in such unremittingly harsh circumstances yet female deeds of heroism generally remain unsung. But the horrendously hard work, the pressure of child bearing and child rearing, of illness, isolation and pain, took their toll. When women like Rosa Praed, Mary Gaunt, Barbara Baynton and Katharine Susannah Prichard wrote about female experience of the bush, they did not romanticise.

For women there were few compensations for the brutal nature of their existence. Not for them the contentment of the campfire, the opportunity to break bread, tell tales, make mates.

This is not to suggest that women were unaware of the freedoms that their rural and pioneering life could afford. Miles Franklin was not alone in extolling the virtues of a horse – and mobility – for Australian womanhood; directly and indirectly, there were women authors who portrayed the absence of 'polite' conventions and painful clothing in a positive light. In comparison to some of their English counterparts who were urged to confine

[1] See Helen Thomson, 1986 and her forthcoming book, *The Mad Woman in the Bush*

themselves to narrow and meaningless lives, many Australian women were able to find a sense of purpose and to gain a sense of worth. When their labour was needed, they were more likely to be valued, although it must be said that there was sometimes a fine line between being necessary and being exploited.

But if work provided a purpose, it also posed something of a dilemma, particuarly for those who aspired to being seen as 'young ladies'. While the number of English roses who were confined to couches could well have been exaggerated, the fact remains that the coveted image of womanhood was frequently one of a fragile soul – often consumptive – who languished away her idle days. Such a model did not fit easily with the realities of a young woman's existence in Australia.

This is one explanation for the Australian heroine who was always trying to reconcile the values of the old country with that of the new; and why she juggled the desirability of enforced leisure with that of necessary (albeit meaningful) work.

Perhaps it was her sense of self which also inspired her spirited challenge to the subordinated status of her sex, for the Australian heroine has a long tradition of seeking independence, self realisation – and creative fulfilment. For more than twenty years before Miles Franklin's Sybylla made her spectacular entry in *My Brilliant Career* (1901) women writers of Australia had been presenting a parade of heroines who would not be satisfied with being the mere appendages of men. Germaine Greer had a heritage of resistance, rebellion and reason on which to draw when she wrote her outstanding analysis of women's position in Western society (*The Female Eunuch*, 1970).

High on the list for criticism of these erstwhile women writers was the institution of marriage which was seen to constrain the existence of women, and there were many writers like Catherine Helen Spence, for example, who suggested that in the interest of women's self realisation, the institution of marriage should be modified, even abandoned. Her novel which put forward alternatives – *Handfasted* – was completed in 1879, but was considered too radical for publication and not until 1984 did it appear in print (see Helen Thomson, 1984).

And she was by no means the only woman writer to examine the pros and cons of marriage, to contrast what a woman gained with what she lost when she became a wife. Like Miles Franklin, there were many women writers who reached the conclusion that the single woman led the better life. When today questions continue to be asked about women's relationship to marriage, and to men, these provocative, often profound and highly popular writers of the past retain their relevance; it is their range of experience and understanding which provides such a rich and rewarding heritage for the modern reader.

However, if the questions about the merits of matrimony, about women's bodies and women's rights, continue to arise, less common now are the concerns about the sins of the fathers being visited upon the sons. It is understandable of course that at a time when Charles Darwin introduced his controversial theories about evolution, the issue would find expression in literary form; there are numerous works of nineteenth century fiction which explore the relative influence of environment versus heredity. But when to this international scientific debate was added the Australian apprehension about the origin of individuals – of whether once a criminal always a criminal, perhaps even producing criminal offspring – the focus on the importance of heredity in national literature is to be expected.

Rosa Praed, for example, was a writer who raised fascinating questions about the way the weakness of one generation might taint the life of the next (see *An Australian Heroine*, 1880); she was genuine in her quest to determine whether a criminal could be rehabilitated, whether a convict could put his past behind him and become a trusted community member. *Policy and Passion* (1881 and 1988), and *Outlaw and Lawmaker* (1893 and 1988) are just two of her novels which explore some of these contradictions which were thrown up in colonial society.

It was partly because the antecedents of many prominent Australian figures could not bear close scrutiny that the practice arose of 'taking people on appearances'; if individuals were wealthy, it was not always wise to enquire too closely into the way their fortunes were acquired. Better to congratulate – and elevate the achievements of 'the self-made-man' than to be concerned with birth or breeding – or so some insisted.

But to women who have always been required to make crucial judgements about the worth and value of a man, the new practical morality of Australia presented a number of difficulties.

How could they take the measure of a man when the yardstick of the old world could no longer be used? This vital question demanded an answer, since the circumstances of women's lives could depend on the choice that was allowed them. Where they would live, how much money they would possess, what freedoms they would enjoy, how many children they would have – even if they were to be happy or ill-used – could all be determined by the character of one man. No wonder this issue was so important; no wonder it has been the theme of so many women's books.

Was it better to marry a rough, rich man, or a poor but noble lord? Was it better to have money in the bank or genteel manners and an impoverished but cultured life? Virtually all the women writers raised these issues as they tried to reconcile the manners of the old world with that of the new, and as they tried to assess the price that women paid for making mistakes. In one novel, *Sisters* (1904 and 1989), Ada Cambridge used the various matrimonial experiences of four sisters to suggest that all marriages (and most men) meant unhappiness for women.

No minor matters, these, in women's lives; they are issues of paramount importance. In the tradition that encompasses Jane Austen, Elizabeth Gaskell and Charlotte Bronte, women writers had asked – what happens to the woman who marries the wrong man? And the Australian novelists continued in this vein. Again and again 'Tasma's' heroines make their matrimonial mistakes; again and again, Ada Cambridge's wives lead lives of distress and misery; and when in Rosa Praed's best-selling novel, *The Bond of Wedlock* (1887 and 1987), Ariana Lomax's husband beats her, the author asks whether the wife has the right to leave.

Some of the problems and priorities of women's existence may remain constant over time, but their expression and the solutions have varied according to period and place. And as Australian women writers tried to reconcile some of the practices of the home country with the pressures of colonial reality, they frequently forged their own refreshing and revitalised forms. So, for example, Ada Cambridge, who was born in England and moved to Australia in 1870, attempted to retain a refining influence in the face of frightening freedom; so Rosa Praed, who was born in outback Queensland, and who moved to England in 1875, attempted to introduce a note of frankness and freshness to the somewhat stultifying London literary scene. Both were influenced by their expansive new world experience at home and abroad; they were but two of the novelists who helped to establish the distinctive and distinguished traditions of Australian women writers.

Finding and formulating this admirable tradition is such a full and fascinating task that it is tempting to go on tracing the common concerns, the creative forces, and the differences too, in interpretation and execution. There have been so many women who have written so many letters, diaries, autobiographies, as well as the genres of journalism, drama and fiction, that the possibilities for locating the links and discerning patterns are virtually never-ending. This is why it can be salutary to find that despite the diversity in women's literary contributions, there is often an identifiable common core. It cannot be simply coincidence that so many of these writers have expressed such a sustained concern for the status of their sex, and such a distrust for the dominance of men. Sometimes it is the subtext, sometimes it is the subject, but invariably women writers have found the power of men problematic.

In Australia, where women have enjoyed a peculiar degree of freedom, they have also been obliged on occasion to take particular precautions. A recurring plot in women's literature is one in which women masquerade as men. Not only does such disguise afford them a certain degree of protection, it also helps to emphasise the distance between the privileges the characters can enjoy when they are permitted to pass as men, and the privations they can be required to endure when they are perceived as women.

One of the reasons that women have – in such numbers – taken up their pen is because it has allowed them to create their own world. It has allowed them to set the conditions of existence – free from the direct interference of men. One of the reasons that women have – in such numbers – taken to reading women's writing is because it allows them a 'safe place' from which they can explore a wide range of experiences of the world, from which they can identify with a range of characters and a variety of existences. This is why women's writing has occupied, and still can occupy, such a significant and central place in women's lives. It is also why women's writing can share much the same disparaged status as women in a world dominated by men.

It is but a brief and broad outline of some of the salient features of women's literary traditions in Australia which has been presented here, and there is much more that could be stated about the nature of women's writing, and its contribution to the cultural heritage. For its influence is not on the wane; far from experiencing a decline, women writers past and present are now enjoying an increasing popularity and prestige.

The reason could lie in the shifts in power in the realms of print, since the information revolution has reduced the importance of the printed word (see Lynne Spender, 1983); men may have moved out to follow the new technologies and thereby allowed greater opportunities for women in print. But regardless of the cause, the reality is that women writers have achieved an impressive record of succcess. There is growing interest in reclaiming some of the lost contributions of the past, and in documenting the nature and influence of the great female tradition.

Some literary studies have a lot to offer in this increasingly technological and often alienating age; it is through the accumulated wisdom of the women writers represented here that the values of the culture can be reflected, and revised, and reaffirmed. While the women writers included in this anthology constitute a good read, collectively they also assume a significance which is greater than the sum of their individual parts; they provide insights, a wealth of understanding, a reservoir of meanings and a basis for discussion. Through *their* eyes we can see a different world, with *their* assistance we can seek to realise the potential of human achievement. In any appraisal of the Australian continent, its people, its place, an appreciation of the writing of its women is essential.

2. Selection Criteria

One of the most upsetting features of putting together an anthology is the number of good writers who must be omitted. Because of the way a collection can become the canon – a declaration of all that has approval rather than an indication of the nature and extent of the vast resource available – the responsibility for determining what should be in and what left out is a disquieting one. If there were no practical problems to consider, no constraints imposed by page budgets, permission fees and sales prices, no doubt an ideal anthology of Australian women writers could make its appearance. But for this anthology, economic realities have prevailed; while the cloth has been cut accordingly, the task has been undertaken with the greatest possible care. Yet with only forty women writers reprinted here, less than 10% of those listed by Debra Adelaide, it is clear that many good women writers must of necessity have been omitted.

Because *The Penguin Book of Australian Women Poets* already exists (see Susan Hampton and Kate Llewellyn, 1986), one of the first major selection decisions was to confine this anthology to prose. However, even within this narrowed band, further unfortunate eliminations had to be made.

Sometimes the decision was made on the basis that the writer was well known and readily available, and so would not be unduly disadvantaged by exclusion: Jeannie Gunn (1870-1961) the author of *We of the Never-Never* (1908) is one example of this fate. Sometimes the decision was made on the grounds that the writer had produced only a slim body of work and should make way for those whose contributions were more substantial; Eve Langley (1908-1974) who wrote *The Pea Pickers* (1942) and *White Topee* (1954) comes into this category. But when one of the fundamental reasons for compiling this anthology has been to reclaim and to present some of the women writers who have slipped into oblivion, and another has been to bring all the women together in order to demonstrate the unity and the diversity of their work, it has often been difficult to leave recently 'discovered' authors in their submerged and silent state, and to risk precluding them from taking a rightful place in the literary heritage.

Another area where awkward decisions needed to be made was in relation to those who qualifed as Australian writers, particularly in the early years. Partly because giving individuals a single nationality is often impossible, where not absurd, no hard and fast rules have applied here. On the one hand, a contribution from the first Victorian novelist, Elizabeth Murray (1820-1877) – who visited Australia from 1852-1859 and wrote the novel *Ella Norman, or a Woman's Perils* (1864, 1985) – has been omitted, while that of Ellen Clacy (n.d.) – who made a brief visit to Australia in 1852-53 and who wrote *A Lady's Visit to the Gold Diggings of Australia* – has been included. The justification for this choice lies more in terms of the overall nature of this volume than in any of the national or literary qualifications of either of the writers; many of the features of Elizabeth Murray's fiction are represented by some of the other women writers whereas Ellen Clacy's account of the goldfields, from the point of view of a woman, and as an example of the genre of travel literature, has few counterparts. So, more for what they wrote than for how they wrote or who they were, one has been given a place and the other has not. In general, however, the issue of Australian content has been as influential as the author's place of residence, especially in the nineteenth century.

But what must be said is that many women writers who deserve to be in a comprehensive collection of Australian literature have been left out. So at the risk of presenting an inventory of the great experiences the reader will miss as a result of these many omissions, I would like to make reference to some of the writers who, because of the pressure of space, have become anthology victims. I do this because I know that it is not usually realised just how wide ranging, extensive and popular have been the contributions of the literary women of Australia. For some of these authors whose achievements will once more be 'eclipsed', it seems that an acknowledgement of their existence and their exclusion is the least courtesy they can be accorded. If their names are known then it is possible that their absence from this anthology, instead of being a problem, might lead to even further interest and study.

It is with regret that I put aside an extract from *The Guardian* (1838), the first novel published on the mainland of Australia and written by Anna Maria Bunn (sometimes referred to as Anna Maria Murray, 1808-1889). And after much deliberation I decided that it would do Caroline Leakey ('Oline Keese', 1827-1881) a disservice to reprint only an extract from her remarkable novel, *The Broad Arrow* (1859), the first novel of Australian convict life[2] – and by and about a women[3]. And the novel of Louisa Atkinson – *Tom Hellicar's Children* – was the last contribution to be cast aside. The first native-born novelist, a botanist and writer who made full fictional use of the Australian setting, and who had scientific reports as well as stories published in the Sydney press during the 1860s, Louisa Atkinson (1834-1872) stands at the start of the distinctive Australian literary tradition. But as there was not enough space to include a complete work,

---

[2] This novel appeared more than a decade before *His Natural Life*, by Marcus Clarke, first published in book form in 1874 and generally taken as the first convict novel.

[3] Extracts from *The Guardian* and *The Broad Arrow* are contained in Lynne Spender, 1988, *Her Selection*.

and as some of her writings are, or will soon, be available[4], her
novel was reluctantly removed.

Among those whom I would have liked to have included is
Georgiana Molloy (1805-1843)[5] a lively letter-writer from
Western Australia; her letters provide a poignant picture of the
young and spirited (and previously protected) woman who, cut
off from family and friends, endures some of the most punishing
pioneering adventures and gives birth and witnesses death under
the most awful of conditions. They show her as a young woman
who is burdened with work but who nonetheless has a passionate
interest in the environment and who despatches letters (and species
samples) to the Royal Society as well as to various members of her
family. In this vein of traditional literature, I also wanted to
include samples from the thirty eight volumes of the diaries of
Annie Baxter (1816-1905)[6], from the journals of Annabella
Boswell (1826-1916)[7] and from the letters of Lady Barker (sometimes known as Lady Broome (1831-1911)) which were published
under the title *Station Life in New Zealand* (1870). But as these
are among some of the works which are, or will be, available
elsewhere, they have been put aside in favour of other contributions.

To have included some of the temperance writing of 'Maud
Franc' (Matilda Jane Evans, 1827-1866), South Australia's second
woman novelist who published nearly twenty volumes of widely
distributed 'moral' fiction, would have been to show some of the
similarities between the anti-drink rhetoric of the nineteenth century and the anti-drug rhetoric of today, and to glean some
valuable lessons in the process. And to have been able to reprint
some of the journalism of Alice Henry (1857-1943), Mary Fullerton
(1868-1946), Marie Pitt (1869-1948) and Charmian Clift (1923-
1969) would have been to have evidence of women's powers of
popular persuasion.

[4] An extract from *Tom Hellicar's Children* has been reprinted in Lynne Spender,
1988, *Her Selection*; Louisa Atkinson's first novel – which she illustrated – will
be reprinted in the Penguin Australian Women's Library; it is entitled *Gertrude
the Emigrant* (1857).
[5] A selection of Georgiana Molloy's letters has been included in Lynne Spender,
1988, *Her Selection*.
[6,7] See Lynne Spender, 1988, *Her Selection*, for examples of their writing.

Catherine Martin (1847-1937)[8], Daisy Bates (1863-1931), Ernestine Hill (1900-1972) and Mary Durack (1913 –) are among the women who have written passionately and compellingly about Aboriginal experience and life in the outback. They have contributed significantly to women's literary traditions and yet, regrettably, they are not represented here. And the number of best-selling women novelists who have been omitted could be used to compile a marvellous anthology of popular fiction: Kathleen Caffyn ('Iota' 1853-1926), the author of seventeen successful novels; Beatrice Grimshaw (1870-1953) the author of forty romances and adventures set in the South Seas; 'Elinor Mordaunt' (1872-1942), who wrote forty works of fiction, many with an Australian setting; Marie Bjelke-Petersen (1874-1969) awarded the King's Jubilee Medal for literature in 1935 for her numerous novels; Helen Bridges (1881-1971) who wrote twenty novels, *The Squatter's Daughter* (1922) among them; 'Sumner Locke' (Helena Sumner Locke 1881-1917) playwright and novelist who died the day after the birth of her son and who gained her literary reputation for the 'Mum Dawson' series of sketches of selection life; Jean Campbell (1906 –) a prolific writer of fiction of which *Brass and Cymbals* (1933) encompasses the multi-cultural experience; Barbara Jefferis (1917 –) dramatist, documentary writer and novelist, whose work enjoys a considerable reputation outside Australia; Ruth Park (1923 –) author of widely acclaimed works of fiction for adults and children; Thea Astley (1925 –) whose work has consistently received praise, and Jessica Anderson (n.d.) who is one of the most outstanding of contemporary writers.

So too can we look forward to anthologies of women's plays which would include contributions by Betty Roland (1905 –), Gwen Meredith (1907 –), Marien Dreyer (1911-1980), Mona Brand (1915 –) and Dorothy Hewett (1923 –).

There will be some who could well suggest that the absence of Helen Simpson (1897-1940) constitutes a grave omission and if quality were the sole criteria for selection there would be grounds for their criticism. For Helen Simpson, novelist, playwright, poet and historian, wrote sixteen remarkable novels (some of them

---

[8] One of her novels, *The Incredible Journey* (1923), an account of the trek of two black women across the desert in search of a stolen son, is a remarkable study and along with her novel, *An Australian Girl* (1890), is now available from Pandora Press.

in partnership with the well known English woman writer 'Clemence Dane') including the outstanding *Boomerang* (1932) and *Under Capricorn* (1937). But again as her work is and will be available, other writers have been given precedence.

To have omitted Ethel Anderson (1883-1958) – whom some would suggest is one of the most talented short story writers Australia has produced – and to compile an anthology in which Jean Devanny (1894-1962) is not represented, is to put aside two of the outstanding contributors to the Australian heritage. But as both women are now enjoying some attention and as much of their work is in print, readers are referred to these other sources to assess the nature of the accomplishments of these two women.

Because preference has been given to some of the unknown women of the past rather than the known women writers of the present, an anthology of contemporary women writers is required to provide a balanced representation of women's achievements over the centuries. Such a volume is planned; with it will come the opportunity to make connections between some of the following writers in the context of women's literature: Elizabeth Jolley, Ruth Park, Thea Astley, Patsy Adam-Smith, Elizabeth Harrower, Glen Tomasetti, Sara Dowse, Barbara Hanrahan, Glenda Adams, Helen Garner, Blanche D'Alpuget, Jean Bedford, Kate Grenville and Jessica Anderson.

Even this list of missing persons is by no means exhaustive. But despite the many omissions, the anthology remains representative of the range of contributions that comprise women's literary heritage. That so many riches are in, when so much has been left out, is indicative of the richness of the tradition.

3. Comparisons and Connections

In order to show the ways in which the writing of Australian women has grown and developed, the contributions have been presented in chronological sequence based on the date of the author's birth. While a number of inconsistencies can occur as a result of such an arrangement, it nonetheless allows for the overall pattern of evolution to emerge and for the tradition to be constructed. On the grounds that most of the major writers since 1940 are likely to be in print and able to enjoy a degree of recognition, the cut-off birth date for contributors has been set (somewhat arbitrarily) at 1939. Unfortunately this means that recent impressive and innovative works which could make a significant contribution to trends of the future (as in the case of Sally Morgan's *My Place* (1987), a powerful autobiographical statement of black experience) must of necessity be omitted.

A further consideration which has been kept in mind is that the material should reflect the range of genres and styles which are embodied in the Australian heritage. For not only is it desirable to be able to see the diversity of the entire tradition, it is also useful to be able to make 'within-tradition' comparisons. When women have used different genres for different purposes (letters and diaries being one such example) then questions arise about the aims and the audiences, the similarities and differences, of the various literary forms. How have women writers used the short story, the play, the autobiography; do all these genres share a common framework, and has each developed along comparable lines?

So that the reader can make comparisons and draw conclusions, the anthology contains a cross-section of genres, from unpublished letters to prize-winning plays. The convict Margaret Catchpole is the first LETTER WRITER to be included and there are examples of the epistolary genre right through to the contributions of the esteemed Dame Mary Gilmore. Taken together, these letters from women of different periods and very different walks of life provide valuable historical and social documentation, along with an indication of the enduring patterns and the individual interpretations to be reflected in this form.

The content of the early nineteenth-century Melbourne DIARY of Georgiana McCrae stands in sharp contrast to some of the letters, but it too is markedly different from that of many other journal entries. The diary of the youthful Ethel Turner not only illustrates the role that a journal can play in ordering the experiences (and recording the secrets) of the adolescent; it also challenges some of the prevailing ideas about permissiveness and progress with its revelations about the opportunities for creative fulfilment and personal freedom that were available to a young woman in Sydney towards the end of the nineteenth century. Extracts from the 'cosmopolitan' twentieth century journal of Nettie Palmer, the critic who did so much to legitimate Australian women's writing and to forge a network of female literary friendships, are but a further example of the viability and flexibility this traditional genre affords.

Then too there are the TRAVEL accounts which no respectable anthology of women's literature could be without. During the nineteenth century English-speaking women defied convention and travelled to all parts of the world, and produced a lively, informative and influential literature which still holds considerable fascination. All these women 'acted', explored, described and explained the new worlds which they visited, their very existence and experience served as a challenge to the protected – and confined – image of idealised womanhood. When Louisa Meredith, Australia's first professional woman writer, wrote her highly popular travel accounts of New South Wales, Victoria and Tasmania, she certainly provided her predominantly English audience with some alarming and amazing tales. She also provided a subversive sub-text in her example of a woman's strength, skill, sense of humour, and power of survival.

And after her adventures and romance in the Antipodes[9], Ellen Clacy returned to England where she published her glowing account of life on the Australian goldfields, and with her particular reference to the pleasures and the problems encountered by women, gave the distinct impression that 'fact' could be even more exciting than 'fiction'. Because the mid-nineteenth century goldfields that Ellen Clacy describes are almost as far removed from contemporary audiences as they were from English readers of the time, it is possible to have some appreciation now of the attractions of this 'on-the-spot' travel reporting.

In the pre-radio and television age, JOURNALISM too was a much more influential genre: it was the medium for conveying information, for defining public issues and shaping opinion. It was also a medium that women used for communicating with each other – sometimes with predictable consequences. When Louisa Lawson began publishing Australia's first feminist periodical, the *Dawn* (1888) it wasn't just her choice of (female) workers which proved to be controversial; her 'copy' also caused adverse comment. It was directed to women and designed to make them think, and to demand a better deal. And although the connections between the writing of Louisa Lawson and Mary Grant

[9] Ellen Clacy fell in love on the goldfields; her return voyage to England became her honeymoon.

Bruce may not at first be apparent, an appraisal of the journalism of Mary Grant Bruce makes it quite clear that she continued in the challenging tradition that the pioneering Louisa Lawson had begun; it is a tradition which continues to this day and is reflected in some of the writing of Germaine Greer, for example.

There must be a conviction about the significance of one's life before an individual can produce an AUTOBIOGRAPHY – which could be one reason that women have a longer tradition of writing about the lives of others than they do of writing about themselves.[10]. While no biographies as such are included here, Faith Bandler's *Wacvie* (1977), a chronicle of her father's life, borders on this category as do many of the fictional treatments of various characters. Autobiography, however, is well represented in an abridged version of Rosa Praed's recollections of her childhood (*My Australian Girlhood*, 1902). Confounding more of the dividing lines between fact and fiction, between autobiography and narrative, is Kylie Tennant's documentation of her experience on an Aboriginal mission (*Speak You So Gently*, 1959). In combination, all these sources allow for consideration and speculation on the needs and nature of women's autobiography.

Even while the seventeenth century playwright Aphra Behn (1640-1689) dominated the Restoration stage[11] it was still widely asserted – often by her male peers – that drama was a genre women simply could not 'do'; and despite the contrary evidence of centuries, the myth sometimes still remains that women cannot write plays. The three outstanding PLAYS included in this collection (two of which have not been published before) will help to put such erroneous and prejudiced beliefs to rest.

Katharine Susannah Prichard may be primarily appreciated for her fine works of fiction yet her lesser known but stark and powerful play, *Brumby Innes* (1940) deserves more attention. And the previously unpublished and prize-winning 'Call Up Your Ghosts' written by Miles Franklin and Dymphna Cusack to satirise the disgraceful reception given to Australian literature simply cried out for inclusion in this collection which assumes the unfair treatment accorded to the writing of Australian women. But even more

---

[10] See Dale Spender, 1987, *Mothers of the Novel.*
[11] See Dale Spender, 1982, *Women of Ideas – and What Men Have Done to Them.*

appropriate, perhaps, for inclusion is the prize-winning and previously unpublished play, 'The Torrents', written by Oriel Gray and which won equal first place with *The Summer of the Seventeenth Doll* in the Playwrights' Advisory Competition of 1955. With its independent heroine, 'The Torrents' stands between the protest of Miles Franklin and the rebellion of Germaine Greer.

Space would not permit the publication in full of Sarah Campion's bold novel, *Mo Burdekin* (1941) which along with Faith Bandler's *Wacvie*, is represented only in extract. But when these two episodes are placed alongside the substantial collection of SHORT STORIES that have been given a place, it becomes possible to distinguish some of the patterns and priorities which have developed in Australian women's fiction. From Catherine Helen Spence (South Australia's first woman novelist) to Olga Masters, women have created a splendid short story heritage which in theme and form reflects some of the realities of women's lives. Among the more famous contributors included here are Barbara Baynton, Henry Handel Richardson, Eleanor Dark and Christina Stead; in addition an introduction to the work of 'Tasma', 'Waif Wander', Mary Gaunt, G.B. Lancaster, Mollie Skinner, Dorothy Cottrell and Antigone Kefala is provided.

Perhaps it is the subject matter itself which has pushed so many women writers to the perpiphery of Australian literary appreciation. Certainly the centrality of black experience cannot be ignored in any collection of women's writing; it is no coincidence that it was a woman, Catherine Langloh Parker, who systematically recorded and edited the first collection of Aboriginal folklore, nor that the significance of this undertaking was appreciated and promoted by Henrietta Drake-Brockman. Some of the LEGENDS, along with an acknowledgement of their importance, are included here, as part of the fabric of women's engagement with the meaning of black experience. From Elizabeth Macarthur to Faith Bandler, from Rosa Praed to Nene Gare, from Mary Gaunt to Katharine Susannah Prichard and Kylie Tennant, women have focussed on the price of inhumanity and the shared experience of sisterhood in their attempt to reflect and resonate the culture's values, and vices. That this particular tradition of censure, subversion and solidarity stands outside the dominant conventions is no doubt a contributing factor in the disqualification of women from the canon.

So too does the concern of women writers with the status of

their sex symbolise a different – and 'deviant' – frame of reference from the mainstream. While women writers remain isolated from one another their calls for rebellion, reform and revolution can readily be rationalised and dismissed. But when they are placed together and it can be seen that it is the norm and not the exception for women authors to raise their voices against female subordination, it becomes increasingly difficult to label feminism as unusual, unreasonable, untenable.

Most of the writers included here have been conscious of their position as women and of the potential of their art; whether this information is to be found in the letters of Mary Gilmore, the diaries of Ethel Turner, the words of encouragement of Nettie Palmer, or the disclosures of Mary Grant Bruce on how and why they became writers, all recognised the crucial role that literature could play in shaping a society. We can show our appreciation for the legacy they left us by acknowledging the value of their words and their vision.

MARGARET CATCHPOLE, 1762-1819

Margaret Catchpole's letters comprise one of the
earliest collections of correspondence of a convict
woman. Born in Suffolk, England, she was first sentenced to death for stealing a horse for her lover (a
notorious local smuggler), and then for escaping from
Ipswich Gaol. Her sentence was commuted to transportation and she arrived in the colony in 1801. A
woman of great spirit, she endured many physical
and emotional hardships, but she seems to have
made a satisfying and self-reliant life for herself;
when it became possible for her to return to England,
she elected to remain in her 'new home'.

Her letters are to be found in the Mitchell Library
(Sydney, New South Wales), they have been
reprinted in a variety of sources, (see *Dear Fanny*,
edited by Helen Heney, 1985) and have been used as
the basis for a number of studies, including the fanciful *The History of Margaret Catchpole*, (1845) by
Richard Cobbold, *The True Story of Margaret
Catchpole* (1924) by G.B. Barton and the novel, *Margaret Catchpole* (1949) by G.G. Carter. In the
interest of clarity, spelling and punctuation have been
modified in the following extracts.

To Mrs Cobbold[1] from Ipswich gaol

Ipswich, May 25th 1801

Honoured Madam,

I am sorry I have to inform you this bad news that I am going away on Wednesday next or Thursday at the longest, so I have taken the liberty, my good lady, of troubling you with a few lines as it will be the last time I ever shall trouble you in this sorrowful confinement. My sorrows are very great. To think I must be banished out of my own country and from all my dearest friends forever. It is very hard indeed for anyone to think on it and much more for me to endure the hardship of it. Honoured madam, I should be very happy to see you on Tuesday before I leave England if it is not too much trouble for you. For I am in great confusion myself now my sorrows are doubled. I must humbly beg on your goodness to consider me a little trifle of money. It would be a very great comfort to your poor unhappy servant,

Margaret Catchpole

To Mrs Cobbold

Sydney, January 21 1802

Honoured Madam,

With great pleasure I take up my pen to acquaint you, my good lady, of my safe arrival at Port Jackson, New South Wales, Sydney on the 20th day of December 1801, and as I was a-going to be landed, on the left hand of me it put me in mind of the Cliff, both the houses and likewise the hills, so as it put me in very good spirits, seeing a place so very like my own native home. It is a great deal more like England than ever I expected to have seen, for here is garden stuff of all kinds, except gooseberries and currants and apples. The gardens are very beautiful, all planted with geraniums and they run 7 or 8 foot high. It is a very woody country for if I go out any distance here it means going through woods for miles. But there are very beautiful and very pretty birds.

[1] Margaret Catchpole had been employed by Mrs Cobbold, who taught her to read and write.

I only wish my good lady I could send you one of these parrots for they are very beautiful, but I see so many die on board it makes me so very unwilling to send you one. But if I should continue long in this country, I certainly will send you something out of this wicked country, for I must say this is the wickedest place I ever was in all my life. The wheat harvest was almost over just as I landed. Here wheat is 8 shillings per bushell. At this time here is 2 crops in the summer, one with wheat and one with Indian corn. The winter is but very short as they tell me.

Madam, I cannot give you much account of the country in this letter. But I will give you more in the next, for I never shall forget your goodness, my good lady, that you showed to me before I left England, and I took everything over with me safe, and it is a great service to me indeed, not that I am in such great trouble at present. But God only knows how it might be for here is many a one that has been here for many years and they have their poor head shaved and sent up to the Coal River and there carry coals from daylight in the morning, till dark at night, and half starved. But I hear that it is going to be put by and so it had need, for it is very cruel indeed.

Norfolk Island is a bad place, enough to send any poor creature with a steel collar on their poor necks. But I will take good care of myself from that. I am pretty well off at present for I was taken off the stores 2 days after I landed so I have no government work to do and they have nothing to do with me except when there be a general muster then I must appear to let them know I am here, and if I have a mind to go up to Parramatta (twenty miles) or Toongabbie (30) or Hawkesbury, I have to get a pass, or else I should be taken up and put into prison, for a very little will do that here.

My dear good lady, I want to say a great deal more but time will not permit for I expect the ship every day, and I have been very bad since I came on shore. I thought I should lose my life but bless be to the Lord I am a great deal better and I was charmingly, all my passage, considering we crossed over the Bay of Biscay and crossed the line very well indeed. But I was tossed about very much indeed but I should not have minded if I was but coming to Old England once more. For I cannot say that I like this country. No horses and very small whiskeys and little chaise carts and passenger boats. My dear madam, I must conclude and send you more accounts the next time.

> from your unfortunate servant,
> Margaret Catchpole

Madam, pray be so kind as to let Dr Stebbing have that side of the letter. I hope these few scrawls will find you and all your good family well and I hope, my good lady, you will write to the first transport ship that comes out, for I shall be very glad to hear from you.

> undated

Dear Sir,

I hope you will be so kind as to write to me by the first ship that comes to Botany Bay and direct for me at Samuel Rolley on the Brickfield No. 40 Sydney.

Sir, we had not one died no, not all the passage out, in so many women.

The crops of wheat is very good in this country for it produces fourteen bushells per acre, it is a very fruitful place indeed for I understand them that never had a child in all their lives, have some after they come here.

Pray sir, send me word if you know how Dinah Parker and her child is.

> May 2 1803

My dear Uncle and Aunt,

I have sent you a newspaper, the only one I could get this time so I hope you will favour me with some of the Ipswich papers when you write to me and send me that when I made my escape out of prison. And send me word if you ever heard or see Mrs Starkes since I left the country and heard Mrs Kid and Lucy, and James and Samuel and my boy Charles, and that is for poor William, I forgot. But I hope they are all dutiful to you in your old days, for I never, for I never wish no one to come here in to such a wicked country. So God in heaven bless you all and good night. I am well beloved by all that know me and that is a comfort . . . they make as much of me as if I was a lady because I am the

Commisariat's cook. So no more at present from your loving cousin,

Margaret Catchpole

I have at this time a man that keeps me in company and said would marry me if I like. But I am not for marrying. He is a gardener. He came out as a botanist and is to be allowed one hundred pounds per year . . . and a man to fetch wood and water and one to go out with him to select seeds and see skins and all sorts of curiosities.

Sydney, October 8, 1806

Dear Uncle and Aunt,

On the eighteenth of April 1806 I was fifty miles up the country and very ill when I had the pleasant news that there was a box from England for me, which it was the greatest joy that I ever felt, after being five years, all but one month from you. Many be the time that I have said to my best friends what I would give to hear from my dear uncle and aunt. I have dreamt of being with you, which I pray to God to preserve your life and mine, to meet once more, which I have no doubt but we shall, as I am, bless God at this time, in good health and happy to hear you are the same. And Lucy and James and Samuel, and my dear boy Charles.

I am seated by the side of a good cask of porter and I wish to see you all before it is out. It will not be tapped till Christmas. This is my daughter's as I call her. She came into the country with me. She has got two fine boys and a girl, and they call me grandmother, for this house is my home when I come to Sydney. For I have been for these 2 years past up the country, at Richmond Hill. I went there to nurse Mrs Rouse, one very respectable person. They came from England free. They respect me as one of their own family for Mrs Rouse, with this last child, she told her husband that she must have died were I not there.

Mr Rouse did live up at Richmond at his farm but the Governor gave him a place to be superintendent and master builder . . . Then I was left overseer at his farm, but it was too lonesome for me so I left.

But I have got four ewes and nine breeding goats, 3 wethers

and seven young ones; that is all my stock at present. Mr Rouse
keeps them and charges me nothing for them. I should have had
six pigs but the place has been so flooded that I thought we must
all be lost. That is how I came to be so very ill, being in the water
up to my middle. As you well know I have a good spirit. I was
trying to save what I could and then I and Mrs Dight and her
three children went up in the loft for safety. We had not been
there above an hour when the first chimney went down, and middle wall went. Then I expected the next chimney to go, and all
the walls, and then to be crushed to death, for the water was about
five feet deep in the house at that time. It was that depth in about
two hours. Mr Dight and his two men were gone to knock down
the pig sties and pig runs, to drive the pigs away, so we were
left alone. But great providence turned up a boat to save us from
a watery grave, came and took us away. I was most frightened
then all the way going over. This happened on the 22nd of last
March . . . Barns and wheat stacks and the Indian corn that was
not gathered, it washed all away before the stream. Some poor
creatures riding on their houses, some on their barns crying out
for God's sake to be saved. Others firing their guns in the greatest
distress for a boat. There was many thousands of head of all kind
of cattle was lost, and so many bushells of all sorts was lost of
grain. So now this place is in great distress for wheat,
livestock . . . and everything is very dear. The wheat is coming
in the ear but the crops look very light.

But my dear Uncle and Aunt, I do not know any want, bless
God, for I have beennursing lying-in women . . . It is a great word
to say but I am well beloved amongst my betters. I never have
known another of punishment since I have been here, only that
I cannot get any tea, that is all the sorrow.

I am very happy to hear of your William's death, for he was
so ill. My dear aunt, I am very happy to hear you grow so lusty
and Lucy so steady, and all do so well. How I did kiss your dear
name, and cry over it for I thought that I had you that minute
in my hand. I have been very happy ever since my dear uncle,
I received yours. I hope you have received letters twice since then
for I always take every opportunity of sending to you and that
you may be well assured I will and I hope you will do the same.
I should be very happy to hear from my aunt and uncle
Led . . . and all my cousins too and if any of them be married
and how many children that have got.

I myself will not have no husband. But here is no women who must have some sort of a man. Some women do very well indeed. Uncle I told you I was going to a farm but I did not. I lived a little while in a letten house on my own. I did not like that so I went to nurse one Mrs Skinner. They are the cherry makers. Then I went to nurse Mrs Rouse and stopped with her one year and then went to Mrs Dight's . . . Then I was left at Mr Rouse, my farm, and from there I went to nurse Mrs Dights here, and from there I went to nurse Mrs Wood and from there to Mrs Rouse again. Now I am going to nurse Mrs Faithfull, Mrs Wood's sister. Their names were Pitt when they came to this country; they were some relation to Lord Nelson, a very good family.

I live very well and much respected. Old Mrs Pitt is very fond of me. But I shall I believe, soon go to live by myself. Mrs Palmer has often time wished me to go to live with her again but the work was too hard for me in this hot country. But I always go to see Mrs Palmer because Mrs Rouse and Mrs Dight was wet nurse to Mrs Palmer.

I might have gone to live with many of the same and might have lived very well but I have no inclination. I have a piece of ground and am thinking to build a house on it or buying a cow. But the price of a cow is from thirty to fifty pounds a piece. That is a great sum of money.

We have got a new governor and the name is Bligh, which I had given in a petition last fourth of June. But if God spare my life I will have a petition in for emancipation and then I will let you know.

My dear uncle, I wish you could see this place for at this time the peaches are all on the trees, the wheat is on the ear. The place is full of wickedness. We are forced to go and get a party together or else we should be robbed and murdered. But I will take good care of myself. My dear Mrs Cobbold is very good to me. She sent me out a box of nice things, some to sell and some to wear. A piece for three gowns, 2 petticoats, 1 white, 1 stuff, 3 muslin handkerchiefs, a cotton shawl, thirteen yards of black lace, six yards of all wide gingham for a gown with borders for capes. 2 collars for capes and a great many more things too many to mention. I hope when you see Mr Stebbing you will be so good as to give the greatest thanks to him for the bountiful present that it was through goodness that Mrs Henrietta . . . of Henly Hall near Ipswich . . . this lady sent me twelve yards of Irish cloth, a bible, prayer book, and four yards of twill and a beautiful letter.

I hope you will see my John Cook and give my love to him and all friends and tell them I am all the same as ever, only I have lost one of my front teeth, and that grieves me. I send Mrs Cobbold the newspapers. I wish you could borrow them after a while. You would like to see them, I well know. I wish you to hear if you can, where Fanny Brookes is, that lived with me at Mrs Cobbold's.

(Letter ends)

Richmond Hill
Sept 2 1811

My dear Uncle and Aunt and Cousins,

This comes with my kind love to you all and happy to hear you are all well as it has me, at this time, thank God for it. And with great joy I received your letters for I thought you had forgot me. But when I saw the date they had been not a long time. They should have come in the *Dromedary* almost two years ago. I received my box on 28th August, 1811, and it makes me very happy to hear my dear cousins are doing so well. A great blessing and comfort to you and a source of happiness to me.

I was very sorry to hear of my aunt Ledders being dead, and poor Susey. Pray give my love to my uncle Ledder, and tell him I am very sorry indeed to hear such news. Give my love to all my cousins Ledders. I should be very glad to hear from my cousin Sarah, so to give my love to Susan, if you should see her and tell her I thought she would not have married.

I am not, and almost fifty years old, nor do I intend. I hope to see home once more and to see dear cousin Charles weigh me a pound of tea for me. And that fine strong young man, Samuel, to make me a pair of shoes, and poor Lucy to thread my needle. For my eyes are not so good as they were. But thank God I do as well as I do. I rent a little farm of about fifteen acres, but half of it standing timber. And the cleared ground, I hire men to put in my corn, and I work a great deal myself. I have got thirty sheep and forty goats, thirty pigs and two dogs; they take care of me for I live all alone, not one in the house. There is a house within twenty roods of me.

I have a good many friends that I go to see when I think proper.
Such as I have nursed when they lay-in, cannot do without me.
I am looked upon very well thank God. I hope to get a few pounds
to come home with. The white frosty morning is just the saving
of us. It has been very cold indeed this winter, but nothing like
your snow – that was very shocking indeed. I am very sorry to
hear that you have lost your friend and I am very sorry that I
have lost a good friend like Mrs Sloorgin, for she sent me this
time twelve yards of Irish cloth, 3 yards of ribbon, 3 good books
and writing paper, and this is some of it.

Mrs Cobbold sent me a very handsome present. Two pieces
for nine capes, four last ones, one just as it came off her own
head which I thought more of than anything. I put it on directly
and many more things too long to mention.

My dear aunt, your hair is kissed and cried over. I will always
keep it and I have the other by me that you sent and hope that
the next time you send you will send some of Lucy's and Charles'
hair. Dear Uncle, you must think I can walk well, for when I
heard there was a box for me I set off and walked fifty miles in
two days. You cannot tell the happiness it gave me. And tell my
friends I was overjoyed to hear of it. Now this will give me great
happiness for a long time and I hope Lucy will always be very
dutiful to her mother as my dear aunt must be getting into years.
For I do not grow younger myself and have lost all my front teeth
[but] I can stir about as briskly as ever and am in good spirits.
Dear Uncle, I hope when you write again you will send me word
of all friends and I thank you for the newspapers, and I wish I
could send you some, but there is no time. The ship is going to
sail directly so I must conclude with my sincere love to you and
all my cousins and pray to God to keep his Bliss upon you all,
and not forgetting myself, adieu

Margreat Catchpole [*sic*]

I am very proud of my dear Charles' letter and sorry I had not
time to answer it but I will the next time. James will soon get
a rich man I think, if he minds Samuel, and I hope will overtake
them. By taking care, this place is getting very plentiful, but everything is very dear. Beef, mutton and pork 15 to 18 pence per
pound, wheat from 12 to 15 shillings per bushell, butter five shillings a pound. On March the fourteenth is my birthday, then I
am fifty years old.

ELIZABETH MACARTHUR, 1769-1850

The letters of Elizabeth Macarthur provide an invaluable and illuminating chronicle of early colonial life from the perspective of an educated woman. While they document some of the differences between convict and free, Elizabeth Macarthur's letters also point to some of the common problems; all the white women in the colony were cut off from family and friends, tyrannised by distance and the tenuousness of the post, and desperately dependent upon letters. Much of their writing was given over to details about arrangements for delivery and with months, sometimes years, between communications, letters tended to be long, records of everyday life written in 'serial' form, added to at intervals as the writer waited for a ship to carry the letter home.

The courageous wife of John Macarthur, Elizabeth arrived in the colony in 1790 and sent home a series of letters which constitute a history of the early settlement as well as a personal account of her own life and admirable achievements. Her writing is characteristic of much of the literary efforts of women in the early years in that it contains descriptions and explanations of the terms of her new existence, and her new self, and speculations of the best ways to relate to the country and its black inhabitants.

The Mitchell Library holds a collection of Elizabeth Macarthur's letters from 1789-1849, and *The Journal and Letters of Elizabeth Macarthur, 1789-1791*, edited by Joy N. Hughes, has been published by the

Elizabeth Farm Occasional Series; the following
extracts have been selected from both sources.

Cape of Good Hope
20th April 1790.

My dear Mother,
   I have the happiness to inform you that we arrived safe, & are
anchored in the Bay from whence I date this on the 14th of this
month after a fine passage of just twelve weeks & three days from
the time we sailed from Portsmouth. I wish I could also add that
we arrived in perfect health, but my poor little Boy is a melancholy proof, at this period, of the Contrary. He has been very
sickly throughout the Passage, & unless a very speedy change
take place I am well convinced he will shortly cease to be an
inhabitant of this world. I believe I told you in Devonshire that
he had nearly cut one of his teeth; I was however, exceedingly
mistaken, for he hath not yet cut any, altho' they appear very
firm in the Gums; & I am in hopes that if once one or two had
made their appearance, he might yet recover & get strength. He
is not near so large as children generally are at four months old,
altho' he is now upwards of twelve. He is very sensible, very lively,
& affords us much pleasure; but the trouble we have had with
so delicate a little creature is indescribable, & I wonder my own
health hath not suffered more from the attention I have been
obliged to pay him. I may justly say with regard to him "that
God tempers the wind to the shorn lamb."
   Mr Macarthur has enjoyed a remarkably good share of health,
ever since we left England, & I trust will continue to do so.
   I was nearly tired with the length of the Passage before we got
into Port, & stood in need of refreshments very much; but now
with the benefit of fresh meat, plenty of fruits & vegetables, I
am quite recovered; & assure my beloved Mother that I never
was in better health, & am in very good Spirits which are only
damped by poor Edward's illness.
   You will expect some account of my Voyage, but I scarcely
know where to begin or what to tell you. I mean to write Miss
Kingdon those particulars; it will be needless for me to repeat
the same in both letters; particularly as I have but little spare time,
being busy in seeing all our Linen washed & got up, & in laying
in stock & refreshment to take with us to Botany Bay. I am also

advised by our Surgeon to spend as much time as possible on Shore, in order to get very strong & prepared for the remainder of the voyage. We are to stay here eight days longer & no more. Tomorrow I go on shore to board during that time. I am to pay a Dollar & a Half a day, & live with a genteel private family. Mr Macarthur cannot quit the ship entirely, but will visit me on shore every day –

If it please the Almighty that we arrive in safety at Port Jackson, I shall write you a long letter by Capt Marshal, but that letter you must not expect till next June, as the Ship is under a Charter to bring tea home from China for the East India Company. She therefore will from Port Jackson go on to China, & from thence return to England which makes the Home Passage very long. Whether I may meet with a Vessel that returns by the nearest way from Port Jackson to England is very uncertain. Indeed I believe it very improbable & therefore you must not expect it. I hope you will receive this in four months from the date, by which time, & long before I trust, we shall be comfortably settled in our New World. We have a good passage from hence, we hope to be at Port Jackson in seven or eight weeks from this time. You may be sure that I shall write to you by every ship that returns, & I pray that you will punctually write to me. *The Guardian*, a 44 Gun Ship, quite new, that was fitted out by Government at an amazing Expense for New South Wales, being laden with provisions & a variety of valuable stores for the Colony is now a wreck at the Cape. The particulars which I have learnt are these. It being summer, she had a good passage from England to this place, where she staid the usual time for water & refreshments, & then proceeded on her voyage, but instead of going the usual track from hence to Port Jackson, the Lieut., who commanded her, took her quite a different one, & proceeded round by Cape Horn, where according to his account he fell in with islands of ice, which entirely impeded his Passage & tore his Ship almost to pieces, so that with great difficulty he brought her back to this place. No lives have been lost, & the provisions have been lodged in Store houses at Cape town, for the use of which the Dutch have the conscience to charge £60 a day. With the cost of unloading her Cargo, & the daily expense of keeping her stores on Shore, it is said she is already sixty thousand Pounds in debt at the Cape, & soon will be as many more.

I have now to desire my particular remembrance to all my

friends, & first of all let me notice my Grandfather. I have in some sort a presentiment that impels me to believe I shall yet see him again. Be that as it may a man arrived at his years, living regularly & so perfectly weened from the things of this world, will meet Death as a friend when he shall appear – Tell him with my love I have not forgotten his Counsel to have ever present to my mind the Duty due by us to our Maker. Believe me,

Y^r affect^e Daughter
Elizth Macarthur

Sydney, Port Jackson, N.S.Wales
March the 7th 1791.

At length we have a prospect of communication once more with our friends by Letter. The *Gorgon* so long wished for and so long expected, is not yet arrived and by her unaccountable delay, has involved us all, in the most mysterious uncertainty, and clouded our minds with gloomy apprehensions for her safety. I hope you will have rec'd my Letter dated Augst 1790; which I sent by the *Scarborough* transport; by way of China. I wrote to my Mother by the same Ship and a second Letter to her, dated a few weeks after the first, I sent by the *Neptune*, who sail'd, I think, some-time in Augst – by those Letters, I think, you will be inform'd of every material circumstance, relative to our Voyage and of what happen'd to us after our arrival till the ship sail'd. I told you of the unfortunate loss of the *Syrius*; a Kings Ship that had been station'd here from the first settling the Colony. She was wreck'd on Norfolk Island – the Ships Company who all escaped with life, but not altogether without hurt; remain'd on the Island, and the *Supply* a small Brig, that sail'd from this place, with the *Syrius*, returned with the news of her sad fate. The provisions of the Colony, at that time being at very low ebb, it was deem'd necessary to take some step lest a supply might not arrive from England in time to prevent a threaten'd famine – every individual of this Colony, was reduced to a very short allowance; & the little Brig was despatched to Batavia under the command of Lieut Ball; there to take up a Dutch ship, and purchase a certain quantity of provisions for this place; with . . . it was to be freighted and despatched hither with all possible expedition. A few Weeks after the *Supply* sail'd, the first Ship *Lady Juliana*, arrived, and brought an account of the loss of the *Guardian*, occasion'd by falling in with Islands of Ice. This ship arrived on the 3rd of June, and came timely to prevent very great distress. On the 21st of June the *Justiana*[sic] arrived, a Store Ship and on the 29th our fleet was safely anchored in the Cove as all those ships were under Contract to return by way of China to take home Tea for the East India Company and there being at that time no Ship station'd here, no way was left to convey a relief to the Inhabitants of Norfolk Island, but by ordering some of those ships to touch there in their way to China. The *Justiana*[sic] and *Surprize* rec'd orders for that purpose; reimbarked a certain proportion of provision for the Island. We had every hope that the supplies might arrive in time to prevent any fatal consequences; yet as we could have no certainty of that till some Ship should first arrive here that might be dispatch'd to know the particulars of their fate; our minds were never perfectly easy on their account, at that time there was with the *Syrius*'s Company the Marines and Convicts near seven hundred persons on the Island, and I can truly say that for upwards of Six Months I never pass'd a day without reflecting on them with pain and anxiety. Week after Week stole away; and Month after Month with little diversity, each succeeding sunset produced among us, wild and vague conjectures, of what could be the cause of the *Gorgon*'s delay – and still we remain'd unsatisfied indeed, indeed all our Surmises have nearly worn themselves out and we are at a loss for new ones: time the great resolver of all events alone can determine this seeming mystery to us. On the 20th of October a general cry prevail'd through the Garrison of the Flags being hoisted (which is a Signal of a Ship appearing off the Harbour) I was preparing myself to receive Mrs Grose and Mrs Paterson being fully persuaded it was the *Gorgon*; however I was soon undeceived, as it prov'd to be the *Supply* from Batavia; she had a very quick passage but had experienced a very sickly one. Mr Ball very soon call'd upon us, and complemented me with many little comforts procured at Batavia, which were truly acceptable. He brought us an account of a Ship, an English Man of War, answering very nearly the description of the *Gorgon* that had been spoken to somewhere about the Equator; and was bound for this port. This intelligence was brought to the Cape of Good Hope, and from thence to Batavia. If this was the *Gorgon* (which yet I hope not) I tremble to think what may have been her fate. The Dutch ship laden with the provisions for the Colonies was not ready to sail when Mr Ball quited[*sic*] Batavia. She did not arrive till the 17th of December. In the dispatches of the Dutch Schelander to Govr Phillips[*sic*] is mention'd something of a Spanish War, having been declared against England in May 1790. The particulars are not well explain'd, or perhaps I should say not well understood, as the Letter is written in Dutch; and no one here understands enough of the Language to transcribe it correctly . . .

I shall begin my relation now of things more immediately occuring[*sic*] to myself, it will be unnecessary to go over the Chit Chat of my last Letter; such as the state of our House the attentions we meet with &c &c. – We pass'd our time away many Weeks cheerfully if not gaily – gaily indeed it could not be said to be. – On my first landing every thing was new to me, every Bird, every Insect, Flower, &c. in short all was novelty around me, and was noticed with a degree of eager curiosity, and perturbation, that after a while subsided into that calmness; I have already described. In my former Letter I gave you the character of Mr Dawes: and also of Captn Tench, those Gentlemen and a few others are the chief among whom we visit – indeed we are in that habit of intimacy with Captn Tench, that there are few days pass that we do not spend some part of together. Mr Dawes we do not see so frequently. He is so much engaged with the Stars, that to Mortal Eyes he is not always visible. I had the presumption to become his pupil, and meant to learn a little of Astronomy it is true I have had many a pleasant Walk to his House something less than a half a Mile from Sydney have given him much trouble in making Orrereyes and in explaining to me the general principles of the heavenly bodies, but I soon found I had mistaken my abilities; and blush at my error. Still I wanted something, to fill up a certain vacancy, in my time which could neither be done by writing, reading, or conversation, to the two first I did not feel myself always inclined, and the latter was not in my power having no female friend to unbend my mind to, nor a single Woman with whom I could converse with any satisfaction to myself the Clergymans Wife being a person in whose society I could reap neither profit or pleasure. These considerations made me still anxious to learn some easy Science to fill up the vacuum of many a Solitary day, and at length under the auspices of Mr Dawes: I have made a small progress in Botany, no Country can exhibit a more Copious field for Botanical knowledge, than this.

I am arrived so far, as to be able to class and order, all common plants. I have found great pleasure in my Study; every Walk furnish'd me with subjects to put in practice, that Theory I had before gain'd by reading but Alas my botanical pursuits were most unwelcomely interrupted by Mr McArthurs being attack'd by a severe illness – In December he got better, and in January we were remov'd into a more convenient House – I shall now introduce another acquaintance Mr Worgan, to you, a Gentleman I have not hitherto named, he was Surgeon to the *Syrius*, and happen'd to be left at this place: when that Ship met with her fate at Norfolk. It is not improbable this Gentleman may himself deliver this Letter to you he is well known to Doctor Cudlipp. I assure you in losing him a very considerable branch of our Society will be lopp'd off. I shall now tell you of another resource I had to fill up some of my vacant hours, our New House is ornamented with a piano-forte of Mr Worgans, he kindly means to leave it with me, and now under his direction I have begun a new study, but I fear without my Master I shall not make any great proficiency, I am told however I have done wonders – in being able to play off God save the King and Foots Minuet besides that of reading the Notes with great facility, in spite of Musick I have not altogether lost sight of my Botanical studies; I have only been precluded from pursuing that Study by the intense heat of the Weather which has not permited[sic] me to walk much during the Summer, the Months of December, and January, have been hotter than I can describe, indeed insufferably so. The Thermometer rising from an 100 to an 112 degrees is I believe 30 degrees above the hottest day known in England – the general heat is to be borne, but when we are oppress'd by the hot winds we have no other resource but to Shut up ourselves in our Houses and to endeavor to the utmost of our power to exclude every breath of Air. This Wind blows from the North, and comes as if from an heated oven. Those Winds are generally succeeded by a Thunder Storm, so severe and awful, that it is impossible for one who has not been a Witness to such a Violent concussion of the Elements to form any notion of it. I am not yet enough used to it, to be quite unmoved, it is so different from the Thunder we have in England, I cannot help being a little Cowardly, yet no injury has ever been suffer'd from it, except a few Sheep being kill'd which were laying under a Tree that was struck by the Lightning, a Thunder Storm has always the effect to bring heavy rain, which cools the air very considerably, I have seen very little rain, since my Arrival, indeed I do not think we have had a Weeks rain the whole time: the consequence of which is, our Gardens produce nothing, all is burnt up, indeed, the Soil must be allow'd to be most wretched and totally unfit for growing any European productions, tho' [word illegible] you would scarcely believe this, as the face of the ground at this moment, where it is in its native State is flourishing even to Luxuriance; producing fine Shrubs, Trees, and Flowers which by their lively tints, afford a most agreeable Landscape. Beauty I have heard from some of my unletter'd Country Men is but skin deep, I am sure the remark holds good in N.S.Wales – where all the Beauty is literally on the Surface, but I believe I must allow it has Symetry of form also to recommend it, as the ground in all the parts that have been discover'd is charmingly turned and diversified by agreeable Vallies, and gently rising Hills but Still those beauties are all exterior. Many Gentlemen have penetrated far into the Country, but they find little difference in the appearance of the Soil. Some rivers have been discover'd to one of which the Govr has given the name of the Hawksbury[sic] it is a very Noble one, and empties itself into the Sea; at a Harbour which Captn Cook in his Voyage nam'd Broken Bay, another River has been discover'd, which some call the Nepean, another the Tench and a third the Worgan, it is supposed by some, that these three are one, and the same River only have been lighted upon by Explorers: at different distances from its source – If the British Government think fit to continue the Colony, those Rivers may be of great Utility; particularly in dry Seasons – as all the fresh Water we have near Sydney is very inconsiderable, tho' we cannot say we have hitherto wanted Water.

I have not yet seen the famous settlement of Rose Hill. I wanted much to have paid it a visit before the Ship sail'd, but have now given up the Idea – the Weather is yet too warm, and Rose Hill has not the benefit of Sea-breezes so much as we have at Sydney. All the ground Works and Farming schemes are carried on at Rose Hill; tho' the head quarters are here. The last harvest was a very one[sic], the Wheat, and Barley not yielding thrice the quantity that was Sown. The Indian corn return'd something more, but it was altogether a poverty struck harvest.

It is very likely my next Letter to you may be dated from Rose Hill Captn Nepean has an Idea that the Govr will remove the remainder of his detachment and Men thither as soon as the Barracks are compleated which are already half finish'd. After the three officers I have already named for Norfolk are gone there will only remain at Sydney Cove Captn Nepean, Mr Townson Mr McArthur and the Surgeon Mr Harris, this would indeed be a very Small Society if it were in danger of losing the Marine Officers, but that cannot be the case till the remainder of the Corps arrive. We shall be pleased to remove any where with Captn Nepean, he is truly a good hearted Man and has I believe a great friendship for Mr McArthur. You will observe I have made no excursion, of any consequence perhaps you will wonder how I should make any in a Country like this. I will tell you how – the Harbour of Port Jackson is universally allow'd to be the finest in the known World from the mouth of which to Rose Hill, they call 16 miles in a Straight direction, then it is so beautifully form'd that I can conceive nothing equal to it, branching out into a number of Arms, and Coves, forming little Islands, and points of Land, so agreeable and romantic that the most fanciful imagination must tire, and I think allow himself to be outdone and yield the palm to reality and simple nature. In a Harbour so form'd and of such extent, a number of pleasant little Water parties might be made to some of those Islands or Bays; and a number I yet promise myself, but hitherto from Mr McArthur's long confinement, and since his recovery from the heat of the Weather, I have been enabled to put but one in execution and that was to a Bay near the Harbours mouth, about 6 miles from Sydney. We pass'd the day in Walking among the Rocks, and upon the sands very agreeably, I look'd carefully for some Shells for you, but could find none better than what you can get at Bude or Widemouth, above this Bay about half a miles distance is a very high Hill which commands an extensive view of the Wide Ocean, on it is placed a Flag-Staff, which can also be seen at Sydney. When a ship appears the Flag is hoisted; by which means we have notice of it, much sooner than we otherways could have, it also conducts the Vessel into the Harbour. There are a few huts near the Flag-Staff, with people in them appointed to keep a look-out, and from thence the Spot has derived the general name of Look-out. Of my Walks around Sydney the longest has not extended beyond three Miles, and that distance I have I believe only ventured upon twice: once to a Farm which Captn Nepean has for his Company, to which we sent our Tea equipage & drank Tea on the turf; and once to a Hill situated between this & Botany Bay, where I could command a prospect of that famous spot. Nor do I think there is any probability, of my seeing much of the Inland country, untill it is cleared, as beyond a certain distance round the Colony, there is nothing but Native paths, very narrow and very incommodious, the Natives are certainly not a very Gallant set of people, who take pleasure in escorting their Ladies, No – they suffer them humbly to follow, Indian file like. As I am now speaking of the Natives, I must give you an account how we stand with them, in order to give you an Idea of this part of our political Government, it will be necessary to carry the Account back to a period some months previous to my arrival. In the Winter 1789 (which you will recollect is Summer in England) a dreadful Small pox was discover'd amongst the Natives, how the disorder was introduced cannot be disover'd. They were found lying in a miserable State some dead and others dying, nor is it to be wonder'd at that this disorder, should in general be so fatal to them, when we consider they are not in possession of a single palliative nor have any means of procuring nourishment for themselves, when their strength no longer permits them to pursue their usual avocations of fishing hunting the Kangaroo, and other little Animals, on which they live. Amongst the unhappy objects that were discover'd was a Boy and a Girl, these were brought in, and from the humanity of the Clergyman, who took the Girl, and of the principle[sic] Surgeon, Mr White who took the Boy, they were both sav'd. The Girl whom I mention'd to you in my former Letters by the name of Abaroo or Booroo, (for it is difficult to catch their exact pronunciation more so to give you an Idea of it by Letters) appears to be about Eleven years old. The Boy (named Nauberry) about nine after they began to learn English, and to make us understand them: it was imagined from their communication, that if a Man or two, could be brought to reside with us, that some valuable information might be obtained, respecting the interior parts of the country – With this view the Govr left no means untried to effect an intimacy, with them; but every endeavor of that sort as before prov'd ineffectual. They accept of his presents as Children do play things; just to amuse them for a moment and then throw them away, disregarded. Despairing to gain their Confidence by fair means, the Govr ordered that two men should be taken by force. This was done, the poor Fellows, I am told exhibited the Strongest marks of terror and

Consternation at this proceeding, believing they were certainly meant, to be sacrificed. When they were taken to the Govrs House and immediately clean'd and Cloth'd their astonishment at every thing they saw was amazing. A new World was unfolded to their view at once; for some days they were much dejected, but it soon gave way to Cheerfulness they were then admitted to the Governors Table and in little time ate and drank every thing that was given to them, they now walk'd about the Settlement as they lik'd, only with a Man who was appointed to attend them, that they might not escape into the Woods, but as they show'd no apparent inclination to do that, the Vigilance of their keeper by degrees abated; which the oldest of the two (named Coleby) soon observed: and in a very artful Manner one night, made his escape: the one who remain'd, and call'd himself Bannylong, till May 1790 and then took himself off without any known reason, having been treated with the most uniform kindness, and appeared highly pleased with our people, and Manners; taking it a great Compliment to be call'd White Man. In the time he was here he acquired English enough, to make himself understood in common matters, and furnish'd our people with the Native names for Animals, Birds, Fish, &c – from this time till after our arrival, nothing was known respecting them, as the Natives whenever they met with any of our people were more shy than ever, and could not be brought to a parley. Nauberry, and Abaroo still remain'd easy and happy expressing no wish to return to the Woods. On the 7th of Septr. Captn Nepean, and several other Gentlemen went down the Harbour in a Boat; with an intention of proceeding to Broken Bay to take a view of the Hawkesbury River, in their way they put in at Manly Cove (a place so call'd from the spirited behaviour of the Natives there at the Governors first landing.) at this time, about two Hundred Natives were assembled, feeding on a Whale: that had been driven on Shore, as they discover'd no hostile intentions our party having Arms went up to them. Nauberry was in the Boat and was desired to enquire for Bannylong, and Coleby, when behold, both Gentlemen appeared; and advancing with the utmost confidence ask'd in broken English, for all their old friends at Sydney. They exchanged several weapons for provisions, and Clothes – and gave some Whale bone as a present for the Governor. Captn Nepean knowing this News would be very pleasing to the Govr dispatch'd a Messenger to inform him of it, and proceeded on towards Broken Bay – The Govr lost no time, but as soon as he was acquainted with the above circumstances order'd a Boat and accompanied by Mr Collins (The Judge Advocate) and a Lieut. Waterhouse of the Navy; repair'd to Manly Cove, he landed by himself, unarm'd in order to shew no Violence was intended. Bannylong approach'd and shook hands with the Govr but Coleby had before left the Spot, no reason was ask'd why Bannylong had left us he appear'd very happy, and thankful for what was given him; requesting a hatchet and some other things which the Govr promised to bring him the next day, Mr Collins and Mr Waterhouse, now join'd them; and several Natives also came forward, they continued to converse with much seeming friendship untill they had insensibly wander'd some distance from the Boat, and very imprudently none of the Gentlemen had the precaution to take a gun in their hand. This the Govr perceiving, deem'd it prudent to retreat; and, after assuring Bannylong that he would remember his promise, told him he was going. At that moment an Old looking Man advanced, whom Bannylong said was his friend, and wish'd the Govr to take notice of him, at this he approach'd the old Man, with his hand extended, when on a sudden the Savage started back and snatch'd up a spear from the ground, and poiz'd it to throw the Govr seeing the danger told him in their Tongue that it was bad; and still advanced; when with a mixture of horror, and intrepidity, the native discharg'd the spear with all his force at the Govr, it enter'd above his Collar bone, and came out at his back nine inches from the entrance; taking an Oblique direction, the Natives from the Rocks now pour'd in their Spears in abundance; so that it was with the utmost difficulty, and the greatest good fortune that no other hurt was rec'd in getting the Govr into the Boat. As soon as they return'd to this place, you may believe an universal solicitude prevail'd as the danger of the Wound could by no means be ascertain'd untill the spear was extracted and this was not done before his Excellency had caus'd some papers to be arranged – lest the consequence might prove fatal, which happily it did not, for in drawing out the spear, it was found that no vital part had been touch'd, the Governor, having a good habit of Bodily health – the wound perfectly heal'd in the course of a few weeks. Since that a Convict game keeper has been kill'd by a spear; but it seems in some measure to have been owing to his own imprudence. Bannylong came many times to see the Govr, during his confinement, and express'd great sorrow, but the reason why the mischief was done could not be learnt, since that period the Natives visit us every day, more or less: Men, Women and Children they come with great confidence, without spears or any other offensive Weapon a great many have taken up their abode entirely amongst us, and Bannylong, and Coleby, with their Wives come in frequently, Mrs Coleby whose name is Daringa brought in a new born female Infant of hers, for me to see; about Six Weeks since: it was wrapp'd up in the soft bark of a Tree, a Specimen of which I have preserved, it is a kind of a Mantle not much known in England I fancy. I order'd something for the poor Woman to Eat and had her taken proper care of for some little while, when she first presented herself to me she appear'd feeble, and faint, she has since been regular in her visits. The Child thrives remarkably well and I discover a softness and gentleness of Manners in Daringa truly interesting. We do not in general encourage them to come to our houses, as you may conceive there are some offensive circumstances, which makes their company by no means desirable unless it be those who live wholly with us. A good deal of their Language (if it may be so call'd) is now understood, but we can learn nothing from them respecting the interior part of the Country, it seems they are as much unacquainted with it as ourselves, all their knowledge and pursuits are confined to that of procuring for themselves a bare subsistence. They chiefly abide about the Sea coast, the Women appear to be under very great subjection, and are employ'd in the most Laborious part of their Work. They fish, and also make the Lines and hooks and indeed seem very little otherways than slaves to their husbands. They weave their Lines from the Bark of a certain tree; which we call May from the perfume the flower has which strongly resembles the White thorn, that blows in that Month in England. Their hooks they grind into form from a shell, they perform this with great dexterity upon any rough stone. Their canoes are made of the Bark of some of their gum trees, taken off in a particular form, for that purpose. Those they paddle about the Coves, and Bays, very dexteriously. The Weapons they use, are a Spear, a wooden Sword, a Stone Adze, or Ax, and a fish gig. The latter is wholly used in spearing the fish in the Water, the Spears which they Aim and discharge with Wonderful ingenuity at a great distance are some of them most dangerous Weapons, having many barbs in them, and sharpen'd Shells; but they are still under such terror of our fire Arms, that a single armed Man would drive an hundred Natives with their spears and we take care not to venture Walking to any distance unarmed, a Soldier or two always attending when we make any excursion. I have never yet met a Single Native in the Woods. I told you in my last, I thought their dialect pleasing; some of their names I think much so. I will give you a few native Names, and begin with the Men, Arrabason, Volahoa, Imerewanga, Boldarry, Werong, Watteval, Erroniba, female names, Milbah, Bood Barangeroo, Cadimang Mooninguru, Worigan, Crewboar. Mr Dawes who has studied the Language, or Jargon, a good deal, has endeavor'd learn[sic] what their notions are of the Deity. It is not discover'd that they Worship the Sun, or any of the heavenly Bodies, and yet they say all who die, go up to the Clouds. Mr Dawes thinks they have a tradition of the Flood among them . . .

My spirits are at this time low very low tomorrow we lose some valuable members of our small Society, and some very good friends. In so small a society we sensibly feel the loss of every Member more particularly those that are endear'd to us by acts of kindness and friendship, from this circumstance, and my former Letters, you may be led to question my happiness, but this much I can with truth add for myself, that since I have had the powers of reason and reflection, I never was more sincerely happy than at this time, it is true I have some wishes unaccomplished, that I [word illegible] would add to my Comfort, but when I consider this is not a state of perfection, I am Abundantly Content.

Adieu, E. McArthur. [sic]

Sydney Port Jackson
New South Wales
18th March 1791.

At length I sit down to assure my dearest Mother that I am in perfect Health, & to add to the pleasure of this circumstance both Mr Macarthur & my little Edward are in full enjoyment of this blessing, & we only want to complete the measure of it to hear that you are equally happy & well. I hope you have received all my former letters regularly. The first was written to you from the Cape of Good Hope – the second from this place giving an account of the voyage, of Mr Macarthur's dangerous illness &

surprising recovery, & of my being, in consequence of fatigue & anxiety, thrown into premature labour, & delivered of a little Girl who lived but for an hour.

In the little friendly meetings that we have in Sydney 'the banks of the Tamar' is a general toast – Many of the Officers having friends & connexions in Devon & Cornwall, the remembrance is pleasing to all. In my last letter I mentioned there being a select number of Officers here, who had been very attentive to us & I am happy to say that we still experience the same attention from them; & however much I may want female society, Mr Macarthur can have no reason to complain. The Governor has been in the habit of sending us some little thing or other every day (Governor Phillip) . . .

The Grape thrives remarkably well. The Governor sent me some bunches this Season as fine as any I ever tasted, & there is little doubt but in a very few years there will be plenty – We have also very fine Melons. They are raised with little or no trouble, the Sun being sufficient to ripen them, without any forcing whatever & bringing them to a great size & flavour. One day after the Cloth was removed, when I happened to dine at Government House a Melon was produced weighing 30 lbs. We have need of cooling fruit in the warm season – particularly when the hot scorching winds set in – but which however are followed by what is termed the Sea Breeze, & this keeps down the temperature of the air, but when they are overpowered by the hot wind the heat is excessive. The same woman is with me that had charge of Edward when I visited you from Plymouth. He has become very amusing to me. He prattles a little, but is backward with his Tongue, as he has always been in every other respect. I hope Mr Pitt has given Mr Macarthur promotion & that by this time he has a Company; in which event our thoughts will be in some measured turned again towards 'Old England'. I have yet great hopes of seeing my Grandfather once more. Tell him so & that he need be under no apprehension for my religion.

(unsigned)

Parramatta N.S.Wales,
22d Augt. 1794

On the 7th of May last I was happily brought to bed of a very fine Boy – to whom I have given his Father's name John. He with the other two – Edward & Elizabeth are in perfect health, & promise fairly to become every thing we could desire.

In November last myself & family all removed to Parramatta, where Mr Macarthur had been the greater part of his time since the departure of Governor Phillip, on account of the employment he holds under Government.

I write to you now from our own House, a very excellent brick building 68 feet in length & 18 feet wide, independent of Kitchen & Servants' Apartments. I thank God we enjoy all the comfort we could desire, but to give you a clearer idea of our present situation I shall make free to transcribe a Paragraph Mr Macarthur's addressed to his Brother, which is now before me.

'The changes that we have undergone since the departure of Governor Phillip are so great & extraordinary that to recite them all might create some suspicion of their truth. From a state of desponding poverty & threatening Famine, that this Settlement should be raised to its present aspect, in so short a time, is scarcely credible. As to myself I have a Farm containing nearly 250 Acres of which upwards of 100 are under cultivation & the greater part of the remainder is cleared of the Timber which grows upon it. Of this year's produce I have sold £400 worth, & I have now remaining in my Granaries upwards of 1800 Bushels of corn. I have at this moment 20 acres of very fine wheat growing – & 80 Acres prepared for Indian Corn and Potatoes, with which it will be planted in less than a month.

My stock consists of a Horse, two Mares, Two Cows, 130 Goats, & upwards of 100 Hogs. Poultry of all kinds I have in the greatest abundance. I have received no Stock from Government, but one Cow, the rest I have either purchased or bred. With the assistance of one Man & half a dozen greyhounds, which I keep, my table is constantly supplied with Wild Ducks or Kangaroos – averaging one week with another, these dogs do not kill less than three hundred pounds weight. In the centre of my Farm I have built a most excellent brick house 68 Feet in front & 18 in breadth. It has no upper story, but consists of four rooms on the ground floor – a large hall, Closets, Cellar etc. – adjoining is a Kitchen, with Servants Apartments, & other necessary offices. The House is surrounded by a Vineyard & Garden of about three acres the former full of Vines & Fruit trees, & the latter abounding with most excellent vegetables. This Farm being near the Barracks, I can without difficulty attend to the duties of my profession.'

E. McArthur.

To Brigid Kingdon

Elizabeth Farm,
Parramatta 1st Septr 1798

Once again, my much loved friend, it is permitted me to sit down under a conviction that the letter I am about the write will be received by you with pleasure. By the Capture of a Ship off the Coast of Brazil we were left without any direct intelligence from Europe for twelve months. We firmly believed that a revolution or some national calamity had befallen Great Britain, & that we should be left altogether to ourselves, until things at home had resumed some degree of order, & the tempest a little subsided. These fears however have by a late arrival proved without foundation.

This Country possesses numerous advantages to persons holding appointments under Government. It seems the only part of the Globe where quiet is to be expected – We enjoy here one of the finest Climates in the world – The necessaries of life are abundant, & a fruitful soil affords us many luxuries. Nothing induces me to wish for a change but the difficulty of educating our children, & were it otherwise it would be unjust towards them to confine them to so narrow a society. My desire is that they may see a little more of the world, & better learn to appreciate this retirement. Such as it is the little creatures all speak of going home to England with rapture – My dear Edward almost quitted me without a tear. They have early imbibed an idea that England is the seat of happiness & delight, that it contains all that can be gratifying to their senses, & that of course they are there to possess all they desire. It would be difficult to undeceive young people bred up in so secluded a situation, if they had not an opportunity given them of convincing themselves. But hereafter I shall much wonder if some of them make not this place the object of their choice. – By the date of this letter you will see that we still reside on our Farm at Parramatta – a native name signifying the head of a river, which it is.

The town extends one mile in length from the landing place, & is terminated by the Government House which is built on an Eminence named Rose Hill. Our Farm, which contains from four to five hundred acres, is bounded on three sides by Water. This is particularly convenient. We have at this time, about one hundred & twenty acres in wheat, all in a promising state. Our Gardens with fruit & vegetables are extensive & produce abundantly. It is now Spring, & the Eye is delighted with a most beautiful variegated landscape – Almonds – Apricots, Pear and Apple Trees are in full bloom. The native shrubs are also in flower, & the whole Country gives a grateful perfume. There is a very good Carriage road new made from hence to Sydney, which by land is distant about fourteen miles; & another from this to the river Hawkesbury, which is about twenty miles from hence in a direct line across the Country – Parramatta is a central position between both – I have once visited the Hawkesbury & made the journey on horse back. The road is through an uninterrupted wood, with the exception of the village of Toongabie, a farm of Government, & one or two others which we distinguish by the name of Greenlands, on account of the fine grass, & there being few trees compared with the other parts of the Country, which is occasionally brushy & more or less covered with underwood. The greater part of the country is like an English Park, & the trees give to it the appearance of a Wilderness of shrubbery, commonly attached to the habitations of people of fortune, filled with a variety of native plants placed in a wild irregular manner. I was at the Hawkesbury three days. It is a noble fresh water river, taking its rise in a precipitous range of mountains, that it has hitherto been impossible to pass. Many attempts have been made altho' in vain. I spent an entire day on this river, going in a boat to a beautiful spot, named by the late Governor Richmond Hill, high & overlooking a great extent of Country. On one side are those stupendous barriers to which I have alluded, rising as it were, immediately above your head; below, the river itself, still & unruffled – out of sight is heard a Waterfall whose distant murmurs add awfulness to the scene . . .

I have had the misfortune to lose a sweet Boy of eleven months old who died very suddenly by an illness occasioned by teething. The other three Elizabeth John & Mary are well. I have lately been made very happy by learning the safe arrival of Edward in England.

We often remember & talk over in the evening the hospitalities which we have both received in Bridgerule Vicarage & happy shall I be if it is ever permitted me to mark my remembrance more strongly than is expressed in these lines.

If you are in the habit of visiting the Whitstone family I pray that you will kindly remember me to them. The benevolence of the Major's heart will dispose him to rejoice at the success which has attended us, & that the activity which was very early discernable in the mind of Mr Macarthur has had a field for advantageous exertion.

How is it my dearest friend that you are still single – Are you difficult to please – or has the War left you so few Bachelors from amongst whom to choose. But suffer me to offer you a piece of advice – abate a few of your scruples & marry – I offer in myself an instance that it is not always with all our wise foreseeings, those marriages which promise most or least happiness, prove in their result such as our friends may predict. Few of mine I am certain when I married thought that either of us had taken a prudent step. I was considered indolent & inactive; Mr Macarthur too proud & haughty for our humble fortune or expectations, & yet you see how bountifully Providence has dealt with us.

At this time I can truly say no two people on earth can be happier than we are. In Mr Macarthur's society I experience the tenderest affection of a Husband who is instructive & cheerful as a companion. He is an indulgent Father – beloved as a Master, & universally respected for the integrity of his Character. Judge then my friend if I ought not to consider myself a happy woman.

I have hitherto in all my letters to my friends forborne to mention Mr Macarthur's name lest it might appear to me too ostentatious. Whenever you marry, look out for good sense in a husband. You would never be happy with a person inferior to yourself in point of understanding – So much my early recollection of you & of your character bids me say.

E. M.

To Miss Kingdon

Parramatta March 1816.
Elizabeth Farm

Edward always recollects you with kindness. I think whenever the soldier has leave of absence & can command a little spare cash he will pay a visit to the neighborhood of Bridgerule.

You may fancy how much I wish to see those dear children, from who I have been so long separated. Edward last quitted about 7 years since – John left this country at the early age of seven years & a half & has not since returned – he is now twenty two. James & William went home with their father & when I last heard of them were with him in Switzerland. John is my faithful & most affectionate correspondent. My Daughters Elizabeth Mary & Emmeline are still with me & a single lady about my own age who shares all my cares.

It is not wealth, nor large possessions that entail happiness; but Health, Industry with the blessing of God effect much.

I am much oppressed with care on account of our Stock Establishments at our Farms at the Cowpastures having been disturbed by the incursions of the Natives. The Savages have burnt & destroyed the Shepherd's habitations & I daily hear of some fresh calamity.

Yesterday the Governor was pleased to order a non commissioned officer & six soldiers out to protect our establishments from further injury.

Two years ago a faithful old Servant who had lived with us since we first came to the colony was barbarously murdered by them & a poor defenceless woman also. Three of my people are now reported to be missing, but I trust they will be found unhurt.

(unsigned)

Parramatta
March 1816.

My dear Eliza
and shall I add my dearest my ever sweetly remembered God Daughter. How shall I express to you in language adequate to my feelings, my delight at receiving your letter? Nor was I less gratefully pleased with one I at the same time received from your Eldest brother and my earliest friend John. Whether I can answer both by this conveyance I am not now certain. But I hope he will believe that I am sincerely thankful for his kindness in relieving my anxiety on my dear Mother's account. To him, to Mrs Kingdon his wife I must ever be obliged. Edward Macarthur was an

invalid under yr. Brother's roof for a short time. He wrote to me such a lively account of their domestic happiness; & indeed gave so animated a description of the family that I concluded the young soldier had left his heart at Markam Church. I am glad that you continue at the home of your infancy – that is while you remain single – because it must be the most natural to you, & I have ever heard the most amiable characters of Mr Kingdon which you so competely confirm.

Your Brother was better acquainted with Mr Macarthur than with me. In our young days, your poor sister, John & Rodger were my intimates & latterly the Bachelor Charles. Thomas was younger & always at school. At a Grammar school he became acquainted with Mr Macarthur & since again the acquaintance has frequently been renewed in London. But if it keep running back I shall never get on. I wish I could see you all & make you acquainted with the old matronly person that now addresses you. I remember every thing connected with your beloved Family – Frank was a very lively boy & very fond of me. We have lately had a heroine in this country who professes a knowledge of the Thomond family. I hope my Mother has taken up her residence again at Bridgerule. I am sure you will be kind to her & I trust she may be comfortable. My cares are many & anxious & I have so long been deprived of assistance from any male branch of my Family that I cannot say I am comfortable or happy. Mr Macarthur has our two youngest sons with him on the Continent, where they are completing an excellent education, which their Father has been able to superintend; & where he is at the same time recovering his health which has been very much broken by the social or political conflicts in which he has in spite of himself been involved. I expect they will shortly return to this country. Glad would I be if you could see them. James I am told is an exact resemblence of what I once was. My son John who is my constant correspondent has finished his law studies & now lives in the Temple –

I know not what I can say of our mode of life that will give you a correct idea of it. It is a mixture of town & country life & yet in many respects unlike anything you can have experienced. Our climate is delightful & we have in much perfection & great abundance the Fruits of warm & cold climates. In our own Garden which is large, we have oranges, lemons, olives, almonds, grapes, peaches, apricots, nectarines, medlars, pears, apples, raspberries, strawberries, walnuts, cherries, plums. These fruits you know. Then we have the loquat, a Chinese fruit, the citron, the shaddock, the pomegranite & perhaps some others that I may have forgotten to mention such as the cherry & guava. We have an abundance, even to profusion insomuch as our Pigs are fed on peaches, apricots & melons during the season. Oranges & lemons we have the whole year round, yet there is a particular season from May to August (our winter) when the trees yield a regular crop. I have I perceive omitted to mention the Fig, of which we have many varities[sic] & an abundance. The Gooseberry & currant have not hitherto thriven at this settlement but at Van Diemen's Land they do well. We grow wheat, barley, oats, we make hay, at least I do, & so does Mrs Macquarie but the practice is not general. We feed Hogs – we have Cattle, keep a Dairy, fatten Beef & Mutton & export fine wool. A variety of avocations arising from these pursuits keeps the mind pretty busily employed. Our Society, as the Country has increased in population, has become more extended. On particular days, such as the King or Queen's birthday there are parties at Government House numbering occasionally 150 persons. I will not say that these assemblies have been very select. However there is a sufficiency of pleasant agreeable persons to visit & to be visited by; to satisfy one who is not ambitious to have a very numerous visiting acquaintance. The Regiment now stationed here is the 46th commanded by Col Molle who is also Lieut Governor. The colonel is a most accomplished, charming man, who has seen much of the world. Mrs Molle is friendly & affectionate & pretty conversant with the same sort of knowledge, but she appreciates it at its true worth. With this family we visit on easy friendly terms which is to us a great consolation. Governor Macquarie is one of the most pleasing men, but then he is the Governor & it is not possible to forget that he is so. Mrs Macquarie is very amiable, very benevolent, in short a very good woman. They have a lovely boy; now ten years old. I am at a loss to say whether this child so ardently desired, so anxiously cherished is to prove a blessing. Altho surrounded with attendants, this dear boy is scarcely ever permitted to be out of the presence of his mother.

A great extent of Territory has been discoverd in the last two years, by three Gentlemen who penetrated thro' a chain of hills which we call the 'Blue Mountains' & which were before thought impassable. The Governor has caused a road to be made which has completely opened the communication. He made an excursion to this new country & was absent an entire month. The Governor has named the chief place of settlement 'Bathurst' which is situated near a large river & upon an extensive plain. Where the river discharges itself & whether it connects itself with other waters is a subject for interesting speculation & after search. I am now reminded that I must close my letter. I hope my mother & my aunt may talk comfortably over old times . . .

God bless you my dearest Eliza,
Your affecte friend,
E.M.

Parramatta 11th December
1817

My dear Eliza

I was favoured with your letter by the *Lord Eldon* Transport, the very same vessel which restored to me your Godfather & my Husband together with our two youngest sons after a cruel separation of nine years. I am yet scarcely sensible of the extent of my happiness & indeed I can hardly persuade myself that so many of the dear Members of our Family are united again under the same roof. Mr Macarthur is occasionally afflicted with Gout, otherwise I perceive little change in him during this length of time. James & William from little boys when they left me returned fine young men James six feet high & stout withal. William more slender, but evidently giving promise of being stout also. They are delighted to return to their native land & breathe not a regret for the gay scenes of the English metropolis. Nothing they saw in France or Switzerland effaced the strong desire they had to return to their native wild woods in New South Wales. So much for the love of country.

I cannot ever express the ardent desire which I have once more to see the place of my Birth – so many & so great have been the obstacles that I have never dared to cherish the hope.

GEORGIANA MCCRAE, 1804-1890

Diarist and portrait painter, Georgiana McCrae was
the daughter of an aristocrat, and received a good
convent education. A competent linguist and musician as well as a talented artist, she initially determined to earn her living from portrait painting. But
she left her easel when she married Andrew McCrae,
and followed him to Port Phillip, where she landed
on March 1st, 1841. The demands of a husband and
ever increasing family frustrated many of her creative
aspirations but even in the most difficult of circumstances she still managed to make her diary entries.
Like so many Australian women who felt isolated
Georgiana McCrae used her diary for much more
than the keeping of a daily record; it was a means of
generating a 'conversation with self', of creating a
reflective space and of maintaining some form of
sanity.

Her journal contains many graphic descriptions of
life and society in early Melbourne; in later years,
Georgiana McCrae returned to her record and added
annotations on the way she and the place had
changed. When editing her work, Hugh McCrae
inserted his own commentary but the extracts
included here contain only the original and sup-
plementary entries of Georgiana McCrae and they
have been selected from the 1983 edition of *Georgiana's Journal, Melbourne, 1841-65*, edited by Hugh
McCrae.

27th As we were trying to enter the heads of Port Phillip, we encountered a fierce gale from the north-west. Sky as black as ink. At last we got into smoother water, and anchored off Swan Pond. On the cliff opposite, saw the foundation walls of a lighthouse. All the buoys adrift, and no pilot within hail. Captain Bunbury remarked what a fine natural position the heads afford for defence, supposing a fort on Point Nepean and a corresponding one on Point Lonsdale, and a chain sunk across the entrance to the bay. Captain Gatenby consulting the chart of the bay and sailing directions, but unwilling to risk the ship and passengers by attempting to go on without a pilot.

Sunday, 28th A clear morning. Wind still north, and fresh, On walking through the cuddy to look at the shore, I surprised Captain Gatenby and Captain Bunbury *tête-à-tête*. As I entered, the former had just said: 'The insurances will hold good', and would have added more had he not become aware of my presence. I immediately told him how much I had heard, whereupon he asked me to treat this 'as a matter, in confidence, between ourselves', and then continued: 'The anchor is dragging, and I fear we shall go stern foremost on Point Nepean. We shall be able to get ashore, but the shock of the ship striking may take you off your feet, so you'd better feign headache and go to your bed, and get the boys to lie down till the wind lulls.' I did as directed, and lay in suspense for a long time, my tin box at hand[1], ready for carrying off. As Mr Cummins had insured my passage and goods for £800 I was less anxious than I might have been. Suddenly, the wind shifted from north to south-west, and we were blown inward. At sun-down the wind fell, and we went on deck to enjoy the fresh air. The mate of a vessel on our larboard bow visited us, and told us that his ship the *Harvest Home* had been weatherbound for several days. He spoke with a Yankee accent and apologized for his captain being too 'grog-sick' to accept Gatenby's invitation.

[1] The box containing her miniatures.

Monday, 1st   Port Phillip.

At 8 a.m., after the anchor had been walked-up to the bows, Tobin, the pilot, came aboard; a man like John Flatt, dresst in a frock-coat and chimney-pot hat. He went straight to the poop, where nobody else was to remain, except Gatenby and a seaman called Adams, but, later on, the captain took George up too, and allowed him to help Adams hold the chart while Tobin steered. Thus George had his share in bring the *Argyle* into port!

About 2 p.m. we anchored in Hobson's Bay off William's Town: a collection of houses, shingled and clap-boarded, and one large stone building.

We lay alongside the *Eagle*, Captain Buckley; and the *York* (seven other ships being in the bay). Captain Gatenby gave us dessert and champagne to celebrate our arrival in Australia, with appropriate toasts. Willie completed his sixth year.

2nd   All kinds of people came on board, chiefly for the purpose of hiring servants; but our emigrants aren't yet at liberty to engage.

3rd   Our cow and calf sold for £100.

4th   Jane Shanks (the maid), the boys, and I went aboard the *Governor Arthur*, a scrubbishy [?] grinding little steamer without any cabin. Half-way up the river the rain began to fall, where-upon I extended the folds of my plaid so as to take in the children and keep them out of the wet. The boat landed us opposite the Yarra Hotel, Flinders Street, and we had to wade through mud and clay, up the hill to Dr McCrae's in Great Bourke Street West. My good London boots, *abîmés!*

7th   Attended service in the wooden church against which are the walls of the stone edifice of St James's in course of erection. In the afternoon we all attended and I stood proxy godmother for little Francis Argyle Bunbury. The clergyman, Mr A.C. Thomson, seeing the group of children gathered round the crockery basin doing duty as a 'font', supposed they were all waiting to be baptized, a natural conclusion since it's a common event for five, or more, in a family born in the bush to be baptized on their first visit to a church. The group consisted of George, eight years;

Willie, six years; Sandy, five years; Farquhar, three years; and Harry Bunbury, two years[2].

8th Went to see our new home, "Argyle Cottage", in Little Lonsdale Street West, consisting of one tolerably large room, with four closets, *called* bedrooms, opening out of it. The walls of wood, about half an inch thick, and the ceiling of the same. The building raised on stumps to about two feet from the ground, and three wooden steps, like those of a bathing-machine, lead up into a French window, which is the front door of the dwelling. At a little distance from the back door is a kitchen hut, *à rez-de-chaussée*. And for this accommodation the rent required by Mr Simpson is £100 per year!

After helping Jane to arrange as much as we could I returned to dine at Dr McCrae's, and met there the Rev. A.C. Thomson, Captain Fyans, and Mr Lloyd Jones.

9th Perambulated the town with Agnes, that is to say, we went up the north side of Collins Street, without any sign of a pavement; only a rough road, with crooked gutters – the shops, built of wood, and raised on stumps.

10th Agnes and the children came to spend the day with us at "Argyle Cottage".

11th Removed our things from Dr McCrae's, and took up our abode at "Argyle", then went to the Union Bank to verify my signature before Mr William Highett[3]. Dined at Dr McCrae's.

12th Jane and I busy all day, unpacking and arranging our cabin-gear.

13th Agnes and the children went to the Doctor's station at Dandenong. Our packages by the lighter were brought up.

14th A fine warm day. At church in the morning.

15th Thermometer 84°. Completed my thirty-seventh year. Busy all day unpacking.

16th The *Argyle* sails for Sydney tomorrow. Captain Gatenby came to say good-bye: sorry he missed the little pilot.

[2] A goodly subject for a photograph.
[3] First manager: beginning service in '38. He died wealthy, and, according to Finn, although the money was unwilled, "it found plenty of legal owners".

17th   Unpacking, arranging.

18th   Called at "Jolimont Cottage"; everything peaceful inside, but the rooms dark, on account of the trellised veranda. While I waited for Madame[4], I smelt flowers in the garden, and listened to a clock on the shelf. *Madame très aimable pour moi... et très myope.*

20th   Went for a ride to try my new saddle. Saw our allotment on the Yarra – nine acres and a half – with a river frontage, the ground thickly covered with boulders of which the house is to be built. Mem.: the direct course of the allotment from the top of Great Bourke Street – twenty-one degrees north of east.

Supplement

At this time there were no houses on the south side of Little Lonsdale Street, only a wattle-and-daub shack, built and inhabited by one, Minifie, a carpenter, and his wife. This building didn't encroach on our view across the flat to Cole's Wharf. In La Trobe Street West (behind "Argyle Cottage"), were two brick houses, numbers 144 and 146, the former occupied by Captain McLachlan and his family; opposite these houses were the Flagstaff and Observatory Hill, with graves of some of the earlier settlers. The burial-place was surrounded by a fence, six feet high, painted black – but the wild bush had penetrated inside. On the hill were she-oaks (so named on account of their likeness to American beefwood trees, called *sheacs*) which echoed the *ramage* of parrots and everywhere about the grass appeared strange flowers, some of which were yellow, while others were white, or turquoise, tinged with green.

Where now stands Hawthorn Bridge and the Punt Hotel, was formerly a road leading to Palmer's Punt, for crossing the Yarra eastward. The nearest house to "Mayfield", southward, was that of Mr Westgarth, in what is now "Menteith Place", Erwin Street. At this time, "Northumberland House" – now a ruin in Flinders Street (between Stephen and Russell streets) – was a cottage of some pretensions[5]. I was told that, in earlier days, the whole population of the settlement, about fifteen persons, had assembled there to drink tea. At the time of my arrival it was occupied by P.W. Welsh and it was there I made my *début*, at

[4] Mrs La Trobe, wife of the Superintendent of the district of Port Phillip.
[5] Stephen Street is now Exhibition Street.

a dinner given in honour of P.W. W.'s sister, after her recent marriage with Mr George Smythe.

After dinner, Mr Meek drove some of us home in his trap: a fearful experience – the horse sent at top-speed through the worst country in the world. At one minute we were completely off the ground, at the next, suddenly down again – gutters, three of four feet deep, and, everywhere, jagged tree-stumps interspersed with boulders!

Moonlight parties gave occasion for tea-drinking, and evening parties to which (since no *trottoir* existed) ladies walked in their husband's Wellingtons over their dress-shoes. During "Dark Moon" a lantern used to be carried in advance by a servant, or one of the gentlemen. Even so late as 1850, Bishop Perry's literary butler used to precede his master, on his return from St Peter's to Jolimont (after Sunday evening service), with a lantern-and-candle.

(1841)

Potatoes at this time cannot be had for less than 6d. per lb.; carrots, turnips, onions, etc., are brought across from Van Diemen's Land[6] and cabbages, grown here, cost 9d. for a very small one. Bream is the only fish I have yet seen. A fisherman comes around occasionally with a basket of these which he takes in the salt-water river.

Water is conveyed from the Yarra in a large barrel mounted on a dray. These loads cost from seven to fifteen shillings, barely enough for a week's supply.

Fortune-du-pot dinners, which were then the vogue, tried my patience and ingenuity. Mutton and beef were to be had at moderate prices, but vegetables and fruit were costly, having to be imported from Launceston. Poultry was exceedingly scarce, and at exorbitant prices. My ever-ready help was Mrs Howe, our baker's wife. Mrs Howe had been a housekeeper in Yorkshire, and, ordinarily, she used to particularize in beef-steak puddings; but when her "big boy" shot a spur-winged plover on the swamp, she would be "brought to table of a game-pie" (Captain Fyans's phrase) – according to Mr McCrae's wish. (The beef-steak puddings cost 5s. each, the pies 7s.) Tarts were out of the question, but, as Ellen always had capital soup ready, we managed pretty well. How she managed to cook at the clumsy fire-hole in the kitchen-hut was a mystery!

6. Called after Anthony Van Diemen, Governor General of the Dutch East Indies, but changed to Tasmania in '55 and '56.

Sold my staircase-carpeting brass rods and eyes to the Port Phillip club for £9 – just what they cost in London. They offer me £26 for my dining-table, and Mr McCrae thinks the Singapore one might do us in the meantime. But I'm resolved not to give up my five-leaved table. Thomas and Stribling were engaged at the current wage to build the house. Thomas, a married man, with three children. Stribling, single, a carpenter.

April

6th   The *Eagle* sailed with our letters for England.

8th   Rain falling in torrents.

9th   Willie laid up with fever, also Jenny. Dr McCrae attending them during the day.

May

3rd   Rode out to fix the site for our house at Carroncarrondall.

5th   Not well. Fainted at tea time.

9th   Dr McCrae to dinner. I fainted in the evening.

11th   Busy drawing the plan and elevation of our house.

15th   Mr Montgomery to dinner.

16th   Mr Elliot Heriot to dinner. During his visit a gale came on with deluging rain which rendered the flat impassable on foot, so that I had to improvise a bed for our guest in the sitting-room.

22nd   A *triste* visit from Agnes McCraw. "All is not gold that glisters." Mr Highett and Mr Ephraim Howe to dinner.

23rd   Tremendous showers of rain. Elizabeth Locke, Mrs Sconce's servant, baptized by the Rev. James Forbes.

30th   A shock of earthquake, while we were in church, made the Rev. Mr Thomson pause in the prayers. The sensation was like when the chain cable runs down and the ship gives a jump. Mr McCrae and Dr McCrae felt the shock while they were walking at Dandenong at the same hour.

June

3rd   The *Duchess of Sutherland* arrived. Captain McCrae landed in the evening and visited us.

4th   Dr McCrae, Agnes, Thomas Anne[7], and I went on board the ship to pay our return-calls to Mrs McCrae. Mrs Thomas, not approving of Mrs M. (tho' of good yeoman ancestry) stayed away. We brought back with us the Captain's children, Maggie, George, and Aleck[8].

5th   Dined at Dr McCrae's, with Captain McCrae and Elliot Heriot.

8th   Little Maggie went home to her mama.

10th   Mr McCrae boarded the *Freshfield*, and hired Ellen Hume as cook, on the recommendation of the ship's doctor. Ellen is from Donegal, and lived in Glasgow with a Mrs Campbell.

11th   Mrs Sconce gave birth to a daughter.

12th   Dinner at Dr McCrae's, and musical evening.

24th   Mr McCrae engaged Robert Lowry, also passenger on the *Freshfield*, as our house-servant.

27th   Mr Deane sent us a native turkey, and invited himself to dine with us. In the evening, another present – a kangaroo tail – arrived from Captain Reid.

28th   Mr John Reeve, from Gippsland, came to early dinner. As he is interested in art, I had great pleasure in showing him my prints and paintings.

30th   Went to town. Met Captain and Mrs Bunbury, and she returned with me to taste the kangaroo soup. We both agreed that, *to our taste*, ox-tail is a superior article. Mr Montgomery, Lauchlan Mackinnon, and the Rev. James Clow to dinner.

July

1st   Took the boys down early to Dr Thomas's to spend the day, as Jane and Ellen wish to carry out a thorough cleaning and re-arrangement of the furniture.

---

[7] Agnes, the doctor's wife; Thomas Anne, the doctor's sister.
[8] Dr McCrae was the son, and Thomas Anne was the daughter, of William Gordon McCrae, of Westbrook, near Edinburgh, Scotland. The doctor, who had been surgeon in the 5th Dragoon Guards, the Inniskillings, arrived in Australia by the *Midlothian* (Captain Morrison): the first ship to come direct to Melbourne.

2nd   Mr and Mrs George Smythe to dinner.

5th   Mr Wentworth, from Vaucluse; P. W. Welsh, and Mrs Meek to dinner.

8th   A lovely morning. Walked to Newtown and had luncheon with Mrs Sconce, and, afterwards, called on Mrs Woolley, Mrs G. Smythe, and Mrs McLachlan.

9th   Pouring rain: a day of rest and needlework. Willie and Farquhar have severe colds.

Sunday, 11th   Captain and Mrs Bunbury came to luncheon. In the afternoon we all went to church to meet the Sconces; I stood proxy for Miss Limond as godmother to Madeline Sconce.

12th   Robert Lowry left with a load of timber, from Mr Kemmis, for Thomas and Stribling to put up huts for themselves, and a stable for the horses.

August

1st   Dr Nicholson will allow Mr McCrae to include the reserve for a road to a future bridge within the fencing of our acres. Learnt that Harry, the bullock-driver, had betted £3 on the fight that came off today during the time of morning service!

2nd   Mr McLure, the boys' tutor (that is to be), came to dine with us. He appears to be fond of young children and has a pleasant way with them. In the evening, an exciting scene took place between Parson Thomson, Sandy Hunter, young Patterson, and young Kennedy – the parson armed with a long pole, and the youths with palings driving intruders out of the cabbage-garden.

3rd   Mr Lawlor came to have a long talk with me.

4th   Dr McCrae completes his thirty-fifth year.

5th   Incessant rain. Grievous for the emigrants camped in miserable thin tents exposed to the south-west wind, while the flats are dotted all over with pools of water. Yesterday, a woman drowned herself in the river, from sheer despair.

6th   Went to the bank for my half-year's pay; quite knocked up on my return from wading through the mud; and my boots – *abîmés*.

7th   Wrote letters for England. Mr and Mrs Browne and Mr Lawlor to dinner. Charmed with Mr B.'s description of the Sandwich Islands.

8th   Mr Goldsmith and Mr Browne to dinner.

9th   Captain Bunbury and Dr Myer to luncheon.

10th   Mr Wentworth called to say good-bye as he was leaving for Sydney. Mr Highett and his brother John came to dinner.

11th   Mr Horsman to dinner. Willie not well. The *Adelaide* sailed with our letters.

12th   A fine frosty morning. The foundation walls of our house at "Mayfield" duly laid.

13th   Busy making suits of tartan for the boys.

14th   The boys suffering from the effects of their damp room. Mr Vignolles, Mr Rawson, and Mr O. Browne to dinner.

15th   Dr Myer brought news that Baby Bunbury is very ill, at Darebin, from teething.

16th   Dr Thomas came to see the boys.

17th   Pouring rain. Completed the tartan suits.

20th   Walked to Spence's to buy bargains of drapery brought from his old shop at Edinburgh. The footpaths were terrible, and the road, all the way, like a bullock-yard.

21st   Poor Baby Bunbury past recovery.

No Date. One day I perceived Major St John riding across the flat towards "Argyle Cottage" with what, at first sight, appeared to be a large green parrot held hawkwise on his wrist. On his arrival at the gate, the major flourished a fine full-grown Cos lettuce in his hand, exclaiming: "One of the first of the kind raised in Port Phillip!" – the lettuce, not inferior to a prime Covent Garden specimen, bound round the middle with a band of grass. A most acceptable present, recalling the green stuff we had been accustomed to have in profusion at Stockwell.

24th   The boys and I went to the burying-ground, to meet the Bunburys who came in their spring-cart with dear little Frankie's coffin. After the burial, the Bunburys drove up to "Stanney", and the Rev. Mr Thomson accompanied us home and stayed to early dinner. Dr McCrae and Agnes came in the evening. Mrs Myer gave birth to a son – her first child.

25th   Mrs and Miss Macarthur, Mrs Thomas, James Grahame and Thomas Anne took me for a long walk in the bush.

26th   Hot wind. The boys and I walked to town.

27th   Mr McLeod and Thomas Anne to dinner. At night, squalls of wind and rain.

28th   Dr McCrae looking ghastly. Thermometer 48°, while yesterday it was up to 65°. A package of vine cuttings arrived from Mr Wentworth, for planting at "Mayfield".

31st   Thermometer 54°. Mr and Mrs Lawlor came to say good-bye, as they resume their voyage tomorrow.

September

3rd   Major Webb and his son to lunch; Captain Webster, Mrs Campbell, George Weir and Mr Goldsmith to dine with us.

4th   Our dog "Pepper" went off (chain, collar, etc.) to hunt ducks and "soldier". Late at evening he came back, shot in the chest and head.

7th   Farquhar's third birthday. Jenny McCrae came to dine with him, and Aunt Agnes gave him a beautiful copy of *Paul and Virginia*, in English, with illustrations.

11th   During a heavy squall the boys' room window was blown in, while the rain poured into the servants' room. The parrot's cage upset, but Ellen rescued the bird from drowning, and nailed a packing-case lid across the boys' window for the night.

14th   Busy cutting out and making chair-covers.

18th   Still very boisterous weather.

19th   Heavy storm of thunder and lightning and rain, with a gale of wind that made the house quiver and creak, the glasses on the shelf ringing with every detonation – then hailstones clattering across the roof to the terror of the children. About 4 a.m. the storm abated.

20th   Mr Octavius Browne and Hunter Ross to dinner. Another night of fearful wind from south-west. Sleep out of question.

23rd   Blowing strong from north. Thermometer 64°. The sky livid. The yard of the flagstaff was unshipped today. [*The flagstaff, on Flagstaff Hill.*]

25th   Captain Lewis, harbour-master, Neil Black, and Captain McLachlan to dinner.

26th   The bullocks let into the garden at "Mayfield", and many cauliflowers and strawberries destroyed. Harry suspected of having done this to spite Osmond the gardener.

30th   Mr O. Browne gave me a sitting for his portrait to send home. He is a brother of Habelot Knight Browne (*Phiz*), the artist who illustrated Dickens's works.

October

1st   Thunder and rain until past 5 p.m.

2nd   Mr Jones Agnew Smith, John McLeod, and Mr O. Browne to dinner.

4th   Martha Cummins twenty-five today. Second sitting from Mr O. Browne.

5th   Mr O. Browne to breakfast. Afterwards, a most satisfactory three hours' sitting.

7th   Mr Browne rode with us to "Mayfield"; the workmen were raising the rooftree – the chimneys, within four feet of their full height. Didn't return till past seven. Mr McCrae pressed Mr B. to take "pot luck" with us; and very bad luck it was. Mr Browne began, like a farmer, drinking his soup with great *éclaboussement*, until he tasted it burnt, when he sent it away. Being half famished, I made my own share palatable with wine.

8th   Busy writing letters for Sydney.

9th   Lovely morning. Saw the smoke from the steamer at Cole's Wharf, and the boys mounted towels on tall sticks by way of farewell signals to their friend "Okitawia Paraone" (Octavius Browne) . . . New Zealanders' pronunciation.

10th   Unpacked George's trowsers – the ones I had made in London: found them already two inches too short.

11th Arranging bills and inventories. Thomas Anne came to tell me that Captain Cole had offered to marry her; she seemed undecided, and was eager for advice. Harry upset our dray and broke it. Mr McLure returned the books he had borrowed, and stayed to dine with us.

14th Visited the Sconces. Robin to be ordained by Bishop Broughton. He was eligible for a fellowship at the time of his marriage; but "fellows" must be bachelors! I feel sad at losing Lizzie.

16th Thermometer 82°. A delightful day. At dinner-time the famous "overlander", Mr Murchison, came in. A sitting from Mr Sconce: to be a present for his sister-in-law, Miss Repton.

20th Another delicious day. I feel all alive.!

21st Thermometer 84°. Sent Jenny Sutherland to learn dressmaking from Mrs Osmond, the gardener's wife.

22nd The first *Quarterly Assembly Ball* to take place this evening.

November

1st A fine clear day. Completed my small needlework.

2nd Hot wind – then thunder with rain. At noon thermometer 85°, and all night at 72°. The closeness of the house and the heat of its wooden walls quite stifling.

3rd Thermometer 75°. Lizzie Cobham and Thomas Anne; also Mr Heriot, and his newly-arrived brother, Ancrum Heriot; and young Baillie Polkemmet to dinner.

4th Final sitting from Mr Sconce, as Mrs Sconce won't allow me to put another touch to the picture, which she considers "perfect", and, as I have painted it *con amore*, I feel pretty well satisfied.

15th Hot wind. Thermometer 85°. Busy writing home. The horse in Pickett's water-cart bolted past the house, with the hose down behind . . . and the water dashing out in the middle of the street.

19th The "Bizzwizzes" (cicadae) making a deafening noise in the gum-trees. George brought two into the house to add to the racket.

Went, *en masse*, on board the *Aphrasia*, to bid good-bye to Robin and Lizzie Sconce.

20th   Thermometer, at noon, 78°. Jane Shanks and Farquhar spent the day at Newtown.

23rd   Captain Fyans and Mr Clark, nephew of Talbot de Mala-hide, to dinner. In the evening, Mrs Thomas, Lizzie, and Thomas Anne to tea: the captain unaware of a rival in the field.

26th   After an early dinner, Mr McCrae started off with Tom Clark on a shooting expedition.

27th   The boys accompanied me to Aunt Maggie's. Heard from her of Thomas Anne's deadly quarrel with Dr McCrae.

Sunday, 28th   Neither Dr McCrae, nor Agnes, at church.

30th   Thomas Anne came to spend the day, and told me her griefs . . . Sandy five years old today.
   Mr McCrae dined at the club. Thermometer 74° with hot wind. Heard distant rolling thunder, or noise underground.

December

1st   First anniversary of Margaret's marriage with Dr Thomas. Mr John Mundy (from Hobart) to tea.

2nd   Lizzie Cobham came to stay with us. Mr McCrae brought Mark Nicholson, a cousin of Dr Cobham's[9] to dinner. I noticed that Mark and Lizzie met as if they had often seen each other elsewhere; wagered Mr McCrae a pair of white gloves that it would be a match, but he pooh-poohed the idea[10].

3rd   Sandy crying for a glass of water, and not a drop to be had . . . Mr McCrae tells me he saw the driver of the[11] cart outside Jemmy Connell's, at twelve o'clock, and then, again, between two and three[12]. Thomas Anne disposed to take my advice, i.e. to accept Captain Cole's offer.

[9] And future M.L.C.
[10] Nicholson occupied Garvoc, in the western district, Panmure, and Cudgee, stretching out so far as Craigieburn. Then, about '49, he bought Wangoom for Manning brothers.
[11] Water.
[12] Jemmy Connell's: Highlandmand Hotel.

4th Thermometer 75°. Thomas and Stribling admit their inability to have the house ready before two or three weeks to come.

6th A letter from Miss Quarry, per *Brankenmoore*, recommending the bearer, Miss Julia Gavan, to our good offices and protection; she and her sister wish to be employed as governesses.

7th Wrote to Miss Julia Gavan, inviting her to come to us until she can find a suitable situation. Mrs Montgomery has engaged Miss Anne; and Miss Emily is engaged by the Thomases at Heidelberg.

9th Lizzie, the boys, and I spent an hour in Mr Carfrae's shop inspecting the fine books brought by him from Edinburgh. Saw Mr Fawkner traipse into the street.

10th Farquhar suffering from an eruption on his face . . . Dr Thomas tells me it is called, in colonial talk, "Dibble-dibble" – a kind of confluent pock – much uglier, and more offensive, even than smallpox. Cloths wetted with diluted chloride of lime must be kept constantly on the child's face to prevent the pock from spreading.

11th Thomas Anne has accepted Captain Cole's offer. Thermometer 80°. She and all the clan go tonight to Mr D. C. Macarthur's ball. Heard of the death of a son of Gordon of Cairnbuly. Had I known the poor fellow came from Sydney among utter strangers his father's son should have had proper attention. Captain Smith of the *Brankenmoore* came early with Miss Julia Gavan. Thermometer 80°, and, in the evening, it rose to 95° with not a breath of air stirring.

13th I engaged the two front rooms at Landall's for one month, at £1 per week, for Jane and the children to sleep there. In the evening, removed my own particular luggage and slept at Landall's.

15th Thermometer 103°. By advice of Captain McLachlan, who lived in Sicily with his regiment, I rolled myself in a blanket and lay outside my bed, to deep cool, until 4 p.m., when a furious storm of wind and rain cooled the air most rapidly.

16th A fine fresh morning. Thermometer 72°. Sponged the boys with vinegar and water. Farquhar's face better.

17th Captain Cole sent invitations to everybody to attend his picnic at Brighton Beach on Tuesday next . . . The match now openly talked of in town.

20th   Looking out things for Thomas Anne's *trousseau*, since the captain begs her to name an early day for their wedding.

21st   Dr and Mrs Myer arrived in their carriage to take me to the picnic, but, on account of the wild-appearing sky, I elected to stay at home, and it was well I did, because at three o'clock a southerly gale sprang up, which continued until five, with such hurricane force that the gentlemen of the party had to hold on to the tent with all their might to keep the canvas from being blown away. Returning at dusk, there were upsets and bruises, even broken limbs . . . yet the Myers and our people escaped unhurt.

22nd   Cutting out work, with Miss Gavan to help me, for our new house, but *je ne suis pas en train aujourd'hui!*

23rd   Lizzie Cobham and I went to Mrs Thomas on purpose to consult with her about the wedding arrangements . . . In the evening, Captain Cole: deafer than usual, and, *en consequence*, most irascible.

25th   Christmas Day: Captain Smith came early for Miss Julia Gavan, and Lizzie Cobham went to keep her engagement at Dr McCrae's.

26th   Frank Cobham returned from the bush, and I engaged Eliza Impey in Jenny Sutherland's stead.

27th   Mr Archibald Cunninghame, of Caddell, to dinner. In the evening I wrote to Mr Crawley a list of commissions for his friend to execute for the bride; at night, tired and breathless.

28th   Robert Lowry brought in a load of firewood from the allotment, and took out some of our packing-cases, and the rabbit-hutch. Thermometer 64°. Lizzie Cobham off to Dr McCrae's picnic at the Moonee Ponds. Thomas Anne and Mr John Mundy came to our early dinner. Captain Cole, to tea, and whether for the sake of prolonging his stay beside his lady-love, or from actual thirst, he took no less than *nine* of our small tea-cups full of tea. While pouring out the seventh cup I could hardly conceal the effects of a twinge of pain, but the captain and Thomas Anne didn't make a move till 10 p.m. The moment they were gone, I hurried off to my room at Landall's and sent Jane for Dr Myer (his house at the end of Great Bourke Street East – Gardner's Cottages). Soon after eleven, Jane and the doctor arrived. At 3 a.m. I gave birth to a fine girl.[13] The doctor, on his way home, tapped at the window of Mr McCrae's bedroom, and told him what had happened while he had been asleep.

29th   Thermometer 85°. My kind neighbour, Mrs McLachlan, came over and took away the boys to spend the day with her family. At night the thermometer fell to 60°.

30th   The boys all day with Mrs McLachlan.

31st   Again the boys go to play with the McLachlan children.

[13] Her first Australian baby: "and it thrave weel, for it sookit weel."

LOUISA ANNE MEREDITH, 1812-1895

Before embarking for Australia in 1839, Louisa Anne
Twamley had already established herself in Birmingham as a writer and artist of renown. With her
passionate interest in botany, and her talent for
description in literary and artistic form, she made a
superb chronicler of the flora, fauna, and the society,
in the colony. The illustrator of some of her own
volumes of poetry and travel, she earnt great praise
for her exquisite paintings of plants and animals, as
well as for her prose. Probably Australia's first
professional woman writer, and the only person to
be awarded a literary pension by the Tasmanian
Government, Louisa Anne Meredith made her
colonial name with *Notes and Sketches of New South
Wales During a Residence in that Colony from
1839-1844* (which was first published in 1844 and ran
into many editions and is now available in Penguin
Australian Women's Library). This was followed by
*My Home in Tasmania, During a Residence of Nine
Years* (1852) and the intention was, as the author
explains in the preface, to provide an English
audience with an accurate and entertaining account
of Tasmanian life. Apart from describing the realities
and difficulties of every day, Louisa Anne Meredith
comments on some of the problems that plagued the
professional writer in colonial times.

One of the most significant and the most neglected
of early Australian writers, Louisa Anne Meredith
remained active in literary and botanical circles until

her death; conservationist, social commentator and
children's writer, her work was well known 'at home'
and 'abroad'. The following extract, from *My Home
in Tasmania During A Residence of Nine Years* has
been taken from the 1852 edition published by John
Murray, London. In it, not only does she describe
the dangers of travel, the delights of Hobart, the distinct advantages of the convict and the servant
system, but Louisa Anne Meredith also provides one
of the first descriptions of the Australian barbeque.

CHAPTER I

*Departure from Sydney – The 'Sir George Arthur' – An Arrest –
Colonial Craftsmen – Opposite Neighbours – 'Dick' – Hippolyte
Rocks – Cape Pillar – Tasman's Island – Cape Raoul.*

The concluding paragraph of my gossiping chronicle of experiences in New South Wales mentioned our departure from Sydney
on our way to Van Diemen's Land; and I now resume the slender
thread of my story where I then broke off.[1]

I returned to the morning of our embarkation, when, in a straggling procession, including the baby, the new nursemaid, the old
pointer, and sundry of our goods and chattels on trucks and hand-
barrows (the main body having been previously shipped), we
proceeded to the jetty, and bade adieu to the friends who came
'to see us out of sight.' I must confess that I felt less regret than
I could have believed possible, at leaving a country which had
been my home for above a year; and if a wistful thought did stray
back to the bright and beautiful gardens, the lovely wild flowers,
the delicious fruits, and the deep blue sky of the ever-brown land,
such a thick hot cloud of dust, flies, mosquitoes, and other detesta-
bilities, rose in imagination before me, as threw a veil over all
such charms; and I parted from them with a stout heart, full of
hopefulness for the future, and rejoicing, above all things, to take
our baby-boy into a more temperate climate, where the fair

[1]Notes and Sketches of New South Wales, during a Residence in that Colony
from 1839 to 1844. London. Murray, 1849.

promise of his infancy might have some prospect of being realized in a life of health, strength, and intelligence.

His good kind-hearted nurse (who, being married, could not leave the colony with us) stood sobbing most piteously as her little charge was borne away in the arms of a stranger, whose domestic ties were as yet unformed, she being a starch, prim spinster, desirous of seeing as much of the world as possible, and of showing it a very tasteful wardrobe in return. I, too, grieved to lose my old servant, for she was as cheerful, willing, earnest, and simple a creature as I ever knew; albeit not perhaps the most dainty waiting-woman in the world – for, to hear her footsteps in the house, one might fancy some tame elephant was pacing about, and I had often found reason to rejoice that all the rooms at Homebush were on the ground-floor – but she was so affectionate and good, that I should have been well pleased if her heavy footsteps could still have followed our own. She had odd quaint notions and expressions, too, that were very droll, uttered as they were with such earnest seriousness. She told me once, that her former master 'was a very learned gentleman, a great scholar – so clever at preaching and doctoring, and talking languages of foreign parts. Indeed, ma'am, he did serve his time at Cambridge College for a parson, only he didn't never take no sort of sitiwation after.'

The vessel had dropped down the stream, and was anchored some distance below the town; and when, at the end of our long pull, we came alongside, the aspect of the *Sir George Arthur* was anything but inviting. (Why will people persist in giving male names to ships?) She, that is, *Sir George*, had been employed in the coal-trade between Sydney and the mines at Newcastle, on the Hunter River, and bore as evident marks of her sooty calling as ever did an old coal-boat on the Birmingham Canal; whilst the air sweeping round her wafted over us a veritable coal-smoke odour, full of murky reminiscences of the good old town. There she lay – as ugly, ill-shapen, slovenly, dirty, black, disreputable-looking a tub as ever sullied the bright blue waves of old Neptune. However, as our present lot was cast in her – no other vessel for Hobarton offering at the time – we went on board the misshapen craft, which seemed to have been built as much as possible after the model of a brewer's vat. The deck was as dirty as the rest, and my cabin, which was tolerably large and convenient, so swarmed with wood-lice that I soon began to have a tolerably vivid idea of another of the plague of Egypt, that of flies having been fully realized during our sojourn in Sydney.

Whilst we were at dinner, a slight disturbance arose from the abrupt entrance of certain subordinate members of the legal profession in search of some considerate friend, who no doubt wished to spare them the pain of parting, and had therefore quietly shipped himself without the ceremonies of leave-taking, unless taking French leave may be so considered; but the affectionate interest of such friends is not easily eluded, and the poor young man was finally compelled to forego his humane intentions, and return to shore with his *friends*, despite the most vehement protestations that he was somebody else.

I had hoped to have been able to remain on deck until we had fairly passed through those great gates, the North and South Heads, and could look back on the grand entrance to Port Jackson which had so delighted me a year before; and many were the subtle deceptions I practised on myself as to the real nature of the indescribable symptoms which were gradually and horribly creeping over me – but all would not do; the approaching misery made a stride with every roll and lurch of the vessel, and a positive leap when she 'went about.' My love for the picturesque waned most lamentably, and I stowed away my sketch-book as an useless incumbrance: cliffs, woods, snow-white beaches, and blue waves were at a deplorable discount, and all sea scenery was so distasteful to me, that I retreated to my berth.

Servants who are engaged to go a sea voyage always declare themselves quite indifferent to sea-sickness – 'never were the least ill all the way from England' – and so protested my new maid; but she proved after all to be quite as poor a sailor as myself. I was compelled, therefore, to make some exertions in taking care of my little boy, who appeared happily unconscious of the prevailing indisposition.

Having a fair and sufficient wind, we expected to have made a quick passage; but, owing to the vessel being (in strict accordance with the usual colonial style of that period) only half-rigged, and wanting top-gallant and studding sails, she progressed very slowly. A singular disinclination to finish any work completely, is a striking characteristic of colonial craftsmen, at least of the 'currency'², or native-born portion. Many of them who are clever, ingenious, and industrious, will begin a new work, be it ship, house, or other erection, and labour as it most assiduously until it is about two-thirds completed, and then their energy seems spent, or they grow weary of the old occupation, and some new affair is set about as busily as the former one, which, meanwhile, lingers on in a comfortless, helpless, useless condition, till another change comes over the mind of the workman, and he perhaps returns to the old work, to which, if a house, he does just enough to enable the impatient proprietors to occupy it; or if a ship, for it to go to sea in a half-fledged condition, which is rarely improved afterwards.

The thoughtful kindness of an old friend of Mr. Meredith's had supplied us with some new novels, as suitable provision for the voyage, and when the horrible sea-sickness had subsided into its second stage of half-dead, half-dreamy, and wholly deplorable stupor and helplessness, I lay and beguiled the weary time by the fictitious miseries of the heroines; though, as their narrated afflictions all happened on dry land, I fear my sympathy was of a very niggardly order, perhaps closely verging on the envious.

Unlike our snug apartment in the *Letitia*, our present rooms were entered from the mess-cabin, the upper portion of the sliding door and a window frame beside it being fitted with Venetian shutters, which, as they could not by any device be induced to shut close, were a perpetual annoyance, and kept my ingenuity constantly at work, devising stratagems to complete the concealment they refused to afford, – but we could not block them wholly, for want of air.

My opposite neighbours naturally attracted some of my attention and interest, as I lay contemplating the outer world of the mess-cabin through the chinks in my shutters. The lady had, like myself, been invisible for some days, but her indefatigable lord was all that time a prey to the most alarming excitement, darting constantly in and out of her cabin in a most distracting manner, and keeping the slide-door vibrating to and fro like a pendulum. Any one who has ever seen a boy with a live mouse

² *currency:* means native-born, as distinct from *sterling*, meaning British-born.

in his hat, covered over with an outspread handkerchief, and remembers the nervous twitchings up of the corner to peep in, and the spasmodic hiding-up again, lest the mouse should jump out, may imagine the daily process of my worthy neighbour 'over the way'. Fifty times a day would he dart out, shove the door violently to – at the imminent peril of his fingers – and after making various stages of one, two, and three yards towards the companion stairs, rush frantically back again, and bolt the door inside in a most decided manner, always limiting the aperture to the smallest possible space that he could thrust himself through, and doing all with the greatest noise possible, until my sufferings from these shocks became so intense, that I could not help pitying those of the young wife to whose solace and benefit they were especially dedicated.

In a berth a little beyond this abode the master of the vessel, the 'captain,' who had remained there invisible for some days, whether really indisposed, or only indisposed to do his duty, I cannot determine; but certain it is, that he refused to go on deck, or to take any part in the command, further than by receiving and giving messages in his cabin. The crew were an idle unruly set, not more than one or two among them knowing anything of seamanship, and those very little; and the owner of the whole concern being on board, chose to stand at the wheel himself a part of each day, and with a knowing wink to such of the passengers as he took into his confidence, informed them that 'the captain's orders *was*, that the wessel should be steered south half west, but I've kep' her away a point or two to the west,' – which accounted for our being rather close in-shore, and must have contributed greatly to assist the invisible captain in determining the ship's position and course. We were fortunate in having had fine weather hitherto.

In condemning the idleness of the crew and servants on board, I must make one memorable exception. There was a smart, active, good-natured boy, about ten or twelve years old, who, if ever ubiquity fell to the lot of mortal form, possessed that property; he was everywhere, doing everything for everybody, and apparently in at least three places at the same time: –

'Dick! take Mr. Smith some hot water.'

'Dick! Mr. Jones wants his coat brushed.'

'Dick! bring a light in the cabin.'

'Dick! go and swab the deck.'

'Dick! peel them 'taturs for cook.'

'Dick! you lazy scoundrel – steward says you've not cleaned his knives.'

'Dick! go and water the sheep' (a whole flock formed part of the cargo).

'Dick! go and help reef topsails.'

'Dick! feed the geese.'

'Dick! take these bones to my dog,' &c., &c., &c.

The cry of Dick – Dick – Dick resounded all day long, and poor Dick seemed really to execute all the multifarious orders given him, with the most unflinching alacrity and good humour. One day Mr Meredith inquired of the owner, if the ubiquitous Dick was an apprentice in the ship. 'Why, no,' drawled forth the broad burly personage addressed; and then he added, with a slow smile overspreading and widening his ample countenance, – 'No – he aint a 'prentice, he's a nevy o' mine, as come aboard for a holiday!'

Alas! for poor relations!

I began to make a 'rule-of-three' statement of the question – if in a cruize [*sic*] for a holiday, Dick has harder work and rougher usage than any other creature on board, required the amount of Dick's sufferings at school? – but my heart failed me – I could not work the sun; and I comfort myself in the thought, that whatever vagrant propensities might attack Dick in subsequent holidays, he would not be likely to indulge them by a voyage with his uncle.

As we neared Cape Pillar, on the tenth day of the voyage, I made an heroic effort to leave my berth, and went on deck for the first time since passing the Heads. Shortly after I had taken my place (on a comfortable steady hen-coop), and had begun to enjoy my return to the upper air and the exhilarating scene around me, a great sensation seemed to arise in the small community – servants ran about and knocked up against each other in the ortho-dox way of people who wish to show that they have no time to lose – then they dived into the cabin in an agitated and impor-tant manner – presently they reappeared, one with a cushion, another with a basket, a third with a cloak – and after spread-ing these about, all again plunged violently below. Another charge accomplished the conveyance on deck of an umbrella, a pillow, a shawl, a book, and another umbrella. Then came, in more slow and stately fashion, bobbing up gradually and fitfully out of the companion, a large easy chair, in and about and round which, as the nucleus of the whole, the other movables were carefully disposed, and both umbrellas opened ready for active service. Finally, after another pause, heralded by a servant, half carried by her vigilant spouse, and followed by two more servants, came the pretty young lady herself, thickly veiled and folded in multitudinous envelopes. She was presently seated in the easy chair, her feet raised on a second chair, and the two umbrellas so carefully arranged that she became again invisible, and my valiant resolve of tottering across the deck, to offer her the common civilities natural between such partners in calamity (our respective husbands being on the most amicable passenger terms) was fairly and finally extinguished. I felt wholly unequal to the perilous task of storming such a citadel of exclusiveness, and remained faithful to my hen-coop and more accessible acquaintances.

It was a most beautiful afternoon, sunny and pleasant, with a fair breeze, and, as we sailed along the picturesque coast of Tasmania, the deep bays, rocky headlands, and swelling hills, formed a charming panorama, which I roughly and hastily sketched as we glided past. The white-cliffed Hippolyte Rocks, commonly called by colonial seamen the 'Epaulettes,' rising squarely, like masses of neat masonry above the sea, had exactly the appearance of a fort, and I almost expected to discern a flag floating over them, or to be startled by the flash and boom of a cannon from their snow-white walls; but a flight of sea-birds rising from the summit was the only token of living residents that the formidable rocks displayed.

The southern promontory of Fortesque Bay appeared to be entirely composed of upright basaltic columns, some of them standing alone, like tall obelisks, but the greater number forming groups of mimic towers and chimneys. The coast rises considerably towards the south, where the mountain-range terminates abruptly in the Cape Pillar, a grand basaltic precipice, or rather an assemblage of precipices, which, seen from the sea, every moment assume some new and more picturesque aspect. Separated from the mainland only by a strait of half a mile in width is Tasman's Island, a scarcely less striking feature in this most grand scenery than the Cape Pillar. Like it, the island is composed of basaltic columns, though on a less stupendous scale, but exceedingly fantastic in form, particularly on the southern side, where the taper spires and pinnacles seem a part of some ancient Gothic edifice, some 'Lindisfarne' or 'Tintern' of bygone glory; whilst, as we gained a broader view of the cape, it assumed the appearance of a fortification – a wall and seaward tower at the north-east end being singularly well defined. When parallel with the strait, we gained through it a fine view of another high basaltic promontory, Cape Raoul, the entrance to Port Arthur being between the two; but this was soon lost, and the island seemed to fold in, as it were, with the westerly cliffs of the cape, until in a south view they formed one towering stupendous mass of dark rocks, most richly tinged with the changeful rose-colour, and purple, and gold of the sunset's glorious hues, which shone forth in still greater lustre from contrast with the deep chasms and ravines which were in almost black shadow, and with the white crested billows of the blue sea, that dashed their glittering spray high over the broken crags. It was a scene never to be forgotten! I have heard much of the grandeur of the 'North Cape' at midnight; but I would not lose my memory of Cape Pillar at sunset for all the icy glitter of that more renowned scene.

One great omission in my meagre descriptive sketch I must here supply, and insert the 'figures,' which well sustained their share in the beauty of the scene. These were a very elegant-looking (but I have no doubt a very dirty and disagreeable) little schooner, which, as she kept still closer in-shore than our shapeless unwieldy vessel could do, gave that life and interest to the sea portion of our view, which a sailing vessel always affords; distance lending enough of enchantment to romancify the veriest tub that ever swam, if her sails look white in the sunshine; and the swarming clouds of 'mutton-birds' continually rising from the sea, where they had floated unobserved, or flying, dipping, swimming, and diving all around us – these would alone have furnished me with ample amusement; as it was, I felt quite busy with so much to enjoy, and only seemed to fear that I could not look about with enough energy to observe everything.

CHAPTER II

Night Alarm – Squall – Storm Bay – Lose Topmasts – Approach to Hobarton – Cast Anchor – Mount Wellington – Scenery round Newtown – Gardens – Hobarton Society – Theatre – Melodramas.

I had been asleep some hours that night, when I was awakened by a strange and terrific noise; and instantly knew, though I had never heard the sound before, that it was the violent flapping of a sail blown out of the ropes. Another and another quickly followed, and buffeted about with a noise like thunder; and the added hubbub of voices and hurried footsteps on deck told me that some serious disaster had occurred. I thought, with fear and trembling, of the iron-bound coast which I had seen so near to us at sunset, and for once found no comfort in my husband's attempts to reassure me, when I knocked at the bulk-head of his cabin to know what was the matter, but helplessly wept over my sleeping baby, expecting each moment some fearful crisis; nor did my instinctive terror much exaggerate the peril we were in. The captain of the vessel had scarcely been seen out of his berth since the day we sailed, and with only half a crew, and those very ignorant of their duty, it may well be imagined that the ship could not at any time be properly worked; but on this particular night, although bad weather had been anticipated, only one man and a boy composed the 'watch'; and both these were shut up in the caboose drinking coffee, when a violent squall struck the vessel, with all her canvas set, blew the sails from the bolt-ropes, and threatened to end our voyage somewhat speedily on the rocks of Cape Raoul, where several vessels with every soul on board had perished before. The night was dark, with a dense fog, and the cliffs were *only a mile to leeward.*

I believe we owe our lives, so far as mortal aid availed, to the promptitude and skill of one of the passengers, Captain Millett (master of an American merchantman), who, when the squall struck the vessel, rushed on deck, and gave all the necessary orders and assistance to restore something like discipline amidst the confusion and riot on board.

At last, for I thought that dreadful night was interminable, the morning dawned; – we were in Storm Bay, which I shall ever think very accurately named; – the weather dark, thick, and squally, with incessant rain. The vessel's deck was so ill-joined that the dirty water dripped through the chinks all over my bed; and, as I lay reading, something dark fell into the border of my cap: thinking it a drop of mud, I snatched off the cap and gave it to the servant, when, to my horror, I discovered that it was an enormous[3] centipede which had fallen upon me, a hideous,

---

[3] Enormous *here*, but I am told these amiable-looking creatures thrive best in India, and there grow to the length of a foot or fourteen inches, and as thick as one's finger!

many-jointed, many-legged green creature, about three inches long, with a forked tail, and a railroad rapidity of progression. My horror in this instance was soon changed to thankfulness that the dangerous reptile had fallen where it did; for my happy little child, on whom it might have dropped, lay sleeping close beside me, and the bite of the centipede is often more venomous and painful than even the sting of a scorpion.

As the weather got slightly better, I went on deck, but all around was very dreary; the fog hung about, and wind and rain came in fitful gusts. Whilst I sat, vainly trying to make out something of the surrounding scenery, Mr. Meredith and several of the other passengers remarked to the captain, who had 'turned out' at last, that another squall was coming; and indeed I could distinctly see the ruffled and foaming water rapidly approaching the ship.

'The masts will go, unless you take in sail,' said some one, growing nervous at the apathetic supineness of the captain, who, lazily gazing aloft, and then resettling himself on a hen-coop, muttered that he 'didn't know – didn't think they would,' and accordingly no change was made.

'*You* had better go below,' said my husband leading, me to the companion, and before I had reached the cabin, there was a loud crash – the rattle of falling rigging and blocks knocking about, quickly followed by a repetition of the same sounds, as the main and mizen topmasts successively went over the side. Such an accident a few hours before would probably have been fatal; but now, being in smooth water, it was only productive of a little bustle and discussion.

The bad weather and total discomfort of the latter portion of our voyage prevented my enjoying the fine scenery of the Derwent, as we approached Hobarton, sailing past Bruni Island and Iron-pot Island Lighthouse.

The situation of the town is the most beautiful that can be conceived – on the rising banks of the noble Derwent, with green meadows, gardens, and cultivated land around it, interspersed with pleasant country residences and farms; and, above and beyond all, the snowy mountain peaks soaring to the very clouds. At length we cast anchor. The rattle of the chain-cable must always be a welcome sound at such a time, but perhaps our recent hair-breadth 'scapes lent a still pleasanter tone to its rough music, which at the moment eclipsed, in my estimation, the choicest concerto ever composed; and we immediately went ashore, most thankful and delighted to step once more on land.

The great difference between Sydney and Hobarton struck me as forcibly during my first ten minutes' walk as after a longer acquaintance; and, in point of pleasantness, I must certainly award the palm to the latter. It is a much smaller place than Sydney, but its home-like English aspect at once won my preference.

Our next fortnight passed happily among relatives whom I had not seen since childhood, and in a cool breezy climate, that reminded us of April in England; the weather was too showery to admit of so much out-door amusement as I could have wished; still, the cool moist greenness everywhere was most refreshing and cheering to me; the little gardens before and between many houses in the middle of the town, with their great bushes of geraniums in bloom, were all full of sweet English spring flowers, looking happy and healthy, like the stout rosy children that everywhere reminded me of HOME; so different to the thick white complexions and tall slender forms so prevalent in New South Wales. The houses, too, at least the few I entered during our short sojourn, were more snug than showy, as if the English attribute of comfort more especially belonged to them. In the streets, carriages and equestrians were less numerous than in Sydney, and I found that here it was not only believed possible, but positively 'fashionable,' for ladies to walk about; an improvement upon Sydney customs, which is in a great measure attributable to the climate. The shops were numerous and good, and the buildings neat and substantial, chiefly of brick, but many of the newer ones of cut stone. Some of the more suburban streets, or rather the suburban ends of them, consisting of good detached houses standing in nice gardens, and adorned by verandas covered with lovely plants, are very pleasant, commanding fine views of the harbour; and from every point I visited, Mount Wellington (or Table Mountain) forms the crowning glory of the landscape. Rising immediately behind the town to the height of 4200 feet, with its summit of basaltic columns covered with snow more than half the year, its aspect is one of ever-varying, but never-decreasing grandeur. Whether it was wreathed in fleecy vapours, dark with rolling clouds, or stood out clear and sunlit against the blue morning sky, I was never weary of gazing on this magnificent object.

A stream flowing from the mountain through a picturesque ravine and valley, supplies the town with water, turning a number of mills of various kinds in its course. To a botanist, Mount

Wellington must be a treasury of gems, many rare and beautiful plants inhabiting its wild and almost inaccessible glens and ravines. The ascent of the mountain is long, and was formerly very fatiguing, but the formation, for a considerable distance, of a road passable for horses, has greatly reduced the difficulty. Several unfortunate persons who at various times have imprudently attempted the ascent without a guide, have never returned, nor has any vestige of them ever been discovered; most probably they have fallen into some of the deep chasms and fissures, and, if not killed instantly, have lingered awhile, and died of starvation. The view from the summit is described as surpassingly grand and beautiful, as indeed it must be, from its great altitude and the varied and picturesque scenery around.

I have been frequently told that the real Waratah is found on Mount Wellington, and have since seen several specimens of the flower mistaken for it – very different and inferior indeed to my gorgeous favourite of the Blue Mountains. The Tasmanian Waratah is a shrub or bushy tree, with handsome dark-green foliage, and bright red flowers of loosely-clustered trumpet florets, scarcely so large as an English woodbine.

We passed the chief part of our sojourn at Newtown, in the environs of Hobarton, where many of the wealthier merchants, government officers, and professional men have tasteful residences. The church and the Queen's Orphan Schools are large and handsome buildings; in the latter, children of both sexes are clothed and educated.

The scenery around Newtown is the most beautiful I have seen on this side the world – very much resembling that of the Cumberland Lakes: the broad and winding estuary of the Derwent flows between lofty and picturesque hills and mountains, clothed with forests, whilst at their feet lie level lawn-like flats, green to the water's edge. But the most English, and therefore the most beautiful things I saw here, were the hawthorn hedges; those of sweetbriar, which are, I think, more general, did not please me half so well, not having so much of common country home life about them.

It seemed like being on the right side of the earth again, to see rosy children with boughs of flowering 'May,' and to feel its full luscious perfume waft across me. Let no one who has always lived at home, enjoying unnoticed the year's bounty of rainbow-tinted blossoms, fancy he knows the full value of English flowers, or the love that the heart can bear for them. I thought I always held them in as fond admiration as any one could do, but my delight in these hawthorn hedges proved to me how much my regard had strengthened in absence; and as I recalled to mind the wide brown deserts I had lately left, with their miles of 'post and rail', or more hideous 'log' and 'deadwood' fences, and then took an imaginary glance over the green hawthorn hedges and elm-shaded lanes of my own beautiful native land, I heartily wished that all dwellers in her pleasant country places could only know and feel what a paradise they inhabit!

I am often glad that I spent the first year of my antipodean life in New South Wales, for now many things which I should not have observed had I arrived here in the first instance, are sources of great delight to me, as being so much more English than in the larger colony, and I could fancy myself some degrees nearer home.

In the Tasmanian gardens are mulberries, cherries, currants, raspberries, strawberries, gooseberries, apples, pears, quinces, medlars, plums of all kinds, and peaches in abundance, growing well and luxuriantly. Our forest trees, too, thrive admirably here, and walnuts, filberts, and hazelnuts are becoming much more common. Vines also succeed in sheltered aspects, but not better than in many parts of England; the summer-frosts to which this climate is liable frequently cut off plants which in Britain can be grown with certainty. Even potatoes are, in some districts, considered a very precarious crop from this circumstance, and, except in situations near the sea-shore, are often nipped by the frost at night, although the weather in the day-time is as warm as in an English June.

The Government Gardens here, although not comparable with those at Sydney, are finely situated on the sloping shore of the Derwent, and charmed me by their verdant and shady aspect. They are – for I must again repeat my oft-used term of praise – they are *English*-looking gardens, not rich in glowing oranges, scarlet pomegranates, and golden loquats, nor stored with the rare and gorgeous blossoms of India, but full of sweet homely faces and perfumes. Great trees of a lovely blush rose were in full bloom at the time of my visit, looking so like the rose-trees of olden days at home, that I could scarcely believe them the growth of the opposite side of the world.

The domain adjoins the gardens, and is laid out in pleasant drives among the groves of native trees. We witnessed there the ceremony of laying the first stone of a new Government House, on a spot commanding views of the Derwent and the surrounding beautiful scenery. A collation was provided on the occasion by the Lieutenant-Governor and Lady Franklin, in a pretty rustic lodge near the site of the new mansion, and some of the guests availed themselves of the presence of an excellent military band to have quadrilles on the grass, or rather in the dust, for the turf was something of the scantiest.

At the period of which I am writing, Hobarton was certainly not in advance of Sydney in point of society or intelligence, and the constant efforts of Sir John and Lady Franklin to arouse and foster a taste for science, literature, or art, were more often productive of annoyance to themselves, than of benefit to the unambitious multitude. The coarse and unmanly attacks made in some of the public papers on Lady Franklin, whose kindness and ability, even if not appreciated at their full value, ought at least to have met with gratitude and respect, were most disgraceful. Unhappily the perpetual petty squabbles and quarrels which seem to form an indispensable part of all small communities, and were especially rife in this little fraction of a world, occupied its attention too exclusively to admit of any great interest being felt in subjects not immediately connected with individual success or advantage. That there might always be found exceptions to this rule is more true, but their good influence, like the light of a few stars in a clouded sky, only served to make the surrounding intellectual gloom more apparent.

Among the young ladies, both married and single, in Tasmania, as in Sydney, a very 'general one-ness' prevails as to the taste for dancing, from the love of which but a small share of regard can be spared for any other accomplishment or study, save a little singing and music; and Lady Franklin's attempts to introduce evening parties in the 'conversazione' style were highly unpopular with the pretty Tasmanians, who declared that they 'had no idea of being asked to an evening party, and then stuck up in rooms full of pictures and books, and shell and stones, and other rubbish, with nothing to do but to hear people talk lectures, or else sit as mute as mice listening to what was called good music. Why could not Lady Franklin have the military band in, and the carpets out, and give dances, instead of such stupid preaching about philosophy and science, and a parcel of stuff that nobody could understand?'

The performances at the neat little theatre in Hobarton are of a better order than the colonies can generally boast, and most romantic and heart-stirring are the titles of the melodramatic pieces usually represented there. I often regretted our distance from town when I saw such announcements as THE MAID OF GENOA, or THE BANDIT MERCHANT, with the celebrated BROAD-SWORD COMBAT and HIGHLAND FLING *in the Second Act'*; – the introduction of apparent anomalies being made much on the pump-and-tub principle of the immortal Crummles. Sometimes half a page of a colonial paper is filled with startling hints of each scene, plentifully peppered with stars, dashes, notes of exclamation, and gigantic italics, quite distracting to read in a quiet country home, amidst peaceful woods; and to know the while, that people in town may go and 'sup full of horrors' with 'The Convict Captain, or the Nun of Messina'; – have their very heartstrings lacerated by 'The Broken Dagger, or the Dumb Boy of the Pyrenees'; – and sit in petrified and agonizing terror to behold of woes of the 'The Bandit's Victim, or the Black Caverns of St. Bruno'!

Perhaps it is scarcely fair to send forth such agitating advertisements into far away nooks of the forest, where their temptations are all unavailing. But wonderful is the serenity with which repeated disappointment enables the mind to endure even such privations! Recently one or two of Shakespeare's tragedies and some good modern plays have been got up very respectably, and last year the announcement of a pantomime sounded cheerily in our ears, like a faint echo of our childhood's laughter; but we afterwards found that its subject was wholly made up of local and personal allusions. The superior success of melodramas over the higher order of dramatic representations, affords an evidence as to public taste which needs no comment. The frightful amount of *snobbishness* which prevails here among those who might really well dispense with the feverish terror of being said or thought to do anything 'ungenteel' or 'unfashionable,' is adverse to the interests of the theatre; and accordingly the patronage vouchsafed by the alarmed exclusives is lamentably small.

CHAPTER III

The Hunt – Public Amusements – Public Decorum and Morality – Prisoner Population – 'Assignment System' – 'White Slavery' – Magistrates – 'Probation System' – Experience in Prisoner-Servants – Their Length of Service – Their Attachment and Good Faith.

As balls must infallibly be popular in a place where everybody dances, so must races claim a large share of patronage where everybody rides, or is in some manner interested in the quality and value of horses; and accordingly Hobarton, Launceston, Campbelltown, Oatlands, and other places in the colony, have their annual meetings, where 'cups', 'ladies' purses', 'town plates', 'sweepstakes', and such like exciting prizes, are gallantly striven for, and fairly won, often by gentlemen-riders, and horses worthy of them.

Hunting is also a favourite diversion, and occasionally the newspapers put forth most grandiloquent narratives purporting to be communications from 'correspondents,' detailing the exploits of the 'field', which usually consist of galloping over rough country after two or three couple of hounds (a kind of 'scratch pack'), which drive before them a poor tame deer, one of the few imported into the colony, and placed at the disposal of the hunt, by owners more liberal than humane. When the poor creature is completely exhausted, it is rescued from the hounds for future torments, and again and again chased to the very verge of existence, by the noble and Christian worthies who enjoy the cruel sport. Perhaps I may be told that deeds quite as cruel are considered 'sport' at home, and encouraged by the highest sanction; but that does not in the least convince me that all the bad habits of an old country should be scrupulously transplanted to a new one, whilst so many of the good ones remain forgotten; and assuredly the absurd custom of *hunting*, with all the show and pretence of earnest pursuit, a gentle tame creature that can scarcely be *driven* away, would be 'more honoured in the breach than the observance.'

One of these cruel exhibitions occurred only a week before our arrival, as I am informed by a person who shared the 'sport' with about sixty others, which ended in the poor tame stag being worried to death by the dogs, its antlers having caught in a low tree, and entangled it: knowing that its longer life would but have led to greater sufferings, I rejoice that it was killed.

A kangaroo is sometimes hunted as a substitute for the old country fox, and, being a wild and swift creature, is said to afford excellent sport.

The dingo of New South Wales, so generally hunted there, is, I rejoice to say, wholly unknown in Tasmania.

Public balls, concerts, regattas, and horticultural shows, are also frequent, and attended fully, and most respectably. I know of no place where greater order and decorum is observed by the motley crowds assembled on any public occasion than in this most shamefully slandered colony: not even in an English country village can a lady walk alone with less fear of harm or insult than in this capital of Van Diemen's Land, commonly believed at home to be a moral pest-house, where every crime that can disgrace and degrade humanity stalks abroad with unblushing front.

The unfounded assertions which have been made and believed in England for some years respecting the moral and social condition of this colony, are most astonishing: how, why, and from whom they have originated, I am at a loss to conjecture; but that they are, for the most part, cruelly, scandalously false, I know.

Not in the most moral circles of moral England herself is a departure from the paths of propriety or virtue more determinedly or universally visited by the punishment of exclusion from society, than in this 'Penal Colony'; nowhere are all particulars and incidents of persons' past lives more minutely and rigidly canvassed, than in the 'higher circles' of this little community; and nowhere are the decent and becoming observances of social and domestic life more strictly maintained. One fact, familiar to hundreds here, may well illustrate this assertion. I select this particular instance, because the parties have now left the colony, and whilst in it occupied a prominent station. A lady, the wife of a military officer of high rank, had for some years held that place in society to which her husband's influential position, and her own right as a gentlewoman, entitled her. She was visited and courted, and might select her own associates from the best families here, until, one unlucky day, there came to the colony a person who professed to be intimately acquainted with this lady's 'birth, parentage, and education', and somewhat officiously proceeded to set forth in various companies a narrative of some long-past error of her early youth; whether false or true, no one paused to ascertain, nor to ask themselves who, amongst them all, could, if similarly attacked, withstand such (possibly) unfounded assertions. Her correct and unblemished conduct during her sojourn here availed nothing: but one and all of her former devoted friends fell away, and refused to hold any further communion with her. Is it possible to believe that this could have been the case, were moral feeling in Van Diemen's Land at the low ebb generally represented?

A residence here for the last nine years, and an intimate acquaintance during that time with the habits and usages of the higher and middle ranks, as well as of the free labouring population of the country places, may, I think, in some measure qualify me to judge how far the sweeping condemnations of the few, are borne out by the demeanour of the many; and now, in all honest faith and truth, I declare them to be every whit as unjust to the people of Tasmania as they would be if cast upon those of the same rank in England. And as, in days of yore, the doughty champion of slandered virtue flung into the lists his mailed gauntlet, or the glorious Bombastes hung aloft his invincible boots, even so, in these modern days of more wordy, but not less mortal strife, do I gently lay down my black silk mitten in the cause of fair and wronged Tasmania!

Nor will I quit the subject thus entered upon, without a few words on behalf of those whose friends are too few in number to allow the silence of one willing voice, however feeble, when aught *can* be said for them. I allude to the numerous prisoners of the Crown, now forming so large a portion of our population, and respecting whom so much discussion has of late arisen, and so little truth been elicited. It was not my purpose to touch upon this matter so early in these pages, because at the time of which I am writing, I had not had the opportunities of forming an opinion which I have since had; but having alluded to the subject, it is perhaps best to anticipate the lapse of time so far, and briefly glance over the general question.

The transportation of British criminals to Van Diemen's Land was, as is well known, continued for many years (and until 1842) under the 'assignment system'; the prisoners brought in each ship being 'assignable' to private service as soon as they arrived. The greater portion of them, therefore, were immediately removed and distributed among different masters in distant places, and with small probability that they would again be brought in contact with their former partners in crime – thus effecting at once the first great step towards reformation, in the breaking up of old and evil connections and associations. The majority became speedily engaged in various ways, chiefly in pastoral or agricultural pursuits, or clearing land; nearly all their fellow-labourers being persons of a like class, but in whom at least a partial improvement had already taken place; and with these they too went on, labouring in occupations or trades they did understand or learning those they did not. They had huts to live in (which were so far superior to the wretched cabins of many labourers at home that they kept out wind and rain), as much fuel as they chose to cut for themselves, abundant rations of good and wholesome food, and a certain allowance of clothing, boots, and bedding, fixed by Government.

After serving thus for three, four, or five years, according to the length of their original sentence, they were, if well-conducted and recommended, allowed a 'ticket-of-leave', which enabled them to quit their first master, if so disposed, and hire themselves for wages to any one else in the colony who was eligible as an employer of convicts; the police magistrate of the district granting them a 'pass' or certificate of permission to proceed to any other specified place. This stage of their punishment appears to have been attended with great success, restoring to them, as a reward for past amendment, enough of independence to arouse their feeling of self-respect and encourage them to continue improving, whilst it reserved power in the hands of the authorities for future rewards or punishments. So manifest are the advantages of this part of the system, that the settlers prefer ticket-of-leave men as servants to any other class, and if the periods of their being such were allowed to arrive sooner and be of longer duration, the change would in most cases benefit the men materially, and tend, by habituating them to the good conduct they then practise, to render more safe and certain their ultimate reformation.

After remaining the allotted number of years in the ticket-of-leave class, the deserving convicts usually received a 'conditional pardon', which permitted them the range of the Australian colonies; and to some was granted a 'free pardon', which generally found them fully prepared to keep and value the liberty it bestowed.

To this system it has of late been fashionable to attach the term 'white slavery', and other opprobrious epithets. Although doubtless susceptible of great improvement, (as what human scheme

is not?) the results were in the main highly satisfactory, and precisely what the Home Government and all humane persons desired
they should be, namely, the conversion, in five cases out of six,
of idle unprincipled outcasts into industrious trustworthy servants,
and the redemption of thousands, who (not strong enough in good
to resist evil entirely, yet with the better impulses of their nature
far over-balancing the worse) would, if they had remained at
home, after a first offence, have been reduced in their degrada-
tion to suffer the contagious influence of spirits more wicked than
themselves, and so have sunk gradually but surely downwards
to the lowest depths of vice. Here, removed from the first crushing grief of disgrace, and seeing before them the prospect of rising
again, and of building for themselves a new character above the
ruins of the old, all the latent good in them springs into action;
and, in very many instances, a life of honest industry and an old
age of decent comfort have succeeded a youth of vice and crime.

For this system to produce its full amount of good in the men,
there must needs be the requisite qualifications of common sense,
probity, and humanity in the masters; and to ascertain and decide
who are and who are not really eligible as such, requires greater
diligence and more impartiality than Government agents are often
found to possess. Bad masters and severe dishonest magistrates
have devoted more men to live as bushrangers, and to die on
the scaffold, than any inherent depravity of their victims. When
the choice of persons to fill the solemn and responsible offices
of justices of the peace was guided, as it *was* here, not by worth,
fitness, or respectability, but by their very reverse – when ser-
vility became the requisite qualification for the man who should
be pleasing to a governor – wretched indeed was the prospect
of the unfortunate prisoner dragged before such a magistrate, and
little indeed had *justice* to do with the proceedings, which wholly
depended on the venal character of the man's master, not of himself. If his master was a useful tool of the governor, he might
fix the precise punishment he chose to have inflicted; if, on the
other hand, he was an honest unpurchaseable person, his servant, however guilty, was either dismissed unpunished, or
removed from his service. Such things, and worse than these,
were of daily occurrence, but are happily now far less frequent;
and I believe the lingering remnants which are still found only
need exposure to insure removal.

In 1842 the old method of 'assignment' was replaced by the 'probation system'; and the prisoners, instead of being taken into private service direct from the ship, were subjected to a probationary period of (supposed) hard labour and instruction, which appears to have been *intended* by the Home Government to advance their reformation, to render them more useful afterwards as servants, and to benefit the colony meanwhile by the great amount of labour available for the execution of public works. These were good intentions, but the officers appointed to carry them out failed signally in their task; some from determined perversity and unpopularity, some from inability, and more from distaste and inattention: and then the herding together of hundreds of criminals of all classes and grades in notorious idleness, made those who were really bad tenfold worse – and even men naturally willing and diligent lapsed into apathetic drones; so that, when they became eligible for service, they were found far less useful and promising than those used to be who were assigned direct from the ships.

To all persons connected with the colony, this will appear an useless repetition of things as familiar as one's alphabet; but I do not write for colonial readers – I can tell *them* nothing that they may not equally well discover for themselves, if disposed to take the pains. I write to communicate such information to general readers in England as I believe many are deficient in, and, not being ambitious of seeming learned myself, would rather repeat many things that everybody knows, than omit one which some require to learn. I wish to convey to others the veritable impressions made on my own mind by the condition and character of the convict population here, and I could not do so intelligibly without some slight sketch of their general position.

I have now lived above nine years in the colony, the wife of a 'settler', and the mistress of a 'settler's' home, and during that time we have been served by prisoners of all grades, as ploughmen, shepherds, shearers, reapers, butchers, gardeners, carpenters, masons, blacksmiths, shoemakers, house-servants, &c., &c., and (with one or two exceptions) served as well and faithfully as we could desire. What more could be said by any farmer's wife at home? Are all English labourers blameless? I can only call to mind one instance of known dishonesty among our many men-servants (that of a groom who stole some wine), and I believe that acts of petty theft are far less common among them than among the generality of servants at home. Many persons here could and would, if required, give the same evidence which I now do; but I prefer adducing a few facts from my own knowledge, as proof that transportation to these colonies *is* – always excepting the probation system – productive of reformation to many who otherwise would, in all probability, have been utterly lost.

Five, ten, and fifteen years are common periods for prisoner-servants to remain in the same service, before and after their conditional pardon; and I lately heard of one who has for *twenty-eight* years lived with another master in a situation of great trust.

My husband's father, Mr. George Meredith, and himself, have now on their estates five old servants, four of whom have been in their family since 1826, and one since 1825, the latter being until lately overseer on a large agricultural farm. One of the four before-named was once an overseer for many years, and now rents a farm and flock from my husband – his wife having joined him eighteen or twenty years ago, with their family, now grown up and married; the second was in like manner gradually promoted from one post to another till he married, became a superintendent, and then a tenant; the third, a good workman in an useful trade, has received a free pardon, is now also a tenant of my father's, and working for himself; and the fourth, after being employed, since he became free, in whaling, sawing, splitting, and divers other avocations, has, for the last eight years, been cook and 'major domo' in our own house, where his faithful attachment and incorruptible honesty are appreciated as they deserve. At the very time I am writing, he and a 'ticket-of-leave' gardener are the only male persons in our lonely house (Mr. Meredith being absent in town), and I feel no more, perhaps even less, fear of attack or molestation, than I should in the middle of London: firstly, because I have no idea that robbers will come; and, secondly, because I know that, if they did, I and my children would be defended to the uttermost by *these very prisoner-servants*; and I think it must be very evident, that the country cannot be the den of horrors it has of late been painted, where a female only *so* protected can sit in her quiet country house, forty miles from the nearest village, with doors and windows left open the whole day through, and sleep safely and peacefully at night, without a bar or bolt or shutter to a single window, every room being on the ground floor.

I have only particularised a *few* instances of long service, but

I could enumerate numbers of men who have lived in the same family ten, fifteen, eighteen years, as trusted and respected servants; some who have grown old and died on the same establishment. Surely such distinct indisputable facts as these are more worthy of credence, and a safer guide to the truth, than the vague generalizing denunciations now so commonly dealt forth by the slanderers of the colony. If I were to note all the corroborative evidence that occurs to me, I should fill my little book with it; in no place that I ever knew at home are houses and families left so totally unprotected and in such perfect safety as here. In a lone cottage, seven miles from our own, there lives, at this very time, a lady, an educated gentlewoman, and her four young children – the eldest only eleven – without even a man-servant in or near the place, all being with their master on a distant farm: all the neighbouring settlers have numerous prisoner-servants, yet she lives undisturbed.

I will now quit this subject for the present, assured that if my counter-statement has no other good effect, it will at least enable my friends to journey on with me more pleasantly than if haunted by those frightful anticipations for my personal safety which the reports of the croakers must have awakened.

Chapter IV

Journey to Swan Port – Restdown – Richmond – 'The Grand Stand' – Colonial Roads – Pic-nic Dinner – A 'Sticker-up' – Jerusalem – Native Names – Halt in the Forest – Free Roads – Road-Gangs – Transit over Gullies – Eastern Marshes – An Invasion – Lonely Houses – Organ of Locality.

Our final destination was Great Swan Port, at the head of Oyster Bay, on the east coast. We commenced our journey thither by a short stage, first crossing the Derwent in the ferry-boats, ourselves in one, and our horses and vehicle in another. Colonial country roads are not calculated for four-wheeled carriages; Mr. Meredith therefore purchased in Hobarton a broad, stout, colonial-built conveyance, an ingenious variety of the gig species, with a seat behind for a servant, which seemed fully capable of enduring all the trying exertions of the journey.

We drove from the ferry to Risdon (properly, I believe, Restdown), a very lovely spot, and the residence of one of my husband's oldest and most valued friends (T. G. Gregson, M.L.C.). I had not seen so beautiful a view, since I left England, as that commanded by the windows of his dining-room. Mount Wellington is here, as in Hobarton, the chief object in the landscape, whilst the broad bright Derwent, enlivened by sailing and steam-vessels, and skirted by green slopes and meadow-like flats, adds greatly to the beauty of the scene. The greater verdure of the forest trees in Van Diemen's Land, than of those in New South Wales, here struck me forcibly.

We lingered so pleasantly with our kind friends, that it was not until the afternoon of the following day that we set forth to make another short stage, and this was a very pleasant one, being for the most part over a fine, newly-made Government road. From the summit of Grass Tree Hill we had a most beautiful view of the town and harbour, bright in the full radiance of the afternoon sun.

Great numbers of the singular 'grass trees' (*Xanthorrea arborea*), of all ages and growths, short, tall, straight, and crooked, each with its long tressed head of rushy leaves, gave a peculiar character to the steep and rocky hills between which we passed, and created an amusing variety in the otherwise monotonous near scenery.

We proceeded to Richmond, a place named, I imagine, in true Antipodean fashion, from its utter lack of all likeness to its charming old-country namesake. It is a squarely-planned township, situated in a flat valley, with a neat square-towered church and square formal houses dispersed about its incomplete streets. A very square many-windowed inn, seeming very new, very roomy, and very empty, looked at us as we passed with as imploring an expression as might be assumed by an inn of its great pretensions and stony dignity; but fortunately we were not destined to test its capabilities, having accepted the proffered hospitality of the then police magistrate of Richmond, who, being a geologist and a virtuoso, afforded us an agreeable evening in the examination of his various collections. Many of the limestone fossils I saw here were new to me, but as their possessor purposed forwarding a characteristic collection either to the British Museum or the Geological Society, the *savans* at home are doubtless acquainted with them ere this.

Our friend's gatherings in the paths of science being somewhat extensive, the room in which my maid slept was plentifully stored with choice and rather bulky fossil specimens, and I had no easy task, next morning, in striving to compose the feelings of the terrified and indignant damsel, who declared she 'had lain all amongst skillintons and dead men's bones, as bad as vaultses under churches'. She had not observed the horrors over night, but was quite positive they *were* 'death's-heads and cross-bones', for she had had such 'horrid odorous dreams'. At length I succeeded in calming her perturbation, and she resumed the charge of the 'young *Erkerluss'* (Hercules), as she termed my bouncing baby.

On setting forth, our kind host directed us to proceed along a new road, or rather track, for some distance, our beacon being 'the grand stand' on the racecourse, which was shortly to appear on our left hand. As we drove on, I carefully looked about for at least a humble imitation of the buildings usually erected for such purposes – some neat little summer-house affair, perhaps, with a white roof stuck aloft on white posts – but no such thing appeared. At length, Mr. Meredith, from his knowledge of the country, was convinced that our route would be wrong, if pursued further in the direction we were then going; and on looking around again most intently, we discovered a small post-and-rail *pen*, of common split timber, neither smoothed nor painted, but bearing a tolerably near resemblance to a temporary pigstye, and this was 'The Grand Stand'! I afterwards remembered having seen the one at Paramatta, which, though far superior to this, was only calculated to hold some half-dozen persons, and was framed in the same rough and unpolished style.

The road now became quite colonial, that is, execrably bad, and the scenery too monotonous to divert my attention for a moment from the misery of the rough jolting we suffered, and from my cares lest every shock should disturb or hurt my baby, whom I dared not trust in the maid's arms for fear she might drop him out whilst saving herself from one of the incessant jolts, which threatened fractures and dislocations at every step.

In the afternoon we reached a solitary public-house, where we purposed resting for an hour, but finding a large party of rather riotous guests already in possession of its wretched little rooms, we hastened on for a short distance, and paused on the next hill, where the horses were tethered to graze, and we soon made a fire to grill our cold meat and warm baby's food; and so, under the shade of some sombre gum trees, had a pleasant pic-nic sort of repast, far more to my taste than a sojourn in the unpromising dingy little hostel we had left.

Here I was first initiated into the bush art of 'sticker-up' cookery, and for the benefit of all who 'go a-gipsying' I will expound the mystery. The orthodox material here is of course kangaroo, a piece of which is divided nicely into cutlets two or three inches broad and a third of an inch thick. The next requisite is a straight clean stick, about four feet long, sharpened at both ends. On the narrow part of this, for the space of a foot or more, the cutlets are spitted at intervals, and on the end is placed a piece of delicately rosy fat bacon. The strong end of the stick-spit is now stuck fast and erect in the ground, close by the fire, to leeward; care being taken that it does not burn. Then the bacon on the summit of the spit, speedily softening in the genial blaze, drops a lubricating shower of rich and savoury tears on the leaner kangaroo cutlets below, which forthwith frizzle and steam and sputter with as much ado as if they were illustrious Christmas beef grilling in some London chop-house under the gratified nose of the expectant consumer. 'And gentlemen,' as dear old Hardcastle would have said, if he had dined with us in the bush, 'to men that are hungry, stuck-up kangaroo and bacon are very good eating.' Kangaroo is, in fact, very like hare.

On this occasion, however, as our basket was town-packed, our 'sticker-up' consisted only of ham. The evening of this day we reached Jerusalem, and, not having any friends in the holy city, took up our quarters at one of the caravanserais, where we were as little uncomfortable as we could expect to be in a place of such limited accommodation. Jerusalem is a township of far less imposing aspect than Richmond, and the neighbouring scenery is very uninteresting.

The absurdity of giving to new little settlements like this the names of old-world places of renown, always seems to me excessive. Not far away from the new Jerusalem are Jericho and Bagdad; whilst English town and country names abound, and the plain farmhouses of settlers are often called after some of the most magnificent palace-seats of English nobles, making the contrast, which cannot fail to occur to one's mind, ludicrous in the extreme. I know only three native names of places in this island – Ringarooma and Boobyalla on the north coast, and Triabunna on the east. In New South Wales many of the settlers have had the good sense and taste to preserve the aboriginal names, which are always significant (when understood), and for the most part singularly musical in sound. Such are Paramatta, Wooloomooloo, Illawarra, Wollongong, Wollondilly, Mittagong, Maneroo, Tuggeranong, Mutmutbilly, Yangalara, and many more; whilst some few, it must be owned, are more grotesque than euphonious, for instance, Jerriconoramwogwog, Jininjininjininderry, and Jinjulluk. Yet even these are preferable to the reiterated old names, and at any rate excite no ridiculous comparison between great old things and little new ones.

Our onward road from Jerusalem was worse than any we had hitherto traversed, being deep loose sand mingled with stones of all sizes, and great masses of rock, over which we bumped and jumped and jolted most perseveringly for some miles; the horses being sufficiently tired in dragging us along at a slow foot-pace, and through as uninteresting a tract of country as can well be conceived. Forests of straggling dingy gum-trees (*Eucalyptus*) were here and there mingled with an equally dingy growth of wattle and honeysuckle-trees (*Acacia* and *Banksia*); the ground bore very little herbage, but was chiefly covered with coarse, harsh, reedy plants, some of which are called 'cutting grass', from the extremely sharp edges of the leaves, which cut like glass; so sharp, indeed, that we have had dogs severely hurt in running through them: other and more numerous kinds are less mischievous.

A large tussock of this grass I have often found a very pleasant resting-place, as, by bending sideways a portion of the upper leaves, and seating oneself upon them, they form an elastic cushion, well backed by the remaining upright leaves, and very preferable to a seat on a log, which usually swarms with ants: it is prudent to *poke* the tussock with a stick, before sitting down on it, as snakes are not unfrequently found coiled within.

On such a primitive kind of ottoman I very gladly rested awhile at our usual mid-day halt in the forest, whilst the smoke of our gypsy fire curled sluggishly upward in the still air, and the horses eagerly rolled themselves in the damp marsh grass that skirted the tiny spring which had made us fix upon this spot for the halt of our little caravan.

Tall gaunt-looking gum-trees, with many straggling far-spreading branches and scanty foliage, towered high above, with streamers of loose bark hanging from all parts of them, sometimes five or more yards long, and waving rustlingly to and fro. At least a fifth part of the trees had either died of natural decay, or been blown down, and lay in all directions; their massive trunks, broken branches, and withered leaves, together with many years accumulation of fallen bark (which these trees shed annually) covering the earth, and scarcely allowing the lesser plants to struggle up amongst them. A few common shrubs grew here and there with pretty but scanty blossoms; and, beside the precious little spring, a gleam of real green brightened the dreary place, and the few poor reeds and shrubs so fortunate as to dwell within its blessed influence, shot up tall and lithe and verdant, amidst that dry, sapless, lifeless-looking forest.

I was pleased to see some fern here, very similar to the common forest-fern or brake at home; but, instead of growing tall and spreading, it seemed stunted and crisped with drought, its leaf-tips all brown and brittle, and the stems hard and shrivelled.

We journeyed on through this seemingly endless region of standing and prostrate gum-trees, frequently walking to spare our poor child the motion of the carriage, and having continually, when driving, to turn aside into the uncleared 'bush', to travel round some enormous tree which had fallen across the beaten track. How little do the good people in England, whom I have heard grumble outrageously at the sixpences extorted from them by the turnpikes – how very little do they know the value of the roads they so grudgingly help to maintain! If they could possibly enjoy, as we did, the delight of making a journey of 120 miles upon one of these free roads, I think turnpikes would ever after beam upon their charmed eyes as the loveliest objects in the landscape, the ever welcome tokens of level roads and easy drives, of Macadam and civilization.

In the district around Hobarton, and on the direct route to Launceston, the roads are reasonably good, and when the probation system rendered the services of so many thousands of convicts available to the local Government for the execution of works of public utility, it was generally hoped that in time our colonial highways would be considerably mended, but such expectation has been signally disappointed. Gangs of many hundreds of men have been located about the island in various places, but, as it would appear, with the most careful determination on the part of the directors that their labour should *not* be beneficial to the colonists. Roads were begun, it is true, but generally in such directions as were rarely traversed, and if one over a more frequented part of the country was commenced and carried on successfully for some time, the gangs were almost invariably removed from it when a little further labour would have rendered it essentially serviceable to the neighbourhood. I know positively of more than one instance where a road between two districts was in the course of formation, which, had it been carried through, would have greatly enhanced the value of certain large properties; but because the owners of these were obnoxious, upon political grounds, to the officer then in charge of the convicts, the work was stopped when within a short distance of the proposed terminus (a portion of the road was left unfinished and wholly impassable), the prisoners' barracks were dismantled and allowed to go to ruin, and the gang removed to a distance, most probably to be kept in idleness; for, as the officer had uncontrolled power, and rather a lengthy list of private feuds, it became extremely difficult to plan a road, in any quarter, which should not either directly or indirectly benefit some of the objects of his undying and vindictive dislike; and hence the very small amount of good effected by a very large amount of power – hence the number of unfinished, almost useless roads and expensive stations and barracks, built at the cost of the Home Government, and left to go to ruin, all over the island – and hence the unpopularity and ultimate failure of the probation system.

A common bush-road cleared of trees and stumps, the latter being too frequently left in the ground, is, if on firm smooth soil, by no means unpleasant, but where rocks intervene, or deep gullies, or the broad stony ford of a river, or a low tract of bog or marshy clay – which the least traffic in wet weather beats up into a slippery tenacious batter-pudding consistency – these, in consequence of no means being adopted for rendering them moderately passable, become serious impediments, and with such obstacles our colonial bush-roads are replete.

How some of the yawning 'gullies' and ravines were passed on our journey, is an enigma to me to this day; for sometimes their banks were so precipitous, that I could with difficulty descend one side and scramble up the other on foot. How the carriage was lowered down and dragged up again, I cannot divine; but my husband and brother, and the good horses, managed it in some mysterious way amongst them, and regularly overtook me as I and my servant walked on before with the child; who, after sleeping through the first three days' easy stages with most exemplary and philosophical indifference to the jolting, now began to intimate that his patience was exhausted, and put in his protest against carriage nursing most determinedly. Still, it was pleasant and comforting to think that we *might* have been far more miserable! and, when growing really weary, distressed, and vexed at our many petty troubles, I used to silence my inward murmurs by the query – *'Would you prefer going by sea?'* and instantly the all-powerful charm of the dry land reconciled me to all present or future annoyances that our journey might present.

Our resting-place, on the fourth evening of our slow and tiresome pilgrimage, was the house of a settler at the 'Eastern Marshes', who, from being the only resident in the neighbourhood, or for miles around, must have his well-known hospitality tried by most of the travellers on this dreary route. Judging from the number we met, these are, fortunately for him, not very numerous; during two days we had only seen two shepherds and their dogs. Our worthy host was an old acquaintance of Mr. Meredith's, and our weary group received every attention and comfort he could possibly provide us; and truly it is no small trial for a quiet little household to be invaded at a moment's notice, or rather with no notice at all, by a whole family party, hungry, thirsty, tired, hot, cold, sick or sleepy, as the case may be, but always troublesome to an incalculable extent, and turning the house upside down to make up cradles for children, and 'shake-downs' for gentlemen, and causing, however reluctantly, multifarious orders to go forth for hot water, cold water, towels, carpet-bags, blankets, driving-boxes, mutton-chops, brandy, milk, slippers, boiled eggs, dry wood, bread and butter, and tea, within half-an-hour driving the bewildered serving-woman nearly beside herself, and making the distracted master glad to escape to the stable to superintend the arrangements for the quadrupedal part of the invading army. Luckily our present kind entertainer was a bachelor, and ourselves not very exacting guests. When there is a wife in the case, I am always trebly grieved at occasioning such a domestic disturbance, being tolerably well able to sympathize in her sufferings. Yet it is not uncommon for such compulsory guests (especially residents in towns), to lay the flattering unction to their souls, that they confer the greatest imaginable favour on an establishment, by turning it inside out; at the same time avowing their conviction that 'people in the country are *always* so delighted to see *anybody*'; which is not exactly the correct construction to put upon the almost universal spirit of kind hospitality which prevails among settlers in the Bush, whether rich or poor; the simplicity and regularity of their lives and occupations rendering such interruptions far more serious than people accustomed to lounge and idle away their days in town can understand. How great a delight it is to welcome to the solitary home in the wilderness, some old and valued friend, and to see the well-known face mingle its silent tales of bygone years with all the newer interests and affections of the present time, can only be known when enjoyed! I believe, in truth, that to appreciate fully and completely the blessings of happy homes, children, friends, and books, a trial of lonely bush-life for a few years is indispensable. Such partial solitude does the spirit good.

I really think that, after seeing the truly lonely houses which we often find in these colonies, I should be puzzled to know where a lonely house could be placed in England! I have in former days seen what I then imagined such, and have read, with an admiring conviction of its truth, my friend Mr. Howitt's eloquent description of 'lone country houses' in general, and of some very fearfully lone ones in particular; but I verily begin to disbelieve the whole theory, and am almost prepared to assert that there is not, and cannot be, a lone house in England, and that there is nobody now living who ever lived in or saw such an one there!

Now this homestead on the Eastern Marshes might with some semblance of truth be invested with the ghostly and robbery qualifications of a 'lonely house': it stands all alone by itself, on an extensive tract of low marsh land, which, even at the time of our visit in November, was all splashy with water, and alive with unimaginable legions of frogs. Beyond the marsh, the forest land, or, to use the settlers' universal term, the 'Bush', commences, and spreads away over miles and miles of inhospitable country used for nothing but sheep-runs, usually called sheep-*walks* at home, but in these young countries we are in such haste to 'advance' and 'go ahead', that, among all other fast things, we must needs have fast sheep, or talk of them as if they were fast, which does as well. Mountains, hills, valleys, ravines – all are wild and trackless as they were thousands of years ago, except where a rude fence of brushwood indicates the boundary-line of different properties, or the narrow thread of a sheep-path winds away amidst the fallen trees and spreading reed-tussocks. No road passes by or anywhere near the place, at least none that I could espy: those travellers who go there, find their way by means of some occult science like divination, appertaining, I presume, to the organ of 'Locality' in its most perfect development, but which

I still venerate in the blindest ignorance; for all forests here, and all parts of them, are to me so exactly alike, that the power of knowing which is the right way to turn round one of many thousand similar trees seems, to my unpractised comprehension, to border on the miraculous.

CATHERINE HELEN SPENCE, 1825-1910

An outstanding literary and political figure of the
nineteenth century, Catherine Helen Spence was born
in Scotland and arrived in Australia in 1839; she
soon became interested in social and political reform.
Committed to obtaining 'Votes for Women', and to
developing a system of proportional representation
which permitted a more equitable electoral outcome,
she was the first woman political candidate in Australia. Her lectures (in Australia, England and the
United States of America), her journalism, and her
fiction, all reflected her feminist/reformist vision; her
novel, *Handfasted*, (a critique of women's exploitation in marriage along with a radical solution), was
considered too advanced for publication during her
own lifetime. The value of some of her writing has
been recognised in recent years and a number of her
novels about independent women are now in print
(*Handfasted* and *Mr Hogarth's Will*, Penguin Australian Women's Library; *The Portable Catherine
Helen Spence*, University of Queensland Press). But
as one of the heroines of Australian women's literature, Catherine Helen Spence deserves even greater
prominence and further study, if she is to be given
her due.

A contributor to the *South Australian Register* and
the *Observer Miscellany*, Catherine Helen Spence
published a wide range of provocative pieces. The
following short story, *Afloat or Ashore*, was published in the *Australasian* July 6 and 13, 1878; while

initially it portrays a woman of spirit, it also depicts
the way in which women can be led to abandon their
independent stance.

Afloat or Ashore

CHAPTER I

Margaret Hope's Views

'You seem to see no drawback to your future happiness, my
dear Lizzie, in the thought that you will have your husband constantly at home with you,' said Margaret Hope to her sister.

'Why should that be a drawback, when Walter and I are so
thoroughly in accord in all things?' returned the younger girl. 'Do
you think we are likely to love each other less than we do now?
It is the very greatest cause I have for congratulating myself on
the life before us that, except for visiting his people – in which
I can, I hope, often bear him company – he will be always with
me. I shall be with him always in his public work, for I shall never
miss a service. In his private studies, in his sermon writing, I shall
be by his side; and all his little tastes and occupations, his gardening and carpentering, will only keep him at home.'

'Well, I only hope you will not bore each other, and tire of
each other before six months are over,' said Margaret.

'You were never in love, Margaret; if you had been you would
know that all this is nonsense. Walter is so thoroughly good, so
fond of me and I of him, that it would be impossible for us to
tire of each other, even if we were constantly together for 50 years.'

'And you are so different from me. I have the weakness of tir-
ing of my friends if I see too much of them, particularly when
there is no opposition, no contradiction.'

'You never tired of me – at least, you never pained me by saying so,' said Lizzie.

'No, because you are so different; and, besides, you allow me
to do exactly as I like. My relation to you has been half-motherly,
and I suppose no mother is ever bored by her child. But marriage is something so different. There is a sudden plunge into the
closest and the most irrevocable union with one absolutely
unknown, as Walter Dunstone was to you six months ago; there
are no ties of blood, no bonds of habit; you begin with such

romantic enthusiastic attachment and it would be terrible to see that Elysian light fade into that of common day, and to feel that the return of the pristine glory is impossible. The man whom I am likely to marry (if I ever do so) is absolutely unknown to me now, and I do not think I can love him enough to bear the constant pressure of alien peculiarities on my own without being either bored or exasperated. I think that most married people feel this, though of course they prudently keep it to themselves.'

'Oh! Margaret, what treason you talk! What can make the life with the choice of your heart other than pleasant? Even if one had to give way a great deal, it is our duty to accommodate ourselves to circumstances.'

'Our duty being always done in this lower world without grudging and without misgiving, and there being no risk of spoiling the party yielded to by indulgence. You are so happy and so confident that I know I am not depressing you by my croaking. I am placing myself in your circumstances, which is a very different thing, as you know, from the actual position.'

'Then what is your idea of married happiness, Margaret — for yourself, I mean?'

'Well, Lizzie, let me see. In the first place, I must love him and he me a great deal to begin with.'

'That is a right beginning, at any rate.'

'Next, he must not be a pottering sort of man, but one with a life's work as different from mine as may be; pretty hard work, and mixing a good deal with all sorts of people, contradictory and perhaps disagreeable. In the third place, he must not interfere at all in my department, or call in question my occupations, my tastes, or my friends; and for these reasons he ought to be a great deal away from home.'

'Then you should have a squatter, not so rich as to live at ease in Melbourne or the suburbs, but who has out-stations to visit, and blundering overseers to scold. Or a commercial traveller, if you could find one warranted steady, and clever enough for you, and, if possible, a gentleman. Or, stay – best of all – a sea captain.'

'Yes,' said Margaret, thoughtfully, 'best of all, I should like a sea captain, either in the navy or in the merchant service. He would be at home with me here for two or three months in the year, and looked for all the rest, with pleasant letters exchanged, quite like love-letters. We should never have time to tire of each other. He could bear with my peculiarities as a pleasant change, a sort of bracing tonic, for a short period, and I should not be exasperated by his. His home would be to him a sort of paradise, and for nine or ten months of the year I should pursue the life I prefer for myself broken in upon by a yearly honey-moon.'

'And you fancy you would have no anxiety in stormy weather; or if you were ill, or he was ill, and you could not nurse and tend each other, or if sorrow or trouble came and you could not sympathise with each other. If you loved your sea-captain as I love Walter, you could never dream of such a thing as rejoicing in long absences.

'People can make up their minds to endure such different things, Lizzie darling. What I could not endure if I loved, would be to feel the love grow less on either side, to feel the companionship which we had hoped would be a joy and a stimulus to all good growing nearly into a bond of custom, dragging down to the commonplace and the conventional – merely the household love which one sees so often, taking the place of what should be both sacred and intense. I scarcely fear this for you and Walter, but look at Jessie Brown and Helen Smeaton, did they ever think of such a flat colourless life during their engagement?'

'They have great happiness and hope in their children, Margaret.'

'No compensation would come to me in children, if I were disappointed in my husband or he in me. So, as I said, I could bear pain, separation, anxiety, as well as most women, but the dreariness of being reduced to insignificance, of boring and being bored, is utterly intolerable to me.'

The two sisters were, indeed, very different, but were very dear to each other. And as they had lost both of their parents and a brother of great promise, who was between them in age, they had been what is called all the world to each other, until the young clergyman, Walter Dunstone, had come, and seen, and conquered the younger of the two. Every one thought he had made a judicious choice, for Lizzie, though only 20, was cut out for a clergyman's wife, whereas Margaret had too many peculiarities to be quite safe. Nevertheless, Mr Dunstone had been first more captivated with Margaret, and with the slightest encouragement on her part would have linked his fate to hers; but she did not at all return his regard. Even as her sister's lover he wearied her a good deal, and to have to sit with the appearance of attention to listen to his young and rudimentary sermons week after week would have been impossible for her, while there was no hope of reorganising them altogether by unsparing criticism. True, as an Anglican, he had not such a high idea of the importance of preaching as she had; the power of the living voice coming to living ears, fresh each week with something, gathered thoughtfully and earnestly given forth, had little or no appreciation from Mr Dunstone. Lizzy fortunately took to the liturgy and the service generally with full satisfaction.

To Margaret it appeared that her future brother-in-law looked on the Anglican Church as rather a great conservative social organisation than a life-giving, spiritual force, and she was exasperated by his ignorance about and his depreciation of all forms of earnestness in other churches, and his thinly-disguised contempt, which he called tolerance, for dissent.

Both sisters were good-looking, both had a small independence quite worth adding to a limited income, and as Mr Dunstone thought Margaret must be lonely when her sister left her, he, as well as Lizzie, had pressed her to make her home with them in their rural parsonage; but this had been firmly though kindly declined. The cottage in the pleasant suburb was sacred by so many memories that Margaret would rather live there on a narrower income than let it to strangers. Frequent visits would be exchanged; but she preferred the old home, and while the lovers pitied her, and her friends wondered that her attachment to her living sister and the excellent young fellow she was marrying should not lead her to sacrifice sentimental notions, and follow them to Landsmere, Margaret was considering if there was no public work she might take up to occupy her leisure. She had one special gift, and that was in finding out what people could do, and in bringing together those who wanted work done, and those who were willing and able to do it; and as one of the oldest residents in Hawthorn she had followed up and indeed enlarged the sphere of usefulness in that way which had been filled by her mother. She knew of a good place for the smart little girl with whom the charwoman wished to begin the world, she knew of needlewomen, sick nurses, governesses, and when they could give satisfaction; and the thought that with more time and more organisation she could be helpful to a greater number. In fact, she had so many tastes and resources that her best friends feared she was cut out for an old maid.

CHAPTER II

Margaret's Views Are Met

Mr Dunstone laughed very heartily at the confidence reposed in him by Lizzie Hope on the earliest possible opportunity as to Margaret's ideas about married happiness for herself. Both lovers were inclined to pity every one who missed such happiness, and had sometimes speculated on what would be done for poor Margaret.

'Well, of the three eligible classes,' said Dunstone, 'I prefer the squatter; – of decidedly Anglican tendencies would be desirable, for Margaret has too much of the old Puritanic leaven in her. No one knows what a squatter may come to. There's Tom Burton, not at all a bad sort, and pioneering now, but as likely to die a millionaire as the richest was at his age. If we want a steeple, or an organ, or windows of the proper kind for Lansmere Church, there's nothing like the squatting connexion.'

But on the following day Walter happened to stumble across Captain Hugh Southam, of the *Australian Queen*, in which he had come out the previous year, just arrived from a specially quick passage. Mutual hearty greetings ensued. Southam congratulated his friend so warmly on his improved appearance that the younger man was tempted to become effusive. He had been fortunate in every way. The Victorian climate had effectually cured the throat affection[*sic*] which had been so annoying in England; he had got a charge in a pretty district about 30 miles from Melbourne, to which he was going in a month, but in the meantime he was pleasantly enough occupied—he was engaged to one of the prettiest and most affectionate girls in the colony.

'Lucky fellow, you,' said Southam. 'Oh! you young clergymen are thoroughly spoiled and petted by all womankind.'

'No more so than you, I am sure. I never saw such a centre for admiration as you are at the head of the cuddy table. What a head you must have to stand it.'

'It needs one,' said Southam. 'But I think it is such hard lines for a woman to be a captain's wife that I have resolved on a single life till I can afford to leave the profession; and it takes a long time to save as much as would secure a comfortable home on shore. Now, a clergyman *ought* to be married, and generally can get a wife who brings a little help. Is it so with you?' asked Southam.

'Well, you are not far out,' replied Dunstone, 'she has what may be considered a nice little fortune; and the Bishop and the Dean have expressed themselves in the most friendly manner about her. Miss Hope was brought up a Presbyterian, but of course goes altogether with me now.'

'Miss Hope?' said Captain Southam. 'Miss Margaret Hope?'

'No, Elizabeth, the younger sister. Do you know anything of the other?'

'I have heard a good deal about her, and seen her likeness, but never saw herself.'

'You must see her, and my Lizzie too,' said Dunstone eagerly. 'You have no engagement for this afternoon?'

'Yes, I have one – a somewhat painful one.'

'This evening then – where are you staying? At Scott's, as before! I shall call for you and take you out with me, and introduce Lizzie to the object of her gratitude, for any one who had any hand in bringing me here she is kindly disposed to, and then you can see Miss Hope too.'

The proposal was acceded to, and without changing his opinion as to the preferableness of the squatter, Dunstone introduced to his sister-in-law the much less eligible sea captain, from his desire to show his own peculiar prize. But Margaret Hope and Captain Southam were interested in each other, and made to fit into each other's peculiarities. It was more remarkable that they should not have met before than that they should be brought together now.

When, accordingly, Mr Dunstone introduced his friend to the Hopes, he could not help seeing that Margaret made the greatest impression. Where had the clergyman's eyes been that he had preferred Lizzie's girlish prettiness to the womanly beauty of the elder, or the acquiescent worshipping attitude of his fiancée to the more original and inspiring conversation which called for thought and challenged discussion? He liked the ease of manner, the air of command which Margaret had naturally fallen into as the head of the little household. Not that Hugh Southam was admiring her on his own account, he never did anything so foolish; but, in the abstract, she was the more admirable of the two. Lizzie had kittenish ways, which Southam did not like; he had seen them in great variety on board the *Australian Queen*, and he associated them with affectation, forgetting that it is quite natural for some girls to be like kittens. But her adoring manner towards the young Anglican, who was sure to be sufficiently spoiled by the female part of his own congregation, was likely to make the fellow good for nothing. A woman like the elder sister might take the conceit out of him, and lead, and suggest, and criticise wholesomely, whereas this girl would think every sermon the best he had ever written, and every little trivial kindness would be praised by her as if it had been a heroic virtue.

'You are very early this year,' said Dunstone.

'Yes, a first-rate run. We got out of the Channel well, and, besides, we made an early start. We, of course, are the first on the berth of the wool ships this year.'

'You will have to wait for the first wool bales three or four months. Rather long for this side of the world.'

'So my mother will think, but I enjoy Melbourne very much, and have many good friends here.'

'You have time this year to fall in love, and get engaged and married,' said Walter, with a little glance at Lizzie. 'I have not been much longer about my little affair.'

'But you are not married yet, and you have a permanent home to take your bride to, and do not need to leave her at the end of the wooing. If I were to propose to take Mr Dunstone back with me, Miss Lizzie, how would you like it?'

'Not at all, and as he would not like it either, there is not much chance of its being done,' said Lizzie.

'It does not suit him, his business does not require it. It is not so much a matter of liking. I think you are a most enviable fellow, Dunstone. You have an honourable and useful profession – I should call it a venerable one, if Miss Lizzie would not object to the implied age for that term. There is a little money on both sides, which makes you pretty independent of the whims of a colonial congregation. You have a temper which will make you pull well with your spiritual heads, and are not viewy enough to get you into trouble with anyone. And you have taken to colonial life from the very first.'

'Other people are not so fortunate.'

Lizzie looked at the speaker with commiseration which slightly amused him, because his envy of Dunstone was more limited than she could imagine it to be.

'How many dying people had you on board this voyage?' asked Dunstone.

'Two died on board,' said Southam gravely. 'Both most hopeless cases when they left England. One was eager to return here to his friends, the other had left every soul he cared for behind. I believe the doctors recommend a sea-voyage as a last resource to get rid of patients, and not with the slightest hope of their surviving it.'

'And the one who was coming home was Mr James Drake,' said Margaret, 'He went to England with you. He wrote to his mother of your kindness and attention.'

'He died off the Cape, poor fellow. I have been to see his people to-day, and delivered over his effects and his last messages. There was a letter for you, Miss Hope, but I left it with the packet at Carlton.'

'We were old friends,' said Margaret, calmly. 'I did not think he could live to come back, and now I think it a great pity that he should have died at sea, for his mother will feel it sorely.'

'I suppose his life was prolonged for six months by the sea voyage. As for poor young Robin, I believe his death was hastened. A second-class passage for a dying man is always a mistake, though we do our best for them. In the case of Mr Drake, I believe he clung to life so tenaciously that he preferred the six months among strangers to an earlier death at home. Some people care nothing for circumstances of pain and discomfort if they can only live, for while there is life they feel hope, and up to the last week Mr Drake thought he would recover. It is difficult for me to understand this feeling. These invalids are a great trial to us. They depress the kind-hearted passengers and provoke the selfish ones, and it is difficult for the master of the ship to show sufficient consideration for them without sacrificing the comfort of others.'

On the following morning the post brought to Miss Hope James Drake's farewell letter, along with a very pathetic note from his mother, with the slight flavour of reproach in it which soothed the old lady's grief. The dying man's letter was full of an invalid's egotism, and yet had a great deal of real tenderness in it. He was so sure that she would be eager to know all about him, and especially how he caught that last cold which had taken such dreadful hold on him; it had been in the tropics too, where no one could have feared anything. Not that he blamed Captain Southam for it, because, of course, he had his other passengers to consider, and the ventilation, which they insisted on having, had been fatal to him; for, with the profuse perspirations he suffered from, the sudden check had fastened on his weak lungs. People had all been very kind indeed, and Captain Southam had done everything in his power, but a ship was not like home for comfort, and now the doctor had said that he could not get over it. Unfortunately he was a young, inexperienced man, not so full of resource as his own medical man in Melbourne, but there was no better advice to be got. He was sure that if Margaret had only married him three years ago he would never have lost his health, for he had been reckless about exposure, and caught cold upon cold till now it had come to this. Still he forgave Margaret from his heart and soul, and wished her health and happiness.

She was sitting with the letter in her hand, with a little amusement curiously mixed up with her real regret, when the visitor of the previous evening appeared. He apologised for his intrusion, asking for Mr Dunstone, who had appointed with him on their way home that if the weather kept up, they should all drive out to the Ferntree Gully, which neither gentleman had seen, and which Miss Lizzie had been describing. It had been fine weather for the last ten days, but it was likely to break soon, and as the place is not seen to advantage when too wet, they proposed to start at once. Walter was not far behind he was sure. There was a quick glance at the letter on Southam's part, and it flashed on Margaret's mind that, as it was not in James Drake's own hand, this might have been the amanuensis, and the covert reproaches and the full forgiveness for both might be as well known by her visitor as by herself.

'So you have got your letter,' he said with a tone of interest.

'Mrs Drake forwarded it to me by post, she was not well enough to come with it. May I suppose that you are aware of its contents?'

'So far I am, because he could not sit up to write, poor fellow, and I offered to write for him, but I felt it was no business of mine, and tried to pay no more attention to it than was absolutely necessary, and to forget it afterwards,' said Hugh Southam, with a little embarrassment.

'I think it is possible you may have misunderstood our relations with each other,' said Margaret. 'My father and his father were great friends, and we were left in Mr Drake's guardianship. We had a good deal of intercourse, and, unfortunately, James fancied I was suited for him, and I knew that he never could suit me. There never was the slightest cause for him supposing that I would or could marry him. There was nothing to forgive me, more than to forgive you. There was nothing in common between us; there were not even the sharp contrasts which often lead to attachment. And he showed signs of great delicacy of health long before the date he speaks of. His father and mother wished it, but the idea of marrying him never once entered my head.'

Captain Southam had heard a good deal more about Margaret Hope than appeared in the letter. All the young fellow's clinging to life had been curiously associated with her, and he had supposed that if he got better she would think differently. She had such strong ideas about health, and that, he was sure, was her only objection. And without telling actual falsehood, he had given his hearer to understand that he had had a good deal of encouragement in his suit. But all these impressions were dissipated at once by Margaret's candid statement, and the more he saw of her the more preposterous it appeared that a poor thing, mentally and physically, like James Drake, could have made any way with such an original and energetic woman.

The excursion was pleasant. The weather kept up until 3 o'clock, when the rain came down in torrents, as the weather-wise captain had prophesied; but they had seen the place in its beauty, the girls were clothed for changeable weather, and they returned to Hawthorn glowing with the exposure and conflict with the elements. During the day the lovers were naturally very much engrossed with each other; during the evening the same thing was continued, and Margaret was left to cultivate the acquaintance of this, to her, most eligible of men, who had hitherto been so impervious to ordinary fascinations. He became somehow interested – not abstractly, but personally – in this handsome woman of 25; and he felt that he was interesting her. After a week or two of this dangerous society – for Dunstone found no difficulty in leading Southam to his suburban cottage on the slightest pretext, where the cosy home feeling of an old house with old furniture, old pictures, and old books, reminded him much more of the nest where his mother and sisters dwelt at Hampstead than any of the newer and rawer, though wealthier, houses he visited – the master mariner began to feel that he must pull up, and to weigh the advantages and disadvantages of running away. This long spell of leisure ought to be turned to account. He might take a trip to Adelaide, or Sydney, or, better still, to New Zealand, and speculate a little in colonial produce. He always tried to do a little business. He had a share in the *Australian*

Queen, and it would be wiser to increase his chances of making a permanent home than to increase his cause for regret that he had not one. But when he mooted his project to Dunstone over a cigar, that young pastor saw no savour in it. He had begun to see the tendency on both sides, and to sympathise with it. When things were going on so swimmingly it would never do for him to get out of the way. He first pressed Southam to stay over his own marriage, which was fast approaching, and then confided his wish that as much happiness might be in store for his friend.

'No such luck for me,' said Southam. 'There are no angelic Lizzies for me.'

'Someone else might suit you as well as she suits me.'

'Ah! but I could not do as well for her.'

'Why not. To tell the truth, there is a curious whim someone has got that she could prefer a husband who would not be always at home.'

'Who thinks that? Not Miss Hope, surely?'

'Yes; she fancies so, at least.'

'That is because she is absolutely fancy free and heart whole. No woman who knew what love was could think so.'

'Just what Lizzie says; but you see for the present it makes you have an advantage instead of a disadvantage. In the first place, you are able to please her; in the second, she will be only too happy to please you. She has the home and everything as she likes it, and a small competency sufficient for her own requirements. You can save as much married as unmarried: and if you want a wife who can submit cheerfully to the drawbacks of your profession she is the very one for you. Besides, you are suited to each other in every way.'

Southam could not help being much surprised that a woman who was capable of a deep and strong passion, as he believed Margaret to be, should have such a strange fancy, for fancy only he was sure it was. He could not imagine a wife who loved him not suffering, as he knew himself would suffer, in the long absences, which, however inevitable and however looked forward to, must be hard to bear. It was only because love to her was merely a thing of imagination that she thought she could bear separation so complacently. First make her in love with him, and then how different her feelings would be. And Southam determined now seriously to try not so much because he could fulfil her ideal of happiness as to convince her how false that ideal was. All his old resolutions which had steeled him to the charms of all sorts of lady passengers, engaged or very much the reverse, who has crossed in the *Australian Queen*, were thrown to the winds. The deprivations and sufferings which he had been unwilling to expose a sensitive wife to, he was determined to make this nonchalant girl feel. He exerted himself to be agreeable; he surpassed himself in his powers of sympathy and his powers of conversation. His reading, his travels, his knowledge of men and of manners, all won his way with a stay-at-home girl who has seen few men so strong, so resolute or so reasonable. Her knowledge that he had been proof to so much fascination, and the cause of his scruples, which Walter Dunstone had communicated to her, made her pride in the conquest equal with his, and the natural result followed with hearts quite disengaged, with every opportunity and circumstance in favour of their becoming attached. There was not the least doubt on the part of Mr and Mrs Dunstone on their first visit to Hawthorn after their little wedding trip, to cheer up poor Margaret, that she had been sufficiently cheered, and that both she and Southam were sufficiently cheerful. But the love was as yet undeclared, though apparent to the practised eyes of the newly married pair. She congratulated herself that he was conquered against his will. He was delighting in the conviction that, when the time of parting came, she would feel how weighty his scruples were; and then the thought came, that without a declaration he would have no right to see her regret.

And it was a matter-of-fact proposal when it was made. Hugh Southam was ashamed of his want of eloquence and enthusiasm. And it was accepted frankly in the same matter-of-fact way, just as if it were a partnership about a vessel, and in the midst of what ought to have been triumph he felt deeply mortified.

'I don't think you know, Miss Hope. I don't think I have expressed myself adequately. I find no words to give you any idea of how dear you are to me.'

'I do not need you to say much. I am quite convinced that you love me far more than I deserve. I have the most perfect confidence in you. I was prepared to esteem and like you. I could not have believed that anyone in so short a time could have won such mastery over me. Perhaps I showed it too openly. You felt you needed no eloquence.'

'It is not that, Margaret; but because I know I have so little to offer.'

'You offer me a good man's name and a good man's heart, and I think that is a great deal.'

'But not such a house as Dunstones – a permanent, settled home.'

'I do not need one. This will be your home when you are on this side of the world. I hope you will like it. I shall try to have it as bright as possible for you. Do you think I would change with Lizzie?'

'Not altogether; but still it will be hard for me to think that my wife is sitting alone here, and I am half across the world – even if she is sitting thinking of me.'

'Which very probably she will be, and you thinking of her, and both of us very happy in the thought.'

'Is it unreasonable in me to think that she should not be very happy.'

'When people have absolute confidence in one another, absence is not so hard, and I mean to have that confidence in you. Try to have the same in me.'

'I do not need to try; I have it. But our sympathy cannot be complete if what causes me regret is an indifferent thing to you.'

'Not quite indifferent,' said Margaret, smiling through tears more charming to Southam's eyes than the smile. 'Why do not you flatter yourself with the thought that I must love you very much if I prefer two months or three months in the year of your society to 12 months of any other man's? Could I go further than that?'

'Perhaps not,' said Southam, doubtfully, 'but – '

'But you suspect my motive; you suspect that there is not a man alive whom I should not prefer on the same conditions, and therefore it is no exceptional compliment to yourself. But just think what these two or three months may be. I have just learned what happiness I am capable of.'

'And so have I, and throw all my scruples to the winds for the sake of it; but that will make the loss of it all the greater.'

'Not the loss of it; only a little change in its form. Both you and I can bear parting bravely enough, but what I cannot bear, and what I am sure you could not bear, is that you should grow to love me less, or that I should grow to love you less. You have been accustomed to hold your dear ones on the conditions you call so hard, and you continue to love your mother and sisters as much as ever, and you will continue to do the same by me. And to them this will make no change. You are with them in England as entirely theirs as heretofore. They lose nothing.'

'And they gain nothing, Margaret. Do you not think my mother will delight in you, and the girls, too? And, as I generally spend the larger part of my land life in England, do not you should be there, within their reach?'

'Oh no,' said Margaret, gently. 'This provides you with two homes; altogether, it is the best arrangement. This place is very dear to me, full of memories of my mother, my father, my brother, and my loving Lizzie. Don't ask me to give this up.'

'No,' said Southam, 'it was very thoughtless in me to speak of such a thing; and this cottage is inexpressibly dear to myself.' And so he dropped the subject, and abandoned himself to so much that was satisfactory about the engagement.

CHAPTER III

The Reality

Hugh Southam had not the slightest cause to complain of any coldness on Margaret's part. Lizzy Hope had not been more affectionate, or more engrossed with her specimen of clerical perfection, than Margaret now showed herself to him. Only the placid way in which she looked forward to the approaching separation, the plans she laid out for her life apart from him, the talks about letter-writing, the little commissions she asked him to execute, as if this was merely a pleasant change and not a deplorable necessity, puzzled, and indeed slightly provoked, him. Along with his love there was awakened a desire for mastery, and he was convinced that she completely mistook her own heart on this point. He had not at first thought of pressing for marriage until after his next voyage, for the present relations were blissful enough; but one day, stimulated by hearing some more of her prettily formed plans for the future, he had the audacity to propose that she should become his wife now.

'Now?' said Margaret, with a hot, sudden flush overspreading her face. 'Surely that is quite impossible – altogether too sudden. I could not think of such a thing.'

Hugh Southam paused, and then said very gravely, 'You see,

my dear Margaret, our chances of companionship are so short and far between that it seems like tempting Providence to neglect an occasion like the present. Take the goods the gods provide thee.'

'Is that with special reference to yourself, or to me?' said Margaret, laughing.

'To both, I hope and believe.'

'Ah, I am not so sure that the gods could provide me any goods better than the present. I thought you were perfectly happy. You said so yesterday.'

'So I was for yesterday, not quite so much so to-day; but certainly very far from likely to be so next month. And the month after that I must go, and you don't seem to care. If you did you would see the reasonableness of my request.'

'Oh! Hugh, I don't mean to say anything disagreeable, but if you only knew how I tremble at any change; the bewildering newness of this happiness we have in each other surely might satisfy you till next year. Think how happy people are in long engagements.'

'You forget our peculiar circumstances, Margaret; and if this is what you call confidence, I think it is very imperfect. I know that the closer and more constant our union is, the more I shall love you. In spite of my imperfections, I believe you are true and tender enough to do the same by me. Why grudge me one short honeymoon this year to throw light on my homeward voyage?'

I am almost ashamed to confess that Margaret, who had hitherto adhered to the resolutions she had formed with the most placid regularity, gave way to Southam in the handsomest manner, and allowed him to set a day that would allow them one month ashore together. He also ascertained that there was no objection to his wife accompanying him home as a passenger, and believed that, once married, she would find it no such easy thing to say farewell.

Lizzie's wooing had been a short one, but Margaret's was so much shorter that Mrs Grundy made some remarks. However, it was set down to the proverbial impetuosity and impatience of a sailor.

It was a bright honeymoon in the most glorious weather. They travelled about for a week, and Margaret saw many places which, although Victorian born, were quite new to her; but even the old places seemed to have a new light on them. Who could point out beauties to her like Hugh, whose memories of English and foreign localities came in to find out resemblances and differences, and to link each new-found scene with his past life in her memory for ever! They came back to their house to spend the rest of the honeymoon where the wooing had been done. Everything went on smoothly. Captain Southam fell into his Australian home as if he had been born to it. When callers came they saw very little changed at the cottage. There was nothing new to admire or criticise. Mrs Southam was exactly the Miss Hope of former times, and even her husband was merely an accident. Not much glory about this marriage: but for the time much happiness.

But the shadow crept on. Margaret had resented the ill-concealed pity of her friends, especially of Mr and Mrs Drake about the approaching parting. She had turned a deaf ear to Mr Drake's suggestion that he could get a tenant for the cottage if she chose to go to Landsmere parsonage, or if Captain Southam could make it convenient for her to take the trip with him. But yet she felt more than she liked to acknowledge it, her husband's regret in view of the approaching parting.

She went with him to the *Australian Queen* which was filling up with terrible rapidity. She saw the arrangements made for her husband's comfort, but he was as independent on his own domain as she on hers. Everything was perfect.

'There seems nothing wanting, Hugh,' said she, just a little disappointed, for she would have liked to contribute somewhat to his appointments.

'Only one thing, Margaret, that is you. Why should you not make this voyage with me? You can, with every comfort. And you will see and become acquainted with my mother and sisters, and we can have another honeymoon in England.'

'Oh no, Hugh. This could not last – it is impossible!'

'What could not last?'

'This happiness – this perfect union. And a captain's wife is always voted a nuisance on board by everyone.'

'Except by himself. Call it our wedding trip: we had just a short one on land.'

'No, dear Hugh, no! I should make such an unaccommodating, disagreeable captain's wife. Don't press me. I cannot go. Let me stay at home and await your return.'

'Yours is a very strange love, Margaret.'

'Perhaps it is, but it is real love. Now dear Hugh, recollect that when you had scruples, it was on your wife's account, not your own. It was how she would feel your absence, not you hers; and if your wife does not mind it, don't blame her.'

'I cannot blame her. My wife can only love me as far as I make myself worthy of her love, as much as I can make her. It is my own shortcoming that is the cause of my defeat.'

'Do you call it defeat that I accepted you at once, that I married you on the earliest possible day, that I shall weary for your return? Oh, Hugh, you have been so spoiled by absolute command on board this *Australian Queen* of yours, that your poor Australian wife must efface herself absolutely to please you.'

'Well, then, I suppose I must submit,' said Southam, 'and try you as well as myself with separation.'

'Let us make the best of what time is left us together,' said Margaret, 'and not spoil it by useless debate.'

'Oh, certainly. I must not forget about your greenhouse: that must be completed before I go.'

Margaret had thought she would not like pottering ways, but this handy sea captain had a knack of liking to do a lot of things about the house and garden, and she found she followed him about as closely as Lizzie could do. He had felt it strange that his wife wanted no money for rent or housekeeping. She would only accept little presents, and he thought the greenhouse, which he could help to put up, was as good a one as he could make.

But the days flew by only too swiftly, and the last good-bye was said, not on board, but at home. Hugh Southam was glad to see his wife crying as bitterly, as copiously, as if she had not views, but even at the last moment she stood firm. Mr and Mrs Dunstone had come to say good-bye: they could not stay, for it was necessary for Walter to be home to give his weekly evening service, and Lizzie could not let him go without her, so they took it for granted that Margaret would accompany them to pay a long visit. But she did not, she promised the visit by and by. She wished to feel the whole of the blow at once, and not to break it in any way. Lizzie's effusive pity dried her tears: she said good-bye to her calmly, and it was not till the united pair drove off to their parsonage that she took in the whole of the situation. There could be no love and no happiness without sorrow; she always knew that a price must be paid for what she had gained, and this was the price she had preferred. Of all the memories that clung round the cottage and the garden, how haunting and how tenacious were those of the new-found, strong, good man who had so recently entered into her life. All the others seemed faint in comparison. As she sat with the book in her hand they had been reading together, or walked through the rooms, or glanced at the garden, or visited the greenhouse, he had left his mark everywhere, the faintest rustle that met her ears was like the sound of his return.

But the great comfort was that the love was in no way worn-out; it was fresh, warm and romantic. It would keep so. She had no fear of his seeing anyone anywhere who would rival her in the possession of his heart. She was far richer than she had ever been, and he must acknowledge the same when he thought over it. She was not to be pitied, no one need pity him. And how would he write? Would he give her details of daily life, or would he give her his inner thoughts, his deepest moods, his fancies, his hopes, his recollections? For herself, it would be the latter kind of letter. She dreaded lest she should bore him on paper with the trivialities of the daily routine which she shrank from encountering by his side, yet when his letters came, after a wearily long interval, really fuller of facts than of sentiment, with sketches of the passengers, and good-natured strokes of satire at their peculiarities; with an account of a calm in the doldrums, when life was a weariness to all but people with some resources, she found it so interesting that she was ashamed of her own reticence, and wrote a different kind of letter from her previous ones in reply, with a good deal of her busy life in it.

Her visits to her sister were pleasant. The young people did not seem to bore each other in the least, but Lizzie's devotion to her husband was in excess of his to her. She waited on him, she anticipated his wishes, she spared him every annoyance and every fatigue that was possible. She would entertain tiresome people to save him from the effort, and go out in the heat, because he was not so well used to the climate, when a visit from her might be supposed to do as well as one from the clergyman. And Dunstone was lazily grateful for her efforts, but did not check them, because it gave Lizzie so much pleasure to do it. Margaret was inclined to protest, but had the good sense to refrain; people must lead their own life, and it was well that Lizzie's idol was not altogether unappreciative. And at the bottom of her heart she acknowledged that she would like to do as much for Hugh if he would permit it, but she liked him better for not permitting it.

When the wind blew hard, Margaret's friends were apt to drop in, and expect her to be anxious when her husband was at sea, but, as Margaret knew something about the laws of storms, she did not disquiet herself till the time came when the *Australian Queen* might be supposed to be within the radius of the barometer at Melbourne. And even then she knew the ship was good, and the captain skilful and experienced, and felt wonderfully at ease.

The second honeymoon, so looked forward to by both, showed no waning in its light. It was ten times better than the first, for it was three times as long, and they knew each other so thoroughly. The absence had added a charm to it, even in Hugh Southam's estimation.

Lizzie was much engrossed with a baby boy, the most wonderful child ever seen, and could stir little from the parsonage, but the Southams were out and about everywhere together, in all kinds of weather, visiting all sorts of places, getting acquainted with country folks, miners, squatters, and merchants. It was now that Margaret fully found out what a circle of friends the popular sea captain had made, and for his sake she received invitations everywhere, and was treated with the greatest kindness.

In the midst of this whirl there was a little pause.

'Margaret,' said her husband, 'I fear I have interrupted your life with my claims. What have you done with all the pursuits and engagements you wrote me last about? I am at leisure when the ship is in harbour, and may be as idle as I please, but you are absolutely at my beck and call, and your protegées may suffer.'

'I got Charlotte Drake to keep up my work for me, for I wanted to have no ties and to be absolutely at your disposal when you are on the Australian side of the world, but would you mind my spoiling your evening a little to-night? There is a poor girl whom Charlotte can make nothing of. She is left destitute by her father's death; she cannot go out as a governess, for she is not educated, and has not the capacity for learning. She sews neatly, and understands the working of one kind of machine, but cannot cut out, and I want to give her some lessons, as Charlotte says she is stupid; and, besides, her pride is hurt at the idea of going out to sew – either by the day or as a permanent needlewoman. Now, Hugh, you could help me by showing this poor Jane Ford the greatest respect, and by pretending to take a deep interest in our cutting lesson, because you know it is really of importance.'

'Of course it is, and my interest need not be pretended but

genuine. I am capable of taking interest in many things besides navigation.'

When Jane Ford came and he saw how she needed to be managed and directed, what patience Margaret had both with her talk, which was very far from brilliant, and with her blunders from nervousness and from conceit – for she displayed both; and how she asked her to return the following morning for another lesson, and declined an excursion they had planned on this account, he could not help saying, after the departure of the young lady –

'You slandered yourself, Margaret, when you said you were disagreeable and unaccommodating to stupid people. You would never see any one on board the *Australian Queen* so trying as this Miss Ford.'

'She is not trying at all, Hugh. I don't think she is very clever or very wise, but yet I don't see why she should not be able to earn her living, and this appears the only possible way at present. Charlotte Drake says she cannot be taught, but that is nonsense. She only needs a little patience on my part and her own. But I knew she was likely to bore you. You will go to-morrow. I did not mean to keep you, but Miss Ford will forget all she learned to-night, if it is not kept up.'

'I shall do a morning's gardening. I am not going to Heidelberg without you, and I, perhaps, can have a prep now and then as unaccommodating wife.'

He thought he had now a sufficient argument to bring against hers. There was still an opportunity for her going to England with him on the second voyage with as much comfort as before, and as he felt certain that her love was greater, he anticipated little resistance.

But no; she would be a trouble to him – she would rather stay and wait for another glimpse of Paradise. It was harder to say no than the first time; she was franker in saying how much she would miss him. She would feel lonelier. Her friends, her tastes, her pursuits were as nothing to her now in comparison to her husband; but the very freshness of their love, the perfectly unalloyed happiness they had during these three months, which she feared would lose so much of its charm if they were constantly together, made her refuse to consent. The meeting was so delicious, it repaid the pain of parting.

His next arrival found Margaret sitting up with a month old baby girl in her arms, and the honeymoon this time was of a quieter description. They had to stay at home a great deal, but, on the whole, they enjoyed it more than the others. Strangers intermeddled less with their life, and the tenderness, the helpfulness, Hugh Southam showed to his wife and little one, his contrivances for their comfort, his quiet home-loving tastes, endeared him all the more to Margaret.

And now a third parting was imminent. The *Australian Queen* was to be over-full of passengers, the principal of whom, in a worldly point of view, were Mr and Mrs Vholes and family, proverbially the most ill-bred, purse-proud people in Victoria, and Hugh felt unwilling to press his wife with a young baby to undertake the voyage, especially as the young baby took ill just before the time of sailing, and was not out of the doctor's hands, though recovering.

'You will not feel so lonely this time with little Dora, though I lose doubly. I did not think life had so much to give me. So far you are right. Three months with you is worth paying the price of three times the absence. I cannot ask you to accompany me this time,' said Southam. The perversity of her sex, or rather, to speak more justly, the perversity of human nature, tempted Margaret now as she had never been tempted before. Just because her husband saw drawbacks to her taking the voyage, she felt inclined to go. Besides, to show Dora to her grandmother was far more incumbent on her than to show herself. But she held back; she felt that she would be disagreeable to those big-wigs, especially to that insufferable Mrs Vholes, whom she had once met and detested. She never could be civil as a captain's wife ought to be. It was easy to bear with poor Jane Ford, but purse-proud arrogance always raised her scorn, and there would be innumerable opportunities of showing up Mrs Vholes's ignorance and ill-breeding which she could not resist. And then Hugh would see her faults of temper, and would love her less: better, far better to stay, and let him go alone.

And she returned to her cottage, haunted more than ever, because the one great object of her daily and nightly cares was his as well as hers, and because he had himself acquainted personally, and by report, with many other people, with whom and for whom she worked. People had given up pitying her now, and supposed that the baby was sufficient for her, and accordingly she took to pitying herself, and to indulging unavailing regrets that it had not been an ordinary lot of passengers. Nay, as the weeks and months passed on, and baby developed one accomplishment after another, she felt that she could have endured Mrs Vholes and the whole family in order that Hugh could watch the wonderful progress and growth, physical and mental, of his darling. She did not believe she could have been so foolish about a baby, and she really acknowledged to herself that she was more absurd than Lizzie, both about Dora and about her husband.

The telegraphic despatch which should announce the safe arrival of the *Australian Queen* was late this voyage. Margaret's eager eyes looked first for that each morning in *The Argus*. 'It was a good ship, a good captain,' she said to herself after each daily disappointment; but when the *Britomarte* which sailed two days after, arrived in London, and the *Claudia*, which sailed ten days after, arrived at Liverpool, and there was no news of Hugh's ship, the very goodness of the ship and of the captain made her more apprehensive. The *Britomarte* must have met with the same winds, and was not so fast a ship. Why had she not been with him instead of suffering this anxiety apart?

At last her eyes caught the name, but coupled with dreadful disaster. – Total loss of the *Australian Queen* on the 18th December by fire, a hundred and fifty miles off Cape Verde. All lives saved. Seven days in open boats. Mails, gold, and ship's papers saved by Captain Southam, the last man to leave the ship. Ship and cargo fully insured. Captain scorched, but not seriously injured.

Her head swam as she read the announcement. She snatched up her baby, and smothered her with kisses and caresses. A hurried ring at the bell announced Mr Drake.

'I came to break it to you, Margaret; but I see you have got it first. How thankful you ought to be that you were not with him, adding to his trouble; but he behaved nobly – did everything that could be done. Telegrams are so unsatisfactory; but Mr Vholes has telegraphed to his agent that Captain Southam's conduct was splendid. I met him at the gate, coming to you. You know all lives are saved, and as the ship and cargo are fully insured, your husband will be no loser. He is sure to get another ship from his owners. It may delay his coming out again for a little, but you have the greatest cause for thankfulness. Why, Mrs

Southam, I thought you were a model sailor's wife: don't give way so.'

'I should have been with him,' sobbed Margaret.

'To be in the way! – with a young baby who is far better here. I am sure. Your whim has served you for once.'

'Oh! if he had died. And think, on the 28th I was at your house, at a party.'

'Of course you could not know, but it was better for you to be at Carlton that night than with him. He would, of course, have saved you first and the little one, and that might have cost somebody's life – probably his own, for he knew his duty and did it.'

'No, no, not me first: me last. Dora first. I should have given her over to Mrs Vholes, with an entreaty to take her to Hugh's mother to comfort her a little, and then, if he had not got off, we might have died together. How selfish I have been to refuse to share his life, his dangers, when he pressed me so hard, but it was not meant for selfishness: and now how long it may be before I can see him. Oh! how much I want to know about that terrible time.

'Wait for his letters: they will come in six weeks or so. He is safe. You ought to be thankful.'

Lizzie Dunstone rushed to her sister as soon as the news reached Landsmere Parsonage, and Margaret felt her sympathy more soothing than that of any one else. Other people, like Mr Drake, congratulated her so on her escape, and on her being no hindrance to her husband's efforts, but Lizzie entered into her bitter regret, and self-reproach, and yet allayed them, because she knew well that Margaret's action had proceeded from no lack of love, but rather excess of it.

When the letters came, the newspapers and the passengers' letters were full of the praise of Hugh Southam – his coolness, his intrepidity, his perfect organisation of the method in which every soul on board was got off: the way he helped every one, carried children and incapable women to the ship's side and got them lowered, saw to the provisioning of the boats, saved wraps and blankets, looked after every one and every thing necessary for their preservation at the imminent risk of death to himself, and bore up until landed on one of the Cape Verde Islands, when he gave way, and was kindly nursed by strangers. That was the hardest blow of all to Margaret.

Southam said little about his own doings in his letter to his wife, but praised his officers and his men, who had one and all behaved with the greatest intrepidity, and had not only obeyed orders but had exceeded them in the efforts they had made for saving the passengers. It was a terrible time, like a nightmare to look back on. He had never thought the wind would keep off, so as to prevent the flames from spreading. There was no certain knowledge of how it originated, but it was suspected it was spontaneous combustion from the wood stored in the hold, as it was there it broke out. He had never hoped to get the passengers all off, and had given up thought of saving his own life. But he was glad she was not there, and so thankful he had not urged it this trip. And as he carried the little children to the boats, he thanked God from his heart that little Dora was safe in the cot he hung for her, to comfort her mother if he should not return. He spoke gratefully of those who had been so kind to him after landing. He was now quite well. His own future was uncertain; the insurance did not cover all his losses; how glad he was that she was not altogether dependent on him for worldly means. The owners were as friendly as possible, so he trusted all would be well. She was a brave woman, she could bear a little more waiting. And he was glad she heard of the escape as soon as of the danger.

Next letter was to the effect that the owners of the *Australian Queen* had offered him a new ship, bigger and finer than the lost one, which was being built, and in that case he could not be out till the very last of the season. He wished he could feel justified in going to Melbourne in the interim, but there were two reasons against it, first the great expense for such a short visit, and also because they wanted him to superintend the building of the ship, as he had some good ideas of his own. He had made up his mind with her, to a certain length of absence, but took badly with its extension. But his owners had made him another offer, which appeared to him handsomer still, even though he could not avail himself of it. They would give him a share in the business itself, as they wanted an active working partner, but he had not sufficient capital to go into it, and besides, even if he had the requisite money at command, she preferred the broken life with its glimpse of Elysium, and loved the house at Hawthorn and the nearness to her sister and her friends. And he would not ask her to give it up, for in case of this partnership with Dart & Co. they must live in London, and lead the humdrum life of city people seeing each other every day.

Margaret started up, put on her bonnet, went to Melbourne, saw Mr Drake, consulted with him as to her affairs, which were in her own power, advertised her house and property in Hawthorn for sale, arranged for the sale of her bank shares and other securities, sent to her banker and ascertained his estimate of her assests, and what he was prepared to advance, went to the office of the P. & O. Company, and then despatched the following telegram: —

'From Margaret Southam, Hawthorn, to Hugh Southam, The Pines, Sussex-place, Hampstead.

'Draw on Bank of Victoria for three thousand pounds. Close with Dart & Co. Dora and I sail – per mail steamer on the 21st.

Humdrum for ever.'

ELLEN CLACY, c. 1830-?

Born in England, (date and place uncertain), Ellen Clacy visited Australia in 1852 when the colony was in the grip of gold fever, and penned one of the best contemporary portraits of life on the goldfields. Her adventures stand in sharp contrast to the accepted image of life for a young Victorian lady, and suggest that 'fact' in the colony could be even more exciting than 'fiction'. More amazing too, than many an imaginative nineteenth century novel, Ellen Clacy's story had a romantic ending; her homeward voyage was also her honeymoon.

Ellen Clacy wrote some fiction; her novellas and short stories are about Australia and deal with bushrangers, blacks and gold-diggings. During the nineteenth century many women went exploring and contributed to the development of an extensive travel literature; the following extract forms part of that impressive tradition.

First published in 1853, *A Lady's Visit to the Gold Diggings of Australia in 1852-1853*, edited by Patricia Thompson, was reprinted in 1963.

A LADY'S VISIT TO THE GOLD DIGGINGS OF AUSTRALIA IN 1852-1853

CHAPTER I

Introductory Remarks

It may be deemed presumptuous that one of my age and sex should venture to give to the public an account of personal adventures in a land which has so often been descanted upon by other and abler pens; but when I reflect on the many mothers, wives, and sisters in England, whose hearts are ever longing for information respecting the dangers and privations to which their relatives at the antipodes are exposed, I cannot but hope that the presumption of my undertaking may be pardoned in consideration of the pleasure which an accurate description of some of the Australian Gold Fields may perhaps afford to many; and although the time of my residence in the colonies was short, I had the advantage (not only in Melbourne, but whilst in the bush) of constant intercourse with many experienced diggers and old colonists – thus having every facility for acquiring information respecting Victoria and the other colonies.

It was in the beginning of April, 185 –,[*sic*] that the excitement occasioned by the published accounts of the Victoria 'Diggings', induced my brother to fling aside his Homer and Euclid for the various 'Guides' printed for the benefit of the intending goldseeker, or to ponder over the shipping columns of the daily papers. The love of adventure must be contagious, for three weeks after (so rapid were our preparations) I found myself accompanying him to those auriferous regions. The following pages will give an accurate detail of my adventures there – in a lack of the marvellous will consist their principal faults; but not even to please would I venture to turn uninteresting truth into agreeable fiction. Of the few statistics which occur, I may safely say, as of the more personal portions, that they are strictly true.

CHAPTER III

Stay in Melbourne

At last we are in Australia. Our feet feel strange as they tread upon *terra firma*, and our *sea-legs* (to use a sailor's phrase) are not so ready to leave us after a four months' service, as we should have anticipated; but it matters little, for we are in the colonies, walking with undignified, awkward gait, not on a fashionable promenade, but upon a little wooden pier.

The first sounds that greet our ears are the noisy tones of some watermen, who are loitering on the building of wooden logs and boards, which we, as do the good people of Victoria, dignify with the undeserved title of *pier*. There they stand in their waterproof caps and skins – tolerably idle and exceedingly independent – with one eye on the look out for a fare, and the other cast longingly towards the open doors of Liardet's public-house, which is built a few yards from the landing-place, and alongside the main road to Melbourne.

'Ah, skipper! times isn't as they used to was,' shouted one, addressing the captain of one of the vessels then lying in the bay, who was rowing himself to shore, with no other assistant or companion than a sailor-boy. The captain, a well-built, fine-looking specimen of an English seaman, merely laughed at this impromptu salutation.

'I say, skipper, I don't quite like that d – d stroke of yours.'

No answer; but, as if completely deaf to these remarks, as well as the insulting tone in which they were delivered, the 'skipper' continued giving his orders to his boy, and then leisurely ascended the steps. He walked straight up to the waterman, who was lounging against the railing.

'So, my fine fellow, you didn't quite admire that stroke of mine. Now, I've another stroke that I think you'll admire still less,' and with one blow he sent him reeling against the railing on the opposite side.

The waterman slowly recovered his equilibrium, muttering, 'that was a safe dodge, as the gentleman knew he was the heaviest man of the two.'

'Then never let your tongue say what your fist can't defend,' was the cool retort, as another blow sent him staggering to his original place, amidst the unrestrained laughter of his companions, whilst the captain unconcernedly walked into Liardet's, whither we also betook ourselves, not a little surprised and amused by this our first introduction to colonial customs and manners.

The fact is, the watermen regard the masters of the ships in the bay as sworn enemies to their business; many are runaway sailors, and therefore, I suppose, have a natural antipathy that way; added to which, besides being no customers themselves, the 'skippers' by the loan of their boats, often save their friends from the exorbitant charges these watermen levy.

Exorbitant they truly are. Not a boat would they put off for the nearest ship in the bay for less than a pound, and before I quitted those regions, two and three times that sum was often demanded for only one passenger. We had just paid at the rate of only three shillings and sixpence each, but this trifling charge was in consideration of the large party – more than a dozen – who had left our ship in the same boat together.

Meanwhile we have entered Liardet's *en attendant* the Melbourne omnibus, some of our number, too impatient to wait longer, had already started on foot. We were shown into a clean, well-furnished sitting-room, with mahogany dining-table and chairs, and a showy glass over the mantel-piece. An English-looking barmaid entered, 'Would the company like some wine or spirits?' Some one ordered sherry, of which I only remember that it was vile trash at eight shillings a bottle.

And now the cry of 'Here's the bus,' brought us quickly outside again, where we found several new arrivals also waiting for it. I had hoped, from the name, or rather misname, of the conveyance, to gladden my eyes with the sight of something civilized. Alas, for my disappointment! There stood a long, tumble-to-pieces-looking waggon, not covered in, with a plank down each side to sit upon, and a miserable narrow plank it was. Into this vehicle were crammed a dozen people and an innumerable host of portmanteaus, large and small, carpet-bags, baskets, brown-paper parcels, bird-cage and inmate, &c., all of which, as is generally the case, were packed in a manner the most calculated to contribute the largest amount of inconvenience to the live portion of the cargo. And to drag this grand affair into Melbourne were harnessed thereto the most wretched-looking objects in the shape of horses that I had ever beheld.

A slight roll tells us we are off.

'And is *this* the beautiful scenery of Australia?' was my first melancholy reflection. Mud and swamp – swamp and mud – relieved here and there by some few trees which looked as starved and miserable as ourselves. The cattle we passed appeared in a wretched condition, and the human beings on the road seemed all to belong to one family, so truly Vandemonian was the cast of their countenances.

'The rainy season's not over,' observed the driver, in an apologetic tone. Our eyes and uneasy limbs most *feelingly* corroborated his statement, for as we moved along at a foot-pace, the rolling of the omnibus, owing to the deep ruts and heavy soil, brought us into most unpleasant contact with the various packages before-mentioned. On we went towards Melbourne – now stopping for the unhappy horses to take breath – then passing our pedestrian messmates, and now arriving at a small specimen of a swamp; and whilst they (with trowsers tucked high above the knee and boots well saturated) step, slide and tumble manfully through it, we give a fearful roll to the left, ditto, ditto to the right, then a regular stand-still, or perhaps, by way of variety, are all but jolted over the animal's heads, till at length all minor considerations of bumps and bruises are merged in the anxiety to escape without broken bones.

'The Yarra,' said the conductor. I looked straight ahead, and innocently asked 'Where?' for I could only discover a tract of marsh or swamp, which I fancy must have resembled the fens of Lincolnshire, as they were some years ago, before draining was introduced into that country. Over Princes Bridge we now passed, up Swanston Street, then into Great Bourke Street, and now we stand opposite the Post-office – the appointed rendezvous with the walkers, who are there awaiting us. Splashed, wet and tired, and also, I must confess, very cross, right thankful was I to be carried over the dirty road and be safely deposited beneath the wooden portico outside the Post-office. Our ride to Melbourne cost us only half-a-crown a piece, and a shilling for every parcel. The distance we had come was between two and three miles . . .

The next few days were busy ones for all, though rather dismal to me, as I was confined almost entirely within doors, owing to the awful state of the streets; for in the colonies, at this season of the year, one may go out prepared for fine weather, with blue sky above, and dry under foot, and in less than an hour, should a *colonial* shower come on, be unable to cross some of the streets without a plank being placed from the middle of the road to the pathway, or the alternative of walking in water up to the knees.

This may seem a doleful and overdrawn picture of my first colonial experience, but we had arrived at a time when the colony presented its worst aspect to a stranger. The rainy season had been unusually protracted this year, in fact it was not yet considered entirely over, and the gold mines had completely upset everything and everybody, and put a stop to all improvements about the town or elsewhere.

Our party, on returning to the ship the day after our arrival, witnessed the French-leave-taking of all her crew, who during the absence of the captain, jumped overboard, and were quickly picked up and landed by the various boats about. This desertion of the ships by the sailors is an everyday occurrence; the diggings themselves, or the large amount they could obtain for the run home from another master, offer too many temptations. Consequently, our passengers had the amusement of hauling up from the hold their different goods and chattels; and so great was the confusion, that fully a week elapsed before they were all got to shore. Meanwhile we were getting initiated into colonial prices – money did indeed take to itself wings and fly away. Firearms were at a premium; one instance will suffice – my brother sold a six barrelled revolver for which he had given sixty shillings at Baker's, in Fleet Street, for sixteen pounds, and the parting with it at that price was looked upon as a great favour. Imagine boots, and they very second-rate ones, at four pounds a pair. One of our between-deck passengers who had speculated with a small capital of forty pounds in boots and cutlery, told me afterwards that he had disposed of them the same evening he had landed, at a net profit of ninety pounds – no trifling addition to a poor man's purse. Labour was at a very high price, carpenters, boot and shoemakers, tailors, wheelwrights, joiners, smiths, glaziers, and, in fact, all useful trades, were earning from twenty to thirty shillings a day – the very men working on the roads could get eleven shillings per diem, and many a gentleman in this disarranged state of affairs, was glad to fling old habits aside and turn his hand to whatever came readiest. I knew one in particular, whose brother is at this moment serving as colonel in the army in India, a man more fitted for a gay London life than a residence in the colonies. The diggings were too dirty and uncivilized for his taste, his capital was quickly dwindling away beneath the expenses of the comfortable life he led at one of the best hotels in town, so he turned to what as a boy he had learnt for amusement, and obtained an addition to his income of more than four hundred pounds a year as house carpenter. In the morning you might see him trudging off to his work, and before night might meet him at some ball or soirée among the élite of Melbourne.

I shall not attempt an elaborate description of the town of Melbourne, or its neighbouring villages. A subject so often and well discussed might almost be omitted altogether. The town is very well laid out; the streets (which are all straight, running parallel with and across one another) are very wide, but are incomplete, not lighted, and many are unpaved. Owing to the want of lamps, few, except when full moon, dare stir out after dark. Some of the shops are very fair; but the goods all partake too largely of the flash order, for the purpose of suiting the tastes of successful diggers, their wives and families; it is ludicrous to see them in the shops – men who, before the gold-mines were discovered, toiled hard for their daily bread, taking off half-a-dozen thick gold rings from their fingers, and trying to pull on to their rough, well-hardened hands the best white kids, to be worn at some wedding party; whilst the wife, proud of the novel ornament, descants on the folly of hiding them beneath such useless articles as gloves.

The two principal streets are Collins Street and Elizabeth Street. The former runs east and west, the latter crossing it in the centre. Melbourne is built on two hills, and the view from the top of Collins Street East is very striking on a fine day when well filled with passengers and vehicles. Down the eye passes till it reaches Elizabeth Street at the foot; then up again, and the moving mass seems like so many tiny black specks in the distance, and the country beyond looks but a little piece of green. A great deal of confusion arises from the want of their names being painted on the corners of the streets: to a stranger, this is particularly inconvenient, the more so, as being straight, they appear all alike on first acquaintance. The confusion is also increased by the same title, with slight variation, being applied to so many, as, for instance, Collins Street East; Collins Street West; Little Collins Street East; Little Collins Street West, &c. Churches and chapels for all sects and denominations meet the eye; but the Established Church has, of all, the worst provision for its members, only two small churches being as yet completed; and Sunday after Sunday do numbers return from St. Peter's, unable to obtain even standing room beneath the porch. For the gay, there are two circuses and one theatre, where the 'ladies' who frequent it smoke short tobacco-pipes in the boxes and dress-circle.

The country round is very pretty, particularly Richmond and Collingwood; the latter will, I expect, soon become part of Melbourne itself. It is situated at the fashionable – that is, *east* – end of Melbourne, and the buildings of the city and this suburban village are making rapid strides towards each other. Of Richmond, I may remark that it does possess a 'Star and Garter', though a very different affair to its namesake at the antipodes, being only a small public-house. On the shores of the bay, at nice driving distances, are Brighton and St. Kilda. Two or three fall-to-pieces bathing-machines are at present the only stock in trade of these watering places; still, should some would-be fashionables among my readers desire to emigrate, it may gratify them to learn that they need not forego the pleasure of visiting Brighton in the season.

When I first arrived, as the weather was still very cold and wet, my greatest source of discomfort arose from the want of coal-fires, and the draughts, which are innumerable, owing to the slight manner in which the houses are run up; in some the front entrance opens direct into the sitting-rooms, very unpleasant, and entirely precluding the 'not at home' to an unwelcome visitor. Wood fires have at best but a cheerless look, and I often longed for the bright blaze and merry fireside of an English home. Firewood is sold at the rate of fifty shillings for a good-sized barrow-full.

The colonists (I here speak of the old-established ones) are naturally very hospitable, and disposed to receive strangers with great kindness; but the present ferment has made them forget everything in the glitter of their own mines, and all comfort is laid aside; money is the idol, and making it is the one mania which absorbs every other thought.

The walking inhabitants are of themselves a study: a glance into the streets – all nations, classes, and costumes are represented there. Chinamen, with pigtails and loose trowsers; Aborigines, with a solitary blanket flung over them; Vandemonian pickpockets, with cunning eyes and light fingers – all, in truth, from the successful digger in his blue serge shirt, and with green veil still hanging round his wide-awake, to the fashionably-attired, newly-arrived 'gent' from London, who stares around him in amazement and disgust. You may see, and hear too, some thoroughly colonial scenes in the streets. Once, in the middle of the day, when passing up Elizabeth Street, I heard the unmistakeable sound of a mob behind, and as it was gaining upon me, I turned into the enclosed ground in front of the Roman Catholic cathedral, to keep out of the way of the crowd. A man had been taken up for horse-stealing, and a rare ruffianly set of both sexes were following the prisoner and the two policemen who had him in charge. 'If but six of ye were of my mind,' shouted one, 'it's this moment you'd release him.' The crowd took the hint, and to it they set with right good will, yelling, swearing, and pushing, with awful violence. The owner of the stolen horse got up a counter demonstration, and every few yards, the procession was delayed by a trial of strength between the two parties. Ultimately the police conquered; but this is not always the case, and often lives are lost and limbs broken in the struggle, so weak is the force maintained by the colonial government for the preservation of order.

Another day, when passing the Post-office, a regular tropical shower of rain came on rather suddenly, and I hastened up to the platform for shelter. As I stood there, looking out into Great Bourke Street, a man and, I suppose, his wife passed by. He had a letter in his hand for the post; but as the pathway to the receiving-box looked very muddy, he made his companion take it to the box, whilst he himself, from beneath his umbrella, complacently watched her getting wet through. 'Colonial politeness,' thought I, as the happy couple walked on.

Sometimes a jovial wedding-party comes dashing through the streets; there they go, the bridegroom with one arm round his lady's waist, the other raising a champagne-bottle to his lips; the gay vehicles that follow contain company even more unrestrained, and from them noisier demonstrations of merriment may be heard. These diggers' weddings are all the rage, and bridal veils, white kid gloves, and, above all, orange blossoms are generally most difficult to procure at any price.

At times, you may see men, half-mad, throwing sovereigns, like halfpence, out of their pockets into the streets; and I once saw a digger, who was looking over a large quantity of bank-notes, deliberately tear to pieces and trample in the mud under his feet every soiled or ragged one he came to, swearing all the time at the gold-brokers for 'giving him dirty paper money for pure Alexander gold; he wouldn't carry dirt in his pocket; not he; thank God! he'd plenty to tear up and spend too.'

Melbourne is very full of Jews; on a Saturday, some of the streets are half closed. There are only two pawnbrokers in the town.

The most thriving trade there, is keeping an hotel or public-house, which always have a lamp before their doors. These at night serve as a beacon to the stranger to keep as far from them as possible, they being, with few exceptions, the resort, after dark, of the most ruffianly characters.

On the 2nd of September, the long-expected mail steamer arrived, and two days after we procured our letters from the Post-

office. I may here remark, that the want of proper management
in this department is the greatest cause of inconvenience to fresh
arrivals, and to the inhabitants of Melbourne generally. There
is but *one small window*, whence letters directed to lie at the office
are given out; and as the ships from England daily discharged
their living cargoes into Melbourne, the crowd round this ineffi-
cient delivering-place rendered getting one's letters the work, not
of hours, but days. Newspapers, particularly pictorial ones, have,
it would appear, a remarkable facility for being lost *en route*.
Several numbers of the 'Illustrated London News' had been sent
me, and, although the letters posted with them arrived in safety,
the papers themselves never made their appearance. I did hear
that, when addressed to an uncolonial name, and with no grander
direction than the Post-office itself, the clerks are apt to appropriate them – this is, perhaps, only a wee bit of Melbourne scandal.

The arrival of our letters from England left nothing now to
detain us, and made us all anxious to commence our trip to the
diggings, although the roads were in an awful condition. Still we
would delay no longer, and the bustle of preparation began. Stores
of flour, tea, and sugar, tents and canvas, camp-ovens, cooking
utensils, tin plates and pannikins, opossum rugs and blankets,
drays, carts and horses, cradles, &c. &c., had to be looked at,
bought and paid for.

On board ship, my brother had joined himself to a party of
four young men, who had decided to give the diggings a trial.
Four other of our shipmates had also joined themselves into a
digging-party, and when they heard of our intended departure,
proposed travelling up together and separating on our arrival.
This was settled, and a proposal made that between the two sets
they should raise funds to purchase a dray and horses, and make
a speculation in flour, tea, &c., on which an immense profit was
being made at the diggings. It would also afford the convenience
of taking up tents, cradles, and other articles impossible to carry
up without. The dray cost one hundred pounds, and the two
strong cart-horses ninety and one hundred pounds respectively.
This, with the goods themselves, and a few sundries in the shape
of harness and cords, made only a venture of about fifty pounds
a-piece. While these arrangements were rapidly progressing, a
few other parties wished to join ours for safety on the road, which
was agreed to, and the day fixed upon for the departure was the
7th of September. Every one, except myself, was to walk, and

we furthermore determined to 'camp out' as much as possible, and thus avoid the vicinity of the inns and halting-places on the way, which are frequently the lurking-places of thieves and bushrangers.

On the Sunday previous to the day on which our journey was to commence, I had a little adventure, which pleased me at the time, though, but for the sequel, not worth mentioning here. I had walked with my brother and a friend to St. Peter's Church; but we were a few minutes behind time, and therefore could find no unoccupied seat. Thus disappointed, we strolled over Princes Bridge on to the other side of the Yarra. Between the bridge and the beach, on the south side of the river, is a little city of tents, called Little Adelaide. They were inhabited by a number of families, that the rumour of the Victoria gold-mines had induced to leave South Australia, and whose finances were unequal to the high prices in Melbourne.

Government levies a tax of five shillings a week on each tent, built upon land as wild and barren as the bleakest common in England.

We did not wander this morning towards Little Adelaide; but followed the Yarra in its winding course inland, in the direction of the Botanical Gardens.

Upon a gentle rise beside the river, not far enough away from Melbourne to be inconvenient, but yet sufficiently removed from its mud and noise, were pitched two tents, evidently new, with crimson paint still gay upon the round nobs of the centre posts, and looking altogether more in trim for a gala day in Merry England than a trip to the diggings. The sun was high above our heads, and the day intensely hot; so much so, that I could not resist the temptation of tapping at the canvas door to ask for a draught of water. A gentleman obeyed the summons, and on learning the occasion of this unceremonious visit, politely accommodated me with a camp-stool and some delicious fresh milk – in Melbourne almost a luxury. Whilst I was imbibing this with no little relish, my friends were entering into conversation with our new acquaintance. The tents belonged to a party just arrived by the steamer from England, with everything complete for the diggings, to which they meant to proceed in another week, and where I had the pleasure of meeting them again, though under different and very peculiar circumstances. The tent which I had invaded was inhabited by two, the elder of whom, a powerfully-built man of thirty, formed a strong contrast to his companion, a delicate-looking youth, whose apparent age could not have exceeded sixteen years.

After a short rest, we returned to Melbourne, well pleased with our little adventure.

The next day was hardly long enough for our numerous preparations, and it was late before we retired to rest. Six was the hour appointed for the next morning's breakfast. Excited with anticipating the adventures to commence on the morrow, no wonder that my dreams should all be *golden* ones.

CHAPTER IV

Camping Up – Melbourne to the Black Forest

The anxiously-expected morning at length commenced, and a dismal-looking morning it was – hazy and damp, with a small drizzling rain, which, from the gloomy aspect above, seemed likely to last. It was not, however, sufficient to damp our spirits, and the appointed hour found us all assembled to attack the last meal that we anticipated to make for some time to come beneath the shelter of a ceiling. At eight o'clock our united party was to start from the 'Duke of York' hotel, and as that hour drew nigh, the unmistakeable signs of 'something up,' attracted a few idlers to witness our departure. In truth, we were a goodly party, and created no little sensation among the loungers – but I must regularly introduce our troop to my readers.

First then, I must mention two large drays, each drawn by a pair of stout horses – one the property of two Germans, who were bound for Forest Creek, the other belonged to ourselves and shipmates. There were three pack-horses – one (laden with a speculation in bran) belonged to a queer-looking sailor, who went by the name of Joe, the other two were under the care of a man named Gregory, who was going to rejoin his mates at Eagle Hawk Gully. As his destination was the farthest, and he was well acquainted with the roads, he ought to have been elected leader, but from some mismanagement that dignity was conferred upon a stout old gentleman, who had taken a pleasure-trip to Mount Alexander, the previous summer.

Starting is almost always a tedious affair, nor was this particular case an exception. First one had forgotten something –
another broke a strap, and a new one had to be procured – then
the dray was not properly packed, and must be righted – some
one else wanted an extra 'nobbler' – then a fresh, and still a fresh
delay, so that although eight was the appointed hour, it was noon
ere we bade farewell to mine host of the 'Duke of York.' . . .

The rain and bad roads made travelling so very wearisome,
that before we had proceeded far it was unanimously agreed that
we should halt and pitch our first encampment. 'Pitch our first
encampment! how charming!' exclaims some romantic reader, as
though it were an easily accomplished undertaking. Fixing a gipsy-
tent at a *fête champêtre*, with a smiling sky above, and all requi-
sites ready to hand, is one thing, and attempting to sink poles
and erect tents out of blankets and rugs in a high wind and pelt-
ing rain, is (if I may be allowed the colonialism) 'a horse of quite
another colour.' Some sort of sheltering-places were at length completed; the horses were taken from the dray and tethered to some
trees within sight, and then we made preparations for satisfying
the unromantic cravings of hunger – symptoms of which we all,
more or less, began to feel. With some difficulty a fire was kin-
dled and kept alight in the hollow trunk of an old gum tree. A
damper was speedily made, which, with a plentiful supply of
steaks and boiled and roasted eggs, was a supper by no means
to be despised. The eggs had been procured at four shillings a
dozen from a farm-house we had passed.

It was certainly the most curious tea-table at which I had ever
assisted. Chairs, of course, there were none, we sat or lounged
upon the ground as best suited our tired limbs; tin pannicans (holding about a pint) served as tea-cups, and plates of the same metal
in lieu of china; a teapot was dispensed with; but a portly substitute was there in the shape of an immense iron kettle, just taken
from the fire and placed in the centre of our grand tea-service,
which being new, a lively imagination might mistake for silver.
Hot spirits, for those desirous of imbibing them, followed our
substantial repast; but fatigue and the dreary weather had so completely damped all disposition to conviviality, that a very short
space of time found all fast asleep except the three unfortunates
on the watch, which was relieved every two hours.

Wednesday, September 8. – I awoke rather early this morning, not feeling over-comfortable from having slept in my clothes all night, which it is necessary to do on the journey, so as never to be unprepared for any emergency. A small corner of my brother's tent had been partitioned off for my *bed-room*; it was quite dark, so my first act on waking was to push aside one of the blankets, still wet, which had been my roof during the night, and thus admit air and light into my apartments. Having made my toilette – after a fashion – I joined my companions on the watch, who were deep in the mysteries of preparing something eatable for breakfast. I discovered that their efforts were concentrated on the formation of a damper, which seemed to give them no little difficulty. A damper is the legitimate, and, in fact, only bread of the bush, and should be made solely of flour and water, well mixed and kneaded into a cake, as large as you like, but not more than two inches in thickness, and then placed among the hot ashes to bake. If well-made, it is very sweet and a good substitute for bread. The rain had, however, spoiled our ashes, the dough would neither rise nor brown, so in despair we mixed a fresh batch of flour and water, and having fried some rashers of fat bacon till they were nearly melted, we poured the batter into the pan and let it fry till done. This impromptu dish gave general satisfaction and was pronounced a cross between a pancake and a heavy suet pudding.

Breakfast over, our temporary residences were pulled down, the drays loaded, and our journey recommenced . . .

Thursday, 9. – This morning we were up betimes, some of our party being so sanguine as to anticipate making the 'Bush Inn' before evening. As we proceeded, this hope quickly faded away. The Keilor plains seemed almost impassable, and what with pieces of rock here, and a waterhole there, crossing them was more dangerous than agreeable. Now one passed a broken-down dray; then one's ears were horrified at the oaths an unhappy wight was venting at a mud-hole into which he had stumbled. A comical object he looked, as half-seas-over, he attempted to pull on a mud-covered boot, which he had just extricated from the hole where it and his leg had parted company. A piece of wood, which his imagination transformed into a shoe-horn, was in his hand. 'Put it into the larboard side,' (suiting the action to the word), 'there it goes – damn her, she won't come on! Put it into the starboard side – there it goes – well done, old girl,' and he triumphantly rose from the ground, and reeled away.

With a hearty laugh, we proceeded on our road, and after passing two or three coffee-tents, we arrived at Gregory's Inn. The landlord is considered the best on the road, and is a practical example of what honesty and industry may achieve. He commenced some nine months before without a shilling – his tarpaulin tent and small stock of tea, sugar-coffee, &c., being a loan. He has now a large weather-board house, capable of making up one hundred beds, and even then unable to accommodate all his visitors, so numerous are they, from the good name he bears. Here we got a capital cold dinner of meat, bread, cheese, coffee, tea, &c., for three shillings a-piece, and, somewhat refreshed, went forwards in better spirits, though the accounts we heard there of the bad roads in the Black Forest would have disheartened many. . .

Saturday, 11. – A dismal wet day – we remained stationary, as many of our party were still foot-sore, and all were glad of a rest. Some went out shooting, but returned with only a few parrots and cockatoos, which they roasted, and pronounced nice eating. Towards evening, a party of four, returning from the diggings, encamped at a little distance from us. Some of our loiterers made their acquaintance. They had passed the previous night in the Black Forest, having wandered out of their way. To add to their misfortunes, they had been attacked by three well-armed bushrangers, whom they had compelled to desist from their attempt, not, however, before two of the poor men had been wounded, one rather severely. Hardly had they recovered this shock, than they were horrified by the sudden discovery in a sequestered spot of some human bones, strewn upon the ground beside a broken-down cart. Whether accident or design had brought these unfortunates to an untimely end, none know; but this ominous appearance seemed to have terrified them even more than the bushrangers themselves. These accounts sobered our party not a little, and it was deemed advisable to double the watch that night.

CHAPTER V

Camping Up—Black Forest to Eagle Hawk Gully

Tuesday, 14. – This morning commenced with a colonial shower, which gave us all a good drenching. Started about eight o'clock; returned to Kyneton; crossed the bridge, and passed several farmhouses. The country here is very changeable, sometimes flat and boggy, at others, very hilly and stony. We were obliged to ford several small creeks, evidently tributaries to the Campaspe, and about ten miles from Kyneton, entered the Coliban range, which is thickly wooded. The river itself is about fourteen miles from Kyneton. Here we camped in the pouring rain. Some of our party walked to the town of Malmsbury, about a mile and a half from our camping place. The town consisted of about three tents, and an inn dignified by the appellation of the 'Malmsbury Hotel'. It is a two-storied, weather-board, and pale house, painted blue, with a lamp before it of many colours, large enough for half-a-dozen people to dine in. It (the inn, not the lamp), is capable of accommodating two hundred people, independent of which there is a large tent, similar to the booths at a fair, about 100 feet long by 30 wide, for the convenience of these who prefer sleeping under cover when the house is full. Being hungry with their walk, our comrades dined here, for which they paid 3s. 6d. a-piece; ale was 1s. 6d. a glass; brandy 2s. per half glass, or 'nobbler;' cheese, 4s. 6d. a pound; bread, 5s. the four-pound loaf; wine, 25s. a bottle. By the time they returned, we had struck our tents, intending to cross a muddy-banked creek that lay in our road that evening, as we were told that the waters might be too swollen to do it next day. The water reached above their waists, and as my usual post was very insecure, I was obliged to be carried over on their shoulders, which did not prevent my feet from being thoroughly soaked before reaching the other side, where we remained all night.

Wednesday, 15. – Rainy day again, so much so, that we thought it advisable not to shift our quarters. In the afternoon, three returning diggers pitched their tents not far from ours. They were rather sociable, and gave us a good account of the diggings. They had themselves been very fortunate. On the same day that we had been idly resting on the borders of the Black Forest, they had succeeded in taking twenty-three pounds weight out of their claim, and two days after, two hundred and six ounces more, making, in all, gold to the value (in England) of about eighteen hundred pounds. They were returning to Melbourne for a spree, (which means to fling their gains away as quickly as possible,) and then as soon as the dry season was regularly set in, they meant to return to Bendigo for another spell at work. On representing to them the folly of not making better use of their hard-earned wages, the answer invariably was, 'Plenty more to be got where this came from,' an apt illustration of the proverb, 'light come, light go.' Two of these diggers had with them their licences for the current month, which they offered to sell for ten shillings each; two of our company purchased them. This, although a common proceeding, was quite illegal, and, of course, the two purchasers had to assume for the rest of the month the names of the parties to whom the licences had been issued. As evening approached, our new acquaintances became very sociable, and amused us with their account of the diggings; and the subject of licensing being naturally discussed, led to our being initiated into the various means of evading it, and the penalties incurred thereby. One story they related amused us at the time, and as it is true I will repeat it here, though I fancy the lack of oral communication will subtract from it what little interest it did possess.

Before I commence, I must give my readers some little insight into the nature of the licence tax itself. The licence, (for which thirty shillings, or half an ounce of gold, is paid per month) is in the following form:

VICTORIA GOLD LICENCE.

N. 1710,   Sept. 3, 1852.

The Bearer, Henry Clements, having paid to me the Sum of One Pound, Ten Shillings, on account of the Territorial Revenue, I hereby Licence him to dig, search for, and remove Gold on and from any such Crown Land within the Upper Loden District, as I shall assign to him for that purpose during the month of September, 1852, not within half-a-mile of any Head station.

This Licence is not transferable, and to be produced whenever demanded by me or any other person acting under the Authority of the Government, and to be returned when another Licence is issued.

(*Signed*) B. BAXTER, Commissioner.

At the back of the Licence are the following rules:

Regulations to be observed by the Persons digging for Gold,
or otherwise employed at the Gold Fields.

1. Every Licensed Person must always have his Licence with him, ready to be produced whenever demanded by a Commissioner, or Person acting under his instructions, otherwise he is liable to be proceeded against as an Unlicensed person.

2. Every Person digging for Gold, or occupying Land, without a Licence, is liable by Law to be fined, for the first offence, not exceeding £5; for a second offence, not exceeding £15; and for a subsequent offence, not exceeding £30.

3. Digging for Gold is not allowed within Ten feet of any Public Road, nor are the Roads to be undermined.

4. Tents or buildings are not to be erected within Twenty feet of each other, or within Twenty feet of any Creek.

5. It is enjoined that all Persons at the Gold Fields maintain and assist in maintaining a due and proper observance of Sundays.

So great is the crowd around the Commissioner's tent at the beginning of the month, that it is a matter of difficulty to procure it, and consequently the inspectors rarely begin their rounds before the 10th, when (as they generally vary the fine according to the date at which the delinquency is discovered), a non-licensed digger would have the pleasure of accompanying a crowd of similar offenders to the Commissioners, sometimes four or five miles from his working-place, pay a fine of about £3, and take out a licence. After the 20th of the month, the fine inflicted is generally from £5 to £10 and a licence, which is rather a dear price to pay for a few days' permission to dig, as a licence, although granted on the 30th of one month, would be unavailable for the next. The inspectors are generally strong-built, rough-looking customers, they dress like the generality of the diggers, and are only known by their carrying a gun in lieu of a pick or shovel. Delinquents unable to pay the fine, have the pleasure of working it out on the roads.

Now for my story – such as it is.

Mike and Robert were two as good mates as any at the Mount Alexander diggings. They had had a good spell of hard work, and, as is usually the way, returned to Melbourne for a holiday at Christmas-time; and then it was that the bright eyes of Susan Hinton first sowed discord between them. Mike was the successful wooer, and the old man gave his consent; for Mike, with one exception, had contrived to make himself a favourite with both father and daughter. The exception was this. Old Hinton was a strict disciplinarian – one of what is called the 'good old school' – he hated radicals, revolutionists, and reformers, or any opposition to Church or State. Mike, on the contrary, loved nothing better than to hold forth against the powers that be; and it was his greatest boast that Government had never pocketed a farthing from him in the way of a licence. This, in the old man's eyes, was his solitary fault, and when Mike declared his intention of taking another trip to the 'lottery fields' before taking a ticket in the even greater lottery of marriage, he solemnly declared that no daughter of his should ever marry a man who had been openly convicted of in any way evading the licence fee.

This declaration from any other man, who had already promised his daughter in marriage, would not have had much weight; but Mike knew the stern, strict character of Hinton, and respected this determination accordingly. The day of their departure arrived, and with a tearful injunction to bear in mind her father's wishes, Susan bade her lover farewell, and Robert and he proceeded on their journey. Full of his own happiness, Mike had never suspected his comrade's love for Susan, and little dreamt he of the hatred against himself to which it had given birth – hatred the more to be dreaded since it was concealed under a most friendly exterior.

For the first month Mike behaved to the very letter of the law, and having for the sum of £1 10s. purchased his legal right to dig for gold, felt himself a most exemplary character. Success again crowned their efforts, and a speedy return to Melbourne was contemplated. In the ardour of this exciting work another month commenced, and Mike at first forgot and then neglected to renew his licence. 'The inspector rarely came his rounds before the 14th; the neighbourhood was considered deserted – fairly "worked out;" he'd never come round there.' Thus argued Mike, and his friend cordially agreed with him. 'Lose a day's work standing outside the Commissioner's tent broiling in a crowd, when two days would finish the job? Not he, indeed! Mike might please himself, but *he* shouldn't get a licence;' and this determination on the part of his 'mate' settled the matter.

In one respect Mike's self-security was not unfounded; the gully in which their tent was now pitched was nearly deserted. Some while previous there had been a great rush to the place, so great that it was almost excavated; then the rush took a different direction, and few now cared to work on the two or three spots that had been left untouched. Like many other localities considered 'worked out,' as much remained in the ground as had been taken from it, and as each day added to their store, Mike's hilarity increased.

It was now the 10th of the month; their hole had been fairly 'bottomed,' a nice little nest of nuggets discovered, their gains divided, and the gold sent down to the escort-office for transit to Melbourne. A few buckets-full of good washing-stuff was all that was left undone. 'Today will finish that,' thought Mike, and to it he set with hearty good-will, to the intense satisfaction of his comrade, who sat watching him at a little distance. Suddenly Mike felt a heavy hand upon his shoulder: he looked up, and saw before him – the inspector. He had already with him a large body of defaulters, and Mike little doubted but that he must be added to their number. Old Hinton's determined speech, Susan's parting words and tears, flashed across his mind.

'You've lost your bonnie bride,' muttered Robert, loud enough to reach his rival's ears.

Mike glanced at him, and the look of triumph he saw there roused every spark of energy within him, and it was in a tone of well-assumed composure that he replied to the inspector, 'My licence is in my pocket, and my coat is below there;' and without a moment's hesitation sprang into his hole to fetch it. Some minutes elapsed. The inspector waxed impatient. A suspicion of the truth flashed across Robert's mind, and he too descended the hole. *There* was the coat and the licence of the past month in the pocket; but the owner had gone, vanished, and an excavation on one side which led into the next hole and thence into a complete labyrinth underground, plainly pointed out the method of escape. Seeing no use in ferreting the delinquent out of so dangerous a place, the inspector sulkily withdrew, though not without venting some of his ill-humour upon Robert, at whose representations, made to him the day previous, he had come so far out of his road.

But let us return to Mike. By a happy thought, he had suddenly remembered that whilst working some days before in the hole, his pick had let in daylight on one side; and the desperate hope presented itself to his mind that he might make a passage into the next pit, which he knew led into others, and thus escape.

His success was beyond his expectation; and he regained the open air at a sufficient distance from his late quarters to escape observation. Once able to reflect calmly upon the event of the morning, it required little discrimination to fix upon Robert his real share in it. And now there was no time to lose in returning to Melbourne, and prevent by a speedy marriage any further attempt to set his intended father-in-law against him. The roads were dry, for it was the sultry month of February; and two days saw him beside his lady-love.

Although railroads are as yet unknown in Australia, everything goes on at railroad speed; and a marriage concocted one day is frequently solemnized the next. His eagerness, therefore, was no way remarkable. No time was lost; and when, three days after Mike's return, Robert (with his head full of plots and machinations) presented himself at old Hinton's door, he found them all at a well-spread wedding breakfast, round which were gathered a merry party, listening with a digger's interest to the way in which the happy bridegroom had evaded the inspector. Mike had wisely kept the story till Susan was his wife . . .

It is not only the diggers, however, who make money at the Gold Fields. Carters, carpenters, storemen, wheelwrights, butchers, shoemakers, &c., usually in the long run make a fortune quicker than the diggers themselves, and certainly with less hard work or risk of life. They can always get from £1 to £2 a day without rations, whereas they may dig for weeks and get nothing. Living is not more expensive than in Melbourne: meat is generally from 4d. to 6d. a pound, flour about 1s. 6d. a pound, (this is the most expensive article in housekeeping there,) butter must be dispensed with, as that is seldom less than 4s. a pound, and only successful diggers can indulge in such articles as cheese, pickles, ham, sardines, pickled salmon, or spirits, as all these things, though easily procured if you have gold to throw away, are expensive, the last-named article (diluted with water or something less innoxious) is only to be obtained for 30s. a bottle.

The stores, which are distinguished by a flag, are numerous and well stocked. A new style of lodging and boarding house is in great vogue. It is a tent fitted up with stringy bark couches, ranged down each side the tent, leaving a narrow passage up the middle. The lodgers are supplied with mutton, damper, and tea, three times a day, for the charge of 5s. a meal, and 5s. for the bed; this is by the week, a casual guest must pay double, and as 18 inches is on an average considered ample width to sleep in, a tent 24 feet long will bring in a good return to the owner.

The stores at the diggings are large tents generally square or oblong, and everything required by a digger can be obtained for money, from sugar-candy to potted anchovies; from East India pickles to Bass's pale ale; from ankle jack boots to a pair of stays; from a baby's cap to a cradle; and every apparatus for mining, from a pick to a needle. But the confusion – the din – the medley – what a scene for a shop walker! Here lies a pair of herrings dripping into a bag of sugar, or a box of raisins; there a gay-looking bundle of ribbons beneath two tumblers, and a half-finished bottle of ale. Cheese and butter, bread and yellow soap, pork and currants, saddles and frocks, wide-awakes and blue serge shirts, green veils and shovels, baby linen and tallow candles, are all heaped indiscriminately together; added to which, there are children bawling, men swearing, store-keeper sulky, and last, not *least*, women's tongues going nineteen to the dozen.

Most of the storekeepers are purchasers of gold either for cash or in exchange for goods, and many are the tricks from which unsuspecting diggers suffer. One great and outrageous trick is to weigh the parcels separately, or divide the whole, on the excuse that the weight would be too much for the scales; and then, on adding up the grains and pennyweights, the sellers often lose at least half an ounce. On one occasion, out of seven pounds weight, a party once lost an ounce and three quarters in this manner. There is also the old method of false beams – one in favour of the purchaser – and here, unless the seller weighs in both pans, he loses considerably. Another mode of cheating is to have glass pans resting on a piece of green baize; under this baize, and beneath the pan which holds the weights, is a wetted sponge, which causes that pan to adhere to the baize, and consequently it requires more gold to make it level; this, coupled with the false reckoning, is ruinous to the digger. In town, the Jews have a system of robbing a great deal from sellers before they purchase the gold-dust (for in these instances it must be *dust*): it is thrown into a zinc pan with slightly raised sides, which are well rubbed over with grease; and under the plea of a careful examination, the purchaser shakes and rubs the dust, and a considerable quantity adheres to the sides. A commoner practice still is for examiners of gold-dust to cultivate long finger-nails, and, in drawing the fingers about it, gather some up.

Sly grog selling is the bane of the diggings. Many – perhaps nine-tenths – of the diggers are honest industrious men, desirous of getting a little there as a stepping-stone to independence elsewhere; but the other tenth is composed of outcasts and transports – the refuse of Van Diemen's Land – men of the most depraved and abandoned characters, who have sought and gained the lowest abyss of crime, and who would a short time ago have expiated their crimes on a scaffold. They generally work or rob for a space, and when well stocked with gold, retire to Melbourne for a month or so, living in drunkenness and debauchery. If, however, their holiday is spent at the diggings, the sly grog-shop is the last scene of their boisterous career. Spirit selling is strictly prohibited; and although Government will license a respectable public-house on the *road*, it is resolutely refused *on* the diggings. The result has been the opposite of that which it was intended to produce. There is more drinking and rioting at the diggings than elsewhere, the privacy and risk gives the obtaining it an excitement which the diggers enjoy as much as the spirit itself; and wherever grog is sold on the sly, it will sooner or later be the scene of a riot, or perhaps murder. Intemperance is succeeded by quarrelling and fighting, the neighbouring tents report to the police, and the offenders are lodged in the lock-up; whilst the grog-tent, spirits, wine, &c., are seized and taken to the Commissioners. Some of the stores, however, managed to evade the law rather cleverly – as spirits are not *sold*, 'my friend' pays a shilling more for his fig of tobacco, and his wife an extra sixpence for her suet; and they smile at the store-man, who in return smiles knowingly at them, and then glasses are brought out, and a bottle produced, which sends forth *not* a fragrant perfume on the sultry air.

It is no joke to get ill at the diggings; doctors make you pay for it. Their fees are – for a consultation, at their own tent, ten shillings; for a visit out, from one to ten pounds, according to time and distance. Many are regular quacks, and these seem to flourish best. The principal illnesses are weakness of sight, from the hot winds and sandy soil, and dysentery, which is often caused by the badly-cooked food, bad water, and want of vegetables.

The interior of the canvas habitation of the digger is desolate enough; a box on a block of wood forms a table, and this is the only furniture; many dispense with that. The bedding, which is laid on the ground, serves to sit upon. Diogenes in his tub would not have looked more comfortless than any one else. Tin plates and pannicans, the same as are used for camping up, compose the breakfast, dinner and tea service, which meals usually consist of the same dishes – mutton, damper, and tea.

In some tents the soft influence of our sex is pleasingly apparent: the tins are as bright as silver, there are sheets as well as blankets on the beds, and perhaps a clean counterpane, with the addition of a dry sack or piece of carpet on the ground; whilst a pet cockatoo, chained to a perch, makes noise enough to keep the 'missus' from feeling lonely when the good man is at work. Sometimes a wife is at first rather a nuisance; women get scared and frightened, then cross, and commence a 'blow up' with their husbands; but all their railing generally ends in their quietly settling down to this rough and primitive style of living, if not without a murmur, at least to all appearance with the determination to laugh and bear it. And although rough in their manners, and not over select in their address, the digger seldom wilfully injures a woman; in fact, a regular Vandemonian will, in his way, play the gallant with as great a zest as a fashionable about town – at any rate, with more sincerity of heart.

Sunday is kept at the diggings in a very orderly manner; and among the actual diggers themselves, the day of rest is taken in a *verbatim* sense. It is not unusual to have an established clergyman holding forth near the Commissioner's tent, and almost within hearing will be a tub orator expounding the origin of evil, whilst a 'mill' (a fight with fisticuffs) or a dog fight fills up the background.

But night at the diggings is the characteristic time: murder here – murder there – revolvers cracking – blunderbusses bombing – rifles going off – balls whistling – one man groaning with a broken leg – another shouting because he couldn't find the way to his hole, and a third equally vociferous because he has tumbled into one – this man swearing – another praying – a party of bacchanals chanting various ditties to different time and tune, or rather minus both. Here is one man grumbling because he has brought his wife with him, another ditto because he has left his behind, or sold her for an ounce of gold or a bottle of rum. Donnybrook Fair is not to be compared to an evening at Bendigo.

Success at the diggings is like drawing lottery tickets – the blanks far outnumber the prizes; still, with good health, strength, and above all perseverance, it is strange if a digger does not in the end reap a reward for his labour. Meanwhile, he must endure almost incredible hardships. In the rainy season, he must not murmur if compelled to work up to his knees in water, and sleep on the wet ground, without a fire, in the pouring rain, and perhaps no shelter above him more waterproof than a blanket or a gum tree; and this not for once only, but day after day, night after night. In the summer, he must work hard under a burning sun, tortured by the mosquito and the little stinging March flies, or feel his eyes smart and his throat grow dry and parched, as the hot winds, laden with dust, pass over him. How grateful now would be a draught from some cold sparkling streamlet; but, instead, with what sort of water must he quench his thirst? Much the same, gentle reader, as that which runs down the sides of a dirty road on a rainy day, and for this a shilling a bucket must be paid. Hardships such as these are often the daily routine of a digger's life; yet, strange to say, far from depressing the spirits or weakening the frame, they appear in most cases to give strength and energy to both. This is principally owing to the climate, which even in the wet season is mild and salubrious.

Perhaps nothing will speak better for the general order that prevails at the diggings, than the small amount of physical force maintained there by Government to keep some thousands of persons of all ages, classes, characters, religions and countries in good humour with the laws and with one another. The military force numbers 130, officers and men; the police about 300.

The Government escort is under control of Mr Wright, Chief Commissioner; it consists of about forty foot and sixty mounted police, with the usual complement of inspectors and sergeants; their uniform is blue with white facings, their head-quarters are by the Commissioners' tent, Forest Creek.

The private escort uniform is a plain blue frock coat and trowsers. It is under the superintendence of Mr Wilkinson; the head-quarters are at Montgomery Hill, Forest Creek. Both these escorts charge one per cent for conveying gold . . .

CHAPTER VIII

An Adventure

Sunday, 3. – A fine morning. After our usual service Frank, my brother, and myself, determined on an exploring expedition, and off we went, leaving the dinner in the charge of the others. We left the busy throng of the diggers far behind us, and wandered into spots where the sound of the pick and shovel, or the noise of human traffic, had never penetrated. The scene and the day were in unison; all was harmonious, majestic, and serene. Those mighty forests, hushed in a sombre and awful silence; those ranges of undulating hill and dale never yet trodden by the foot of man; the soft still air, so still that it left every leaf unruffled, flung an intensity of awe over our feelings, and led us from the contemplation of nature to worship nature's God.

We sat in silence for some while deeply impressed by all around us, and, whilst still sitting and gazing there, a change almost imperceptibly came over the face of both earth and sky. The forest swayed to and fro, a sighing moaning sound was borne upon the wind, and a noise as of the rush of waters, dark massive clouds rolled over the sky till the bright blue heavens were completely hidden, and then, ere we had recovered from our first alarm and bewilderment, the storm in its unmitigated fury burst upon us. The rain fell in torrents, and we knew not where to turn.

Taking me between them, they succeeded in reaching an immense she-oak, under which we hoped to find some shelter till the violence of the rain had diminished; nor were we disappointed, though it was long before we could venture to leave our place of refuge. At length, however, we did so, and endeavoured to find our way back to Eagle Hawk Gully. Hopeless task! The ground was so slippery, it was as much as we could do to walk without falling; the mud and dirt clung to our boots, and a heavy rain beat against our faces and nearly blinded us.

'It is clearing up to windward,' observed Frank; 'another half-hour and the rain will be all but over; let us return to our tree again.'

We did so. Frank was correct; in less than the time he had specified a slight drizzling rain was all of the storm that remained.

With much less difficulty we again attempted to return home, but before very long we made the startling discovery that we had completely lost our way, and to add to our misfortune the small pocket-compass, which Frank had brought with him, and which would have now so greatly assisted us, was missing, most probably dropped from his pocket during the skirmish to get under shelter. We still wandered along till stopped by the shades of evening, which came upon us – there is little or no twilight in Australia.

We seated ourselves upon the trunk of a fallen tree, wet, hungry, and, worst of all, ignorant of where we were. Shivering with cold, and our wet garments hanging most uncomfortably around us, we endeavoured to console one another by reflecting that the next morning we could not fail to reach our tents. The rain had entirely ceased, and providentially for us the night was pitch dark – I say providentially, because after having remained for two hours in this wretched plight a small light in the distance became suddenly visible to us all, so distant, that but for the intensity of the darkness it might have passed unnoticed. 'Thank God!' simultaneously burst from our lips.

'Let us hasten there,' cried Frank, 'a whole night like this may be your sister's death and would ruin the constitution of a giant.'

To this we gladly acceded, and were greatly encouraged by perceiving that the light remained stationary. But it was a perilous undertaking. Luckily my brother had managed to get hold of a long stick, with which he sounded the way, for either large stones or water-holes would have been awkward customers in the dark; wonderful to relate we escaped both, and when within hailing distance of the light, which we perceived came from a torch held by some one, we shouted with all our remaining strength, but without diminishing our exertions to reach it. Soon – with feelings that only those who have encountered similar dangers can understand – answering voices fell upon our ears. Eagerly we pressed forward, and in the excitement of the moment we relinquished all hold of one another, and attempted to wade through the mud singly.

'Stop! halt!' shouted more than one stentorian voice; but the warning came too late. My feet slipped – a sharp pain succeeded by a sudden chill – a feeling of suffocation – of my head being ready to burst – and I remembered no more.

When I recovered consciousness it was late in the morning, for the bright sun shone upon the ground through the crevices of a sail cloth tent, and so different was all that met my eyes to the dismal scene through which I had so lately passed, and which yet haunted my memory, that I felt that sweet feeling of relief which we experience when, waking from some horrid vision, we become convinced how unsubstantial are its terrors, and are ready to smile at the pain they excited.

That I was in a strange place became quickly evident, and among the distant hum of voices which ever and anon broke the silence not one familiar tone could I recognize. I endeavoured to raise myself so as to hear more distinctly, and then it was that an acute pain in the ankle of the right foot, gave me pretty strong evidence as to the reality of the last night's adventures. I was forced to lie down again, but not before I had espied a hand-bell which lay within reach on a small barrel near my bed. Determined as far as possible to fathom the mystery, I rang a loud peal with it, not doubting but what it would bring my brother to me. My surprise and delight may be easier imagined than described, when, as though in obedience to my summons, I saw a small white hand push aside the canvas at one corner of the tent, and one of my own sex entered.

She was young and fair; her step was soft and her voice most musically gentle. Her eyes were a deep blue, and a rich brown was the colour of her hair, which she wore in very short curls all round her head and parted on one side, which almost gave her the appearance of a pretty boy.

These little particulars I noticed afterwards; at that time I only felt that her gentle voice and kind friendliness of manner inexpressibly soothed me.

After having bathed my ankle, which I found to be badly sprained and cut, she related, as far as she was acquainted with them, the events of the previous evening. I learnt that these tents belong to a party from England, of one of whom she was the wife, and the tent in which I lay was her apartment. They had not been long at the diggings, and preferred the spot where they were to the more frequented parts.

This awakened my curiosity, and I would not rest satisfied till fully acquainted with the how, when and where. Subsequently she related to me some portion of the history of her life, which it will be no breach of confidence to include here.

Short as it is, however, it is deserving of another chapter . . .

CHAPTER IX

Harriette Walters

Harriette Walters had been a wife but twelve months, when the sudden failure of the house in which her husband was a junior partner involved them in irretrievable ruin, and threw them almost penniless upon the world. At this time the commercial advantages of Australia, the opening it afforded for all classes of men, and above all, its immense mineral wealth, were the subject of universal attention. Mr Walters' friends advised him to emigrate, and the small sum saved from the wreck of their fortune served to defray the expenses of the journey. Harriette, sorely against her wishes, remained behind with an old maiden aunt, until her husband could obtain a home for her in the colonies.

The day of parting arrived; the ship which bore him away disappeared from her sight, and almost heart-broken she returned to the humble residence of her sole remaining relative.

Ere she had recovered from the shock occasioned by her husband's departure, her aged relation died from a sudden attack of illness, and Harriette was left alone to struggle with her poverty and her grief. The whole of her aunt's income had been derived from an annuity, which of course died with her; and her personal property, when sold, realized not much more than sufficient to pay a few debts and the funeral expenses; so that when these last sad duties were performed, Harriette found herself with a few pounds in her pocket, homeless, friendless, and alone.

Her thoughts turned to the distant land, her husband's home and every hope was centred in the one intense desire to join him there. The means were wanting, she had none from whom she could solicit assistance, but her determination did not fail. She advertized for a situation as companion to an invalid, or nurse to young children, during the voyage to Port Philip, provided her passage-money was paid by her employer. This she soon obtained. The ship was a fast sailer, the winds were favourable, and by a strange chance she arrived in Melbourne three weeks before her husband. This time was a great trial to her. Alone and unprotected in that strange, rough city, without money, without friends, she felt truly wretched. It was not a place for a female to be without a protector, and she knew it, yet protectors she had none; even the family with whom she had come out, had gone many miles up the country. She possessed little money, lodgings and food were at an awful price, and employment for a female, except of a rough sort, was not easily procured.

In this dilemma she took the singular notion into her head of disguising her sex, and thereby avoiding much of the insult and annoyance to which an unprotected female would have been liable. Being of a slight figure, and taking the usual colonial costume – loose trowsers, a full, blue serge shirt, fastened round the waist by a leather belt, and a wide-awake – Harriette passed very well for what she assumed to be – a young lad just arrived from England. She immediately obtained a light situation near the wharf, where for about three weeks she worked hard enough at a salary of a pound a week, board, and permission to sleep in an old tumbledown shed beside the store.

At last the long looked-for vessel arrived. That must have been a moment of intense happiness which restored her to her husband's arms – for him not unmingled with surprise; he could not at first recognize her in her new garb. She would hear of no further separation, and when she learnt he had joined a party for the Bendigo diggings, she positively refused to remain in Melbourne, and she retained her boyish dress until their arrival at Bendigo. The party her husband belonged to had two tents, one of which they readily gave up to the married couple, as they were only too glad to have the company and in-door assistance of a sensible, active woman during their spell at the diggings. For the sake of economy, during the time that elapsed before they could commence their journey up, all of them lived in the tents which they pitched on a small rise on the south side of the Yarra. Here it was that our acquaintance first took place; doubtless, my readers will, long ere this, have recognized in the hospitable gentleman I encountered there, my friend's husband, and, in the delicate-looking youth who had so attracted my attention, the fair Harriette herself.

MARY FORTUNE,
('WAIF WANDER', 'W.W.' ETC.), N.D.

Very little is known about this remarkable woman
writer who has been credited with being the first
woman writer of detective fiction in Australia – and
certainly one of the first in the world. Morris Miller
(1940) lists *The Detective Album; Tales of the Australian Police by W.W., Reprinted from the
Australian Journal* (1871) as the first collection of
detective stories in Australia and Henry Mitchell (in
the *Australian Journal*, Vol 15, May 1880, p487–8)
commends 'Mrs Fortune' for her originality and un-
equalled achievement as a fiction writer of Australia.
But despite her productivity and the praise that was
given her, she probably ended her life in penury;
there is an undated letter in the Moir Collection, La
Trobe Library, signed M. H. Fortune, written in the
period 1905–1910, in which she complains of the
difficulty in selling her work and infers that she is
living in poverty (see Elizabeth Webby and Lydia
Wevers, 1987, p241).

Clearly committed to earning her living by her
pen, Mary Fortune's stories are often directed
towards the widest possible market; but in some of
her fiction her women characters show a surprising
degree of independence. The following short story,
'Kirsty Oglevie', is taken from the *Australian Journal*
(16 June 1866, no 42, pp661–3) and reveals a female
victim as well as a spirited heroine.

KIRSTY OGLEVIE

Mrs Oglevie – as you might surmise from the name – was a Scotchwoman, and, as the world judges, a most respectable person indeed. She was a widow, the undisputed possessor of one of the finest stations on the Murrumbidgee, and the reputed owner of fifty thousand pounds in bank deposits besides. So you will readily perceive that Mrs Oglevie was indeed a lady of great consideration. Picture to yourself a coarse, very stout, awkward, largely built woman, with low beetling forehead, and features altogether expressive of the lowest standard of intellectual organization; a figure formless, and most untidily habited; a mop of unkempt grey hair, half covered by a dirty net-cap, with a profusion of border – a cap which was always on one side, and never by any chance straight. Picture to yourself such a person, with the air of a virago, and a look of *suspicious* authority, as if she was always upon the watch for some infringement of her sway, and ready at a second's notice to punish it; and when you have the idea of such a person's appearance in your mind, you have that of Mrs Oglevie's. Upon her own ground she could truly have exclaimed, like Robinson Crusoe, 'I'm monarch of all I survey,' were it not for one exception, and that a momentous one – she certainly had no control whatever over her only child, Miss Oglevie. Christina Oglevie – or, as her mother always called her, and most people, too – Kirsty Oglevie, was a young lady of mayhap twenty years, and as good a specimen of a certain class of 'young Australia' as you would be likely to find in a long summer day's search. Fortunately for her she had been blessed with a father who, though an ignorant man himself, had sense enough to appreciate the great advantages of even a 'little learning', and, consequently, Kirsty had been obliged – much against her inclination, it is true – to pick up a desultory sort of information – sometimes at a temporary school, perhaps opened for a time in the neighbourhood, or sometimes from a stockrider or domestic servant, who happened to know a little more than simply how to read and write. It was fortunate, as we have said, for poor Christina that her father had lived to secure her even so much, for her mother was decidedly averse to instruction of any sort whatever, unless it had something to do with the making or saving of money. She was wont to remark that she 'didna see what mair Kirsty needed than her mither afore her. I canna write my ain name, as a' body kens, an' if Kirsty makes her way as weel i' the world as I've dune, she needna grumble.' Mrs Oglevie would twenty times rather see her daughter going through the wet grass with her 'coats kilted,' to drive home some stray cow or calf, than see her indulging in a book; and, to do Miss Christina justice in that matter at any rate, she agreed with her mother, for a book was her thorough abomination.

About two years before the opening of our story, Mr Oglevie, good man, died; and he left his daughter a perfect picture of health, although no beauty, with a good, warm heart, and spirits overflowing with fun and frolic, still with really good sense to counterpoise both them and her mother's unfavourable influence. Certainly she was bold and forward in her manners, and most unlike what a young girl in her position would have been in an older country; but anything to the contrary could not be expected from a training such as hers had been; and, of course, her accomplishments were in keeping. She could with difficulty mend a tear in her dress, but could saddle a horse and back it as well as any man on the station. No better or more spirited stockrider was in that part of the country; in bringing in a mob of cattle she was second to none of her mother's hired stockmen, while she could 'give' the longest stock-whip on the station with a vigour and effect that would have done credit to a stronger arm. But Kirsty's great rage – next to horsemanship – was dancing; nothing could tie or hold her if there was a ball, however rowdy, within forty miles of her; and her mother knew it.

Upon one or two occasions earlier in Kirsty's life, maternal authority had been tried to prevent her attending some frolic or other, but all in vain; to the stables would go Christina, flourishing her whip in dangerous, though of course accidental, proximity to her mother's red nose; and she would be heard of, twenty or thirty miles away, flying along the road at a breakneck pace, just as likely without a hat as with one, and certainly not alone – for Kirsty had a beau, who was just as good a horseman as *she* was.

Christina's lover, Ned Goldie, was a young neighbouring farmer, one of that class which Mrs Oglevie delighted to call 'Cockatoos.' He was as different in disposition from Miss Oglevie, as a husband intended is generally from his intended wife. A quiet, steady, unassuming young fellow; he found it as difficult to say 'no' as his lady love did to say 'yes,' and fortunately was it for him that his tastes led him to avoid all society whatever, as he would have been sure to have become the tool of the first designing scoundrel he met. Nevertheless he went with Kirsty anywhere and everywhere, and that without the maternal wishes being at all consulted in the matter; and Kirsty repaid his attention by taking care that – as she herself was wont to express it – he did not make a fool of himself, which meant, as everyone knew, that others did not make a fool of him.

The homestead of Mrs Oglevie's cattle station was neither very comfortable nor very ornamental, that good dame despising every attempt at luxury that surpassed mere animal enjoyment; so Christina's private room was simply a shingle-covered log erection, lined with calico, and fitted up with the barest necessities of bedroom furniture; and it was there one evening, as our story begins, that the young lady was occupied when we wish to introduce her personally to our readers. A tall, robust girl, with an abundant figure, totally ignorant of corset or crinoline (crinoline! you had better mention such a thing to natural Kirsty Oglevie!) and a perfect mass of fair hair, gathered 'anyhow' into a net; a good-humoured face, lighted up with a flashing pair of bright, clear eyes; and that is the appearance of Christina. She was at the time intimated engaged in a more womanly occupation than she was often to be seen indulging in – viz., in opening out the voluminous folds of a piece of bright-coloured *barége*, which she was busily measuring into skirt lengths; and in the middle of this employment enters Mrs Oglevie.

'What are ye aboot, Kirsty? what's a' this? As sure's I'm a leevin woman this day if she's no gaun to the ball at Garse's!'

'Deed is she, mother!' replied the self-possessed girl, deliberately holding up the bright fabric to the light. 'You've hit the right nail on the head for once. Kirsty's *just* going to the ball at Garse's!'

'Ye're an ill-behaved, shameless lass! an' that's weel kenned thro' the country. Kirsty Oglevie's name's a byeword for fifty miles roun'; but tak' my ae last word for it, Kirsty Oglevie, an' ye tak' up wi' yon shaughled cockatoo, Goldie, ye'll never get a saxpence o' mine gin ye were starvin'!'

Kirsty flung her drapery on the bed, and, without deigning to her mother any reply save a look, which, however, her favourite servant – Irish Ellen – declared was 'as good as a summons any day,' she went out past her angry maternal relative, humming the refrain of a song she had learned from the said Ellen, with which, too, Mrs Oglevie was well acquainted –

Of all the old women that ever I saw,
Oh, a sweet bad luck to my mother in-law!

Of course, it is unnecessary to say that such conduct was highly unbecoming in a daughter. Our readers are quite aware that we are merely portraying Mrs and Miss Oglevie as they really existed; and we assure them, in addition, that we are far from wishing to hold up either as a pattern to the mothers and daughters of Australia.

Christina, then, made direct for the stable, and led from thence her favourite horse. It was something worth looking at to see with what groom-like alertness and 'savey' Kirsty threw the saddle upon her steed's back; and now, with knee against the animal's side, she drew the girths as tight as a drum. Meanwhile, affecting not to notice her mother, who had followed in sheer desperation of anger, for she was too much afraid of Kirsty to venture upon interfering with her. That she did notice her, however, was quite apparent from the wicked twinkle of her eyes as she made her horse move suddenly with a sudden twitch of the bridle, bringing thereby his heels rather close to the old lady. 'Take care, mother,' she said, then, looking to see if her stockwhip was coiled in its accustomed place at her saddle-bow, and gathering up the bridle in her left hand preparatory to a spring into her seat, 'take care! Terry doesn't like any one too near his heels!'

'Augh, ye bad, worthless quean!' shrieked Mrs Oglevie, mad with passion, 'bitterly ye'll rue the day ye began to ride rough shod ower ye're mither!'

Kirsty vaulted into her saddle and was off like a shot. She 'took' the three-railed fence of the home paddock with the greatest ease in life, and alighted on the grassy 'run' beyond, singing again at the top of her voice,

Of all the old women that ever I saw,
Oh, a sweet bad luck to my mother-in-law!

The pent-up rage in Mrs Oglevie's breast exploded in an ejaculation of,

'Hech, sirs!' as she stood, with clenched fist and scarlet visage, watching the wild girl scouring over the plains. Her mother saw her detaching the coiled stock-whip from her saddle-bow, and uncoiling it with a decided report that made the ears of all within hearing ring again; and the first crack was followed by another and another, each successive one serving as an increased stimulus to her charger, that soon bore her out of sight, away in the direction, as Mrs Oglevie well knew, of Goldie's farm. 'Hech, sirs!' repeated the squatteress again, turning to vent her ill-humour upon some of her domestics, when she perceived that Casey O'Connor stood behind her.

'Mr O'Connor,' as he dearly liked to be titled, had entered the service of Mrs Oglevie a few weeks before as a sort of general overseer; and whispers were already afloat among the observant servants that he was successfully trying to make an impression upon the soft heart of the ancient widow. However that might have been, it is quite certain that the tall, brawny Irishman was treated with great consideration by his mistress, and treated her in return with a respectful insinuation of manner that was laughable to every one excepting the good dame herself.

'Hech, Casey,' added the matron, on observing her admirer, 'hech, Casey, my heart's fairly sair wi' that awfu' lass!'

'An faith, Mrs Oglevie, mine is sore, too, pitying ye!' was the sympathising reply. 'Sure anyone can see the way its tellin' on ye! Ye're not like the same woman from one day to another.'

''Deed its true, man! I dinna feel as weel as I used when Oglevie was here. The management o' that harum-scarum neer-do-weel o' a bairn is over muckle for me. Hear till her! thae whip-cracks are for Goldie. There, ye can hear him answerin' back wi' his the noo.'

'Well, it must be heartbreakin' for a mother like you, sure enough, to see the child you wasted your time over payin' no more attention to your advice than if you was the worst mother in the world. God knows, my heart bleeds for ye, Mrs Oglevie, to see a fine woman like you, in the prime of your days, frettin' yourself to a shaddy, is enough to make a feelin' man mad!'

This great sympathy apparently greatly overcame the good lady; she detected a weakness which obliged her to seat herself upon a log near by – an operation which she certainly did not effect without difficulty, but it was a difficulty occasioned by a too great protuberance of person – and then with a great sigh she leaned her broad back against the fence, and made an attempt to straighten her dirty cap upon her grey head.

'Weel, Casey, its something at ony rate to hae a freen to speak wi'; its a grate relief to the hairt to open ane's mind wi' somebody.'

'It's a proud man I am the day,' replied the blarneying Irishman, taking off his hat to let the widow have the full effect of a fine mass of curly hair, unthinned by time, of which he was the vain possessor, 'to hear ye say that Casey O'Connor's a comfort to ye! Well, ye know, Mrs Oglevie, that if ye weren't above me in a way o' money and the like, I'd a said more long ago, although the Casey O'Connors (thank God) have no reason to be ashamed of their family.'

To see the palpable effect of this flattery upon the old woman was 'cakes and ale' to Casey. Personal vanity in a woman, at what age *does* it die out? Mrs Oglevie was fifty if she was a day, and ugly, and coarse, and unwomanly in every portion of her character; and here she was believing that O'Connor's affected admiration for her person was real and quite natural. That Casey did admire the widow's plethora of purse was certain; *that* almost anyone would have done. But that her odious old figure could create anything but disgust or merriment in the bosom of any young man, it assuredly required more than the ordinary amount of female vanity to credit. Yet credit it most certainly did Mrs Oglevie.

'Ony freen,' she replied, with a little affected purse of her lips, 'ony freen' may surely speak his mind to ane he thinks weel o'; an' deed I'm muckle in need o' advice aboot that crazy lass. Sae if ye'll come ben the hoose the nicht, Casey, my man, after a' the wark's through, we'll hae a talk ower it an' maybe be baith the better o' it.'

Didn't Casey O'Connor watch the corpulent lady going away into the house with a delight he could scarcely conceal. Casey O'Connor, Esquire, owner of Oglevie's station, eh? He thought he could swallow the old woman along with that, although she was a tough morsel sure enough.

It was nearly dark on that fine summer evening when Christina returned, and she came back considerably quieter than when she went away. After stabling her horse and giving him his feed, she entered the open door quietly, with the intention of going to her own room, where she was to get the assistance of Ellen that night in the fabrication of the dress for Garse's ball. Passing the closed door of the common sitting-room, she heard the subdued voices of her abomination, Casey O'Connor, and her mother, and a little pause convinced her that she herself was the subject of a not very flattering conversation between them. Kirsty's ire was aroused in an instant; she took a driving-whip from a nail in the entrance hall, and with a swift step, made a *detour* that brought her to another door leading to the parlour occupied by her mother and her Irish admirer.

Fortunately for Kirsty this second door was ajar, and most unfortunately for the owner in prospect of Oglevie's station. He was at that very moment winding up a point-blank proposal of marriage to the squatteress, with an assurance that, in addition to everything else, he would relieve the mind of his intended wife of all trouble upon her daughter's account. The interesting pair sat at a small table and were indulging themselves in a glass or two of 'auld Glenlivet,' the fair widow having made a complete gala night of it; grapes of various kinds flanked the decanters and glasses, and upon her own head she had actually placed considerably less awry than usual, her Sunday cap; and altogether the complacent lady was beaming with good humour and whisky.

'Not a throuble ye'll have, me darling,' iterated the grinning Casey. 'I'll do everything for ye! Aud never fear, I'll break in that young dame that's aggravatin' ye to death! She's playin' on ye're soft, kind, heart, and wearin' the flesh af ye're bones; but my word for it, I'll tame her into dacent behaviour!'

'You will – will you?' shouted Kirsty, bounding into the room like a young panther. 'Crack' went the whip around his shoulders and 'crack!' again. 'You'll break *me* in, will you?' – crack! crack! '*You* will, will you?' – crack! crack! crack!

Casey roared and cursed, and skipped about, until he got a chance to bolt out of the door, and then he did, carrying away the livid marks of Kirsty's whip, which remained with him for keepsakes for some time after. Not from any cowardice did Casey run away – oh, no! He felt like tearing the young tigress in pieces; but he dared not venture upon touching her. Much as her mother complained of Kirsty, he doubted whether she would take in good part a personal attack upon her, while on the contrary, she could hardly help feeling that she owed much to the man who had suffered such an indignity upon her behalf.

'But only wait, *Miss!*' he soliloquized, as he rubbed his shins in his own room; 'just wait 'till I have her safe, and if I don't pay you off my name's not – ' He *did* repeat a name here; but, strange to say, it was not Casey O'Connor.

After he had fairly run for it, Kirsty turned to her horrified and stunned parent. She stood before her in a defiant attitude, the very picture of a young fury, drawing the lash of her whip through the fingers of her left hand, with an absolute *longing* to lay it about her shoulders – a longing so fully expressed in her blazing eyes that Mrs Oglevie began to feel more uncomfortable. But she restrained herself did Kirsty, with a great difficulty it is true, and *only* because she was her mother.

'You old fool!' she said, with clenched teeth; 'you abominable old fool! Is that the man you're going to put in my dead father's place? Is *he* to get the hardly-earned fruits of an honest man's labour? – a wretch that has gallows in his face as plain as a pikestaff! Faugh!' And Kirsty turned upon her heel and marched out, leaving her mother a great mass of agitated flesh, incapable of replying one word.

Miss Oglevie bounced into her own room with a great determination boiling up in her bosom; not another night would she sleep under the roof with such a pair – Kirsty was off to Goldie; and so lighting a candle which stood upon her table, she pulled a sheet off the bed, and commenced tossing all her possessions of any value into it. They were not very numerous – first of all, the ball-dress fabric, and then her dresses, hats and linen, a few little ornaments, and poor Kirsty's trousseau was all told. She tied the corners of her impromptu portmanteau together, and swinging the bundle over her back, she walked out to the stable once more, without a single regret for the home she was leaving, or the mother she was leaving in it; and then once again saddled Terry, and fastening her bundle on his back, she turned back to seek Ellen. She found the young Irish girl in the kitchen, and telling her she wanted to speak to her, Ellen followed Kirsty, who, leading Terry, took her way out to the plain and stopping under a tree, she explained to Ellen what she was going to do and why.

'Oh, Lord save us!' ejaculated the impulsive Irish girl, 'are you going to run away, Miss Kirsty? an' will the old mistress marry that – that blackguard Casey O'Connor? Oh! what'll we do at all, at all?'

'I'll tell you what you must do, Ellen,' replied Christina hurriedly; 'go right in and pack up your traps, and come along with me. You'll be just as well at Goldie's farm as at Casey's station, *I* know; and, besides, it won't do for me to go poking over in the night to Ned, although his mother does live with him. Now, off you go, and I'll wait for you at that piece of bush.'

Ellen waited for no further instructions, and half an hour had barely elapsed when the two young girls might have been seen crossing the lonely dark plain, leading in turn the horse which carried what Christina laughingly termed their 'swags'.

Almost as soon as she was missed upon the following morning, the news of Kirsty's elopement had reached the station. She had been seen, accompanied by Ned Goldie, passing through a township some miles distant at full gallop. They were on their way to be married, and were no doubt united before Mr Casey O'Connor and her mother had settled in their minds what to do in the matter. In this case public opinion was in favour of the high spirited Christina. Ned Goldie was respected through the neighbourhood as a steady, hard-working man, and Kirsty's home was known to be made anything but a comfortable one by the unmotherly conduct of Mrs Ogelvie; so if the young woman preferred the little farm to the wide station, it was her own business, and sensible people respected her choice. And then again, the news of the old dame's intended marriage with Casey O'Connor created nothing but the greatest disgust through the whole country side. Every reported preparation, as it flew upon the strong wings of rumour from one household to another, only created fresh sneers and scandal. Great preparations were nevertheless going on at the station for a hurried wedding – preparations which, however, consisted chiefly in the providing of showy dress, etc., for the occasion. A flashy new buggy was purchased by Casey himself (out of Mrs Ogelvie's money of course), and the master of the station in prospect gave himself so many airs in anticipation of his coming elevation that he made himself ten times more disliked than ever. Oh, wasn't it 'a great day for Ireland entirely' when Casey drove the resplendent bride to the township where the important ceremony was to be performed. Mrs Oglevie was robed in a bright-coloured satin, and decorated with a gossamer shawl, resembling nothing save a web of woven rainbows. From her youthful hat floated long white nodding plumes, showering over her face an ample white-lace veil, behind which her red face looked for all the world like a red rising morning sun seen dimly through a curtain of floating mist. And Casey O'Connor himself? Oh! vain were an attempt to describe him! Vainglory and pride shone out of every crease of his new habiliments; and the very radiation of the well-varnished, swiftly-revolving wheels of the new buggy was of a piece with all the rest of the splendour.

Before they reached the residence of the clergyman, however, the bride and bridegroom must have felt considerably crestfallen, for, in spite of all existing laws in force, every digger turned out

of his hut, or tent, or hole, or store, or wherever he happened
to be, and 'joed' them with all his might. Hoots, and jeers, and
laughter rang before and behind them, until positively even brazen
Casey felt regularly ashamed of himself. The stake was one worth
enduring for, however, and Casey drove on, alighting at last
before the house where they were to be married in the very middle
of a crowd collected for the occasion. There was not much noise
indulged in there, it is true, the laughter being subdued; but the
opinion of the mob was plainly enough expressed in their disrespectful grins and whispered sneers. Now, as the intended Mrs
Casey O'Connor's person was of no small dimensions naturally,
and as its amplitude was most considerably increased by the most
voluminous of crinolines, it took some little time for her to extricate herself from the carriage; and as Casey was assisting her to
do so, two policemen stepped from the crowd, and one of them,
tapping him upon the shoulder, arrested him in the Queen's name!

The intended owner of Oglevie's station, with an oath, let go
of his fair bride, and made an ineffectual attempt to bolt – but
he was too late; in a moment a pair of glittering handcuffs were
clasped over his wrists, and a precious crestfallen object he was,
with his large white-gloved hands crossed before him and
ornamented with so unexpected a pair of bracelets.

It was some time before the crowd understood this affair; but
when they did, their delight knew no bounds. Cheer and hurrah
followed each other in succession, and ribald jokes nearly withered
the humiliated 'Mother Oglevie.' There she stood, with open
mouth, leaning in helpless abundance against the wheel of her
buggy, quite incapable of crediting her misfortune, until the shouts
and cries of the excited mob informed her that she had very nearly
bestowed her precious person and fine property upon 'Lanty Gor-
mon,' alias Molly, alias Jim Snap, a convicted burglar and thief!

Some one who pitied the old lady, perhaps more than she
deserved, pushed her into the buggy and drove her home. But
not before the more immediate of the impolite crowd had torn
her fine veil to pieces in attempts to get 'one glimpse of the young
bride.'

Although Mrs Goldie laughed when she heard of this
scene – laughed until she was obliged to 'lie down to it,' as she
said herself, and clapped her hands and danced about for very
joy at the discomfiture of Casey O'Connor, she was the very first
to fly over on horseback to the disappointed and humiliated old

woman. Kirsty found her seated disconsolately and in more than usual dishabille, in her disordered parlour. She was chewing the dirty string of her awry cap, and looked the image of chagrined mortification.

'Never mind, mother,' shouted Kirsty, bounding into the room; 'you're well rid of the wretch, I'm sure. Don't bother any more about it. As for the people, who cares for them? You can buy them all out, and be rich after. Come, put on your bonnet, and I'll drive you over to Goldie's. Bless your heart, mother, it's the nicest little place in the world!'

Cunning Kirsty Goldie! How well she knew the best plaster for her mother's bruised feelings. Buy them all out? Of course she could; and she permitted herself to be persuaded. So it was Kirsty's own hands that harnessed a horse, and brought a vehicle round to the door, and drove the soothed squatteress upon a visit to her new son-in-law.

ADA CAMBRIDGE 1844-1926

Novelist and poet, she was born in Norfolk, England
and published some pious books in her youth. In
1870, she married the cleric, George Cross, and they
left for Australia; as a country clergyman's wife (who
courageously resisted some of the conventional
demands of the position, see *Thirty Years in Australia*, 1903), she lived in a number of rural parishes in
Victoria before settling in Melbourne. The first Australian woman poet of significance, Ada Cambridge's
international acclaim rested primarily on her fiction.
She began writing novels in 1873 – ostensibly to
boost the family income – and in 1875 *Up the Murray* was serialised in the *Australasian*. After this
came a steady stream of stories (some appearing in
serial form) and her list of published novels numbers
more than twenty. *A Marked Man* (1890; Pandora
1987) helped to consolidate her fame and her fortune
and to establish her reputation as a critic of the
female condition.

While remaining well within the realms of polite
fiction, Ada Cambridge was able to plant many
doubts about the desirability of marriage and the
reliability of men. In her work the institution of marriage is often used as a symbol of the old order and
many of her Australian heroines reveal some of the
contradictions – and the disappointments and the
despair – that accompanied the demands of trying to
reconcile the old and the new: they could articulate
their conflict even if they felt powerless to change
their circumstances.

Among some of her many deceptively romantic and often disquieting novels are *A Mere Chance* (1882), *The Three Miss Kings* (1891 and Virago, 1987), *Not All in Vain* (1892), *A Marriage Ceremony* (1894), *Materfamilias* (1898), *Sisters* (1904 and Penguin, 1988), *A Platonic Friendship* (1905 and forthcoming, Penguin) and *The Making of Rachel Rowe* (1914). Her poetry includes *Unspoken Thoughts* (1887) and *Hand in the Dark and Other Poems* (1913).

The following novel, *A Girl's Ideal*, was first serialised in the *Age* in 1881 and has not since been reprinted. It gives a good indication of the author's scope and style.

A GIRL'S IDEAL

CHAPTER I

First Impression

The *Devonshire*, after lying for a day and a half in Plymouth Sound, took the last of her passengers – a mother and her two daughters and half a dozen miscellaneous men – on board, and set forth, in tow of a steam tug, on a voyage that was not expected to end under two or three months at least, and that might take four or five if the elements were not propitious. Some of the people who leaned over the poop railing for a pensive last look at the peaceful landscape, melting into the lustrous haze of sunset that glorified sea and sky, would almost as soon think of going to and from England in a fishing boat as in the *Devonshire*, now, though she is just as good a ship as she was then, and probably better; but in those days Orient liners had not 'come in,' and sailing vessels of the higher class still enjoyed a modest popularity.

The mother and daughters above-mentioned were not leaning over the railing with the rest. The eldest daughter did not feel very well, and already her chair had been unfolded for her, in which she sat, looking pale but pretty, at a convenient distance from the companion doorway; and her mother and sister were in devoted attendance upon her.

'Darling, do you think you can keep up?' said the mother anxiously, clinging to the back of the chair with furtive apprehension, as the treacherous deck heaved and swayed beneath her feet. 'Shall Mary run and get a pillow for your head?'

One of the miscellaneous men was standing by with his hands in his pockets, an ordinary wholesome-looking, broad-shouldered man, with a sun-browned face and a brown beard to match, evidently a returning colonist. He wheeled half round at the sound of the lady's voice.

'If Miss Hamilton will take my advice,' he said, in a tone that was a little blunt, but not disrespectful, 'she won't *think* of going below. Not until you are in the last extremity,' he added, looking at the girl with a twinkle of humour in his clear, rather cold, blue eyes. 'You have no idea, unless you are used to being at sea, how you would precipitate misfortunes.'

Mrs Hamilton herself was growing rapidly paler and paler; but she was able to lift her head and compress her grey lips into an expression faintly signifying disapproval of this young man's interference. He was a worthy young man, she had no doubt. He had been of service to her in Plymouth, where she had met him for the first time only a few hours ago, helping her to make terms with extortionate boatmen, and he would doubtless be of service to her again before the voyage was over (men were bound to be of service to unprotected women); but, as a stranger of unknown antecedents, whom accident had introduced to her in an irregular manner, he could not be permitted to address her daughters – and particularly Nina – in that haphazard and familiar fashion. 'What do you think, dear?' she inquired, ignoring him.

Nina, however, after the manner of daughters, who have so little gratitude, did not seem conscious that any liberties had been taken. She looked up at him with a vague but friendly smile, and assured him that she would try to stay on deck as long as possible. Then she half turned her pretty head, and whispered faintly, 'Pillows, Mary.'

Her sister immediately dashed through the doorway near her, went almost headlong into the saloon below, and came up again, like a flash, with an armful of pillows. These were arranged under Miss Hamilton's head and shoulders; and, being picturesquely wrapped in a red shawl, the invalid lay back in her chair for about ten minutes, an object of admiring interest to all beholders. She was an extremely pretty girl – openly, almost obtrusively, pretty.

She was slight in figure and delicately shaped; she had hair like golden-spun silk; she had a skin like a blush rose, and large eyes like pale sapphires; and her features, from those eyes downwards, were of nature's most finished modelling – the mouth especially, which was very small and very smiling and soft and red like the mouth of a child. Hypercritical people, who never failed to point out the defect of a high and narrow forehead, used to wish she had 'more in her;' but, as everybody knows, a pretty face can do very well on its own merits, its possessor seldom suffering neglect from an absence of intellectual charms. Nina was like a bit of Sèvres porcelain, Mrs Hamilton was fond of saying to her intimate friends, who nearly always agreed with her; and the mother occasionally implied that Mary, by comparison, was an earthen pot. The good women did not know how excellently discriminating she was in this judgment of her daughters. She was naturally ignorant of the fact that a bit of Sèvres porcelain, transparently fine and delicate as it is, with its jewel-like tinting and its exquisitely painted flowers and figures, is seldom to be compared, for real artistic worth and beauty, with a ruddy-coloured clay pipkin of primitive classic mould.

At the end of ten minutes, there was a sudden and hurried descent to the lower regions. Mrs Hamilton retired first, and the favorite daughter, begging the arm of the gentleman who had been snubbed on her behalf, followed quickly after. In ten minutes more all the ladies who had been so anxious to see the last of 'the old country' had disappeared from public view – that is to say, all but one.

Mary Hamilton stood, still and straight, like a strong young sapling, with her head in the air and her hands locked behind her, apparently unaffected by the prevailing sense of insecurity. She looked as if no sea, nor anything else in this world, could shake her off her balance. A tall, upright girl, in the rudest health, who at a very recent period had been an angular, gawky hoyden, but who was likely, in a year or two more, to be a generously-developed, if not a nobly proportioned and majestic woman; a girl with an intelligent, interesting, irregular face, of which, like her sister's, the chief feature was its mouth – a wide, sweet mouth, full of decision and determination – and with the grace of a wild animal in a rather large-limbed figure, which had had room to grow everywhere after nature's directions, and had done its growing vigorously. The brown-bearded unknown, sitting musingly on the skylight, left off looking at the blue mist into which the distant land was fast resolving itself, and looked at her instead – for she stood very nearly in his line of vision; and, though he was no artist, he took note of the flawless shape, encased in its loose envelope of dark blue serge, of the reposeful power and independence of the girl's unstudied attitude, and the intent, wide-eyed earnestness of her face; and he was suddenly inspired with the conviction that she was not only a 'fine girl' to look at (though not to be compared with her sister, of course), but a girl whose acquaintance – in the prospective dearth of congenial society – it might be interesting to cultivate. He edged himself off the skylight, and sauntered to her side.

'You bear the parting very well, Miss Hamilton,' he said, feeling that it was an awkward speech, but not able at the moment to improve upon it.

'The parting?' she inquired, looking at him with frank surprise and much self-possession. 'What parting?'

'I mean the parting from your native land.'

'Oh, I beg your pardon. I did not understand you. But it is not my native land. Australia – the land that I am now going back to – that is my native land. And I am not Miss Hamilton,' she added, with an abrupt little smile; 'I am – Miss Mary.'

He bowed a little stiffly. *Did* she suppose he was the kind of man who, if not forewarned of consequences, would be likely to call her 'Mary,' he wondered? It seemed to him that she, too, was snubbing him; and he did not like it. She was too young a woman to give herself airs with a man of his age; if her mother liked to do it, that was another matter. He was not going to be taught his place by a schoolgirl.

'Your sister – who, I presume, *is* Miss Hamilton – seems to feel the motion of the ship a great deal,' he remarked, bluntly and coldly, after a short pause. 'Don't you think she would be glad of your help – she and your mother? You seem so well, and they have only you to wait upon them – '

Then he realised what a cruel and vulgar revenge he was taking for the pin-prick to his vanity, when suddenly she lifted a pair of earnest, troubled, puzzled eyes. She was more easily hurt than he had expected. She seemed to wince almost as if he had struck her, and her face flushed crimson.

'Mother sent me up again,' she replied hurriedly; 'she wished me to come back. But – yes, you are right – I ought to have insisted on staying. I was thinking – I was full of my own thoughts, and forgetting them. I will go at once.'

He opened the door for her mechanically, angrily conscious that he was a rude and unfeeling brute, and ashamed of himself, now that it was too late.

'Don't go,' he entreated. 'If your mother sent you back, it is all right. Miss Mary, you can do no good, and will only get upset yourself. Stay on deck – the tug is going to cast us off directly – '

But she was gone.

At the close of that day, when the ship was driving through the starlight with a fair wind, and all the lonely night was silent around her, save for the swish and ripple of the water at her bows, the people who have been mentioned were giving their first impressions 'in confidence' – Mr Macleod, to his sister, of the Hamilton family; and the Hamilton family, to one another, of him.

Mr Macleod's sister, at present a stranger to the Hamiltons, having come on board in London, was sitting on deck with a shawl over her dressing gown, unwilling to go to bed until she was obliged. She had been indisposed, like the majority of the female passengers, but was recovering again in the freshness of the night air; and she was pleased to interest herself about the lately joined party, and anxious to find out whether they seemed to be desirable acquisitions or otherwise.

'The mother is an old cat,' said Mr Macleod, in a tone of calm conviction, giving forth his sentiments in instalments, as he puffed placidly at his pipe. 'She gives herself airs enough, but I don't believe she is anything more than a good imitation of a lady. She never could have been born one – with such a tone of voice as that. You should have heard her, in the midst of her daughters and her baggage, abusing old Joe Smith – you know old Joe! as decent an old waterman as ever breathed – because he wanted a shilling or two more than some friends of hers had told her she ought to pay. She was glad enough when I came along and offered to share the boat with her, and to have me to look after all her handboxes and parasols; but after I had seen her settled in her cabin, and there was nothing more I could do for her, then she sent me about my business. She doesn't, apparently, wish for the honor of my further acquaintance.'

'Well, why do you make yourself so cheap? I'm always telling you – and you always will do it. What are the daughters like?'

'The eldest seems very nice. Indeed, she's quite a little beauty. I don't know when I have seen such a pretty girl. Not a bit like her mother – gentle, courteous, speaking softly – a nice girl all round, it appears to me. Of course you can't tell,' he added prudently, 'what she will turn out when you come to know her.'

'I hope,' replied the lady, with a pathetic sigh, 'that when you come to know her it won't turn out that you make an idiot of yourself. Now, pray don't, Don – for my sake – while we are travelling together. A man by himself can do what he likes, but you must remember you have to take care of me.'

'I should think your mind might be easy about that,' he remarked, 'seeing that I have attained the mature age of 35 and have never been entangled, as you call it, yet. I have not kept out of it all these years,' he went on, less deliberately, as if he were thinking the suggestion over, and it irritated him a little – 'I have not been knocking about the world for over thirty years, amongst all sorts of women, to fall a victim to a casual pretty face in thirty minutes – though it *is* a pretty face – I don't care who says it isn't. It strikes one like a pretty picture – that's all. Thirty minutes!' he broke out warmly, after yet another cogitative pause; 'it was hardly ten. For I couldn't see her in that hideous blue veil that she came on board in.'

The lady laughed, and stroked his coat sleeve with her white hand. 'Poor, dear Don!' she murmured, mockingly, 'Never mind. What about the other girl? There is another, didn't you say?'

'Oh – she! It's hard to tell. A sort of overgrown schoolgirl – big, with a large mouth – one of those uncompromising young women, you know – gives one the idea of having spent all her time on the cricket field with a lot of brothers – doesn't know what you mean unless you speak the very plainest of plain English, and full of prickles if you don't take her the right way. That's how she strikes me.'

'The kind of young woman I particularly dislike. And who are they, I wonder? Victorians going back, did you say? Hamilton – Hamilton; there are so many Hamiltons. Can they be the people who had Wattle-bank before Fred took it, do you suppose? The widow and children went to England when the father died.'

'Very likely. There are two girls, I believe, and the mother took them home to some of his people. That was nine years ago. I remember old Hamilton died just after I came back from Ceylon, that time I went to look after Charlie. Poor old Hamilton, what an old good-for-nothing he was! and he left his family hardly anything. The bank got Wattle-bank when he died, you know. Fred bought the place off the bank.'

'We'll ask Mr Lorimer. He would know anyone who had ever belonged to the neighbourhood. Mr Lorimer!' she called, raising her voice suddenly.

A very small and wizened old man, wrapped, this mild June night, in a long-skirted overcoat, shuffled across a little strip of dim white deck, and peered into her face.

'Mrs Lepel!' he cried, in a high, thin, cracked voice; 'my dear lady, I am delighted to see you are able to come upstairs again. I didn't recognise you in the darkness.'

'Mr Lorimer, tell us – those people who came on board this afternoon, are they the Hamiltons who used to live at Wattle-bank?'

'The same,' he replied, whispering confidentially; 'the very same. It was a great surprise to me to see them, for I had not heard they were coming back, and that they should come in this ship too – a curious coincidence, is it not? and as handsome as ever,' the old man went on – 'apparently just as young. I was speaking to her just now. You noticed me speaking to her, perhaps?'

'No, I didn't. Why, dear me, you are as bad as Don. Don has been raving about Miss Hamilton's beauty.'

Mr Lorimer chuckled and simpered, 'Miss Hamilton is a very nice-looking young person,' he said; 'but I was not referring to Miss Hamilton. I spoke of the elderly lady, Mrs Lepel – of the mother.'

'Oh – the mother!' Mrs Lepel vaguely remembered having heard something of an old love affair belonging to the days when this parchment-faced bachelor was supposed to have been young. 'Is the mother very handsome? Don, you didn't tell me that Mrs Hamilton was a beauty as well as her daughter.'

'I didn't think she was.'

'Ah, you are a young man, sir. And you did not see her thirty years ago, when she was Miss Butler. She *was* a handsome girl, if you like. Somehow girls don't grow up so handsome in these days – nor young men either, for that matter – present company excepted, of course, Mr Donald.'

Mr Donald gave a grunt, and went on smoking placidly. Mrs Lepel, who was a lively person, amused herself with a congenial topic.

'And you mean to tell me I am not so handsome as the girls used to be, Mr Lorimer? Well, I always thought till now that you were one of my admirers.'

'My dear lady! – *you!* I never for a moment – I was speaking of girls – young girls – '

'And you don't reckon me among the young ones? – I see. But let me tell you, Mr Lorimer, I am only twenty-seven. And one doesn't expect to be altogether past one's youth and beauty at twenty-seven. Don, I appeal to you.'

'Oh, dear, dear!' cried the old man, with a feeble gesture of distraction.

'Well, never mind. I don't object to rivals of thirty years ago. Tell me about her, Mr Lorimer. Was she much run after when she was Miss Butler?'

Mr Lorimer made an ineffectual attempt to explain that Miss Butler was not nearly so much run after as Miss Macleod had been, before Mr Lepel was so fortunate as to win her hand; but he described Miss Butler as having had an unusual number of admirers.

'And I suppose you were one of them?' the lady suggested, much amused with what seemed to her a very comical idea.

'Mrs Lepel, I was – I was.' And the old man dropped his little gallantries, and spoke with fretful energy, 'I have never made any secret of it. Yes, I was one of the many she had to choose from. And, if I may say so without vanity, I am the one she ought to have chosen, and not that old rascal of a Dick Hamilton, who was the worst of the lot. However, I forgive her – I forgive her,' he added, in a thin, tremulous, angry falsetto. 'She is punished for her foolishness. She is left to scrape and pinch on two or three hundred a year, instead of being one – a – ahem! I let my tongue run on too fast. You will excuse me, my dear lady. Seeing her again so unexpectedly, after many years' absence – it upsets me a little.'

'Oh, don't mention it, Mr Lorimer. I am very much interested, I assure you, and I will get you to introduce me to her in the morning. But I think it must be nearly time for the candles to be put out, so I'll say good night.'

She went downstairs to the cuddy, leaning on her brother's arm, with her handkerchief held to her mouth. 'I could not have stayed another minute,' she whispered, chuckling violently under her breath. 'I should have laughed in his ridiculous old face. The preposterous old creature – he must be 80 at the very least. O dear me, we shall get a little fun after all! Mr Lorimer and Mrs Hamilton, and you and the pretty daughter.'

'I don't see much to laugh at myself,' said Mr Macleod. 'It rather strikes me the other way. I've known the old fellow since I was born, and I never thought he was anything but a machine for grubbing mony. It touches me to see him showing a bit of human feeling after all. And to think of him keeping the memory of an old love green in such a barren desert of a life. Poor old Lorimer!'

'Oh, I heard ages ago that he had had a disappointment. But, bless me, he ought to have got over it long before this time!'

'Who, of your rejected suitors, will think you the handsomest woman in the world when you are 50 or 60 do you suppose?' Mr Macleod inquired, stopping at his sister's cabin door, and looking an affectionate rebuke at her upturned face – a girlish, piquant, careless, laughing face.

'There – don't begin,' she responded hastily, lifting deprecating hands. 'I do wish you wouldn't always be so dreadfully in earnest about everything. It's a mistake, Don, as I am always telling you. Amuse yourself, and don't moralise, if you want to have a comfortable life. That is my theory. Good night, dear old boy. Go and have another pipe on deck, and meditate upon the charming Miss Hamilton.'

'Bother the charming Miss Hamilton.'

'Hush! They'll hear you.'

Meanwhile, Miss Hamilton had gone to bed. She was lying in the most comfortable of the two small bunks which lined the cabin, propped up with pillows. Her spun-gold hair, shaken out of chignon and braids, had been brushed from her face, and knotted up at the back of her small, narrow head. She looked particularly delicate and pretty, and, like Mrs Lepel, had evidently become somewhat accustomed to the motion of the ship. She was nibbling a biscuit, and sipping a glass of weak brandy and water, over which she made many grimaces. Watching with much solicitude, the mother lay, supporting herself on her elbow, on the opposite bed – the bed which would get all the drip from the port window whenever seas were rough. Mrs Hamilton was but partly undressed; she could nòt retire altogether until she had seen her darling comfortably settled and asleep. By the door, still in the old blue frock in which she had come on board, Mary sat at the foot of her sister's bunk, leaning her straight back against the venetians behind her and swinging her feet in space. She, poor girl, had to share a stern cabin with three strange women; and she was lingering until the last moment, dreading to face the unknown discomforts that awaited her.

'One is a fat old lady, Nina, very bad with asthma, and another is a young one, with a baby – quite a small baby – and no nurse. They represent three generations of one family, I believe. The third – or rather, the fourth – is that girl we saw on deck with a green feather in her hat and a long curl hanging over her left shoulder.'

'How dreadful!' murmured Nina, with a little shudder. 'But you need not speak to them, you know, dear.'

'Not speak to them! Why, how can I help speaking to them, sleeping in the same room? Oh dear me, why do people have such nasty ways on board ship? One would never think of doing such things on land. How I wish I might sleep on the floor here, between you. May I not, mother? I don't want any regular bed, my own pillows and the possum rug would do for me. I shouldn't be a bit in the way, and I could wait on you and Nina. You would like to have me here to wait on you in the night. And I would get up very early, and you could use my bunk to put your clothes in.'

This proposition, though eloquently urged, was not, of course, entertained for a moment. She was sent off to her distant quarters (where she 'waited on' the asthmatic old lady and her daughter, cheerfully nursing the baby for them for the greater part of the night), carrying with her sundry superfluities of Nina's wardrobe to stow away in the meagre space allotted for her own. But, before she went, they discussed their fellow passengers who had just been discussing them.

'I find out that he is Mr Macleod – Mr Donald Macleod,' said Mrs Hamilton, in reply to a question from her eldest daughter. 'He is brother to that Mrs Lepel, whose husband bought Wattlebank after we went home. I was so surprised when Mr Lorimer told me. I thought he was – well, I couldn't tell who he might be; but the Macleods are a very good family, I believe. They used to have Bungil, Nina, that nice place with the beautiful garden and family pictures – but you were too young to remember it – that your poor father was always wishing for. This young Mr Macleod has it now.'

Here Nina contributed the information that Mrs Lepel was on

board. Mr Macleod had mentioned that his sister was travelling with him, and that he feared, by the manner of things, that she was not going to be a good sailor. This was very interesting intelligence. Mrs Hamilton sat up in her bunk, looking quite alert and bright, as she indulged in desultory reminiscences of Mrs Lepel's early youth, and congratulated herself and Nina upon having someone of their own class to speak to on the voyage, contrary to her most sanguine expectations.

'I remember her well – a pretty, graceful child. She was but a child when I saw her last. She rode over to Wattlebank with her father one day, and stayed to lunch. You two girls were little things in the schoolroom then. I remember she asked poor papa to give her one of old Sappho's puppies, and made Mr Macleod carry it home for her on his saddle, done up in a bag. Such work he had with it! The old man spoiled her a good deal. She was the only daughter, so of course it was natural, and it did not seem to hurt her. She had very pretty manners – quite like a little woman. I remember there were some boys, but I can't recollect seeing any of them. This Donald was the eldest, I suppose – taking Bungil and the family pictures . He is a fine young man. And not married, Mr Lorimer says, which I rather wonder at, considering his position, and that he is not altogether in his first youth. How attentive and obliging he has been to us to-day!'

'Very,' said Nina. 'And he was so nice to me after you had to go down.'

'I see a great look of his father in his face, now I come to think of it,' pursued Mrs Hamilton reflectively.

'He has a very striking face,' murmured Nina.

Whereupon Mary, who had been swinging her feet in a meditative manner, and gazing into vacancy with her steadfast eyes, suddenly broke in: – 'A striking face! Oh, no, Nina! He has a most commonplace face. As plain a person as I ever saw.'

Her sister laughed, with a light touch of elder-sisterly disdain. 'O yes, I suppose he would be plain to *you*. But he is a very good-looking man for all that. What shoulders he has! What a splendid beard!'

'I hate beards – nasty, dirty things.'

'Of course,' retorted Nina, still smiling, with her head on one side. 'You like lean, shaved cheeks, and a sandy moustache – '

'Sandy!' echoed Mary, turning round fiercely, in a blaze of wrath. '*Sandy*, indeed!'

'But then you see, my dear, you are not everybody. Other people have their views, and *I* don't think a man is half a man without his beard.'

'It is very useful when he has an ugly mouth that he wants to hide,' said Mary, defiantly; but she was confused and flushed. 'That's how it is with Mr Macleod – if his mouth is anything like his nose.'

'Why, what is the matter with his nose. A good, honest, solid nose I call it. You wouldn't have a broad man with a nose like a knife-blade?'

'There's a difference between a knife-blade and a thing like that.'

'True,' assented Nina, with a mocking sigh; 'but unhappily we can't all be modelled after the antique. Because one man – '

'Who is Mr Lorimer, mother?' Mary hastily interrupted, jumping from her seat and beginning to gather her bundle together. 'He seems to think he knows you very well. Nina says he looks like a disreputable Jew pedlar. Didn't you, Nina?'

'So he does, exactly. And how dirty he is! He must have inherited his clothes from a long line of ancestors – particularly his great coat.'

'His appearance is peculiar,' said Mrs Hamilton, smiling a little; 'but he is a very important person, notwithstanding. He is Lorimer, of Lorimer and Lovett, the great brokers. I knew him when I was a girl. He is quite an old friend, indeed; and I hope you will remember that, Mary, and not laugh at him, nor be rude to him, my dear.'

'Mother! *am* I rude to people?'

'Sometimes you are, though I do not think you mean to be. You are brusque, and off-hand and thoughtless – that is being rude. And I notice that it is always to the wrong people. I wish you both – you too, my Nina – to be attentive to Mr Lorimer, and not mind his little eccentricities. He seems to have every wish to be kind and useful to us.'

'Why should he?' protested Mary. 'We don't want people to be kind and useful to us – unless it is a big man who will carry our parcels and he can't do that. He looks as if he wants to be carried himself.'

'Well, go to bed, child. It is nearly ten o'clock, and they will be calling to us to put the lights out. Moreover, Nina wants to get to sleep.'

CHAPTER II

Before Breakfast

Mrs Lepel occupied a cabin with her maid, next door to Mrs Hamilton and Nina, in a favourable position near the centre of the ship. Mr Macleod enjoyed the luxury of a similar apartment all to himself, adjoining that stern cabin so terribly unsuited to ladies with delicate digestions, the fourth part of which was assigned to Mary. In the middle of the night he woke up with a monotonous wailing sound in his ears. Such were what Mary would have called the 'nasty ways' of people on board ship, that he could hear the voices of his neighbours on the other side of the partition quite distinctly if they were not careful to subdue them, and this voice was only too surely recognisable.

'Hang that brat!' he muttered with all the energy of which a bachelor of mature age was capable. 'How is a fellow to sleep if he's to have a baby squalling within a foot of his pillow, I should like to know? They should have a nursery somewhere, if they must take them on board, and not let passengers be annoyed in this way?'

He tossed about a little, fuming and fretting; he tried, by burying his head in the bedclothes, to put himself to sleep again. But he was hopelessly wide-awake, and the baby cried piteously. He resisted a strong temptation to protest audibly in the popular manner. 'Keep that child quiet can't you?' for he was a reasonable man, though he was a bachelor; and he set himself to wait until the 'row' as he termed it (speaking of it to his sister the next day), was over, with such spartan fortitude as he could command. By-and-by he heard the asthmatic old woman gasping and wheezing; then he heard the young mother sighing and moaning; she was evidently very sick and very tired; and they raised their voices at intervals in ineffectual remonstrance to the baby, which wailed on steadily as if it had no intention of stopping.

'Pleasant, this,' he remarked to himself grimly. 'However,' he reflected magnanimously, 'I suppose it is worse for those poor women than for me.'

Then there was a brief lull, and in the lull he heard the soft pat of footsteps, slowly marching up and down. Somebody was trying to soothe the baby to sleep in the regulation fashion; and, as he listened, he marvelled how anyone could walk so firmly on that see-sawing stern-cabin floor. It could not be the mother, nor yet the grandmother – he was quite sure of that. Was it the young lady who had worn the green feather and the long curl, whom he had seen at the door of the stern cabin the day before, when possessing himself of his own apartment? If so, appearances had been even more deceptive than usual, and he would never believe in instinct and intuition again. Presently, still listening, he heard her voice. It was singularly serene and cheerful; the voice of one blessed with admirable patience and temper, whoever she was. 'There, there, there – bye, bye, bye – hush, hush, hush.' She was patting the baby's back and keeping time with her pats and footfalls. 'Hush, hush, hush – bye, bye, bye – there, there, there.' It almost persuaded him to go to sleep himself. Certainly it had a most tranquilising effect upon his irritated nerves. There was no tune; there were only these meaningless words; but the tender sing-song lullaby, every subdued note clear and pure as those of a lark on a spring morning, was delicious. Any baby that could resist it, he thought, must indeed be incorrigible. This baby, at any rate, could not. Slowly, but surely, it yielded to the charm, breaking out into its paroxysms of passion or pain at longer and longer intervals, and with fainter and fainter energy, and permitted itself to be comforted. It ceased at last even to whimper, and for the rest of the night was heard no more. But when the baby was gone to sleep, the nurse still walked up and down for awhile, singing very softly, but with the same delicate clearness, fragments of songs and waltzes, little airs of the street, here and there blended with hymn tunes, which seem to suggest themselves unconsciously, like vocal thoughts, and Donald Macleod, no longer restless and irritable, lay awake on purpose to listen to her. It was a wonderfully charming voice, and he could not help puzzling himself with conjectures as to what sort of person it belonged to. He had a theory about voices. He used to say – and he was rather a dogmatic man, though more open to reason than men of that sort usually are – that the voice was an unfailing keynote to the character of him or her to whom it belonged, and particularly he insisted that its quality was the test of good breeding, or the reverse, no matter what education had done, or failed to do, for it. But his theory was not often put upon its trial so fairly as now. For, to the best of his belief, he had never seen the girl, or woman, to whom this voice belonged. It suggested a girl, young and refined, and gentle and sweet, and the only person on board, that he knew of at all answering to that description was the pretty Miss Hamilton, whose voice he had been reluctantly compelled to admit, was thin, flat and disappointing. He almost forgot how much he admired the pretty Miss Hamilton, in the interest that he took in this invisible lady, whose acquaintance he imagined he had yet to make. 'For I'm certain she is a lady, though she may turn out to be a nursemaid,' he finally concluded, summing up his impressions before he went to sleep.

In the morning he was out very early, as every man had to be who wanted to get his bath before he dressed himself – a luxury that could only be obtained in the *Devonshire* on open deck, from the hose of an obliging sailor; and when the ordinary dressing bell summoned the ladies from their beds – which summons the greater number of them disregarded – he had been walking the poop for more than an hour and was wondering how much longer he would have to wait for his breakfast. He was so hungry that, in the absence of more substantial satisfaction, he thought he would solace himself with a pipe; and he ran downstairs to fetch his matchbox, which he had left below. The cuddy was showing signs of life and animation. Stewards were bustling to and fro with armfuls of crockery and table linen. Dejected looking lads, who had not yet found their sea-legs, were crawling from door to door with their little flat-bottomed water cans. The sun was shining down through the skylight upon the still fresh and fragrant bouquets of English flowers that bloomed on the swing trays amongst the bottles and tumblers, and reflected their fair faces in the mirrors over the sideboard. The place looked bright and cheerful; it was untarnished yet by the stains of the sea. None of the passengers were about. The men who had made a point of their morning bath were enjoying the air, as he had been doing; and it was too soon to dream of seeing ladies.

But as he swung himself off the bottom step of the staircase into the comparative gloom at the back of it, the door of the stern cabin opened before him, and Mary Hamilton came out. For a moment she paused on the threshold with the light from her own window behind her, and he could not see her very distinctly. Then she closed the door, and came towards him. There was a kind of alert response in the expression of her figure moving through the shadow swiftly, with large, easy strides. When she came into the light he saw who it was, and knew that it was she whom he had heard through his cabin wall. She still held the baby – it was a little thing in long clothes – close to her breast, in one strong hand, while with the other hand she gathered up her old blue skirt. At the moment of recognising her he told himself that his first impression had been a wrong one. She was looking as fresh as the morning, with glossy, wet hair, and the bloom of youth and health in her face. There was a smile in her eyes and at the corners of her large, but distinctly womanly, mouth, that had something of the sweetness of her singing voice about it. He wondered how it was that she seemed so changed since yesterday.

'Good morning, Miss Mary,' he said, pulling off his cap, 'are you up already?'

She bowed a little distantly, and then suddenly seemed to warm to the unexpected greeting.

'Oh, Mr Macleod – good morning. Yes, I have been up some time.' He noticed the refined intonation of all her syllables now, though he had not noticed it before. 'Is that a baby you have there?' he made bold to inquire – for the sake of saying something that would keep her where she stood for a minute, with the light from the stairway on her face. 'Yes. I am going to take him for a walk on deck until my mother and sister want me. I think the air – it seems so fresh and lovely this morning – will do him good, poor little fellow. Isn't it a mite to be knocked about on board ship?' looking down on the small bundle compassionately. 'He is not four months old yet.' Mr Macleod glanced furtively at the baby's half-concealed face, and remarked that it seemed pretty comfortable. Then he made polite inquiries after the health of Mrs Hamilton and Nina.

'I have not seen them yet,' said Mary, with one foot on the step of the stairs. 'Mother told me not to go to them too soon, as I might disturb my sister. Their cabin is over yonder,' nodding vaguely into the space behind him. She was so tall that she could very well look over his shoulder.

'And the baby – is he of your party?'

'O dear, no! The baby is – well, I really don't know their names yet. I have to share their cabin. They are very kind; I don't mind it now. Indeed, it is very fortunate I am there, for I can help them in many ways. I am able to do things, and they are not. His mother,' stroking the child's swathed head with a large, brown hand, 'is very ill this morning. She had such a bad night. I have been wondering whether, if I could find the doctor, he would be able to give her anything. Do you think he would? Do you know where he is?'

Of course Mr Macleod volunteered at once to look for the doctor, and in due time found him and sent him to the stern cabin. Going on deck afterwards, having forgotten his match box, he took a retired seat near the main deck, and amused himself watching the powerful young woman marching up and down the poop with her baby, and thought he had never seen a plain girl that had so interesting a face, or looked so vigorous, so capable, and so perfectly contented and happy. She was giving the baby a walk in such a businesslike manner that he perceived she did not want to be talked to, and therefore left her unmolested; yet he had an inclination to talk to her. She was not the kind of girl he had thought her yesterday, there was a wholesome and kindly and companionable air about her, and no prickles at all. It seemed to him, moreover, that she was one of the few to whom a man *might* talk, with comfort and safety. Not like the pretty sister, with whom conversation, in spite of its superior charms, would be fraught with certain perils and dangers, that he would have to put himself to trouble to guard against; but rather like a 'good fellow' of his own sex, who would give and take on equal terms. This was the first modification of his conception of her character – the beginning of rapid changes.

CHAPTER III

After Dinner

Neither Mrs Hamilton nor Nina appeared in public that day. Mrs Lepel came upstairs for a little while, and lay, in shawls and pillows, on the skylight; but her maid sat by to wait upon her, and Mr Macleod was not called upon to exert himself on her behalf. So he spent the day in watching Mary, who interested him more and more.

At breakfast she was the only lady who ventured to brave the aroma of savory dishes. Having tried in vain to tempt her mother and sister with delicate morsels of various kinds, she sat down exactly in front of him, and not only smelt, but ate, sausages and fried potato with a placid zest that spoke volumes for the excellence of her digestive organs. Looking at her at intervals he was struck with the value of physical health to one's personal appearance. This girl, he remarked to himself, could not be called pretty – certainly not – with so unformed a manner, and with those masculine jaws and that immense mouth, but the warm colour and clearness of her skin, the dewy brightness of her large straightforward eyes, and, above all, the superb outlines of her figure, made her very pleasant – even attractive – to contemplate. So fresh, so wholesome, so charmingly natural, in the best sense, she was. 'After all,' he said to himself – and said afterwards to Mrs Lepel 'you can hardly call a woman, with a shape and complexion like hers, *plain*. She mayn't be pretty, but she has much the same effect on you as if she were.'

After breakfast, Mary Hamilton went to her mother's cabin, where she spent an hour. Then she appeared on deck again with the baby, which she presently introduced to Mrs Lepel – to whom Mr Macleod introduced her. Having walked the child to sleep, she carried it back to the stern cabin, and reappeared with its frail-looking mother hanging to her arm, whom she placed in a folding chair and waited upon with much assiduity, the doctor being also in attendance. Then she disappeared for a while, and by-and-by was seen carrying basins of arrowroot about for her various patients – ignoring the servant lads, who trotted vaguely after her. Then she took the old asthmatic grandmother for a turn up and down the deck; then again brought up the baby; then escorted the mother downstairs, after which she did not show herself any more until the bell rang for dinner – a meal served on board the *Devonshire* at three o'clock.

At dinner she appeared in her place, with some slight – very slight – attempts at embellishment about her; and several sickly ladies being present, she looked more fresh and blooming than before. Watching her quiet devotion to the demands of an extremely healthy appetite, Mr Macleod reproached himself that he had not taken his seat beside hers for the voyage, and wondered whether it was too late to change it. What a comfortable neighbour she would have been! And he could have talked to her between the courses, at any rate.

When dinner was nearly over, he lifted a bottle, round the neck of which hung one of his own visiting cards, from the swing tray above him, and handed it to the nearest servant, with a whispered direction, and a surreptitious nod towards the young lady opposite. The man glided round the long table, stooped over Mary's shoulder, and held the mouth of the bottle to a wineglass. 'Mr

Macleod wishes for the honor of a glass of wine with you, Miss.'

It was a successful and satisfactory little manoevre. She looked up from her pudding quickly, as if for a moment she did not understand the message; and meeting Mr Macleod's eyes fixed upon her, she smiled a frank and modest smile that charmed him. She had an immense mouth, no doubt, but what a sweet mouth it was, in spite of its size. And, oh, *what* teeth! 'Do you mind if I take water?' she asked, laying the palm of her hand on the top of her wineglass. 'I am not a total abstainer, but I am not used to wine, and don't like it.'

'Certainly,' he responded promptly, 'But won't you have anything else?'

No, she wouldn't have anything else; she preferred water. The servant poured some out for her, and she lifted and drank it, with a little bow to her new friend that was full of simple grace.

Though she had refused his wine, she was evidently pleased that he had asked her to take it. And he wondered what had made him think her raw and unformed – the kind of girl who might have lived in the cricket field with larrikin brothers. That was a great mistake. She had very pretty manners.

And by and by, when the long meal was quite over, and he had had his saunter and his smoke – when the brilliance of the blue June day was growing soft and misty on the quiet sea – he saw her sitting down at last, with nobody near her, and saw the opportunity he had now begun distinctly to desire for making her closer acquaintance. She was occupying an end of one of the fixed benches surrounding the deck, which served not only for passengers to sit upon, but for coops for the poultry dedicated to the saloon table. It was very rarely that she sat in an arm chair or indulged in lounging attitudes. She was lounging a little now, however. Her elbow rested on the railing and the crown of her head in the palm of her hand, the other lying listlessly in her lap. Her feet were crossed; there was a droop about the shapely shoulders and the straight strong back, she was looking down upon the sea with dreamy brooding eyes. She reminded him of Story's statue of Cleopatra – the air of brief repose pervading a figure too full of power and vigor for the restful attitude to mean fatigue.

'This is the first time I have seen you sitting down to-day, except at meal times,' he said, stepping up beside her, and leaning his arms on the rail. She started at the sound of his voice; evidently she had fallen into a brown study, 'I don't often sit down. I don't get tired,' she replied absently.

'No, you don't look as if you did. And you are never sea-sick?'

'Never,' she said proudly. 'I am never sick at all, either on sea or land.'

'What a lucky person. And yet I see you can feel for those who are less fortunate. You have been quite a sister of mercy to the invalids. By the way, how is Miss Hamilton to-night?'

Mary explained that her sister was very unwell, and was not going to get up at present; and, having regard to the sympathy and concern that such an announcement was sure to call forth, she discoursed about Miss Hamilton in a frank and friendly manner – the delicacy of her constitution, the necessity that she should be spared as much of the fatigue of travel as possible, her beauty, her cleverness, and her importance generally – much to Mr Macleod's edification and amusement. Notwithstanding her little dignities she was the most approachable young person he had ever attempted to gossip with after a few hour's acquaintance. Evidently she was very young in worldly experience, even for her years. She talked to him with no apparent consciousness that he was a man or a stranger – giving him all the information about herself and her family that he was curious to possess, but would not have dreamed of asking for – with the utmost candor.

'You know we have been poor people since my father died,' she said, after telling him that their going home had been a great mistake, and that she, for her part, was delighted to be returning to Australia; and she made the statement cheerfully, looking at him with her remarkably straightforward eyes.

'How should I know?' he inquired, smiling. It was impossible not to smile and yet he was seriously interested.

'Because you know all about us, Mr Macleod,' was her calm rejoinder. 'Oh yes,' – putting up her hand as he showed signs of protesting – 'I know you do. I heard you talking to that old Jew man this morning; his voice, small as it is, is so sharp that it seems to penetrate every corner of the ship, and whenever he mentions the word 'Hamilton' I am sure to hear it. And so I am certain you know *that*. We were well off at Wattlebank when I was a child; but when Wattlebank was sold we had only a little over £200 a year left to live on. That is all we have had since. My mother thought it would not matter so much if only we could live in England, in some kind of association with my father's family, who had a position, she said, that money, or the want of it, could not affect. But the relations we thought most of had been dead for hundreds of years, and the only remnant of the family was Uncle Joseph, a canon of Eastwold. No; we always called him 'the canon' before we went home, but he was only a minor canon, and that is an immense difference, you know. He had a little parish in the city, but he was always in residence in his prebendal house. It was such a sweet old house – almost as old as the cathedral itself; but *he* – oh, what a horrid man he was! He didn't want us living at Eastwold – He said nasty things of mother behind her back – he called Nina 'colonial' – he snubbed us and sneered at us – he was one of the most insulting men I ever knew. How mother managed to stand it all those years I don't know, especially when dear old Uncle Peter was always writing to ask us to come back. Do you know my Uncle Peter – Mr Peter Butler?' she inquired, abruptly. 'He is manager of the Bank of Australasia at Abercorn.'

'Butler? Is old Butler your uncle?' Mr Macleod exlaimed with lively interest. 'Oh yes, I know him, of course. I live only a few miles from Abercorn. I know him well; he's a capital fellow; he often does business for me.' Business, indeed, was the only bond that had ever existed between Mr Butler and Mr Macleod, but it was made the most of. 'I have known him for years, and I like him awfully. But how odd that he should be your uncle! Are you going to see him when you get back?'

'We are going to live with him,' said Mary. 'He has been asking us ever since my father died, and now at last Mother has consented. He is a widower, you know, and mother can keep his house. Of course that is very nice,' she added reflectively; 'for it will be comfortable for him to have his sister. And Nina – well, *she* must be taken care of, whatever happens. And Mother can better afford her what she wants, she need not be any great tax on him. But I – I – oh, Mr Macleod, you don't know what I wouldn't give if I could persuade my mother to let me earn my own living for myself. I could do it somehow – I know I could – if only I might be allowed to try. Doesn't it seem disgraceful to have all this health and strength,' and she stretched out her noble arms slowly, with a gesture that spoke eloquently of the physical and moral forces at her command – 'and do nothing but prey upon one's family; people who are *not* young and strong, and who have no more than enough to feed and clothe themselves? Ah, Mother and Nina are always telling me that I ought to have been a boy – I wish to goodness I had been! No-one wants to stop a boy from working when he has the will and ability to work.'

Mr Macleod had his opinions upon this subject; which were, substantially, that women should keep, and be kept, in their place, and certainly that they should not work for a living while there was anything in the shape of a man to do it for them; but he did not express his opinions just now. He looked at the girl beside him, who had no consciousness of the impropriety in giving him these curious confidences, whose intelligent face was all aglow with a grave enthusiasm for a cause that evidently lay very near her heart, and he felt himself very much in sympathy with her.

'What would you do,' he asked, 'if your mother would let you work?'

'I would do anything that turned up,' she replied promptly. 'Not art work, for, unfortunately, I have no gift that way, but anything else that ordinary men can do. I don't want a distinguished profession,' she explained, with a sudden sweet smile. 'I should be content to scrub floors and clean windows, if that was the only walk of life open to me. I should like to be taken into the bank, and be uncle Peter's clerk, for I am capital at figures – or to have charge of a telegraph office – or to keep a shop – I shouldn't care what, if it was anything I could do well and earn money by. But there it is – Mother sets her face against my doing anything. It's the only thing I have against mother,' the girl sighed, quaintly; 'I *don't* think she sees these things from a broad enough point of view. All she thinks of is that it is unladylike, and that it would somehow disgrace us. Now *my* feeling is, that those people who would look down on a girl because she worked to support herself and help her family, would be too contemptible to take any notice of. I would not care for their opinion, I know. What do you think?' she enquired suddenly, turning her large eyes upon her companion.

Mr Macleod looked a little puzzled, 'Well,' he said, hesitatingly, 'of course, I have always considered that a woman's work should be in her home, which is her natural sphere, and where there is always so much that she can do – '

'Ah,' she interrupted sharply, jumping up from her seat with such vehemence that the cocks and hens dozing in the shadow of her petticoats awoke in a fright and began to cluck and scuffle violently, 'Ah, you are just like all the rest of them! You have one rule for everybody. Women should do this – women should do that. And you don't take into account that there is as much difference between the circumstances of one woman and another as between those of a woman and a man – every bit as much.'

'But Miss Mary, look here – '

'No, I don't want to look; I know everything you are going to say before you begin. You think I am one of those horrid "woman's rights" people that you men are always primed for; and I don't happen to be one them – far from it. I am only a strong useless girl that wants to help her family, because there is no father or son to do it. Mother and Nina can cook and mend the stockings,' she added, laughing a little, but with a sort of entreating earnestness in her face and voice, 'but they cannot earn money, nor do I want them to try. That is where it is, Mr Macleod – they cannot earn money, though they want it so badly, and I can – I could, if I might.'

She had turned round and was standing with her back to the railing and her arms loosely folded. There was a childlike ease and grace in the unconscious attitude which would have enchanted a sculptor; but it struck Mr Macleod, looking at her with a sympathetic stir of emotion in his veins, that she had the makings of a noble woman in her.

While he looked, the most curious change came over her face. The half indignant passion died out of her eyes, which grew dark and soft; there was a sudden droop and relaxation of invisible muscles, transforming her features into an expression of tender wistfulness; her mouth, which had been set in a strong line, parted over her pretty white teeth into a slow, sweet, absent smile. He was going to speak to her, but she put up her hand hastily, and whispered 'Hush!' And then, wondering what had affected her so strangely, he heard the thin, sharp wail of a violin rising into the breezy twilight from the main deck behind him. Listening for a few minutes, he made out, with some difficulty, the air of an old waltz that he had often heard played by barrel-organs in the street.

'That must be the tune the old cow – '

'Oh, hush!' she interrupted, 'Don't speak. I love to hear it.'

But while they listened together – he, untouched by the strains of an instrument that he irreverently designated a fiddle; and she, palpitating visibly under some mysterious spell that they cast upon her – the captain brought the performance to an untimely end.

The captain, by the way, had an uncertain temper and not much ear for music.

Stop that caterwauling, will you?' he bawled out, almost in Mary Hamilton's ear.

'Oh!' she exlaimed passionately, 'Why didn't he let him finish it? Mr Macleod, did you ever hear that waltz played by a military band? Did you ever *dance* to it?'

'I am not sure,' he replied. 'But it is an old thing, and I have waltzed a good deal in my day. I suppose I must have danced to it at some time or other.'

'O, no, I know you havn't [sic],' she said quietly, but still with a sort of repressed excitement about her. 'If you had, you could never have forgotten it.'

CHAPTER IV

Acquaintance

A select little group of saloon passengers sat on deck next morning with an awning over their heads, Mrs Hamilton, looking a year or two older than when she came on board, but otherwise convalescent, stitching at some fine embroidery intended for Nina's adornment. Mrs Lepel, very gay and elegant in mustlins [sic] and ribbons, showing her white and jewelled fingers to great advantage as she played with a tatting shuttle and a ball of thread; Nina lying back in her chair languidly, saying nothing, but looking pale, pensive and pretty. Mr Macleod in the middle of them, sitting on the skylight with his legs dangling and his arms upon his knees. They were making each other's acquaintance rapidly.

'Dear Wattlebank! It is so nice to know that it is not in the hands of total strangers,' Mrs Hamilton was saying. I am sure Mr Lepel would keep it up nicely. And you who were accustomed to such a lovely garden at Bungil, you will have taken care of my fernery, and the roses and the creepers on the verandah? I have often wondered how my dear Wistaria was getting on. It used to curtain the west gable completely.' And she proceeded to make many inquiries as to what rooms in the west gable (and then what all the other rooms) were used for; whether the drawing room chimney smoked still; whether the new dairy had been built, that was so badly wanted; and so on.

Mrs Lepel was very communicative. She gave the required information freely, and a full description of the changes and improvements that had taken place of late years at Wattlebank. 'But you must come and see for yourself,' she concluded pleasantly. 'I suppose you will be visiting the old neighborhood when you get back?'

'I don't think so,' said Mrs Hamilton. 'My brother, Mr Butler, who lives at Abercorn, has persuaded us to pay him a visit before we settle ourselves. It will be very dreary, I am afraid, after Eastwold – a bush township after the society of an English cathedral city – but we must try to put up with it for a little while.'

'Well, we must do what we can to make it cheerful for you,' said Mrs Lepel. 'Abercorn is not a bad little place, as townships go. And I know Mr Butler; he seems a very nice man.'

'I don't mind roughing it for myself,' proceeded Mrs Hamilton confidentially, 'but I feel for the girls who are at an age to suffer so from that kind of thing. At home they always had the palace and the deanery to run in and out of and all the society of the close, which was so particularly refined and select. And their uncle, the canon – of course his house was like our own. And there was Lord Chester's pretty place close by. Ah, Nina, no more Dunchester balls for you now, my dear!'

'I wonder you left Eastwold,' remarked Mr Macleod in a tone of voice that made his sister look at him suddenly, and furtively knit her brows.

'It was for this dear child's sake,' said Mrs Hamilton, indicating Nina; 'her health would not stand the English winters. Indeed, she ought to have come away long ago, but we had not the heart to leave all our people and banish ourselves to the colony again, until we were really driven to it. I daresay you understand the feeling yourself, Mr Macleod being of an ancient family too.'

'Oh no, I don't,' he responded coolly. 'I am a colonial born and bred, and though I like to take a visit to Europe now and then, I'd rather live in Victoria than anywhere on the face of the Earth.'

'But when you are at home, where generations of your ancestors lived and died – '

'But you see I haven't any ancestors,' he interposed, studiously ignoring the shadow on his sister's face. 'The only ancestor I ever professed to lay claim to was my good old father, who, when I first made his acquaintance, was a shepherd, and afterwards rose to be a bullock driver, and made his fortune carting stores to the diggings.'

'Your name speaks for itself,' said Mrs Hamilton graciously, 'and all the early gentlemen settlers did rough work, of course. My own dear husband thought nothing of it.'

'Oh, if you come to names,' said the aggravating young man, 'there's my coachman – he's a Macleod too. And, for what I know, he's just as much kin to Rorie Mhor as I am. I don't set any store by names.'

'And what about the Bungil family portraits?' suggested Nina, smiling.

'The Bungil family portraits, Miss Hamilton, are apocryphal, I assure you. When the poor old governor got rich – it's a weakness with people who make their money in the colonies, as you may have noticed – he thought he'd set up a pedigree.'

'Donald, I'm ashamed of you,' interrupted Mrs Lepel, angrily. 'How can you speak so of Papa? Don't you suppose he knew more about his family than you?'

'Now, Jenny, you know as well as I do – didn't he go pottering all over Scotland, and whenever he could get hold of a Macleod, male or female, that he could get a fellow to daub a copy of for a five pound note – '

'Don't listen to him, Mrs Hamilton; he's only saying all that to tease me,' said Mrs Lepel, trying to laugh off her vexation.

'I know it,' said Nina, looking at him archly with her coquettish smile. 'And I don't believe a word he says.'

Here Mrs Lepel espied a figure quietly pacing up and down the deck on the other side of the skylight to which their backs had been turned, and she was glad of the opportunity it suggested to change the conversation.

'Here is your daughter, with that charming little baby. Come here, dear,' beckoning to Mary, 'and let us have a look at him.'

They all turned round, Mr Macleod with sudden interest, amused but eager; Nina and her mother with displeased surprise.

'Baby!' exlaimed Mrs Hamilton sharply. 'What baby? Mary, what in the world are you doing with that child?'

Mary came round to where they were sitting, slowly, with her long, light, graceful stride. The baby was in her left arm, lying on her breast, with its little face peeping over her shoulder. She was steadying it with a turn of her powerful wrist and the tips of her long fingers. With the other hand she held a parasol over its head and her own.

'It is our stern-cabin baby, mother. Mrs Brown and Mrs Jenkins are neither of them able to carry it about at present, and they have no nurse.'

'Well, my dear, I don't choose to see you making yourself their nurse. Go and take it back to them immediately.'

The girl looked from one to another with a face full of indignation and grief. Her eyes rested at last upon Mr Macleod, with an expression of appeal he could not resist. 'The poor little beggar looks awfully happy,' he remarked shyly, 'it seems a pity to disturb it, doesn't it?'

'I have already asked you, Mary, not to have anything to do with the stern-cabin passengers,' said Mrs Hamilton, severely.

'But she never can resist a baby, Mr Macleod, no matter whose it is,' broke in Nina, laughing. 'At Eastwold we never met a dirty little wretch in the street that she did not want to take it in her arms and kiss it.'

'Very kind of her, I'm sure,' said Mr Macleod. He did not laugh in response, as he was expected to do; and he began to notice at this moment that Miss Hamilton's forehead was too high and narrow, and to feel satisfied about Miss Mary's mouth, that it was *not* too large for a woman made on such a liberal scale.

'At any rate, this is not a dirty little wretch,' exclaimed the young nurse, letting the baby down from her shoulder and displaying it to the company.

'Isn't he a darling?' appealing to Mrs Lepel, who had no children of her own, but was wildly anxious to have them and who had shown a kindly interest in the youngest of the *Devonshire*'s passengers. 'And, oh, mother, it *does* do him so much good to get out of that stuffy cabin and into the fresh air. He sleeps so well after it.'

'Let her do it if she is so anxious about it – at least until the mother is able to attend to the child herself,' pleaded Mrs Lepel. 'It would be a pity to let the little thing suffer more than we could help – such a mite as it is to come to sea. And when you are tired,' she added, looking at Mary, who fell in love with her there and then, 'bring him to me and I will nurse him for a little.'

'Oh, how good – how kind you are!' the girl responded with a kind of rapturous gratitude, for she saw at once that the intercession of this distinguished personage had spared to the poor

little infant its pleasant airings, and to herself the delightful satisfaction of doing something to help other people. 'I am sure not
to be tired, but I will bring him to you to show how much good
his walks do him. See how bright he looks since I brought him
up this morning! He does love the sunshine so, bless his little heart!'

That night Mrs Lepel and her brother compared notes of the
day's experience, and with respect to the Hamilton family, came
to much the same conclusion.

'I don't approve of that woman,' the young matron declared,
in her light and pleasant voice, as if she were criticising a bonnet.

'She's as vulgar as she can be,' said Mr Macleod forcibly.

'But she is going to live near us, so it is just as well to be civil,
Don. I hate to have enemies. I like even the butcher to come to
his shop door when he hears my ponies in the street and beam
on me as I go by. I couldn't bear to think there was anybody
in Abercorn who disliked me and said nasty things of me.'

'There are plenty who do, you may depend.'

'O, no, there are not. And I don't mean to begin with Mrs
Hamilton. All the same, I think she is an absurd woman, and
of course she will have to be kept in her place. And the eldest
girl – your beauty, Don – she is not what *I* call good style, if you
do.'

'I never said anything about her style. I only said she was pretty,
and rather amiable. So she is. A vast improvement on her mother.'

'Well, I wouldn't say that. I think she gives herself airs. No,
the only one of them worth cultivating – and I mean to cultivate
her – is that big girl, Mary, whom you run down so cruelly.'

'I'm sure I don't run her down. I think she's a splendid creature.'

'Oh, Don! Why you made me think she was – I don't know
what!'

'If I did, I didn't know what I was talking about. She is as much
a lady as her mother is the other thing. I suppose she must have
got some good blood from that old scamp of a father of hers.
He wasn't a bad sort, I believe, when he was sober.'

'And yet you sneer at ancestors! Oh, Don, how could you tell
those tales about poor papa and about the pictures? They will
set it all about Abercorn that we are nobodies; and how annoyed
Fred would be!'

'You didn't suppose I was going to talk brag with Mrs Hamilton, did you? You must send Fred to see her; he'll remove any
stains that I may have cast upon the honor of our house.'

'Fred has a proper respect for his wife's family,' said Mrs Lepel, tossing her pretty head. 'And I won't have my husband sneered at behind his back.'

CHAPTER V

An Old Waltz

In the saloon one evening, a day or two later, Mrs Hamilton and Mr Lorimer sat together, chatting amicably of old days over a game of bézique. Mrs Lepel was at the piano, playing Beethoven's sonatas – very softly, that she might not disturb the whist players; and Mary was leaning over the back of her chair, listening in a dreamy silence – quite oblivious of everything, apparently, but the music and her thoughts. Mr Macleod was restless, wandering upstairs and down. He had smoked enough for a little while, the cuddy was close and hot, and he was in no mood for cards. He did not know what he wanted, but in his heart he was wishing that Mary Hamilton would lift her great, dark eyes to his face as he passed the piano, and give him an opportunity to sit down and talk to her. He did not notice pretty Nina, standing at her mother's shoulder, in a dainty, pale-pink Sèvres-china looking dress, until Nina at last, not liking to be neglected, compelled him.

'Is it a fine night, Mr Macleod?' she inquired gently, when he came within speaking distance.

'A beautiful night, Miss Hamilton,' he replied, rather absently. 'No moon, you know, but clear and starlight, with a nice steady wind. We are going along at a very fair pace. I wish we may keep it up.'

'And it is not cold?'

'O dear no – quite mild.'

'I daresay Mr Macleod would be kind enough to take you up for a breath of fresh air before you go to bed,' here Mrs Hamilton interposed. 'It would help her to sleep, Mr Macleod; she is such a poor sleeper.'

'Certainly – most happy,' said Mr Macleod.

'Only wrap yourself up well, darling.'

Then Mr Macleod found himself slipping past the piano, with a slim hand on his arm, and a golden head, veiled in some soft black lace, almost touching his shoulder, feeling uncomfortably

conscious of Mrs Lepel's observation. Mary did not look up, and
Nina never for a moment dreamed of calling her sister to come
and get a breath of fresh air too.

On deck it was very peaceful and lovely. The great dome of
clear, dark sky overhead was so infinitely vast and solemn, and
so was the mystery of heaving sea below, dimly shining through
the soft obscurity of a most tranquil summer night. The light of
the stars, which seemed to be sprinkled amongst the rigging,
showed the ship, with all her sails set, sweeping swiftly and steadily before the gentle wind – as majestic a spectacle, perhaps, as
the art of man can show. There was no sound to break the sacred
stillness but the hissing gurgle of water at her bows, the creaking
of a spar, the measured footfall of the officer of the watch quietly
marching up and down, and the faint hum and tinkle of the
piano.

'How sweet,' ejaculated Nina, with a little sentimental sigh.

Mr Macleod did not immediately respond. He felt sentimental, too, but he was not in sympathy with his companion, young
and pretty maiden though she was. He marched her round and
round the poop for a few minutes, in a brisk and businesslike
manner, aware that several cigars at the stern railing were turning their red tips, erewhile directed seaward, towards him, and
then he said carelessly, 'Your sister seems very musical.'

'My sister, musical!' echoed Nina, with her thin little laugh.
'Oh dear no, she doesn't understand music at all. Poor dear child,
she has some very excellent qualities, but anything in the shape
of a fine art is altogether beyond her.'

'She told me so,' said Mr Macleod, rather stiffly. 'But I think
she underrates herself. She must have the artistic temperament
in some measure, or she could not sit and listen to Mendelssohn
and Beethoven, as she has been doing for this last hour.'

'She doesn't know what she is listening to, Mr Macleod. I assure
you she hardly knows one tune from another – except that horrid old Faust waltz. And she *is* rather mad about that.'

'And why is she mad about that?' asked Mr Macleod quickly.
He remembered that it was the old Faust waltz that the violinist
of the second class had attempted to play – the waltz that Mary
had told him he could never have danced to, or he would not
have forgotten it.

'Ah,' simpered Nina, with an affected little shake of the head,
'thereby hangs a tale.'

'Oh, indeed, I beg your pardon. Of course I didn't want to pry into Miss Mary's affairs.'

'There is no secrecy about it. Everybody in Eastwold knew, I suppose. It is just the old story of so many girls' waltzes, Mr Macleod.'

'A special partner, I suppose?'

'Yes, a special partner. It was almost her first ball, poor child, and he did pay her a great deal of attention certainly.'

'She danced with him to that waltz?'

'Yes, as if she could never stop. It was the last dance before we left. She waltzes very well, though you would not think it; those big clumsy people do sometimes.'

'Who was he?'

'A Captain Armstrong. He was a friend of Lord Chester's, and was staying at Dunchester, and this was one of the Dunchester balls. They said he had been invalided from India, but he didn't look very ill. He was a tall man, and rather good-looking – fair, but bronzed, with a very straight nose and his hair parted in the middle. He had a large light moustache, and wore an eyeglass. All the Eastwold people raved about him. I didn't think him anything out of the way, but he had that haw-haw air, you know, as if he didn't think we were good enough to speak to, which led people to imagine he was a person of great importance. His taking up Mary was very funny – nobody could understand it, but I believe it was just to spite the pretty girls, who expected attentions. He could see that Mary never expected anything – anybody can see that she is not the kind of girl to attract men; and by taking up with her he saved himself all trouble. He didn't think we were worth taking trouble about, I suppose,' Nina added, rather tartly.

'Perhaps he admired your sister,' suggested Mr Macleod.

'That is not very likely, though, to be sure, there is no accounting for tastes. Oh, no, he was too much a man of society for that. Poor Mary, dear, good girl though she is, is such a very rough diamond, and she would be a mere child from his point of view. It was just as a child that he treated her. However, she didn't understand it, somehow, and let him turn her head.'

'Do you think Miss Mary could be mistaken for a child? It seems to me that she is particularly womanly.'

'Ah, that is only because she is so big. Is she not an enormous creature? She is stones and stones heavier than I am, though she is two years younger. How much do you think I weigh, Mr Macleod?'

This question indicated a new departure in the conversation, which for a while addressed itself almost exclusively to Nina's own history and affairs. She told her companion how much, or rather how little, she weighed – told him various interesting particulars of her Eastwold life, and of the Canon, her uncle, and of Lord Chester, her friend (who was evidently suffering many pangs of regret for her departure from the neighborhood of Dunchester); and then asked him questions about Bungil, about Wattlebank, and about Abercorn, and hazarded *naive* conjectures as to what sort of existence she would be able to make of it at the Bank of Australasia. Mr Macleod listened with an appearance of interest, and made intelligent comments and replies – wondering at intervals what time it was, and when he would be expected to resign his young charge to her mother. And then there was suddenly the sound of a fresh, sweet voice, coming up the stairs, and Mary and Mrs Lepel appeared, arm in arm.

'Where are you, Nina?' called Mary; 'mother says you are not to stay up any longer, unless you put on warmer things.'

'Stuff,' responded Nina, pettishly. 'I am as warm as possible.'

But the *tête-à-tête* was interrupted, and the pair were divided for the present. Nina, very anxious to be on good terms with Mrs Lepel, who was showing Captain Armstrong's singular inclination to make a favorite of her sister, joined that lady for the few minutes that they all remained on deck; and Mr Macleod somehow found himself giving a 'breath of fresh air' to Mary. He did not march *her* round and round the poop; he enticed her forward until they reached the rail that divided them off from the main deck, and there he paused until she sat down, and then sat down at the top of a companion ladder at her feet. He did not say much to her, nor she to him. She leaned her head in the palm of her hand, with her elbow on the railing, in the Cleopatra attitude, and she looked down upon the main deck, roofed in with spars and inverted boats, with thoughtful eyes that did not seem to see anything, the light from a lantern that hung below them shining softly up into her face. He was content to sit and watch her from under the brim of his slouch hat – to sit still at her feet until she chose to speak to him. The starlight above and the lamplight below showed him all her noble outlines against the dusk behind her; they were more lovely in his eyes every time he looked at them. And he lost all consciousness of the largeness of her mouth and the masculine firmness of her jaws, of the irregularity of her nose, and the obviousness of her cheekbones, as he studied her face now in the shadowy light, and in its dreamy and tender and thoughtful repose. It was a face whose beauty lay deep, but the beauty was there, and plenty of it; and to-night, in the illumination of Captain Armstrong's story, he saw it more distinctly than he had ever done before.

CHAPTER VI

A Ballroom Idyll

'It was about six months ago, while there was a great party staying at Dunchester for Christmas. And he was amongst the guests.'

Mary Hamilton was sitting on deck one moonlight night – when the *Devonshire* lay becalmed in the tropics – with her head on Mrs Lepel's knee. Mrs Lepel had carried out her intention of 'cultivating' the young girl, who was, to her mind, much the nicest of all her female fellow passengers; and Mary had responded with an ardent, headlong devotion that was very gratifying to both of them. Tonight, in the stillness and the moonlight, they had fallen into confidential talk; and Mary was giving her friend, who had already had some hints of it, the history in outline of the Armstrong romance.

'It was about six months ago,' she said, softly. 'I went to Cathedral service one afternoon by myself. Service began every day at four o'clock, you know, and already the daylight was gone; the east end of the cathedral was lit up, and all the nave and aisles were dark. I went in at the west door, and there was the Dunchester party, about a dozen of them, straggling about, with some of the Palace people with them. Lord Chester had brought them in to Eastwold to show them the cathedral. That was the firt time I saw – him. I noticed him, because he was very tall, and carried himself differently from the other men: it was too dark to see his face. Afterwards they stayed to service, and he sat opposite to me in the chancel. Then I saw him distinctly.'

'And was he very handsome?' inquired Mrs Lepel in a sympathetic voice, stroking the head on her knee.

'Very – very. He had the sort of look that you would think a king should have. He towered up in his stall in such a proud, serene way, with his chin lifted a little, you know. There was a light just at his shoulder, and it shone on his moustache, and the little rings of hair on his forehead. He had a wide beautiful forehead, and his moustache had long, drooping ends, the color of – Oh, the color that your hair is sometimes, a golden, auburn color. I couldn't help looking at him, and thinking how different he was from all the Eastwold young men.'

'And he looked at you, I suppose?'

'Oh! no he didn't. I don't think he knew I was there. It never occurred to me then that he would ever take any notice of me. Besides, the stalls were full of the grand Dunchester ladies, who had come with him.'

'Well?' said Mrs Lepel persuasively; for here Mary came to a long pause.

'Well,' waking up from her reverie, 'after church they went away to the bishop's palace. I think they dined there. And I walked home. And there I found Nina full of her preparations for the ball. She was talking to Miss Morris, a young lady we knew at Eastwold – our doctor's daughter – who was going too. And Miss Morris told us about Captain Armstrong – that he had come from India and had been in the Abyssinian war, and that he was very charming and a great favorite with everybody, and that all the ladies of Eastwold were looking forward to dancing with him. How well I remember it. How full of him they were – a great deal more so than I was.'

'And then came the ball?'

'Yes, and then came the ball – two nights afterwards. It was one of those big things that Lord Chester gave every year or two, when he invited everybody in the neighborhood – all his tenants and all the Eastwold people – "tag, rag and bobtail," Uncle Joseph used to say; and somebody told him about us, and we had cards for it. It was the only time we ever went to Dunchester; they never asked us to their other parties of course, and we were not on regular visiting terms with them,' explained Mary, naively.

Mrs Lepel smiled, and patted the girl's innocent brown head. She was intensely amused and interested. 'Go on, love,' she muttered. 'Tell me all about that ball.'

'It was a bitter cold, frosty night,' said Mary, 'and very dark. We and the Morrises clubbed together for a fly, and the Morrises called for us at eight o'clock, for it was rather a long way to go. Mostly I stayed at home to keep house when mother and

Nina went out; it was too expensive getting evening dresses for all of us. But mother thought this was a special occasion, and that it would be a great treat for me; so she bought me a new white muslin frock, and I made myself some trimmings of ivy leaves – those nice, shiny ivy leaves, you know, with the light veins in them.'

'Yes! I know. And what did Nina wear?'

'Oh, Nina looked lovely. She had her dress made by the best dressmaker in Eastwold; it was the finest, faintest-blue tarlatan, with a wide sash to match, and pale-pink roses about it; and she had mother's pearl cross and earrings. She looked beautiful.'

'Well?'

'So we wrapped ourselves up and set off. And when we reached Dunchester – oh, how splendid it all was! I never saw anything like it. The entrance hall was as big as all our house put together, and full of flowers and statues and footmen, and a great carved staircase, with rows of lamps up both sides of it. I felt so shy and nervous about going in. But Dr Morris had often been there, and he led the way; and we went, we ladies, into a charming dressing-room, where there was a big delicious fire, and arm chairs, and hot tea and coffee; and we got a good warm, and a lady's maid settled up our skirts, while he talked to some of his friends in the hall. Then we went into the ballroom – Dr and Mrs Morris and mother first, then Miss Morris and Nina, and then me.'

'"Mary Beaton and Mary Seaton, and Mary Carmichael and me,"' murmured Mrs Lepel.

'I don't think I ever was really conscious until then how enormously big I was,' the girl went on. 'I towered over Miss Morris and Nina, and, walking all by myself, I felt so conspicuous, and so hot and so awkward, my face was the color of a peony, I do believe.'

'Child, you would look beautiful with that color in your face.'

'Oh, Mrs Lepel!'

'And I hope you had your neck and arms uncovered?'

'No, I hadn't. Nina had; but I wore my dress high to my throat, and my sleeves nearly to my wrists.'

'Ah, well, I know you must have looked very nice. And I don't wonder at Captain Armstrong. Did he see you when you went in?'

'Not just at first. There was a great crowd about the doorway. Lady Chester shook hands with us, and Lord Chester gave mother his arm, and found her a seat. Nina got a partner directly; some of the Eastwold men had asked her beforehand. And I caught sight of Mrs Clarke, our curate's wife, who sat in a quiet corner, and I sat down with her, while mother walked about the room a little and talked to people. I did not expect to dance much, for I hardly ever went out, you know, and I knew so very few people there; but I liked to sit and watch the others dancing – it was very pleasant and amusing, and I had Mrs Clarke to talk to. However, presently I began to long to be dancing too. There was a splendid band playing – that kind of clanging, swelling music, beating time with such beautiful precision, that makes you throb and tingle all over; and I could hardly bear it – I felt as if it was impossible for me to sit still. They were having a waltz, and I watched them – it seemed so delicious. I had never waltzed myself – not to speak of, you know – except with Nina at home, to keep her in practice; but I saw the step in a moment, and I felt that, if only someone would give me a chance, I could do it so well. And, amongst the couples that went flying and swimming past us, I saw Captain Armstrong and Lady Craven – Lady Craven was Lord Chester's sister – and I said to myself that, of all men in the room, I would like best to dance with him. None of them danced – none of them looked and moved – like him. It was the very last thing I ever expected, though.'

'Well?'

'Well, when the waltz was over, to my surprise, Mr Greville came up and asked me if I was engaged for the next Lancers. He was the archdeacon's son, quite a young man, with spectacles, an undergraduate at Cambridge. We used to call him Verdant Green at Eastwold. He was a shocking dancer, but I didn't care for that. I was delighted to get him, and to be moving about with the rest; and for Lancers it did not matter. So we stood up, when our time came. I had left off feeling shy – I was wild to dance – I was very happy. And there, in our set, *vis-à-vis* with me, was Captain Armstrong; and when I looked at him he was looking very hard at me – not rudely, not boldly, but as if he liked to look at me, somehow. I had been feeling that I was very plain and commonplace beside the other girls, and that my dress was nothing to theirs; and yet something in the way he looked across at me made me feel that I was all right – the sort of feeling you know you have when your clothes suit you. He seemed to think I looked nice. I suppose gentlemen don't consider what things cost, as ladies do.'

'Gentlemen have much the best taste, my dear, and white muslin and ivy leaves would suit you charmingly.'

'He was the first man who had ever looked at me with any particular interest,' proceeded Mary softly, 'and, being the man he was, I could not help feeling it. It seemed to warm me all over in the strangest way. I suppose it was very silly, but I couldn't help it. I had an instinct that we were attracted to each other, ridiculous as it seemed that he should think of such a girl as I, and that we both knew it. Whenever I passed him in the dance I seemed to know he felt it and liked it as well as I; and when we came to the grand chain at last – '

'Oh, Mary, he didn't squeeze your hand, I *hope*?'

Mary was silent for a few seconds, and made her confession in a tremulous voice. 'He – he held it a little, and looked into my face – '

'My dear, that was very improper. I'm afraid he was just one of those horrid, handsome male flirts who make a regular business of breaking silly girls' hearts. You are not up to their ways; I am. I know them well.'

'I don't think so,' said Mary, with quiet confidence.

'And before he had been introduced to you. It was not respectful. You shouldn't ever make yourself so cheap to a man, love, as to let him take those liberties.'

'Why not?' demanded Mary, with a sudden flash of her forcible earnestness. 'People cannot make themselves too cheap to those they love. I would not have allowed anybody else to do it.'

'But you didn't *love* him, at that early stage?'

'Yes, I did. Or, if I did not, I knew I was going to.'

'Well,' said Mrs Lepel, with a smile and a sigh, 'when the Lancers were over, what happened then?'

'Then I found mother and Nina, and Mr Greville left me with them. And, ten minutes afterwards, I saw Lord Chester coming up to us with Captain Armstrong. Nina leaned forward, looking very pleased; she thought, of course, they were coming to her. But, when Lord Chester had introduced him and left him, Captain Armstrong stooped over me and asked me for the first waltz I could spare. I knew that was what he wanted, though at the same time I could hardly believe in it. Like a stupid, I gave him my card. Of course he saw how empty it was; and he wrote his initials in three places – all for waltzes – before he gave it back to me. I had a great scolding from Nina afterwards for letting him have my card; but I am glad I did – oh, I am so glad I did! It is my only visible memento of him, and I have it to keep now that he is gone. "R.R.A.", those were his initials; I have no idea what the two R's stand for – I never heard his Christian name.'

'And he took his three waltzes, by force of arms, did he?'

'Yes,' said Mary, simply. 'The first one we hardly danced at all. I was so confused and so trembling; I made a bad beginning. We went half way round the room and I could not catch his step exactly. I felt that he was disappointed and thought I couldn't dance, and that made me worse. I blundered horribly. And then he slackened and stopped, and asked me if I would mind sitting out the rest of it with him, because his head ached. He had had a fall from his horse in India which had hurt his head – it was for that he had been invalided home; and he said the doctors had ordered him not to dance much. So we went away to a refreshment lobby and had some cup, and then he took me to a long gallery, where there was hardly anyone but ourselves, and we sat down on a sofa in a recess, and talked.'

'And what did you talk about?'

'Different things. He told me some particulars about his accident. A vicious horse threw him when he was out hunting, and far away from his companions. And they thought he had gone back to the station, and did not find him for hours afterwards, and he had been lying in the sun, insensible all the time. It was a "narrow squeak", he said; but it had gained him his furlough, so he didn't care. And then he looked at my ivy leaves, and asked me where they grew; he said he had never seen any quite like them before. And he asked me a little about myself; and I was so anxious that he shouldn't make any mistake about me – that I shouldn't seem to be sailing under false colors – that I told him who we were, and where we lived, and that we were not regular Dunchester visitors. I told him about Australia too, and that we were thinking of going back there soon. And he said he had heard of Melbourne from some brother officers, who had spent leave there; and that they had told him it was a very jolly place. And he said perhaps he should turn up there himself some day, and would meet me in the street when I least expected it. I seemed to know him quite well when we had had that talk. It was a very pleasant talk.'

'So it seems. And he came for his next waltz?'

'Oh, yes. I asked him to come. I said to him frankly, "I know you think I can't dance, Captain Armstrong; but I am sure I can. You have not given me a fair trial. You will come for No. 11, won't you?"'

'And what did he say?'

'He looked at me steadily for a second or two, and then he said, in a very quiet voice, "Rather!"'

'Oh! And how did you get on that time?'

'We were unfortunate that time, too, though in a different way. For it came just about supper time. We had two or three turns, and had fallen into our step, and found out that we could go beautifully together, when Lord Chester led off some old lady to the supper-room, and the more important of the guests followed them, and he said we might as well go too.'

'He took you in to supper then?'

'Yes; and we had a nice place, and he was very attentive and amusing. I saw lots of people looking at him, but he didn't take any notice of anybody – only me. He gave me all kinds of nice things, but I couldn't eat, I was too excited and happy – though generally I have appetite enough; and he talked to me about India and about the Abyssinian campaign. And he said he wished we would go out to Australia by the mail he was going to take, and that we would stop at Galle and come on to Bombay with him for a month or two, and see something of India. Ah, shouldn't I have liked that! But of course I told him we could not afford to come by the mail at all – still less to take such a trip as that.'

'And after supper what did you do? Did you have your third waltz, then?'

'There was one quadrille first; then we had it. I was sitting in the conservatory, between the ballroom and the drawingrooms, with Dr Morris, who had danced the quadrille with me, when I heard the band begin that lovely air – that lovely Faust waltz that I shall never forget – never, so long as I live! I was so afraid he would not know where I was that I asked Dr Morris to take me into the ballroom; and in the doorway I met him, coming to look for me. "This is ours," he said, and he held out both his hands and in a moment we were dancing it together, dancing perfectly – we were both so tall, and this time I had no trouble to catch his step – we seemed to be in the air, and not on the common ground. O me, how sweet it was!'

'It didn't make his head ache this time?'

'No; I asked him that as we were going round and round. He only said he didn't want to stop until I did – that he could go on all night. And so we did – almost. We paused for a minute, now and then, but only for a minute – he did not let me go; and we danced until everyone else had left off, and we were dancing alone, with a great ring of people standing round and looking at us. Then all at once the music ceased – it came on me like a shock. We stopped, and I slipped out of his arms. I saw the people staring. The room seemed to be going round with me. Then Captain Armstrong said, "Come out and get cool; you have made yourself giddy." And we went out of the ballroom, and through the conservatory, and along a passage, and down some steps – he seemed to know all the nooks and corners of the house – until we came to a little lobby, with a great window in it, and the moon was shining through some stained glass at the top of the window. There was a deep window seat, and we sat down there.

'Wasn't the lobby lit up, like the other places?'

'No.'

'Were there no other people about?'

'No.'

'Well, what did you do there?'

Mary Hamilton kept silence for a few minutes.

'Nothing,' she said presently.

'He didn't make love to you?'

'No, Mrs Lepel.'

'He didn't kiss you?'

'No.'

'We sat there for about five minutes, until I got over my giddiness; then I knew I ought to go back – oh, I don't like to talk about it! He took my hand to lead me through the dark places; and he said he should never hear the Faust waltz again without thinking of me. That was all.

'Was that really all?'

'Yes.' She spoke with a little hesitation, and paused. Then she went on hurriedly: – 'Mrs Lepel, I will tell you a secret. He *would* have kissed me if I had let him. I don't mean that he asked or offered to kiss me. I only *felt* that he wanted to do it. It frightened me a little; I hurried back to the ballroom, not to give him any opportunities to say or do anything of that sort. And he did not – of course he did not. I could not have permitted it. But – but,' the girl broke out, lifting her head with sudden passion in her dark eyes, 'but now that he has gone to India, and I am here, and the chances are that I shall never see him again, I wish – I can't help wishing – that I had let him kiss me that once! It would not have done anybody any harm, and oh, what a memory it would have been!'

'Dear child, you were quite right not to allow it,' said the young matron, gravely. 'It would have done you harm.'

'Why, why?' persisted Mary. 'I cannot see it. He was going away. He was not going to marry me. I did not dream of his marrying me. It would not have compromised him, and how could it have hurt me, when I already cared for him enough to wish that I *might* let him do it?'

'He would have thought you a fast, immodest girl, dear.'

'I should have liked him to think me only exactly what I was,' said this strange young woman quietly. 'It was quite as bad to wish that he might kiss me as let him do it.'

'Oh, no, Mary! When you are older you will know better than that.'

'I would never pretend, Mrs Lepel, and I think if I had let him kiss me when he – when we both – wanted, that he would have understood. At any rate, I don't think I should have been ashamed of it now. He singled me out from a host of grand and rich and beautiful ladies – he made me very happy. Perhaps – perhaps it would have been spoiled; if it had gone on. I didn't ask for it to go on. I did not want any vulgar love making; I did not want to catch him. But for once in my life,' clasping her hands round her knees, and lifting her face to the mellow moonlight – 'for once in my life I have known what it is to be perfectly happy, and as long as I live I shall be thankful to him for giving me that experience.'

'Well!' exclaimed Mrs Lepel, in a tone of shocked dismay, 'I never heard of anything so extraordinary as that a girl like you should surrender herself at a moment's notice to that extent, and, O, dear me, as if men were not bad enough already!'

'Men!' echoed Mary, quickly and sharply, with a flush in her excited face, 'We are only talking of one man, Mrs Lepel. Don't suppose I am likely to let anyone do and be to me again what he was. I am *not* a fast girl, nor immodest, though you may think it.'

'Dear child, I don't think it. But I think you are too innocent for anything. You will be always getting into trouble – you will always be in danger.'

'In danger! I don't understand you,' the girl responded haughtily.

This suggestion, which to Mrs Lepel seemed quite as inoffensive as several others that had been made, evidently displeased her deeply.

'I mean that you are so honest yourself and so terribly unsuspicious, that you will never see through the wiles of those dreadful creatures.'

'Men, do you mean? I shall have nothing to do with their wiles, because I shall have nothing to do with them. I shall be quite safe,' said Mary, cooling down.

'And you are going to dedicate yourself to Captain Armstrong's memory?' Mrs Lepel asked, after she had succeeded, at considerable trouble, in effacing the unpleasant impression she was so surprised to have made. 'Are you going to live a life of celibacy for his sake?'

The girl was silent for a while. Then she lifted a wistful face, wet with tears, and laid her large arms around her friend's slim waist.

'Perhaps,' she whispered, 'perhaps, some day – who can tell what will happen? and I have all my life before me – some day I may see him again.'

'Have you never seen him since that night?'

'No.'

'And what you have been telling me – was there nothing more? was that all?'

'Yes; that was all.'

'And you really look for him to come back to you?'

'No; I don't look for anything. But he said – he said he might turn up in Melbourne some day, and meet me in the street when I least expected it.'

CHAPTER VII

Mr Macleod and I

When Mary Hamilton had finished her story she begged that Mrs Lepel would consider herself entrusted with a sacred secret, not to be breathed to anybody. Mrs Lepel cheerfully assured her young friend that she would not dream of violating the confidence that had been reposed in her – as few of us hesitate to do under similar circumstances, and she did not tell her brother all about it (with strict injunctions to him to let it go no further) for nearly three weeks.

During these three weeks, though the voyage from a social and domestic point of view, was tedious and uneventful to a degree seldom experienced in these days, much happened to affect the welfare and destiny of the little group of passengers with whom we are concerned. Mrs Hamilton sedulously cultivated a renewal of intimacy with her old friend and admirer, Mr Lorimer, who, though shunned a good deal by the saloon company as a par- simonious old bore, with habits (particularly at table) that were little short of disgusting, and violently disliked by Mary, whose constitutional honesty forbade her to dissemble her dislike, even to please her mother, had still a perfunctory respect accorded to him, by virtue of his commercial position. Mrs Hamilton did not feel that she imperilled her gentility by consorting with the 'old Jew pedlar,' as her youngest daughter persisted in styling him, whose manners would have disgraced a respectable servants' hall; though she would not have 'anything to do with' the meek mother and grandmother of the stern cabin, coming back with their baby to the home of a well-to-do Bourke-street storekeeper, for the world. She treated the old man with a queenly and gracious and tender condescension that was massively entertaining to Mrs Lepel; and the ancient bachelor gave himself all the airs of an old beau, toddling after her upstairs and down, paying her elaborate compliments in his penetrating falsetto voice, and gener- ally devoting himself to her service in a public and impressive manner.

'I do believe she will marry him,' whispered Mrs Lepel on one occasion, stuffing her handkerchief into her mouth. She was watching the pair as they perambulated the deck in front of her; the comely widow who marched along with a firm tread, had accepted the arm of her feeble and shambling cavalier, whose head was about at a level with her shoulder, and the effect was certainly comical. 'I do believe she means to marry him, Don. Otherwise she would never make herself look so ridiculous.'

'She is quite capable of doing it, I imagine, if he will let her,' responded Mr Macleod, disgustedly. 'But I don't think he will, Jenny. He'll keep all his money in his own dirty old hands as long as he has life in him.'

'He would have married her once, you know.'

'Yes, he was not a crystallised miser then.'

'But he has always admired her evidently. And he is getting into his second childhood now,' concluded the young matron rashly. 'I don't believe in any woman not being able to wind an old man round her finger, if she likes.'

'Well, we shall see.'

And in the course of time they did see.

Nina behaved herself to her potential stepfather with the sweetest decorum and amiability; though she, too, called him an old Jew pedlar continually behind his back. Nina, however, had her own affairs to attend to. In the little handful of passengers occupying the saloon, there were far more men than women, and these – supplemented by the ship's officers – tacitly elected her the belle and queen of the party. She flirted with them all, after her subtle and gentle manner, and lightened the tedium of the voyage considerably by means of this occupation. But, partly from the inevitable perversity of human nature – nowhere so flagrantly evident as in these matters – and partly from prudential motives she set her affections upon, and laid her matrimonial snares for, the only one amongst them who took not a particle of interest in her. Mr Macleod, as we know, had had a superficial admiration for her personal charms, but even this had evaporated after a few days acquaintance; and now, though she expended all her resources of fascination upon him, she was chilled, through a very thick cloak of vanity, by an unmistakable sense of failure. And she was not conquered by her failure, but rather stimulated to long and strive the more for the thing that she desired. Oh, to be mistress of Bungil, to be sister-in-law at Wattlebank, to be 'settled' so comfortably, so luxuriously, so safely, with no more need for shifts and pinchings! That was the great prospect that tantalised and fascinated her. But, besides this, she hungered, with such hunger as her shallow and selfish little heart was capable of, for the respect and regard, and the personal passion of this fine, strong, honest, manly gentleman, whom – as anyone could see – a woman might trust in, rest on and look up to with perfect security, in every vicissitude of life. So she flattered him and courted him, patiently, in all sorts of wily ways, keeping her faith in the potency of her own attractions, and her hope in the chances that the coming day might bring forth, in spite of all discouragement – not as yet knowing that her sister was of sufficient importance to be reckoned an obstacle in her way.

And Mr Macleod, ever the least conceited of men, and now himself absorbed in an independent interest, knew nothing of all this. He did not see that the belle of the ship was 'setting her cap' at him (though a few others did, including of course Mrs Lepel) and he took no more notice of her than the exigencies of common politeness demanded. The greater part of his time and thoughts was taken up in watching Mary Hamilton, which he did from morning till night, and sometimes, between night and morning, he was watching too – for the sound of her voice, singing the baby to sleep.

She would have been a pleasant study to anybody interested in the human subject, let alone a man who was deliberately and consciously falling in love with her. The struggle between her insatiable inclination to be always doing something and helping some one, and the duty imposed on her by her mother's wishes and prejudices, was an apparently endless one; and in every fresh phase of it, it seemed to Mr Macleod, to present her character in a more admirable and touching aspect. The baby difficulty fell into the background after a few days. Young Mrs Brown became tolerably well and strong, and struck up friendly relations with a little clique of female passengers, who did not belong to the Lepel and Hamilton set; and these ladies were anxious to take their share of the baby, which chanced to be the only child in the saloon. Mary snatched it when she could, prompted by Mrs Lepel's participation in the proceeding; but it was no longer her special charge except at night, when, as a matter of course, she did whatever was required for it, that those who were less strong than she might be undisturbed.

Having lost this special mission, however, she was not long in finding another.

One hot afternoon, when the saloon passengers were making themselves comfortable under the awning in their lounge chairs, she was sitting on the bench overlooking the main-deck, watching some second-class children with wistful eyes, as if longing to go down and play with them. Mr Macleod, sauntering up and down the poop, which he preferred to sitting still, amused himself, as usual, with the contemplation of her beautiful shape and pose, which were always suggestive of the classic ideal so long as her face was out of sight – sweet, honest, womanly face, that wanted no Greek lines to make it more charming than it was to him. Presently she heard his step approaching her, and, without raising her head, called him – a thing she had never done before – 'Mr Macleod, come here a moment.' Of course he came, with the utmost alacrity, and she directed his attention with a grave little nod, to a distant corner of the main deck. 'Do you see that woman there, sitting in a shawl, and leaning her head against the bulwark?' she inquired. 'I have been watching her for some time, and she seems so dreadfully ill. She has been trying to sew but she cannot get on with it, and every now and then she coughs such a terrible cough.'

Mr Macleod leaned his arms on the rail, and looked at the person indicated. She was a poorly-dressed woman, with a patient and rather refined face, who appeared to be in the last stages of consumption. 'The doctor said he had only one real invalid on board – a woman in the second class – that must be she,' he said. 'Poor soul; she looks very bad, doesn't she?'

'She is the wife of that long, thin man, who appears so delicate too,' proceeded Mary; 'and I have found out that it is he who plays the violin. And these little ones are theirs,' pointing to a couple of happy children tumbling about just below them. 'They seem to be very poor, and I'm afraid she has not much comfort down there. Oh, dear, how I wish I might go down and speak to her! She looks so lonely, sitting there, doesn't she? And how hard those horrid planks must be to her poor tired back. I would give anything if I had one of the nice chairs that these healthy, lazy people are sprawling about in, to carry down to her. But I haven't a chair of my own, and if I had mother wouldn't let me lend it.'

'She shall have mine,' said Mr Macleod. 'I'll send my chair down to her,' and he turned round as if to go and fetch it.

'Oh!' exclaimed Mary, flushing brightly, 'how good you are! How kind you are! But, Mr Macleod' – laying her hand for a moment on his arm – 'Won't you just go down and speak to her first! You are a man; you *may* go into the second class. Say that the doctor told you about her, and that you came to ask her if she feels better, and mention the chair casually – you know? And if there is anything I *could* do for her – oh, do find out, if you can, whether there is anything I can do for her that I might be allowed to do; will you?'

'All right,' responded Mr Macleod. He was glad, as he always was, of an opportunity to serve a woman in need, but he was profoundly grateful for the chance that enabled him to serve Mary

Hamilton at the same time.

She watched him descend the ladder, and thread his way round to the spot where the woman was sitting, with eager expectation in her eyes. He knew how she was watching him; he seemed to feel her eyes at the back of his head. And he acquitted himself with signal credit. The little ceremonious air of respect with which he approached the humble invalid, and the attitude in which he stood to talk to her, indicated to Mary's quick perception that her new friend was a born gentleman; and for the first time she began to be conscious of a distinct partiality for him. 'I wonder which of the other passengers would have done it?' she asked herself, and then was laid the foundation of a special trust in him, that became a lifelong habit.

After speaking to the woman, who had risen to receive him, for a few minutes, Mr Macleod introduced himself to the husband. They were all standing together, when simultaneously they turned and looked up at the girl watching them from the poop above. The woman smiled shyly, with a faint flush in her thin white cheeks; the husband took off his hat with an elaborate obeisance. Mr Macleod's proceedings indicated that he was giving his young friend the credit of having originated the little enterprise in which he was engaged. Mary was deeply touched. She rose to her feet, flushed and embarrassed, and then, with a headlong impulse, she jumped down the ladder, ran across the main deck and joined the group.

'Are you feeling better?' she inquired eagerly, holding the hand of the sick woman firmly in both her own, with an infinite pity and friendliness in her sweet, hurried accent. 'I am so sorry to see you looking so ill. And we – Mr Macleod and I – are troubled to think you are sitting uncomfortably, when you ought to be resting all you can; and Mr Macleod wants you to have his chair. You will, won't you? Oh, please do; he doesn't want it; men don't want chairs; and it would make him so happy to see you using it. Would it not, Mr Macleod?'

Mr Macleod had sent a servant into his cabin for the chair; and as Mary spoke, it was brought – one of Silver's lightest and easiest deck lounges; and he himself put the invalid into it with a peremptory air that forbade protest – not that any protest was meditated.

'I am indeed most grateful to you, sir,' murmured the musician, humbly.

'I can never thank you, sir – nor you, Miss,' added the sick wife, whimpering.

'Nonsense, nonsense,' interrupted Mr Macleod. 'As the young lady says, men don't want chairs. It was mostly in my cabin, always lying in the way, for me to tumble over. I'm glad to get rid of it.'

'And we shall hope to see you sitting in it every day,' said Mary. 'And Mr Macleod will come and see you sometimes – won't you, Mr Macleod? And you will send me a message by him if there is anything I can do for you? I should be so glad to come myself, and sit with you, and read to you, and help you with the children – but I mustn't. Mother doesn't like me to leave her.'

'Then, my dear, pray go back,' urged the invalid, casting a timid, frightened glance towards the little circle of fine ladies above her. 'I thank you for all your kindness, but don't vex your mamma on my account. Pray go back.'

So Mary went back, refreshed in spirit, but troubled and saddened in her sympathetic heart. She was afraid to reappear on the poop directly from the main deck, and went into the saloon by one of the doors that stood wide just now to let the warm air blow through, stopping on her way to kiss the second-class children all round, who were much astonished by the proceeding. Her coadjutor followed her in, after a prudent interval; he was immensely satisfied with the situation. 'Mr Macleod and I' – they were associated together in an undertaking that was certain to develop intimacy, and he found the prospect very charming. 'Mr Macleod and I' – how naturally the phrase had occurred to her, and how persistently it haunted him!

CHAPTER VIII

A Surprise

The invalid of the second class did not want the chair for long. About a week after Mary Hamilton and Donald Macleod had made her acquaintance – during which time they paid her a great many surreptitious attentions – she disappeared from public view; and the doctor, being interrogated, informed them that a fresh phase of her illness had arrived, and that he did not think it likely she would live to see the end of the voyage.

It was a very wild night, with a storm threatening. All day

long the barometer had been falling steadily, and the ship's officers consulting it frequently with anxious eyes. Hatches were battened down and dead-lights screwed up; sailcloth was conspicuous by its absence, and even yards had vanished. The bending masts creaked in their sockets; the stout timbers groaned; the wind whistled and howled through the network of rigging. All around the leaden sea heaved heavily and ominously under a leaden sky. Neither moon nor star was visible. Nina Hamilton, cold and nervous, had gone to bed, accompanied by her devoted mother; and Mary, left to her own devices, was standing on the poop, clinging to a railing, with her petticoats flapping about her, looking, with eyes full of solemn elation, at the wild and noisy night. No other lady had ventured upstairs, and very few men. Of those few Mr Macleod was one, and he it was who brought the doctor's report to her.

'He says Mrs Dubois is very bad to-night. She has been coughing incessantly, but now she has left off. He has been ordering her everything he can think of, but she seems now as if she couldn't eat. At least it is no good her eating; she is more sea-sick than she was when she first came on board. He has been talking to the captain about her, and they are going to move her into a better cabin tomorrow. To-night she is too ill to be moved.'

'Take me down to see her,' demanded Mary, quickly.

'What, so late as this?'

'Never mind, I must go; I couldn't go to bed and not know whether I mightn't do something to make her night easier. Oh, such a night for her, too. Take me down, Mr Macleod; I want to see those women that live there with her, and ask them what can be done. They will help, I am sure, but I should like to talk to them myself.'

'All right,' said Mr Macleod, 'come along then.'

They went down the ladder to the main deck, arm in arm, clinging together in the wind and the darkness; and after stumbling forward a few paces, were joined by the doctor, who was on his way to see his patient. The three had a short consultation, when it was decided that Mary should go down to the second class cabin with the doctor, and that Mr Macleod should not go.

'You stay here and wait for me,' said the girl, to whom no scruples of conventional propriety ever occurred, unless other people suggested them. 'If we all go it will be too many. I will not keep you long.'

So she went away with the doctor, himself a newly-fledged hospital student, with the down of youth upon his chin, and Mr Macleod squatted on the top step of the companion to wait for her return. He had to wait a long time but it did not seem long to him. He had some interesting reflections to occupy his mind while he sat solitary, watching the rapid rising of the wind and the sea.

'Was that young Miss Hamilton who was there just now?' inquired the captain, rather peremptorily, coming up behind him.

'Yes,' her friend reluctantly admitted. 'She wants to do something for Mrs Dubois.'

'She has no business to be gallivanting about the ship with young men at this hour, after her mother is gone to bed.'

'No; but she is all right,' said Mr Macleod. 'I will take care of her.'

'If you are taking care of her, just fetch her back, will you? And tell her I can't permit it.'

'Very well. But she will be back directly.'

The captain marched to and fro a few times, gave some orders, and went down to the cuddy for a game of whist. Three-quarters of an hour later Mr Macleod still dreamed on his windy perch, and there was no sign of Mary Hamilton.

Presently, when it was ten o'clock, and he was thinking he ought to go and fetch her, he saw her coming back to him. Dark as it was, he recognised the outlines of her beautiful figure, and her confident, light stride. The doctor was not with her; she was returning alone. As soon as he made sure of this, he ran down the ladder, and met her at the foot of it; and then his greeting died upon his tongue, for he saw that she was crying bitterly.

'Don't go in yet,' he urged, in a tone of grave concern, as she made an effort to brush past him. 'Come up on deck and sit quietly for a few minutes, until you feel better. Come and tell me all about it. Is she so very ill?'

'Oh, Mr Macleod,' the girl broke out, passionately, when they had reached the railing at the extreme end of the ship, where (as he saw, though she did not) they were safe from observation; 'it is so terrible – I don't know how to bear it! She cannot breathe one easy breath. She cannot do anything for her children, and she looks at them as if her heart were broken! She has been trying to make them lots and lots of clothes, so that they may not be in rags and untidy when she is dead, and there they lie, unfinished – she will never be able to sew for them any more! The doctor says she will perhaps be dead before this time to-morrow night. And she is only thirty! What years more of life and happiness she might have had!'

'Not if it was consumption. There is no cure for that, you know.'

'But she has been too poor to make any fight for her life, as she might have done. Her husband plays the violin in orches-tras, and he can't earn much. She has had to work hard when she was weak; she has not had good food, and the things she wanted; and her great chance, her best chance – getting out to an Australian climate – she could not take till it was too late. And now, and now,' sobbed the excited girl, laying her arms on the railing, and her face upon her arms – 'now she has the agony of dreading what will become of her children, added to all her pain. Oh, what wouldn't I give to be rich! Not for myself, for I am strong, and strong people should work, but that I might help poor women, and poor little children, who cannot. Think of Mr Lorimer, with thousands and thousands that he never wants, and will never use! He would not miss what would make her mind easy. Yet he will keep it all, and those little things will struggle and suffer and lose health and life, perhaps just as she has done. It is enough to make one turn Communist to think of such things.'

Mr Macleod stood by, silently, for a few minutes. It was not the time to discourse of political economy and the rights of men. He did not know what to say. 'I wish to heaven I had not let you go down there,' he remarked at last, gloomily, 'you take things too hard.'

'No,' she said, lifting her head; 'no, don't say that. For it did her good to see me, and I was able to help her. I told her I would do her sewing for her. To-morrow morning I am going to get the little frocks and things, and do as much of them as I possibly can before we land. It was piteous to see her so anxious about the sewing. 'Their father will do his best to house and feed them,' she said, 'but he can't make their clothes, and no one else would take the trouble to keep them tidy and nice, and warm in the cold weather.' I have not asked mother yet, but surely, *surely*, she will not object to my doing it. I can sit in my cabin, if she likes; I need not let anybody know what work it is. And, Mr Macleod, I made another promise. I hope you will not be vexed with me; but I did so long to comfort her all I could.'

'I vexed with you?' he exclaimed, almost angrily. 'What a preposterous idea! If the promise was at all on my behalf, you know well that I will redeem it, "to the half of my kingdom" – or the whole, for that matter – gladly.'

'Would you? – really?' She paused for a few seconds, and he felt that she was looking gravely at him. 'You don't mean so much as that,' she said, simply, 'but you are very, very kind. I do think you are the kindest man I ever knew.'

'Nonsense. Tell me what you promised.'

'I said I would look after her children – that I would see them whenever I could, if Mr Dubois would let me know where they were. And then, *after* I had said so, I recollected how helpless I should be, perhaps. Mr Dubois looks for employment in Mebourne, and I shall be up at Abercorn, so far away. So I said, I thought – I felt almost sure – that you would see them for me, if you were going to town often, and I could not get there. You do not mind? I thought I might say it – you had been so good to her. It is not to do anything for the children; only to tell me how they are. It was such a comfort to her to think there might be some kind of friend to turn to, if they wanted a friend, poor desolate little mites! You do not mind?' she repeated, lightly dropping her fingers for a moment upon his arm.

'Mind!' he replied quickly, in a low, hurried voice, keeping her hand fast. 'You have honored me with – with what I should like to go down on my knees to thank you for. Let me do what you wish for the children, and everything else in the world for you – let us do things together always, as we have been doing these last few days! You know what I mean? I didn't intend to have spoken of it till I was at Bungil, and you settled at your uncle's house, but I can't wait – and you may as well know it first as last –'

At this moment a sudden swell lifted the ship and hurled her over almost on to her beam ends. They had been too much preoccupied to notice the gathering wrath of sea and sky, and were for the first time conscious that the storm had burst upon them. Mr Macleod flung his arms round his companion and pinned her to the railing, to which he clung literally with the grasp of a drowning man. It was all he had time to do. They lost their footing as the planks slid from under them, but held on to each other and to their support until the ship righted herself, which she did with a violent rebound and the crash of a heavy sea over her decks; and then, while they were both drenched, and blinded and gasping, Mr Macleod folded his lady-love to his heart, and in the pitch darkness kissed her streaming face and hair in a way that made everything he said, and had not said, intelligible.

And Mary Hamilton was too utterly stunned and astonished to make any resistance.

CHAPTER IX

Mr Macleod's 'Intentions'

That night, when the storm was at its height – when the ship was, not running, but lying hove-to helplessly, under bare poles, rocking like a cradle in the winds and waves – when seas were breaking in, through smashed skylights and ineffectual hatchways, upon the closely prisoned passengers, huddled together in frightened groups, washing the floors under their feet, and soaking them in their beds and dressing-gowns – in the midst of tumult and confusion and wretchedness – Mrs Dubois died. She was supposed to have gone to sleep, and they tucked her in her poor bunk, and watched beside her that she might not tumble out; but when the gale abated, and a gleam of morning suffused the fetid darkness of the stifling den, they wanted to wake her to give her some medicine, and she was cold and stiff.

Mrs Lepel was lying outside her bed in a quilted wrapper, with an opossum rug over her knees, and a novel of Rhoda Broughton's in her hand, trying to get a little rest, as she expressed it, after the terrible night she had gone through, when her brother tapped at her door, bringing the news that was making a subdued commotion all over the ship.

'Come in, Don,' she called, in her pleasant, gay voice. 'Oh, my dear boy, did you ever know anything like it? My cabin things, of course, were ruined long ago; but Ellen has just been turning out my dresses and the only ones I have to depend on are so stained that I shall never be able to put them on again. I shall not have a rag to land in. The water splashed all over Ellen's bunk, and dripped through even into the tin boxes – how, I can't imagine. And you never came to help us. How did you get on your self? You look very seedy, somehow. What have you been doing all night?'

'I have been up and down. I didn't regularly go to bed. It has been a terrible night. That woman who was so ill, you know – she died between three and four o'clock this morning.'

'You don't say so? Poor thing! Why, I thought the doctor said she would live a long time yet. O, dear me, if there is one thing I have a horror of more than another it is a death on board ship. I did so hope nothing of that sort would happen. To feel there is a corpse close to you, when you are going about the same as usual – it makes me cold all over.'

'You won't feel it long. She is sure to be buried to-day.'

'And then there will be the funeral on the main deck – the dreadful-looking object, done up in that barbarous way, and the splash of it when it is thrown into the sea – oh, don't let me see or hear anything of it, Don! Tell me when it is going to be, and I'll lock myself up here till it is all over. It would give me the horrors so that I could not sleep at night.'

'I thought you would come out presently, and talk to Mary Hamilton, perhaps. She is awfully cut up about it.'

'Poor dear child! Why *should* she make herself miserable over other people's troubles, as she does. I never saw such a girl. She wants to take the world on her shoulders. If she goes on like this, what a life she will have! She ought to take a leaf out of her sister's book. There was that girl lying tucked up, warm and cosy, last night, while her mother dabbled about, barefooted, baling the water out of her cabin. Ellen saw it with her own eyes.'

Mr Macleod leaned his back against Ellen's bunk, which was piled with her mistress's clothes, and gazed at the port-hole fixedly, with his hands in his pockets. 'She has been doing a lot for that woman,' he remarked, presently; 'and now she is heart-broken about the husband and children. I don't think Dubois is worth her pity – a good-for-nothing loafer he seems to me; but, of course, it is rough on the children. And she feels it. I can't bear to see her so cut up, and I wish you'd come out and talk to her.'

'Now, Don, you know I am no good at that, when people are miserable. I hate to see people miserable, and I hate to be made miserable myself. I'd rather keep out of it when I possibly can. If she leaves off crying, and seems inclined to cheer up, send her in to me here – for really it is too wretched to get up when everything is wet and messy, and one is tired after a bad night, as I am. Tell her I should like to see her, and send her in. Dear girl, I am very fond of her; she's the only creature in petticoats I care to speak to, except Ellen. She is a girl without a bit of sham or nonsense in her; and I do like to help her to hold her own against that genteel mother and sister of hers. But sometimes she is too much for me. She excites herself about things; she takes little trifles so terribly to heart; she is uncomfortably serious and moral about everything. And it upsets me, Don, and makes me low-spirited. Why don't you talk to her yourself?' she added, when she became aware that her brother was still gazing at the porthole as if he could see through it, apparently lost in thought.

'I? I have said too much already, I'm afraid.' 'Oh, Don!' lifting herself into a sitting position, with anxious eagerness in her face, 'What have you said? You have been great chums with her, I know, but you have not been making love to her, have you? Oh, I hope not! Remember, they are coming up to live near us at home – and think of Mrs Hamilton's relations! It is not so bad as if it were Nina, who seemed to have smitten you at first; but still it won't do, you know. Dear old boy, you wouldn't, after all these years, take up with a nobody-knows-who – you, the head of the family, and the owner of Bungil – would you?'

'I would take up, as you call it, with Mary Hamilton, for good and all, if I could, though I were the Prince of Wales.'

'Ah, but you can't,' said Mrs Lepel, in an altered tone. 'I was forgetting Captain Armstrong.'

'What about Captain Armstrong?'

'Don't you know? He is the man she has given her heart to. He amused himself with her at a ball six months ago. As far as I can make out, he treated her much as he would have treated a young dressmaker, or a pretty parlor-maid who had taken his fancy for an hour or two, certainly he never dreamed of courting her in any orthodox manner – no more, for the matter of that, did she. Nevertheless, not being able, I suppose, even to flirt at a ball except in deadly earnest, she has bestowed her young affections upon him; and she means to dedicate herself to his memory – all of him that she is ever likely to get, I imagine.'

'Did she tell you that herself, Jenny?'

'Yes; she told me all about it,' Mrs Lepel responded, triumphantly. And she then proceeded to describe the Armstrong episode in its minor details – to which her listener gave a rapt attention; winding up with the remark that the story had been told her in strict confidence, and that therefore he was not to speak of it again.

'Mind *you* never speak of it again,' Mr Macleod retorted, with a touch of peremptoriness that Mrs Lepel was not used to, and did not like. 'She is young; she trusts everybody to be what she is herself; she has had no sympathy in her own family; and she unburdened her heart to you because you were kind to her. When she is older she will be wiser with her confidences; she will be more reticent about matters of this sort. Jenny, you said just now she was coming up to live near us. Take care of her secret, when she is there; don't let the gossips of Abercorn get hold of it.'

'Her sister talks of it openly.'

'No; she only tells what she saw; that was nothing. I am sure she doesn't know what you know. Look here, Jenny, I have learned her ways a little; and I know just how it was that that fellow got hold of her; and I know how she will stick to him. But I am going to get the better of him some day or other, I hope. At any rate, I am going to try. So make up your mind to it, will you? and don't attempt to hurt her, nor to hinder me. It would not do the least bit of good, and would only make things confoundedly unpleasant. I have never seen the girl I wanted to marry before, but I have met her at 'last. And have her I will, in spite of anybody, if she is by any manner of means to be had.'

Mrs Lepel was silent for a moment, considering painfully. She was a reasonable little woman, and she knew exactly what this meant. 'To think that, after waiting all this time, you should make no better choice!' she sighed protestingly. 'She is a good child – but *such* a child! And she has no beauty, no manners, no culture, no money, no anything! and you will have to marry the whole family, and not her only! and, after all, perhaps she will keep you dangling years and years, for the sake of that Armstrong man, and never take you at all!'

Mr Macleod smiled a little, as he stood, with his arms folded, filling up the little cabin with his square and solid bulk. Then he stooped down and kissed his sister, who flung her arms round his neck, with a little whimper of mingled love and vexation; and they parted, without another word, the best of friends. Mrs Lepel settled herself afresh in her pillows and opossum skins, and, after sighing pensively once or twice, and wondering whether Mary Hamilton might not be made to look distinguished and aristocratic by dressing her properly, returned to her novel, where she speedily became as interested in a reckless heroine and an impecunious hero as the heart of author could desire. Mr Macleod went away to seek his love, who was rushing about, with streaming eyes, in pursuit of her many devices for gratifying the supposed wishes of the dead woman, and for comforting the bereaved little family; he looked very strong and quiet and determined about it, but very silent and sad.

The funeral took place in the afternoon, as he had anticipated. The sea was still turbulent, with a heavy underswell, but the day was bright and tranquil, and at this time – between dinner and tea – the sun was sinking and the sky aflame with its divinest colors. Most of the saloon ladies either shut themselves in their cabins, like Mrs Lepel, or stood on the poop, looking down with grave, pale faces and almost frightened eyes; but Mary stood on the main deck, in the character of a chief mourner, clad in a rusty old black silk gown, holding her prayer-book in both hands, while her tears fell fast on the open leaves; and when the service began, and Mr Macleod stepped quietly up and stood beside her, she did not move or shrink. She offered him a share of her book, seeming to accept his companionship still as a matter of course.

After that most solemn of rites was over, and while the sound of the splash, that Mrs Lepel had so dreaded, was echoing in her ears, she was, as Mr Macleod expressed it, 'cut up' to an extent that was altogether unreasonable and unaccountable to everybody but her lover, who understood the nature that took things so 'hard.' She went away to her cabin, and lay in her bunk and sobbed, with her head buried in a pillow, until night came, and her mother arrived to scold and remonstrate and bid her come out and behave herself. After which she appeared at the tea-table, with a face swollen and disfigured, and tried to eat, but could not. And then, at a little before bedtime, she stole upstairs to her favorite post at the stern railing to soothe and refresh herself with the night air and the solitude; and there Mr Macleod found her, and found the opportunity he had been impatiently longing for for twenty-four hours.

CHAPTER X

Good Friends

'Miss Mary, I hope you are going to forgive me.'

'For what, Mr Macleod?'

'For what I said, for what I did, last night.'

'Forgive; that is not the word for you to use. It is I who shall want to be forgiven.'

'I ought not to have surprised you unawares. I shocked you and frightened you. I had no business to take such a liberty until you had given me some sort of leave. It came to me, somehow; I could not help it. That is my excuse.'

'If it was because you could not help it,' she said gently, 'then there is no need to make excuses. We are not to be blamed for what we cannot help.'

'And you don't blame me?'

'I? How could I blame you? I am the very last person. You are not a man to do such a thing without meaning it; and, doing it, you paid me a great, great honor – the greatest any man could pay me.'

'Women don't generally look at things in that way.'

'I don't know how other women feel. But all last night I was thinking of it, and thinking how much it was – how much it might have been – and wishing that I deserved it.'

'You understood me, then?'

'Yes; of course I understood.'

'You knew that I was asking you to marry me – to be my wife at Bungil by-and-by – to let me give you all I have, so that you could help people like poor Mrs Dubois as much as you liked?'

'Yes, I knew. I was very grateful to you, Mr Macleod.'

'You didn't seem so. I thought you were terribly angry. I was afraid I had offended you, so that you would never speak to me again.'

'Oh, how could you imagine that! It was only that I could not accept what you wanted me to have. That was not your fault. But it forced me to stop you. I couldn't let you go on, thinking what would have been a mistake.'

'Are you sure you could not accept it?' he asked, after a long pause. They were standing together in that friendly proximity to which both had grown accustomed, and their *tete-à-tete* was so trustfully frank and kindly still. He could not believe that he was in the position of her rejected lover, while she treated him in this way. 'Are you sure you could not take me?'

'Oh, yes. I am quite sure of that.'

'Dear, tell me why?'

She was silent for a little, not in the least offended by the question. She was staring out to sea with her thoughtful eyes; he saw them in the darkness, shining steadily; he saw her resolute mouth, looking gravely sweet, but so certain of what it was going to say. 'Oh, what is the use of asking why?' she exclaimed at last. 'Wasn't it enough for you to see how things were? You saw I could not do it; explaining why does not alter anything.'

'A man can't be so easily satisfied.'

'But, Mr Macleod, you would not wish to have anybody who did not want to have you, would you? I am sure you would not.'

'I have always said I would never ask a woman twice – that I would never have her unless she gave herself freely –'

'And you were quite right,' she interrupted quickly.

'But now – I don't know – circumstances alter cases.'

'No – oh, no they don't. People should never marry unless they both know from the first that they naturally belong to each other.'

'Sometimes they don't find it out at first – especially when they have only known each other for such a little while as we have; and they find it out afterwards.'

'Well, when they do find it out – that is time enough.'

'You talk as if you had had a great deal of experience,' Mr Macleod remarked, in an aggrieved tone; 'and you cannot have had a tenth part of mine.'

'But I know what I feel. I don't go by other people's experience. I know how it should be. If I had been meant for you, Mr Macleod, I should have know it last night. I should have known it in a moment – and so would you. I should not have run away from you; I should have stayed as long as possible. I should have kissed you just as you kissed me.'

'Oh,' said Mr Macleod, drawing a deep breath; 'would to Heaven you had! That would have been a moment worth living for.'

'Somebody will,' she said gently, laying her hand on his coat sleeve; 'some day somebody will. But a woman who doesn't do that, and yet takes you and marries you – she will do it for the sake of living at Bungil, or for the sake of having plenty of money, or perhaps merely for the sake of a home of her own and children, and a good husband – which every woman wants, of course.'

'You will want all that, Mary. You are the last woman in the world who should be an old maid.'

'I do not want to be an old maid,' she said; 'but I will not marry merely to save myself from that. You would not like me to take you simply because, if I did, I should be what mother calls 'settled,' would you.'

'Most certainly I should not.'

'And because you are well off?'

'You would never marry a man for his money, I know – though heaps of girls do it every day.'

'No, I never would. I would sooner marry a poor man and work for him. But I will never marry anyone,' she added presently, with a soft but resolute deliberation, 'unless I love him best of all the world.'

Mr Macleod stood by the railing, leaning his arms upon it. He understood her quite well. 'And you do not love me best,' he said, after a long silence.

'No. I can't help it – it is not my fault.'

'Do you think you would have done, if you had met me first?'

'Perhaps. We have been good friends. We have suited each other in many things. You have done more for me than any man ever did – and I think have cared for me more.'

When she said this, he wondered whether it would be wise to attempt the storming of the Armstrong fortress, in which he perceived more than one weak place. A little consideration decided him that it must be attacked with caution by and by, but that for the present it would be best to leave it alone. 'Yes, we have been good friends,' he said. 'It has been very pleasant. But I suppose even that must come to an end now.'

'Why need it come to an end?'

'A rejected suitor is generally expected to make himself scarce, isn't he?'

'I can't see why he should, unless he has behaved badly, or the lady has behaved badly to him. Have I behaved badly to you, Mr Macleod? I feel that I have, but I am so sorry for it – you don't how sorry!'

'You? – you couldn't behave badly. No girl ever sent a fellow away more kindly and sweetly. It makes it fifty times harder to leave you, though.'

'Then why need we quarrel? Cannot we be good friends without marrying each other? I will never say a word about it, if you do not. Can't we forget that this has happened, and be just as we were before?'

'You can forget it, I dare say. But every time I see you, or speak to you, I shall be wanting to ask you to be my wife.'

'If you think you will do that, you must not see me. But, O
dear me, I have been thinking how pleasant it would be, when
we were settled at Abercorn, to see you riding up the street now
and then! It is a great disappointment. Why did you think about
me in this way, Mr Macleod?'

'Didn't I tell you? Because I couldn't help it.'

'You won't try to help it now – now that you know it is useless.'

'Certainly I won't until I see you married to somebody else
before my eyes. But,' he added, as she slowly lifted herself up
from her lounging posture, with a gesture of dignity that he felt
in the darkness rather than saw, and that indicated a sudden
change in her attitude towards him and the matter under discussion, 'but do not be afraid that I shall persecute you. I am not
that sort of man. I will never worry you about it. I will be guided
by your wishes when you come to Abercorn. I will only permit
myself as much intercourse with you and your family as you care
to allow me. You can trust me about that can't you? Mary, give
me your hand, and say you trust me.'

She gave him her hand immediately. 'It is very late,' she said,
under her breath. 'I think it must be bedtime.' And the next instant she was gone.

Soon after this conversation, which practically resulted in the
restoration of a semblance of their old relations, the *Devonshire*
sighted a trail of brown seaweed, and then a far-off faint blue
cloud, and the passengers congratulated themselves that their
voyage was nearly over.

It was falling dark on a lovely spring evening when the ship
sailed up to her anchorage in the bay. It was too late for her to
find her berth at the pier till morning, but boats came out in the
moonlight to fetch off several people whose friends had been on
the watch for them. The first to go was Mr Lorimer. His partner
came to meet him, full of business information; and the old man
was too eagerly and anxiously absorbed in his commercial affairs
to think of offering anybody a share of his roomy boat, or even
to say good night to Mrs Hamilton. Then Mr Lepel and Mr Butler
appeared together – the former a very short, stout, red-faced man,
with a loud voice and the airs of a field-marshal; and the latter
an elderly, grey, diffident person, whom Mrs Hamilton and Nina
greeted with subdued, almost condescending affection and Mary
with many endearments. The two families left the ship together,
travelled to town by the same train, and parted in the yard of

the Hobson's Bay station, where an imposing carriage was in waiting to convey the Lepels and Mr Macleod to their hotel.

The Hamilton ladies were squeezing themselves into their cab, and Mary, standing with her foot on the step, struggling with an armful of wraps and bags, when Mr Macleod came round to say good night.

'You will be up at Abercorn soon, I suppose?' he suggested inquiringly, promptly appropriating the wraps and bags.

'O yes; as soon as the things are out of the Customs. I can't leave my business long,' said the banker.

'Good-bye, then, for the present.' He lifted his hat to Mrs Hamilton and Nina, put Mary into the cab, and then offered his lady love his hand silently.

'Mr Macleod,' she whispered, holding it, and stooping down, 'you will come and see us soon?'

'May I?' he replied, in the same tone. 'Thank you, dear.'

CHAPTER XI

Abercorn

Abercorn was a good sized bush township; having said which, we have, perhaps, sufficiently described it. The Australian reader will at once picture to himself the one long, wide street, with its irregular row of buildings on either side – its old established stores, running back into by-lanes, under low zinc roofs and broad verandahs; its white-faced banks, apparently so much bigger and grander than, in such a locality, they need be and so strikingly out of harmony with the unpretending simplicity of the dwellings surrounding them; its numerous public houses, with the inn where the coach puts up standing conspicuous among them for the roomy comfort of its wide-spreading premises; its half-a-dozen little churches, all within a stone's throw of one another; its modest police station, with the lock-up isolated in the backyard; its neat post office, its shire hall, its mechanics' institute, its State school – all the apparatus of civilisation that the name to colonial ears suggests. And Abercorn had not been enterprising or original in arranging its material conditions; it was just a middle-sized bush township of the typical pattern – neither more nor less.

The Bank of Australasia stood in the middle of the street, lifting two stories of plate glass and stucco above the heads of its

neighbours, to the great pride of the townsfolk, who had no particular eye to the picturesque. Mr Butler, who had been manager
there since 'the early days,' when it was opened, was that honorable institution in Abercorn, 'our old and most respected
townsman,' and was much looked up to at public meetings and
relied on by struggling and impecunious church committees. The
late Mrs Butler had been the daughter of a retired tradesman in
the neighborhood, and as Mrs Butler had been a leader of society in Abercorn. Evidences of her taste and culture remained in
the appointments of her house – chiefly in wool-work cushions,
beadwork chairs and a profusion of miscellaneous antimacassars.
The drawingroom at the Bank of Australasia was upstairs – a
rigid apartment, which no one entered save to receive visitors,
or to sweep and dust, except on the occasion of a ceremonious
party. Its highly ornamental chairs were to look at and not to
sit upon – except on the edge, very gingerly, while in one's Sunday clothes; and the only table was not available for use, inasmuch
as it was thickly covered with books (to be looked at and not
read), photographic albums, shells, Chinese boxes, and other articles of 'bigotry and virtue,' ranged round a gigantic glass shade
in the middle, which enshrined the vase and the bouquet of white
flowers and silver leaves that had once crowned Mrs Butler's wedding cake. The marble mantle-piece supported a gold clock, also
under a glass shade, flanked by brilliant vases – always in
pairs – and finished off with cut-glass lustres, intended to hold
candles, which never were put into them, at the corners; and the
hearth, which might have done something to redeem the prevailing
inhospitable gentility of the room, was invariably fireless, and
filled with paper shavings or something equally detestable.

Into this drawingroom came Mrs Hamilton and Nina, and
effected a revolution that shook Abercorn to its social and domestic foundations. Their long residence in Eastwold had at least
taught them what a drawingroom was for, and that this time-
honored system of decoration was susceptible of improvement.
So they covered some of the easiest of the beaded chairs with
a modest-patterned chintz, and turned the stiffest and hardest ones
out altogether, substituting their own folding chairs of the voyage,
made luxurious with a little stuffing, in which Nina, who loved
comfort, could nestle. They took down some terrible red curtains,
and hung up dainty cretonne in their place; they spread a big
crumb-cloth of unbleached linen on the floor, as the only mode

of effacing the barbaric splendours of the carpet; they cleared away all the antimacassars and nine-tenths of the ornaments; they burnt the gilded shavings on the hearth, and substituted logs of sheoak and redgum, which were lit whenever there was an excuse for a fire, and were ready to light at all times. They surrounded themselves with roomy low tables; they had the newspapers brought up; they sewed, and read, and wrote letters, and drank tea there; and from the windows looked down upon the life of the little township – the people going in and out at the stores and hotels, the men gossiping on the footpaths, the occasional buggies and bullock-drays rumbling by – as from a higher sphere.

Mary, who was not in the drawingroom very much, was furiously indignant at the liberties that were taken with it. Never mind if it was furnished with sackcloth and ashes, or skulls and crossbones, or deal benches and three-legged stools; it was poor Aunt Butler's own room, and all her little treasures ought to be respected and left, as she had arranged them, reverently, for Uncle Peter's sake. Mary's protest was disallowed, of course; and all she could do to save her uncle's feelings was to persuade him that the chintz and the crumb-cloth were intended to protect the precious fabrics that were too good for dailywear, and that the exclusion of the ornaments would ensure their safety from injury and breakage. Mr Butler, who was a meek man, and a little in awe of his sister, who had married into a class above his own, made no protest himself. He sighed as he placed the vase of orange blossoms and the glass shade on the top of his own chest of drawers, and ranged the despised little knick-knacks on his bedroom chimney-piece; but, as he went about the streets afterwards, doing Mrs Hamilton's commissions, he gave his fellow-townsmen to understand, with evident pride, that his sister was a superior woman, with superior tastes, and that things which did for most people would not do for her.

The ladies of Abercorn, when they came to call, took voluminous notes of the new arrangements. They, as well as Mr Butler, deluded themselves with the belief that economy had inspired the idea of the chintz and the crumb cloth, until their hostess took occasion to refer, with a shudder, to the tasteless vulgarity that she had had to cover from her sight; and then they were much exercised in their minds and had great and solemn discussions amongst themselves. They all agreed in disapproving of Mrs Hamilton's taste, as she had disapproved of theirs,

and thought that tea in the afternoon was a mischievous inno-
vation; *very* bad for the nerves of young people; at the same time
they had a disquieting secret impression that a lady who had been
living in intimate friendship with lords (a fact that was communicated to the public without loss of time) would be sure to know
'what was the fashion' better than they could do. And in due course
they also set up afternoon teacups of minute size and elaborate
pattern, and got into the habit of asking her advice when they
meditated a purchase of furniture. The men of Abercorn, though
not much in it, fell at once in love with the new drawingroom
at the bank – men generally having truer tastes and instincts in
all these matters than women of the same grade of intelligence.
Heads of families referred to it as a model of comfort and cheerfulness, which they compared to their own prim reception rooms
to the great disparagement of the latter; and the young bank clerks
and idle youths of the town always liked to gossip on the opposite side of the street, whence they could get a full view of the
window where Nina had a special chair and table, and where she
displayed her pretty self, in charming costumes, to an admiring
public nearly all day long.

Men and women, however, were alike in their desire to show
hospitality and attention to the new comers. As soon as it was
intimated from the bank that Mrs Hamilton was 'settled,' they
called in a body – wives of lawyers and doctors, police magistrate and clergymen, and of two or three of the more prominent
storekeepers and men of business in the town, the husbands, as
a rule, being represented by their cards; and a number of little
evening parties immediately ensued before the half of the calls,
about which Mrs Hamilton exercised much deliberation, were
returned. A 'few friends' in a clerical household began them. Half-
a-dozen people arrived at the parsonage at nine o'clock, and sat
in a circle in a square room, exchanging small and stiff remarks
upon trivial subjects – the only kind of conversation possible
under such conditions – until half-past eleven, when biscuits and
wine were served, and the company went home. Then there was
a 'musical evening'. This was at a lawyer's house, and was a more
considerable gathering; but the entertainment was conducted upon
the same depressing system. The guests sat round the room in
solemn silence, twiddling their thumbs, while one after another
performed on the piano, also solemnly, as if going through some
religious rite, and, naturally, with a good deal of nervousness

and fluster – for three mortal hours; when a profuse and jovial supper made some amends for the boredom that everybody had endured. Other musical evenings followed, of much the same kind; and then the police magistrate, who was a cultured gentleman, with some sense of the spirit as well as the letter of hospitality – the kind of man at whose house no guest was ever received on a chilly day in a fireless room – gave a little party, where people wandered about, and talked and laughed and amused themselves, in a comfortable room containing plenty of tables, and plenty of nooks and corners, and where music discharged its proper functions naturally, and not under artificial pressure; which party Nina declared reminded her more of dear Dunchester and the Bishop's palace than anything she had experienced since leaving England. There were also a few dances, which, inasmuch as they were unpretentious and inexpensive in their arrangements, and as the Abercorn people, like Australians in general, were light hearted and easy-going, and by no means inclined by nature to take their pleasure sadly, were the most successful and satisfactory of the entertainments; though, to be sure, Nina was much disgusted to see how the ladies, one and all, decked themselves with artificial flowers – apparently considering them the distinguishing feaure of a correct ball-dress.

Mrs Hamilton and her daughters – daughter, rather, for Mary had no voice in such matters – accepted the hospitality that was shown them on all these occasions, not without giving their entertainers a distinct impression that it was very kind of them to do so. They always arrived late, when the chief of the arm chairs was vacated for Mrs Hamilton, who took it graciously, but as a matter of course; and they always departed early. Mrs Hamilton, during the interval, was the object of special attentions from host and hostess; and Nina, placid and graceful, conscious of superiority in beauty and in 'style,' looking, to do her justice, very refined and charming in her faintly-tint̀d, Sèvres-china dresses – was the queen and goddess at whose feet bank clerks bowed down (and Nina did not disdain bank clerks when nothing better was available). Mary, who had an inveterate habit of taking up with, as well as of snubbing and neglecting, the 'wrong people,' always squeezed herself into corners, and either found an old maid, or some other indifferent person to talk to, or yawned openly, and made it evident to anyone who took the trouble to notice her (and Abercorn was not so ready to do that as Mr Macleod had

been) how insufferably bored she was. She liked the dances, into
the life and fun of which she entered with all the ardor of her
youth and her wholesome nature, but she hated the prim little
parties with the same characteristic vehemence. The Abercorn
people voted her a rather disagreeable girl in those early days,
before they knew her well enough to ask her to 'drop in' when
she felt disposed, and, when she did, to make her free of the
homely life of the family sittingroom.

She did not see her friend of the voyage for a considerable time;
and she missed him a great deal. He was not, of course, to be
compared with her captain, whose image was ever present to her
thoughts, the glorified type and pattern of everything that a
gentleman and a soldier and a lover should be; but then neither
were the men of Abercorn for a moment to be compared with
him. How often, at the dull little parties, when she yawned and
sighed for the evening to be over, did she wish she could see him
walk in at the door, with his brisk, downright, peremptory tread,
looking so square and strong and so full of quiet energy. She
thought she was anxious for news of the Dubois children – and
so she was; but she was far more anxious for a sight of her rejected
lover's face, and to be assured afresh that he was her good friend
as he promised to be.

It was by no means his fault that she did not see him sooner.
He called at the bank almost immediately after his return to Bungil, and found all the ladies out; and he left a message that he
would come again on the following afternoon, as he was anxious to see them. This gratifying message Nina received from the
servant, and did not communicate to her sister, whom, next day,
as soon as lunch was over, she despatched on a series of shopping expeditions, and when Mr Macleod arrived he was ushered
up to the drawingroom, where he was entertained with much
hospitality by Mrs Hamilton and her eldest daughter only. He
stayed a long time; he looked at some photographs of Eastwold
and of Nina's English friends – which included those of her dear
Lord Chester and the bishop and the dean; he took great interest
in the description of Eastwold life which the photographs suggested, and apparently he took great interest in Nina herself, for
he stared at her a good deal, noticing the soft delicacy and purity
of her skin, and how well her faint-blue muslin dress, with the
pink roses at her throat, became her. He even drank some tea
out of the lilliputian cups, and ate some thin bread and butter,

served by Miss Hamilton's beautifully white hands; he sat at Nina's window and looked up and down the street, giving her little sketches of the characters and histories of the passers-by. Finally, he took out his watch – with an air intended to imply that, beguiled by all these pleasant things, he had totally forgotten how the time was passing – remarked that he was making an unconscionable visit, and that he should be late for dinner if he lingered any longer, and, with genuine reluctance, departed, leaving his two entertainers in high good humor with themselves and things in general and Mary came toiling home, hot and dusty, with an armful of parcels that she had insisted on carrying herself, in time to see him riding at full speed out of the town. When she was told by the servant that Mr Macleod of Bungil had been to call, she marched up to her bedroom without speaking, and felt strongly disposed to cry.

Then Mrs Lepel came, driving her little basket phaeton and a pair of Shetland ponies. Her visit was very short, for she had a great deal to do whenever she came into Abercorn, and this was her first appearance after a long absence. She had to speak to her devoted butcher, and inquire after his wife and his children, and to chat with sundry other shopkeepers, all of whom she extensively patronised in the way of business, and who waited upon her as she sat in her carriage with eager assiduity, regarding her not only as the great lady of the neighborhood, but as the most affable 'that ever they had to do with.' Nina, watching her royal progress up and down the street, began to fear that she was not coming to the bank at all; but the little woman ran up the steep staircase to the cheerful drawingroom, in time for twenty minutes brisk chat and a cup of tea, and left the Hamilton ladies as much pleased, and, as the mother expressed it, 'refreshed' by her congenial society, as they had been by her brother's a few days before. She was profuse in her praises of the new chintz and cretonne, and sympathised cordially in the condemnation of the late Mrs Butler's taste – 'only, poor thing, she never went out of the colony, hardly out of Abercorn, you know; she had no chance of seeing anything better.' Mrs Hamilton smiled serenely, feeling that there was a special bond of union between Mrs Lepel and herself, who had seen better things, and were acquainted with the habits and customs of the great world. When their visitor departed, Mrs Hamilton and Nina, true to their little code of etiquette, remained upstairs and rang the bell for the maid-of-all-work to open the door, an intimation, which that damsel, a native of Abercorn, never properly comprehended; but Mary ran down to the hall to let her friend out, and into the street to help her to tuck herself into her carriage comfortably.

'Dear child,' said Mrs Lepel, patting the girl's beautiful shoulder as she stooped before her, 'I am so glad to see you again! Mind you come and see me soon.' And she flicked her little ponies and rattled away, bowing brightly from side to side in acknowledgement of the beaming faces watching to see her go, thinking to herself that, if Don was fated to make a fool of himself with 'those people,' it was a blessed chance that led him to choose the one member of the family who had any claim to be called a lady.

Mr Butler hired a buggy, and drove his sister and his eldest niece to Wattlebank to return Mrs Lepel's call, as soon as Mrs Hamilton's sense of what was proper permitted (Mary, to her bitter disappointment, was not allowed to go, because it 'looked absurd to see a whole family carting itself about, like cheap excursion people,' Nina said); and this expedition, on which they set forth with some elation, was not so satisfactory as it might have been. Wattlebank was a charming country house, improved and refined out of all likeness to its former self; and, upon her arrival, its ex-mistress found herself by no means so cordially welcomed as she had expected to be. The little party was shown into a room and left to wait, with nothing to amuse them but the sound of merry laughter from a lawn where a number of people were playing Badminton; and then Mrs Lepel came in hastily, in a garden hat, with her racquet in her hand. She sat for about half an hour, talking small talk, pleasantly, but with an abstracted air – her husband, whose loud and lordly tones were distinctly audible from the garden, not appearing at all; and then, when Mrs Hamilton rose, she exclaimed, 'Oh, must you go?' and said good-bye cordially, but with obvious relief. All the same, the two ladies returned to Abercorn full of delight with their visit, apparently; and Mary, for the first time, was shy about asking if Mr Macleod had been there, yet thought he must have been, if it had been so pleasant.

She met her lover at last, however, to the great satisfaction of both of them. One afternoon, at about five o'clock, when she had been busy all day helping the maid-of-all-work to clean the numerous bank windows – her mother and sister being con-veniently engaged in repaying the civilities of some out-of-town neighbors – she put on her hat and set off for a long solitary walk, taking the road that led to Bungil as the shortest route to the open country. About half-an-hour later Mr Macleod mounted his horse to ride into Abercorn; and they consequently met – under particularly happy circumstances. The man was jogging along meditatively, in the lovely early summer sunset light and stillness, thinking over a design for a new sheepwash that he intended to have before another year – the girl had paused to lean her arms on the top rail of a fence to look at the sky and wonder what Captain Armstrong was doing – when they became aware of each other's presence.

'Oh, is it *you*?' cried Mary, with unmistakable welcome in her surprised face and voice. And, 'I thought I couldn't be mistaken in your figure,' said Mr Macleod. And then they stood silently for a few seconds, clasping each other's hands, while the horse put his delicate velvet nose over his master's shoulder and sniffed at them.

'I thought I was never going to see you again,' said Mr Macleod, looking her over with critical, satisfied eyes, and thinking that if Nina's diaphanous raiment was elegant, this unstarched brown holland was classic in its refined simplicity, clothing the noble shape that never seemed more noble than now. 'Tell me what you have been doing with yourself all this long while. Oh, doesn't it seem a long while?'

'It does,' said Mary, simply. 'But I have been very busy, without much leisure to think of it.' And then they turned and walked along the empty road together; and she gave him a tolerably detailed account of what she had done since she had seen him last, and of her impressions of Abercorn. 'I am very busy,' she repeated, contentedly. 'We have only one servant, and I can help her in so many ways that I never need to be idle. I do most of the cooking, and I trim the lamps, and I iron Nina's fine things, and I mend Uncle Peter's socks, and – oh, lots of things. I like living with dear Uncle Peter so much better than being at Eastwold. But I'm afraid – I can't help being very much afraid – that we shall be a great expense to him, no matter what I do to help.'

Then they talked of other subjects. Mr Macleod told her how he had been to town, and had hunted up the Dubois children; how he had found them tolerably well and happy, their father having got employment at one of the theatres, which brought him in enough to support them comfortably. 'And I fancy, by the look of things, that they'll have another mother before long,' said he, lightly. 'There was a strapping young woman on a visit to their lodgings when I was there – a ballet-girl, or something of that sort – and she was feeding the little brats with lollies, and he was very attentive to her.'

'What,' cried Mary, in indignant horror, standing still, and looking at him fixedly with tragic eyes. 'Oh, the wicked, heartless, indecent brute! To think of those poor, dear little creatures – worse than orphans fifty times! To think of that poor, sweet, patient sufferer, who slaved and died for him – only a few weeks dead! Mr Macleod, *what* did you say to him? Didn't you tell him how wicked, how terrible it was?'

'No,' said Mr Macleod, smiling a little. 'I didn't think that was my business. And, besides, I rather liked the look of the girl's face – an honest, sensible, wholesome face it was, though the paint hadn't improved it. She looked as if she would be kind to the kids, and maybe it will be a good thing for them if he marries her.'

'Oh, to think of it! – so soon as this!'

'Soon! If he doesn't want to wait for love of his wife, why should he wait for the mere look of the thing!'

'It is for love of his wife he should wait – wait always,' said the girl, passionately. 'But he never loved her, of course.'

'Oh, I don't know that I would say that – '

'People who have loved properly can never want to love a second time,' said Mary, almost defiantly.

'How do you know? my dear, you haven't lived long enough to be so certain about anything – least of all about that.'

'I know what I feel myself,' she said, still speaking excitedly. 'I can't imagine anyone loving a second time.'

'Child, don't say it – don't be so terribly positive.'

'I do say it.'

'I hope you will live to find yourself mistaken then.'

'How can I be mistaken! A woman can have but one true mate.'

'But it isn't always an easy matter for her to identify him,' said Mr Macleod.

Neither of them were thinking any more of Mr Dubois and his late and future wives.

CHAPTER XII

'Except one Person'

From this time Mr Macleod and Miss Mary Hamilton met very frequently, and were more or less 'talked about' in connection with one another. They met accidentally on lonely roads, the girl, being an energetic pedestrian, usually taking her walks abroad by herself, and the man riding about the country, apparently for no other purpose than to look for her; and great was the sensation when they were observed by passers-by from Abercorn, sauntering comfortably along the roadside together, absorbed in confidential talk. Then Mr Macleod was seen about the streets of the township, as he never used to be seen in the old days, before his trip to Europe (when he was thought to hold himself too much aloof from those who, if not landowners, were men and brothers, and quite as good as he); and it was noticed that his horse was hung up at the bank more often than was consistent with the theory of business engagements. The young bank and Government clerks used to stand on the other side of the street and stare up at the drawingroom windows when he was there, and could not believe but that he was 'after' their golden-haired paragon of perfection, and merely using the sister as a go-between. An impression, by the way, that was shared by Miss Nina herself for a considerable length of time. Then the owner of Bungil – who had erewhile restricted himself in the enjoyment of his social pleasures to a particular sphere, lying wholly outside the range of these entertainments – appeared at the little parties and musical evenings that were so much in vogue in Abercorn, having, it was presumed, previously ingratiated himself in an altogether abnormal manner with the heads of the household in which hospitalities were dispensed. As he had never been seen amongst them in this familiar way before, the Abercorn gossips were a good deal agitated, and set themselves to find out the special strong reason that must have induced him so to break through the traditions of his family, and the reason was not far to seek: it lay spread out before their very eyes, so that a child might see it. At first they were only certain that it was one of the Hamilton sisters, and could not make up their minds which. Both would brighten up when he entered the room; both would look at him expectantly. Nina would blush and smile, and look conscious and coquettish; Nina nearly always was the first to speak to him, and would call him to her side if she had the chance, and Nina, in everybody's estimation, was the natural choice for a man like him to make. But always he drifted to Mary sooner or later, and always Mary received him with a quiet, bright contentment; and though, more often than not, they did not begin to talk immediately, there was that in the look of them when they subsided together, on one sofa or on contiguous chairs, that indicated to anybody possessing a grain of intelligence that there was a bond and an understanding of some sort between them. Finally, the public mind was set at rest by the fact that he had been heard to address her as 'dear' - and in a whisper too - when helping her down the churchyard steps after service on a dark Sunday night. 'Take care, dear,' he had said. Mrs Jones was close behind him, perfectly satisfied in her own mind that he had not come all the way from Bungil to attend service at night - and a wet night too - for the first time within the memory of man, for a proper purpose, and she heard him say it with her own ears; and apparently the girl was accustomed to hearing him call her 'dear,' for she made no protest - she just went down the steps cautiously, holding his hand, and on reaching the footpath took his arm and walked off with him in the rain, with her head under his umbrella, as bold as you please.

After this, Mrs Jones, who was the strong-minded wife of a solicitor, and the mouthpiece of public opinion in Abercorn - or had been, rather, before Mrs Hamilton's arrival - felt it her duty to call at the bank and acquaint the deluded mother with what was going on. To those - and they were many - who were privy to the mission, and who watched Mrs Jones anxiously when she went out and when she returned home, there were dark indications that that powerful woman had not been so victorious in her friendly encounter with Mrs Hamilton as she was wont to be in her many generous efforts to set her neighbors right and to regulate the conduct of their affairs; but that her errand had been, in the main, successful, was speedily apparent to all. In the first place, Mr Butler and Mrs Hamilton went alone to Bungil (the man at the hotel told the Jones's groom that that was where the single buggy, hurriedly ordered by the banker, had gone to, which interesting and significant intelligence was conveyed, through the Jones's housemaid, to Mrs Jones); and they did not return until 'all hours.' Then Mr Macleod, for two or three days, almost lived at the bank, so constantly was he seen going in and out; and once Mrs Lepel came and carried off Mary for a *tete-à-tete* drive in her pony carriage (which was a feature of the proceedings that nobody could understand); and then, all at once, Macleods and Lepels were seen no more in Abercorn – but only Nina, looking wretchedly ill and cross, and Mary, grave and pale, with that determined set in her mouth, holding her head up and giving herself airs; and Mrs Hamilton, flustered in manner, but smiling in face, going about telling everybody that Mr Macleod, of Bungil, had proposed to her youngest daughter, and was dying to have her, but that Mary, stupid child, had refused him, which, as the Abercorn ladies said to one another, was a tale for the marines, and not for *them*.

A long time after this – when the Hamiltons had been more than a year in Abercorn, and public opinion was quite unanimous to the effect that they had attempted to 'hook' the marriageable man of the neighborhood, and had failed – a mysterious circumstance occurred. It was on the occasion of a public holiday and a certain race meeting, a few miles off, which annually emptied Abercorn of its inhabitants. All the buggies in the place, packed with gaily-dressed holidaymakers and their well filled luncheon baskets, had been gone for some hours; banks and stores were closed; the streets were deserted, save that here and there a servant peered out at a door or over a gate to look for another servant to talk to; and Mary Hamilton, who had given up her seat in the family conveyance to a lady more anxious to go to the races than she, was keeping house with only an old maid friend for company, when Mr Macleod came riding into the township and stopped at the Bank of Australasia.

Mary and her friend were upstairs in the drawingroom, very busy over some homely needlework, when the door bell rang. The old maid, Miss Masters by name, put her head out of the window and recognised the aristocratic lineaments of the horse tied by the bridle to a post outside. 'Oh, my dear, I do believe it is Mr Macleod, of Bungil!' she murmured, in an awestruck whisper.

Then Mary ran to the window and looked down, with a flushed face and beating heart. 'So it is,' she said, with a catch of her breath. 'That is his Lapwing. He never allows anybody to ride her but himself. And we have sent Jane out!'

'I'll go down and let him in,' said Mary, hurriedly; and she went out of the room like a flash, leaving her friend to gather up, in frantic haste and excitement, all the snips and litter that their unfashionable occupation had produced.

Mr Macleod stood on the doorstep, rapping his leggings with his riding whip. The heavy hall-door, with its complicated fastenings, opened, and Mary stood before him, with an anxious, startled, wistful face – not a face of welcome, but certainly not a face of reproval or reproach. They clasped hands silently, and looked at each other.

'You didn't expect to see me to-day?' he suggested, with a little embarrassment.

'No, Mr Macleod, I didn't expect to see you at all. But to-day – to-day, I thought you would certainly be at the races.'

'That wasn't why you stayed at home, was it?'

'No. I stayed because there was not room for me in the waggonnette very well, and I didn't care about it. But you are a judge or something, aren't you?'

'Only a steward. I have been to the races; I have just come away. I shouldn't have gone if I hadn't hoped to see you; and when I saw you were not there – then I thought I would come and look for you.'

'Why? What is the use? It only makes everybody miserable.'

'I had a reason for wanting to see you today particularly. You don't mind my coming like this, do you?'

'Only that mother is out. Nobody is at home except Miss Masters, who is spending the day with me.'

'Where is Miss Masters?'

'Upstairs.'

'I don't want to see anybody, but you. Let me come into the dining room, may I? Just for five minutes, Mary.'

She hesitated, and then stood back a little, and he came into the hall and shut the door; and then they entered the dull and rather shabby little diningroom together. Neither of them sat down.

'I am going away,' said Mr Macleod, abruptly. 'I can't stand this sort of thing any longer, Mary, and I am going to travel again. Nothing wants me at Bungil, and it's too deadly dull and solitary living there all by myself. I've got sick of the whole thing, and restless, and I'm going to try a change. And I thought I would like to see you again before I went.' She stood before him, leaning against the table, supporting herself upon the edge of it with her hands – an attitude showing all the lovely lines of her flawless figure to perfection, and he thought, as he looked at it, and at her downcast face, that she was the most beautiful woman he had ever seen. 'I thought at least you'd like to say good-bye to me,' he added, as she kept silence, with her eyes fixed on the toes of his boots.

'I don't like it!' she burst out, passionately; 'I hate to say good-bye. I can't bear you to go away – to go away like that, as if I were driving you from your home!'

'Well, if you'll tell me to stay, I'll stay fast enough.'

'You ought to look after your property and your tenants, and the interests of your country – a great landowner like you.'

'I have a splendid manager, and the best of overseers; and I have no vocation for politics.'

'And aren't there any girls in the world but me? If you would only make up your mind to it – if you would only settle down and look out for a nice wife of your own rank – you *might* be so happy, if you would!'

'My dear child,' interrupted Mr Macleod, gently, 'you needn't waste your breath going over all that old ground again. You know there is only one woman in the world for me, and that I can't be happy without her.'

'You won't try.'

'No; I won't try. Simply because I know it is no use trying.'

'Haven't I to try? And it helps me. If I gave way as you do – I, who never have anything, though I would be content with so little – life would be too dreary to put up with. Think how it used to be with you before you saw me; and what chances a man has with money and position and splendid health and strength like yours! Mr Macleod, do try – to comfort me.'

'I wish you wouldn't always call me Mr Macleod,' he interposed, rather sharply.

'Don – I feel so impertinent when I call you Don – Don, stay at Bungil to work, and try to make yourself happy, won't you? Let me help you where I can; let me be your friend, your sister.'

'No, I won't have you for a sister. I want bread. I don't want a stone. The time for compromises of that sort is long gone by. I must either have you as I want you, or I must clear out altogether, where I can't be tantalised beyond all bearing as I am now.'

'I like you so much,' said Mary, sweeping her handkerchief over her shining eyes. 'I like to know you are at Bungil, even if I never

see you. I like you more than I can say – though the way mother
and Nina are always abusing me for not marrying you would
be enough to make me hate you if you were anybody else. I love
you,' she added suddenly, 'for it is more than liking; I love you
better than any man in the world, except – except one person.'

'Yes, except one person – one shadow, one ghost, one dream.
Are you always going to give yourself to that person, Mary, who
never comes to ask for you – who will never want you as I do?'

'Perhaps he will come some day. If not – I cannot help it, but
I feel that I must still wait for him. Oh, don't you see how it is?
Just as you can't help choosing me, I can't help choosing him.
He is my first love – I think he will be my last, and I cannot marry
anybody else. I wish I could – I wish I could.'

He drew her hands from her face, and drew her to him, as he
stood before her, with his back to the empty hearth. She made
no resistance, but laid her face on his shoulder and wept there.

'I will go away for a little while,' he said gently, with an
unsteady intonation of voice. 'It will be best for us both. But I
will come back before long. And, Mary, if you think you owe
me any compensation for what I am suffering for your sake,
promise me something that will comfort me.'

'What? I will promise anything.'

'To let me know all that happens – to let me help you if you
get into any trouble – not to shut me out of your life altogether
because you have refused to marry me – to let me be a sort of
father and brother rolled in one, if I mayn't be your husband.
You wouldn't let conventional nonsense prevent you from doing
that? I will give you my agent's address in London.'

'Is that all?' she responded readily. 'No, I wouldn't be afraid
to do that. I would sooner tell you things than anybody.'

Five minutes later, Miss Masters, leaning over the banisters on
the landing above, witnessed the parting at the hall door. She
saw Mr Macleod take the girl in his arms and kiss her; and she
distinctly heard Mary say, as she held her handkerchief to her
eyes, 'O, Don, I wish you would not go!'

She wished he wouldn't go! And she called him Don! Things
were coming to a pretty pass, thought the scandalised old maid.

CHAPTER XIII

A Letter

While Mr Macleod was away on his travels, he received the following letter from Mrs Lepel: —

Dear old Boy, –

'How are you getting on? Do you feel any better for having seen the Yosemite Valley? and does Salt Lake City comfort you at all? We are all moped to death here for want of you, if that is any consolation to you in your affliction – and I suppose it is. People crossed in love like to make everybody belonging to them as miserable as they can, I notice; and the innocent always have to suffer for the guilty in this world. I never see that girl, striding along the road like a six-foot grenadier, with her hat on the back of her head and her petticoats barely reaching to her ankles, that I don't want to get down out of the carriage and go and box her ears. However, I don't do it; I return good for evil, and treat her with the most exemplary kindness. Indeed, I was driven to take her up – more than I need have done by the strict terms of my bargain with you – because I found that those Abercorn people were rather nasty to her after you were gone. They said she had thrown herself at your head – or your feet, I forget which – and, aided or abetted by her family, had implored you to have her, and that you were obliged to go away out of the country to escape from her importunities. Of course I wasn't going to let that sort of thing go on. So I went in and invited the whole family to Wattlebank (much to Fred's disgust, who left me to entertain them while he took a day's shooting at Bungil); and after that I drove Mary about the town with me whenever I went in. I also – though I admit it was gall and wormwood to do it – made a call on Mrs Jones, and took occasion to hint at the real state of the case. So I have done my duty by you, have I not? And I expect to be thanked accordingly.

'But, O dear me, there have been such changes since then! Mrs Jones has something else to talk about now. You know I told you we were going to town for the races? Well, we got nice rooms at Scott's, and went down a few days beforehand (for I wanted to see about my dresses and things)! and next morning I was shopping, and I met Mrs Redwood, and as usual we had a gossip. And she said presently, "Who do you think has bought our place at Kew? Old Mr Lorimer, of all people! What do you suppose he is going to do with a large house like that?" "Oh," I said carelessly, "let it, or sell it again. He saw it was a bargain, I suppose, and he is sure to make a profit out of it somehow" I assure you the thought of Mrs Hamilton never for a moment entered my head. He left the *Devonshire*, you know, without even saying good-bye to her; and, never hearing any more of him, I thought he had forgotten all about her as soon as he was back with his money bags. Imagine, then, my utter astonishment when, getting out of our carriage at the races (it was the first day, and the Redwoods went with us), I saw, going up the steps to the terrace in front of us, Mr Lorimer, Mrs Hamilton and Nina Hamilton, apparently making a party by themselves. It was Fred called my attention to them. "Do look at old Lorimer," he said; "I really believe he has invested in a new suit of clothes at last!" And when I looked, and was struck, just as Fred had been, by the unusual smartness of his appearance, Mrs Hamilton turned round, and I recognised her. She, too, was very smart, and so was Nina – who wore a pale pink dress trimmed with white lace, and looked a perfect sylph. All at once the whole thing flashed across me. "O, Fred," I said, "don't you see what it means? He is going to marry Mrs Hamilton and set up housekeeping at Kew." "A likely thing, at this time of day!" said Fred. "I'm certain of it," I said. "I'll bet you anything you like he doesn't," said Fred; "he's too cute." "Bet me a Turkey carpet for the diningroom that he doesn't," I said. "Done," said Fred. And my dear Don – though you mayn't believe it – he has had to order me that carpet, as I knew he would, and a pretty penny it will cost him, too. It will teach him not to be so positive about everything, thinking he knows better than anybody else.

'Well, we let them get ahead a little way, for Fred didn't want me to speak to them; and, as the first race was coming on, we ladies got nice places on the stand with some people we knew, and Fred and Mr Redwood went down to the saddling paddock. And then we saw our young lovers parading up and down the lawn. They *did* look so comical! Mrs Hamilton was sweeping along, dragging an immense train of flounces over the grass behind her, carrying herself proudly, like a Queen of Sheba; and Nina went mincing and tripping, with her little airs and graces – looking, to do her justice, really very pretty and stylish (I heard lots of people asking who she was). And between the two, that poor, dear, absurd little man, toddling along like an elated child – evidently as delighted with the situation as he could be! It was really too preposterous. I avoided them successfully until lunch time, when, their carriage happening to be put up next to ours, I was in a manner driven to speak to them. I didn't say much; just enough for bare civility, and to satisfy my curiosity on one or two points. I was too disgusted with them – and besides Fred was so afraid they would hang on to us if we gave them any encouragement. But I told Mrs Hamilton I was surprised to see her in Melbourne, and asked her when she had come down. And she replied, very affably and sweetly, that dear Nina had not been well, and had seemed to want a change, and so she had brought her to town for a few weeks to see if that would set her up. And then I asked for Mary, and was told that she was keeping house for her uncle at home. Mary was always strong and well; happily there was no need for any anxiety about *her*; and then I chaffed Mr Lorimer a little about his holiday making; and he was quite confused – the absurd old idiot! – and said he thought he had done enough hard work in his life to entitle him to a little rest and recreation in his old age. 'Oh, you must not talk about old age yet,' said Mrs Hamilton, smiling at him like a young flirt in her teens; and then she turned to me and explained that her old friend was so very kind to her and her dear child, taking them about and giving them so much enjoyment that they could not have had, being two lone women, but for him. I saw them several times afterwards, always the three together. They were at the races every day, and at the theatres every night. Fancy Mr Lorimer spending his time like that! And when we came away from town we left them there; they were driving about Collins-street in a very nice carriage, Mr Lorimer still in his new suit of clothes, at eleven o'clock in the morning. When I pointed them out to Fred, as we were going to the station, he made use of unparliamentary language. He began to wonder then, I expect, what Turkey carpets cost.

'As soon as we got back to Wattlebank, I determined to go and see Mary, and find out how much she knew. So I drove in to Abercorn the very next day; and there was the dear child, as busy as a bee, making gooseberry jam, with her sleeves turned up over her elbows. She was as happy as possible, and as ignorant of what her mother and sister were doing as a baby. She had just taken her jam off the fire, and she washed her hands and came and sat down with me, and we had some tea and a nice long talk. She said Nina had not been well, and her mother had suddenly decided to take her to Melbourne for a change. They had written to say they had arrived safely, and had not been heard of since. Meanwhile she (Mary) and Mr Butler were very happy and comfortable by themselves. She was making her uncle some shirts; she had done up the garden; she had helped Jane to take up all the carpets and thoroughly clean the house. Evidently she had scope for the gratification of her inordinate desire for work, and, therefore, was enjoying herself. So I went home, and waited to see what would turn up. And by and by Mrs Hamilton and Nina came back, and very soon there was an explosion. The impending marriage was announced, and Mary, they told me, was almost beside herself with indignation, and grief and rage. I was afraid to go near, until the storm had blown over; but one day I met her having one of her furious walks, and I took her up in the carriage and made her tell me all about it. Poor, dear child, I really was sorry for her! She seemed quite heartbroken. She was looking as if she had had a month's illness, and she burst out crying the moment I spoke to her. 'If it was anybody mother cared for, if it was a proper marriage, I wouldn't mind a bit,' she said. 'I would have liked mother to be happy in her own way – I would never have set myself against her marrying again. But Mr Lorimer! It is too shocking to think of her marrying him! She says it is for her children's sake; but why should she sacrifice herself in that horrible manner for us? It is not for me, she knows; it is for Nina. But Nina has all she wants, and by and bye she will marry herself and be well off – she is so pretty, she is sure to have husbands to choose from – if she will have a little patience. And I would work for them night and day, thankfully. Oh, Mrs Lepel, it is too dreadful that mother should let herself down to do such a thing as that!'

'However, Mrs Hamilton did it. And, having made up her mind to do it, she was wise and did it quickly. The old man came up, and they were married quite quietly, in Abercorn; and the bride and bridegroom, taking Nina with them, have gone back to Melbourne – where, Mrs Redwood says, Mrs Lorimer is buying furniture for her house at Kew, regardless of expense. Mary is left with her uncle – a very prudent arrangement. Her stepfather shakes in his shoes at the mention of her name; and her mother and sister would be seriously incommoded by her presence under their roof in these early days. Poor Mary! I have not seen her since the wedding. Fred went to the bank yesterday, and he says she looks like a tragedy queen. I am going to fetch her out for a few days, if she will leave her uncle; perhaps that will cheer her. They *do* say (but they say all sorts of preposterous things) that Mr Butler is paying attentions to the doctor's sister. There are indeed no fools like old fools. If he *should* marry again, like Mrs Hamilton, then what will become of Mary? Dear old boy, I think you shouldn't be away long.

'I have no more news to give you – not any, at least, that will interest you after this. Fred is writing to tell you about the horses and dogs and things, and I send you papers up to date. Take great care of yourself and come home soon, and don't forget any of my commissions. – Ever your loving sister, JENNY LEPEL.'

CHAPTER XIV

Seven Years After

Seven years after the event communicated by Mrs Lepel to her brother, when he was travelling in America and elsewhere, in a vain search after happiness, the Melbourne papers announced one morning that Mr Lorimer, of Lorimer and Lovett, was dead. 'On the 18th inst., at Dunchester House, Kew, George Leigh Lorimer, son of the late George Lorimer, Esq., of London, and great grandson of the late Major-General Leigh, of Leigh Stanton, Devonshire, England, aged 82,' was the imposing announcement penned by his disconsolate widow.

He survived his marriage with Mrs Hamilton for seven years – which was about four years longer than anyone had expected. At first, the change in his domestic circumstances rejuvenated him amazingly. He had really loved, as well as he could love anybody, the handsome Miss Butler of his youth, and had kept her memory green as a tender oasis in the desert of his narrow and sordid heart; and when, at the age of seventy-five, he made her his wife, and flattered himself that there was the same reciprocity of sentiment between them as there might have been thirty years before, he did so with the avowed intention of reaping in his old age the reward of all the toil and privation in which he had spent his life. So, in the first glow and intoxication of his little romance, he bought a big house, gave *carte blanche* for furniture and fittings, set up a carriage and staff of servants, and showed a spirit of liberality that was totally at variance with all his known habits and customs, and that was very grateful to the feelings of his wife and his step-daughter, who had hardly expected to begin their new career so favorably. For awhile, everything seemed to go well. Mrs Lorimer's fine establishment, her husband's reputed wealth, and her own clever management, speedily secured her a good place in that society which spells itself with a capital S, and which – wisely, perhaps, in a small community – does not pry too closely into the character and composition of a household possesed of these eminent qualifications. Pretty Nina, with her graceful manners and her charming taste in dress, carrying the aroma of Dunchester about with her, like scent on her pocket-handkerchief, wherever she went, was a host in herself – winning the favor of soft-hearted fathers of families as well as the ardent admiration of their sons. And Mr Lorimer, clothed by a fashionable tailor, and taught to give his arm to lady guests and not to eat with his knife and drink with his mouth full, performed the duties appointed to his position with wonderful credit and cheerfulness. But after awhile, the poor old man, shuffling about draughty entrance halls and corridors in attendance on his wife, caught a bad cold, and was laid up with a severe attack of bronchitis. And then his little romance came to an end; the semblance of a happy marriage crowning his old age, that he had imagined himself blest with, dissolved in thin air like the dream that it was. He was very ill and feeble, and his wife would not stay at home to take care of him. She contented herself with ordering his gruel and his beef tea, and when he grew worse she hired a nurse from the hospital. While he lay wheezing painfully on his bed, feeling too weak to lift his trembling old hand to his poor old grey head, she went about to parties, with her daughter, just as usual, enjoying herself even though he might be dying, as he said to Mr Lovett, when his partner – almost as old and grey as he – came one day to sit with him, and to tell him how the business was going on. 'Enjoying herself while I am dying, Lovett, and spending the money like water that I have toiled all these years to earn. I see how it is now! She doesn't care for me – she only cares for the money.'

He recovered from his illness, but only partially; a man on the verge of seventy-eight very seldom does recover entirely from a sharp attack of bronchitis. He left his room, and he discharged his nurse; but he remained weak and shaken, and he no longer frequented the haunts of fashion as he had done. Mrs Lorimer and Miss Hamilton – the latter, who was looked upon as something of an heiress, being at this time engaged to a rising young barrister – went to parties and entertained their friends, apparently without being in any need of his assistance; and he, when the days were fine, went to his office, which had resumed all its former charms, and when the weather was unfit for him to go out, shuffled mournfully about his big house, lamenting the expenditure of precious money, in which he no longer took any pleasure, and the terrible waste that he discovered in all directions.

And then Mary, who, hitherto, had only paid flying visits to her mother, at the rate of two in the year, came to live in Melbourne. Uncle Peter (who had not married the doctor's sister, nor thought of it, but had been supremely contented with his young housekeeper) was removed from the bank at Abercorn to a higher sphere in Gippsland; and Mrs Lorimer took the opportunity to recover her daughter, with a view to getting her 'settled' now that Nina was provided for. Mary went with the utmost reluctance. She adored her uncle; she loved Abercorn, where by this time everybody was her friend, and every child and every sick old man and woman looked up to her as a sort of guardian angel; she had choirs, and night schools, and sewing classes, and all sorts of thriving institutions depending on her as the corner-stone of their support; she was earning her own living, and making people happy; she was having just the homely, simple, useful life that her soul loved. However, being bidden to give this all up, and to make her home under Mr Lorimer's roof – that she might be present at her sister's wedding, and a comfort to her lonely mother when the pet child was gone – she obeyed, though it was a sore trial to her to transplant herself, and she had not been long in the Kew house before she discovered a new vocation. She was bewildered a little, at first, by the bustle and excitement that she was not used to – the constant shopping, and calling and receiving of guests, and the publicity of the life that her mother and sister led; but when this had worn off, she saw her place in the household, and established herself in it – she became the companion, caretaker and champion of the deposed head of the family, the poor 'old Jew pedlar,' whom once she had despised, but whose helpless condition appealed to her now as the helplessness of the ship baby, whose mother was too ill to look after it, had done in earlier days.

Many people – Mrs Lepel and Donald Macleod amongst the number – said that but for her the old man would never have lived to be 82. Certainly, if he had not enjoyed the happiness he had looked for in his wife, he tasted the joys of paternity before he died. Physically and morally, his youngest stepdaughter was the prop of his declining years. For twelve months or so after she came to Kew – and while her mother was much taken up with Nina, now Mrs Jennings, who lived close by, and was always in more or less delicate health – the tall young woman was constantly seen, when the mornings were bright, marching slowly up and down the quiet roads and about the public gardens, with the feeble old man clinging to her strong arm; or driving him, muffled in overcoats and comforters, in a little basket carriage, to and from his office in Flinders-lane. After that, he had a slight stroke of paralysis, and could walk no longer; and then she coddled him up at home, dragged him about the garden in a bath chair (as easily as if he had been a baby in a go-cart), and lightened his hours of fractious restlessness by adding up interminable accounts for him – which soothing occupation, intended to ease his mind of a constant fear that he was becoming insolvent and would leave the world a beggar, seemed to do him more good than anything. Then he had a second stroke, which deprived him of speech; and, when a nurse was hired, and he showed a violent dislike of her ministrations, and an evident desire to have no one but Mary by him, the girl insisted on taking the charge of him altogether; and for nearly two years – long, weary years, that stole some of the bloom from her sweet and comely face – she made herself a slave and prisoner that he might have all the comfort his pitiable state permitted. Her mother protested against the extravagance of such a sacrifice; but her excessive devotion consoled the wife, conscious of her own shortcomings, and she was permitted to sacrifice herself. Then, at last, the third stroke came, and the old man was taken; and when he was gone no one wept for him except his young nurse, to whom he had never been anything but a burden upon her hands.

As soon as he heard that Mr Lorimer was dead, Donald Macleod, who was at Bungil, set off to town, to see if there was anything he could do for Mrs Lorimer, as a friend of the family – to see, that is to say, if he could help or comfort Mary. Mary Hamilton was his beloved still, though he was just as far from winning her as he had ever been; the only difference was that as years went on, and she approached more and more to his ideal pattern woman, he loved her more and more. And he never lost an opportunity for serving her – or for seeing her – that came in his way.

He did not go immediately to Kew; he went to see Mr Lovett, who was supposed to know more than anybody of his late partner's affairs. Mr Lovett was not a communicative man, but he told his visitor a surprising piece of news. 'He has left a good bit,' said the old broker; 'nearly as many thousands as he was years old when he died. But he has not left it as they expect.'

'Hasn't he?' said Donald, rather alarmed. 'He made his will when he was married, did he not?'

'Yes; leaving everything to his wife. But he made another about three years ago, only he kept it dark, to save unpleasantness. Mrs Lorimer won't get much out of that, I fancy.'

'Why, you don't mean to say he's gone and endowed colleges and things?'

'You'll see tomorrow, Mr Macleod. The will is to be read tomorrow, and you'll see who has got the money. You'll say, as I do, that she deserves it.'

'Mary Hamilton!'

'I won't tell you. You'll see tomorrow.'

'If he has left it to the person who deserves it, he has certainly left it to Mary,' said Mary's lover, feeling a little stunned.

CHAPTER XV

A Streak of Light

He waited for a day, and then he went to see her, and to see what had happened.

Mr Lorimer was buried, and the blinds were all up again at the Kew house. There was a cheerful air about the white walls and the shining windows, and about the well-kept garden, now full of April roses, in that delicate freshness of such an autumn morning as hardly any country but Australia can show. There was no look of mourning anywhere about; certainly not in the face of the damsel who answered his ring at the door bell, and who informed him smilingly, in response to his inquiries, that Mrs Lorimer was pretty well, 'considering,' but that she was not at home.

'Not at home?'

'She is gone to see Mrs Jennings, Sir. Mrs Jennings was very much cut up about poor mother's will yesterday, and the servant came to say she had been very ill all night. So missus went at once, and said she might not be back till evening.'

'And Miss Hamilton?'

'Miss Hamilton is at home, sir.'

'Ask her if I may see her for a few minutes, will you. Stay – where is she?'

'In the little breakfastroom, sir.'

'I'll come in,' said Macleod, walking into the hall coolly. 'She expects me, I think; I will announce myself.'

He crossed the tesselated floor with a ringing stride, marched up a little passage and tapped at a closed door.

'Come in,' responded a clear voice within.

He opened the door into a cheerful sittingroom, where the morning air blew in through open windows, and a bright fire blazed upon the hearth; and there he found his sweetheart, sitting idly, in the old Cleopatra attitude, with her elbow on the back of the chair and her head leaning in her hand, gazing dreamily into the fire – resting herself, at last, after many weary days and sleepless nights. He paused on the threshold for a moment to look at her. She had changed a good deal – as who does not? – in seven years; but every change, in his estimation, had been for the better. In figure she was magnificent. It was delightful to him to rest his eyes, vexed with the daily sight of narrow shoulders and pinched waists, and limbs constrained and distorted to suit the exigencies of fashionable costume, upon the full and sweeping lines of her perfect shape, never broken by frills and frivolous trimmings, and never spoiled by steel or whalebone. Some day, probably, she would be one of those enormous women who have a difficulty in getting up and downstairs, and who break the springs of their husband's buggies; but now, between twenty-nine and thirty, she was a Venus of Milo, with large, round arms, perfect – the rare instance that her lover was acquainted with, of a nineteenth century female figure, modelled 'after the antiques,' after nature's original and flawless pattern. Her face too, which had never claimed any relation to the Greek type, was changed and ennobled by the experience of seven years of earnest, vigorous life. It was no longer the face of an impulsive girl, ready to talk about her sweetheart to the first sympathetic listener; there was a grave response and dignity about the frank eyes and large, firm mouth – an expression that indicated a strong and steadfast nature, not subject to the winds and waves of passion and caprice.

After the slight pause, she turned her head a little, and saw her lover in the doorway. 'Don!' she exclaimed, jumping up. 'I did not know it was you. I am so glad! I have been wishing so much that you would come.'

He advanced a few steps into the room, and she went to meet him. They were a tall and noble pair, when they stood together. He too had altered in seven years; his face had a slight furrow here and there, and his beard was grizzled. He was broader and squarer, and evidently rode a stone or two heavier than he used to do when his mare Lapwing carried him to and from Abercorn so often. He was going to be stout, perhaps obese, in his old age, as well as she; but to-day he looked, to all but the veriest schoolgirl eyes – certainly in the eyes of his love, to whom he was the first and best of friends, and only just short of being the first and dearest of men – vigorous, well built, powerful, a strong man in his prime, to whom anything weak might trust for protection – after all, the essential charm and beauty of manhood, for lack of which nothing can compensate.

'And you are all alone?' he said. 'I did not expect that. May I stop a little while and talk to you?'

'Do,' she said, sitting down in her chair by the fireside, and pointing to another near her. 'It is just what I am wanting.'

He did not take a seat immediately; he put an elbow on the mantelpiece, and stood on the hearthrug looking down at her. 'Is it true,' he said, 'that you are to have all that old fellow's money, Mary?'

'Yes,' she answered quietly, without lifting her eyes. 'It is between £70,000 and £80,000, and he has left it to me – all except £600 a year for mother during her life, and a few legacies to servants.'

'You take it very coolly,' he said; 'did you know he was going to do it?'

'Certainly I didn't, Don; it was a tremendous surprise to me, as well as to poor mother and Nina. He used to say sometimes that I was good to him, and that I should be rewarded for it; but I had no idea that he meant this. I thought, as everybody else did, that he had settled his affairs when he married. But I have got over the shock of it now,' she added, gently. 'I have

realised what it all means. But I did want very much to see you.
It is such an immense fortune for a single woman; I want to know
if you think what I have made up my mind to do about it is right.'
'What have you made up your mind to do? Not to give it all
to your mother and Nina, I hope. It would be just like you.'
'Now, Don, would it be like me?' she inquired, looking up at
him with a smile. 'You think I am always ready to do wild things
on the impulse of the moment, as I used to be. You forget how
old I am getting.'
'Oh, do I? I should have to forget my own grey hairs, then.
But, seriously, have you given it away?'
'Not a penny of it.'
'I am glad to hear it. But now you must tell me why you *haven't*
done that,' he said, seating himself beside her; 'for I am sure it
must have been a terrible temptation to you.'
'Well,' she began, leaning her head back and folding her hands
on her knee, 'I was tempted, just at first. Mother was so very,
very angry; and Nina and her husband, with three little children
to provide for, were so terribly disappointed – I could hardly bear
it. But by and bye, when they saw how sorry I was for them,
Mother said she knew that I would not allow such an iniquitous
will to stand – that, if poor Mr Lorimer had wronged them, as
she said he had, I would rectify the wrong. And she proposed
to me to divide the money in three equal parts.'
'And you wouldn't? Well, Mary, if anyone had asked me to
bet on it, I would have staked all I am worth that you'd have
jumped at the chance of dividing it.'
'Do you think I am selfish to keep the whole? All the others
think I am a monster of selfishness.'
'My dear, I know you better than they do. But still I can't understand what made you refuse them. Tell me.'
'Well, it came to me like a sort of instinct that I ought not to
do it, even before I had taken time to think it over. But the more
I thought of it the more I felt sure it would be wrong. In the first
place, my poor old man, though he is dead, has his rights; he
wished me to have charge of his money, and the spending of it.
I hardly look upon it as my own to give away outright like that;
and it would not do mother or Nina any good. Nina's husband
is clever, and works hard, and if he goes on working some day
he will be a judge, perhaps; at any rate, he will live the life a
man ought to lead. But if he had twenty or thirty thousand

pounds, he would grow idle and useless, and his life would be spoiled. They are very well off as they are; he has a comfortable income, and their home is nice; and of course I will never let them be troubled by any real want of money. And mother – mother will always live here, and will have no expenses. She will have every comfort, she knows. And, Don, I hope it isn't an undutiful thing to say, but I think I can use my poor old man's money to better purpose than she would do.'

'I have no doubt of that,' said Mr Macleod.

'I should like him really to be rewarded, as far as I could reward him, for the sacrifice he made in getting it. Do you know what I mean? – to do him good, doing good with the money which, up to the present, has been of so little use in the world, as money ought to be – to make his barren labors fruitful, so that his poor life, spent in that sordid way, should not be altogether spent in vain, you know?'

'Yes, I know,' assented her companion, a little grimly. 'I see what you are after now. You are going to squander a magnificent property in pauperising the whole place and encouraging vice and improvidence. I thought it wouldn't be you if you didn't do something of that sort.'

'No, I am not,' she said, smiling. 'You know I don't mean to do that.'

'You don't *mean* to do it, but that's what the generosity and self-sacrifice of you charitable women come to. You don't know anything of political economy; your tender hearts are touched, and you go spending yourselves and your money on a lot of thankless imposters, who only make fun of you behind your back.'

'I am not going to do that, Don.'

'Aren't you going to give your money to the poor?'

'No; not directly.'

'You are going to spend it in some philanthropical, regenerating schemes for the amelioration of the sorrows of your fellow creatures.'

She looked at him with grave amusement. 'I have no schemes,' she said; 'but I am going to do what I can. I'll not encourage pauperism, if I know it, but I will look for poor women, like Mrs Dubois, and for little children who are neglected and miserable, and when I find them I will help them. I have some notion of political economy, though you don't think it, and I dare say I shall often be imposed upon and cheated. I don't care. Nothing can explain away the terrible responsibility that we have, who roll in luxury, for the wretchedness and crimes of those who have not enough to eat, If I did not do something – if I did not do what I could – I should never know what it was to sleep in peace.'

'My dear, you were born before your time. The golden age is a long way off yet.'

'I know it is, Don. But some day I think it will come. Every hundred years shows a difference. And we may as well help it to come as soon as possible.'

He was silent for a few minutes, looking in the fire; and she rose softly, and went out to give some order to a servant. When she came in again, he was standing with his back to the chimney-piece, waiting for her; and she walked up to him and laid her hand on his arm.

'Don,' she said, 'I have not told you everything. There is something else I am going to do – not for others, for myself.'

'What is that?' he asked, patting his hand on hers.

'I don't know how to tell you, yet I think you will not be surprised, and I will not keep you in the dark. I am going to let Captain Armstrong know.'

'What? – that you are rich? Good heavens! Mary, you are indeed mad about that fellow. Do you mean to say you will actually entice him to come and marry you for your money, when he has never made a sign of wanting you for yourself – and after ten years?'

'It was when I was a poor girl – poor, and dressed commonly, and with no attraction to equal those of the women he was used to meeting – that he singled me out,' she said, with a little suppressed passion in the wavering intonations of her voice, and a flood of blushes all over her face. 'And officers in the army – they are nearly always poor, too, and cannot afford to marry if they would. Perhaps he has been too poor. I am not going to send him a message, of course; I am only going to write to an old friend of mine who is in India, and who knows him, and knows that he is acquainted with me. She will tell him – that is all. But I would not do it without letting you know first.'

'He isn't married yet?'

'No. He is at Bangalore. He has been fighting in Afghanistan. He is a major now. Oh Don,' she broke out, suddenly, touching his coat sleeve with her face for a moment, 'You have been more good to me than any man ever was to any woman in this world, and I am always making you suffer for it!' He was silent for a moment, and then he took her in his arms and kissed her. 'My love, you can't help it - no more can I,' he said.

And soon after that he went away with a heavy heart, not seeing that a streak of light had dawned in the horizon of his future at last.

CHAPTER XVI

Major Armstrong

Mary Hamilton naturally became an important personage. Society suddenly awoke to a full perception of her charms, physical and otherwise, and wondered how it was that so fine a creature had been hidden in obscurity for so long. People all began to see that her face, though irregular, was full of character and breeding; that her figure was faultless; that her manners were reposeful and dignified; that her taste in dress, though peculiar, was refined, the men being unanimous in their admiration of it. She bore herself in company with a kind of majestic serenity that might have been considered 'airs' in a poor woman, however large or tall, but which in a wealthy person of her proportions was in the highest degree proper and charming. Nevertheless, society lamented that she was 'odd,' and wished very much that she had been more like other people.

She lived in the Kew house with her mother, who, naturally, governed the establishment as before. Mrs Lorimer, indeed, always assumed a right to the property which had passed out of her hands. That Mary had legal possession of it, by accident of an old man's imbecility, did not in the least affect the fact that she was morally entitled to it - as she was in the habit of remarking frequently. So she kept house in a lavish manner, much more to the advantage of Mrs Jennings than of its real mistress; she received and entertained, as of old, with Nina's more than ever indispensable assistance; and whenever the family carriage was seen dashing about the streets and suburbs, it was sure to contain the mother and the eldest daughter, and, perhaps, a grandchild or two, and seldom or never the person to whom it, and everything appertaining to it, belonged.

Mary's home life was anything but happy in those days. She was regarded by her family as 'a monster of selfishness,' because she would not allow them to set aside her stepfather's will; and her mother and sister sympathising in each other's pecuniary misfortunes, shut her out of their confidence and of all intercourse with them, except just so much as was required for the maintenance of domestic and social decency. Mrs Lorimer, to do her justice, was more resentful of her husband's treatment of her on her pet child's behalf than on her own; and Nina, pitying herself much more than anybody else, embittered the maternal heart with her silent air of patient suffering, her pathetic acceptance of injustice and ill-usage against the fortunate sister, who had, as she maliciously hinted in her soft voice, 'secured everything.' Mary bore it very meekly and sweetly, though she by no means allowed herself to be crushed by it. She was of a nature too large and generous to take account of petty annoyances, as some irritable small souls must do; and little personal indignities, which most of us feel so hard to bear, such as she had daily, as mistress of the house, to put up with, did not in themselves cause her the slightest pang of mortification. She was hurt to the heart that she was so wholly misunderstood, but she was not in the least hurt that she was superseded in her authority over her own house and servants. That was nothing (and where she did value her authority, she was quite able to maintain it, regardless of unpleasant circumstances). She walked about town, while others drove in her carriage, wearing her plain and simple dresses as she had always done, only that now they were better made and of finer material; and wearing ever, in face and mien, the expression of her faith that life was too solemn and important to be muddled away in trifles. With her dim but confident foresight of a golden age afar off, and her sense of what tremendous and appalling changes and reformations had to be fought through to reach it, her sense, above all things, of her personal responsibility as a factor in the great schemes that were to make the world better – she was not exactly what a member of good society was expected to be, and she certainly, with all her horror and avoidance of the appearance of philanthropical eccentricity, laid herself open to the charge of being 'odd.'

'And have you spent all your money yet?' Mr Macleod inquired, when one day he met her coming from the children's hospital, with a suspicious redness about her eyes.

'I would give every penny of it away this moment,' she replied passionately, 'if I could keep the little ones from the suffering and trouble that poverty brings on them – them, who have never deserved to suffer!'

'You are always breaking your heart over the children, Mary.'

'Yes, Don. How can I help it?'

'Has it ever occured to you,' he asked, after a pause, when they were walking along the pavement, side by side – observed with much curiosity from the cabs and carriages in the road – 'has it ever occurred to you, Mary, that a certain person, if he turns up, will probably want to spend your money in quite a different way?'

'Yes,' she said.

'And would you, with your peculiar views about the responsibilities of wealth, think it right to marry a man who might squander it, so that it would do nobody any good?' He did not openly remind her, but he intended her to remember that he had offered to let her do what she wished with it if she would marry him.

'We cannot look so far as that,' she replied, after a pause. 'We can only do what is in itself right – right for everybody all round – and take the consequences. And to me it seems right, above all things, that people who love each other should marry, no matter what comes of it.'

'Well,' he said, sighing, 'your code of morals has, at any rate, the merit of simplicity.'

'It is what I *feel*,' she insisted, gently.

'And have you heard from India yet?' he inquired, after a moment's gloomy silence. 'The mail is in to-day.'

'Not yet,' she replied. 'And, Don, I don't know that I expect to hear very much. Ten years – . I think sometimes I have forgotten what an immense long time it is.'

She shook hands with him presently at the railway station, and they parted to go their respective ways to lunch. It seemed to him that she was unusually dispirited, and he wished more fervently than he had ever done – and he had wished it pretty often – that the man who had spoiled her life for half-an-hour's amusement had been shot in Abyssinia, or Afghanistan, or somewhere where he had been within reach of legal bullets.

But, half an hour later, Mary felt that her harvest time, for which she had waited so many years, had come. She was alone in her big diningroom, sitting with untasted dishes before her. Like Mandle – or was it Postlethwaite? – with his lily, she held

a letter in her hand, which supplied nourishment enough even
for that midday meal to which she was accustomed to bring a
particularly healthy appetite. Her eyes glistened, her face was
flushed, her large white hands trembled, with a shock of excitement such as seldom disturbed her strong and steadfast
organisation. Of course, the letter was from India. It was from
the 'friend' whom she had mentioned to Mr Macleod. No other
than the Miss Morris who had accompanied her to the memorable Dunchester ball, and who a year or two thereafter (for which
reason Mary had maintained with her a constant correspondence)
had married a cousin in the Indian civil service, whose professional duties had brought him at last into contact with Captain
Armstrong's regiment. This lady, who had heard at the time all
about the 'flirtation,' as it was called, between the military man
of the world and the unsophisticated girl with whom he danced
three times at her first ball; and who, being herself a matron,
took an intense interest in the prospective fate of all single women
of her acquaintance, had faithfully fulfilled her friend's unex-
pressed injunction – as Mary was sure she would if only she were
favored with an opportunity.

'I saw Major Armstrong soon after I received your letter,' wrote
Miss Morris that was, 'and I told him the astonishing news about
your great fortune. He was deeply interested. He said he remembered you perfectly. "I had good reason to remember her," he
said, looking at me rather strangely, as if he wanted to say more.
And then he asked if you were married yet; and when I told him
"No" he said he wondered at that, for that you were such a very
charming and attractive young lady. We talked a good deal about
you, and he reminded me of your beautiful waltzing, and said
you had the prettiest trimmings on your dress (he meant the ivy
leaves) that he ever saw. He seemed to be thinking it all over
a great deal; and when he went away he forgot to say good-bye
to me until he was outside, and came back to apologise. A day
or two afterwards, just as I was beginning to write this, he came
to call quite early, and it was on purpose to give me a message
for you. "If you are writing to Miss Hamilton this mail," he said,
"will you tell her that I wished her to know how much I rejoiced,
as an old friend, in her good fortune, which I am sure no one
deserves more – that I am deeply grateful to her for doing me
the honor to remember me so well after all these years – and that
perhaps I may have the pleasure of thanking and congratulating

her myself very shortly." And when I asked him what he meant by that, he explained that his leave was due, and that he had been thinking of taking a run to Melbourne and seeing the exhibition. I told him I had heard he was going to England for his leave, but he said he had changed his plans on account of the exhibition. I asked him when he thought of going, and he said in about a month or two; but last night he sent round to tell me that he was going to leave the station in two days, and that he would sail for Melbourne by the next mail. So, my dear Mary, you will see your old admirer just a fortnight after you get this letter. He said I was to remind you that he told you at Dunchester he should come to Australia some day, and he says he would have done it long ago if he had had the chance. He is dreadfully afraid you will find him so altered from what you remember him, but I told him, of course, that he would be no more altered than you. And, my dear, he is just as handsome as ever he was, whatever he may think. All the ladies say he is the handsomest man in Bangalore, just as they said he was the handsomest at Dunchester that night of the ball. He is neither stout nor grey nor bald; but, indeed, why should he be? He is but a young man. The only difference you will see is that he is browner, and that he has a sword-cut across his temple that he got from some of those wretched Afghans. Perhaps his moustache is not quite so golden and silky, but it is a lovely moustache still.'

All that night Mary Hamilton lay awake in her bed, tossing restlessly – too deeply stirred and too happy to sleep – weighing all these precious sentences, and counting the minutest grains of meaning that could possibly be extracted from them. The whole description of him, and of his conduct towards herself, given by her friend, harmonised perfectly with her preconceived ideas of his character – only now he had the prestige and the scars of gallant battle to ennoble him in her imagination. How delicate was his message of congratulation; how gracefully he acknowledged the 'honour' to himself of her remembrance of him. He must have remembered her too, despite his long silence and absence, to recall so accurately the very trimmings of her dress. He remembered how well she waltzed – ah, that delicious waltz! He had 'good reason' to remember her, he had said; and he was coming to her now, not because she was rich, but because he had never had the chance before. She saw him again, in his stall in the cathedral, with the light shining up into his face – saw him in the Dunchester ballroom, looking across at her, as she stood opposite to him in the Lancers, with Mr Greville, her youthful first partner. She thought of the little vestibule, with the big window, and the moon shining in; and how he would have kissed her there, and she would not let him. Were all these visions, that had mocked and tantalised her, day and night, for the ten best years of her life, going to become living realities at last? With such possibilities to think of, it was not likely that she could sleep.

In a little while Mr Macleod heard what had happened, and he immediately made arrangements to stay in town until the fortnight was up. And two days after the arrival of the mail steamer he wrote to Mrs Lepel, who had found the name of Major Armstrong in the list of passengers from Bombay, and who was in a fever of excitement at Wattlebank, as follows:—

'I have seen that fellow, Jenny, and I don't think he is much good.'

CHAPTER XVII

Realisation

Mr Jennings, representing his mother-in-law and the family – who, in their anxiety to do honor to an imperial officer of distinguished rank and reputation, and a friend of Lord Chester's, smothered any anxieties they might have had on behalf of Mary's fortune – was sent to call upon Major Armstrong as soon as he arrived; and the young barrister, who was an amiable, good fellow – even to Mary, when left to his own devices – returned from his expedition, apparently delighted with his new acquaintance.

'A splendid man,' he said, enthusiastically. 'You'll like him awfully. No end of a swell, I can tell you, and yet not a bit stuck up. He chatted away to me as if he had known me for years, and said what a pleasant welcome it gave him our hunting him up so soon. He'll have plenty of people after him, you'll see – a fellow like that. He is as handsome as he can be, and he's got that Afghan wound that will make all the women admire him fifty times more than they would have done. And that he is every inch a born gentleman anybody can see.'

Mr Macleod, who called upon the distinguished stranger subsequently, came, as we know, to quite another conclusion.

Mary did not see him for a few days; and when they met at last, it was not exactly in a crowd, but it was with several pairs of keen and curious eyes upon them. Mrs Lorimer thought it proper to give a dinner party as being a suitable way of receiving him herself, and of introducing him (in the character of her and Lord Chester's mutual friend) to Melbourne society, and it was on this occasion, when all the guests were assembled, Mr Macleod amongst the number, that the supreme moment arrived. Major Armstrong, tall, spare, athletic and soldierly, with a well-bred, straight-nosed, handsome face, was standing on the hearth-rug in a lordly attitude, but chatting with sprightly ease to Nina, who gratefully reclined on an ottoman in front of him, when Mary, who had lingered in her room, struggling until the last moment for her customary composure, opened the door noiselessly and came in. She was looking her best, in at least one person's estimation, with an unwonted fire in the depths of her eyes, and a flush of excitement in her strongly expressive face. She had dressed herself much more richly than she had ever done before, though she was all in black, and had not discarded her characteristic style; and she had left her magnificent neck and arms, which were her most striking attractions, so slightly veiled with cobweb lace that the perfection of their shape and whiteness was sufficiently apparent. She had evidently intended that her beloved should see her to the very best advantage.

But when he looked at her, Mr Macleod, who was watching him, did not like his look. There was no disappointment in it, as there reasonably might have been – for was not she yet turned thirty, and (in the estimation of young matrons like Nina) an old maid? He had eyes to see and appreciate the noble physical development of the woman whose girlhood had charmed him with the promise of it, and he was himself past the age for the worship of bread-and-butter misses. But there was a certain cool and watchful criticism, an entire absence of anything like emotion or embarrassment, in the way he glanced across the room at her as she entered, which enraged the jealous lover whose pulses throbbed at the mere sound of her distant footstep. 'I thought as much,' he said to himself bitterly. 'He is no more in love with her than she is with me. He has only come for her money.' For the briefest instant, Mary, too, did not like his look. She saw, with a swelling heart, that he was as splendidly handsome as she had ever imagined him – more handsome, with his bronzed cheeks and his scarred temple, than he had been in his younger and more dandy days; and that his eyes had a welcome for her, as the eyes of King Ahasuerus for Esther when she 'obtained grace and favor in his sight.' Yet there was something – what, she did not understand – that was more, or less, than she had expected, a subtle change in him that chilled her vaguely with the sense that she had not fully known him. It was but for a moment, but it was enough to cool her excitement and calm her nerves for the ordeal upon which she entered when she opened the drawingroom door.

'How do you do?' he said, striding forward to meet her with an ardent greeting in voice and gesture. 'I am so glad to see you again.'

She gave her hand silently, too much moved to speak. The company exchanged significant glances, and opened an irrelevant conversation amongst themselves.

'What a long time it is, isn't it?' he went on, holding her hand, and looking down smilingly. 'You must have thought I was never going to redeem my promise to come to Australia. Had you not quite given me up?'

'Almost,' she said, under her breath.

'It was so good of you not to forget me altogether. And you are looking so well. I am so glad to see you looking so well! I have often thought about you – though you didn't know it – since that night at Dunchester, when we had those charming waltzes together.'

They were sauntering towards the watchful circle about the hearthrug, who were pretending not to watch them; and when he made that early and public reference to the sacred secret that should have been for ever between themselves, all her blood seemed to rush into her face, and, dying as quickly, left her looking white and shocked. She did not know what had happened; but Donald Macleod, seeing it all, with every sense sharpened, began to comprehend – began to see the streak of light which had dawned in his own horizon.

After the first minute or two, she recovered her outward serenity and self-possession. She exchanged a few conventional ideas with Major Armstrong respecting his health, his voyage, his furlough, and the exhibition he was supposed to have come to see, looking at his shirt-front while he looked very steadily at her face; she greeted her other guests at the same time, and made inquiries of Nina after the welfare of nephews and nieces.

Then she stood on the hearthrug, quietly, but drawing her breath a little quickly, and looking round with a vague, dazed air.

'Sit down, won't you,' said Donald Macleod in an undertone. She glanced at him a moment, wistfully, and took the chair he placed for her in silence. The actions of both were trifling, but significant. During dinner, though he did not sit beside her, Major Armstrong paid a particular attention to his younger hostess – delicately, in that he did it in a polished and graceful manner, but, in Mr Macleod's opinion, too obviously to the public company for good taste. He turned to her for her opinion upon every subject that was started; and she never spoke that he did not immediately assume a deferential, listening attitude. His eyes wandered towards her incessantly, watching her keenly when she was not looking at him, and looking what Nina described as 'unutterable things' when she was – looking, at any rate, more tenderly, and more confidently, than his rival thought he ought to have done, under the circumstances, highly favored and privileged though he was.

As soon, however, as the diningroom door closed upon the ladies he laid aside his charming manners as if putting off his dress coat. There was no father of the family to propitiate – only men as young and younger than himself, and he took his ease accordingly. He criticised the wine freely, and called some of it 'beastly stuff,' remarking that Miss Hamilton's taste in that direction sadly wanted cultivating – which, however, did not prevent him from drinking a great deal of it. He entertained his companions with highly-flavored anecdotes bearing upon Indian domestic life and social matters generally, embellishing the conversation with many barbaric adjectives. He smoked his cigarette at leisure, while the younger bachelors fidgeted to be going, with his chair tilted on its hind legs, and one knee above the level of the table. Mr Jennings, and most of Mr Jennings's friends, voted him a fine fellow and capital company; but Donald Macleod, sitting a little apart, looking on, and listening, was immensely disgusted.

When at last they returned to the drawingroom, Major Armstrong was as polished and graceful as soldier and gentleman need be – only rather more brilliant in conversation and impressive in his attention to Mary than he had shown himself before dinner. He had not been many minutes in the room before he sought her out, where she sat on a retired sofa, and took a seat beside her; and the jealous eyes that watched them then found them a curious study. The man had flung himself into an easy posture, had crossed his long legs and rested his elbow on a cushion close to hers, and by-and-by he fingered, with a sort of subtle familiar caress, a ribbon of her gown that touched his knee. The girl, at first flushed and fluttered, grew, by slow degrees, but steadily, quiet and grave and pale; and she seemed to stiffen imperfectly into majestic and rigid attitudes. Presently she rose hastily – apparently to her companion's annoyance and surprise – and walked across the room towards a group of unattended matrons. On her way Mr Macleod intercepted her; and she stopped and looked up at him, wistfully, absently, inquiringly, with a new and tragic sadness in her eyes.

'Do you mind if I say good night, Mary?' he said coldly. 'I have some business to see after to-night, and I am going home by the early train.'

'Are you going back to-morrow?' she asked hastily.

'I must. I have stayed down here too long already. But I thought I should like to see you happy before I left.'

She looked at him with a strange smile that had the same effect on him as tears. 'Thank you,' she said, gently. 'Good night. I am sorry you are going.'

And so she was – much more sorry than she knew, or he either. She passed on hurriedly, with close shut mouth and a lump in her throat, longing for night to come, that she might sleep in peace. And he slipped out of the room and down the stairs, as strongly and strangely stirred as she, saying to himself, half in anger, half in triumph, 'She is disappointed already. He is not the man she expected to see.'

CHAPTER XVIII

The Touch of a Vanished Hand

Donald Macleod went home to Bungil, and Major Armstrong had the field to himself.

It was more than a week before Mary Hamilton and her beloved had an opportunity for anything like confidential intercourse. Mrs Lorimer and Mrs Jennings were delighted with their new visitor, who – as they had confidently anticipated – became one of the chief ornaments of Melbourne society, which was entertaining a good many distinguished strangers just now, and whose intimacy with their family was very advantageous to themselves; but they concluded, after some discussion, that Mary was not to be encouraged to suppose that he had come to Australia to see her. They could not bring themselves to keep so desirable an acquaintance at arm's length; at the same time, they agreed that it would be highly injudicious to allow Mary, who was very happy as she was, to receive attentions from him, or from any other man, which might lead to matrimony, and to the taking of her fortune 'out of the family.' So, when Major Armstrong paid his calls, he was entertained and made much of by the married ladies of the house – as, indeed, was only proper; and the wealthy mistress of it talked to him about the weather when she happened to have a chance to get in a word. As his leave was limited – which the mother and sister knew quite as well as he – this system of intercourse did not commend itself to Major Armstrong. Nor, if the truth must be told, did it commend itself to Mary. And the man, who had a calm conviction that the ground was firm beneath his feet, took a short and ready way to extricate them both from their embarrassments. He came to play tennis one afternoon, a select party having been asked to meet him, and when he went away he slipped a note into Mary's hand. She was standing a little apart, and he was able to do it unperceived by the company around them; but if all the world had witnessed the action she could not have dyed herself in deeper blushes, or looked more shocked and startled.

'What a child she is still,' he reflected, as he walked towards the railway station. 'It can't be that she has lived to her age and never had a love-letter on the sly before – a girl so ready to be made love to! Yet she looked as innocent as if she had never heard of such things.'

Mary, when he was gone, ran upstairs to dress for dinner half an hour before the time, and locked herself in to read her letter. It was a closely written half-sheet of notepaper, folded lengthwise twice, and twisted into a knot, and it had no address on the outside of it. She did not know why she experienced a pang of regret that it had not had a whole sheet given to it, and been put into an envelope and conveyed to her in the ordinary way, through the post office; but she did experience that pang, very distinctly. The pleasure – which, though not unmixed, was very great – of having a written communication from her hero and idol, whose 'R.R.A.' in an old ball programme had been her only tangible memento of him – or of any man – for ten or eleven of the best years of her life, was curiously counteracted by the mode in which she had received it – curiously, considering that the mere departure from conventional usage was not the thing to offend her. The contents of his letter were as follows: –

'Dear Miss Hamilton, – I am very anxious to see you alone. I can get no opportunity to speak to you in these family visits, and I have much to say that I am impatient for you to hear. Is it too much to ask you to come out early tomorrow, and meet me at the exhibition before the place is crowded? Say at a quarter-past ten, under the dome, or, as that would be rather public, in the picture gallery. I will be waiting for you near Colin Hunter's Salmon Fishers, and I do not think you will disappoint me – Yours always, R.R.A.

The next morning, looking pale, grave and restless, and much as if she had not been to bed, Miss Hamilton took an early breakfast, and sallied out on foot before her mother came downstairs. She walked through the garden – her garden – in the fresh sunshine of an October morning, with a deliberate step and her head poised proudly as if defying the world and Mrs Grundy to accuse her of clandestine proceedings. She wore a simple, short dress of dark-blue linen, made (as she was very careful now to have all her garments made) to fit her superb shape exquisitely, and a little creamy Indian muslin round her neck, and round her close straw hat; no frills, no ornaments, no mantle over her shoulders. She looked, to the eyes of the multitude of men crowding the platform of the railway station, on their way citywards to business, the picture and pattern of a modest and noble woman, though perhaps few of them formulated the idea.

She took her place amongst these men in a well-filled carriage – an unprotected maiden lady, singularly becoming that undignified position – serene in her majestic consciousness of being perfectly able to take care of herself; and on reaching Melbourne, she streamed away with the crowd into the crowded streets, walking in almost a straight line along the pavement, amongst the hurrying men and youths, carrying her parasol over her shoulder, to shade her stately head, with the air of a princess.

She did not want to keep her lover waiting for her, and did not mind, in her anxiety to avoid that, running the risk of reaching the Salmon Fishers before him. Her pride did not happen to lie in things of that sort. Nor did it lie in a contempt for omnibuses, one of which she hailed as it passed her, when half-way to her destination.

This plebeian but convenient vehicle deposited her at the gates of the Exhibition as the town clocks were striking ten; and it did not occur to her to hide herself amongst Worcester china and Doulton pottery until Major Armstrong had come in and gone to keep his tryst. She gave up her parasol, and ascended at once to the picture gallery, where she took her place before Colin Hunter's picture, standing still to look at it with eyes that were too full of dreams and visions to comprehend half its beauty. There she stood, ticking off the passing moments with her loud-beating heart, for at least half an hour, wondering – with no sense of personal affront, and a little alarm lest anything had 'happened' to him – why he kept her so long waiting for him, who should have been waiting for her.

Then she saw him striding hastily towards her. He was looking exceedingly handsome, even at a distance too far for eyes less sharpened than hers to recognise his features; and she was vulnerable to that potent charm, like the rest of her sex. In his height and his soldierly carriage, in his dress, in his generally distinguished air, he was, she said to herself – as she had said the night when she first saw him towering up in his cathedral stall, with the 'dim, religious light' irradiating his face – a man apart from other men, a king amongst common mortals, and her heart swelled with pride and welcome as he approached.

'Oh, how sorry I am – how glad I am!' he began breathlessly, holding his hat in one hand and her hand in the other.

'Both at once?' she said, gently, with a self-possession that belied her throbbing heart.

'So glad you have come, and so sorry not to have been here first. It was an accident. I hope you will forgive me. You do forgive me; don't you?'

'Of course,' she said hastily, 'we can't help accidents. I came here because you wished me to come, Major Armstrong, but – but why did you not ask me yesterday to give you an interview at home? I could have done that very well.'

'I wanted you away from your people – I wanted you to myself,' he replied, looking down at her with ardent significance in his by no means bashful eyes. 'I wanted to get you right away from everybody. You know, you don't want to ask. I wish to goodness I *could* get you right away from everybody,' he added sharply, glaring at some inoffensive country folks who were strolling by, as if they hadn't just as good a right to pay an early visit to the pictures as he. 'Come into the German court, won't you? It is quiet and comfortable there, and there are those nice seats, where we can sit down.'

'Don't you want to look at some of these pictures while you are here?' she inquired, in a cool, level voice, but with a burning color in her face. 'Have you noticed how queerly this one is painted – all thick and ridgy, as if the paint had been put on, like mortar, with a trowel? And yet how beautiful the effect is at a little distance. Stand back here, and you will see how deliciously breezy that Loch Fyne looks, and what a delicate distance ever so far off it has.'

'Oh, yes; but I don't want to look at pictures. I want to look at you. Come into the German court, won't you? I want to sit down on one of those cosy lounges and have a long talk about old times.'

After a moment's hesitation, she turned, with a smile, and they walked together to the German court, the most truly comfortable nook that was to be found within exhibition precincts; and they sat down side by side on a restful semi-circular ottoman, with a well-cushioned back, Major Armstrong reclining sideways that he might study the form and features of his companion at his leisure.

'You ought to be modelled,' he remarked presently, after a slightly embarrassed pause. 'Do you know you have a splendid figure.'

'Yes, I know I have,' she said simply, looking round at him with a pleased smile. 'It is my only beauty, and therefore I appreciate it.'

'Your only beauty – nonsense! It is by no means your only one, but it is your most striking one, I think. It was your figure that struck me first at Dunchester that night.'

'Was it?' There was, to sensitive ears (not to Major Armstrong's), a faint accent of disappointment in her voice.

'I remember seeing you come into the room, looking so tall beside the other people of your party. I had Lady Craven on my arm, and she noticed you too. "Who is that tall girl," she said, "in the white dress, with the holly berries in her hair?"'

'I had no holly berries,' interposed Mary quickly; 'and nothing in my hair. 'I wore ivy leaves on my dress.'

'I mean ivy leaves. "Who is that girl in white, with the ivy leaves?" she said. "What a fine creature she is; and what a splendid woman she will be when she is a few years older." And so you are,' he added impressively.

'It was very kind of Lady Craven,' said Mary, still a little chilled.

'She was a fine woman, too. Do you remember her? She was awfully pretty. Always had a whole string of lovers after her. A fellow had to make a regular fight to get hold of her at all. A distracting little flirt she was – but no wonder, considering the sort of husband she had. Did you ever see Craven? He *was* such a dreadful little beast.'

'I never saw him that I know of. I did not go to Dunchester in the regular way. That night – that night of the ball – was the only time I ever was there,' said Mary, looking a little stiff and grave.

'Ah, that was a jolly time we had that night; wasn't it? Didn't you enjoy yourself that night, Mary? I know you did. You don't mind my calling you "Mary," do you?' he added, touching her smooth shoulder with the tips of his fingers. 'It is not as if we were strangers, you know.'

She did not answer for a moment, and somehow – strange as it may appear – she did not like the question.

'And I don't even know what your name is,' she said, presently. 'I suppose you have a Christian name, as well as other people, have you not?'

'What! Don't you know my name? Good gracious! Fancy my never telling you my name. But somehow I thought everybody knew it. It is Reginald – Reginald Reeve Armstrong. Reeve was the name of an old brute of an uncle of mine, who was to have left me a fortune, and didn't. Rex is what they call me at home. I wish you would call me Rex. Will you?'

'Why should I,' she responded, just a little haughtily. 'It is only fast women who call men by their Christian names. I am not a fast woman. I never do it.'

'I heard you call that Macdonald – Macpherson – what's his name – by *his* Christian name the other night.'

'Oh, Don – he is different.'

'Different! Do you mean to say that fellow is more to you than I am?'

'He is an old friend – one of the best, the truest of friends. And you – you' –

'I am an older one, at any rate, if not a better one. Yes, and
I am a better one too, and you know it, Mary. You understood
me that night at Dunchester; did you not? You have been faithful to me – faithful ever since – have you not?'

She turned her face away and looked at a lead Adonis on the
opposite wall in silence. Her heart swelled with a vague indignation, that made her firm mouth quiver and her eyes glisten. Why
did he press her like this, when as yet he had never declared himself, and whether *he* had been faithful or not? Until within a few
days, she had never thought of concealing from him – whenever
he wanted to know it – that she loved him, and had watched and
longed and waited for him. She was not the woman who would
have made her lover drag a reluctant confession out of her, though
she was – perhaps, rather *because* she was – as delicately modest
and maidenly as a good and true woman could be. Her pride
would never have prevented her from laying herself freely at his
feet, as well as in his arms; indeed, her pride itself was of a kind
that would have prompted her to do it. But now, for some as
yet, to her, inexplicable reason, she longed, and every moment
longed more and more, to keep her secret hidden from his eyes.
The conventional idea occurred to her, for the first time, that
she had 'made herself cheap,' and that he thought lightly of her
in consequence. The deeper feeling out of which that idea had
grown had not formulated itself into any conscious sense of his
unworthiness, and of the mistake that she had made – not yet.
She only knew that in some way her expectations had disappointed her.

'You have been true to me, have you not?' he repeated, tenderly,
resting, not his finger tips, but the palm of his hand on the slope
of her beautiful shoulder. 'That is what I have been counting on
all these years – that is why I have come to Australia, Mary.'

She sprang to her feet suddenly, and drew herself to her full
height, not with any look of offence, but with a proud air of dignity and composure that gave her companion an unpleasant
shock. There was a moment's pause, during which he, too, rose,
slowly and gracefully, saying to himself, 'Now, how could I have
made that blunder? After all, she is a woman of thirty now, and
a great heiress into the bargain. She knows her own value, of
course.'

'Have I vexed you?' he inquired aloud, with the most delicate
air of respect and contrition. 'I am very sorry.'

'I am not vexed, Major Armstrong,' she said gently, looking beyond him as she spoke and drawing her breath quickly, 'but I might be, if you went on talking to me in that way.'

'In what way?'

'Never mind. It is time for me to be going home, I think. It is eleven o'clock, and I have not seen my mother to-day yet.'

'Oh, *don't* go yet. Why, you have only just come. Walk round the place with me, won't you? I want you to show me the pictures and things.'

To this reasonable request she naturally acceded, for she did not want to leave him, and had no violent longing for her mother's society; and for another hour they sauntered about amongst artistic trifles and treasures, she acting as *cicerone* and pointing out the things she most admired, while he looked and listened in a polite but rather absent manner, bestowing many surreptitious glances on her dress, her face, her hands, her hair – evidently finding more to interest him in them than in all the contents of the Exhibition put together. Then she suddenly demanded her parasol and said she must be going.

'*Must* you, really? But you will let me see you home?'

'Oh no! It is too far. And I am accustomed to going about by myself.'

'You ought not to be accustomed to it then, and I certainly shall not allow you to go home alone.' So he called a cab and they drove all the way out to Kew together. And when she reached home she took out her watch and saw that it was nearly lunch time.

'You will come in and see my mother?' she said, standing on the gravel before the open hall door. 'And you will have some lunch with us, won't you?'

'Thank you,' he responded, with alacrity. And he followed her in, the door was closed behind them, and they entered the drawingroom together.

'Tell Mrs Lorimer that Major Armstrong is here,' said Mary to her parlor maid, seeing that the room was empty.

'She is out, Miss,' the girl replied. 'She went out shopping with Mrs Jennings after breakfast. But she would be back to lunch, she said.'

Mary walked into the drawingroom, in silence, with her heart beating rather quickly. It was a cheerful apartment, with no gilding or satin about it, but furnished luxuriously and substantially in sober colors, and with the object, before any other, of making those who used it comfortable. Mrs Lorimer had had experience, and some natural sense of the fitness of things, to guide her in arranging its appointments; and Mary herself, who could not tolerate a sham of any sort or kind, was essentially a woman of good taste, in the genuine meaning of the term. The chief charm of any room (when it was not absolutely midsummer weather) adorned this one conspicuously – a bright and hospitable fire of resinous logs, crackling cheerfully on a capacious open hearth. All the windows were open to the balmy airs of spring; but, because the fire was not needed to warm cold hands and feet, it did not therefore fail to commend itself as a graceful indication of a housewife's generous and genial instincts. It suggested to Major Armstrong, as he sauntered round, looking at pictures and ornaments, that Mary Hamilton's home was a pleasant place.

'I see you have the correct brick-red in this dado,' he said. 'It is a regular Morris kind of thing, isn't it? Pretty too.'

'Do you like it? Mother had it done about two months ago. The old dado was rather staring; it killed the carpets.'

'Nice carpets. Turkey, aren't they?'

'Yes; mother bought them some years ago. She is very fond of Eastern carpets. She is going to buy some more out of the Exhibition.'

'Does the house belong to your mother, then?'

'Practically it does. Legally, it is mine.'

'All the property is yours, isn't it?' speaking carelessly.

'Nearly all.'

'For your own use absolutely, as the lawyers say?'

'Yes.'

He stood in the middle of the floor, looking round. She stood beside him, with her hat in her hand, her heart full of the sense of the barrenness of this harvest season, that was to have borne fruit enough to compensate for eleven years of famine.

'What a capital room it would be to dance in!' he remarked, after a pause. 'Have you ever given any balls here?'

'Yes, a few.'

'I wish you would give another. I want to dance with you again,' he said, dropping his eyes to her face, which was immediately suffused with her girlish blush. 'What a beautiful dancer you were long ago, Mary. I never had such a partner, before or since. Do you remember that waltz?'

She looked at him eloquently.

'How we kept it up, didn't we? It was the one perfect waltz of my life. I never hear the old Blue Danube without thinking of it.'

'O no – it was not the Blue Danube! I don't believe they had the Blue Danube so long ago as that. It was the waltz from Faust, don't you remember?'

'Was it? I'm sure I always thought it was the Blue Danube. I haven't much ear for music, I must confess. "God save the Queen" is about the only tune that I should feel it safe to swear to. But I am sure I remember that waltz, whether it was the Blue Danube or whether it wasn't.'

'This was how it went,' said Mary. She opened the piano, near which she stood, dropped on the music-stool and played a few bars of the air that had haunted her night and day for so many years. The sound of the soft notes which often before had stirred her to weep over the memories that were embalmed in them touched her heart in its susceptible mood, and set free magnetic currents that she had been trying to hold in check. She played a few bars, and she could not play any more. She rose hastily, biting her lips, and shut up the piano.

Major Armstrong had been standing behind her, and was so close that when she turned round she touched him. He did not move away; he looked at her intently and inquiringly, with his bold eyes, and saw that hers were full of tears. In another moment she was lying in his arms, sobbing and crying, with her hands on his shoulders and her face lifted to his, taking and giving that kiss of which in dreams she had had a foretaste that the reality never would equal.

It was not the passion of the hour that overmastered her; it was the pent-up store of lonely years that had filled her heart too full – her woman's heart that had loved so well, and, never having had its natural expression, demanded some relief.

CHAPTER XIX

What Will She Do

Donald Macleod reached Bungil late in the evening of the day after Mrs Lorimer's dinner-party, at which he had witnessed the meeting between Mary and Major Armstrong, that had con-

founded so many anticipations. As he drove his light buggy up
the avenue of English trees that was one of the far-famed beauties of the grounds around his house, the aspect of the place that
for many years had represented little more than board and lodging had a new charm in his eyes. Certainly he had been away
for a long time; and Bungil, notoriously one of the prettiest, as
it was one of the oldest, residences in the district, was glorified
by the light and color of a wonderful sunset, and by the beauty
and verdure of the loveliest season of the year. It was a mellow
brick house, with the original weatherboard peeping out here and
there from a dense drapery of ivy and blossoming creepers; it
had low, wide windows framed in bougainvillaea and banksia
roses; it had a hospitable abundance of substantial chimneys, from
which, even on a mild October night, the grey smoke of bright
log fires streaked the transparent opal-green of a truly Australian
sky. There was never a weed on the gravelled garden paths, nor
on the lawns and tennis courts, mowed and rolled as regularly
as the weeks came round, that were so seldom used or looked
at. It was a tradition that flowers grew in the Bungil beds and
borders when other people had none; and to-night, in the flower
season, the glory pea was a blaze of color, and the thickets of
white and purple lilac saturated the air with perfume. But the
master of the house, looking up and down, and round and round,
sniffing the dewy atmosphere, had a sense of being at home that
was unusually pronounced, and it was not altogether on account
of long absence or because the house looked its best in spring
time. He began to regard his property – a fine property, though
it was his – with the eye of a mistress, and not as the master only.
That was the subtle difference that he did not analyse or understand. There was a new charm about the place; it was irradiated
with that streak of light that had come into his horizon with the
coming of Major Armstrong.

Usually, on his return home after an absence, his housekeeper,
an old servant of the family, who had once been his nurse, awaited
him on the doorstep, with anxious, maternal inquiries after his
health and welfare. To-night a youthful figure – Mrs Lepel was
a woman who would look young till she was fifty – stood on
the threshold, with the hall lamps shining on her fair-haired head.

'What, – Jenny!' he exclaimed, recognising her. 'Why, where
have you come from?'

'From Wattlebank,' she replied, running out to meet him. 'I

heard that your buggy had gone to meet the coach, and I got Fred to send me over. I am so glad to see you, dear old boy! How are you? And how' – pulling him down and whispering in his ear – 'are things going on?'

'I'll tell you by and by,' he whispered back. 'Are you going to stay here to-night? Where's Fred?'

'I left Fred at home. I wanted to have a good, long quiet talk, you and I by ourselves. You are to drive me back to-morrow.'

'All right. You must let me have some dinner first, though, before you ask me any questions.'

'Do you want your dinner? That is a good omen. And you are looking very well, Don. Go and get ready then – don't dress. We'll dine at once, and have a long evening.'

As the night was falling, the lamps were lit in the diningroom, a spacious, low-roofed apartment, wainscotted in cedar, and hung all round with the mythical family portraits that were the chief pride and glory of the house; and brother and sister sat down to their soup with an evident contentment in each other's society. Donald, to his companion's great satisfaction, ate a hearty meal with placid zest, chatting cheerfully about the exhibition, about 'Grand Flaneur' and 'Progress,' about the movements of 'the Duke' and things in general that were going on in Melbourne until the last course was removed. Mrs Lepel trifled with the wing of a chicken and a spoonful of curry, watching him and dissembling her impatience. As soon as the servant had left the room she jumped up and ran round to her brother's chair.

'Now, come along to the smoking room,' she said, persuasively, with her arms round his neck. 'You don't want any more wine, and I have rolled you a quantity of lovely cigarettes. Come along, and tell me all about Mary and that mysterious major of hers. I am dying to hear what he is like and how she takes him.'

Mr Macleod rose, stretched himself, and suffered his sister to lead him to his smoking-room and sanctum, to place him in his own special easy chair, with his cigarettes, his matches, his coffee, and all he could want or wish for, on a table beside him, and prepared himself to give her the information that she desired. She, with a little shawl round her shoulders, sat down on the threshold of an open French window, between the firelight within and the moonlight without, propping herself against the framework, and clasping her hand round her knees, looking extremely youthful and pretty in her white gown, with a great bush of pale pink tamarisk behind her.

'And so you don't think he is much good?' she began, when they had made themselves comfortable.

'No, I don't, he replied, with promptness. 'I came to that conclusion the moment I set eyes on him.'

'But you had made up your mind already. You were prepared to think so.'

'I was prepared not to like him, of course. But I judged him fairly – at least I think I did – as I would have judged any other man.'

'Where did you see him?'

'I was down on the pier when he landed. That was where I saw him first. And I heard him too – he was slating an unfortunate beggar who was carrying some of his luggage, in remarkably choice terms. I wonder the fellow stood it.'

'Oh, I don't think they mind – if a man is only a *genuine* "swell," and does it effectively. And it is a habit of Indian people, with their black servants that want kicking to make them stir themselves. I suppose he is really what you would call a swell, isn't he, Don?'

'I suppose so. He is a major, with a lot of clasps and things. And a major fresh from Afghanistan, with the honor and glory of a real wound, has a right to give himself airs.'

'Is he as handsome as Mary said?'

'He's an uncommon good-looking fellow,' Mr Macleod generously admitted. 'Tall and sinewy, and as straight as a dart. His face has got the same clean-cut look, and a fine color, like an old meerschaum. It is half-covered, though, by a ridiculously long moustache, and he stares at you through his eye glass as if you were the dirt beneath his feet.'

'Dear me, he must be very charming,' said Mrs Lepel musingly. She was particularly struck with the last-named peculiarity, and began to feel a new respect for Mary's taste. 'What made you think he was no good, Don?'

'Many things – everything.'

'Did he put on the swell with you?'

'O dear no!' – drawing himself up. 'He has given me no offence – no direct offence. And he is a talkative, get-at-able fellow, in his high and mighty style. I called on him at his hotel, and you would have thought he had been my intimate friend all those years, instead of my enemy.'

'Did he talk about her?'

'Yes. He asked me if I knew her, and wanted to get out of me whether her fortune was *bona fide* and under her own control. I saw what he was driving at, and, needless to say, I gave him no information.'

'You might have bamboozled him a little.'

'No – I'll do nothing of that sort. There shall be fair play all round.'

'Honesty isn't *always* the best policy in this world, my dear boy.'

'That is a matter of opinion, Jenny. It is the only policy for me. I said I would win her from him if I could, and so I will; but I'll do it in open fight, and not by strategy.'

'And do you *still* think you will win her from him! That is what I want to know, Don. How is it with her now – now that her ideal has become an actual fact? Is he what she expected? Or is she disappointed?'

'She is disappointed, Jenny.'

'After all! Well, I do pity her, though I am glad – and though it is no more than I expected from the first.'

'Yes; I know she is, I saw it in her face. The man doesn't care a rap for her; he has come to marry her for her money – if he can. I knew it before I had been half an hour in his company, and she is bound to know it too, sooner or later.'

'She will not see him with your eyes.'

'She will find him out, nevertheless. She has begun to find him out already.'

'Then what will she do? Oh, dear me, why didn't you stay in Melbourne, if things are likely to go that way? This is not to win her in open fight – to come away and leave her alone with him. Why, he will trap her into an engagement before she has had time to find him out – while he still wears the glamour of that old romance, and she thinks she adores him as she has always done; and when she has given her word, then it will be too late to interfere. Her high sense of honor will compel her to marry him, even if she sees that it is a mistake.'

'No, Jenny. The sense of honor of an ordinary woman might prompt that course – Mary knows better. She'll never marry him after she has found him out, engagement or no engagement.'

'You are trusting to that?'

'I trust in her,' he said, simply, staring thoughtfully into his moonlit garden. 'I won't hang round her, prying into her intercourse with him. I'll bide my time here for a little while. She knows where I am. And I think I shall know when it is time for me to go back.'

'How will you know? *Anything* might happen, and you never know a word of it!'

'She will let me know.'

'Mary! Oh, good gracious! There's not one of you men even *begins* to know what a woman is made of! Do you think *any* person with a grain of self-respect – let alone Mary – would say to a lover who had been treated as she has treated you, "I have been disappointed in the man I have been wanting all my life, so I don't mind making shift with you." Mary would die before she would degrade herself and insult you by calling you back – by offering you Major Armstrong's leavings.'

Mr Macleod had finished smoking, and was leaning forward in his chair with his arms on his knees. His face was close to his sister's, and he looked into her bright eyes with a slow, grave smile. 'Mary and I understand one another, Jenny. I don't think we are quite like other people,' he said.

Which was true.

CHAPTER XX

What She Did

Donald Macleod stayed at home at Bungil, and 'bided his time.' Not that he expected Mary, literally, to send for him, or that he made sure of having secured her. It was a point of honor and delicacy with him to withdraw himself from her neighborhood at this juncture; and, though his heart was sore for her, thinking of what she had to go through, to look on at her suffering and humiliation – until he had the right and the power to help her and himself – was more than he could bear. And he trusted her to need no exhortation from him, even if he could bring himself to give it, to encourage her to be true to her best self and he knew that, if she were true to herself, his time, though perhaps not yet, would come. He could do nothing to hasten it while Major Armstrong was in possession of the field and when Major Armstrong was no longer in possession, he felt sure he should soon know it. So he stayed at home, though all the world was flocking to Melbourne, and attended to his business diligently.

But Mrs Lepel was anxious and restless. Womanlike, she felt that to leave things alone was practically to give up the game, or at any rate, to court certain failure. Now that there was the blessed hope of a happy adjustment of this long and most unsatisfactory love affair, which had kept the family in constant difficulties, and made Don an old man before his time, why, in the name of goodness, shouldn't it be seized and cherished, and the advantages of the position legitimately followed up? She did not believe that Mary, left to her own devices, would act like a sensible woman now – particularly with reference to a military hero who stared at other people through an eyeglass 'as if they were the dirt beneath his feet,' after acting like a fool for a dozen years; and she had no faith in any man's ability to take proper care of himself and his best interests. In her perplexity, she took counsel with her Fred – a thing she was not in the habit of doing when serious questions had to be decided, and Fred was a great comfort to her.

'Rubbish, rubbish!' exclaimed the little man, fussing and fuming. 'Don is an idiot – he always was, where that girl was concerned. Four or five years ago, he ought to have let her alone – and then he wouldn't; now there is about sixty thousand pounds at stake, and he throws up his hand! With these bad times too, and Bungil mortgaged to half its value! You must look after things, Jenny; you must use your clever little brains, my dear. We will go down to town at once, and you shall keep an eye on her and give her advice, and prevent her from throwing herself away. That Armstrong fellow will soon be at the end of his furlough – he has only got six months; you must get at her Jenny, and stave him off. Stave him off till his leave is up – that's the thing to do.'

Mrs Lepel thought so too. She was supported, as she expected to be, in her own convictions. She quite agreed with her husband, moreover, that if the intervention of 'the family' was to do any good, it must be brought to bear at once. She kissed him affectionately; sat down and wrote to Mrs Redwood, to say that, after all, Fred found he would be able to get away at once, if it would be convenient to receive them – urging her friend, by all the sacred ties of friendship, to hurry the milliners and dressmakers who were preparing for her arrival in town; and then bade her maid pack up for an immediate departure.

Donald, busy in his woolshed and in his rose garden, had a

message from Wattlebank to the effect that his sister and brother-in-law had gone to town a little earlier than they expected, and would look for him, of course, to join them there for the race week. A day or two later he had the following letter from Mrs Lepel: –

'Dear old boy, –

'We got down all right. Trains overflowing, of course, and crowds everywhere. I never saw Melbourne so full. Mrs Redwood was at Spencer-street, waiting for us. People are indeed fortunate who have friends like her just now, for the hotels and lodging-houses are choked. You will have to look out, if you want to get a bed for the race week.

'I sent a message up to Mary at once to let her know I had come, and Mrs Redwood asked her for lunch next day. Don, I told you how it would be – you had no sooner turned your back on them than they got *engaged*. The moment I set foot in town that was what I heard – that Miss Hamilton was engaged to Major Armstrong, and that Mrs Lorimer was in a terrible state of mind about it. I can't say I was surprised, but I was very much upset, for I knew what a blow it would be to you. Oh, why *didn't* you stave him off till she had time to understand and realise how things really were! He took her unawares – just as I expected he would, if she were not looked after – and now it is too late to help it. And she is not happy, anybody can see; I don't believe she *meant* to do it. Major Armstrong is very charming; I admire him excessively. But he is a terrible *viveur*, and it is so plain that he does not care for her. He treats her in an easy sort of way, as if he quite understood that he had only to throw his handkerchief. Somebody has told him about her infatuation, I am certain, by the manner of him. He doesn't disguise his conviction that she has been hopelessly worshipping him in secret and keeping single for his sake – though he is polite and charming to her as to everybody. I dare say he is accustomed to being hopelessly worshipped; and I am sure I don't wonder. I really can quite understand, now I see him for myself, how an ignorant and romantic country girl might fall over head and ears in love with him after receiving a very moderate amount of his attentions; he is *most* fascinating. And I suppose it would not have been like Mary, having once fallen in love, to fall out again comfortably, like other people. But her constancy will cost her dear, I am afraid. Already he is spending her money, they say. He lost a great deal at cards one night when he was not very sober, and borrowed of her to pay. Mrs Redwood says he gave a cheque with her name on it, without taking the trouble to transfer it to his own account first, but we know what Melbourne gossip is, and I daresay that is not true. The suspicion that he has borrowed her money is bad enough, however, and that I belive, is a fact. Mary has all the look of things having gone wrong. I saw it in her face as soon as she came in. She came by herself, but Major Armstrong fetched her after lunch. She was pale, and looked worried and tired. She said she had a headache. Fancy Mary with a headache! "It's a new thing for you to set up," I said to her, making a joke of it; but she blushed as if I had accused her of stealing something, and I was sorry I had spoken. She was not like herself at all. She was stiff and prim, even with me, and wouldn't talk about anything except the exhibition and theatres and things. She did not ask about Abercorn, though generally she takes my breath away with her questions; and she hardly mentioned you. And then Major Armstrong came in, looking so lordly and handsome, with his beautiful manners. He really is the most captivating man I ever met, I think. Mrs Redwood says everybody is running after him and making a fuss with him, and I don't wonder at it. He stayed for half-an-hour, and talked to Mrs Redwood and me – to me particularly, and Mary sat by, in a dull sort of stately patience, waiting till he had done, and hardly joining in at all. I looked at her several times, to see what she was thinking of; but I could not read her – and she always used to be like an open book. The only thing I could see clearly was that she was out of heart, and unhappy. Nothing was said about her engagement until they were going away. But I was determined to get something out of her, so I went up to help her put her bonnet on; and, while we were alone, I made a kind of attempt at congratulation – not a very cordial one, I fear. "Oh," she said quickly, with a little cold air of restraint – so unlike her! – "there is nothing settled. It is too soon for good wishes yet." "But everyone says you are engaged," I declared; "Major Armstrong publishes it everywhere." She shut her mouth down in that obstinate way that she has sometimes, and I thought she was not going to say anything more. Then she put her hand into mine, and turned to come downstairs. She made me come downstairs, though I was burning to have a nice, long, comfortable talk. "There are a great many difficulties," she said, "Major Armstrong doesn't quite understand. My mother is very much opposed to my marrying. It is possible that she may not give her consent." After that I said no more. Mary Hamilton is the best of daughters, but when did she ever let her mother stop her doing anything she had set her mind on? When Mrs Lorimer did her best to plague the very life out of her because she wouldn't marry you, what effect had it? She might as well have talked to a post.

'They went away then, he and she together. I stood at the hall door to see them go; they were bound for the exhibition, where a party of people were waiting for them. As they stepped into the street, she turned quickly, as if with a sudden thought, and came back to me. "Is Don quite well?" she asked abruptly, looking at the bridge of my nose. And when I assured her that I had left you very full of business, and in the best of health, at Bungil, she rejoined her young man, and they marched off. A fine-looking couple they were, he so soldierly and distinguished-looking, and she with that magnificent straight figure, both so tall and both dressed so perfectly, walking along together with that light level stride (no one but a man can walk with Mary properly); but to think of him, charming as he is, as a mate for her, is preposterous. Why, Nina, though he is worlds too good for her, would have suited him far better.

'It is a grievous pity that you went home, but it is no use talking about that now. I leave it to you to decide what is best to be done. O dear me, what a contrary world it is!

'Lovingly yours,

Jenny Lepel.'

'P.S. – Tell me if I can do anything for you, dear old boy. Mrs Redwood says that any time you come down you can have a truckle bed in her husband's dressingroom.'

Mr Macleod read this letter twice over very carefully, and then packed up his portmanteau.

CHAPTER XXI

The Last Straw

Most of the readers of this story, I imagine, remember the Melbourne Cup day of 1880 – the lovely day that it was, and the brilliance of the festival that was held on the Flemington course. No rain, no dust, no wind, no cold, as so often before had taken the fine edge off the charm and enjoyment of that great public holiday, but a canopy of sweet blue sky, bathed in the exquisite light and warmth of Australian spring time, over the heads of the 120,000 happy and orderly people, who thronged the stand, the lawn and the hill, to witness the memorable triumph of Grand Flaneur. It was a perfect day, as far as weather was concerned; and, in other respects, perhaps the greatest Cup day yet registered in Victorian racing annals. It was also, to Mary Hamilton and all belonging to her, a day of large events – evermore to be remembered as isolated from common days.

Her carriage left the house at ten o'clock to join the great tide that was setting out of town. It was a roomy, open carriage, as such a morning demanded, comfortably appointed, with the coachman in a new suit of livery, and a big luncheon basket strapped behind. Mrs Lorimer lay back in the cushions, looking serene and satisfied, *vis-à-vis* with her charming but objectionable son-in-law that was to be – or that she imagined was to be – having laid aside anxieties and animosities for the occasion. She was very fashionable, in sage-green, touched up with splashes of old-gold satin, and held a gold-lined umbrella over her head with much state and dignity. Mary, classically simple in her equally fashionable attire, sat beside her mother, until they were joined by Mr and Mrs Jennings, and then, as the unmarried and youngest woman of the party, she took her place, with her back to the horses, by her gallant lover's side. She was not looking well – she who had always been so full of life and vigor; and Major Armstrong, critically studying her face, said to himself that she was certainly a very fine woman, but could not hide her age. It was beginning to occur to him, also, that she was a trifle dull, if not perhaps even a little stupid.

The carriage pulled up at Nina's garden gate, the grounds of the little villa not admitting of a 'drive' to the front door: and Major Armstrong jumped down with alacrity to fetch out his prospective sister-in-law, with whom, in spite of her strong objection to him as Mary's possible husband, he was on the best of terms. It was some time before he made his reappearance. Carriages, buggies, cabs, with a four-in-hand drag every now and again, dashed in a continuous stream along the sunny road; and Mary and her mother watched them – making feminine comments upon striking bonnets and parasols, and greeting familiar faces – and waiting patiently. Then when Mrs Lorimer was beginning

to fidget and to think of getting down to see what was keeping
Nina, Mr Jennings came trotting along the garden path, dapper
and spruce, with his member's card in his buttonhole, and his
field-glass slung over his shoulder. He came to the side of the
carriage to greet his relations; and over his head Mary watched
her lover and her sister, who followed him at a considerable distance, and very much at their leisure. The young matron – she
looked much younger than Mary today – was a vision of Cup
day beauty, as she stepped daintily into the sunshine, in a soft
glistening dress of palest Sèvres China pink, with a white veil
over her face, and her golden hair shining. 'Doesn't she look
lovely?' sighed Mrs Lorimer, with a pathetic, subdued ecstacy.

'She always does,' said Mary.

Nina paused for a few seconds on the garden path, as if to give
them all an opportunity to admire her properly; and Major Armstrong took a pink parasol out of her hand, opened it and held
it over her feathery little pink bonnet carefully. They dawdled
down the path in this way for a short distance, he talking gaily
to her, and she laughing – her prim little soft laugh – as she
glanced up at him archly from under the pink parasol; and then
they paused simultaeously and looked at a rose-bush. Nina
touched a crimson bud with the tip of her gloved finger; and
Major Armstrong, giving her the handle of her sunshade, took
out a pocket-knife, cut off the flower and trimmed the stalk,
and – Mary became as red as the rose itself when she saw it –
he held it for an instant against Nina's cheek before he gave it
to her. Nina snatched it quickly and stuck it into the soft lace
that draped her throat and bosom; but she laughed on, and
Major Armstrong took the parasol from her hand again and held
it over her.

'How do you do, Mother dear? Isn't it a delicious morning?
Well, Mary. Oh, good gracious, why, you wore that dress on
Saturday, Mary! Major Armstrong, why didn't you make her
wear her pretty new Indian silk? I thought that was on purpose
for Cup day.'

Mrs Jennings, after a few of these remarks, settled herself in
her place of honour, and repossessed herself of her parasol. As
Major Armstrong took his seat opposite, she glanced at him with
a little arch significance, and began to laugh again. 'He is a very
naughty man, Mary,' she exclaimed, nodding her small head,
'Don't look at me like that, Major Armstrong – you know you

are very naughty. If I were Mary, I wouldn't have anything to do with you.'

'Mary is not so unkind as you are,' responded the Major, not turning to his betrothed but gazing with his handsome bold eyes into the unusually animated face before him.

Mary said nothing; she sat very uprightly in her place, with her head half turned away, and looked at the passing carriages. The sweetness was missing from her strong and steadfast mouth, and her eyes lacked the sunshine of interest and enjoyment that was reflected all around her. 'She is cross,' said Nina to herself, with a little shrug. 'She is jealous because he admires me.' And then it occurred to her forcibly that it would be an excellent thing to make her still more jealous, and, if possible, provoke a breach between the engaged pair before the major's leave was up. Mary was becoming very touchy about her dignity now-a-days, and her lover was far from showing that anxiety about the safety of the Lorimer fortune that might have been expected. Mr Jennings would not mind if she (Nina) 'carried on' a little – supposing he noticed it, which was not in the least likely – for the furtherance of so desirable an end as the keeping of £60,000 in the family; and she had the profoundest belief in the potency of her powers of fascination when she chose to put them forth. Moreover – but this was an unformulated motive – he *was* so handsome and so charming! And Mary did not know how to appreciate such a man, after all the fuss she had made to get him.

Poor Mary! That 'look of things having gone wrong' was very plain to read. Things were going all wrong to-day. When her lover came to Kew after breakfast he was preoccupied with racing news and prospects, and not with thoughts of her. When she came downstairs, in her quiet, refined dress, over the adjustment of which she had taken as much trouble as Nina over her laces and embroideries, and found him alone in the drawingroom, he began to tell her about the horses she ought to back, and never noticed that her dress became her. And now he was flirting with Nina, chaffing and joking and talking vulgar nonsense, and apparently not seeing, nor caring to prevent her from seeing, what bad taste it was. Her hero of the Dunchester ballroom was fading away – he was another person from this. And in place of that deified image, her imagination was vaguely occupied with a vision of Bungil house, nestling sweetly and peacefully in its bosky garden, and of Don, lonely and miserable, trying to bear the burden of a life that she had emptied and spoiled.

'There go the Redwoods,' called Mr Jennings, from his box-seat, as a light landau rolled past them. 'That's Lepel, with the grey hat.'

Mary turned round eagerly. There were Mrs Redwood and Mrs Lepel, sitting side by side; they bowed to her in passing with the stately serenity that became a couple of distinguished women whose dresses would be chronicled in to-morrow's newspapers. Mr Lepel took off his hat; Mr Redwood also. But Don's square figure was missing from the group – Don's strong, stern, kind, good face, that she would have given anything to see. Was he too sad and sore even to come to see the Cup race? It was a terrible thought.

They drove along the sunny road, three of them in high spirits and good humor, bantering each other gaily, and one dispirited and out of tune, confused with her secret perplexities. And by and by they arrived at the great racecourse, were admitted to the carriage enclosure, and turned out upon the terrace steps, to be swallowed up in an immense throng of gay people, the 'rank and fashion' of combined Australia, sprinkled with foreigners of all nations, exhibition commissioners, naval officers, and distinguished strangers of miscellaneous kinds. They made their way along the crowded terrace, and struggled for precarious standing room on the staircases of the grand stand, where sitting room there was none by this time; and Mary had the pleasure of seeing her sister wedged in the crowd a few steps below her, and protected from the crush by Major Armstrong's arm, while she stood, like a tall pillar, protecting herself. Then the Governor came along, driving his own four-in-hand, with the Duke of Manchester beside him; and in the ensuing disturbance on the staircase, where room had to be made for the vice-regal party to get into its box, the two disappeared; and while Mr Jennings hunted for them – as for two infinitesimal needles in a gigantic bottle of hay[sic] – Mary and Mrs Lorimer kept one another company till lunch time.

'Well, I see nothing of them,' said Mrs Lorimer, rising from a seat on the lawn, where she and her youngest daughter had betaken themselves, thinking to waylay the wanderers. 'But I suppose they will find us at the carriage. We had better go and see after the lunch, my dear; everybody seems to be going to lunch.

'It is awkward being without either of our gentlemen. Ah,

there's a pink dress – that's Nina! No it isn't. How tiresome!'
'Take my arm, Mother,' said Mary. 'We can do without our
gentlemen until they want us. It is not very crowded in the carriage paddock, and John will be there, you know.'

The two ladies went in search of their vehicle and coachman,
Mrs Lorimer leaning on the arm of her tall daughter, who walked
along with great majesty, carrying her nose very much in the air.
Mary was a superior woman to most women, but she was a
woman all the same; and to have a handsome *fiancée*, and be
left to walk without an escort in the face of all her friends and
acquaintances, was a trial even to her sweet temper. They found
John looking out for them, with his hamper unstrapped and his
glass and crockery set out. Mrs Lorimer stepped into the carriage and drew off her gloves. Mary was about to follow, having
investigated the condition of the oyster patties and meringues,
when the truants appeared – Nina tripping daintily over the grass,
her laces fluttering and her bangles jingling, laughing apparently
more joyously than ever, with her husband on one side of her
and Major Armstrong on the other.

'Oh, *there* you are!' cried Mrs Jennings, sweetly, with great surprise. 'Why, where *have* you been? We have been looking for
you everywhere!'

'We couldn't think where on earth you had made off to,' said
Major Armstrong, in a tone of concern.

Mary disdained to take any notice of these flimsy protestations.
Mrs Lorimer, who began to share Nina's views as to the advisa-
bility of bamboozling the gallant major, if possible, and had the
mother's serene confidence in her pet daughter's discretion, ral-
lied them cheerfully, without any reproaches. Then they went
to lunch: the ladies sitting in the carriage, the men standing round
the open door, joined occasionally by other men; and the rapid
popping of champagne corks mingled with the buzz of merry
voices and laughter all around them. They drank their champagne,
picnic fashion, out of tumblers, and Major Armstrong drank a
great deal, and grew reckless and hilarious in consequence. He
'chaffed' Mrs Jennings with an easy familiarity that, though it did
not offend her – nor Mr Jennings either, who was himself affected
more than usual by the heat of the midday sun – was terrible to
Mary, in the way that it debased her ideal hero and gentleman
and outraged her fine sense of propriety.

'Look how solemn Mary is!' cried Nina, laughing, with her lips to her tumbler. 'She's shocked to see us all so giddy. Never mind, my dear, you will have plenty of time to reform him presently. Let him enjoy his liberty while he can.'

'I have not the slightest wish to interfere with Major Armstrong's liberty,' replied Mary, drawing herself up proudly.

And then it occurred to that gentleman that he was playing a little too fast and loose with £60,000; he suddenly became sedate and sober – or tried to appear so – and set himself to propitiate his *fiancée*. This also she resented – far more than she had resented his neglect.

The crisis came about two hours afterwards. They were walking up and down the brilliant lawn, he and she together, he endeavouring to make amends for previous shortcomings, and she doing her part of the little conversation that circumstances permitted in the vaguest monosyllabic fashion. The sun was very strong by this time, and she was tired of the crowd and glare – wishing the long day to be over, that she might get to her own cool room, put on her dressing gown, and shut herself in with her sad thoughts. 'Phew!' ejaculated her companion, 'It's as hot as India. Don't you feel it very hot?'

Mary suggested that perhaps having had lunch and champagne in the open air made it seem hotter than it was at noon; and then they passed the lower end of the grand stand where a crowd of people were jostling each other round a gigantic bar. There was a sound of popping corks and the bubble of effervescing waters.

'Aren't you awfully thirsty?' inquired Major Armstrong earnestly. 'Wouldn't you like some soda? They've got some over there. I could get it for you in a minute.'

'Oh no, thank you' said Mary quickly. The crowd looked eager and restless and just a trifle rough in its thirstiness, squeezing and scuffling each for his turn to be served.

'Really. Nor yet lemonade? Perhaps I could get you some tea there. Shall I see if they've got some tea?'

'Not anything, thank you,' said Mary, with decision. 'But don't let me keep you, if you'd like anything for yourself,' she added, seeing that he lingered.

Major Armstrong confessed that he was parched with thirst, but refused to quit her side merely for his personal gratification. Whereupon Mary desired him, rather imperiously, to go at once and not think of her; and he – making the fatal mistake of taking her at her word – apologised profusely, promised to return immediately, and went. And as it was not an easy matter even for a lordly major to get waited on, at such a time and place, as he was accustomed to be waited on, Mary stood for a few seconds, looking after him, and then discovered that she was alone.

Alone in the crowd on Cup day! It was too much. She had told him to leave her, certainly; but what woman ever considered *that* a justification for her desertion under such circumstances? She saw him drawn into the crowd that surged round the bar counter, and, tall as he was, swallowed up out of sight; and then, spurred by the sudden sense of her disappointment and desolation, she lifted her head, turned round, and with close-shut mouth and dilating nostrils, set forth alone to find her way back to her mother and sister, whom they had left at the other end of the lawn. All along the terrace she marched, with her proud unhurried step, her parasol held well back over her shoulder, so that her face, scorning to hide itself, was visible to all. People gazed after her, in amazement and consternation, they looked down on her from the closely-packed stand; then stared at her when they met and passed her – so imposing a figure amongst other women, so well known to almost everybody – and audibly wondered how in the world it could have happened that she had been left to walk amongst them with no friend or escort at her side. And then just when she was beginning to feel that the ordeal she had encountered was almost more than she could bear, a big, brown-bearded man came shouldering his way through the crush towards her, and a voice said, very distinctly, very gently – 'Mary, do you want anything?' It was Don.

CHAPTER XXII

One Lesson Learned

He had been sitting between Mrs Redwood and Mrs Lepel, whom he had joined on the racecourse, on an upper seat on the grand stand, when his quick eye caught sight of his beloved, far away, marching up the terrace. He lifted his glasses, gazed at her steadily for a few seconds, saw that she was alone, saw even in her stately carriage the indication of the spirit that had led her to defy appearances; and he laid his hand on his sister's arm.

'I see Mary, Jenny – I am going to her,' he said briefly, as he rose from his seat.

And before Mrs Lepel could get breath for any enquiry or remonstrance he was out of earshot, forcing his way powerfully through the crowd that packed the stairs.

Mary, do you want anything?' he said, when Mary came up to him, breasting the human tide that at that time was setting strongly in the direction of the carriage paddock, with her stiff proud face held high in the air.

In a moment the color rushed into her cheeks and the light into her eyes. Her lips parted and began to quiver. She held out her hand with an eager gesture. She looked for a moment as if she had a hard struggle to control the sudden emotion that leaped up in her at the sight of his dear and welcome face. He did not wait for her to speak, and he asked no more questions; instinctively he understood the situation. He quietly put her hand within his arm.

'Now where do you want to go, dear? Would you like to go home?' he inquired gently. 'There's a man there who will take a message to your people, if you tell him where they are; you need not wait for them, if you are tired. Wouldn't you like to go home?'

Oh how nice it was to be taken care of like this again! Of all things she longed to go home, she said; she had lost sight of her party, and the sun had made her head ache – she was tired of the crowd and noise, and of standing about. It was with a little tremulousness in her voice that she made these feeble explanations; but by the time they were half way down the terrace again she had collected herself, and recovered the self-possession that had been so nearly lost.

Fortunately, they did not see Major Armstrong, though they passed the very spot where she had parted from him, and though he was already beginning an anxious hunt for her; in a crowd of that magnitude, it was much easier to miss him than otherwise. Mary looked steadily before her, still with her parasol held back over her shoulder; she heard the popping of the soda-water corks at the bar, but she took no heed whatever. No doubt Major Armstrong would be considerably alarmed by her disappearance, but it would not last long. He would know where to find Mrs Lorimer and Nina, and they would tell him what had become of her.

'I must not take the carriage,' she said, as they came to the top of the steps, 'even if it could be got out – which would be impossible until some of the others were gone.'

'We don't want the carriage; we'll go by train,' replied Mr Macleod cheerfully. 'There are trains always going, and they won't be very crowded yet.'

Accordingly they strolled to the station and finding a train about to start, conveyed themselves into town thereby very comfortably. They sat *vis-à-vis*, and Mary looked out of the window and made comments on the landscape, which, however, was pretty well shut out by the lines of empty carriages standing in readiness for racecourse use; and Mr Macleod, though he did not notice much else, studiously refrained from looking at her. From Spencer-Street [sic] they walked until they found a cab and therein drove out to Kew – where their arrival caused some astonishment to the solitary domestic left in charge of the house.

'I was tired, Jane,' Mary explained as she stepped into the hall; 'and Mr Macleod has kindly brought me home.'

Then she turned to Don, who had left the cab at the gate, but did not look resigned to his departure. He stood on the doorstep, with his hat in his hand, Jane's hospitable face invited him to follow her mistress. For a few seconds Mary stood silent and irresolute; then she said carelessly, 'Come in and have some tea with me, Don – if you don't despise tea. Jane get some tea as quickly as you can. And bring some soda water and – what will you have with it Don? Sherry or brandy? And lots of ice, Jane.'

She walked into the drawingroom [sic] which was cool and quiet, with its drawn blinds and inviting chairs and lounges; and Mr Macleod followed her, and shut the door gently behind him.

'How nice it is to get out of the sun, isn't it?' she said hurriedly, standing in the middle of the room and beginning to unfasten her bonnet.

'But it has been a lovely day for the Cup, hasn't it? I am so glad of that, it would have disappointed so many people if it had rained as it did on Saturday. What an enormous crowd it was! I never saw so many before. The duke must have been surprised to see such a gathering, and to see how orderly and well managed everything was. I should think from all I have heard, that very few English races pass off like ours, with no need for a policeman. And what a wonderful horse that Grand Flaneur is, isn't he, Don?'

Don was quite silent. He would have no part in this transparent pretence, the very first pretence that either of them had been guilty of in their intercourse with one another. He waited until she had done speaking; and then he walked up to her, took her bonnet out of her hand, and laid his broad palms heavily upon her shoulders.

'My love,' he said solemnly, looking into her eyes, which were scarcely below the level of his own, 'My love, you are not going to have any false pride with me?'

For an instant she stood quite still, with a sort of shiver running through her, then she put hands to her face and began to cry bitterly.

'What can I say?' she sobbed. 'You know how it is with me. O, Don, I have been making mistakes – terrible mistakes – all along, and now I am punished for it?'

He took his hand from her shoulders, and drew her within his arms. 'There is one mistake you can rectify,' he said, holding her close to his throbbing heart. 'Just think for a moment of all you have made me suffer, and the time you have made me wait – you can at least make amends for that. Never mind *him*; we'll think of him presently. Never mind appearances, we don't care for Mrs Grundy. Kiss me, my love – kiss me before Jane comes in. O Mary. Mary, you were always so truthful – don't have any false pride now!'

And she did not have any. She did not protest her unworthiness, nor grovel for forgiveness, nor do any of the things that conventional propriety demanded. She took her rest – before Jane came in – in the arms that had so long been open for her, and braved the consequences with a strong heart.

THE END

LOUISA LAWSON, 1848-1920

Journalist, editor and publisher, she was born Louisa
Albury, in Mudgee, New South Wales. She was married at eighteen to Norwegian sailor, Peter Larsen
and experienced numerous hardships and difficulties
as she tried to rear her five children. In 1883 she
moved to Sydney and was able to give rein to her
passionate interest in politics and intellectual debate.
Given the obstacles, she enjoyed an extraordinary
degree of success on political/literary scenes, becoming the editor of the *Republican* (1887) and the
founding editor of *The Dawn*, (1888-1905), Australia's first feminist periodical which she published,
wrote for and edited, for almost twenty years. She
became a prominent figure in the feminist movement,
an activist for women's suffrage and an ardent supporter of job opportunities for women, particularly
in the world of print. She published son Henry's first
collection, *Short Stories in Prose and Verse* (1894).

She contributed numerous articles, stories and
editorials for *The Dawn*, sometimes under her own
name, sometimes under a pseudonym. Her writing,
often aimed at awakening women to their disadvantages and urging them to action, was highly
influential and helped to establish the tradition of
women's political journalism which produced such
outstanding figures as Mary Gilmore and Mary
Grant Bruce.

The following articles from *The Dawn*, 1 April
1904 and 1 October 1904, give some indication of the
author's style of commentary and commitment.

THE DECLINE OF THE BIRTHRATE

Fearful and wonderful are the theories put forth by men as to the cause of the decline of the birthrate. Verily, as Olive Schreiner said, 'If women were the inhabitants of Jupiter of whom you had happened to hear something, you would pore over us and our conditions day and night, but because we are before your eyes, you never look at us.' If men had not been so blinded by self-complacency and conceit they would have seen plainly with the naked eye, what was apparent to every woman in the land twenty years ago. Woman for perfect motherhood requires what man promises at the altar to give her, and then straightaway goes away and forgets. She requires the love and magnetism of a true man, and this her babe participates in to a fuller and more beneficial extent than does she herself. The marriage bond, all honour to it, whether of civil or sacred origin is the preliminary to a contract, arduous or otherwise as the temperament of those concerned decide. Let us, for the sake of argument, sink the sacredness of it, for in far too many cases this element is not apparent. Let us deal with it only from its civil aspect. Do all men conform religiously to their part of the bargain? No, they do not. And why do they not? Because of the selfishness of their natures, – self-ishness acquired through ages of despotism. Wherever there is despotism there is injustice, and wherever there is injustice there is consequent suffering, and wherever there is suffering there is resentment. Do men know that they are selfish? No, and yes. The majority do not, but the thinkers, those who extend a helping hand to their sisters to betterment, do. Not the scholarly follower of the meek and lowly Jesus, who goes holidaying at a salary of £1000 per year all told, and a purse of sovereigns in his pocket. Not he, he only proclaims the frivolity of the women who support him, and preaches to them the necessity of subjection. Such an one the other day held up his hands in holy horror when it was suggested that he form a league of his women for the purpose of returning good men to Parliament to make laws for them and their children. Oh, no. If just men were put at the head of affairs in Church and State he might find his office gone. Is it, then, the self-satisfied seers who sit in Royal Commissions at an awful cost to our already impoverished revenue, largely paid by women? We say, it is these, impotent men in many instances, or the husbands of barren women? For they are childless, some of them who sit in judgment upon the mothers of men, and talk of their frivolity and love of dress? No. Nor did the love of frivolity and dress actuate the women of a savage tribe on the West Coast of Africa, who, dissatisfied with the treatment accorded them by their husbands and sons, suddenly left in the night and sought the protection of an alien tribe until their demands for justice were recognised, whereupon they returned to a womanless camp. Love of decent dress does not always mean extravagance. The dowdy woman is far more extravagant than she who loves pretty things for her husband's sake. The dowdy one who cares nothing for dress buys good material so that it may last, and plenty of it so that she will have enough; and gives it to the nearest dressmaker to spoil, perhaps, for she does not care. But the dressy woman often finely tucks a shilling remnant, and with a half-penny worth of silk or cotton feather-stitches it into a dressy garment; and knows how to wear it with a whisp of tule at her neck, and a two-penny string of pearls worn above a bunch of honeysuckle pulled from the nearest fence. 'Ah, my word,' we heard a wise man say of such an one. 'She would make a good poor man's wife. She would keep him poor.' Awfully clever, wasn't it? Poverty does not deter childbirth. It does not in the case of the drought-stricken selector, it does not in that of the duffered out digger, both of whom are proverbial for the size of their families, and who, if they have not peace and plenty have plenty of peace; and no hawkers to wake the baby, and no neighbours to be irritated by its crying. Deliberate prevention is cited as one of the most telling causes of the decline of the birthrate. In most cases that reach the public, man suggests the operation, and in most cases man performs it, and in nine cases out of ten a man informs upon the other two. And if the sinner is a female, who taught her her trade? Why, some unscrupulous male medico, a publisher of obscene literature, or manufacturer of patent medicines, all of whom expect and demand that women keep to the letter of the law her part in the matrimonial contract, while they play ducks and drakes with theirs.

What man does not know at least a score of capable, modest, and industrious women who do not marry. Why? They know nothing of the marriage lottery? Don't they! Why, where have they been all their lives? Studying the marriage question in their own homes, of course. Studying the selfishness of their brothers,

and turning their thoughts and affections to the large family of
humanity. 'No, poor mother's lot was enough for me. Father
drank,' etc. And so it is that women feeling insecure and unsup-
ported, do not feel themselves justified in having a large family.
It is put forward that in the country the decline is not so apparent. Just so, because a man is more of a companion to his wife
in the bush, and the nearest corner pub is too far for him to con-
veniently visit, so he stays with his wife, and the children help
to keep them company and drive loneliness away. And so it should
be. But the woman who doesn't marry – doesn't she want babies?
God pity her, yes. Does she want the strong true love of a good
man? Does she? Just ask old Mother Nature and see her smile.
And the sooner man has learnt to be a law unto himself and above
all to be true to himself and his pledges the sooner this vexed
question of the decline of the birthrate will cease.

WOMAN VERSUS MAN QUESTION

From the time when Adam made the first paltry charge against
Eve, men have been ever found ready to indulge in a querulous
gerimede against the sex. Eve got the apple, and woman-like, gave
Adam a bite, after which Adam went and told, putting all the
blame upon her. Eve left Eden and the apples (and went to look
for oranges, perhaps) and, like a sensible woman, forgave her
mate and let the matter drop. But Adam keeps on telling and telling and Eve simply says, 'Pooh! What I get in future I'll keep for
myself.' This makes Adam more mad, and he flies to the daily
Press and tells. But unfortunately for him everybody is not so
sure that his motives are quite disinterested. It is not known that
he ever pulled an apple and gave Eve half and said nothing about
it. Nor was he ever noted for stepping aside to give Eve any plums
that fell to his lot in the way of light billets or good pay, etc.
No; but he has been known to eat all the plums himself, and all
the banquets too, for that matter, allowing Eve, sometimes, the
privilege of looking on while he gorged. Now, Eve considers herself quite as good as Adam, so she says, 'Oh! yes,' to his cheap
and nasty advice. 'One word for me and two for yourself, old
man I can look after myself. Keep your protection. It is not worth
a quarter the price you put upon it. We like working in factories
because our time is our own when not at work, and if we work

well we will be experts and command good pay; and we will not have to sell ourselves body and soul for protection. We'll be all right if you'll keep out of the way. You are the cause of all the bother, and you always were. We won't go to service, either – well, not until we know just what we are expected to do, and get reasonable hours, like you do. Because you make those you protect unhappy and we get mixed up in it; and worry takes the strength from us and we can't work, and you run and tell. You're an old hen-wife, and we don't want your interference. Go and mind your own business, and take the mote out of your own eye. We won't alter to suit service – but you are in power, and can alter service to suit us, there now!' But still Adam keeps on talking, with a view to keep woman's horizon bounded by four walls called home, thus cramping her mind and aspirations, and making her a creature far removed from what God made her. But she is learning to be true to herself, to know her own value; better still, to take man at her own, not his fictitious valuation. She will thus create a new heaven and a new earth, whose conditions will be better for her and her children, and better a thousand-fold for man, for she cannot better her own condition without improving his.

JESSIE COUVREUR, ('TASMA'), 1848-1897

While many of her heroines have Australian connections, and many of her works of fiction have Australian settings, Jessie Couvreur was more concerned about the exploitation of women than with explaining the peculiarities of Australia to an English audience. Much of her writing about women's plight originated in her own marital experience; born in London, Jessie Catherine Huybers arrived in Tasmania in the 1850s and in 1867 was married – unhappily – to Charles Frazer. In 1883 she took the unusual step of obtaining a divorce, partly because of her husband's gambling and infidelity. She then proceeded to support herself primarily by her pen.

After her divorce she married Auguste Couvreur, a Belgian journalist and politician, and on settling in Europe she was associated with a variety of social/political causes and with a series of lectures on Australia. On the death of her husband in 1894, Jessie Couvreur became the Belgian correspondent for the *Times*.

At a time when Australian literature was associated with the imagery of the outback, the relationships between solitary men, and the ethos of egalitarianism, Jessie Couvreur was exploring the effects of city life, the inter-connections and tensions within families, and the social divisions created by wealth and birth. Women – and sexual inequalities – were at the centre of much of her

292 Jessie Couvreur ('Tasma')

work, and her fiction, widely acclaimed at the time, constitutes a challenge to the conventional version of Australian literary history.

  Uncle Piper of Piper's Hill: An Australian Novel was first published in 1889 (and is now available in Pandora's Australian Literary Heritage series) and should stand as a classic of Australian fiction. *In Her Earliest Youth* followed in 1890, and *The Penance of Portia James* (1891) (now available Penguin Australian Women's Library), *A Knight of the White Feather: Incidents and Scenes in Melbourne Life* (1892), *Not Counting the Cost* (1895) and *A Fiery Ordeal* (1897). 'An Old Time Episode in Tasmania' (included here) was first published in *Coo-ee: Tales of Australian Life by Australian Ladies* (1891, edited by Mrs Patchett Martin), and is indicative of her concerns with women's position in society.

AN OLD-TIME EPISODE IN TASMANIA

The gig was waiting upon the narrow gravel drive in front of the fuchsia-wreathed porch of Cowa Cottage. Perched upon the seat, holding the whip in two small, plump, ungloved hands, sat Trucaninny, Mr Paton's youngest daughter, whose straw-coloured, sun-steeped hair, and clear, sky-reflecting eyes, seemed to protest against the name of a black gin that some 'clay-brained cleric' had bestowed upon her irresponsible little person at the baptismal font some eight or nine years ago. The scene of this outrage was Old St. David's Cathedral, Hobart, – or, as it was then called, Hobart *Town*, – chief city of the Arcadian island of Tasmania; and just at this moment, eight o'clock on a November morning, the said cathedral tower, round and ungainly, coated with a surface of dingy white plaster, reflected back the purest, brightest light in the world. From Trucaninny's perch – she had taken the driver's seat – she could see, not only the cathedral, but a considerable portion of the town, which took the form of a capital S as it followed the windings of the coast. Beyond the wharves, against which a few whalers and fishing-boats were lying idle, the middle distance was represented by the broad waters of the Derwent, radiantly blue, and glittering with silver sparkles;

while the far-off background showed a long stretch of yellow sand, and the hazy, undulating outline of low-lying purple hills. Behind her the aspect was different. Tiers of hills rose one above the other in grand confusion, until they culminated in the towering height of Mount Wellington, keeping guard in majestic silence over the lonely little city that encircled its base. This portion of the view, however, was hidden from Trucaninny's gaze by the weatherboard cottage in front of which the gig was standing, – though I doubt whether in any case she would have turned her head to look at it; the faculty of enjoying a beautiful landscape being an acquisition of later years than she had attained since the perpetration of the afore-mentioned outrage of her christening. Conversely, as Herbert Spence says, the young man who was holding the horse's head until such time as the owner of the gig should emerge from the fuchsia-wreathed porch, fastened his eyes upon the beautiful scene before him with more than an artist's appreciation in their gaze. He was dressed in the rough clothes of a working gardener, and so much of his head as could be seen beneath the old felt wide-awake that covered it, bore ominous evidence of having been recently shaved. I use the word ominous advisedly, for a shaven head in connection with a working suit had nothing priestly in its suggestion, and could bear, indeed, only one interpretation in the wicked old times in Tasmania. The young man keeping watch over the gig had clearly come into that fair scene for his country's good; and the explanation of the absence of a prison suit was doubtless due to the fact he was out on a ticket-of-leave. What the landscape had to say to him under these circumstances was not precisely clear. Perhaps all his soul was going out towards the white-sailed wool-ship tacking down the Bay on the first stage of a journey of most uncertain length; or possibly the wondrous beauty of the scene, contrasted with the unspeakable horror of the one he had left, brought the vague impression that it was merely some exquisite vision. That a place so appalling as his old prison should exist in the heart of all this peace and loveliness, seemed too strange an anomaly. Either that was a nightmare and this was real, or this was a fantastic dream and that was the revolting truth; but then which was which, and how had he, Richard Cole, late No. 213, come to be mixed up with either?

As though to give a practical answer to his melancholy question, the sharp tingle of a whip's lash made itself felt at this instant across his cheek. In aiming the cumbersome driving-whip at the persistent flies exploring the mare's back, Trucaninny had brought it down in a direction she had not intended it to take. For a moment she stood aghast. Richard's face was white with passion. He turned fiercely round; his flaming eyes seemed literally to send out sparks of anger. 'Oh, please, I didn't mean it,' cried the child penitently. 'I wanted to hit the flies. I did indeed. I hope I didn't hurt you?'

The *amende honorable* brought about an immediate reaction. The change in the young man's face was wonderful to behold. As he smiled back full reassurance at the offender, it might be seen that his eyes could express the extremes of contrary feeling at the very shortest notice. For all answer, he raised his old felt wide-awake in a half-mocking though entirely courtly fashion, like some nineteenth century Don César de Bazan, and made a graceful bow.

'Are *you* talking to the man, Truca?' cried a querulous voice at this moment from the porch, with a stress on the you that made the little girl lower her head, shame-faced. 'What do you mean by disobeying orders, miss?'

The lady who swept out upon the verandah at the close of this tirade was in entire accord with her voice. 'British matron' would have been the complete description of Miss Paton, if fate had not willed that she should be only a British spinster. The inflexibility that comes of finality of opinion regarding what is proper and what is the reverse, – a rule of conduct that is of universal application for the true British matron, – expressed itself in every line of her face and in every fold of her gown. That she was relentlessly respectable and unyielding might be read at the first glance; that she had been handsome, in the same hard way, a great many years before Truca was maltreated at the baptismal font, might also have been guessed at from present indications. But that she should be the 'own sister' of the good-looking, military-moustached, debonair man (I use the word debonair here in the French sense) who now followed her out of the porch, was less easy to divine. The character of the features as well as of the expression spoke of two widely differing temperaments. Indeed, save for a curious dent between the eyebrows, and a something in the nostrils that seemed to say he was not to be trifled with, Mr Paton might have sat for the portrait of one of those jolly good fellows who reiterate so tunefully that they 'won't go home till morning,' and who are as good as their word afterwards.

Yet 'jolly good fellow' as he showed himself in card-rooms and among so-called boon companions, he could reveal himself in a very different light to the convicts who fell under his rule. Forming part of a system for the crushing down of the unhappy prisoners, in accordance with the principle of 'Woe be to him through whom the offence cometh,' he could return with a light heart to his breakfast or his dinner, after seeing some score of his fellow-men abjectly writhing under the lash, or pinioned in a ghastly row upon the hideous gallows. 'Use,' says Shakespeare, 'can almost change the stamp of Nature.' In Mr Paton's case it had warped as well as changed it. Like the people who live in the atmosphere of Courts, and come to regard all outsiders as another and inferior race, he had come to look upon humanity as divisible into two classes – namely, those who were convicts, and those who were not. For the latter, he had still some ready drops of the milk of human kindness at his disposal. For the former, he had no more feeling than we have for snakes or sharks, as the typical and popular embodiments of evil.

Miss Paton had speedily adopted her brother's views in this respect. Summoned from England to keep house for him at the death of Trucaninny's mother, she showed an aptitude for introducing prison discipline into her domestic rule. From constant association with the severe *régime* that she was accustomed to see exercised upon the convicts, she had ended by regarding disobedience to orders, whether in children or in servants, as the unpardonable sin. One of her laws, as of the Medes and Persians, was that the young people in the Paton household should never exchange a word with the convict servants in their father's employ. It was hard to observe the letter of the law in the case of the indoor servants, above all for Truca, who was by nature a garrulous little girl. Being a truthful little girl as well, she was often obliged to confess to having had a talk with the latest importation from the gaol, – an avowal which signified, as she well knew, the immediate forfeiture of all her week's pocket-money.

On the present occasion her apologies to the gardener were the latest infringement of the rule. She looked timidly towards her aunt as the latter advanced austerely in the direction of the gig, but to her relief, Miss Paton hardly seemed to notice her.

'I suppose you will bring the creature back with you, Wilfrid?' she said, half-questioningly, half-authoritatively, as her brother mounted into the gig and took the reins from Truca's chubby hands. 'Last time we had a drunkard *and* a thief. The time before, a thief, and – and a – really I don't know which was worse. It is frightful to be reduced to such a choice of evils, but I would almost suggest your looking among the – you know – the – *in-fan-ti-cide* cases this time.'

She mouthed the word in separate syllables at her brother, fearful of pronouncing it openly before Truca and the convict gardener.

Mr Paton nodded. It was not the first time he had been sent upon the delicate mission of choosing a maid for his sister from the female prison, politely called the Factory, at the foot of Mount Wellington. For some reason it would be difficult to explain, his selections were generally rather more successful than hers. Besides which, it was a satisfaction to have some one upon whom to throw the responsibility of the inevitable catastrophe that terminated the career of every successive ticket-of-leave in turn.

The morning, as we have seen, was beautiful. The gig bowled smoothly over the macadamized length of Macquarrie[*sic*] Street. Truca was allowed to drive; and so deftly did her little fingers guide the mare, that her father lighted his cigar, and allowed himself to ruminate upon a thousand things that it would have been better perhaps to leave alone. In certain moods he was apt to deplore the fate that had landed – or stranded – him in this God-forsaken corner of the world. Talk of prisoners, indeed! What was he himself but a prisoner, since the day when he had madly passed sentence of transportation on himself and his family, because the pay of a Government clerk in England did not increase in the same ratio as the income-tax. As a matter of fact, he did not wear a canary-coloured livery, and his prison was as near an approach, people said, to an earthly Paradise as could well be conceived. With its encircling chains of mountains, folded one around the other, it was like a mighty rose, tossed from the Creator's hand into the desolate Southern Ocean. Here to his right towered purple Mount Wellington, with rugged cliffs gleaming forth from a purple background. To his left the wide Derwent shone and sparkled in blue robe and silver spangles, like the Bay of Naples, he had been told. Well, he had never seen the Bay of Naples, but there were times when he would have given all the beauty here, and as much more to spare, for a strip of London pavement in front of his old club. Mr Paton's world, indeed, was out of joint. Perhaps twelve years of unthinking acquiescence in the flogging and hanging of convicts had distorted his mental focus. As for the joys of home-life, he told himself that those which had fallen to his share brought him but cold comfort. His sister was a Puritan, and she was making his children hypocrites, with the exception, perhaps, of Truca. Another disagreeable subject of reflection was the one that his groom Richard was about to leave him. In a month's time, Richard, like his royal namesake, would be himself again. For the past five years he had been only No. 213, expiating in that capacity a righteous blow aimed at a cowardly ruffian who had sworn to marry his sister – by fair means or by foul. The blow had been only too well aimed. Richard was convicted of manslaughter, and sentenced to seven years' transportation beyond the seas. His sister, who had sought to screen him, was tried and condemned for perjury. Of the latter, nothing was known. Of the former, Mr Paton only knew that he would be extremely loth to part with so good a servant. Silent as the Slave of the Lamp, exact as any machine, performing the least of his duties with the same intelligent scrupulousness, his very presence in the household was a safeguard and a reassurance. It was like his luck, Mr Paton reflected in his present pessimistic mood, to have chanced upon such a fellow, just as by his d – d good conduct he had managed to obtain a curtailment of his sentence. If Richard had been justly dealt with, he would have had two good years left to devote to the service of his employer. As to keeping him after he was a free man, that was not to be hoped for. Besides which, Mr Paton was not sure that he should feel at all at his ease in dealing with a free man. The slave-making instinct, which is always inherent in the human race, whatever civilisation may have done to repress it, had become his sole rule of conduct in his relations with those who served him.

There was one means perhaps of keeping the young man in bondage, but it was a means that even Mr Paton himself hesitated to employ. By an almost superhuman adherence to impossible rules, Richard had escaped hitherto the humiliation of the lash; but if a flogging could be laid to his charge, his time of probation would be of necessity prolonged, and he might continue to groom the mare and tend the garden for an indefinite space of time, with the ever intelligent thoroughness that distinguished him. A slip of paper in a sealed envelope, which the

298 Jessie Couvreur ('Tasma')

victim would carry himself to the nearest justice of the peace, would effect the desired object. The etiquette of the proceeding did not require that any explanation should be given.

Richard would be fastened to the triangles, and any subsequent revolt on his part could only involve him more deeply than before. Mr Paton had no wish to hurt him; but he was after all an invaluable servant, and perhaps he would be intelligent enough to understand that the disagreeable formality to which he was subjected was in reality only a striking mark of his master's esteem for him.

Truca's father had arrived thus far in his meditations when the gig pulled up before the Factory gate. It was a large bare building, with white unshaded walls, but the landscape which framed it gave it a magnificent setting. The little girl was allowed to accompany her father indoors, while a man in a grey prison suit, under the immediate surveillance of an armed warder, stood at the mare's head.

Mr Paton's mission was a delicate one. To gently scan his brother man, and still gentler sister woman, did not apply to his treatment of convicts. He brought his sternest official expression to bear upon the aspirants who defiled past him at the matron's bidding, in their disfiguring prison livery. One or two, who thought they detected a likely looking man behind the Government official, threw him equivocal glances as they went by. Of these he took no notice. His choice seemed to lie in the end between a sullen-looking elderly woman, whom the superintendent qualified as a 'sour jade,' and a half-imbecile girl, when his attention was suddenly attracted to a new arrival, who stood out in such marked contrast with the rest, that she looked like a dove in the midst of a flock of vultures.

'Who is that?' he asked the matron in a peremptory aside.

'That, sir,' – the woman's lips assumed a tight expression as she spoke, – 'she's No. 27 – Amelia Clare – she came out with the last batch.'

'Call her up, will you?' was the short rejoinder, and the matron reluctantly obeyed.

In his early days Truca's father had been a great lover of Italian opera. There was hardly an air of Bellini's or Donizetti's that he did not know by heart. As No. 27 came slowly towards him, something in her manner of walking, coupled with the half-abstracted, half-fixed expression in her beautiful grey eyes, reminded him of Amina in the *Sonnambula*. So strong, indeed, was the impression, that he would hardly have been surprised to see No. 27 take off her unbecoming prison cap and jacket, and disclose two round white arms to match her face, or to hear her sing '*Ah! non giunge*' in soft dreamy tones. He could have hummed or whistled a tuneful second himself at a moment's notice, for the matter of that. However, save in the market scene in *Martha*, there is no precedent for warbling a duet with the young person you are about to engage as a domestic servant. Mr Paton remembered this in time, and confined himself to what the French call *le stricte nécessaire*. He inquired of Amelia whether she could do fine sewing, and whether she could clear-starch. His sister had impressed these questions upon him, and he was pleased with himself for remembering them.

Amelia, or Amina (she was really very like Amina), did not reply at once. She had to bring her mind back from the far-away sphere to which it had wandered, or, in other words, to pull herself together first. When the reply did come, it was uttered in just the low, melodious tones one might have expected. She expressed her willingness to attempt whatever was required of her, but seemed very diffident as regarded her power of execution. 'I have forgotten so many things,' she concluded, with a profound sigh.

'Sir, you impertinent minx,' correct the matron.

Amelia did not seem to hear, and her new employer hastened to interpose.

'We will give you a trial,' he said, in a curiously modified tone, 'and I hope you won't give me any occasion to regret it.'

The necessary formalities were hurried through. Mr Paton disregarded the deferential disclaimers of the matron, but experienced, nevertheless, something of a shock when he saw Amelia divested of her prison garb. She had a thorough-bred air that discomfited him. Worse still, she was undeniably pretty. The scissors that had clipped her fair locks had left a number of short rings that clung like tendrils round her shapely little head. She wore a black stuff jacket of extreme simplicity and faultless cut, and a little black bonnet that might have been worn by a Nursing Sister or a '*grande dame*' with equal appropriateness. Thus attired, her appearance was so effective, that Mr Paton asked himself whether he was not doing an unpardonably rash thing in driving No. 27 down Macquarrie[*sic*] Street in his gig, and introducing her into his household afterwards.

It was not Truca, for she had 'driven and lived' that morning, whose *mauvais quart-d'heure* was now to come. It was her father's turn to fall under its influence, as he sat, stern and rigid, on the driver's seat, with his little girl nestling up to him as close as she was able, and that strange, fair, mysterious presence on the other side, towards which he had the annoyance of seeing all the heads of the passers-by turn as he drove on towards home.

Arrived at Cowa Cottage, the young gardener ran forward to open the gate; and here an unexpected incident occurred. As Richard's eyes rested upon the new arrival, he uttered an exclamation that caused her to look round. Their eyes met, a flash of instant recognition was visible in both. Then, like the night that follows a sudden discharge of electricity, the gloom that was habitual to both faces settled down upon them once more. Richard shut the gate with his accustomed machine-like precision. Amelia looked at the intangible something in the clouds that had power to fix her gaze upon itself. Yet the emotion she had betrayed was not lost upon her employer. Who could say? As No. 213 and No. 27, these two might have crossed each other's paths before. That the convicts had wonderful and incomprehensible means of communicating with each other, was well known to Mr Paton. That young men and young women have an equal facility for understanding each other, was also a fact he did not ignore. But which of these two explanations might account for the signs of mutual recognition and sympathy he had just witnessed? Curiously enough, he felt, as he pondered over the mystery later in the day, that he should prefer the former solution. An offensive and defensive alliance was well known to exist among the convicts, and he told himself that he could meet and deal with the difficulties arising from such a cause as he had met and dealt with them before. That was a matter which came within his province, but the taking into account of any sentimental kind of rubbish did *not* come within his province. For some unaccountable reason, the thought of having Richard flogged presented itself anew at this juncture to his mind. He put it away, as he had done before, angered with himself for having harboured it. But it returned at intervals during the succeeding week, and was never stronger than one afternoon, when his little girl ran out to him as he sat smoking in the verandah, with an illustrated volume of *Grimm's Tales* in her hands.

'Oh, papa, look! I've found some one just like Amelia in my book of Grimm. It's the picture of Snow-White. Only look, papa! Isn't it the very living image of Amelia?'

'Nonsense!' said her father; but he looked at the page nevertheless. Truca was right. The snow-maiden in the woodcut had the very eyes and mouth of Amelia Clare – frozen through some mysterious influence into beautiful, unyielding rigidity. Mr Paton wished sometimes he had never brought the girl into his house. Not that there was any kind of fault to be found with her. Even his sister, who might have passed for 'She-who-must-be-obeyed,' if Rider Haggard's books had existed at that time, could not complain of want of docile obedience to orders on the part of the new maid. Nevertheless, her presence was oppressive to the master of the house. Two lines of Byron's haunted him constantly in connection with her –

> 'So coldly sweet, so deadly fair,
> We start – for life is wanting there.'

If Richard worked like an automaton, then she worked like a spirit; and when she moved noiselessly about the room where he happened to be sitting, he could not help following her uneasily with his eyes.

The days wore on, succeeding each other and resembling each other, as the French proverb has it, with desperate monotony. Christmas, replete with roses and strawberries, had come and gone. Mr Paton was alternately swayed by two demons, one of which whispered in his ear, 'Richard Cole is in love with No. 27. The time for him to regain his freedom is at hand. The first use he will make of it will be to leave you, and the next to marry Amelia Clare. You will thus be deprived of everything at one blow. You will lose the best man-servant you have ever known, and your sister, the best maid. And more than this, you will lose an interest in life that gives it a stimulating flavour it has not had for many a long year. Whatever may be the impulse that prompts you to wonder what that ice-bound face and form hide, it is an impulse that makes your heart beat and your blood course warmly through your veins. When this fair, uncanny presence is removed from your home, your life will become stagnant as it was before.' To this demon Mr Paton would reply energetically, 'I won't give the fellow the chance of marrying No. 27. As soon as he has his freedom, I will give him the sack, and forbid him the premises. As for Amelia, she is my prisoner, and I would send her back to gaol to-morrow if I thought there were any nonsense up between her and him.'

At this point demon No. 2 would intervene: 'There is a better way of arranging matters. You have it in your power to degrade the fellow in his own eyes and in those of the girl he is after. There is more covert insolence in that impenetrable exterior of his than you have yet found out. Only give him proper provocation, and you will have ample justification for bringing him down. A good flogging would put everything upon its proper footing, – you would keep your servant, and you would put a stop to the nonsense that is very probably going on. But don't lose too much time; for if you wait until the last moment, you will betray your hand. The fellow is useful to him, they will say of Richard, but it is rather rough upon him to be made aware of it in such a way as that.'

One evening in January, Mr Paton was supposed to be at his club. In reality he was seated upon a bench in a bushy part of the garden, known as the shrubbery – in parley with the demons. The night had come down upon him almost without his being aware of it – a night heavy with heat and blackness, and noisy with the cracking and whirring of the locusts entombed in the dry soil. All at once he heard a slight rustling in the branches behind him. There was a light pressure of hands on his shoulders, and a face that felt like velvet to the touch was laid against his cheeks. Two firm, warm feminine lips pressed themselves upon his, and a voice that he recognised as Amelia's said in caressing tones, 'Dearest Dick, have I kept you waiting?'

Had it been proposed to our hero some time ago that he should change places with No. 213, he would have declared that he would rather die first. But at this instant the convict's identity seemed so preferable to his own, that he hardly ventured to breathe lest he should betray the fact that he was only his own forlorn self. His silence disconcerted the intruder.

'Why don't you answer, Dick?' she asked impatiently.

'Answer? What am I to say?' responded her master. 'I am not in the secret.'

Amelia did not give him time to say more. With a cry of terror she turned and fled, disappearing as swiftly and mysteriously as she had come. The words 'Dearest Dick' continued to ring in Mr Paton's ears long after she had gone; and the more persistently the refrain was repeated, the more he felt tempted to give Richard a taste of his quality. He had tried to provoke him to some act of overt insolence in vain. He had worried and harried and insulted him all he could. The convict's constancy had never once deserted him. That his employer should have no pretext whereby he might have him degraded and imprisoned, he had acted upon the scriptural precept of turning his left cheek when he was smitten on the right. There were times when his master felt something of a persecutor's impotent rage against him. But now at least he felt he had entire justification for making an example of him. He would teach the fellow to play Romeo and Juliet with a fellow-convict behind his back. So thoroughly did the demon indoctrinate Mr Paton with these ideas, that he felt next morning as though he were doing the most righteous action in the world, when he called Richard to him after breakfast, and said in a tone which he tried to render as careless as of custom, 'Here, you! just take this note over to Mr Merton with my compliments, and *wait for the answer.*'

There was nothing in this command to cause the person who received it to grow suddenly livid. Richard had received such an order at least a score of times before, and had carried messages to and fro between his master and the justice of the peace with no more emotion than the occasion was worth. But on this particular morning, as he took the fatal note into his hands, he turned deadly pale. Instead of retreating with it in his customary automatic fashion, he fixed his eyes upon his employer's face, and something in their expression actually constrained Mr Paton to lower his own.

'May I speak a word with you, sir?' he said, in low, uncertain tones.

It was the first time such thing had happened, and it seemed to Richard's master that the best way of meeting it would be to 'damn' the man and send him about his business.

But Richard did not go. He stood for an instant with his head thrown back, and the desperate look of an animal at bay in his eyes. At this critical moment a woman's form suddenly interposed itself between Mr Paton and his victim. Amelia was there, looking like Amina after she had awoken from her trance. She came close to her master, – she had never addressed him before, – and raised her liquid eyes to his.

'You will not be hard on – my brother, sir, for the mistake I made last night?'

'Who said I was going to be hard on him?' retorted Mr Paton, too much taken aback to find any more dignified form of rejoinder. 'And if he is your brother, why do you wait until it is dark to indulge in your family effusions?'

The question was accompanied by a through and through look, before which Amelia did not quail.

'Have I your permission to speak to him in the day-time, sir?' she said submissively.

'I will institute an inquiry,' interrupted her master. 'Here, go about your business,' he added, turning to Richard; 'fetch out the mare, and hand me back that note. I'll ride over with it myself.'

Three weeks later Richard Cole was a free man, and within four months from the date upon which Mr Paton had driven Amelia Clare down Macquarrie[sic] Street in his gig, she came to take respectful leave of him, dressed in the identical close-fitting jacket and demure little bonnet he remembered. Thenceforth she was nobody's bondswoman. He had a small heap of coin in readiness to hand over to her, with the payment of which, and a few gratuitous words of counsel on his part, the leave-taking would have been definitely and decorously accomplished. To tell her that he was more loth than ever to part with her, did not enter into the official programme. She was her own mistress now, as much or more so than the Queen of England herself, and it was hardly to be wondered at if the first use she made of her freedom was to shake the dust of Cowa Cottage off her feet. Still, if she had only known – if she had only known. It seemed too hard to let her go with the certainty that she never did or could know. Was it not for her sake that he had been swayed by all the conflicting impulses that had made him a changed man of late? For her that he had so narrowly escaped being a criminal awhile ago, and for her that he was appearing in the novel rôle of a reformer of the convict system now? He never doubted that she would have understood him if she *had* known. But to explain was out of the question. He must avow either all or nothing, and the all meant more than he dared to admit even to himself.

This was the reason why Amelia Clare departed sphinx-like as she had come. A fortnight after she had gone, as Mr Paton was gloomily smoking by his library fire in the early dark of a wintry August evening, a letter bearing the N. S. Wales postmark was handed to him. The handwriting, very small and fine, had something familiar in its aspect. He broke open the seal, – letters were still habitually sealed in those days, – and read as follows: –

'SIR, – I am prompted to make you a confession – why, I cannot say, for I shall probably never cross your path again. I was married last week to Richard Cole, who was not my brother, as I led you to suppose, but my affianced husband, in whose behalf I would willingly suffer again to be unjustly condemned and transported. I have the warrant of Scripture for having assumed, like Sarah, the *rôle* of sister in preference to that of wife; besides which, it is hard to divest myself of an instinctive belief that the deceit was useful to Richard on one occasion. I trust you will pardon me. – Yours respectfully,

'AMELIA COLE.'

The kindly phase Mr Paton had passed through with regard to his convict victims came to an abrupt termination. The reaction was terrible. His name is inscribed among those 'who foremost shall be damn'd to Fame' in Tasmania.

Rosa Praed, 1851-1935

Rosa Praed was an outstanding nineteenth century
novelist, who was born Rosa Caroline Murray Prior
in the area now known as the Gold Coast, Queensland. She lived on a number of isolated, outback
stations and in the absence of formal education was
primarily self taught; when, not long after her
mother's death, her father became Post Master
General of the new state of Queensland, she moved
to Brisbane and enjoyed many of the benefits of its
social and political life. In 1872 she married Campbell Mackworth Praed and before the couple moved
to England in 1876, she lived for a brief and harrowing period on Curtis Island.

In London, Rosa Praed achieved astonishing success; without the aid of wealth or patronage she
found herself a recognised place on the popular literary scene. Her first two novels – *An Australian
Heroine* (1880) and *Policy and Passion: A Novel of
Australian Life* (1881) – presented an exciting perspective on Antipodean life and established her
reputation as a writer; when *The Bond of Wedlock*
was published in 1887 (in which the assumption that
a wife should stay with her violent husband was
challenged) and proved so popular that it was soon
adapted for the West End Theatre, her literary success was assured.

Twenty of her more than forty novels were set in
Australia and drew extensively on her Queensland
experience; she created the fictional state of

Leichardt's Land as the backdrop for some of her
political dramas, psychological and social explora-
tions, and colonial adventure stories. Firmly
committed to the development of a distinctive Australian literature, she focussed on many distinguishing
Australian characteristics in her work. She was consistently concerned with the plight of Aborigines and
with the position of women.

But if she enjoyed literary success, she also
experienced many personal disappointments and
pains; her own marriage was unhappy and her children all predeceased her. For twenty eight years of
her life she lived with Nancy Harward, a spiritual
medium with whom she collaborated on some of her
'psychic' novels.

The merit of her work has become more widely
recognised of late and after decades of unavailability
some of her novels are now in print; *An Australian
Heroine* (forthcoming in Penguin Australian Women's
Library); *Policy and Passion* (forthcoming from
Virago); *The Bond of Wedlock* (Pandora); *Outlaw
and Lawmaker* (Pandora), *Lady Bridget in the Never-
Never Land* (Pandora); more are likely to be
reprinted.

My Australian Girlhood (1902) is Rosa Praed's
account of her early life and reveals some of the
social and emotional forces which helped to shape
her values; this account also contrasts starkly with
some of the conventional encoded images of the outback. While many of her attitudes to blacks would
be unacceptable today, her familiarity with and
championing of black culture made her a radical in
her own time. The first part of *My Australian Girlhood* is reprinted here in full, and is taken from the
1904 edition published by Fisher Unwin, London.

MY AUSTRALIAN GIRLHOOD
CHAPTER I
The Young-Old Land

I often wish that, like the late Mr du Maurier's *Peter Ibbetson*, one could live one's childhood over again in dreams. For some of us, what a delightful contrast they would present to the smug English conventionalities! My own childhood certainly had in it no playmate counterpart of the exquisite Duchess of Towers, and its crude romance – of a sort – would probably not appeal to well brought up folk. Yet after thirty years of civilised existence, that wild youth 'down under' comes back to me in all its unforgettable charm, and I am grateful to it for having brought to bear on my life at least one mighty influence – one passion from whose thrall I have never wished to escape. My Australian girlhood taught me to love Nature, and to find in the old Nurse ever my best friend.

It is an odd, but a very real thing – the nostalgia of the gumtrees. Even still, I never see a white-barked eucalyptus, whether it be in a flourishing plantation about Cannes or a sickly denaturalised clump on the Roman Campagna or some melancholy sucker in a hothouse, without being seized by an untranslatable emotion. I never smell the pungent, aromatic scent, which for twenty-two years was as the breath of my nostrils, without being carried back to the old, vivid world of untrodden pastures and lonely forests, without falling again under the grim spell of the bush.

I have heard people say that they can remember distinctly events which took place when they were three years old. I can't remember events so far back as that; I can only see pictures. These make in my mind a little gallery of scenes following one upon another – imperfect, phantasmagoric, like the shadows thrown by an unpractised performer upon a magic-lantern sheet.

The first picture which flashes upon the sheet shows my grandmother and her boxes. Perhaps it is because the old lady taught me to read from those boxes – thus opening to my baby mind an enchanted world of Bible stories and fairy legends – that my grandmother stands out foremost on the memory page. In my picture she seems rather an awesome person, with a long upper lip, grave, piercing dark eyes, and four shiny black curls, two on each side of her face, which is framed by the border of a huge straw bonnet with a quilling of brown ribbon in the inside. She wears, besides, a mantilla with large sleeves, and a gown of brown-and-white checked stuff having three wide flounces edged with narrow velvet. When she smiles, her face ceases to be severe, and the tones of her voice, which were low and pleasant, linger like the sound of a lullaby. My grandmother's boxes were black wooden trunks, some flat, some rounded, and on the tops and sides of them, there was painted in thick white letters, a legend which set forth that Colonel Thomas Murray Prior had taken passage in the *Roxburgh Castle* from Southampton, Engand, for Bungroopim Station, Logan River, Brisbane Water, Moreton Bay, Australia. In addition to this lengthy inscription, were foreign addresses telling of former wanderings, while the names and addresses of the owners of the vessel and of their agents in Sydney were duly recorded, so it will be seen that there was sufficient alphabetic material on those boxes to enable me to take elementary lessons in grammar.

That was nearly fifty years ago, when Moreton Bay was still a penal settlement, and the colony of Queensland not in existence; when Brisbane was only a river village called Brisbane Water, and its Houses of Parliament – in which later, I used often, for private and personal reasons, to listen anxiously for the turn of a debate – were not dreamed of.

It was in the beginning of things Australian. And first let me say that my only excuse for these scattered memories and impressions of Australian life is that they belong to an order of things which has passed away. To a girl born now in the bush, the old pioneering times would be as the tale of a vanished dream. Everything has changed; but I can look back upon the start of a colony – I speak of Northern Australia, which I venture to predict will have a prominent part in the making of future history. A bold boast, but my own countrymen and women will forgive it. The climate and products of Queensland give it a distinctive position in the Federated Commonwealth, and its scrubs and fastnesses and wild coast-line have afforded a last foothold to the dispossessed. So, remembering the little war of my childhood, after the Frazer murder, between the squatters and the Blacks, I may almost say that I was an outside spectator of the sweeping away of the old race from the land.

I love the Blacks. Some of them were my play-fellows when

I was a child at Naraigin, up in the then unsettled north; and truly, I think that the natives have not deserved their fate nor the evil that has been spoken of them. It was mainly the fault of the Whites that they learned treachery, and were incited to rapine and murder. But this comes into another chapter.

In one of my grandmother's boxes – one of those from which I learned my alphabet, and which, after half a century and much journeying has returned to me again – are a pile of old papers – some ancient family documents of quaint spelling, that concern not these pages – and near the top of the pile, a bundle of tattered letters – square blue sheets folded into an oblong, the outer one of each inscribed with hieroglyphic marks and 'Paid Ship Letter' in red ink doing duty for a postage stamp. These are my father's accounts of his landing and early experiences in Australia, carefully kept by the old people, Death having played the postman for these and other letters, bringing them at last into my possession, as well as some pages of manuscript – jottings of pioneering days, dating back over sixty years. In 1839 the voyage out in sailing ship took five or six months. From a storm outside, the vessel passed between Sydney Heads, and the young emigrant writes: 'It is a strange sensation to be anchored in a smooth, beautiful, apparently landlocked bay, with trees growing down to the water's edge, and not a house in sight.' What a different scene now! Villas and gardens on every headland, and marking the semi-circle of each sandy bay.

I remember a certain wild morning when I too passed out of a grey, heaving sea – heaving with the swell after a great storm – into blueness and peace. I can see the narrow break in the purple line of cliff, the two huge profiles of the Heads, a lighthouse on the boldest, and the ocean, dashing spray against the rocky rampart. There was the faint dip showing Cunninghame's Gap, where once a ship, mistaking it for the opening of the harbour, dashed straight against the rocks, and every soul, save one, on board was drowned within sight of the lights of home. A little boat with a reddish sail raced our big steamer and won the race, rising like a cockle-shell on the waves, and rounding the North Head before us. Then we came into still water, a blue basin with indented sides, and a background of town and suburbs. We could see a flotilla of yachts – it was Saturday afternoon – dancing round the points.

There rises in my memory another entry into Sydney Harbour, this time a night one, after a voyage from Tasmania, and I recall the thrill with which we heard out of the darkness, as a boat pulled up to the steamer, the news that Prince Alfred had been shot by Farrell the Fenian. Then next day, the mingled excitement and horror of seeing Sydney placarded with posters offering '£1,000 reward' for any of the accomplices of Farrell.

I turn to the pioneering jottings and string them on my own thread. For the stringing, however, I must go back to the time when Australia beyond Botany Bay was unexplored, save by a small band of adventurers, of whom the ill-fated Leichardt was chief. There is mention of him in one of the letters that came out of my grandmother's box.

'I was delighted to learn yesterday that Leichardt had arrived safely after accomplishing his long and tedious journey to Port Easington, one of the most daring and successful expeditions which has yet been attempted. I have not heard particulars, except that there is a most splendid country and some navigable rivers. I shall write to Leichardt and congratulate him on his coming to life again. I hear that he intends publishing a work, and that a large subscription has already been made for him. He certainly deserves a grant from the Government, for they will be the principal gainers by his travels.'

The story of Leichardt is too well known to be repeated here. It has been written by an abler Australian pen than mine – that of Mr Archibald Meston. Leichardt's charm of manner, the result of a varied foreign education; his artistic nature, his cultivated mind, and his passionate attachment to Miss Nicholson; above all, his love for his adopted country, and frequently expressed determination to die, if need were, for Australia, have made him a hero of romance to those who, like my father, were his comrades, and to such as myself, who remember the interest he inspired, and the wild rumours which from time to time were afloat concerning his end.

For a long time it was believed that he might still be in existence, a prisoner among the northern Blacks. As it is, no one knows how or when he died.

There were no roads then from one colony to another. Only the coast-line had been explored. It was known that New Holland, as it was called, stretched over 2,500 miles from east to west, and nearly that distance from north to south, but it could but be conjectured that beyond the inhabited – or, rather, habitable – rim, extending inland some hundred or two of miles, lay a vast Sahara fatal to man and beast.

The squatters of those times were a brave, reckless band. Quick to love and quick to hate, full of pluck and endurance, dauntless before danger, iron in physique and nerve, and ready for any difficult or dare-devil feat – their adventures, escapes, jokes, and carouses would have furnished rich material for an Australian Lever or Fenimore Cooper.

In the very early forties a party of these men left Sydney, and pushed north into the country which is now called Queensland. The Government gave extensive grants of land to pioneers, and hitherto undiscovered country was thrown open. The outside Blacks had never seen a white man or a horse, and they took the first mounted stockman for a kind of centaur, and called him 'Yarraman Dick' – 'yarraman' being their word for a horse.

The pioneers led a following of ticket-of-leave men and convicts on term, whom the Government lent out. When the pioneer was about to start for a new country he would get his convicts together and talk to them after such fashion as this: 'Lads, we are going into the interior. If any of you jib at the job, let me know like men, and I'll turn you in and get others; but if you stick to me I'll stick to you, and give you good rations and twenty pounds a year as long as you behave yourselves.' Very few did jib at the job, some of them showed the true hero stuff, and many a one got in this way his ticket-of-leave, and ultimately, his freedom.

It was as in the days of the patriarchs. Men travelled with their flocks and herds, and, like Abraham and Lot, fought the tribes for land and water. Then legislation stepped in, granted licenses and defined boundaries. A Land Commissioner was appointed, who ruled the land with a rod of iron. 'King Tom,' the first Land Commissioner, had a Prime Minister familiarly styled 'Unbranded Kelly.' For in those days all animals, which at the age of twelve months were still unbranded, became by law the property of the Crown, and were impounded and sold. Kelly, with a company of policemen and blackboys, would make raids upon the stations and bring the unbranded calves in triumph to the Pound. A lady reigned as housekeeper over the Commissioner's household, and ruled the Commissioner also. It was she who became the owner of those confiscated calves at a nominal price. No one dared bid at the Pound against her.

Words fail for painting the loneliness of the Australian bush.

Mile after mile of primeval forest; interminable vistas of melancholy gum-trees; ravines, along the sides of which the long-bladed grass grows rankly; level, untimbered plains alternating with undulating tracts of pasture, here and there, broken by steep gully, stony ridge, or dried-up creek. All wild and utterly desolate; all the same monotonous grey colouring, except where the wattle, when in blossom, shows patches of feathery gold or a belt of scrub lies green, glossy, and impenetrable. I know nothing so strange in its way, as to travel for days through endless gum-forest. Surely there never was tree so weird as a very old gum, with its twisted trunk, the withes of grey moss which hang from its branches, and the queer protuberances upon its limbs in which wild bees hive. It was a great thing when we camped out if the black boys found and chopped down a 'sugar-bag' so that we could season our damper with native honey. A white gum has spotted, scaly bark; from a red 'iron-bark' the gum oozes and drops like congealed blood. Then, see the odd, expectant way in which the tree will slant along the side of a ridge, and the human look of its dead arms, when it is one that has been 'rung' or blasted by lightning! There is nothing pretty about a gum-tree. It seems to belong to antediluvian nature. Often, a laughing jackass, the big kingfisher of Australia, is perched in the fork of a bough shrilling its devilish merriment, or an iguana will be dragging its unwieldy length up the trunk – a land crocodile which seems antediluvian too; as does a kangaroo which may be starting upon a series of eccentric boundings, its uneven legs and long tail flapping in the air, with, perhaps, a baby marsupial peeping from its pouch. And talking of antediluvian animals, is there anything more curious than a platypus, which has fur like a seal, a bill like a duck, and which lays eggs and nurses its young, when they are hatched, with the milk of its breasts? Naturalists say that the platypus represents a very early stage of mammalian evolution. Yes, indeed, the bush seems a kind of primeval survival, and like nothing else in the known world.

It is told that there was once an old, old country, and that when the priests of Sais talked to Solon and rebuked him for boasting of the great age of his nation, – assuring him that before ever Greece and her heroes were, a mighty race of men existed, which had built a city of golden gates and cultivated a land spreading where the Atlantic Ocean now rolls, – they spoke of the lost Atlantis which has been written of in other places.

But before Atlantis was, old books say that the world had shaped itself into a great and different land, which was Lemuria. And of Lemuria the largest part that remains to this day is Australia.

This is what certain records tell, but of the truth of them who can speak with knowledge? Yet also, who can see the land in its hoariness, and the convulsions that have torn it, and the curious mammals that are upon it, and upon no other land, and the gum-trees of such weird conformation unlike all other trees that are – who can see these things and ponder over them, without pondering too and greatly wondering over the story of the lost Atlantis and of Lemuria that was before, and over the rebuke of the priests of Sais, and the legends and the myths which have come down through the mists of many ages!

I was thinking something of this sort during a three days' ride I took not so very long ago, among gum-trees so twisted, bleached, and ancient that they seemed the ancestors of all Australian gums. A sudden rebreathing this was of the old wonder and wildness: a dream journey through a witches' forest. For was there ever anything more ghoulish than these hag-like white-limbed trees? My ride was across the high tableland of New South Wales, out of the sides of which enormous slices have been torn in some far-back convulsion of nature, leaving gigantic chasms strewn with huge boulders and overgrown by scrub that has never been trodden by human foot. It is over such walls of rock and down such chasms that the Fitzroy and Belmore Falls dash and sweep.

The ranger at the Fitzroy Falls had, it is almost certain, never heard of Atlantis nor of Lemuria, nor of the priests of Sais. But he had lived among the gumtrees, and their strange fascination had wrought itself into his being, for he too seemed to brood in his own fashion upon these things.

'It's a queer country, this Australia!' he said. 'I've often wondered as I've been going along what was the beginning of it. Talk of its being new! Seems to me that it's as old as the world before Adam, and that it was just forgotten, when the Creator parcelled out men afresh, after the Flood.'

'It's creepy-like,' the ranger went on. 'As you walk on and on, there's a feeling comes over you that you've gone back to Genesis. Curious, that for all you may dig and look, there's never a trace of men, or old monuments and things, like Egypt and

America and the other places. And no animals to speak of except kangaroos – and they're just monstrosities – and no trees but those old gums.'

He pointed to the edge of the great gorge where the gums stretch out their twisted arms, while skeleton trunks that have been hurled down by flood or tempest, lie on seamed and blackened boulders, their roots wrenched up into air, their branches embedded in loose stones and washed-down soil. It is desolation indescribable. The chasm falls in jagged precipices over a thousand feet deep, and down in the bed, is a torrent fed by the waterfall – one knows that it roars because the water of it is churned white, but the sound cannot be heard.

'There must have been a terrible big earthquake here sometime,' the ranger said, 'for down there the rocks are all black as if they had been fired. No, you wouldn't believe that patch of green was a forest of enormous trees, would you? You've got to go to the bottom to see them.' He flung a stone over the cliff. It fluttered in the air and sank, sucked inward, falling noiselessly upon another green forest patch.

'Never a man that I heard of got into that bit,' said the ranger. 'I've tried this many year, and couldn't force a way. I don't believe there's been a human being among those trees since the beginning; and fire can't touch them, for it's too damp for flames to run. And so they've growed and gone on from the beginning.'

'I don't wonder,' he added ruminatively, 'that shepherds and stockmen go mad living all their lives among the gum-trees.'

In old days, the stockmen's huts stood each in a clearing, leagues and leagues from any other dwelling – in a plain if possible, near water, and as far as might be from a scrub, for there the Blacks would have their lair when they wanted to do mischief. The hut was built of logs and rough slabs, and roofed with sheets of bark held fast by cross-laid saplings. The big slab fireplace was like a little square room added on to the end; and sometimes spears would come whizzing down through the great open chimney. The stockman had no bolt to bar his door, for what would have been the use of a lock when a blackfellow could so easily crawl on to the roof, and set fire to the bark, or drop unawares down the chimney? He had to depend for his safety upon his quick hearing, his good aim, and the excellence of his carbine. And on cloudy nights he knew that he had not much to fear, for the natives have a superstitious dread of going out in darkness, so they never make an expedition from the camp except on moonlight evenings or with an illumination of fire-sticks.

One night long ago, at the Nie-Nie station, the spears whizzed in. The hutkeeper was lying wrapped in his blanket, dead asleep. The spears did not wake him, and presently the Blacks crept down the chimney and battered his skull with a nulla-nulla before he awoke to know that his last hour had come. Then in the district other murders followed. Maybe the carrying off of some dusky Helen had provoked them. Such thing was then, and is now, and has been since woman was first the desire of man. It is for this cause that most of the Blacks' crimes have been committed.

The squatters of the place roused up and went out, but they found only deserted camps. There was that rocky region of cavern and waterfalls and ravines at the head of the rivers, and here the blacks bided. By and by came a detachment of the mounted police and stalked a camp. They took some prisoners, who were driven before the soldiers to Sydney, and with all the formalities of the law were committed for trial. But the formalities of the law required identification of the accused as a preliminary to conviction, and who could identify the black, clothed and cowed in the dock, with the naked tatooed savage who might or might not have hurled a spear. Law is a beautiful and subtle thing. The crime could not be proven, and so the prisoners were discharged. They had had a very good time in gaol. It was winter, and at that season the Black is more or less comatose, and only asks for his 'possum rug and a mess of bandicoot. He was given blankets and roast beef and a pack of playing cards, which he learned to use and to love.

How often have I watched the Blacks gambling in their camp, a blanket spread out on the ground and six or eight of them sprawling round it, and playing with a very dirty pack of cards for the pool in the middle, to which each had contributed after his means and kind – one a screw of tobacco, another his belt, a third a pinch of flour or sugar, a fourth perhaps his tomahawk!

That imprisonment in Sydney was the savages' first peep at civilisation.

'My word, corbon budgery that fellow gaol!' said the criminals, returning exultant to their tribes. 'Plenty blanket, plenty patter. No white men coola; budgery play about,' which being interpreted is, 'Gaol is a very good place; there is a plenty of food and blankets, the white men are not angry, and one has lots of

fun.' They were quite impressed with the notion that in the event
of a war between black and white, that 'big fellow Gubbernor
along-a-Sydney,' would hang the white man and let the black
go free. They could not understand why white justice should not
be meted according to black canons, which allows the relatives
of a slain man to avenge his death by killing any member of the
tribe to which the murderer belongs, and the victim is sometimes
chosen by the chance settling of a fly from the body of the deceased
upon some bystander.

Then again the squatters of the north rose up in fury. They
surprised the camp and killed many natives, taking many others
prisoners. They went mad as men do when they catch the fever
of slaughter, and shot down men, women, and children, building up a great pyre of wood and burning the bodies upon it, and
there were some who said that all the bodies were not voiceless.

This was called the Myall Creek tragedy. It made a great stir.
Seven of the squatters were brought to Sydney, tried for murder,
found guilty, and sentenced to death. Party feeling ran high in
the Legislative Assembly. Mr Wentworth, pleading for the accused
and at daggers drawn with Mr Plunkett, the Attorney-General,
hotly defied the Government to carry out the sentence. Mr
Plunkett, determined upon the defeat of his adversary – and it
is to be hoped from higher motives also – swore that not only
should these men be hanged, but that any white man who could
be proved to have killed a blackfellow not in self-defence, should
be held guilty of murder. New South Wales was then a Crown
colony, and the Attorney-General, officially a member of the
Council, had great power. The seven men were executed; and
while in office, Mr Plunkett carried out his resolve to the best
of his ability. He was detested by the squatters, and the wish was
frequently expressed, in language more forcible than becoming,
that the Attorney-General could change places for six months with
a shepherd on the Myall.

All hail to thee, Plunkett! Had there been more like thee, the
national conscience would have less cause for self-reproach.

Of course, however, there was the squatters' side of the
question.

CHAPTER II

The Dispossessed

Long after this, there stayed at our huts an old man who had
been a stock-rider on the Myall Creek district at the time of the
tragedy. He had suffered at the Blacks' hands, for his face had
been battered in by the blow of a nulla, and he was lame from
a spear wound. 'Old Waddy,' he was called. A bullock driver
once told us that he was so named because he was a dry old stick
– waddy being the Blacks' word for stick. Perhaps his appearance had something to do with it, for he was wizened and
shrivelled, with a corrugated skin that did truly resemble a piece
of dead bark. He had another sobriquet, 'Greenhide Sam,' for
which there was a practical reason. He was extraordinarily quick
and clever in cutting strips of greenhide and turning them into
stockwhips, leg-ropes, and so forth. All the greenhide work on
the station used to be kept for wet weather and Old Waddy. He
made Tommy his first stockwhip, which was at the time when
Wetherby, of Leura Creek, was charged with and convicted of
the murder of King Billy. Whereby Old Waddy was moved to
deep sorrow and wrath. He had his own views on the subject,
which were not sentimentally humanitarian as regards the blacks.
While he plaited the thongs of greenhide, and the half-made stockwhip wriggled like a snake between his knees, he would unburden
himself to Tommy and me about the evils of humanitarianism
upon the part of a government, instancing the disastrous effect
of Plunkett's pro-Black policy, and invariably preluding his discourse with the story of his spear wound, and of a certain gory
episode connected with a dead blackfellow's hand, which last
impressed the whole thing word for word upon my memory.

As a rule, we were bidden to keep clear of the stockmen's huts,
but the authorities made an exception in the case of Old Waddy,
for he held women, girls, and boys in deepest reverence, and never
in our hearing used swear-words of stronger quality than 'By Gum'
or 'Darn,' or 'Blazes.'

This was how the story went. 'You may have heard the boss
tell of old Pipeclay, Miss – a flea-bitten grey – and I never see'd
a better horse. The niggers knew him too, and had an uncommon down on him and me, for we'd often fell across one another.
Well, that day I'd been showing some travelling swells the short
cut to the Macintyre Brook, and coming back, old 'Clay' gives

sign that a Black is close handy – by Gum, that horse could scent a darkey! – and before I'd time to unstrap, a big blackfellow slews round an iron-bark tree and puts a spear into my side. I didn't feel much, but there was the spear sticking out of my thigh, and I thought it was all up with me. 'Anyhow,' I says, 'I'll settle that darkey,' so I ups after him; and by Gum, he brings me clean through a camp. Lor, such a hullabaloo! They takes me for a Debil-debil; and the chap was too blown to give tongue, or else they could easily have settled my business. On, old 'Clay gets to my man, and the Black – he shies into a clump of brigalow and shindies up a tree. But I bring him down flop; and then I cuts off his hand and takes it along with me slung on to the dees of my saddle, so that Pipeclay's side was red and streaming with the nigger's blood. I believe the old horse knew what I was after, and in consequence went more spry. You see we chaps had our dander up over those seven whites that was hanged for the Myall Creek business; and those swells I took along the short cut was magistrates. So I goes after them with my bloody hand and flips it down agen the Johnny-cakes they was cooking at their camp, and shows them my spear-wound that was smarting pretty hard by then. 'Report me if *you* like,' I says, 'and the Governor and the Attorney-General may hang me if *they* like; and if only one of them was on this run stock-keeping, and the other on the next, my word, they'd sing another tune before the year was out! Darn them chaps,' I says, 'that sleep safe in beds and drink claret instead of quart-pot tea, and calls us murderers and hangs us because we protects ourselves.'

'There was a Jackeroo chap on the Namoi as I've had many an argument with,' Old Waddy went on, 'as plucky a devil for a new chum as ever lived, and always preaching kindness to the blacks. My word! he used to kill a bullock for them every week or so because he said we'd taken their country and were bound to provide their grub. Then, by Gum, one evening as he sits smoking outside the hut, without a moment's warning, he finds a spear in his chest! Darn'd, but he would have been a blue duck if I hadn't ridden up that very moment and scared the natives off. He had some narrow shaves, that chap; for one night, when he was camping out with his own black-boy, he feels a tommyhawk come down by his head, close-up cutting his ear off, and when he fires his revolver, the black-boy makes off and never was seen after. He comes to me for sewing up his cuts – cool as blazes. 'Be quick about it,' says he, 'don't you be afraid of hurting me; just fancy you're stitching up a ration-bag.'

'I tells you what it is, Miss. Here's a man has to look after a herd and wants to do his duty by his master; and then, just when he's got the cattle quiet on their camps, they gets a rush, because of a black's spear thrown among them, and away they goes – especially in winter time – and he's got all his work to do again, and maybe this happens over and over. At first he takes it quiet-like, but when he's had it pretty often, by Gum, I wouldn't be a black-fellow in his way! And that's Nature! I could have told things to the bosses in the settled districts – the cattle speared, and some hocked, and just the kidney fat took. And then, when a chap might come home at nights – as I've done – and find his mate lying killed and all his swag gone, well, who's going to say what that chap'll do if his dander's up, except another in like circumstances; and maybe *he* wouldn't do the same. I never did want to hurt anything myself. If I seed a living creature crawling my way I'd step aside – except it was snakes. I've done hot work in my day, 'cause I've been put in the middle of it. But I never did nothing that lies hard on my conscience. I don't say the same of some I've knowed, or even of those Myall Creek men as was hanged. That was a dirty job all round. But what I says is, that the way you've got to deal with the Blacks is to keep your word and give 'em what you've promised, whether it's a blanket, or baccy, or a bullet. And when two colours gets to contrarieties, one agen the other, and anger and fear is up, you ain't going to have things run as easy as this 'ere stockwhip.'

And it always seemed to me that Old Waddy summed up the matter pretty fairly. The Blacks were more certain than ever that the 'big fellow gubbernor' was their friend when they heard of the hanging of those seven men; and outrage followed outrage so thickly that the humanitarian policy had to be squashed, and Major Mills, with a picked corps of men from the regiments, was sent up to fight the natives. He had some Black troopers in his force, and these renegades seemed to take a fiendish delight in the betrayal and slaughter of their own kindred. One of them – a good tracker – led the soldiers to the stronghold of the tribe, and the Blacks, hemmed into a gorge from which the only outlet was a waterfall, were all shot down or leaped the precipice and were dashed to pieces. After it was all over, the betrayer of his people proudly held out his blood-stained sword. 'My word! Corbon

budgery this long fellow knife,' he said, 'plenty mine been num-
kull ole fellow Mammy belonging to me. I been marra cobra
belonging to that old woman!'

He was gleefully relating how he had cut off his own mother's
head! It is horrible to think that young blackfellows were taught
to track and kill their own people! Of Major Mills's regiment half
of the troopers were Blacks. In this guerilla warfare formalities
were usually dispensed with, but sometimes they were observed
after a tragi-comic fashion. There is in the breast of every Englishman a very proper aversion to shooting a human being in cold
blood, which here struggled with the instinct of the sportsman.
One day Major Mills and his party were riding back to the camp
after a long and so far fruitless man-hunt. Suddenly a white
trooper espied a black-fellow who, hoping to escape the observation of the dreaded Maamie (chief of the police), had climbed
into the fork of a high gum-tree. The sergeant reported to the
major.

'Blackfellow up a tree, sir.'

'Order him down,' said the major.

'I have done so,' replied the sergeant. 'He won't come, and I
cannot climb the tree.'

'Go again,' said the major, 'and order him down three times
in the Queen's name.'

'And supposing Her Majesty don't fetch him?' asked the
sergeant.

'Then *bring him down*,' grimly answered Major Mills.

The sergeant advanced with carbine pointed. 'I say, you nigger, come down in the Queen's name!'

'Ba'al mumkull!' (don't kill me), shrieked the Black in abject
terror, not understanding one word of English, and only realis-
ing that he was in peril of his life.

Said the sergeant, 'I orders you again in the Queen's name to
come down.'

Still piteous cries of 'Ba'al mumkull.'

'I orders you a third time in the Queen's name to come down,'
repeated the sergeant. 'Then if you ain't a-going to obey Her
Majesty's orders, I must obey mine.'

His hand was upon the trigger. A shot; a thud; and the 'big
game' fell at his feet.

Who can wonder that to the blackfellow the white man was
a fierce beast of prey to be destroyed before it could pounce!

The black troopers who witnessed that occurrence took the lesson to heart, and I used to hear a story of one, who on his own responsibility brought down his man. Having omitted the official formula, he exclaimed, as the wounded black dropped, 'Tsch! Tsch! Altogether mine lose-him Queen's name' (I quite forgot to say, 'In the Queen's name'). Then a happy idea striking his brain – it being quite immaterial to him whether the incantation, as he considered it, was addressed to the dead or the living – he cried –

'Come down in Queen's name one time. Come down in Queen's name two time. Come down in Queen's name three time. That budgery now' (that's all right now).

It is sad but true that the Australians were apt pupils in the art of treachery. The native tracker was always the most bloodthirsty in a fray and the keenest in hunting down his own tribe.

A stratagem conducted on the principal of 'Set a thief to catch a thief' brought this early campaign to a close. It had lasted for some time; the tribe had been hunted hither and thither, and the remaining ringleaders had hidden themselves in that broken country at the head of the Fitzroy River, which was extremely difficult of access.

The native police, under white officers, had been out for several days upon a fruitless search, and were about to leave that part of the district. Towards sundown, they came upon a track which led them to the borders of a scrub. It was now time to camp, and the blackboys went forth in search of bandicoot for supper. One of them heard in the distance the sound of a tomahawk, and following its guidance, came unseen upon a wild Black chopping an opossum out of a hollow tree. The trooper watched him to the camp, then after consulting with his own mates went to their chief. 'Maamie,' said he, 'you pidney; plenty boy been woolla. Metancoly Myall Black nangry camp. Suppose, Maamie, you go, directly blackfellow mel. No good boots – too much noise.'

The interpretation of which is, 'Master, you understand, these boys have been talking over the matter. There are a great many wild Blacks at the camp. If you go, they will see you at once. Your boots make too much noise.'

Metancoly is the Black's expression for a great number. The Australian natives only count to five: one, kimmeroi; two, bulla; three, bulla-kimmeroi; four, bulla-bulla; five, bulla-bulla-kimmeroi. After that, the term is metancoly.

The boy then suggested that he and his companion should take
off their clothes, steal down to the Myall's camp, and with their
rifles lie there concealed till dawn. 'Then,' continued he excitedly,
'murrai early, when Myall first wake, Euroka ba'al get up; close
up ogle eye that fellow; blackfellow make fire; then boy mel-mel;
shoot along-a daloopil and I believe, plenty catch him.' (Very
early when the Myall first wakes, the sun is not up, and it is nearly
dark. The Blacks make a fire, then we boys see them, and shoot
them with our guns.)

The plan was adopted. At early morn it was dark and cold
and the fires had burned out during the night. Though the stars
were still shining, there was already a chorus of magpies: the
laughing jackasses were saluting day, and there were the strange
twitterings and multitudinous murmur of insect life that may be
heard before sunrise in the Australian bush and that now covered
the stealthy movements of the watchers as they got their guns
ready for action. One by one, the sleepy blacks came out of their
gunyahs. They scratched themselves, and jabbered unsuspiciously
to each other as they blew upon the half-burnt firesticks. Soon
a blaze illuminated the camp and the shiny forms stood revealed
in the glow – easy targets for the marksmen. Each trooper covered
a Myall and fired. A volley echoed through the scrub. Panic seized
the Blacks: they knew not where to turn, and hardly one escaped.

In Moreton Bay, the depredations of the Blacks were more or
less regulated by the yield of the bunya forests. In the good bunya
years, there were always a great many more murders; and in
bunya-feast times the squatters went in fear, and the women
stayed about the house and all the men looked well to their
weapons. The great ranges between our two rivers, the Auburn
and the Logan, were covered with bunya forest. It is beautiful
to ride through a bunya scrub, where a track has been cut, to
see the huge yellowing cones hanging, each one larger than a man's
head, and to watch the light falling in curious, pointed shafts from
the dark pyramid tops of the tall trees, and glinting in diamond
sparks upon the glossy green leaves of the lower branches, beneath
which all is gloom, and only creeping things move. When the
great cone is quite yellow, the nuts are ripe, and they are very
sweet and palatable, cooked, as the Blacks know how, in the ashes
of the camp fire. For miles and miles, the tribes assemble, and
there is peace among the braves, for till the bunya-feast is ended,
open strife and warfare are not. The tribes may gather and eat

their fill of the bunya, but the opossums and dingoes and wild animals of their neighbours' pasture they may not trap, for that would be breaking the law of savage hospitality.

Then the kangaroos, iguanas and other beasts and reptiles of the bush are sacred, but the cattle are the white man's and may be speared and eaten; and the white man – if he be alone and has not his gun ready – may be speared also, and roasted and eaten, to still the craving for flesh food, which seizes men after long abstinence. Sometimes the white man was too vigilant, and the cattle were well guarded, and the craving became greater than could be endured; and then an unsuspecting stranger from some outside tribe would be led to a quiet spot and bidden to look at a snake in a water-hole, or at the red sky, or at something moving in the grass; and while he looked, a warrior behind would strike him a blow on the back of his neck with a waddy, and that night there would be horrible feasting. Or else some plump young lubras,[1] doomed beforehand and guessing their doom, would be sacrificed to the need.

On the Great Range close to our station, a party of riders came one day upon a nauseous place. It was a small gorge with bunya scrub on one side of the slope, and a very big rock on the other. The rock was a curious shape, quite bare and difficult to climb, and apparently flat on the top. The party did climb the rock, and then they found that the flat top was in reality a shallow hole, and that in the hole were quantities of human bones, relics probably of the bunya-feasts.

But there are those who say that the cannibalism of those times is not due to the longing of the carnivorous animal, but to some religious observance. How this may be I don't know, and it does not seem to matter. Old Jimba of the Donga used to relate how after a 'corbon big fellow fight and Corroboree,' a conquered foe who had fought very vigorously would be eaten by his conquerors, because there was a notion that thus the victor would assimilate some of the fighting qualities of that man of valour. Only Old Jimba put the matter in a way that even to us then required a good deal of elucidation in more intimate conversations with the blackboys and Billabong Jenny, our half-caste nurse.

It is the Korradgees or medicine men who guard the religious mysteries of the Blacks. One finds it very hard to get them to

[1] Young, unmarried black women.

tell anything about their religion. But that there are mysteries which have been handed down for ages, and that they do perform secret rites, is certain. They acknowledge the power of a great Spirit of a superior grade to the popular Debil-debil; and they believe in a heaven or happy hunting ground, and in a hell which a Logan Black described as 'one big fellow flat altogether prickles,' a plain covered with Bathurst burr, being the especial detestation of unclad natives.

In some tribes there is a kind of Nature worship. The sun and the moon are mighty deities: there is Munduala the fire-god, who in the end of all things will burn up the earth, and the men sing and dance to gain the favour of the Pleiades, the senders of rain. There is Yo-wi, the dark spirit who roams the earth at night, and Wa-wi the snake spirit, and Buba, the legendary progenitor of kangaroos; and it is easy to trace a shadow of Rosicrucian lore in the belief in Turong, or water-spirits; and in Pot-koorook and Tambora, elves and gnomes.

Sometimes one speculates whether in the far ages there ever dwelt a white man-god among them who taught the people knowledge of some things good and evil, and delivered to them the marriage ordinances and the Mystery of the Bora. What was Baiàmé the Great Ruler, and whence came the tradition of him as a glorified man? 'Corbon big fellow like-it gum-tree,' a Namoi Black used to say: and he would describe Baiàmé as always lying down, with his head resting upon his right hand, and his arm buried in the sand of the sea, so deep that he could not lift himself. And the sea came up and brought fishes into his mouth; and by and by the arm would rot away, and then Baiàmé would be free and would rise up in his might and destroy Whites and Blacks upon the land. I thought of the legend of Baiàmé, in one of the cave temples in Ceylon, where a colossal Buddha lay in Blessedness, his head resting upon his great bent arm; and I wondered whether in the dawn of the mythologies there had ever been an association between the sleeping Baiàmé and some pre-Buddhic idea of the Nirvanic Rest. For it is curious how, in some of the Blacks' traditions, one comes across traces of the eastern doctrines of reincarnation and metempsychosis, and the threefold division of man into body, soul, and spirit, made by the mediæval mystics. With the Blacks, there are the Bunna, or fleshly body, the Tohi or Soul, and the Wunda which is disembodied spirit. The Tohi, they hold, comes back from time to time, to the world, sometimes in the form of a beast if the previous life has been a degrading one, or may be, as animating a being of higher order, if its former ways have been brave and virtuous. 'When black-fellow altogether budgery, he go bong' – that is to say, dies – 'and then he jump up white man,' an old man in the camp used to tell us; and it was pathetic to find that for him, nothing loftier existed in the scale of creation than the enemy of his race. Had the white man, when he came among the Blacks, but realised the native ideal, who knows that there might not have been a new kind of Divine dynasty after the model of that of the Children of the Sun! They were brave, honourable, and reverent of the higher human qualities, those original barbarians. They did not become mean and false and cruel till civilisation set them an example, and their women were not unchaste until white men taught them immorality.

We knew a half-caste woman married to a fencer on the Logan who had been taken from the Blacks as a little girl, and brought up in a squatter's family, and she liked talking about her early life and the tribal laws and ways. She would tell how she had seen an unfaithful gin speared in the camp by her husband, the elders applauding; and another frail gin taken out by her brother and beaten with a nulla-nulla till she was almost dead, while the injured husband, who had a soft heart, sat by and wept at her shrieks, but dared not interfere.

She would tell, too, about the Blacks' belief in God and in spirits, and among many old superstitions, how the old men had a notion that their passage to heaven would be in some way facilitated by the cutting off of one of their fingers – it was the third finger, I remember, which was usually missing among the aged people of the camp. I recollect, too, one old blackfellow on the Logan, whom Mary Macdougall, of Wooroot, helped through a bad illness, and who, to her distress, insisted, as soon as he got better, upon going away alone to a certain water-hole, that he might hold commune with spirits. He said they often came to him there, and had told him that he should 'close-up go bong' (nearly die), 'but that Debil-debil would not catch him that time.'

According to the half-caste gin, her camp had its light, romantic side as well, and there were story-tellers who used to sit in front of the gunyahs and tell tales, 'Oh, very interesting,' she said; 'all about love.' Yet there did not seem a great deal of sentiment about the way in which the braves conducted their courtship, it being the custom for a young man in search of a wife to walk up to a camp where, among her kindred, squatted some lubra who had taken his fancy, and to throw his boomerang into the midst of the family circle. Then, if it were picked up and returned to him, he had to fight a rival for the possession of the fair one, who was delivered over to the best man; but if the boomerang were allowed to lie he might step in and claim his bride without further preliminaries. No doubt, however, there had been ogling and sighing, and perhaps tremors, fears, and heartburnings before this culminating point was reached. It is only in the setting, after all, that the eternal drama alters. The main motive is always pretty much the same.

There was a spot on the Logan which was regarded with great veneration because it was a Bora ground. It was a large circle, marked out and hollowed in the centre, with a raised mound of earth all round, in which were two openings giving entrance, as it were, to the circus. We could never have made out what the Bora really was, and I don't imagine that any European knows its true meaning, though in his valuable book Mr Meston has given a very detailed, interesting description of the rite. Still, I never before heard or read of a white man witnessing it, except one Murrell, who lived with the Blacks seventeen years, but his report only touched remotely on the occult side of the Bora. Yet sometimes when they were sitting round the camp fire, after the horses had been hobbled, and the pipes lit, and a pannikin of grog poured out, the 'Boss' used to question his black-boys as to this great mystery, but though they were communicative enough about minor affairs of the tribe, they would always become grave and shake their heads when asked about the Bora, and would answer: 'Suppose mine pialla you, altogether black-fellow mumkull mine' (If I were to tell you, the Blacks would kill me).

It was the Divine Ruler, they say, who commanded the Bora, and the mystery is curiously connected with other mysteries of other nations and ages, by the use of a magic wand, the original wand having been delivered, according to tradition, by the Great Ruler himself, and possessing no doubt, some occult significance. In these days, the wand is a stick carved with some device, and sent from one tribe to another as the summons to the ceremony.

The trees round the Bora ground are marked with nature-symbols, and devices of animals, and there appears to be something peculiarly emblematic in the effigy of an emu. The main object of the rite is the initiation of the youths of a tribe into its secrets, and their admittance as warriors to the privileges of manhood.

As neophytes they enter the sacred circle by one of the openings in the outer mound, the old men put armlets of kangaroo skin upon their arms, a fillet round their heads, and a band round the waist crossed back and front, and they pass out at the other opening, kippers, or accepted braves. But before and after the rite there are ordeals to be undergone, and they must live apart for a time in the bush, abstaining from food, and are not allowed to see a gin.

Our half-caste had nothing to tell about the Bora, for no woman may participate in it. Talking about these rules for food, there are among the Blacks laws regulating the diet of men and women, something, after the manner of those laid down in Leviticus. Marroon Station on the Logan, where we lived, got its name from the breaking of one of these regulations. The legend is that a young lubra went out hunting with her father and brother, and ate of iguana at a forbidden season. Whereupon the Great Spirit was angry, and a storm arose and so frightened the girl that she confessed her crime. The Great Spirit was not appeased by her confession, for while she was making it, the earth toppled over and buried her, and the mountain that covered her was Mount Murrun, and the name of that place is to this day Marroon or Murrun, which in the Blacks' tongue is Iguana.

CHAPTER III

Out of My Grandmother's Box

Another bundle of torn, faded, and often weather-stained papers came out of my grandmother's box. They are the love-letters of a young pioneer squatter on a station called Bungroopim in the scarcely settled Moreton Bay district, and a girl living on the Parramatta River near Sydney. The year 1841 is the date on the letters. It was when Sir George Gipps was governor, and the Constitution Act granting New South Wales a measure of self-legislation had just been passed by the Imperial Parliament.

They give their own picture of life as it was over there sixty years ago – these old love-letters. They had to travel a distance which I covered by road and rail, not very long ago, in about the same time that it takes to get from London to the French Riviera, and sometimes they were five months on the way. For in one of them the wooer says that 'her welcome letter of February the 17th reached him on July the 30th: and then only through a chance meeting with its bearer at the Bay,' where he was delivering a mob of bullocks to the butcher.

In all the correspondence there is the same story of loss and delay, and long periods seem to have passed without any communication between the lovers. 'I am indeed thankful to know by the sight of your handwriting at last,' she writes with mirthful seriousness, 'that you have not been murdered by bushrangers or eaten by Blacks.' There's something very pathetic in the look of these old letters, their big, square sheets, yellow-stained so as to be almost illegible, muddy marks sometimes at the foldings, and the address in the centre oblong of the outer leaf, as the way was then, almost effaced. Evidently no post went anywhere near the Logan, for not one of them shows sign of stamp or postmark.

The very touch of the time-worn paper has a personal and tender interest. It is so curious to think of the many days they may have travelled in some dead and gone bushman's pocket; and if they could speak, what comic and thrilling incidents of the wilds they might tell; how they must have been handed from one to another, coming into the keeping, maybe, of some desperate character, or stirring the sympathies of some rough cattle-drover, so that perhaps an extra day's ride was taken, or a butcher kept waiting, or a fray with the police braved, because a girl wanted her lover to know that she thought of him, and was true.

They were very different from the love-letters a girl would write to-day – these closely-crossed sheets traced in a delicate, pointed handwriting, and expressed with a quaint sobriety, a certain sweet stiffness which gives them an odd charm savouring of the last century, of Jane Austen, and the days of short waists and beaver hats – all curiously out of keeping with the savage passions let loose in the bush. The pretty, sloping penmanship never commits itself to anything more effusive than 'My dear Mr Prior' at the beginning and 'Your sincerely attached' at the close of each epistle. He appears to have complained a little of her maiden reserve, for she answers in mild reproach, 'You call my letters cold, my dear Mr Prior, but I must beg you to believe that there is no abatement in the warmth of my feeling, and have I not given you the best proof of my affection and confidence in consenting to share your fortunes?' And she goes on to tell him that 'Mama' is teaching her housekeeping, and so she thinks their marriage had better not be hurried, 'for what will it matter after we have been together many years, whether our wedding was a month or two sooner or later.' And she adds that she does not regret, as he does, that he has so little of the world's wealth, for if they ever become '*even* rich (the italics are hers) what happiness it will be, knowing that they have shared the bitters as well as the sweets.' This is the most emotional declaration in the letters, and one can fancy that it might have been just the least bit unsatisfying to the ardent lover in his backwoods hut, chafing impatiently against separation, and the limitations of their correspondence.

Yet through all the gracious propriety of diction, there exhales from these sixty-year-old documents a fragrance of sentiment that imparts poetry to such homely cares as appear to have occupied even the courtship of these two. On his part, the difficulty of keeping his working horses shod and in good condition, the number of travellers going by 'who eat,' the expense and labour of sending rations to the distant camps, and, above all, the doubt of being able to get together that £200 which was to start the young couple with, as he puts it, 'a clean score' – to say nothing of his troubles with myall (wild) Blacks. On hers, deep anxiety lest her future husband should cripple himself through his efforts to provide for her comfort, and such quaint remonstrances as this – 'And now, my dear Mr Prior, I must express my regret that you should have parted with your bullocks to such disadvantage on my account, for I know it is solely on my account that you have engaged the builders. Let me beg of you to make no such sacrifice again, but to discharge those builders, and when I come, let me be your assistant in improving your hut, for indeed I should like to have it in my power to prove that I could be happy with you *anywhere*.'

And she is in distress over the calamities of her own household. There is drought on their station; their 'bush' has been burned down; their waterholes are almost dry, and every day dying horses and cattle have to be carried out of bogs from which they have no strength to extricate themselves. The distress, too, is of a more intimate kind. 'Papa,' while his bush is burning and his beasts are perishing, sits 'in the little parlour writing poetry.'

'He is now writing a piece on Life,' she says, 'which is very pretty, but mama does not like his confining himself so much to the little parlour, for besides injuring his health, poetry also makes him neglect the station.' 'But papa,' she mournfully adds, 'was never cut out to be a bushman; he is much fonder of writing poetry than of riding after cattle.'

Then there is the eldest brother, Thomas – another cause of woe. Thomas, who was 'our favourite brother, and papa's favourite child;' Thomas, who 'had great talents, and most endearing qualities,' but who was always making papa angry and disturbing the serenity of poetic composition in the little parlour, thereby plunging his sisters into grief. In vain does the lover at Bungroopim assure his fiancée that 'Thomas, in spite of his wildness, has really excellent principles and a good heart,' and that it will not be his – the lover's – fault if Thomas does not become a steady fellow. But Thomas appears to be incorrigible; Moreton Bay does not content him; he insists upon roving – first to Ceylon, then in the South Seas, where, before he is twenty-one, he gets himself wrecked and murdered.

The burdens of Thomas, and of papa's poetry, which lie heavily in these love-letters, are lightened occasionally by accounts of Sydney gaieties – the Homebush Races, a review, the sight, from a window in George Street, of people going to the Governor's levee – 'the barristers in their wigs and gowns, the clergymen in their gowns also, and the Catholic bishop finer than any of them.'

There is a ball to which she goes 'because Elizabeth wishes her company,' but which she scarcely enjoys since the 'one person for whose society she cares is absent.' As an engaged girl, she refrains from either waltzing or galloping, which perhaps may account partly for the lack of enjoyment. There she sees for the first time the new dance called the polka and hears 'the new railroad gallop,' 'an excellent imitation – at least every one says so, and I am sure it must be, for it is like the setting off of a steamer.' Steamers were not too common then in Botany Bay. Yet they seem to have had cheerful times in Sydney sixty years ago, though in the farms outside convict servants occasionally gave trouble. I don't know which governor it was who, as here related, made such an affecting farewell speech at this particular ball that nearly all the ladies present were moved to tears.

Even then, too, Sydney had its opera-house, for in the letters comes gossip about a fancy ball that took place in it, and which, seen from the upper boxes, was 'a most gorgeous scene, too dazzling to be described.' I am not quite sure whether this was the very house in which I, a twelve-year-old bush girl, heard my first opera. It was 'Lurline'; Lucy Escott sang in it, and to those unsophisticated eyes a fairy world was opened.

But the chronicle of Sydney gaieties is a short one. Before very long the pair are married and settle down in what was then 'Out Back.' By and by the girl-wife writes from Bungroopim to the mother-in-law in England, giving an italicised description of her 'wild man of the woods,' who has 'an immense pair of whiskers, a moustache, and a beard that is not fully grown, but will be *very fine* when he comes back from his next camping-out trip,' and 'whom his mother would surely not recognise in his bush-man's dress – his blue shirt and blue-and-white guernsey, a pair of trousers *of my making*, and enormous leggings – and who is indeed, I can assure you, a *very handsome man.*'

She goes into innocent raptures over their rough home – the slab hut with its bark roof and earth-floored verandah, which has gum-sapling posts, round which roses, passion-flower, and sweet verbena grow. She tells minutely of the garden sloping down to the water-hole – the grass plat with three beds, a trumpet-tree, bearing its strong-scented, bell-shaped flower in the centre one; vines along the fence, and oranges and lemons, pomegranates and fig-trees, and many lilies. It sounds idyllic, this bush garden. Below it lay a fearsome lagoon – fearsome because of the Bunyip tradition that clung to it – and gloomy with melancholy she-oaks and flooded gums. This Bunyip tradition was fairly well authen-ticated. A girl wandering in maiden reverie by the lagoon's banks, saw the monster, flew and told a graphic tale. She described it as an immense, slimy creature with a calf-like head and the body of a great serpent. I can myself testify that the Blacks held Bun-groopim waterhole in direst awe. They said 'Debbil-debbil sat down like-it that place,' and not one of them could ever be per-suaded to swim from bank to bank.

There must have been some foundation for the many Bunyip legends. No doubt, a creature unclassified by naturalists did once exist in the creeks and lagoons till, scared by civilised intruders, it hid itself and pined, dying out at length like the dodo and great auk. Just as in the golden age, fauns and nymphs, and the great god Pan, and Apollo himself, walked the pagan forests, so fabulous monsters dwelt in the primeval bush. The Bunyip, perhaps, was the last survival of Lemurian mythology – for is it not said that Australia is a remnant of that prehistoric continent, and that the monoliths on Easter Island are the work of Lemurian builders? How that may be I know not, but I can well imagine that only monsters could have inhabited those gruesome pools locked in the grotesque arms of hoary gums and shadowed by she-oaks – the most dismal of trees, with their straight, black stems and thin, drooping foliage, which whispers mysteriously in a light breeze and gives piteous moans when the wind swells into a blast. I know just such a place – they called it the Moongar Water-hole, and long ago I used to camp by it. Picture the scene as in my mind I see it. A dray, loaded high – the tarpaulin slung tentwise over it – drawn up by a bleak stretch of water – a tiny lake, narrowed at one end, where it is slushy and rank with weeds and rushes, in which wild ducks have their home. The surface is inky black, except where the moon strikes it: the shallow bend is full of dead logs and floating twigs, but at the sides, the banks shelve steeply into deep water, darkly clear. Close round are she-oaks, ti-trees, the swamp oak with its leprous-looking trunk and the flooded gums, round which drift and wrack have gathered, showing where, in rainy seasons, the lagoon has overflowed. Grass of the kind called 'blady' grows in coarse tussocks, and near the pool lies the bleached corpse of a huge gum-tree, one side of it blackened and hollowed where camp fires have been lighted.

The fire of my picture blazes brightly, the billy hung over it for quart-pot tea, the ashes raked ready for the baking of a batch of Johnny-cakes; Paddy Mack, the bullock driver, is kneading. Do you know how to make a Johnny-cake? Let me tell you, in case you ever go to the bush, far enough west for Johnny-cakes to be possible. First, you must cut a small sheet of bark from a gum-tree near, and heap on it a mound of flour, in which you must hollow a hole and fill it with water, then work up the mass into a dry dough, which you must cut into thin cakes. All this time, the blackboy, or somebody else, has been piling small sticks on the fire, so as to make a bed of ashes, which is spread out, the cakes are laid upon it, and dexterously turned till they are cooked. It may seem a simple process, but yet it is difficult to make a real Johnny-cake. A large part of the art lies in mixing the dough, a still larger part in preparing the fire. For if the ashes be not properly prepared, the Johnny-cake will be heavy and no longer a Johnny-cake; it is then a 'Leather-jacket,' or it is a 'Beggar on coals,' when little bits of the sticks are turned into charcoal and make black marks on the dough.

Have you ever tasted bush pot-au-feu? Here it is – an iron pot or a large billy slung on a forked stick over the camp fire, into which each stockman dips for his dinner. A lucky pot – a sort of fishpool from which you may land half a wild duck, a whole parrot or pigeon, a lump of kangaroo tail, a slice of salt junk as they call it – or a bit of pork – through all, a miscellaneous flavouring of store salt, a pinch of pepper, a suspicion of the aromatic gum-bark or bitter leaf – for the pot should be stirred with a twig from some handy tree – maybe a bunch of wild parsley, and edible fungus – who knows that? The mess is very excellent, I assure you – when it has simmered long enough – better than the best French ragout you could get in some wayside cabaret in France, and that is saying a good deal.

But you can't enjoy the bush pot-au-feu without a draught of quart-pot tea. I will give you the receipt, though it is not practicable in England. For you must boil quart-pot tea and drink it in the bush. You must boil it over a fire lighted in the hollow of a dead log, and you must drink it out of a battered and blackened pannikin. When the water in your billy is at boiling point, you must empty into it, out of a dirty ration-bag, a good handful of store tea. After that, from another ration-bag, dirtier and very sticky, you must put in some cakes of soft 'hut' sugar, stirring the mixture with a bit of stick – also from a gum-tree. Now you must cover the quart-pot with another one, and let the tea draw, and afterwards, you must cool it by pouring it from one quart pot into the other. Next, divide it among the pannikins put in readiness, and drink it in the company of your mates. You will find it better than any tea you ever tasted.

But to produce a satisfactory result, the conditions must be complied with. You must have the quart pots, the pannikins, the ration-sugar, the gum-tree stick, and above all, the mates. These things can only be got together in the bush.

In the camping-out scene I am picturing, one blackboy is preparing the fire for baking; the other had gone after wild duck into the bend. I can hear the ping-ping of his gun, the swish of wings; almost the sizzle of soft mud as he plunges through the reeds and bog. The fancy sets me thinking of times when I have followed a sportsman by moonlight a little way across the Home Swamp. Then our feet would make a 'kr – rsh – kr – rsh' as we trod – soft at first, and louder with the wetness of the ground. The water would rise over our ankles and leak into our boots, and one would feel goose-flesh down one's backbone – so eerie a sensation that the natural impulse is to switch a stick behind to scare off anything uncanny that might be following. There would be all kinds of strange noises – curlews giving their mournful wail, the gurgling 'gr – rr' of a 'possum up a gum-tree'; the rustling of rushes, making a silky 'tr – rrse,' and the cracking of dead reeds. And now alarmed cries from waterfowl, the whistling of their wings filling the air . . . A shot, and the frogs would stop croaking and every living thing hold itsef on the alert. Even the cluster of flying foxes hanging from a branch and looking in the moonlight like some monstrous black fruit, would break up, a horrible smell tainting the night breeze. Then would I turn and fly, never halting till I had reached the paddock sliprails. But only cheerful bush noises sound round the camp I remember. Our horses clank their hobbles and tinkle the bells hanging from their necks – they couldn't get far if they tried to break home. Some of the men are spreading grass-tree tops, which they have cut for out-bedding, beneath the tarpaulin, and two or three others – drovers who have been waiting for rations – are yarning over an adjacent camp fire of their own. They have been telling Bunyip stories. 'I don't know much about the Bunyip,' drawls one, 'but I can tell you there's a water-hole where I wouldn't camp by myself at night – no, not if – ' A native dog drowns the rest in his howl. I have taken a billy to dip for water. There's a ripple on the blackness of the lagoon . . . A snake has wriggled down from the bank. Sirius's reflection spreads and wobbles, and the pointers of the Southern Cross begin to dance. Presently the pool is still again. I sit down on a log, and wait till the snake has gone further.

Echoes come back to me of the men's talk. Harry, commonly called the Liar, has made a surprising statement.

'That's a sneezer, Harry.'

'My word, it's true. Mailman Bill told me,' says Harry.

'I sa-ay, is Bill going to get the mail contract again next year?'

'I do-on't think so' (how to reproduce the bush sing-song?)

'Jack Cameron has tendered; he's £10 less than Bill. . . .'

'I sa-ay. . . . Why didn't you ride that mare the Boss gave you? . . . No! oh no, *she's* not wild, I used to ride her on camp.'

'We-ell! I shouldn't think she'd be much of a camp horse. Too long in the back. And as soon as you take a pull at her bridle, up goes her head. Give me a horse that you can snatch about in a mallee scrub, no matter how thick it is. Those star-gazing brutes run up agen a tree in no time. There was old Mooney on Seaforth, came a buster yesterday when a *myall* brute of a heifer cleared while he was cutting him out of a mob of scrubbers. Seaforth started bucking, and run 'im agen a colibah-tree and knocked 'im off and left 'im hangin' on to his stirrup leather. . . .'

That's how they always talked by the camp fire, whenever I listened to them. I never heard stockmen, whether in their huts or out in the bush, discuss any subject but cattle and horses.

I'm not specially interested in the men's yarning; the moon makes such ghostly shadows. She's near her full, and pales the stars. But the Pleiades are always visible. Venus has risen over the tops of the trees, and now Mars is shining; the Milky Way is making a track right across the heavens. . . . The dear old constellations fix themselves even now – I can never get accustomed to the Great Bear and the signs of the north. I am in the south once more, living again the wild, familiar life. Out beyond that great block of flats opposite, against the trees of the park, I can see the camp fire by the water-hole, and through the roar of London traffic I hear the night cries of the bush.

It is a big jump back to Bungroopim, but of such mind-flights is life made. The young couple start matrimony on a herd of cattle, and horses, and two hundred pigs, and the bridegroom fetches in wood from the scrub to build a slaughter-house. They have visions of a boiling-down establishment, and of boiling all the fat cattle which there are no butchers to buy or settlers to eat. Of society they have practically none. 'Some day,' the young pioneer writes, 'this will be a flourishing country; its capabilities are greater than any of us know, and our descendants may be building towns on this wild land which we have reclaimed from the wilderness.' A true prophecy. Now, all that riverside is dotted with selector's homesteads; there are townships everywhere, and a railway brings, in a few hours, the supplies which bullock drays were often twelve weeks carrying from Brisbane-town to Bungroopim. Sometimes the station was entirely cut off from the world. 'For two months,' writes its mistress, 'the river has been bank high, and four drays are encamped the other side waiting to cross.'

Occasionally they take a trip to Tamrookum, the nearest station, in a cart with one horse, and two bullocks as leaders; and
they break down at the last creek, being obliged to cross by a
log and make for the head-station on foot. The girl who saw the
Bunyip has married and gone to live at Tamrookum. The place
is bound up in later memories of my girlhood. Many a time I
have wandered through the scrub near that crossing which the
old log still bridged. There were unromantic ticks in the scrub,
but we didn't much mind them when we were young; it was rather
an excitement pulling them out when we got home. To be sure,
if one tick were left in, it festered and made a most uncomfortable sore; but that didn't often happen, and was not to be weighed
in the balance with scrub joys. One of these was a huge Moreton Bay fig-tree, which gave us more delicious fruit than any we
could get in the garden. Then there were mulgams – native raspberries, peculiar to the Logan; and there was the chucky-chucky,
a most pleasant-tasting wild plum, which had a way of hanging
tantalisingly over the water, so that if the pool were deep, there
was a little difficulty in gathering it. The geebong was not quite
so nice – its fruit was slimy and rather sickly, yet not unpalatable.

I recollect the chestnut-trees with their brilliant orange blossoms and their long pods, which we made boats of, and raced
where the stream ran swiftly. I had forgotten the quandong-trees,
the berries of which contained decorative stones that gins and
children used to string for necklaces. There is no end to the delights
of a scrub. Later on, I should like to write a whole chapter about
scrubs. A Ceylon or Malayan jungle is very beautiful, and I have
driven through one for a day at a stretch; but, on the whole, I
prefer an Australian scrub. If more tame, it is more practicable
as a solitary haunt, for at least there are no tigers or panthers
straying round to pounce upon the unwary.

It was by the banks of Tamrookum Creek that 'our poet,'
Brunton Stephens, composed his 'Convict Once.' We read it in
manuscript, and begged that it might appear in the *Marroon
Magazine*, and we thought it a slight upon that periodical – the
outlet for local literary ambition – when it was sent to England
instead. To the astonishment of everybody it was published by
a great London house, and praised in the *Saturday Review*, and
after that we thought more of our poet, though most of us
preferred his 'Tamrookum Alphabet' in rhyme, to any of the
higher flights of his genius. Indeed, the Tamrookum boys thought

very small beer of the poet, because he preferred to sit and read Xenophon by the lagoon to running in wild horses out of the scrub.

Tommy came into the world before I did, and his birth is duly announced to the old lady of the boxes. 'Having neither doctor nor nurse,' the young mother writes, 'and knowing that I might die before there was any hope of medical assistance, I endeavoured to prepare my mind for leaving this world.' Poor little bride of nineteen! The trembling characters of this short letter – the rest of which is a sort of Magnificat – all maternal rapture – show how weak she still was; and there breathes an intensely living note from the young husband's postscript, telling of the danger she was in – about which she herself says nothing – of his frantic despair at the thought of losing her, how there was no doctor within sixty miles, and how in any case none could have been got to the station as the rivers were up. Indeed, it had been in preparing the hut for flood-bound travellers that her trouble was brought on sooner than it was expected.

Things did not go altogether well with the young couple. There were few people to eat the fat cattle, and the boiling-down establishment does not seem to have paid. Three of us, I think, had come into the world when Bungroopim had to be given up, and there was nothing for it but, as the old hands would have said, 'to up swag and shift further out.'

So father went north – almost as far north as any one could then go. He bought Naraigin – the pretty native name was afterwards changed to Hawkwood – and from there he writes to my mother that he is getting ready for her coming, that he had been very anxious, having been told that the Blacks were bad, but that he had found them quieter than he expected; that he has got in the posts for the new humpey, and will try and send to Sydney for glass windows for the sitting-room. I don't fancy, however, that the windows ever came, for I can remember nothing but rough slab shutters. He tells her, too, that he has begun to purify the place, and that the stench from the boiling-down pots will not be so bad after a little while. I have a vision of those big, black, boiling-down pots, of the heaps of dry bones, which make one think of a chapter in Ezekiel, and of the tall, fat-hen plants growing up all round the spot. He bids her have grass cut for packing, and the harness of the American waggon oiled, and she is to do her best to get strong for the journey.

CHAPTER IV
Naraigin

Almost the first thing which I can remember in any consecutive fashion is that journey through the bush. It seems to stand out like a sort of hegira in these insignificant annals. Scenes rise from it, vividly illuminated for an instant, and the next a blur – vistas of giant gum-trees and of a buggy toiling among them along a bush-track with a small retinue of blackboys and packhorses before and behind, and two figures always prominent in the picture – one a dark-whiskered, bronzed, and resolute person of picturesque, not to say buccaneering, aspect, who is mixed up in my child's mind with a bright Crimean shirt and poncho, a carbine, and with long cantos from 'Childe Harold' and 'Mazeppa,' which he taught us to recite of evenings by the camp fire; the other a frail, delicate-complexioned being, helpful and gay, dimly photographed on the memory page against a background of forest, wearing a large hat, bending over pack-bags, and holding horses, with us two babies clinging to her skirts – the queen, as the dark-whiskered, buccaneering man is king – of my phantasmagoric world.

Associated with the recollection of that long journey is a vague terror – the terror of wild Blacks, blending in imagination with the eldritch shapes of the old gum-trees, the grey moss draping their twisted limbs, and the red gum dropping like stalactites of blood from gashes made by the Blacks' tomahawks in their branches. Distinctly do I recall the delight of gathering those ruby-like droppings, and the disappointment of tasting, and finding exceeding bitterness.

There are shifting glimpses of great plains, of stony hills and gullies, and of lonely bark huts. Then there's a vision of rain and of roaring waters – we were stuck up for weeks by floods – and by and by, out of the mist of waters, comes the picture of a white horse with its forefeet caught in a crevasse between stretches of lichen-covered rock – the scales of the lichen clear as in a pre-Raphaelite painting; more vague, the silhouettes of men and blackboys holding supports of saplings under the horse's body to prevent it from falling further – there were caves beneath, which, in fancy, lent a touch of mystery to the business; and then all the rest becomes blank again. I have only a hazy notion of our camping in the caves, and, mixed up with the horse incident, comes the tragic impression of an accident of which the details are all lost.

A break came in the journey, while the horses were spelled at a station called Taabinga, which, as compared with Naraigin, was as the flesh-pots of Egypt deserted for the wilderness. Here *David Copperfield*, with the original illustrations, was, to a child of six, an epoch-making experience. Odd are the things that stick in a small mind. A bit of *Byron*, with sonorous rhythm, 'The Assyrian came down like a wolf in the fold,' is fixed by the explanation that a wolf – hitherto a legendary monster – was no more than a kind of dingo, which I knew came out of the scrub and pounced upon lambs, and for which squatters laid strychnine baits. It was the first touch of disillusionment, but had its consoling points, for when camping among the gumtrees the sound of dingoes howling always brought up a romantic picture of cohorts gleaming with purple and gold, and the ever-present dread of attack by Blacks translated itself into splendid anticipation of assault by an armed band of magnificent Assyrians.

After a bit, the sense of moving ends. . . . We had reached Naraigin – and the next scene on my magic-lantern sheet is half comic, half sentimental – a kangaroo flying in ungainly leaps over the hurdle fence of a cleared patch by the stockyard, where lucerne and pumpkins and fat-hen plants grew, and where seated on a stump the delicate-faced being in a large hat read the story of *The Ugly Duckling* from Hans Andersen's fairy tales to three little children, agape with interest. So it has happened that whenever I used to read by an English fire, Hans Andersen to another set of children, I have seen fat-hen plants instead of the duckling's burdock leaves, and the picture of the kangaroo taking his constitutional poised grotesquely above the fence of hurdles in the picture.

Narcotics sometimes play queer tricks with the brain in rolling out grey matter folds, or whatever it is that means memory. Once, when a doctor had given me a dose of opium, I had an odd experience in the matter of piecing together these broken child-recollections, which I had not been able – try as I would – to fit into a whole. No effort would bring back a picture of Naraigin; all was blank except for such whimsical snatch as the kangaroo and the fat-hen patch, or a glimpse of paddock sliprails dropping into a bog which the horses made passing through when they were run up to be saddled. Everything inside and outside the sliprails was blank.

But that night, as I lay in a drugged half-doze, there came the lifting of a curtain, and with it the most curious sense of a dual personality. I seemed to see myself, a small child dressed in a holland overall with rows of wavy red braid upon it and a sun-bonnet dangling from my bare neck, perched with Tommy upon those very sliprails that dipped into the bog, and with the whole scene behind and before, spread out as distinct as a painted land-scape. And the strange thing was, that I seemed to know it was all perfectly real and true, and that there could be no question at all about the place having looked exactly as I saw it. There was the lagoon with blue lilies upon its surface, and that deep, dark, clear look lagoons have; and the blacks' gunyahs and camp fires by the edge of it, and the cart track leading up to the woolshed and losing itself over the stony pinch among the iron-bark gums. There was Naraigin humpey and the sugar-loaf shaped hill behind, with long, brown, blady grass, and bare white trunks of dead gums. I could see the blackened log on the very top of the hill, and the heap of smaller logs and twigs with which mother used to make the signal fire that told our father all was well when he was out with the squatters taking vengeance on the Blacks after the Frazer murder.

'Yes, it is all just like that,' the inert, mature self, watching the child, seemed to be saying, while the child-self swung herself from the sliprails and played with Tommy, and jabbered to the picaninny who came up from the lagoon. 'Oh! yes, I remember Waggoo. And I know that squatter riding up the track – 'Mon-seer Jacks,' as they called him, from Boompa; and he'll have store-sugar toffee in his swag that Gritty Macalister will have made for us. I remember his poncho; it was longer than father's and flapped just that way on to the horse's crupper.' So go the com-mentaries of that other self. And I notice 'Monseer Jacks's' carbine, and a pair of little revolvers which we were always told would bite, when he laid them down beside him on the verandah. All the men we used to know in those days carried revolvers that bit little children. But the men were all very kind to the little chil-dren, and if they hadn't store goodies to give us – which depended upon whether the drays had lately come up – they would bring us emu-eggs or tufts of yellow cockatoo feathers and such-like, or perhaps a tame wallaby for a play-thing.

'Monseer Jacks' stops and asks us questions before going on

to the humpey, and Tommy and I have a good deal to tell him. . . . 'Yes, I remember every word. It's all just as it happened.' 'Monseer Jacks' - presently I will tell you how he got the nickname - takes me on the saddle in front of him, and we ride through the sliprails and up to the humpey together.

Everything is quite clear now. I can see the slab hut with its sloping bark roof fringing raggedly over the verandah eaves. The slabs stand apart as though they had not been introduced to each other, but you don't notice that inside, for the walls have been lined with canvas. The verandah has an earthen floor and log steps, and is supported by gum saplings on which the bark has been left. All along it are rough squatters' chairs and slab settles, and there are saddles and bridles and stockwhips hanging from nails in the wall, and a canvas water-bag slung from one of the rafters. These rafters, and those in the parlour, I recall as the home of tarantulas, centipedes, and sundry uncanny reptiles, as well as of frogs which had an uncomfortable way of flopping down upon one in rainy weather. Centipedes used to live, too, between the canvas and the slab wall, where they would in their perambulations make eerie scratchings; and many a long hour have I lain awake in cold terror, listening to the sound of the hundred feet on their travels, and getting as near to the outer side of the bed as was possible. For in the bush there we slept mostly on bunks made of sawn saplings nailed against the slabs.

We were always told never to go to sleep with our hands touching the canvas, and one of the boys I recollect had a finger bitten in that way by a centipede, which finger turned black and gave him great pain.

There were no windows to the humpey, only rough slab shutters imperfectly meeting. One of my earliest Naraigin memories is of a black's face, with its very white eyeballs and shining eyes, peering in out of the darkness between the half-closed shutters. It was strange that a spear did not come whizzing in through the aperture, for mother has told me the tale of how she was alone in the hut, father being out after the Black murderer of an out-shepherd whom the native police were hunting, and how she was in the kitchen with Tommy, and Baby Lizzie, and me. . . . I can see the earthen-floored room with its big slab fireplace and mother setting bread in a camp oven when the blackfellow looked in - and how this was the murderer, reconnoitring no doubt, and how father, coming home while the bread was still setting, captured him as he skulked outside, handcuffed and tied him to a tree; and how before the native police arrived next morning, the man had wriggled himself out of the ropes and had broken loose into the bush again. That was before the Frazer murder and the Squatter's Raid, which was an epoch in those Naraigin days.

Somehow, in odd connection with the glistening white eyeballs of the blackfellow, there comes into my mind the melancholy eyes of a stately 'Time,' looking out of the foreground of a queer seventeenth-century painting that hung in the parlour, above a settle covered with a red blanket. The room had an earthen floor like the rest, and I don't remember any furniture in it, except rough chairs and a big table and this wide settle, on which stray bushmen camped when the beds were all occupied. Time, robed in red and blue draperies after the fashion of the St. Peters and St. Pauls of Italian pictures, seemed strangely incongruous with the settle and with the bushmen. He was in a big canvas, unframed, that hung between the two doors, back and front, which in summer were always open. There were other paintings too – mostly unframed. One, a Dutch School representation of the disciples, showed them in flat caps and blue blouses hauling up a truly miraculous draught of what seemed red mullet and very lively eels. There were, too, some Dutch interiors and some other Scriptural pieces, a Christ in Gethsemane and meek-faced Madonnas surrounded by wonderful wreaths of flowers that might have grown in the Garden of Paradise, so unfamiliar were they on the Burnett River, where, except for the yellow pumpkin blooms and such-like commonplace things, we had only the lagoon lilies, the wattle, the sandalwood and wild blossoms of scrub and bush. I did not care for the Madonnas and the Dutch disciples; but the 'Time' picture seized my child's imagination, and I remember how I used to sit and gaze at it, pondering upon its mysteries. For I had been told that it was an allegory and symbolical of the different stages of man's destiny on earth; and I found it hard to reconcile the ruined castle in the background, the big tree of knowledge overshadowing Time and his death's head and hourglass – a tree on which grew such rosy apples as I had never dreamed of. I used to long in those days to see real apples! – the groups of fantastically-dressed youths and ladies and knights in armour on rich-caparisoned horses, the mummers, jesters and all the mediaeval pageantry there exhibited – with crude bush life as it unfolded itself to a little herd of Australian children.

CHAPTER V

The Blacks' Camp

The woolshed is fixed in my imagination as the most delightful playground that the heart of child could long for, with its many pens, its empty wool-bales and presses, its slanting log floor, and all its queer nooks and corners. I think of it only as a playground, for we were never allowed to go within earshot of the place in shearing-time, lest our baby ears should be polluted by the shearers' oaths. Outside the woolshed were two great pits dug in the ground and filled with tallow, those vilely odorous, three-legged, rusty iron boiling-down pots being put again to their ancient use.

And thereto hangs a tragedy. The scab broke out among the sheep. They died by hundreds and thousands, and were boiled down for the tallow; and so it came about that the poor pioneer was almost a ruined man again. He re-stocked with cattle; and we had to abide on at Naraigin afterwards, through many troublous years.

One time there was a strike among the shearers, and the young men on the river tackled the shearing themselves, and got back-aches as well as sprained wrists, where the sinews give out with the heavy work of the shears. And they didn't do their shearing well, for the word 'Tar' became a by-word and an opprobrious epithet then at Naraigin. The reason is, that in those days – now we shear by machinery – there was always a spare hand or two in the woolshed carrying pots of tar; and whenever a sheep was cut, through unskilful use of the shears, there would rise a cry of 'Tar,' the spare-hand with the tar-pot dashing forward thereat and dabbing the wound. I know of this because I used to hear the 'chaff' at such times, and because there seemed to be many 'spare-hands,' and we ran short of tar.

The ground near the boiling-down pots was so fertilised that here millet flourished, pumpkins grew to gigantic proportions, and fat-hen was unusually succulent.

Well for us that this was so, for there happened a time of famine, when the drays were stuck up for months by a flooded river, and the store was empty of flour, tea, and sugar, so that we had to live on mutton and pumpkin for many months.

The lagoon was another great feature in that childlife, and also the Blacks' camp beside it, where Billabong Jenny, our black nurse, used to take us, when mother had things to do or went out riding on the run with the gentlemen and left us in Jenny's charge. The dogs would rush out barking as we approached, and the blackfellows sprawling on the 'possum rugs by their fires, with their dirty bits of cooked bandicoot or snake or iguana beside them – I can smell the burnt flesh now – would slap at the dogs, calling 'Eoogh! Eoogh!' which in the camp means that there's nothing to get into a fuss about. Then we would stand by the gunyahs, taking care not to put ourselves on the 'possum rugs, or to go too close to the gins and picaninnies. This was forbidden when we visited them in the camp – for the gunyahs were populated not by human inhabitants alone – but we were allowed to play with the Blacks in the open after they had had a dip in the lagoon. We used to love watching old Jimba as he fashioned a spear from a brigalow sapling, first digging out the shaft and roughly rounding it with his tomahawk, then screwing round his foot and making a kind of socket for his spear between his big toe and the ball of his sole, while he scraped it smooth with a bit of broken glass or sharp stone.

The gins and the picaninnies were always in the lagoon, which facilitated our intercourse. They used to dive under the blue water-lilies and pluck up the roots, that were like small yams. When roasted in the ashes, these bulbs became yellow and powdery, and were as dear to our semi-civilised palates as they were to the stomachs of our savage companions the picaninnies. Gastronomically speaking, I learned a good deal from the Blacks, particularly from a certain half-caste boy called Ringo, who was the first object of my youthful affections. Indeed, there was serious thought of an elopement to the scrub with Ringo, but upon going into the question of the marriage laws of the race, we discovered that he, being a Cuppi, was bound to wed with a Dongai, or undergo the penalty of excommunication, and perhaps death. So reflecting that as I was not a Dongai, though living near the Donga Creek, we should probably both be knocked on the head with a nulla-nulla and then eaten after a corroboree, we thought better of the elopement. Ringo taught me also to find and appreciate a fat, white grub, the native name of which I forget, though I should like to recommend it to European and Australian epicures. I also made acquaintance, under Ringo's auspices, with the flesh of the iguana and that especial delicacy, the eggs of the black snake. I learned, too, at the camp to plait dilly-bags, to chop sugar-bags (otherwise hives of native bees) out of trees, to make drinking vessels from gourds, and to play the jew's-harp; but English life is not adapted to the display of these accomplishments.

The camp Blacks were not considered domesticated, and were migratory, coming and going about the stations, and just staying as long as they found themselves comfortable. They were only pressed into service when shepherds were scarce, or 'rung' trees – that is, gums which had been barked and allowed to wither – required felling. But we had several blackboys in regular employment, and these lived in a hut, wore clothes, and had adopted, as far as possible, the customs of the white men. These were Bean-Tree Dick, Freddy, and Tombo. They would not do anything except stock-keeping work, but used to ride among the cattle, looked for lost sheep, and brought up the horses. Their moleskins were always white; they wore Crimean shirts, with coloured handkerchiefs knotted above one shoulder and under the other, and sang songs in their own language set to operatic airs – they had learned them from a musical officer in the Native Police of the district. The effect was curious. And even now, the sound of Verdi's popular airs, either at the Covent Garden Opera-house or on a barrel-organ, will call up a picture of Tombo with his woolly hair, his beady eyes, and glistening teeth. Tombo was a splendid mimic. There lived with us at Naraigin a sentimental German, Dr Lanhaus by name, who recited English poetry with the strongest German accent and the most absurd gestures. Edgar Allan Poe's 'Raven' was one of Tombo's show pieces, and he would stand in an attitude, by the camp fire, one hand on his hip, the other upraised, and spout forth strangely pronounced lines, one or two of which linger –

'Sitting on my sh . . amber dooer . . .
. . . Quoth the ra . . aven "Nevare moor!"'

Poor Tombo! In after years he forsook the paths of virtue, rejoined his tribe, met a missionary, and became demoralised in a township. He caused one of his child playfellows considerable embarrassment once in Brisbane, on occasion of a foundation-stone being laid by the Governor, or something of the sort. The child was a grown young lady then, and very proud of herself, as in the wake of a political personage she marched towards the daïs for privileged spectators. But lo! from beneath the sawn wood erection, a blackfellow rushed forth, scantily clad, the tattoo-marks visible, extremely tipsy, and with a clay pipe thrust through his woolly locks. He took her hand; his greeting was effusive.

'Hallo! Budgery you! Sister belonging to me. Tsh! ts . ch!' making the Blacks' click of tongue and teeth expressive of admiration. 'My word! Ba'al you been wear-im frock like-it that long-a-Naraigin! You pidney? (understand). What for you no glad to see Tombo? Plenty mine been brother belonging to you. Plenty mine been show you crack-im stockwhip. Plenty mine been carry you over creek,' and so on, through a list of humiliating reminiscences.

Our camp Blacks at Naraigin never stayed with us long, but would move on up or down the river, as soon as they were tired of us or we of them.

They had gradually got into intercourse with the Whites through bringing fish from the creek and things from the bush to the stockmen's huts, and had learned to love the stray presents they got, such as a pinch of flour, or sugar, or tobacco, the remains of any carcases of beasts that were killed at the yards, or a 'White Mary's' cast-off petticoat. Very often they would be at variance with the tribe – perhaps for having transgressed the strict marriage laws, which prohibit union within certain degrees of relationship – and then they would come and put themselves under white protection. Billabong Jenny and her husband Mundo were outcasts of this kind, he being a Hippi, and she a Cuppi or Combo – I forget how it exactly works out – and forbidden to wed. Anyhow, they took the law into their own hands and escaped from the tribe. But Mundo was superstitious, and the terror of this evil that he had done worked upon him, and he fell ill and was like to die. When a blackfellow falls ill he believes that an enemy has cut off a piece of his hair while he slept and has buried it under a gum-tree, and that as the hair rots away so will his strength decline, till Debil-debil at last takes him to his own place. Mundo was convinced that this spell had been wrought upon him, and sent for 'that fellow White Massa' to tell him that he, Mundo, had disobeyed the law, and was about to 'go bong.' Billabong Jenny bewailed her approaching widowhood, and there was a mournful scene in Mundo's gunyah.

Then the 'White Massa' considered how he might save Mundo, for it is not to be gainsaid that superstitious fear kills as surely, if a little more slowly, than the dreadful *daloopil*, as the Blacks call the white man's firearms.

So the next day he went again to the gunyah, his face cheerful with smiles, and Mundo eyed him with trembling hope, for they all had faith in the 'White Massa' medicine man, he having cured them with simple drugs, of colic and influenza.

'Name, name,' cried Mundo, which is the Black way of saying, 'Tell us all about it.'

'My word, Mundo, directly budgery you,' said the medicine man (You will be all right soon). 'Mine been mel-mel Debil-debil and pialla that fellow like it dream last night.' (I have seen Debil-debil and talked with him in a dream last night.) 'Debil-debil been show me grass from cobra belonging to Mundo, close-up gum-tree. Debil-debil been marra grass, put him along-a fire and burn altogether. Ba'al that fellow rotten now. Ba'al Mundo go bong.' (Debil-debil showed me the hair from Mundo's head under the gum-tree. Debil-debil took away the hair and burned it, so that it will not go rotten, and Mundo will not die.)

And Mundo rose up, and recovered from his sickness.

Several years after that, White Massa sent messages and tried to persuade the chiefs to forgive Mundo and Billabong Jenny, and to admit them again into the tribe. He thought that he had succeeded; but the law of the Blacks is not lightly to be set aside, and in due course there came a command to Mundo to attend a great corroboree. Then Mundo was afraid, though he still felt that a white medicine man who could pialla Debil-debil in a dream might have power with the native elders. He was begged to disobey the order, but Mundo only shook his head.

'Ba'al you pidney, Massa,' he said. (You don't understand, Master.) 'Blackfellow not like-it white man. Suppose altogether Black chief say come to corroboree – when like-it that, blackfellow must go.'

So he went sorrowful; and there came shortly afterwards a message for Billabong Jenny telling her that Mundo was dead. Then arose a howling from the camp such as had never been heard. The next day when we went down to the Lagoon, Billabong Jenny was seated under a gum-tree alone uttering dismal cries, and gashing herself with a knife, so that blood mingled with her tears. After that, she lay in her gunyah, her head bound up with dirty rags, her face hidden as she crouched with it against the earth. She would not speak when we spoke to her, nor did she break silence for many days till the time of her mourning was ended.

Oh yes, in the Blacks' camp, as in the squatters' humpey, there are the human affections and the common emotions which men and women, and even the beasts, share. There, too, the gins mourn their mates, and the mothers love their babies. On the Burnett, though in summer the sun scorches, and parching winds bring sandy blight, and flies torture, and drought is a terror; yet in winter the same wind pierces chill to the marrow of unclad creatures, and there are autumn rains which stream through into the Blacks' gunyahs. Bad it is for the gin who has no 'possum rug, and is burdened perhaps with a puling hybrid picaninny – a reproach to her among the men of her tribe, so that she is desired of none of them. There was Nunaina at our camp, who had a sickly yellow baby. She had come from a tribe on the Milungera side, and she had lived in a Chinese shepherd's hut, and had learned to speak English. She was a very pretty gin, with smooth hair and large, soft eyes and lissome limbs, but she had fretted herself thin because the child was ailing. It had rained; after the rains came a cold wind, and food was scarce, and Nunaina shivered, and the baby cried, tugging at empty breasts. That was when the lagoon overflowed and joined the creek and the men crossed in tubs to take rations to the shepherds on the other side. This happened in later Naraigin days – there is no need for keeping to chronological sequence. Ah Tat, the Chinese gardener, sat up half the night watching the water creeping over his sweet potatoes and lamenting that they would 'all go lotten,' and had his swag rolled up beside him, prepared to flit to the highest gum-tree in the cultivation paddock. It was when the waters went down that a little procession came out of the camp, following Nunaina and the child, which they laid under a gum-tree to die. Nunaina's face brightened as the little thing seemed to revive with the weak spirit and water that was poured down its throat, but she was bitter and very sad. 'How I make that fellow warm?' she said. 'Ba'al me got plenty blanket.' Then there was a great wail, and an old gin picked up the dead child. Nunaina threw herself upon the ground and put dust upon her head, and the other gins went back to the camp weeping. In the evening they made a hole for the little picaninny under the gum-trees, and then they shifted camp, for Blacks will not stay where one of them has been buried, believing that the spirit of the dead haunts the spot. A few days afterwards Nunaina came back, worn almost to a skeleton with grief; and she dug up the child's body and wrapped it in her blanket, and carried it away up along the Donga to bury it in the country of her own tribe.

But who cares now about the joys and sorrows, rights and wrongs of savages who cumber the earth no more! There has been no one to write the Blacks' epic; not many have said words in their defence; and this is but a poor little plea that I lay down for my old friends.

CHAPTER VI

The Challenge of Donga Billy

There was a white man on the river, who one morning looked out and saw a great mob of Blacks camped before his head station. He did not know what they had come for, but he was afraid, and he parleyed with them from his house door. He told them that it was Christmas time – a time at which all men, black and white, feasted, that there were flour, sugar, plums, good things in plenty, in the store; and that his White Mary would make them a great and pleasant mess – and all should eat and be filled. And the Blacks did eat, and on the next day there was much weeping among those who were left in the camp, for there had been death in the pot.

It was after this thing had been done that the Burnett district became noted as one in which the Blacks were dangerous.

Young's station, Mount Larcombe, near Gladstone, had been bailed up, and several of the hands murdered. Folson of Balloo Creek was speared in his verandah, and another squatter was tomahawked while camping under his bullock dray. Up to this time, however, there had been no murders near Naraigin. But now a feeling of insecurity was creeping up among the squatters. Four men were killed at Dykehead, not many miles from Boompa, and a flock of sheep had been stolen from the Frazers at Hornet Bank. People began to suspect that the Blacks meant wholesale mischief: and this was indeed the case. Had the tribes been capable of sustained action, they must have swept the country. Fortunately for us Whites, it was their habit, before any important enterprise, to have a great Woolla (council of war), then a corroboree, at which there was much urging to bloodshed on the part of the gins, and afterwards a certain number of braves had to be selected for the war-path. That gave time for hints of their intentions to reach their enemies.

It was a great bunya year; and there were rumours down in the camp of tribal wars and corroborees which meant the seething of foul blood and the unchaining of wild passions. And the Government in its wisdom had seen fit to disband a number of the Native Police, so many of the dismissed troopers joined in with the Blacks of the district and became dangerous ringleaders – far more dangerous than the wild Blacks, for they understood firearms and the ways of Whites, and had got over the superstitious fears of their brethren. The squatters began to feel uneasy, and the women practised at targets with firearms, and the men would ride home from their work with a sinking at their hearts, fearing for their wives and children. Often have I heard father describe how each evening coming in from the run he used in cold fear to mount the hill overlooking the humpey, and draw free breath again when he saw it lying quiet and unharmed.

Boompa was the nearest station to us, and there lived Monseer Jacks, the same who had interviewed Tommy and me at the sliprails. A certain glory of the French Imperial Court rested upon Monseer Jacks. A few years before this time, he had gone on a trip to Europe, had visited Paris, and there had been presented to Napoleon the Third, and invited with his wife – who was talked of on the river as having been a most stately and brilliant person – to one of those often described Imperial houseparties at Compiègne.

Mr Jackson was fond of narrating the incidents of this memorable visit, and had a way of making casual reference to the opinions of the French Emperor and Empress, implying his intimacy with these august personages, for which foible he was unmercifully chaffed by his fellow-squatters, so that because of it, and a certain Continental polish of manner that he affected, as well as his Napoleonic cut of moustache and beard, he was known along the river as Monseer Jacks. We children loved him, because he brought us goodies from his store, and old *Illustrated News* pictures to paint over, and during the flour famine, he saved his last half-sack, and ordered Gritty Macalister, his housekeeper, to bake a weekly loaf for the 'Naraigin picaninnies.'

I have seen many ugly women, but I never saw any one quite so ugly as Gritty Macalister, and she gloried in her ugliness and used to remark devoutly in her broad Scotch, 'Praise be to the Lord, A'm no weel favoured, and whiles there's a gin in the camp neither the stockmen nor the Blacks will be casting eyes at an auld hag like me.'

But alack for Gritty! One day Donga Billy broke into her kitchen and 'bounced' her for rations. Gritty coolly threw a damper and a bit of salt junk into his dilly-bag, and proceeded with her ironing, showing no sign of alarm, though Donga Billy was a murderer of Whites and the greatest warrior of his tribe. Then Donga Billy, struck with admiration, cried out as he departed –

'Corbon budgery you. Directly ba'al white man sit down long-a Donga Creek. Altogether, Black mumkull that fellow. Altogether cramma White Mary like it gin. Mine marra you. Budgery you gin belonging to me.'

(I like you. Soon there will be no white men upon the Donga Creek, the Blacks will kill them all. I will take you, you will be a very good gin to me.)

And no longer could Gritty make the boast that she had never been looked upon with eyes of longing by any man, and she went to and from her washing tubs and the kitchen, dogged by a great fear.

Monseer Jacks came one evening to Naraigin, and told us that Gaythorne, his stockman, had heard from one of the boys about the place that the Blacks were talking of bailing up Milungera, the Scotts' station, and Hornet Bank, the Frazers' place, and were waiting till full moon to carry their plan into execution.

The story of the Frazer murder is told in all Australian records, but I must tell it again, or these Naraigin memories would be very incomplete.

Naraigin, Hornet Bank – where the Frazers lived – and Milungera, the Scotts' station, lay west, making an unequal triangle. Hornet Bank was two days' journey from us: and beyond, the country was practically unexplored. Only a little while before Monseer Jacks brought us this news, the Widow Frazer, two daughters, and two sons had ridden down the river, spending a few days at Naraigin and also at Boompa. They came to buy bulls, and having accomplished their object went back to their home. I never visited Hornet Bank, but know that it was the usual bush hut, with a verandah and bark roof, and was divided into three main rooms – the parlour, the store, and a chamber in which Mrs Frazer and her three daughters slept. Sylvester Frazer and a younger brother had their bunks in the store, while an elder brother, with the tutor, slept in the skillion room off the verandah. Two shepherds occupied the 'men's hut,' a little way from the family house. All these, with the exception of Sylvester and the elder brother, who was absent getting stores, were massacred by a mob of about a hundred Blacks.

I don't remember Mrs Frazer, but I have a clear picture of the eldest daughter – a girl of nineteen, red-haired, blue-eyed, with a very pretty Scotch face and a trim figure, which showed to particular advantage in her well-fitting habit as she sat upon a fine chestnut horse. I see her now, as the party drew up in front of our sliprails. I see her, too, in the evening, when we all lounged in the moonlit verandah, and she and her sister sang Scotch songs to a Jew's harp and concertina accompaniment. She was engaged to be married to a squatter in the Wide Bay district, and Monseer Jacks told us that the clergyman had been written to, the date fixed, and that her trousseau was in the drays her brother was bringing up.

Milungera was a greater distance from us than Hornet Bank, and had fewer hands. It is not so long ago that I sat in a pretty drawing-room talking to a very handsome and sweet-faced old lady with white hair, who had been playing delightfully on her piano the Sonata in A minor which we all know. I never heard a more exquisite touch on the keys than that of Mrs Scott, and I asked her how she had contrived to keep up her music during those wild years which she spent on the Burnett.

'Mine was the very first piano of the Burnett,' she said, 'but that wasn't till long after you had all left it, and in the meantime I suppose the music was bottled up inside me just as I had carried it away from my English home. Ah! can you remember back to those dreadful times, and do you recollect how you came over with your father and your dear mother, when they were frightened about us, and rode all the way from Naraigin to try and persuade us to go back with them till the Blacks had got quieter.'

'And you wouldn't go?'

'It was impossible. Mr Scott was laid up with fever and ague, and every second day 'the shakes,' as they used to say, came upon him, and he was perfectly unfit for the journey. Your father saw that it was useless, and so then he said very little about the danger from the Blacks, but tried to make light of the trouble. I was making a garden, and after we had had dinner, he came out while your mother took care of Mr Scott, and planted some rows of cabbages for me. He noticed a white thing stuck up on the hurdles, and asked me what it was, and I told him it was a target, and that I practised for an hour every day shooting at it with bullets. Of course I took care that the Blacks about the place should see me. Ah! my dear, in those times I should never have dreamed of going along the covered way from the house to the kitchen, without my loaded revolver ready in my belt. Well, your father cried scorn upon my shooting, and so to test it, I made him put his hat on the post of one of the hurdles, and each time I fired, a bullet went through the crown. I really believe it was my being such a good shot that saved us at Milungera. The Blacks were afraid of me and used to tell each other, 'That fellow White Mary at Milungera ba'al muskeeto.' (That white woman at Milungera never misses.)

'Oh! what heartrending things happened then! I recall as if it were yesterday how we got the news of the Frazer massacre, and I remember Mr Jackson riding up one evening when my husband and I were at tea, and his terrible agitation as he rushed in and blurted out the news. I was pouring out the tea, and stopped, with the tea-pot in my hand, unable to take in the horror of it all. That fine old lady, and the children and those nice girls! . . . It's too dreadful even now to talk about. . . . I suppose I must have looked like fainting, for I saw my husband making signs to Mr Jackson not to say any more. . . . No wonder the squatters were roused to take vengeance at last! I remember what Yeppoi used to say – he was quite a civilised blackboy and very fond of me, and used to tell me things about his tribe. . . .

'"Suppose," he said, "white man mumkull blackfellow, plenty blackfellow cry, but suppose blackfellow mumkull brother belonging to you, ba'al you cry.' And he couldn't understand our easy way of taking things when white men were speared. . . .

'Somehow I've always felt that if we had only appealed to the Blacks from their own point of view, and roused their generous feelings, we shouldn't have had all those horrible massacres. But it's just the British want of sympathy in dealing with savages. . . .' And then Mrs Scott branched off to less remote and more burning questions of colonisation. But presently she got back again to the Donga Creek troubles.

'. . . Danger never seems to come home to Englishmen till it's a question of their women being killed – and worse. They didn't trouble as long as it was only shepherds and stockmen and out-

side squatters who were murdered. And the wonder was that the
stations were so unprepared. I don't believe there was a charge
of gunpowder at Boompa till Mr Jackson borrowed a pound from
our store. . . . And yet,' she went on after a moment or two, heaving a deep sigh, 'I do think those wild days were the happiest
I have ever known. Life was so full and so utterly real; you *lived*
every hour and every minute of it. There was no opportunity
for sentimentality or self-analysis or worrying over one's neighbours' concerns. One had to do all the time with fact – and that
was pretty grim sometimes. But it was so varied. If there was
tragedy, there was plenty of comedy as well.' She paused and
presently began to laugh. 'Such odd incongruities! A funny thing
came into my mind at the moment. One evening a trooper arrived
with two prisoners, and he wanted Mr Scott, who was a magistrate, to judge them there and then, and give him authority for
taking them down to gaol. And there were my husband and I
very busy indeed, washing up dishes after our dinner – of course,
as you know, we had no servant – and I was wiping the plates,
and he had a greasy cloth tied to a stick and was cleaning the
frying pan. I can see him now – you remember what a particularly dignified looking man my husband was – dropping the frying
pan and putting on his coat, and then going to judge the prisoners.
After that, he came back to the frying pan, and I set to work
and cooked a second supper for the troopers. . . .'

No need for Mrs Scott to ask if I remembered. Those journeys
through the bush, and those nights of camping out between the
earth and open heaven are just the things of which in all my life
I am gladdest, and that are most real and closest cherished. I can
see the narrow flat, grown with gum and wattle, where we made
our camp. And dear Aldebaran and the shifting Southern Cross
and the curved Scorpion – how familiarly they come back once
more! The camp fire throws leaping lights upon the trunks of the
gums, so that the naked branches gleam gaunt and appear to move
against the shadow, in shape of beckoning arms. Here, the leaves
look all of a light quiver, and there, a dead black blur. The white
shreds of bark hanging down are like phantom garments, while
the thickening bush seems one vast array of unearthly forms melting into the gloom of night. And the noises breaking that
mysterious stillness! – So furtive, such strange shrieks at uneven
intervals, such wails, such stealthy creepings and burrings!
Nobody is speaking – not even the blackboys at their camp.

Father, sitting silently in the fire-smoke, is plaiting a thong for his stockwhip.

Presently Tombo creeps up.

'Massa, mine been see fire-stick, I believe Myall Black look out.'

From among the ghost army, steps a living Black, naked, a girdle of kangaroo skin round his waist; his breast and arms and thighs tattooed and painted in white and red and blue, a big bone amulet shining on his chest. He is erect; there is something frank and fearless in his aspect, and though he is armed with spear, boomerang and nulla-nulla, it is clear that his immediate purpose is not warlike.

Father sees the Black, but makes no movement towards his gun, and the Black speaks.

'White Massa!'

'Yohi' (yes), father says, nodding his head.

'Mine Donga Billy. You nidney. Blackfellow been woolla, you coolla belonging to me.' (I am Donga Billy; you understand. The blackfellows have told me that you are angry with me.)

'Yohi; mine corbon coolla belonging to you' (Yes, I am very angry with you), said Father.

'You been pialla (tell) Black, suppose Donga Billy come humpey belonging to you, you shoot that fellow. What for?' said the blackfellow.

Then Donga Billy's misdeeds were enumerated, and they were many and great.

'Bugery,' he replied. 'Ba'al mine jerron. I come Naraigin. Suppose you coolla, you marra daloopil. I man-him spear, waddy, nulla-nulla. Which fellow budgery? Which fellow mumkull? Ba'al mine jerron.' (Good. I am not afraid. If you are angry you shall take a pistol. I will have a spear, a waddy, and a nulla-nulla. We shall see which is the best man, which will kill the other; I am not afraid!)

And so Donga Billy delivered his challenge.

'Yohi,' father said, 'Mine pidney, now yan' (go away).

'Budgery,' said Donga Billy; 'mine yan.'

And he went away.

There were cries from Tombo in the early morning.

'Massa, Massa. Come along-a camp. Woolla (talk to) Captain Payne ba'al mine Boompa-Boney. Mine Tombo. Naraigin boy. Plenty mine been take care of white man,' and then there was the sound of voices raised in regret and laughter. Captain Payne, commandant of the Native Police, explained the cause of the disturbance. He was there with his band, a tall, grim-looking man, short in speech, and ready in action.

'I'm after Boompa-Boney. 'Twas he speared Folson. He's about these parts. I sneaked your blackboy's camp, making sure I'd got him. What on earth are you doing here?'

Father said he was on his way to Milungera to try and get the Scotts to go back to Naraigin.

'They won't go,' said the commandant. 'Scott's bad with the shakes; but Mrs Scott's plucky as blazes and the best shot in the district. I tell you what it is; you squatters will have to arm a corps of your own if this murdering business gets hotter. There aren't enough of us to do the work. Goodnight. Budgery you, Tombo. Hi!' throwing him a fig of tobacco, 'suppose mine been mumkull Tombo plenty mine cry. You take it apology belonging to me, Tombo.'

And Captain Payne made the blackboy a magnificent bow.

'My word Massa close up ba'al more you been see Tombo,' said the boy. 'Police been think-it Boompa-Boney sit down along-a mine camp. My word! Budgery Captain Payne. That fellow Maamie (chief) close up like it Gubbernor; 'pologise to Tombo same as gentleman.'

It was the proudest memory of Tombo's life that he had once received an apology from the commandant of the Native Police.

I think it was upon the return journey from our expedition to the Scotts – but am not quite certain – that the half-caste Polly became a member of our family. Polly – she was duly christened – gave us so much trouble in after years, down south, that the subject of her adoption was not often mentioned, and so I am a little hazy as to times and seasons. For in spite of much fruitless endeavour on the part of the home authorities to instil into her the first principles of truth, honesty, and righteous dealing – to say nothing of the Catechism, the alphabet, and the art of washing herself – Polly took up first with a married bullock-driver, which ended in a fight, and brought disgrace on the head station, and afterwards made off for the bush with a blackfellow of one of the Logan tribes, and never again emerged into civilisation. I connect her with the Scotts because her mother came from Milungera and used to wear a striped gown of Mrs Scotts, slung over one shoulder and beneath the other arm. She was a good-looking gin, and had been the victim of a misplaced attach-

ment to a Chinaman, by whom she had been told to
'yan' – otherwise depart. Polly was a little Black-Mongolian
picaninny trotting by her side. Beantree Dick, our blackboy, in
whom Black Eliza – she had taken Mrs Scott's christian name as
well as the striped skirt – found her ultimate fate, shook his head
over the picaninny.

He was a blackboy of European prejudices imbibed in the
Native Police force, though I don't fancy he would have minded
if the creature's father had not been a Chinaman. He was quite
an attractive person, with a good voice, which the commandant
had trained, teaching him to sing white-black doggrel and native
ugals to operatic airs; and when we were camping out, he would
stand up by the fire, a picturesque figure with his white teeth and
gleaming eyes, very spick and span in moleskins and a Crimean
shirt with the red silk handkerchief, which was always his
Christmas present, twisted round his waist, while he trolled
forth –

> 'Wheelbarrow break 'im,
>   Walla tumble down,
> Ba'al Massa give-'im flour,
> Blackfellow got-'im none.'

Translated 'The drays are broken. The rain is falling. Master
gives me flour, and the blackfellows have none.'
Or,

> 'Yurù dhári nie! Yurù dhári nie!
> Dūla ranja burūla! Yarù dhári nie!'

Which is a ugal sung to the accompaniment of waving fire-
sticks, in order to scare away the spirits of the dead.

Black Eliza, with her picaninny, stuck us up in the bed of a
creek, and told a piteous story, to the effect that the tribe was
going to have a corroboree the next night, and meant to kill and
eat the luckless Polly.

It was quite common for the Blacks to dispose of a half-caste
in this way, and naturally the White Missus' heart was moved
to pity. Moreover, she had for some time cherished the notion
of catching a black lubra young, and training her to be a house
servant. Accordingly a bargain was struck. Black Eliza received
a clasp-knife and a fig of tobacco, on condition that she waived
all claim henceforth to the picaninny, and Polly was temporarily

delivered into the keeping of Tombo. A large handkerchief was tied round her head and she was put naked, but for a swathe of calico, into one of the saddle bags.

A fray had taken place at a deserted out-station where we camped that night. The station hands had been getting in scrubbers, and the carcases of wild bullocks lay in the stockyard, not far from the unburied bodies of dead Blacks. Here Polly was washed in a tub of warm water, her head shaved, and she was laid to sleep in a blanket in a far corner of the earthen-floored chamber. In the middle of the night father, who had lain down at the edge of the bunk, dressed, with his pistol beside him, was roused by the sound of stealthy footsteps, and stepping on to the floor with his pistol levelled called, 'Who's there?' prepared to fire in the direction whence he momentarily expected a boomerang to be hurled.

But a whining voice cried, 'Massa, ba'al mine find 'im blanket.'

It was poor little Polly, who, accustomed to sleep with her mother and the dogs by the camp fire, heaven's blue above her, had risen forlornly and was groping round the four walls by which she was cabined.

After a few days, Black Eliza put in appearance at Naraigin, and was welcomed by Beantree Dick. The White Massa performed the marriage ceremony after this fashion. Seeing Black Eliza at Dick's camp, he went down.

'Dick,' he said, 'I believe you like Eliza for gin belonging to you?'

'I believe corbon budgery that fellow,' replied Dick, thus intimating that she was superior to all other gins in his estimation.

'Eliza, you take Dick for Benjamin belonging to you?' he asked solemnly.

I can't get at the derivation of 'Benjamin' as the black equivalent for husband, but this boots not.

'Yes, massa,' the fair one answered with alacrity.

'Budgery! Eliza, I give Dick for Benjamin belonging to you. Dick, Eliza gin belonging to you. Now I been marry you all right like-it white woman.' Then there was delivered a homily to the pair on the whole duty of matrimony, and Eliza was bidden go no more to the camp, but take up her abode in the blackboy's quarters.

CHAPTER VII

'Cry Havock'

The moon was near the full. One day, Waggoo told me, under strict bond of secrecy, that there was going to be a corroboree that evening across the river, and promised that if I were willing, he and Tombo would take me to a spot from which I might look on unseen.

There was a horrible fascination in the prospect. I had listened with bated breath to Waggoo's tales of wonderful corroborees, and for months – years – had yearned after the sight. I trembled and longed, but dared not ask for permission, which I knew would certainly be refused. Towards dusk, I sneaked surreptitiously out of the humpey, and Tombo and Ringo conveyed me across the river to a little stony pinnacle on which was a patch of scrub, whence we had a good view of the lightly timbered flat where the Blacks were assembled in a wide circle illuminated by many fires.

The fires burned at regular distances, and in rows of three or four deep, there were gathered, in line, first the naked forms of many warriors pipe-clayed and painted, their heads bristling with parrot and cockatoo feathers, their necks wreathed with rush beads, their spears brandished above their heads; then the old men, and behind them the gins, who kept up a monotonous, discordant chorus to the accompaniment of a kind of tom-tom and a few jew's harps and the beating of boomerangs and waddies.

Now the chant dies in a long wail; now it swells into a fierce shout of triumph. The chiefs in the front seem to direct the performance. Some of them are painted to represent skeletons, others in spiral stripes as though huge snakes were coiled round their bodies. They wave their spears and utter harsh cries. Presently a little party of braves steps into the arena. They hold their shields in front of them, make sinuous movements, glance from one side to the other, vigilant and cunning, stoop as beneath imaginary doorways, and whisper together.

Clearly it is the rehearsal of a night attack upon some white man's station. Then there is a dash sideways upon a cluster of mock sleepers, who rise with drowsy gestures, give signs of horror and alarm, and after offering a feeble show of resistance, beg for mercy. A pantomimic struggle follows. Spears are pointed, nulla-nullas aimlessly hurled. The gins break their chant with infuriated yells. The circle closes in; the old men clash their boomerangs together in time to quick music, and the gins sway to and fro in a sort of drunken ecstasy.

Then the dance begins. More logs are thrown upon the bonfires, which blaze up high, and the whole scene is a lurid terror. The black forms thread the flames, bending this way and that in rhythmic motion, and the maddened faces with distended eyeballs and glistening teeth are as the faces of demons.

Now the chant becomes slow and mysterious, as if it were an invocation. There are three wild shouts, and four or five rude effigies of women, made of saplings and draped with red blankets, are dragged in to the circus and stood upright. They are saluted with screams of horrible laughter, and the warriors, painted like skeletons, mock them with gestures of derision. Then the black forms thicken round them. They are thrown down, stamped upon, and beaten with nulla-nullas, and at last hurled upon the central bonfire. The boomerangs clash louder, the saturnalia is fiercer. But I feel faint and sick, for I am convinced that a human sacrifice is about to be offered, and I turn and flee. Tombo and Waggoo follow and lead me back to the humpey, where I creep into my bed and lie shuddering. I do not dare go to my parents, who, believing us all long ago in bed and asleep, are in the verandah watching the red glow. I have often thought that had I described to them the ghastly performance I had witnessed, the Hornet Bank tragedy might have been averted.

One evening when Captain Payne, with a very small band, was camping on the Donga, Sylvester Frazer, a lad of seventeen, came to the camp on foot. He had a great weal on his forehead where a nulla-nulla had struck him; he was dazed and seemed drunk; but he was only drunk with horror.

He said that he had been asleep in his bunk the night before, and that he had been awakened by a noise, and while reaching up for a loaded gun that hung over his bed, had got a blow on the head which stunned him; then he had fallen between the bunk and the slab wall and had lain there insensible. He did not say how long he had been unconscious, and no one ever asked him what he had heard and seen. He said that the Blacks had murdered every one, that he had waited till they were gone away, and had then taken a revolver which he found, and walked ten miles to where he knew the Police were camping.

Now Captain Payne rode to Hornet Bank, and he saw, all in

a row, the dead women, the men and boys and two little children, lying as the murderers had placed them. And of the horror that he found, he too afterwards spoke little. He buried the bodies, and then with his band, rode on in hot haste and overtook one division of the tribe camped with the plunder in a narrow valley edged in on either side by rocks. There they were feasting, and shouting, and making merry, acting in abominable travesty the deeds of the night. One of them, who was a disbanded trooper, had a gun, and as he paused to take aim at a crow in a gum-tree near, Captain Payne covered him and gave the word, and the pursuers fired. But the sun was going down, and in these parts, twilight closes quickly, therefore many Blacks escaped into the scrub. After that, they took refuge in the bunya country, where it is difficult for man and horse to follow after prey.

A blackboy piloted father one moonlight night over Zen-Zen Plain, and told him that he had been one of those who had attacked Hornet Bank Station. Then when father pledged himself for the boy's safety that night, he gave in his own fashion the horrible story.

He explained what had puzzled the Whites on the Burnett, and said that the station dogs had not barked and given the alarm, because a black employed to fetch wood and water on the place, and whom they knew, had quieted them. Then he told how the Blacks had made their way to the store where young Frazer and the tutor slept, and how young Frazer, disturbed by the noise, had come out, to find Boompa Boney leading in his men, and had asked him what they wanted.

'Boney tell him "Altogether mumkull! Altogether marra White Maries"' (To kill every one and to take all the white women), the Black related. 'My word corbon that fellow ask Boney, ba'al mumkull; ba'al marra White Mary. Altogether ration, blanket, tobacco, everything belong to blackfellow, but ba'al marra White Mary.' Then blackfellow plenty pialla (talk), and by and by other blackfellow come behind and hit that whitefellow along-a waddy and mumkull (kill). Directly, that fellow tumble down, and altogether, blackfellow come up and mumkull schoolmaster. Then,' went on the boy, 'blackfellow been yan along-a White Mary's room, and plenty ole Missus talk. "Boney, what for you mumkull? Plenty you been brother belonging to me. Plenty I been give you flour, sugar, blanket, Boney ba'al mumkull! Ba'al marra (seize) White Mary, picaninny belonging to me." . . . I believe

Boney ba'al (not) want to mumkull old Missus,' the narrator added, 'but blackfellow corbon woolla (made great talk) and then altogether mumkull. . . .'

All night the Blacks held high and dreadful revelry. There were two shepherds in the huts who had come in the day before to be settled up with, and who knew nothing of the doings of the night. 'When Piggi jump up, two fellow white man come outside along-a cooliman,' the blackboy continued. (When the sun rose, two white men came up with their pitchers.) 'My word, plenty white men sleep. Ba'al they pidney (know) blackfellow along-a humpey. Directly blackfellow mel-mel (see), Boney sing out, "White fellow! White fellow! Make haste mumkull (kill)."' And so the two were chased and killed. 'When Piggi good way,' the blackboy ended, 'altogether blackfellow yan.' (When the sun was well up, all the Blacks went away.)

After this, word went down the river, and some bushmen met in Boompa verandah and held a council of war. There were Jackson of Boompa, and Murray of Naraigin, and Scott of Milungera and Gaythorne, Overseer of Gurrum Downs, and Carmichael of Zen-Zen. And it was decided that Gaythorne should take a message along the river and to the districts beyond Zen-Zen Plain and Donga Creek, that arms and ammunition should be collected and a corps formed, and that the little army should collect at Naraigin after dark that day week, and start forth on its raid.

And so one evening, the Naraigin sliprails were kept down and there was a passing in of many men and horses, and all the men were armed, and each squatter had his following of stockmen and trusty boys. That night, they all camped in Naraigin verandah, but there was little sleep and much counsel. Gaythorne believed that the Blacks had a deep-laid plot to exterminate the Whites, and urged that vengeance for the late massacre should be taken, not upon individuals, but upon the race, and that all males should be slaughtered. Some of the party were for destroying women and children also, and Tombo and Freddy and Beantree Dick, the blackboys who had been brought into the council, urged this course with a logic that was incontrovertible. 'Suppose you no kill picaninnies,' they said, 'that fellow by and by jump up kipper (young man) and mumkull (kill) you. Suppose you shoot Black Maries ba'al more picaninnies.'

But the party held firm to the traditions of British warfare. Sylvester Frazer was with Captain Payne's band; and these were scouring the heads of the Burnett, Sylvester conjecturing that the rest of the Blacks, ignorant of the 'Maamie's' (commandant's) whereabouts, would make for that broken country, which was their favourite place of refuge.

'It's my belief,' said Gaythorne, 'that he's wrong. They'll double back through Boompa Scrub, and if we look sharp we shall catch them in the Wild Man's Gorge, biding their time to attack the station. They'll be in no hurry for a bit, for they're bound to have a corroboree before taking any decisive step. They've threatened Boompa, and setting aside the loot, there's Gritty Macalister, and Donga Billy has been boasting that he is going to take her into the bush for his gin.'

So the next morning the irregular corps set forth. The first battle took place at the Dead Finish Flat close by Boompa, for Gaythorne's supposition had proved correct. The Boompa head-station was badly situated from the strategical point of view. Not far from the men's huts, the river ran through a narrow valley bordered by precipitous banks, along which one might ride for miles without being able to reach the river-bed. Here there was a large Blacks' camp. At sight of the camp, the army divided. One half cut off the Blacks from retreat by the river and opened fire, the other half rode round to the hut, which was barred and barricaded, and within which sat Gritty Macalister, grim and desperate, awaiting her fate. When the relieving force appeared she threw open a door behind and admitted her master, Gaythorne, and some of the others. But even as she did so, a mob of Blacks which had fled from the camp battered down her barricade and rushed in for shelter. They were met by the guns of the white men. Shrieks and groans echoed through the hut, and blood flowed freely upon the earthen floor of Gritty's kitchen.

'Take your wull on them, gentlemen,' she cried out. 'Never heed an auld woman. And for the Lord's sake put an end to Donga Billy!'

The combat to which Donga Billy had challenged the white man, took place here, and Gritty was delivered from the terror of abduction by her fierce admirer. Donga Billy was one of the few Blacks who would turn and face their opponents in open fight. He stood forth bravely and fought as a brave should. But the daloopil (carbine) was greater than nulla-nulla and spear, and Donga Billy was gathered to his fathers.

One skirmish was very like another. They have all been fought

over again, not once only, on winter evenings in front of the great
slab fireplace when the hot grog was mixed and the bushmen
gathered round the blaze; also amid clouds of tobacco-smoke on
the verandah, when the insects buzzed and the flying ants made
for the lamp within, and there was a great and clammy heat,
when, maybe, sheet lightning played on the horizon, and the
heavy clouds were brassy, and there was no breath of air, for
the season of drought did not wane. . . .

And we children, sprawling on the verandah, listened to the
squatters' talk, and saw in imagination vivid pictures of fierce
and bloody fights.

It went on for a time, the irregular warfare. Day after day the
trackers rode ahead, and every now and then would pass back
the word 'Mandowie' (footmarks), but no Blacks were sighted.
Hour after hour, they rode – in scrub and through scrub – I can
feel the gloom and tangle of it! Then, out of scrub once more,
all along the grey-green gum-tree wolds, and by desert and sandy
creek. At last, when the horses have plunged into another dense
scrub and carbines have to be carried carefully, Bloodhound Joe,
the finest tracker on Donga Creek, turns round on his horse, his
eyes agleam, 'Scht! Scht!' he mutters. 'Myall (wild Black) sit down.
Mine close-up camp.'

And the bushmen press forward and hold their breath and strain
their eyes, peering through the darkness of bunya boughs and
the shadow and blot of vine and undergrowth. We used to hear
them tell the story. . . . 'Yes . . . There they are . . . By Jove!
At last! . . . The camp dogs bark and the carbines are levelled.
A great naked Black gets up from his 'possum rug and rubs himself, looking this way and that. He sees the glint of a gun and
the head of Gaythorne's flea-bitten grey. He stoops for his spear
and calls to his fellow braves. The gins and picaninnies screech
in alarm and run in and out of the gunyahs . . . You see it all
in little bits . . . here a head: there a body: . . . arms . . . legs
. . . heads . . . again . . . all misty . . . all confusion. Now we
make a rush. Hoorray! At them, Tombo. . . . Down with them,
Dick. . . . Bang! Bang! . . . Whiz . . . Whiz! . . . On goes the
storming of the camp. . . . Then quiet – no black shapes remaining. . . . Time it's taken – perhaps three minutes. . . . We're off
horses examining the conquered camp. . . . Blankets, 'possum
rugs, dilly-bags, tomahawks, bits of raw and cooked bandicoot
and snake. There's a very old gin with a rifle-ball through her

chest, lying in her last gasp, and you feel bad as she looks up at you with glazing eyes. A picaninny that has its leg broken is squalling, and a baby lies on the ground smothered, with its head under a fallen gunyah. The only man left is a wounded warrior whom Beantree Dick has taken prisoner.

'Casualties, Tombo missing; but by and by he comes back with a broad grin on his black face.

'"Well, Tombo? Blackfellow all gone?'

'"Yowi (yes)," says Tombo. "Mine been knock down three fellow big blackfellow. My word, look here!" and he triumphantly produces three gory trophies, which are the right hands of three of his own tribe.'

There are other incidents of that raid spoken of in whispers, and at such times the men in the verandah become silent and look very grave. They shake the ashes from their pipes and cut up more tobacco.

The war did not last a great many months. The fighting Blacks were almost all killed, and those which remained pushed northward.

Thus the Frazer murder was avenged, and for a while afterwards the land was at peace.

Will the bush ever give up the secrets of its dead, and of the many lonely tragedies that have been played out under the gum-trees?

There was a green valley between two ranges thickly covered with scrub that lay a good way from us up the river. 'Cobra belonging to white man's skull sit down here' (There's a white man's skull here,) said Tombo the blackboy, as we rode through the valley. And there the bleached skull lay with two or three other human bones which had been torn by dingoes, probably from a hastily made grave. It was that unburied skull with its eyeless sockets and grinning jawbones which made Time's death's-head in the altarpiece of childish memories, an actuality of life to me. Afterwards at Naraigin, a very old shepherd, who was 'short of a sheet of bark,' as they say in the bush of one not quite bright in his wits, told the tale of the skull, in which he himself had been an actor.

Long, long ago, one of the very first settlers, with his mate, went out with a gun and compass and provisions, seized by the longing to explore new country. They found the green valley and were satisfied, and stayed there to camp, but one day riding through the scrub, the settler's gun caught in a creeper, and went off, wounding him badly in the back. His mate got him to the camping place, and he lay half paralysed for two or three days, his one anxiety being that the mate, who was a stupid creature, should learn the compass before he died, as otherwise how would he get back to civilisation? So the sick man tried to teach his companion, till from very feebleness, the stick he was using to point with, dropped from his hand. When he was a little stronger, he had the fire rekindled and took his knife up to point with, as he went on with the lesson. But the knife got magnetised somehow and twisted the compass. 'Look,' said the man with a puzzled stare, and died, and the mate never could make use of the compass after all. He fell in with a tribe of the Donga Blacks, and they did not kill him and eat him – perhaps because he was half starved and showed no fight, his gun and ammunition being lost. He stayed with them for eight months, and at last made his way down Donga Creek and got among white men again.

Once, a drover for whom I was weighing out meat gave me a pocket-book he had found with some human bones away out in unexplored country. There were only three or four leaves in it, and one had a list of rations and some small sums jotted down, and on another was part of a letter out of which a jagged bit had been torn. The words that were left seemed a clue to the heap of bones.

'. . . alone in the bush . . . separated from . . . dearest. . . . Camp about sixteen hundred miles. . . . Many birds, emus, ducks, . . . others very beautiful. . . . Camps of Blacks, but seem harmless and suffering from . . . Off day of fever . . . Shakes awful . . . I suppose not used . . .'

The rest was gone. Who was the letter meant for, I wonder; and did the friend or sweetheart ever learn its writer's fate, and get the comfort of knowing that probably God's hand had dealt death, and not a Black's spear?

There were some marks below the list of rations which made me fancy he might have been a surveyor. That was a hard life then and now – when a man might wander alone 'out West' for miles and miles over barren plains with never a tree, except for a burnt patch of scrub or the withered gums along an empty watercourse – perhaps with his water-bag giving out, and his horses maybe lying down quietly to die, after a dry stage.

I remember, during one drought, two men travelling north and coming back a few days later after they had nearly died of thirst, so that the experience was still fresh upon them. They knew there was a water-hole sixty miles from their starting place; and they got it right enough, but there was no water in it. They reached it in the evening, and all the water in their water-bags had been drunk hours before, and the horses were knocked up. Either way, backwards or forwards, death stared at them. They knew that by going on, they might strike the river; and the river up in that part will branch out into many threads running beside each other perhaps for a hundred miles, and though the channels will be dry, one of them may run to a 'dead head,' which means finding a water-hole. But it means, too, that you may be going along one dry bed, and water may be in another a few hundred yards from you and you won't know it.

The men went forward, and their sufferings became terrible. The horses tried to graze but could not, and the men smoked in dismal silence, till by and by one of them began to rave – quite quietly, fancying that he was riding in Sydney Domain, and talking a great deal about his wife. But after a big he got wilder, and tore off his clothes, which is what a man always does when the thirst madness seizes him; and when he is beyond that, he lies down and the blue ants get at him. How often have I heard bushmen, in their verandah talks, tell the harrowing details! About sundown, the horses suddenly cocked their ears and staggered along with a little fresh heart. There was a water-hole ahead, and men and horses drank and wallowed in it. I remember well their describing the taste and smell of that water as something Paradisaical, and how it seemed to find its way down to finger-tips and toes, as through the pores of a sponge.

In truth, all the flimsinesses of life are torn into shreds by the wild forces of nature which reign in the bush. One of the most horrible things I remember, happened – not in those childish days, but later when I was grown up and married, and living on an island in the same Wide Bay district. There is no pretence, however, in these disconnected memories, to keep to times and places in proper order, beyond a general outline of events, and I may as well tell the story here.

It is a grievous little tale, and I was not mixed up in it beyond the fact that Cousin Will, who told it to me, was one of the search party, and knew all about it. A woman, her husband, a mate, and a child started from a tiny bush township, to which they had come in coaster and bullock dray, to look for work. They had 'humped bluey' and were 'on the wallaby track' in Australian vernacular, which means that they walked and carried with them their earthly goods on the men's backs, rolled up in a blue blanket. Of course they were new chums – and very new ones, or they would have taken water-bags. But they did not, and very soon they got thirsty: and they were in sandy gum bush – nothing round them but stringy-bark and grass-trees – which is a sign of bad country – and no water anywhere. The child cried and became heavy in the woman's arms – it was a toddling thing of two or three, and had to be carried except for small spells when it walked, supported by its mother's hand. They went on through the flat forest of gums – I know the country – the ground whitey-brown and hard: the grass hard too and brown also, the gum-trees lean and lanky, with hard, greyish leaves, that whizz in the scorching wind like plates of tin. On to the limbs and stems of the trees there clung strange ghosts of grasshoppers, pallid and motionless – the cast-off husks of locusts, which, vigorous now in their new casing, make a maddening, metallic whirr in the upper foliage. And the grass-trees! What weird things they are, with their uncouth black trunks and dreary bunches of a gigantic kind of grass, out of which uprise brown cones, long and slender and about the size and thickness of a Black's spear. One might fancy them a scattered cohort of monstrous beings, standing with weapons poised. There are dead twigs strewing the earth, and fallen logs, and in patches, a wiry undergrowth, peopled with curious insects – if one stopped to look. For instance, the brown praying mantis, its arms upraised and hands folded, beseeching grace. Here and there is a big ant-bed, with little trails extending on every side, as the streets of tombs went out of ancient Rome – for in an ant-bed in the bush one may find a likeness to the great old cities and the dead empires of the world! The ants made their raids in search of food and thirst of conquest. The Romans did the same.

The men 'humping bluey' had no ideas of that kind: they only thought of finding water. But there was not a sign of even a dry gully or hidden spring. All was parched and arid: a brassy sun overhead.

The men were sure there must be a water-hole somewhere near, and proposed that they should explore for it, while the woman

and child remained on the track. The two disappeared among
the gumtrees, and the woman and her baby waited. Some time
passed: the men did not come back, and the woman grew frightened. She fancied that she heard her husband calling, and
supposed that he was not able to see her in the labyrinth of gums.
She moved a little way, but was afraid to leave the child lest it
should wander out of sight. By and by, it cried itself to sleep.
No angel descended, as to Hagar in the wilderness, and the poor
woman, desperate with terror, thirst, and anxiety for the child,
determined to go herself and look for water.

So she tied the sleeping child to a gum-sapling with a piece of
cord she had with her, and set on her quest. She walked on
through the forest; it seemed to her certain that she would easily
find her way back. Had she been a bushman, she would have
marked the trees and so 'blazed a track!' But that did not come
into her mind. The thickening trees closed her in all alike; not
a landmark to guide her. And after a while, she knew that she
was lost in the bush.

The men on their fruitless search for water, were lost too – they
had taken no precautions either, and were without a compass
to give them any clue to their position. For a day and a night
they roamed in the bush, and at last found themselves again at
the little township. Search parties were sent out for the woman
and child: and very soon, by the side of the track, the child was
found; but the horror of the thing was that soldier ants had
attacked the defenceless baby, and before it died the poor mite
had gone through the torture to which Red Indians used sometimes to condemn their enemies. It skin was literally eaten, and
they buried what remained under the gum-sapling to which it
had been tied. In the meantime the mother, perishing with thirst,
had been found by a shepherd near the township. He brought
her there, and she told her story. The search party returned, and
a blackboy, riding ahead, met her and blurted out the news of
what they had discovered. On hearing it, the woman lost her
reason, and died soon afterwards, in the asylum of the district.

These are some of the things which happen in the bush.

Mr Henry Lawson, the Australian Kipling as they call him,
has written a pathetic little story of bush life called, 'No place
for a woman.' Truly it was no place for a woman – that Naraigin country. Had there been no Blacks and no tragedies, still heat
and insects were always with us – except, perhaps, for a month

or two in the brief winter. Often in the hot days of summer we used to amuse ourselves by frying birds' eggs on a sheet of zinc, by the sun's rays at midday. Then the water in the casks was as though it had been boiled, the lagoon gave us an undesired warm bath, and whatever one touched, whether made of wood or metal, seemed to be burning. As for the insects, there were myriads of them. The legs of the dining table had to be put in pint pots filled with water, to prevent the white ants from climbing up and devouring our food. This, to be sure, did not hinder the winged ants from flying down upon it, and they had an uncanny trick of leaving their wings behind them at seasons, like a certain white lizard which, when one catches it, escapes by simply detaching its tail. Of these simpler pests, flies were abominable and maddening, and to endure them at all, one had need to be stifled in a shuttered room, or encumbered with an iron framework about the head, from which hung a tent of mosquitoe netting. It was a particular kind of fly which caused sandy blight, and drove shepherds in their huts and women in the headstations blind and wild with pain while it lasted. Those dark-lashed blue eyes of the girl-wife at Bungroopim – Irish eyes which were so large and soft – became contracted and watery, and spoiled by reddened lids, and thinned lashes from the frequent use of lotions. For two years she had to live in a room from which every particle of light had been excluded, by hanging up blue blankets over the windows – the only curtains procurable in the bush. Then besides the blight, and not counting in snakes, there were centipedes and scorpions, which were sometimes brought in with the wood for the kitchen fire, and sometimes made holes and crawled out from behind the canvas lining of our slab walls. I remember how I was bitten one night in one of the fingers, as I lay in my bunk, how the finger swelled and turned black, causing excruciating pain, and how our father cut it with his razor and sucked the poison, relieving the pain with arnica and bread poultices. I don't think any of us were sorry when we were obliged to leave Naraigin, though impending ruin was the cause of our selling the station. Bad times came with the scab among the sheep and the treading down of those green, thick-leaved fat-hen plants (of which very good spinach could be made) in an access of activity round the disused boiling-down pots. We had the foul smell intensified when the wind set towards the humpey, and a cloud of depression rested upon the head-station. Naraigin had been an extravagant venture, bought with the disadvantage of a heavy mortgage – heavy, that is, when borne by an almost penniless young couple, burdened as well with several babies.

The disappointed pioneer writes: 'I will boil down fifteen hundred wethers and as many cattle as I can find fat enough, for a sop to the Bank. A debt of £10,000 at 10 per cent. interest is no light matter. Alas! I have reaped the covetous man's reward.'

Reflecting on the rate of interest on money in these days, the covetous man's mouth may well water. A loan at 10 per cent. meant on the whole favourable terms: it was the ordinary Bank rate, and the safest investment might be expected to return 12 per cent. on the capital put out.

So Naraigin was sold. We bade goodbye to Monseer Jacks, and Tombo, and Black Eliza – who showed no grief at parting with Polly – and Ringo and the rest of our dusky friends, who had sheltered themselves at the camp by the lagoon during the squatters' raid, and had remained on Donga Creek ever since. It was all over – that bit of wild life.

CATHERINE LANGLOH PARKER, c. 1855-1940

The first person to undertake systematic collection and collation of Aboriginal tales and legends, Catherine Langloh Parker was born in South Australia and spent her early years on a property in Queensland. As the wife of K. Langloh Parker (under whose name she primarily published, although she also published as Catherine Stowe), she lived on stations in New South Wales and Queensland where she used her proximity to black culture and folklore to constructive and compassionate purpose. *Australian Legendary Tales; Folklore of the Noongahburrahs* was published in 1896 and went through many subsequent editions; Catherine Langloh Parker also published *The Walkabouts of the Wur-Run-Nah* (1918) and *Woggheeguy; Australian Aboriginal Legends* (1930) along with *The Euahlayi Tribe; A Study of Aboriginal Life in Australia* (1905).

Like many Australian women writers, Catherine Langloh Parker was concerned to understand and value Aboriginal people and culture; although such understandings as those expressed by her have changed since she recorded some of the aboriginal lore, there can be no doubting the sincerity of her concern and her motives.

The following legends have been taken from the 1954 edition of *Australian Legendary Tales* which was illustrated by Elizabeth Durack and edited by Henrietta Drake-Brockman, who was herself an

impressive writer in her own right. Henrietta Drake-
Brockman (1902-1968) supported and promoted the
work of many other Australian women writers and
shared their commitment to an appreciation of
Aboriginal life; part of her introduction to Catherine
Langloh Parker's work is included here to contextualise the legends.

ABOUT THESE STORIES

These legends are important.

They were collected more than fifty years ago by Mrs Langloh
Parker, who as Catherine Field grew up amongst the aborigines
then living on her father's station. As a child she was saved from
drowning by natives; as a married woman she continued to live
amongst them at Bangate Station on the Narran River, N.S.W.
To her, they were first of all playmates and friends. Later-
developed, more scholarly interests were never allowed to chill
the warmth of human relationship. It is her own sympathetic yet
completely objective attitude which helps to make these legends
and tales so vivid, so dramatic, so alive with the breath of the
dark people who first recounted them. For Australians, there is
added charm in fresh images that yet seem familiar, like the stars
of the Southern Cross. The legends possess a poetic quality, childlike in its simplicity despite their adult wisdom, that should endear
them not only to children but to the young in heart. Clear-cut
character drawing and shrewd understanding of basic human
behaviour and motive, is both delightful and amusing. It would
be difficult to find a better concise comment on social snobbery
and maternal vanity than in 'Dinewan the Emu and Goomble-
Gubbon the Turkey'. The idea of family limitation for economic
reasons, though savage in application, suggests how old in human
reckoning much cherished 'modern' thought may be! Nor is gentler insight lacking. The story of the little duck who, captured
by a vicious water-rat, hatched forth a platypus, is a parable of
lonely motherhood as pathetic as it is brave. Serious readers will
discover that these legends, taken as a whole, create an astonish-
ingly vivacious picture of life in Australia 'as it was in the
beginning'.

Mrs Langloh Parker believed her *Australian Legendary Tales*, published in London in 1896, to be the first considerable collection of aboriginal legends and tales . . .

Mrs Parker was in fact one of the first people to write exclusively of the Australian aborigines as fellow creatures. Perhaps she was, indeed, the first to set forth, to any noteworthy extent, their own vision of themselves and their conditions of living, so far as she was able to reproduce their thoughts and speech forms in written English. However well-intentioned earlier serious writers may have been, there remains in their work a hint of patronage, of 'outside' observance, of 'case-book' approach . . .

Mrs Parker makes her original intention clear in her first preface: 'A neighbour of mine exclaimed, when I mentioned that I purposed making a small collection of the folk-lore legends of the tribe of blacks I knew so well living on this station, "But have the blacks any legends?" thus showing that people live in a country, and yet know little of the aboriginal inhabitants. . . .'

Fifty years on, the majority of us remain ignorant of this lovely legendary world they created, a magic world, a world of myth woven about the characters of our own trees and birds and beasts – which are entirely different to any others in the world – and about our hills and rivers and stars. These are indeed Australian stories that belong to Australia and to all Australians – dark, white, or newly arrived! No other country has stories quite like these. I, too, have lived amongst aborigines, and respected them as fellow humans. Nevertheless, when I read National Library copies of Mrs Parker's legends, I was filled with regret that I had not known them all my life.

Perhaps, I thought, she had felt as a child as I felt – that she did not wish continually to read stories about European, American, Asiatic, or even African, flowers and fairies; about castles she had never seen, or strange minarets; about witches and princes and hobgoblins and genii. She, too, I thought, may have longed for satisfying tales about the soft bush creatures, the wicked snakes, the gay or spiteful birds. She, too, must have wanted to know if the dark people who lived here before we came, loving the land as we now love it, had made up fables like those handed down from the Greeks and Romans, or like the myths and sagas of the Norsemen who were amongst our own ancestors. Surely, I used to think, if a country is to be loved, it is necessary to have stories and poetry about its own soil and creatures. The older such stories are, the more they are founded on natural facts and behaviour observed for centuries, the better; no matter how supernatural they may eventually become. It seemed to me that we had none; that we were doomed to wait till some were manufactured. Yet, all the time, here were these fascinating legends languishing out of print.

In this new Australian edition a selection has been made from four books. Some of the stories are 'woggi-gai', or fairy-tales pure and simple, as told for the piccaninnies. Many explain also the beginnings of things, and were believed in the same way that Europeans once believed the world was flat, and that the sun, moon and stars revolved overhead. But some were not told to the children, or even to their mothers. Many of the longer stories, especially those about Baiame, the All Father, who lived in his Sky Camp, were religious, and so sacrosanct; in the same way that Bora, or initiation, ceremonies were, and in some districts still are, as sacred to aborigines as church services to us . . .

Yet another reason for regarding these legends as important, is that they so pleasantly enlarge not only appreciation of natural Australian environment, but also realization of human affinity with the original Australians. Being at home is knowing all about a place. Feeling at home is feeling at ease. To be at home in the deepest and best sense, we would be wise to learn to feel at ease with the people who lived here before us, knowing Australia more intimately, though in a different way. If the aborigines had possessed a written language, or spoken one only, instead of many, I think our coming would have been less tragic: as it was, they had not only many different tribes and languages, but also a secret sacred life, and sacred phrases for many of their legends too esoteric to be passed on to any but the fully initiated. For that reason, the first white people could not understand many of the things they saw, and too quickly believed that the aborigines were a people without imagination or beliefs – an idea easily refuted by such legends as these.

But the legends show also how much the aborigines were, and in outlying districts still are, haunted by magic and superstition. And how much of their lives had to be spent in arduous food-hunting, and how callous they were by our standards; though by theirs, we were, and still frequently are, worse than callous in our disturbance of their traditional hunting grounds and hallowed places. The way of the future should be a way of mutual understanding and respect. For that reason I am happy to have the opportunity to help in handing on Mrs Parker's admirable collection, once again, on behalf of the original dark authors.

To conclude, the Euahlayi people, of whom Mrs Parker writes, had a charming habit of singing charms over their babies to help them to be good, or to grow strong or clever, or to preserve them from danger. Perhaps one such, sadly abused in the past, can be recalled now at a moment of national growth. It was always sung to a child who was just beginning to make his own way in the world, and reaching out for everything.

Kind be.
Do not steal,
Do not touch which to another belongs;
Leave all such alone.
Kind be.

H. DRAKE-BROCKMAN

Perth, W.A.
1953

AUSTRALIAN LEGENDARY TALES
DINEWAN THE EMU AND GOOMBLE-GUBBON THE TURKEY

Dinewan the emu, being the largest bird, was acknowledged as king by the other birds. The Goomble-gubbons the turkeys, were jealous of the Dinewans. Particularly was Goomble-gubbon, the mother, jealous of the Dinewan mother. She would watch with envy the high flight of the Dinewans, and their swift running. And she always fancied that the Dinewan mother flaunted her superiority in her face, for whenever Dinewan alighted near Goomble-gubbon, after a long, high flight, she would flap her big wings and begin booing in her pride, not the loud booing of the male bird but a little, triumphant, satisfied booing noise of her own, which never failed to irritate Goomble-gubbon when she heard it.

Goomble-gubbon used to wonder how she could put an end to Dinewan's supremacy. She decided that she would only be able to do so by injuring her wings and checking her power of flight.

But the question that troubled her was how to effect this end. She knew she would gain nothing by having a quarrel with Dinewan and fighting her, for no Goomble-gubbon would stand any chance against a Dinewan. There was evidently nothing to be gained by an open fight. She would have to effect her end by cunning.

One day, when Goomble-gubbon saw in the distance Dinewan coming towards her, she squatted down and doubled in her wings in such a way as to look as if she had none.

After Dinewan had been talking to her for some time, Goomble-gubbon said, 'Why do you not imitate me and do without wings? Every bird flies. The Dinewans, to be the king of birds, should do without wings. When all the birds see that I can do without wings, they will think I am the cleverest bird and they will make a Goomble-gubbon king.'

'But you have wings,' said Dinewan.

'No, I have no wings.'

And indeed she looked as if her words were true, so well were her wings hidden as she squatted in the grass.

Dinewan went away after a while and thought much of what she had heard. She talked it all over with her mate, who was as disturbed as she was. They made up their minds that it would never do to let the Goomble-gubbons reign in their stead, even if they had to lose their wings to save their kingship.

At length they decided on the sacrifice of their wings. The Dinewan mother showed the example by persuading her mate to cut off hers with a kumbu, or stone tomahawk, and then she did the same to his.

As soon as the operations were over the Dinewan mother lost no time in letting Goomble-gubbon know what they had done. She ran swiftly down to the plain on which she had left Goomble-gubbon, and, finding her still squatting there, she said, 'See, I have followed your example. I have now no wings. They are cut off.'

'Ha! ha! ha!' laughed Goomble-gubbon, jumping up and dancing round with joy at the success of her plot. As she danced round she spread out her wings, flapped them, and said, 'I have taken you in, old stumpy wings. I have my wings yet. You are fine birds, you Dinewans, to be chosen kings, when you are so easily taken in. Ha! ha! ha!'

And, laughing derisively, Goomble-gubbon flapped her wings

right in front of Dinewan, who rushed towards her to chastise her treachery. But Goomble-gubbon flew away, and, alas, the now wingless Dinewan could not follow her.

Brooding over her wrongs, Dinewan walked away, vowing she would be revenged. But how? That was the question which she and her mate failed to answer for some time.

At length Dinewan mother thought of a plan and prepared at once to execute it.

She hid all her young Dinewans but two under a big salt-bush. Then she walked off to Goomble-gubbon's plain with the two young ones following her. As she walked off the morilla, or pebbly ridge, where her home was, on to the plain, she saw Goomble-gubbon out feeding with her twelve young ones.

After exchanging a few remarks in friendly manner with Goomble-gubbon she said to her, 'Why do you not imitate me and only have two children? Twelve are too many to feed. If you keep so many they will never grow big birds like the Dinewans. The food that would make big birds of two would only starve twelve.'

Goomble-gubbon said nothing, but she thought it might be so. It was impossible to deny that the young Dinewans were much bigger than the young Goomble-gubbons, and, discontentedly, Goomble-gubbon walked away, wondering whether the smallness of her young ones was owing to the number of them being so much greater than that of the Dinewans. It would be grand, she thought, to grow as big as the Dinewans. But she remembered the trick she had played on Dinewan, and she thought that perhaps she was being fooled in her turn. She looked back to where the Dinewans fed, and as she saw how much bigger the two young ones were than any of hers, once more mad envy of Dinewan possessed her.

She determined she would not be outdone. Rather would she kill all her young ones but two.

She said, 'The Dinewans shall not be the king birds of the plains. The Goomble-gubbons shall replace them. They shall grow as big as the Dinewans, and shall keep their wings and fly, which now the Dinewans cannot do.'

And straight away Goomble-gubbon killed all her young ones but two.

Then back she came to where the Dinewans were still feeding. When Dinewan saw her coming and noticed she had only two young ones with her, she called out, 'Where are all your young ones?'

Goomble-gubbon answered, 'I have killed them, and have only two left. Those will have plenty to eat now, and will soon grow as big as your young ones.'

'You cruel mother to kill your children. You greedy mother. Why, I have twelve children and I find food for them all. I would not kill one for anything, not even if by so doing I could get back my wings. There is plenty for all. Look at the emu-bush how it covers itself with berries to feed my big family. See how the grasshoppers come hopping round, so that we can catch them and fatten on them.'

'But you have only two children.'

'I have twelve. I will go and bring them to show you.'

Dinewan ran off to her salt-bush where she had hidden her ten young ones.

Soon she was to be seen coming back – running with her neck stretched forward, her head thrown back with pride, and the feathers of her booboo-tella, or tail, swinging as she ran, booming out the while her queer throat-noise, the Dinewan song of joy; the pretty, soft-looking little ones with their striped skins running beside her, whistling their baby Dinewan note.

When Dinewan reached the place where Goomble-gubbon was, she stopped her booing and said in a solemn tone, 'Now you see my words are true, I have twelve young ones, as I said. You can gaze at my loved ones and think of your poor murdered children. And while you do so I will tell you the fate of your descendants for ever. By trickery and deceit you lost the Dinewans their wings, and now for evermore, as long as the Dinewan has no wings, so shall a Goomble-gubbon lay only two eggs and have only two young ones. We are quits now. You have your wings and I my children.'

And ever since that time a Dinewan, or emu, has had no wings, and a Goomble-gubbon, or turkey of the plains, has laid only two eggs in a season.

HOW THE SUN WAS MADE

For a long time there was no sun, only a moon and stars. That was before there were men on the earth, only birds and beasts, all of which were many sizes larger than they are now.

One day Dinewan the emu and Brolga the native companion were on a large plain near the Murrumbidgee. There they were, quarrelling and fighting. Brolga, in her rage, rushed to the nest of Dinewan and seized from it one of the huge eggs, which she threw with all her force up to the sky. There it broke on a heap of firewood, which burst into flame as the yellow yolk spilt all over it, which flame lit up the world below, to the astonishment of every creature on it. They had only been used to the semi-darkness, and were dazzled by such brightness.

A good spirit who lived in the sky saw how bright and beauti-ful the earth looked when lit up by this blaze. He thought it would be a good thing to make a fire every day; which from that time he has done. All night he and his attendant spirits collect wood and heap it up. When the heap is nearly big enough they send out the morning star to warn those on earth that the fire will soon be lit.

The spirits, however, found this warning was not sufficient, for those who slept saw it not. Then the spirits thought they must have some noise made at dawn of day to herald the coming of the sun and waken the sleepers. But for a long time they could not decide to whom should be given this office.

At last one evening they heard the laughter of Goo-goor-gaga the laughing jackass ringing through the air.

'That is the noise we want,' they said.

Then they told Goo-goor-gaga that, as the morning star faded and the day dawned, he was every morning to laugh his loudest, that his laughter might awaken all sleepers before sunrise. If he would not agree to do this, then no more would they light the sun-fire, but let the earth be ever in twilight again.

But Goo-goor-gaga saved the light for the world.

He agreed to laugh his loudest at every dawn of day; which he has done ever since, making the air ring with his loud cack-ling, 'Goo goor gaga, goo goor gaga, goo goor gaga.'

When the spirits first light the fire it does not throw out much heat. But by the middle of the day when the whole heap of fire-wood is in a blaze, the heat is fierce. After that it begins to die gradually away until only red embers are left at sunset; and they quickly die out, except a few the spirits cover up with clouds, and save to light the heap of wood they get ready for the next day.

Children are not allowed to imitate the laughter of Goo-goor-gaga, lest he should hear them and cease his morning cry.

If children do laugh as he does, an extra tooth grows above their eye-tooth, so that they carry a mark of their mockery in punishment for it, because well the good spirits know that if ever a time comes wherein the Goo-goor-gagas cease laughing to herald the sun, then the time will have come when no more Daens are seen in the land; and darkness will reign once more.

THE SOUTHERN CROSS

In the very beginning when Baiame, the sky king, walked the earth, out of the red ground of the ridges he made two men and a woman. When he saw that they were alive he showed them such plants as they should eat to keep life, then he went on his way.

For some time they lived on such plants as he had shown them; then came a drought, and plants grew scarce, and when one day a man killed a kangaroo rat he and the woman ate some of its flesh, but the other man would not eat though he was famished for food, and lay as one dead.

Again and again the woman told him it was good and pressed him to eat.

Annoyed, weak as he was, he rose and walked angrily away towards the sunset, while the other two still ate hungrily.

When they had finished they looked for him, found he had gone some distance, and went after him. Over the sandhills, over the pebbly ridges they went, losing sight of him from time to time. When they reached the edge of the coolabah plain they saw their mate on the other side, by the river. They called to him to stop, but he heeded them not; on he went until he reached a huge yaraän, or white gum-tree, beneath which he fell to the ground. As he lay there dead they saw beside him a black figure with two huge fiery eyes. This figure raised him into the tree and dropped him into its hollow centre.

While still speeding across the plain they heard so terrific a burst of thunder that they fell startled to the ground. When they raised themselves they gazed wonderingly towards the giant gum-tree. They saw it being lifted from the earth and passing through the air towards the southern sky. They could not see their lost mate, but fiery eyes gleamed from the tree. Suddenly, a raucous shrieking broke the stillness; they saw it came from two yellow-crested white cockatoos flying after the vanishing tree. Mooyi, they called them.

On went the Spirit Tree, after it flew the Mooyi, shrieking loudly to it to stop, so that they might reach their roosting-place in it.

At last the tree planted itself near the Warrambool, or Milky Way, which leads to where the sky gods live. When it seemed quite still the tree gradually disappeared from their sight. They only saw four fiery eyes shine out. Two were the eyes of Yowi, the spirit of death. The other two were the eyes of the first man to die.

The Mooyi fly after the tree, trying always to reach their roost again.

When all nature realized that the passing of this man meant that death had come into the world, there was wailing everywhere. The swamp oak trees sighed incessantly, the gum-trees shed tears of blood, which crystallized into red gum.

To this day to the tribes of that part, the Southern Cross is known as Yaraän-doo, the place of the white gum-tree. And the Pointers are called Mooyi, the white cockatoos.

So is the first coming of death remembered by the tribes, to whom the Southern Cross is a reminder.

BARBARA BAYNTON, 1857-1929

While there is some ambivalence about Barbara
Baynton's origins, it would seem that she was born
Barbara Lawrence of fairly humble parents, in Scone,
New South Wales, and that she later gave herself
embellished antecedents. Divorced from her first husband and with three children to support, she was
never in danger of romanticising women's experience
of life in the bush. Later, married to Thomas Baynton, and relieved of some of the pressures of
providing for her family, she turned to writing and
produced a small but starkly brilliant body of work.
Her depiction of the outback as oppressive, brutalis-
ing and unremittingly cruel, particularly for women,
stands in sharp contrast to some of the sentimental
male imagery of the time.

Only recently accorded some of the acclaim her
work deserves, Barbara Baynton's fiction is now in
print in *Portable Australian Authors: Barbara
Baynton*, edited by Sally Krimmer and Alan Lawson
and published by University of Queensland Press
(1980); the following short story has been taken from
this edition and is representative of her perspective
and her style.

SQUEAKER'S MATE

The woman carried the bag with the axe and maul and wedges;
the man had the billy and clean tucker bags; the cross-cut saw
linked them. She was taller than the man, and the equability of

her body contrasting with his indolent slouch accentuated the difference. 'Squeaker's mate' the men called her, and these agreed that she was the best long-haired mate that ever stepped in petticoats. The Selectors' wives pretended to challenge her right to womanly garments, but if she knew what they said, it neither turned nor troubled Squeaker's mate.

Nine prospective posts and maybe sixteen rails – she calculated this yellow gum would yield. 'Come on,' she encouraged the man; 'let's tackle it.'

From the bag she took the axe, and ring-barked a preparatory circle, while he looked for a shady spot for the billy and tucker bags.

'Come on.' She was waiting with the greased saw. He came. The saw rasped through a few inches, then he stopped and looked at the sun.

'It's nigh tucker time,' he said, and when she dissented, he exclaimed, with sudden energy, 'There's another bee! Wait, you go on with the axe, an' I'll track 'im.'

As they came, they had already followed one and located the nest. She could not see the bee he spoke of, though her grey eyes were as keen as a Black's. However she knew the man, and her tolerance was of the mysteries.

She drew out the saw, spat on her hands, and with the axe began weakening the inclining side of the tree.

Long and steadily and in secret the worm had been busy in the heart. Suddenly the axe blade sank softly, the tree's wounded edges closed on it like a vice. There was a 'settling' quiver on its top branches, which the woman heard and understood. The man, encouraged by the sounds of the axe, had returned with an armful of sticks for the billy. He shouted gleefully, 'It's fallin', look out.'

But she waited to free the axe.

With a shivering groan the tree fell, and as she sprang aside, a thick worm-eaten branch snapped at a joint and silently she went down under it.

'I tole yer t' look out,' he reminded her, as with a crow-bar, and grunting earnestly, he forced it up. 'Now get out quick.'

She tried moving her arms and the upper part of her body. Do this; do that, he directed, but she made no movement after the first.

He was impatient, because for once he had actually to use his strength. His share of a heavy lift usually consisted of a make-

believe grunt, delivered at a critical moment. Yet he hardly cared
to let it again fall on her, though he told her he would, if she
'didn't shift'.

Near him lay a piece broken short; with his foot he drew it
nearer, then gradually worked it into a position, till it acted as
a stay to the lever.

He laid her on her back when he drew her out, and waited
expecting some acknowledgement of his exertions, but she was
silent, and as she did not notice that the axe, she had tried to
save, lay with the fallen trunk across it, he told her. She cared
almost tenderly for all their possessions and treated them as
friends. But the half-buried broken axe did not affect her. He wondered a little, for only last week she had patiently chipped out
the old broken head, and put in a new handle.

'Feel bad?' he inquired at length.

'Pipe,' she replied with slack lips.

Both pipes lay in the fork of a near tree. He took his, shook
out the ashes, filled it, picked up a coal and puffed till it was alight
– then he filled hers. Taking a small firestick he handed her the
pipe. The hand she raised shook and closed in an uncertain hold,
but she managed by a great effort to get it to her mouth. He lost
patience with the swaying hand that tried to take the light.

'Quick,' he said, 'quick, that damn dog's at the tucker.'

He thrust it into her hand that dropped helplessly across her
chest. The lighted stick falling between her bare arm and the dress
slowly roasted the flesh and smouldered the clothes.

He rescued their dinner, pelted his dog out of sight – hers was
lying near her head, put on the billy, then came back to her.

The pipe had fallen from her lips; there was blood on the stem.

'Did yer jam yer tongue?' he asked.

She always ignored trifles he knew, therefore he passed her
silence.

He told her that her dress was on fire. She took no heed. He
put it out, and looked at the burnt arm, then with intentness at her.

Her eyes were turned unblinkingly to the heavens, her lips were
grimly apart, and a strange greyness was upon her face, and the
sweat-beads were mixing.

'Like a drink er tea? Asleep?'

He broke a green branch from the fallen tree and swished from
his face the multitudes of flies that had descended with it.

In a heavy way he wondered why she did sweat, when she was

not working? Why did she not keep the flies out of her mouth
and eyes? She'd have bungy eyes, if she didn't. If she was asleep,
why did she not close them?

But asleep or awake, as the billy began to boil, he left her, made
the tea, and ate his dinner.

His dog had disappeared, and as it did not come to his whistle, he threw the pieces to hers, that would not leave her head
to reach them.

He whistled tunelessly his one air, beating his own time with
a stick on the toe of his blucher, then looked overhead at the sun
and calculated that she must have been lying like that for 'close
up an hour'. He noticed that the axle handle was broken in two
places, and speculated a little as to whether she would again pick
out the back-broken handle or burn it out in his method, which
was less trouble, if it did spoil the temper of the blade. He examined the worm-dust in the stump and limbs of the newly-fallen
tree; mounted it and looked round the plain. The sheep were straggling in a manner that meant walking work to round them, and
he supposed he would have to yard them to-night, if she didn't
liven up. He looked down at unenlivened her. This changed his
'chune' to a call for his hiding dog.

'Come on, ole feller,' he commanded her dog. 'Fetch 'em back.'

He whistled further instructions, slapping his thigh and pointing to the sheep.

But a brace of wrinkles either side of the brute's closed mouth
demonstrated determined disobedience. The dog would go if she
told him, and by and bye she would.

He lighted his pipe and killed half an hour smoking. With the
frugality that hard graft begets, his mate limited both his and
her own tobacco, so he must not smoke all afternoon. There was
no work to shirk, so time began to drag. Then a goanner crawling up a tree attracted him. He gathered various missiles and tried
vainly to hit the seemingly grinning reptile. He came back and
sneaked a fill of her tobacco, and while he was smoking, the white
tilt of a cart caught his eye. He jumped up. 'There's Red Bob goin'
t'our place fur th' 'oney,' he said; 'I'll go an' weigh it an' get the
gonz' (money).

He ran for the cart, and kept looking back as if fearing she
would follow and thwart him.

Red Bob the dealer was, in a business way, greatly concerned,
when he found that Squeaker's mate was "avin' a sleep out there

'cos a tree fell on her'. She was the best honey strainer and boiler that he dealt with. She was straight and square too. There was no water in her honey whether boiled or merely strained, and in every kerosene tin the weight of honey was to an ounce as she said. Besides he was suspicious and diffident of paying the indecently eager Squeaker before he saw the woman. So reluctantly Squeaker led to where she lay. With many fierce oaths Red Bob sent her lawful protector for help, and compassionately poured a little spirits from his flask down her throat, then swished away the flies from her till help came.

Together these men stripped a sheet of bark and laying her with pathetic tenderness upon it, carried her to her hut. Squeaker followed in the rear with the billy and tucker.

Red Bob took his horse from the cart, and went to town for the doctor. Late that night at the back of the old hut (there were two) he and others who had heard that she was hurt, squatted with unlighted pipes in their mouths, waiting to hear the doctor's verdict. After he had given it and gone they discussed in whispers, and with a look seen only on bush faces, the hard luck of that woman who alone had hard-grafted with the best of them for every acre and hoof on that selection. Squeaker would go through it in no time. Why she had allowed it to be taken up in his name, when the money had been her own, was also for them among the mysteries.

Him they called 'a nole woman', not because he was hanging round the honey tins, but after man's fashion to eliminate all virtue. They beckoned him, and explaining his mate's injury, cautioned him to keep from her the knowledge that she would be for ever a cripple.

'Jus' th' same, now then fur 'im,' pointing to Red Bob, 't' pay me, I'll 'ev t' go t' town.'

They told him in whispers what they thought of him, and with a cowardly look towards where she lay, but without a word of parting, like shadows, these men made for their homes.

Next day the women came. Squeaker's mate was not a favourite with them – a woman with no leisure for yarning was not likely to be. After the first day they left her severely alone, their plea to their husbands her uncompromising independence. It is in the ordering of things that by degrees most husbands accept their wives' views of other women.

The flour bespattering Squeaker's now neglected clothes spoke

eloquently of his clumsy efforts at damper making. The women
gave him many a feed, agreeing that it must be miserable for him.

If it were miserable and lonely for his mate, she did not complain; for her the long, long days would give place to longer
nights – those nights with the pregnant bush silence suddenly cleft
by a bush voice. However she was not fanciful, and being a bush
scholar knew 'twas a dingo, when a long whine came from the
scrub on the skirts of which lay the axe under the worm-eaten
tree. That quivering wail from the billabong lying murkily mys-
tic towards the East was only the cry of the fearing curlew.

Always her dog – wakeful and watchful as she – patiently waiting for her to be up and about again. That would be soon, she
told her complaining mate.

'Yer won't. Yer back's broke,' said Squeaker laconically. 'That's
wot's wrong er yer; injoory t' th' spine. Doctor says that means
back's broke, and yer won't never walk no more. No good not
t' tell yer, 'cos I can't be doin' everythin'.'

A wild look grew on her face, and she tried to sit up.

'Erh,' said he, 'see! yer carnt, yer jes' ther same as a snake w'en
ees back's broke, on'y yer don't bite yerself like a snake does w'en
'e carnt crawl! Yer did bite yer tongue w'en yer fell.'

She gasped, and he could hear her heart beating when she let
her head fall back a few moments; though she wiped her wet forehead with the back of her hand, and still said that was the doctor's
mistake. But day after day she tested her strength, and whatever
the result was, silent, though white witnesses, halo-wise, gradually circled her brow and temples.

"Tisn't as if yer was agoin' t' get better t' morrer, the doctor
says yer won't never work no more, an' I can't be cookin' an' workin' an' doin' everythin'!'

He muttered something about 'sellin' out', but she firmly refused
to think of such a monstrous proposal.

He went into town one Saturday afternoon soon after, and did
not return till Monday.

Her supplies, a billy of tea and scraps of salt beef and damper
(her dog got the beef), gave out the first day, though that was
as nothing to her compared with the bleat of the penned sheep,
for it was summer and droughty, and her dog could not unpen
them.

Of them and her dog only she spoke when he returned. He
d – d him, and d – d her, and told her to 'double up yer old broke

back an' bite yerself'. He threw things about, made a long-range feint of kicking her threatening dog, then sat outside in the shade of the old hut, nursing his head till he slept.

She, for many reasons, had when necessary made these trips into town, walking both ways, leading a pack-horse for supplies. She never failed to indulge him in a half-pint – a pipe was her luxury.

The sheep waited till next day, so did she, then for a few days he worked a little in her sight; not much – he never did. It was she who always lifted the heavy end of the log, and carried the tools; he – the billy and tucker.

She wearily watched him idling his time; reminded him that the wire lying near the fence would rust, one could run the wire through easily, and when she got up in a day or so, she would help strain and fasten it. At first he pretended he had done it, later said he wasn't goin' t' go wirin' or nothin' else by 'imself if every other man on the place did.

She spoke of many other things that could be done by one, reserving the great till she was well. Sometimes he whistled while she spoke, often swore, generally went out, and when this was inconvenient, dull as he was, he found the 'Go and bite yerself like a snake,' would instantly silence her.

At last the work worry ceased to exercise her, and for night to bring him home was a rare thing.

Her dog rounded and yarded the sheep when the sun went down and there was no sign of him, and together they kept watch on their movements till dawn. She was mindful not to speak of this care to him, knowing he would have left it for them to do constantly, and she noticed that what little interest he seemed to share went to the sheep. Why, was soon demonstrated.

Through the cracks her ever watchful eyes one day saw the dust rise out of the plain. Nearer it came till she saw him and a man on horseback rounding and driving the sheep into the yard, and later both left in charge of a little mob. Their 'Baa-baas' to her were cries for help; many had been pets. So he was selling her sheep to the town butchers.

In the middle of the next week he came from town with a fresh horse, new saddle and bridle. He wore a flash red shirt, and round his neck a silk handkerchief. On the next occasion she smelt scent, and though he did not try to display the dandy meerschaum, she saw it, and heard the squeak of the new boots, not bluchers.

However he was kinder to her this time, offering a fill of his cut tobacco; he had long ceased to keep her supplied. Several of the men who sometimes in passing took a look in would have made up her loss had they known, but no word of complaint passed her lips.

She looked at Squeaker as he filled his pipe from his pouch, but he would not meet her eyes, and, seemingly dreading something, slipped out.

She heard him hammering in the old hut at the back, which served for tools and other things which sunlight and rain did not hurt. Quite briskly he went in and out. She could see him through the cracks carrying a narrow strip of bark, and understood: he was making a bunk. When it was finished he had a smoke, then came to her and fidgeted about; he said this hut was too cold, and that she would never get well in it. She did not feel cold, but submitting to his mood, allowed him to make a fire that would roast a sheep. He took off his hat, and fanning himself, said he was roastin', wasn't she? She was.

He offered to carry her into the other; he would put a new roof on it in a day or two, and it would be better than this one, and she would be up in no time. He stood to say this where she could not see him.

His eagerness had tripped him.

There were months to run before all the Government conditions of residence, etc., in connection with the selection, would be fulfilled, still she thought perhaps he was trying to sell out, and she would not go.

He was away four days that time, and when he returned slept in the new bunk.

She compromised. Would he put a bunk there for himself, keep out of town, and not sell the place! He promised instantly, with additions.

'Try could yer crawl yerself?' he coaxed, looking at her bulk. Her nostrils quivered with her suppressed breathing, and her lips tightened, but she did not attempt to move.

It was evident some great purpose actuated him. After attempts to carry and drag her, he rolled her on the sheet of bark that had brought her home, and laboriously drew her round.

She asked for a drink, he placed her billy and tin pint besides the bunk, and left her gasping and dazed to her sympathetic dog.

She saw him run up and yard his horse, and though she called him, he would not answer nor come.

When he rode swiftly towards the town, her dog leaped on the bunk, and joined a refrain to her lamentation, but the cat took to the bush.

He came back at dusk next day in a spring cart – not alone – he had another mate. She saw her though he came a roundabout way, trying to keep in front of the new hut.

There were noises of moving many things from the cart to the hut. Finally he came to a crack near where she lay, and whispered the promise of many good things to her if she kept quiet, and that he would set her hut afire if she didn't. She was quiet, he need not have feared, for that time she was past it, she was stunned.

The released horse came stumbling round to the old hut, and thrust its head in the door in a domesticated fashion. Her dog promptly resented this straggler mistaking their hut for a stable. And the dog's angry dissent, together with the shod clatter of the rapidly disappearing intruder, seemed to have a disturbing effect on the pair in the new hut. The settling sounds suddenly ceased, and the cripple heard the stranger close the door, despite Squeaker's assurances that the woman in the old hut could not move from her bunk to save her life, and that her dog would not leave her.

Food, more and better, was placed near her – but, dumb and motionless, she lay with her face turned to the wall, and her dog growled menacingly at the stranger. The new woman was uneasy, and told Squeaker what people might say and do if she died.

He scared his missus at the 'do', went into the bush and waited.

She went to the door, not the crack, the face was turned that way, and said she had come to cook and take care of her.

The disabled woman, turning her head slowly, looked steadily at her. She was not much to look at. Her red hair hung in an uncurled bang over her forehead, the lower part of her face had robbed the upper, and her figure evinced imminent motherhood, though it is doubtful if the barren woman, noting this, knew by calculation the paternity was not Squeaker's. She was not learned in these matters, though she understood all about an ewe and lamb.

One circumstance was apparent – ah! bitterest of all bitterness to women – she was younger.

The thick hair that fell from the brow of the woman on the bunk was white now.

Bread-and-butter the woman brought. The cripple looked at it, at her dog, at the woman. Bread-and-butter for a dog! but the stranger did not understand till she saw it offered to the dog. The bread-and-butter was not for the dog. She brought meat.

All next day the man kept hidden. The cripple saw his dog, and knew he was about.

But there was an end of this pretence when at dusk he came back with a show of haste, and a finger of his right hand bound and ostentatiously prominent. His entrance caused great excitement to his new mate. The old mate, who knew this snake-bite trick from its inception, maybe, realized how useless were the terrified stranger's efforts to rouse the snoring man after an empty pint bottle had been flung on the outside heap.

However, what the sick woman thought was not definite, for she kept silent always. Neither was it clear how much she ate, and how much she gave to her dog, though the new mate said to Squeaker one day that she believed that the dog would not take a bite more than its share.

The cripple's silence told on the stranger, especially when alone. She would rather have abuse. Eagerly she counted the days past and to pass. Then back to the town. She told no word of that hope to Squeaker, he had no place in her plans for the future. So if he spoke of what they would do by and by when his time would be up, and be able to sell out, she listened in uninterested silence.

She did tell him she was afraid of 'her', and after the first day would not go within reach, but every morning made a billy of tea, which with bread and beef Squeaker carried to her.

The rubbish heap was adorned, for the first time, with jam and fish tins from the table in the new hut. It seemed to be understood that neither woman nor dog in the old hut required them.

Squeaker's dog sniffed and barked joyfully around them till his licking efforts to bottom a salmon tin sent him careering in a muzzled frenzy, that caused the younger woman's thick lips to part grinningly till he came too close.

The remaining sheep were regularly yarded. His old mate heard him whistle as he did it. Squeaker began to work about a little burning off. So that now, added to the other bush voices, was the call from some untimely falling giant. There is no sound so human as that from the riven souls of these tree people, or the trembling sighs of their upright neighbours whose hands in time will meet over the victim's fallen body.

There was no bunk on the side of the hut to which her eyes turned, but her dog filled that space, and the flash that passed between this back-broken woman and her dog might have been the spirit of these slain tree folk, it was so wondrous ghostly. Still, at times, the practical in her would be dominant, for in a mind so free of fancies, backed by bodily strength, hope died slowly, and forgetful of self she would almost call to Squeaker her fears that certain bees nests were in danger.

He went into town one day and returned, as he had promised, long before sundown, and next day a clothes line bridged the space between two trees near the back of the old hut; and – an equally rare occurrence – Squeaker placed across his shoulders the yoke that his old mate has fashioned for herself, with two kerosene tins attached, and brought them filled with water from the distant creek; but both only partly filled the tub, a new purchase. With utter disregard of the heat and Squeaker's sweating brow, his new mate said, even after another trip, two more now for the blue water. Under her commands he brought them, though sullenly, perhaps contrasting the old mate's methods with the new.

His old mate had periodically carried their washing to the creek, and his mole-skins had been as white as snow without aid of blue.

Towards noon, on the clothes line many strange garments fluttered, suggestive of a taunt to the barren woman. When the sun went down she could have seen the assiduous Squeaker lower the new prop-sticks and considerately stoop to gather the pegs his inconsiderate new mate had dropped. However, after one load of water next morning, on hearing her estimate that three more would put her own things through, Squeaker struck. Nothing he could urge would induce the stranger to trudge to the creek, where thirst-slaked snakes lay waiting for some one to bite. She sulked and pretended to pack up, till a bright idea struck Squeaker. He fastened a cask on a sledge and harnessing the new horse, hitched him to it, and, under the approving eyes of his new mate, led off to the creek, though, when she went inside, he bestrode the spiritless brute.

He had various mishaps, any one of which would have served as an excuse to his old mate, but even babes soon know on whom to impose. With an energy new to him he persevered and filled the cask, but the old horse repudiated such a burden even under Squeaker's unmerciful welts. Almost half was sorrowfully baled out, and under a rain of whacks the horse shifted it a few paces, but the cask tilted and the thirsty earth got its contents. All Squeaker's adjectives over his wasted labour were as unavailing as the cure for spilt milk.

It took skill and patience to rig the cask again. He partly filled it, and just as success seemed probable, the rusty wire fastening the cask to the sledge snapped with the strain, and springing free coiled affectionately round the terrified horse's hocks. Despite the sledge (the cask had been soon disposed of) that old town horse's pace then was his record. Hours after, on the plain that met the horizon, loomed two specks: the distance betweeen them might be gauged, for the larger was Squeaker.

Anticipating a plentiful supply and lacking in bush caution, the new mate used the half bucket of water to boil the salt mutton. Towards noon she laid this joint and bread on the rough table, then watched anxiously in the wrong direction for Squeaker.

She had drained the new tea-pot earlier, but she placed the spout to her thirsty mouth again.

She continued looking for him for hours.

Had he sneaked off to town, thinking she had not used that water, or not caring whether or no.

She did not trust him; another had left her. Besides she judged Squeaker by his treatment of the woman who was lying in there with wide-open eyes. Anyhow no use to cry with only that silent woman to hear her.

Had she drunk all hers?

She tried to see at long range through the cracks, but the hanging bed clothes hid the billy.

She went to the door, and avoiding the bunk looked at the billy. It was half full.

Instinctively she knew that the eyes of the woman were upon her. She turned away, and hoped and waited for thirsty minutes that seemed hours.

Desperation drove her back to the door, dared she? No she couldn't.

Getting a long forked propstick, she tried to reach it from the door, but the dog sprang at the stick. She dropped it and ran.

A scraggy growth fringed the edge of the plain. There was the creek. How far? she wondered. Oh, very far, she knew, and besides there were only a few holes where water was, and the snakes; for Squeaker, with a desire to shine in her eyes, was continually telling her of snakes – vicious and many – that daily he did battle with.

She recalled the evening he came from hiding in the scrub with a string round one finger, and said a snake had bitten him. He had drunk the pint of brandy she had brought for her sickness, and then slept till morning. True, although next day he had to dig for the string round the blue swollen finger, yet he was not worse than the many she had seen at the 'Shearer's Rest' suffering a recovery, now there was no brandy to cure her if she were bitten.

She cried a little in self pity, then withdrew her eyes, that were getting red, from the outlying creek, and went again to the door. She of the bunk lay with closed eyes.

Was she asleep? The stranger's heart leapt, yet she was hardly in earnest as she tip-toed billy-wards. The dog, crouching with head between two paws, eyed her steadily, but showed no opposition. She made dumb show. 'I want to be friends with you, and won't hurt her.' Abruptly she looked at her, then at the dog. He was motionless and emotionless. Beside if that dog – certainly watching her – wanted to bite her (her dry mouth opened), it could get her any time.

She rated this dog's intelligence almost human, from many of its actions in omission and commission in connection with this woman.

She regretted the pole, no dog would stand that.

Two more steps.

Now just one more; then, by bending and stretching her arm, she would reach it. Could she now? She tried to encourage herself by remembering how close on the first day she had been to the woman, and how delicious a few mouthfuls would be – swallowing dry mouthfuls.

She measured the space between where she had first stood and the billy. Could she get anything to draw it to her. No, the dog would not stand that, and besides the handle would rattle, and she might hear and open her eyes.

The thought of those sunken eyes suddenly opening made her heart bound. Oh! she must breathe – deep, loud breaths. Her throat clicked noisily. Looking back fearfully, she went swiftly out.

She did not look for Squeaker this time, she had given him up. While she waited for her breath to steady, to her relief and surprise the dog came out. She made a rush to the new hut, but he passed seemingly oblivious of her, and bounding across the plain began rounding the sheep. Then he must know Squeaker had gone to town.

Stay! Her heart beat violently; was it because she on the bunk slept and did not want him?

She waited till her heart quieted, and again crept to the door.

The head of the woman on the bunk had fallen towards the wall as in deep sleep; it was turned from the billy; to which she must creep so softly.

Slower, from caution and deadly earnestness, she entered.

She was not so advanced as before, and felt fairly secure, for the woman's eyes were still turned to the wall, and so tightly closed, she could not possibly see the intruder.

Well, now she would bend right down, and try and reach it from here.

She bent.

It was so swift and sudden, that she had not time to scream when those bony fingers had gripped the hand that prematurely reached for the billy. She was frozen with horror for a moment, then her screams were piercing. Panting with victory, the prostrate one held her with a hold that the other did not attempt to free herself from.

Down, down the woman drew her prey.

Her lips had drawn back from her teeth, and her breath almost scorched the face that she held so close for the starting eyes to gloat over. Her exultation was so great, that she could only gloat and gasp, and hold with a tension that had stopped the victim's circulation.

As a wounded, robbed tigress might hold and look, she held and looked.

Neither heard the swift steps of the man, and if the tigress saw him enter, she was not daunted. 'Take me from 'er,' shrieked the terrified one. 'Quick, take me from 'er,' she repeated it again, nothing else. 'Take me from 'er.'

He hastily fastened the door and said something that the shrieks drowned, then picked up the pole. It fell with a thud across the arms which the tightening sinews had turned into steel. Once, twice, thrice. Then the one that got the fullest force bent; that side of the victim was free.

The pole had snapped. Another blow with a broken end freed the other side.

Still shrieking 'Take me from 'er, take me from er,' she rushed to and beat on the closed door till reluctantly Squeaker opened it.

Then he had to face and reckon with his old mate's maddened dog, that the closed door had baffled.

The dog suffered the shrieking woman to pass, but though Squeaker, in bitten agony, broke the stick across the dog, he was forced to gave the savage brute best.

'Call 'im orf, Mary, 'e's eating me,' he implored. 'Oh, corl 'im orf.'

But with stony face the woman lay motionless.

'Sool 'im on t' 'er.' He indicated his new mate who, as though all the plain led to the desired town, still ran in unreasoning terror.

'It's orl er doin',' he pleaded, springing on the bunk beside his old mate. But when, to rouse her sympathy, he would have laid his hand on her, the dog's teeth fastened in it and pulled him back.

MARY GAUNT, 1861-1942

Born in Chiltern, Victoria, Mary Gaunt was one of
the first women students at the University of
Melbourne. From an early age she was interested in
pursuing a literary life and choice gave way to necessity when after a short period of marriage
(1894-1900) she sought to earn her living by her pen.

Her first novel, *Dave's Sweetheart*, was published
in 1894, and *The Moving Finger* (a volume of short
stories) in 1895; in 1897 she published *Kirkham's
Find*, her novel of women's independence (and available in Penguin Australian Women's Library). The
second stage of her literary success came after 1910
with the publication in England of her extremely
popular *The Mummy Moves* and this was followed
by a series of 'thrillers' and travel documentaries
(based on her journeys and residences in Africa,
China, the West Indies and Italy, where she finally
settled). The author of more than twenty works of
fiction and of half a dozen works of non-fiction,
Mary Gaunt achieved a prominent place in London
literary circles in the early twentieth century; her
work however has remained largely unknown,
abroad and at home, over the last fifty years.

'Dick Stanesby's Hutkeeper' is taken from the 1895
edition of *The Moving Finger* (Methuen) and is a
stark tale of sexist and racist double standards which
raises some of the harsh questions of colonisation.

DICK STANESBY'S HUTKEEPER

'Hallo! Dick. You here! Why, I thought you were away up tea-planting in Assam.'

'And I thought you were comfortably settled down on the ancestral acres by this time.'

'No such luck. The ancient cousin is still very much to the fore. Has taken to himself a new wife in fact, and a new lease of life along with her. She has presented her doting husband with a very fine heir; and, well, of course, after that little Willie was nowhere, and departed for pastures new.'

'Make your fortune, eh! Made it?'

'Of course. Money-making game riding tracks on Jinfalla! Made yours?'

'Money-making game riding tracks on Nilpe Nilpe.'

The two men looked at each other, and laughed. In truth, neither looked particularly representative of the rank and aristocracy of their native land. The back blocks are very effectual levellers, and each saw in the other a very ordinary bushman, riding a horse so poor, the wonder was he was deemed worth mounting at all. Both were dusty and dirty, for the drought held the land in iron grip, and the fierce north wind, driving the dust in little whirls and columns before it, blew over plains bare of grass and other vegetation as a beaten road.

Around them was the plain, hot and bare of any living creature, nothing in sight save a low ridge bounding the eastern horizon, a ridge which on closer inspection took the form of bluffs, in most places almost inaccessible. Overhead was the deep blue sky, so blue it was almost purple in its intensity, with not a cloud to break the monotony. Sky and desert, that was all, and these two Englishmen meeting, and the shadows cast by themselves and their horses, were the only spots of shade for miles.

'Sweet place!' said Guy Turner, looking round. 'Warmish too. Wonder what it is in the shade?'

'In the shade, man. There ain't any shade, unless you count the shadows of our poor old mokes, and mine's so poor, I'll bet the sun can find his way through his ribs. I've been in the sun since daybreak, and I reckon it is somewhere about boiling point.'

'I suppose it must be over 160°. What the dickens did you come out for?'

'Well, seeing it's been like this for the last three months, and is likely to go on for three more, as far as I can see; it ain't much good stopping in for the weather; besides there's this valuable estate to be looked after. But to-day I rode over for the mails.'

'What, to the head-station?'

'Lord, no! The track to Roebourne passes along about twenty miles off over there, and I get the boss to leave my mail in a hollow tree as he passes.'

'Trusting, certainly. There's some good about this God-forsaken country.'

Dick Stanesby, or, to give him his full name, Richard Hugh De Courcy Stanesby, shrugged his shoulders scornfully.

'Evidently, Dick, that mail wasn't satisfactory. Has she clean forgot you, Dick, the little white mouse of a cousin, with the pretty blue eyes? She was mighty sweet on you, and – '

But there was a frown on Dick's usually good-tempered face. He was in no mind to take his old chum's pleasantry kindly, and the other saw it, and drew his own conclusions therefrom.

'Chucked him over, poor beggar, I suppose. Hang it all! Women are all alike; once a man's down, he's forgotten,' but he did not speak his thoughts aloud. He looked away across the sweltering plain, and said casually,

'Where do you hang out, old man?'

Stanesby pointed east in a vague sort of manner, that might indicate South Australia, or far distant New South Wales.

'Got a shanty on the creek there,' he said laconically.

'Creek, is there a creek? The place looks as if it hadn't seen water since the beginning of the world.'

'Oh, there's a creek right enough. I believe it's a big one when it rains, but it hasn't rained since I've been here, and there ain't much water in it. Just a little in the hole opposite the hut. The niggers say its permanent. Springs, or something of that sort.'

'Niggers! That's what I've come over about. They've worried the life out of us on Jinfalla. Taken to spearing the cattle, and the men too if they get a chance. Old Anderson thinks we ought to have some 'concerted action,' and settle the matter once for all.'

'H'm. Wipe 'em out, I suppose he means?'

'It's what a squatter generally means, isn't it, when he talks about the blacks? Sounds brutal, but hang it all, man, what the devil is a fellow to do? They're only beasts, and as beasts you must treat 'em. Look here, there was a young fellow on our run, as nice a boy as you'd wish to see – his people were something decent at home, I believe, but the lad had got into some scrape and cleared out, and drifted along into the heart of Western Australia here. He was riding tracks for old Anderson about two hundred miles to the west there. He didn't come in last week for his tucker, so they sent word for me to look him up.'

'Well?' for Turner paused, and drew a long breath.

'Well – same old nip, of course. His hut was burnt, and he and his hutkeeper – I tell you, Dick, it won't bear talking about – he was a lad of twenty, and the hutkeeper was an old lag, might have been seventy to look at him, but when I found their bodies down by the creek, I couldn't tell which was which.'

'It's bad,' said Stanesby, 'very bad. What did you do?'

'Buried 'em, of course, my mate and I, and shot the first buck we came across skulking in the bush. What would you have us do?'

'It's all bad together,' said the other man, with an oath. 'The blacks about here are tame enough if you let 'em alone, but these young fellows get meddling with their women, and – well – '

'That's all very well, but you didn't find a mate too ghastly a corpse to look at, or you wouldn't take the matter so coolly. You'd have done just as I did. Something must be done, old man, or the country won't be habitable.'

They had been riding along slowly, side by side, one man eager, anxious, interested, the other evidently with his thoughts far away. The mail he had got that morning was stuffed into his saddlebags, and the news it brought him made him think longingly of a home in far-away England, a creeper-covered house, and a cosy room with a bright fire, and the rain beating pleasantly on the windows. Rain – he had not seen rain for three long years. Always the hard blue sky and the bright sunshine, always the dreary plain, broken here and there by patches of prickly bush and still more thorny spinifex, always the red bluffs marking the horizon, clean cut against the cloudless sky.

Habitable? Such a country as this habitable? It had given him bread for the last three years, but – but – he felt burning in his pocket the letter summoning him home – telling of the death, the unexpected death, of his young cousin, that made him master of that pleasant home, that filled his empty pockets. What did anyone ever dream of living in such a country for – driving the unlucky niggers back and back? What need for it? What need? Far better leave it to the niggers, and clear out altogether.

Had Gladys forgotten? He wondered. The little white mouse of a cousin, as Turner called her, who had cried so bitterly when he left, and even now answered his letters so regularly, those letters that had come to be written at longer and longer intervals as home ties weakened, and the prospect of seeing her again slowly died away. Had she forgotten – had she? She looked like the sort of woman that would be faithful – faithful – well, as faithful as anyone in this world could be expected to be, as faithful as women always are to their lovers in distant lands. Turner had been sweet there once too, curious he should meet him just now; he had forgotten her surely, or he would never have referred to her so casually. Yes, Turner had forgotten, and yet he had been very bad too – strange how completely a thing like that passes out of a man's life. Could he take up the broken threads just where he left off – could he? So sweet and tender as she was, so quiet and restful. There was that other one, who loved him after her fashion too, but – pah, it was an insult to Gladys to name her in the same breath – she – she – The country was *not* habitable – a doghole unfit for a European; what was Turner making such a song over the niggers for?

'Old man,' said Turner, he had been telling to unlistening ears the tale of how the blacks had speared, in wanton mischief, a mob of two hundred cattle on Jinfalla, not fifteen miles from the home station, 'old man, you see it would be just ruination to let this go on. Either they or we must clear out. We can't both live here, that's certain.'

'Always the same old yarn wherever the Englishman goes, always the same old yarn. Poor niggers!'

'Well, what'd you have? ' said the other warmly; 'something's got to be done.'

'I'm going to cut it all.'

'What?' Turner stopped his horse and looked his companion full in the face. 'Cut it all?'

'My cousin's dead.'

'John Stanesby?'

'John Stanesby.'

'And Heyington's yours?'

'And Eastwood too.'

'Good Lord!'

There was silence for a moment. Then Turner said again:

'You can marry Gladys Rowan now.'

'Yes.'

Then he added, as if as an afterthought, 'If she'll have me.'

'No fear of that,' said Turner with a sigh. Then he turned to his old chum, and stretching over laid a kindly hand on his arm, 'I congratulate you, old chap.'

'Thank you.' And they rode on in silence, the one man thinking bitterly that if ever he had cherished a spark of hope of winning the woman he had loved he must give it up at last, the other trying to realise the good fortune that had come to him. And an hour ago he had been as this man beside him – only one little hour ago!

'How far do you reckon it to the headstation? Fifty miles?'

'Fifty? Nearer eighty I should say.'

'Then I guess I'll put up at your place. How far's that?'

'About ten miles.'

'All right. Lead on, master of Heyington.'

To refuse a man hospitality in the bush – such a thing was never heard of, and, though Stanesby said no welcoming word, it never occurred to Turner to doubt that he was more than welcome.

'It's right out of your way.'

Turner stared.

'Good Lord! What's ten miles, and we haven't met for years. I must say, old chap, you don't seem particularly pleased to see an old chum.'

'I – they ain't so plentiful I can afford to do that. No, I was thinking of going in to the station with you.'

'Right you are, old man, do you? Only we'll put up at your place for the night – my horse's pretty well done – and go on in the morning.'

Stanesby said nothing, only turned his horse's head slightly to the left. Save the red bluffs away to the east there was nothing to mark the change of direction. There was no reason apparently for his choosing one direction rather than another.

They rode in silence, these two who had been college chums and had not met for years. Possibly it was the one man's good fortune that raised a barrier between them. It was not easy for Turner to talk of present difficulties and troubles when, as Stanesby said, he was going to 'cut it all'; it was not easy for him to speak of bygone times when the other man was going back to them, and he would be left here without a prospect of a change. And Stanesby said nothing, he could only think of the great difference between them; and yesterday there was nothing he would have liked better than this meeting with his old friend, which to-day fell flat. No, he had nothing to say. Already their paths lay wide apart.

An hour's slow riding brought them to the creek Stanesby had spoken of. There was no gentle slope down to the river, the plain simply seemed to open at their feet, and show them the river bed some twenty feet below. Only a river bed about twenty yards wide, but there was no water to be seen, only signs, marked signs in that thirsty land, that water had been there. Down where the last moisture had lingered the grass grew green and fresh, and leafy shrubs and small trees and even tangled creepers made this dip in the plain a pleasant resting-place for the eye wearied with the monotony of the world above it.

'By Jove!' cried Turner, surprised.

'Told you so,' said his companion, 'but it ain't much after all. Fancy calling that wiry stuff grass in England, and admiring those straggly creepers and shrubs. Why we wouldn't give 'em house-room in the dullest, deadest corner of the wilderness at home.'

'Lucky beggar!' sighed the other man. 'But you see they're all I'm likely to have for many a long year to come. Hang it all, man, I bet you'd put that shrub there, that chap with the bright red flower, into your hot-house and look after him with the greatest care, or your gardener would for you.'

'It'd require a d – d hot house,' said Stanesby laconically, wiping his hot face.

They did not descend into the bed of the creek, the ground was better adapted for riding up above, and a mile further along they came upon a large blackfellows' camp stretched all along the edge of a waterhole.

'The brutes,' said Turner; 'bagging the water of course.'

'They'd die if they didn't, I suppose. This, and the hole by my place is the only water I know of for forty miles round. After all they were here first, and if I had my way they'd be left to it.'

'All very well for you to talk,' grumbled Turner. 'Do they look worth anything?'

Certainly they did not. The camp was a mere collection of breakwinds made of bark and branches, more like badly-stacked woodheaps than anything else, and the children of the soil lay basking in the sun, among the dogs and filth and refuse of the camp, or crouched over small fires as if it were bitter cold. The dogs started up yelping, for a blackfellow's dog doesn't know how to bark properly, as the white men passed, but their masters took no notice. A stark naked gin, with a fillet of greasy skin bound round her head, and a baby slung in a net on her back, came whining to Turner with outstretched hands. She had mixed with the stockkeepers before, and knew a few words of English.

'Give it terbacker along a black Mary. Budgery[1] fellow you,' but he pushed her away with the butt end of his whip.

'My place's not above a mile away now,' said Stanesby, as they left the precincts of the camp behind them.

'I wouldn't have those beggars so close, if I were you. Some fine morning you'll find yourself – '

'Pooh! They're quite tame and harmless. I've got a boy from them about the place, and he's very good as boys go. Besides, I'm off as soon as possible.'

'Well, I bet you the man who takes your place thinks differently.'

'Very likely.'

'Got a decent hutkeeper?'

'What? Oh yes. Pretty fair.'

Clearly Stanesby was not in the mood for conversation, and Turner gave it up as a bad job. It was about two o'clock now, the very hottest hour of the day, and all nature seemed to feel it. Not a sound broke the stillness, not the cry of bird or beast, nothing save the sound of their horses' hoofs on the hard ground was to be heard.

'By Jove!' said Turner, 'this is getting unbearable. I vote we get down and shelter for a spell under the lee of the bank.'

For all answer, Stanesby raised his whip and pointed ahead.

'There's the hut,' he said. 'Better get on.'

It was hardly distinguishable from the surrounding plain, the little hut built of rough logs, and roofed with sheets of bark stripped from the trees which grew in the river-bed. Down in the creek there was a waterhole, a waterhole surrounded by tall reeds and other aquatic vegetation which gave it a look of permanence, of freshness and greenness in this burnt-up land. But that was down in the creek, round the hut was the plain, barren here as elsewhere; no effort had been made to cultivate it or improve it, and the desert came up to the very doors. The only sign of

[1] Means 'good'.

human life was the refuse from the small household – an empty
tin or two, fragments of broken bottles, and scraps of rag and
paper, only that and the hut itself, and a small yard for horses
and cattle, that was all – not a tree, not a green thing. The bed
of the creek was their garden, but it was not visible from the house;
its inmates could only see the desolate plain, nothing but that
for miles and miles, far as the eye could see. So monotonous,
so dreary an outlook, it was hardly possible to believe there was
anything else in the world, anything but this lonely little hut, with,
for all its paradise, the waterhole in the creek below.

Turner said nothing. It was exactly what he expected; he lived
in a similar place, a place without a creek close handy, where
the only water came from a well, and undiluted, was decidedly
unpleasant to the taste. No, in his eyes Stanesby had nothing to
grumble at.

The owner of this palatial residence cooeed shrilly.

'Jimmy; I say, Jimmy!'

A long, lank black boy, clad in a Crimean shirt and a pair of
old riding breeches, a world too big for him, rose lazily up from
beside the house, where he had been basking in the sun, and came
towards them.

Stanesby dismounted and flung him his reins, Turner following suit.

'All gone sleep,' said Jimmy, nodding his head in the direction
of the hut, a grin showing up the white of his regular teeth against
his black face.

'Come on in, Turner.'

The door was open and the two men walked straight into the
small hut.

It was very dark at first coming in out of the brilliant sunshine,
but as Turner's eyes grew accustomed to the light, he saw that
the interior was just exactly what he should have expected it to
be. The floor was hard earth, the walls were unlined, the meagre
household goods were scattered about in a way that did not say
much for his friend's hutkeeper, a shelf with a few old books and
papers on it, was the only sign of culture, and a rough curtain
of sacking dividing the place in two, was the only thing that was
not common to every hut in all that part of Western Australia.

'Howling swell, you are, old chap! Go in for two rooms I see.'

'I –'

The curtain was thrust aside, and to Turner's astonishment,

a girl's face peered round it. A beautiful girl's face too, the like of which he had not seen for many a year, if indeed, he had ever seen one like it before; a face with oval, liquid dark eyes in whose depths a light lay hidden, with full red pouting lips, and a broad low brow half hidden by heavy masses of dark, untidy hair, which fell in picturesque confusion over it. A beautiful face in shape and form, and rich dark colouring, and Turner started back too astonished to speak. Such a face! Never in all his life had he seen such a face, and the look turned on his companion was easy enough to read.

'Come here, Kitty,' said Stanesby in an unconcerned voice. 'I want some dinner for this gentleman.'

Then she stepped out, and the illusion vanished. For she was only a half-caste, beautiful as a dream, or he who had not seen a woman for many a long day – he never counted the black gins women – thought so, but only a despised half-caste, outcast both from father's and mother's race.

Not that she looked unhappy. On the contrary, she came forward and smiled on him a slow, lazy smile, the smile of one who is utterly contented with her lot in life.

'Whew! So that's our hutkeeper, is it?'

'Dinner, Kitty.'

The girl took a tin dish from the shelf and went outside. She walked well and gracefully, and Turner followed her with his eyes.

'By Jove!' he said, 'talk about good looks. Why, Dick, you – '

'Hang it all, man,' said Stanesby. 'I know well enough what you're thinking. The girl *is* good-looking, I suppose, for a half-caste. The boss's sister, old Miss Howard, found her among the tribe, a wild little wretch, and took her in and did her best to civilise her; but it wasn't easy work, and the old lady died before it was done.'

'And you're completing the job?'

Stanesby shrugged his shoulders.

'I saw her, of course, when I went in to the head-station, which wasn't very often, and I suppose I told her she was a good-looking girl. She mayn't understand much, but she understood *that* right enough, trust a woman for that. Good Lord! I never gave her a second thought, till I found her at my door one night. The little beggar had had a row with 'em up at the house and came right off to me. It wasn't any use protesting. She might have done worse, and here she's been ever since. But she's got the temper of a fiend, I can tell you, and it ain't all skittles and beer.'

The girl entered the room and Stanesby began turning over his mail letters, making his companion feel that the subject had better be dropped between them. He had explained the girl's presence, he wanted no comments from his old friend.

He filled his pipe and sat down on the only three-legged stool the hut contained, watching his friend seated on a box opposite and the girl passing in and out getting ready the rough meal. She was graceful, she was beautiful, as some wild thing is beautiful, there was no doubt whatever of that. Her dress was of Turkey red; old Miss Howard had had a fancy for dressing all her dark *protegées* in bright colours, and they had followed in her footsteps up at the station, and Turner mentally appraising the girl before him, quite approved her taste. The dress was old and somewhat faded, but its severe simplicity and its dull tints just set off the girl's dusky beauty. Shoes and stockings she had none, but what matter? any touch of civilisation would have spoiled the picture.

Stanesby apparently took no notice of her, but began to read extracts from his letters and papers for his companion's benefit. He was hardly at his ease, and Turner made only a pretence of listening. He could not take his eyes from the girl who was roughly setting out the table for their meal. 'The temper of a fiend,' truly he thought it not unlikely, judging by the glances she threw at him whenever she took her eyes from Stanesby. She could hardly have understood what he read, but she listened intently and cast angry glances every now and then on Turner. He and these letters, she seemed to feel, were not of her world, they were taking this man away from her. Yes, he could well believe she had the temper of a fiend. But she said nothing. Her mother had come of a race which from time immemorial had held its women in bondage, and she spoke no word, probably she had no words in which to express her feelings.

The table was laid at last, and a piece of smoking salt beef and a great round damper brought in from outside and put on it.

'Dinner,' said the girl sullenly, but Stanesby went on reading, and paid no attention, and Turner felt himself watching to see what would happen next. He caught only snatches of the letter, just enough to know it was a description of a hunt in England, of a damp, cold, cloudy day, of an invigorating run – the contrast struck him forcibly – the stifling, hot little hut, and the jealous, half-savage woman standing there, her eyes aflame with anger at the slight she fancied was put upon her.

She stole over and touched Stanesby lightly on the arm, but he shook her off as he would a fly and went on reading calmly.

The other man watched the storm gather on her face. She stood for one moment looking, not at Stanesby but at him; it was very evident whom she blamed for her lover's indifference; then she stretched across to the table and caught up a knife. Her breath was coming thick and fast and Turner never took his eyes off her, in between her gasping breath he heard his friend's voice, slow and deliberate as ever, still telling the tale of the English hunting day, still reading the letter which put such a world between him and the girl standing beside him. Then there was a flash of steel, Turner felt rather than saw that it was directed at him, and, before he even had time to think, Stanesby had sprung to his feet and grasped her by the arm.

'Would you now? Would you?' He might have been speaking to a fractious horse. Then as Turner too sprang to his feet and snatched the knife from her hand, he flung her off with an oath.

'You little devil!' He sat down again with an uneasy laugh, and the girl with an inarticulate cry flung herself out of the open door. In all the half hour that had elapsed, she had spoken no word except when she called them to their dinner; but in that inarticulate moan the other man seemed to read the whole bitterness of her story.

'I told you,' said Stanesby, he seemed to feel some explanation or apology were necessary; 'I told you she had the temper of a fiend. I hope she didn't hurt you, old man?'

'No, no. She meant business, though, only you were too quick for her. But I say, old man, it isn't well to have a good-looking young woman fix her affections on you in that ardent manner. There'll be the devil to pay, some day.'

The other laughed, and then sighed.

'I tell you it was no fault of mine,' he said.

'Come on and get something to eat. There's whisky in that bottle.'

Virtually he had dismissed the subject; with the disappearance of the girl he would have let the matter drop, but he was not at his ease, and his old chum was less so. It was all very well to talk of old times, of college days, of mutual friends, each was thinking, and each was uncomfortably conscious that the other, too, was thinking, of that dark-eyed, straight-limbed young savage who had forced her personality upon them both, and was so far, so very far, removed from the world of which they spoke. There was another thing too, a fair-haired, blue-eyed girl, as different – as different as the North Pole from the Equator – each had loved her, to each she had been the embodiment of all earthly virtues, and each thought of her as well, too – the one man bitterly. Why should this man, this whilom friend of his, have everything? And the other man read his thoughts, and unreasoning anger grew up in his heart against his old chum. It has nothing whatever to do with Dick Stanesby's hutkeeper, of course, nothing whatever; but it is nevertheless a fact, that these two old friends spent what should have been a pleasant afternoon, devoted to reminiscences of old times and a renewal of early friendship, in uncomfortable silence. The monthly mail, which Stanesby had brought in, contained many papers, and after their meal they lighted their pipes and read diligently, first one paper and then another. At first they made efforts at conversation, read out incidents and scraps of news and commented thereon, but as the afternoon wore on, the silence grew till it became difficult to break it. The sunlight outside crept in and in through the open doorway. There were no shadows because there was nothing to cast shadows, save the banks of the creek down below the level of the plain and the red bluffs, thirty miles to the eastward. But the sun stole in and crossed the hard earthen floor, and stole up the wall on the other side, crept up slowly, emphasising the dull blankness of the place. So did the sun every day of the year, pretty nearly; so did he in every stockkeeper's hut on the plains of Western Australia; but to-day he seemed to Turner to be mocking his misery, pointing it out and emphasising it. Such his life had been for the last three or four years; such it was now; such it would be to the end. He could see no prospect of change, no prospect of better things: always the bare walls and the earthen floors for him; unloved, uncared for he had lived, unloved and uncared for he would die. And this man beside him – bah! it would not bear thinking of. He pushed back the stool he had been sitting on, and strolling to the door looked out. Nothing in sight but the black boy, who wasn't a boy at all, but a man apparently over thirty years of age, lolling up against the verandah post, like one who had plenty of time on his hands.

Stanesby got up and joined him. The hot wind that had blown

fiercely all day had died down, and now there hardly seemed a breath of air stirring. It was stupid to comment on the weather in a place where the weather was always the same, but Turner felt the need of something to say, so he seized on the well-worn topic.

'It's getting a little cooler, I think.'

'Confound it, no.'

Stanesby looked round discontentedly. The untidy, uninviting remains of their midday meal were still on the table, pushed aside to make room for the papers they had been reading; it gave the place a dishevelled, comfortless air, which made its dull blankness ten times worse.

Turner noticed it, but he did not feel on sufficiently good terms to rail at his friend's hutkeeper, as he would have done in the morning. He only shrugged his shoulders meaningly when Stanesby called out.

'Boy! I say, Jimmy, where's the girl?'

Jimmy turned lazily and showed his white teeth.

'Sit down along a creek, you bet.'

'Go and fetch her.'

Jimmy showed his white teeth again, and grinned largely, but he did not stir.

'My word! Baal[2] this blackfellow go.'

'Much as his life is worth, I guess,' said Turner grimly, 'judging by the specimen of her temper the young lady gave us this afternoon.'

Stanesby muttered something that was hardly a blessing under his breath, then he caught up his hat and went down the bank to the waterhole. The other man felt more comfortable in his absence. He sat down, lighted his pipe, and taking up the paper again, began to read with fresh interest.

Half an hour passed. The sun sank below the horizon, gorgeous in red and gold, and Turner watched the last rosy flush die out of the western sky. Darkness fell, and he sat on smoking and thinking sadly, till his comrade loomed up out of the gloom.

'Is that you, Stanesby?' he called out.

'Who the devil should it be?' Then remembering his hospitality, 'Why you're all in the dark! Why didn't you light a candle!'

The girl did not make her appearance, and Turner did not comment on her absence. Stanesby said nothing. He lighted a candle, and calling Jimmy to his assistance, began clearing the table and washing up the dirty plates and pannikins. Turner offered to help, but was told ungraciously that two were enough, and so went on smoking and watched in silence. He did not feel on intimate enough terms to comment; but he knew well enough Stanesby had gone out to find the girl, and either failed to find her, or at any rate failed to bring her back. It was no business of his any way, and he sat smoking till he was called to the evening meal, which was a repetition of the mid-day one, with milkless tea instead of whisky for a beverage.

Stanesby apologised.

'I'm clean out of whisky, I'm sorry to say.'

'It's all right, old man. I don't often manage to get it at all on Jinfalla.'

They discussed station matters then, discussed them all the evening, though Turner could not but feel that his host's thoughts were far away. Still they lasted, they interested the man who was bound to live on here, till at length Stanesby got up with a mighty yawn and suggested they should turn in.

There was a bunk fixed against the wall, and he threw his comrade's blankets into it.

'It's all I can do for you to-night, old man. Come to Heyington next year, and I'll treat you better.'

'Thanks,' said Turner. 'No such luck for me.' Then he spoke the thought that had been in his mind all the evening.

'I say, that girl hasn't come in.'

'She's all right, she can sleep out then. I can't say it'll cool her temper, for it's as hot as blazes still. Good night, old chap.'

Turner lay awake long after the light was out, staring up at the unceiled roof, at the faint light that marked the open doorway and the window, thinking, thinking, wondering at his own discontent, thinking of the fair-haired, blue-eyed girl he had loved so well and so long. It was all over between them now, all over; there had never been anything except on his side, never anything at all, and now it was not much good his even thinking of her. She would marry Dick Stanesby and never know, never dream – His thoughts wandered to that other girl, it was no business of his, but it worried him nevertheless, as things that are no concern of ours do worry us when we lie wakeful on our beds, and the girls' beautiful, angry face haunted him. He thought of her there down by the creek, alone in her dumb pain, so young, so ignorant, so beautiful. There was something wrong in the scheme of creation somewhere, something wrong, or why were such as she born but to suffer. His life was hard, cruelly hard, he had known better things; but she – she – hers had been hard all along. Had she known any happiness? he wondered. He supposed she had if she cared for Dick Stanesby. When first she came, unasked and unsought, he had been good to her; he knew his friend, he had known him from a boy, easy-going, good-natured, with no thought for the future for himself, how could he expect him to think for another? He had been good to her – oh, yes, he knew Dick Stanesby – very good to her, but he had taken no thought for her future any more than he would for his own. He would go into the head-station with him to-morrow morning, he very much doubted if he would come back. He would intend to at first, but it would be very much easier to stay, and he would stay, and the girl – what would become of her? He found himself saying it over and over again to himself, what would become of her? What could become of her? till he fell into an uneasy doze and dreamed that he was master of Heyington and had married Gladys Rowan, who was no other than Dick Stanesby's hutkeeper, and crouched in the corner with a long, shining knife in her hand. Then he awakened suddenly and heard the sound of voices, a woman's voice and Dick's, Dick's soft and tender. He could not hear the words, but the tones were enough. It was the same old Dick. He did not want her, he would rather be without her: but since she was there, he must needs be good to her. So she had come back after all! He might have known she was sure to come back. Why couldn't she stop away? Why couldn't she join her relatives down by the creek? Alas! and alas! The barrier between her and them was as great as it was between her and the white man. Greater, if possible. Poor child! poor child! How was it to end? He tossed and turned and the voices went on softly murmuring. He thought of Gladys and grew angry, and finally, when he had given up all hope, he felt fast asleep.

Next morning he found that peace reigned. The girl came in and quietly cleared away the remnants of last night's meal and began making preparations for breakfast. Her mind was at ease evidently. She had no doubts about the permanency of her heaven; and when she saw him she smiled upon him the same slow, lazy, contented smile with which she had first greeted him, apparently forgetting and expecting him to forget all disagreeable episodes of the day before. How long would this peace last? asked Guy Turner of himself.

The meal done, Stanesby called to his black boy to bring up the horses, and touching the girl on the shoulder drew her aside, evidently to explain that he was going into the head-station and wanted provisions for the journey.

'We'll take a packhorse between us,' said he to Turner, 'it'll save trouble; and I'll show you a decent camping-place for to-night.' Then he followed the girl outside, and his companion began rolling up his swag.

He came back a few moments later, the girl following, and Turner could not but note the change in her face. It was not angry now, there was hardly even a trace of sullenness on it. Fear and sorrow seemed struggling with one another for the upper hand, and she was sobbing every now and then heavily, as if she could not help herself.

'Good Lord! Stanesby, what the dickens have you been doing to the girl?' he said.

Stanesby looked at him angrily.

'You seem to take a confoundedly big interest in the girl,' he said.

'Well, hang it all, man, she looks as if she had been having a jolly bad time, and really she's only a child.'

'A child, is she? A child that's very well able to take care of herself. I haven't been beating her, if that's what you're thinking. I suppose I may be allowed to go into the head-station occasionally without asking my hutkeeper's leave.'

'Oh! that's the trouble, is it? Depends upon your hutkeeper, I should say. I don't ask mine, but then – '

Turner paused, and Stanesby answered the unspoken thoughts with an oath.

'Oh, if you feel that way,' began Turner, but his companion flung himself out of the hut angrily.

Then the girl turned round, and Turner wondered to himself if she were going to repeat the performance of last night. But no, she was quiet and subdued now, as if all hope, all resentment even, had left her.

'Going to the head station?' she asked, and her voice was soft and low and very sweet, with just a trace of the guttural enunciation of her mother's race; but she spoke good English, far better than her appearance seemed to warrant, and did no small credit to old Miss Howard's training.

'Yes, yes, of course. We're going to the head station, but Stanesby'll be back in a day or two,' he added soothingly, because of the sorrow on her face. And then he hated himself for saying so much. What business was it of his?

She stepped forward and laid both hands on his arm.

'Don't take him away, don't, don't!' she pleaded.

Her big dark eyes were swimming with tears, and there was an intensity of earnestness in her tones that went to the young man's heart. Besides, he was young, and she was very good to look upon.

'My dear child,' he said, his anger against his old friend growing, 'I have nothing in the world to do with it. He must go into the head-station sometimes. He must have gone often before.'

She dropped her hands and leaned back wearily against the wall.

'No,' she said, 'no, not when the myalls are down along the creek.'

'Good Lord! Those d – d black fellows! I never thought of them. But they won't touch *you*.'

She looked up and smiled faintly, as if amused at his ignorance.

'Kitty tumble down,' she said, relapsing into the blackfellows' English.

'Oh! come, I say,' said Turner, 'this'll never do.' And he went outside in search of Stanesby, whom he found strapping their swags on to the packhorse.

'Look here, I say, old man, that poor little beggar's frightened out of her wits of the myalls down by the creek there.'

Stanesby shrugged his shoulders.

'All bunkum! I know her ways. She wants to get me to stop. She seems to guess there's something in the wind. The myalls! pooh! They're as tame as possible. They steal any odds and ends that are left about – that's about their form.'

'But the poor child is frightened.'

'Frightened! Get out. There wasn't much fright about her when she took the knife to you last night! She knows very well how to take care of herself, I can tell you.'

'But those myalls. On Jinfalla we – . Well, it really seems to me risky to leave her all alone. Even if there isn't any danger – the very fact of being alone – .'

'Pooh! Considering she tramped from the head-station here all the eighty miles on foot, just because of some breeze with the cook there, she must be mightily afraid of being alone. However, if you don't like her being left, it's open to you to stop and look after her. I'm going to start in about two minutes.'

'Oh, well, if you think it's all right – '

'Of course it's all right. There's Jimmy got your horse for you. Come on, old chap.'

Turner mounted, and Stanesby was just about to do the same, when with a quick cry the girl ran out of the hut and caught his arm.

She said no word, and before he, taken by surprise, could stop her she had wound both her arms around his neck and laid her face against his breast.

Turner put his spurs into his horse, and rode off smartly. It was no affair of his. The whole thing made him angry whenever he thought of it.

As for Dick Stanesby, though usually never anything but gentle with a woman, he was thoroughly angry now; he had felt angry before, but now he was roused, which did not often happen, to put his anger into words.

'Confound you, Kitty! Do you hear me? Don't be a fool!' and he roughly shook her off, so roughly that she lost her balance, staggered, and fell. He made a step forward to take his horse, which was held by the stolid black boy, but she was too quick for him and, grovelling on the ground at his feet, put out her arms and held him there, murmuring inarticulate words of tenderness and love. Stanesby stooped down, and caught her wrists in both his hands.

'Get up!' he said roughly, and dragged her to her feet. She stood there, leaning all her weight on his supporting hands, looking at him with reproachful eyes.

They were beautiful eyes, and there was need enough for her sorrow had she only known; but what Stanesby was thinking of was the awkwardness of the situation. He did not mind the black boy, he counted him as so much dirt – but Turner! Already this girl had made an exhibition of him, and now it was worse than ever. Every moment he dreaded he would turn round, and even though he did not it was equally bad, he kept his face purposely averted.

The girl broke out into passionate prayer to him not to leave her, then, seeing he was still unmoved, she began to call him every tender name her limited vocabulary contained, though there was little enough need to do that, her eyes said enough.

'Kitty, go back to the hut this moment! For God's sake, don't be such a fool! One would think I was going to murder you.'

'The myalls will,' she said. Then she paused, and added solemnly, 'to-morrow.'

'What confounded rot!'

He let go her hands suddenly, and she fell to her knees and tried to put her arms round him again; but with a quick movement he stepped backwards, and she fell forward on to her face. He pushed her aside roughly, angrily, with an anger that was not all against her, and mounted hurriedly, snatched the pack-horse's rein from the black boy, and was off at full gallop after his friend before she could regain her feet. But she did not try to, once she realised that all hope was gone. He had left her, it was all over with her, she might just as well lie there.

At the sound of the galloping horses behind him Turner looked round. Through the haze of the early morning, the haze that promised fierce heat later on, he saw the horses coming towards him, and beyond, half-veiled by the dust they made as they passed, a dusky red bundle flung carelessly out on the plain, of use to no one. The black boy walked away, it was no business of his. There was the lonely hut and the far-reaching plain, nothing in sight but the bluffs far away to the east, nothing at all, only that red bundle lying there alone and neglected.

He had no words for his comrade when he did come up. That dusky red heap seemed to fill all his thoughts, and about that silence was best. Stanesby checked his horses, and they rode on slowly as men who have a long journey before them. The sun climbed up and up to the zenith, but there was no shelter, no place for the noonday rest. Then away in the distance arose a line of trees raised up above the horizon, and Stanesby pointed it out to his companion.

'We can spell there a bit,' he said. 'It's only that beastly prickly bush, for all it looks like a forest of red gum at the very least from here, but there'll be a scrap of shade, and I'm getting tired. There's water there sometimes, but it was dry as a bone last time I passed.'

'It's a grand country!' sighed Turner.

'By George!' said Stanesby, 'I never will come back this way. Why should I, now I'm free to do as I please?'

Why, indeed? And Turner's thoughts immediately flew back to the dark-eyed girl, and the solitary hut as he had last seen it through the haze of the morning, with that red heap lying there carelessly flung aside, and the black fellow stalking away. Why should he go back? Why indeed? Only to have that scene repeated. Better go straight on to England, and home, and pretty, fair-haired, blue-eyed Gladys Rowan.

So they lay there in the scanty shade and spelled, and built a small fire of dry sticks, and filled the billy from the waterbag that hung at each horse's neck, and boiled their tea, and ate their humble mid-day meal, and dozed the afternoon away, lazily watching the hobbled horses as they searched on the still damp edges of the shallow clay pan for such scanty grass as the moisture induced to grow there. They hardly spoke, they had nothing in common now; once they reached the head-station, they would part never to meet again. Each felt it instinctively, and each was thankful that it should be so. The sooner the parting came, the better now.

The shadows of the thorny bushes began to grow longer and longer as the sun sank in the west, and they mounted their horses and started off again. Then the sun went down, and the colour faded out of the sky as the stars, bright points of light, came out one by one. The new moon was a silver rim clear cut in the west, and not a sound broke the stillness. How lonely it was, how intensely lonely! Turner thought of the poor girl alone in the hut miles behind them, and wondered if his companion too were thinking of her. After all, surely the very loneliness gave safety. At any rate, she was safe at night. If the blacks did not attack at dusk they would leave her alone for the night. But the morning – next morning! Was it right to leave her? He himself had no faith in the myall blacks, they were treacherous, they were cruel. Had he not come over to arrange some plan of campaign against them? And yet he went away and left that girl at their mercy, completely at their mercy. He felt strongly tempted to turn back. If they could not stop with her, at least they might have brought her along with them. She was defenceless; her blood was no protection, rather the reverse. And then, when he turned to speak to Stanesby, the recollection of his scornful, 'It's open to you to stop and look after her,' tied his tongue. After all, it was not likely Stanesby would have left if there was the slightest danger; he had lived among these blacks, he understood them thoroughly; it was an insult to the man he had known all his life to suppose anything else; and yet the thought of the girl's loneliness haunted him. The moon set, and by the starlight they saw looming up ahead some rocks, isolated rocks, roughly piled together by some giant hand.

'We'll camp there, ' said Stanesby, 'there's a little water down under the rocks – about enough to keep life in the horses; there's some grass and a bush or two to make a fire. What more could the heart of man desire?'

Out in the bush not much time is wasted, and soon after they had halted their blankets were spread, and they were asleep, or lying, if not asleep, staring up at the bright starlit sky of the southern hemisphere.

But Turner could not sleep, it was worse than it had been the night before. Why should he be haunted in this way? Why should he take Stanesby's sins on his shoulders? The girl was all right, she must be all right; why should she haunt his dreams, and keep him wakeful on his hard bed, when he had a long journey still before him? Stanesby was sleeping peacefully as a child. He could hear his deep breathing; if there was anything to be feared he would not sleep like that. It was hot still, very hot. This was an awful climate, a cruel life, and Stanesby had done with it all. No wonder he slept soundly.

He sat up restlessly. A sound in the distance broke the stillness, then he started, surely it was the trotting of a horse. He rubbed his eyes. Their own three horses were there close beside them, he could see them vague and indistinct in the gloom. They were there right enough. What could this be? Who could be riding about at this time of night? They were still a good forty miles from the head-station, and this horse was coming from the opposite direction.

He put out his hand, and shook his companion awake.

'Some one's coming,' he said shortly.

'Some one! Gammon! Good Lord! – '

There was no doubt about it, and he rose to his feet. It was the other side of the rocks, and they walked round quietly. They were only curious, there was nothing to fear. In the dim starlight they saw a man on horseback advancing towards them.

'Hallo!' called out Stanesby, as he came quite close, 'who the devil are you?'

The horse was done. They could hear his gasping breath, and the man bent forward as if he too had come far and fast, but he did not answer, and as he came closer Turner saw he was a blackfellow.

Stanesby saw it too, and saw more, for he recognised his own black boy Jimmy.

'Good God! Jimmy, is it you?'

There must be something wrong, very wrong indeed, that would bring a blackfellow, steeped in superstitious fears of demons and evil spirits, out at dead of night.

'Jimmy!' Stanesby caught him by the shoulder, and fairly pulled him from his horse, 'What's the meaning of this?'

Jimmy did not answer for a moment. He was occupied with his horse's bridle, then he said carelessly, as if he were rather ashamed of making such a fuss about a trifle.

'Myalls pull along a hut.'

'My God!' cried Turner. It seemed like the realisation of his worst fears.

But Stanesby refused to see any cause for alarm.

'And you've ridden like blazes, and ruined the mare, to tell us rot like that. What if they do come up to the hut? They've been there before.'

The answer was more to his companion than his servant, but Jimmy answered the implied reproach.

'Blackfellow burn hut,' he stated.

'Nonsense!'

'This fellow sit down along a bush,' he went on stolidly.

'Well – if you did! I wish to heaven you had stopped alongside your confounded bush before you ruined my mare.'

'Bungally you!' said Jimmy, who was no respecter of persons, meaning 'you are very stupid.' 'Blackfellow put firestick in humpy and – '

'Good God! Stanesby, I knew it. The myalls are going to burn down the hut, and this beggar's got wind of it.'

Jimmy nodded approvingly.

'All gone humpy,' he said, stretching out his hands as if to denote the deed was done.

'But the girl, Jimmy, the girl!'

'Poor gin tumble down.'

'I – Jimmy,' Stanesby caught him by the shoulder, and shook

him violently, and Turner knew by the change in his voice that his fears were roused at last, 'how did you know this? When did you hear it?'

'Sit down along a bush,' said Jimmy again. His vocabulary was limited.

'But when – when? It must have been all right when you left?'

'Blackfellow pull along a humpy to-night,' said Jimmy, nodding his head solemnly, feeling that at last he had got a serious hearing, and hoping to hear no more about the mare.

'But the girl – the girl! Where's the girl?'

'That one myall hit him gin along a cobra big fellow nulla-nulla? Gin tumble down.'[3]

'But – my God! what'd you leave her there for?'

'Myall got 'em nulla-nulla for this fellow.'

'You brute!' cried Turner, 'why didn't you bring her with you?'

'Only got 'em one yarramen,' said the blackfellow nonchalantly. There was only one horse, he had taken it and saved his skin. He had come to warn the white man of the destruction of his dwelling, but he did not count the half-caste girl of any value one way or another. The blacks would attack the hut at sundown when they saw the coast clear. The white man would be angry at the destruction of his hut, he had ridden after him to tell him, and also because safety lay with the white man; but the girl – if there had been a horse in the little paddock, he might possibly have brought her out of danger, but even as a blackfellow he looked with contempt on a half-caste; and as a woman – well, a woman was worth nothing as a woman. There were plenty more to be got. He lay down on the ground, and lazily stretched himself out at full length. There was nothing more to be got out of him.

Stanesby kicked him, and went for his horse.

'This is terrible!' he said, in a hoarse, husky whisper. 'That poor child! Old man, I ought to have taken your advice. My God! Why did you let me leave her?'

Turner was saddling his own horse, and asking himself the self-same question. That girl's blood was on his head he felt, and yet – and yet – it was no business of his. Stanesby had declared all safe.

---

[3] A blackfellow has hit the woman over the head with a big stick or club. The woman is dead.

'What are you going to do?'

'Going straight back, of course.'

'We'll be too late. Jimmy certainly said at sundown.'

'He may be wrong, you know; besides, there's no trusting these devils. They might have changed their minds. You'll help me, old man, won't you?'

'Of course.'

It took but a few moments to prepare for that journey back. Each man saw that his revolvers were loaded, saddled his horse, and they were ready. The horse Jimmy had ridden was done.

'Shall we leave him?' said Stanesby, contemptuously stirring him with his foot.

'No, by Jove! no,' said his companion, 'we must have him. He knows all the sign.'

So they forced the reluctant Jimmy to mount the packhorse, and distributed his load between them, taking only what was absolutely necessary.

When they were quite ready Stanesby looked at his watch.

'Ten o'clock,' he said. 'We must be there before daylight if we want to do any good;' and Turner could not but note that there was a more hopeful ring in his voice. Evidently he thought that perhaps all would be well after all.

They rode in silence, each man busy with his own thoughts. They had to ride judiciously too, for their horses were poor, and they had done forty miles already that day. Could they ever get back to the out-station before breakfast? Could they? And would they be in time if they did? Turner asked himself the question again and again, and he felt that his companion was doing the same thing. Whenever he touched his horse with the spur till the poor beast started forward with a fresh burst of energy, his companion felt he was thinking that the girl's life was forfeit by his carelessness, was wondering would they ever be in time.

Dawn would be about six o'clock. Forty miles to go, and eight hours to do it in. Forty miles straight ahead, with absolutely nothing to break the monotony except the little patch of prickly bush where they had spelled that afternoon. They went farther before they spelled to-night, and they did not stop then till it was very evident to both that the horses must have a rest, if it was only for half an hour. Turner lay on the ground and stared up at the starlit sky, and listened to the deep breathing of the black boy, and the restless pacing up and down of his companion. Then he fell into a doze from which he was aroused by Stanesby, and they were on their way again.

'We can't stop now till we get there,' he said. 'Old man, we must be in time. We must!'

But the other man said nothing. He could not judge, he could only hope. And now at the end of the journey, weary and tired, his hopes had gone down to zero.

The first faint streaks of dawn began to show themselves in the eastern sky, and Stanesby drew a long breath.

'My God! we're still a mile away.'

'If they weren't there last night we'll be in time.'

'Poor little girl! How thankful she'll be to see us. It's all right, it must be all right.'

And the light broadened in the east, the rosy light grew deeper and deeper, then it paled to bright gold, and behind, and all around, the world looked dark against that glowing light. Up came the rim of the sun, and Stanesby, urging his tired horse forward, said, 'We ought to see the hut now. The confounded sun's in my eyes.'

Turner rubbed his own. But no, against the golden glowing rising sun the horizon was clean cut as ever, only the boundless plain, nothing more.

'Jimmy!' Stanesby's voice was sharp with pain and dread.

Jimmy raised his head sullenly. He was tired too, and considered himself ill-used.

'All gone humpy,' he said.

Brighter and brighter grew the sunlight, another fierce hot day had begun. And there was nothing in sight, nothing. The plain was all around them, north, south, west, only in the east the red bluffs.

'All gone humpy.' Their haste had been of no avail. The tale was told. They had come too late.

What need to ride for all they were worth now? But so they did ride, revolver in hand. And when they arrived at what had been Dick Stanesby's hut, an out-station of Nilpe Nilpe, there was nothing to mark it from the surrounding plain but a handful of ashes; even the hard earth showed no sign of trampling feet.

Stanesby flung himself off his horse like a madman.

'She may be all right. She must be all right. It may have been an accident. She is hidden down by the creek.'

Turner said nothing. What could he say? His thoughts flew

back to the lonely hut, and the girl lying there on the hard ground
in her dusky red dress, alone, cast off, a thing of use to no one.
Well, she was dead, he expected nothing else, and she was
avenged. Surely this home-coming would haunt the man who
had left her all the days of his life.

He laid his hand heavily on the black boy's shoulder.

'Track, you devil!'

And Jimmy led the way down towards the waterhole.

They followed him in silence.

The tall reeds looked green and fresh after the hot dry plain,
but they also suggested another idea to Turner, and he tried to
check his companion's headlong career.

'Look out! You don't know. They might be in those reed beds.'

'All gone blackfellow,' said Jimmy, and stolidly went ahead.

Then at last he brought them to what they sought. Dead, of
course. Long before they started on that mad ride back her sufferings had been over. Dead! and Turner dared not look his
companion in the face. No peace, no tenderness, about a death
like this. It was too terrible! And this man had left her; in spite
of her prayers he had left her!

They avenged her. The blacks had not gone far, but they could
not follow them up that day. They spent it in the shade down
by the waterhole, and Turner did not try to break his companion's silent reverie. Then when their horses were recruited they
set out for the head-station of Nilpe Nilpe. There they told their
tale. It was not much of a tale after all. Only a half-caste girl
murdered, and a hut burnt. Such things happen every day. But
the blacks must be punished, nevertheless, and half-a-dozen men
rode out to do it, Stanesby at their head.

He was very silent. They said at the station, coming into a fortune had made him stuck-up and too proud to speak to a fellow,
only Turner put a different construction on his silence. And the
vengeance he took was heavy. They rode down among that tribe
at bright noonday, led by Stanesby's black boy, who had been
one of themselves, and when evening fell it was decimated, none
left but a few scattered frightened wretches crouching down among
the scanty cover in the creek bed, knowing full well that to show
themselves but for a moment was to court death swift and certain. So they avenged Dick Stanesby's hutkeeper.

They count Dick Stanesby a good fellow in his county. He is
a just landlord, well beloved by his tenants. He is a magistrate

and staunchly upholds law and order; and withal he is a jolly good fellow, whose hunting breakfasts are the envy and admiration of the surrounding squires. His wife is pretty too, somewhat insipid perhaps, but a model wife and mother, and always sweet and amiable.

There have been found men who were Goths enough to object to Mrs Stanesby's innocent, loving prattle about her eldest boy and her third girl, and the terrible time they had when her second little boy had the measles, and they were so terrified for the first twenty-four hours lest it should turn to scarlet fever; there have been men, I say, who have objected to this as 'nursery twaddle,' but their womenkind have invariably crushed them. They believe in Mrs Stanesby and in Dick Stanesby too.

'Their story is too sweet,' says Ethel De Lisle, his sister's sister-in-law. 'It reminds one that the chivalry of the olden times has not yet died out among true Englishmen. Only think, he loved silently because he was too poor to speak. He went away to Australia, and he worked and waited there all among the blacks and all sorts of low people, and at the end of four years, when his cousin died and left him Heyington, he came back faithful still and he married her. I call it too sweet for words.'

But Mrs De Lisle has never met Guy Turner. He is still 'riding tracks' on Jinfalla, and consequently she knows nothing of Dick Stanesby's hutkeeper, or of a solitary grave by the Woonawidgee creek.

MARY GILMORE, 1864-1962

Mary Gilmore was born Mary Jean Cameron, near
Goulburn, New South Wales, and many of the
details of her life are contained in the first letter
printed here. Her correspondence reveals her consum-
ing interest in education, justice and literature; for
twenty-three years she gave expression to her widely
read and influential views as editor (and writer) for
the women's page of the *Sydney Worker*. During her
lifetime she published more than ten volumes of verse
as well as memoirs and reminiscences (such as *Old
Days, Old Ways*, 1934 and *More Recollections*,
1953). Honoured for her contribution to Australian
society and the world of letters, she was a firm supporter of women's rights and a tireless worker in the
interest of the validation of Australian literature. She
helped to establish the reputations of those writers
whom she believed worthy of recognition.

The collection of letters included here has been
taken from *Letters of Mary Gilmore*, selected and
edited by W. H. Wilde and T. Inglis Moore
(Melbourne University Press, 1980); the selection has
been made with the intention of revealing some of
her links with other women writers.

To W. A. Woods[1]

'Burnside', Strathdownie E. via Casterton Vic.
11 June 1903

Amigo,
What sort of auto. notes do you want? Bald facts, or nice little items that will 'frill', or both 'em?

Anyhow here goes for a sort of personal – but you know what sort I am, so why can't you fix it up?

I was born near Goulburn, N.S.W. Mother, N.S.W. native of N. of Ireland parentage, highly strung, nervous, bright woman, without either fads or superstitions. I was born when she was barely twenty. Father; fine looking man of splendid physique, talent for the mechanical, *very* Highland. When he was about forty he met his equal at scratch pulling; I have an idea he and the other man sat and pulled all night without advantage on either side. My father never pulled again. He was too proud to risk a beating. He had all the Highland superstitions – though he always *said* he didn't believe in 'em. I have them too, and I always say I don't believe in them, nor do I intellectually, but in the bedrock of my soul the belief is there.

In my young days I was considered a prodigy of learning because I could write a fine angular hand and read a newspaper article at the age of seven. One of my earliest recollections is as a child of three sitting on my maternal grandfather's knee and spelling out of the old Family Bible 'In the Beginning was the Word'.

My mother's people were Wesleyans of the rigid Presbyterian kind. Indeed it was simply accident that called my grandfather anything so mild as Wesleyan. No weekly newspaper was read inside his doors on Sundays, and no wicked secular music was ever heard inside his gates. One of my uncles learned in secret to play two hymn tunes on that instrument of evil – the fiddle. As a surprise, he played them to his father, but the old man never

---

[1] As Walter William Head, he was a founding editor of the labour movement newspaper, the *Hummer* which later became the *Worker*. After disappearing to avoid imprisonment for debt, he reappeared – with aliases ('Walter Alan Woods' and 'William Ashe Woods' etc), becoming a member of the Tasmanian Parliament in 1906 and from 1925-1931, speaker of the House of Assembly.

spoke, indeed except from the setness of his look one would not think he heard. Yet he was one of the best men I ever knew. He had the sense of contract, which means so much, and is so sure an indication of character. He served the Lord even in his smallest actions, but he held his head on a level with the throne. My father was something the same in his 'face to face with God' attitude, but he was more of the 'The Sabbath is the Lord's and Let Him not encroach' – on the other days. (If this isn't autobiog., it is at least the springs of my beginnings.)

I went to school in Wagga in due time and found that I had constantly to explain myself to my fellow pupils. 'You use such long words' they used to say. I was surprised; I had no intention of using out-of-the-way language. I was a voracious reader, and spoke like a book. At this school (I was ten) I was put into a low class because I could not add up, but in six months I was in third class, and considered an exceedingly quick child. In third class we had composition and I recollect almost invariably my slate was kept to show round to the teachers. I did not think of it myself. The other girls drew my attention to the fact. When I was eight or nine I would sit for hours writing 'letters' on a slate; no one ever read them – not even myself, and as quickly as one was written it was cleaned off and another begun. At the little Brucedale (near Wagga) school I used to spend all my dinner hour at this, eating my lunch as I wrote. Then I went to school in Wagga. I was ten, and we, my brother and I, had a three-mile walk. I was a thin, tall, delicate child, and the hours of school took so much from my vitality that many and many a time I walked home with the calves of my legs pushing to the front in a state of nervous terror at the imaginary *something* that might be behind. In the morning there were no terrors, only in the evening. I was a child that constantly craved the affection of its nearest, or the signs of it, and because I would not sue I got, or fancied I got, least of it. It is the child that leaps on your lap and kisses you that gets the kiss, not the one that sits in the corner and longs for it, yet the first probably only kisses for love of kissing.

After Wagga School I went to Downside School a few miles away. Here I was a bad girl. The poor old pedagogue, for pedagogue he was, used to keep me in and go to his dinner. I used to climb out the window and over the fence, have my dinner and be back again before he remembered me. At the inspection held here the report read 'So and So'; 'One pupil excellent' – which was *ME* no less, though I didn't know it till years later. Fifteen years later I found the widow of my old master in Sydney. She did not know me; I told her who I was. She flung her arms round me – 'Ah!' she cried, 'When I saw those wicked eyes I felt there was something I ought to remember'. She told me Mr – had talked about me up to the day of his death, that he had always been so proud of me, &c., &c. You know there is something in that kind of thing which makes you feel so much. At the time you didn't think of anything, didn't know you deserved anything, and afterwards when you *know* you were different someway from the general run, you find the recognition was there all the time – unknown and unthought of. And, here, the poor old man was dead and I could not tell him how his kindness touched me.

After that I went to school in Cootamundra and later at Bungowannah, near Albury – a small country school among farms, where I had a bed made up in the school quite away from the house, because there was no spare room for me in the residence, where I used to lie awake in the moonlight nights trembling and cold with nervous fear, listening to the cry of the morepork in the hills, and the melancholy wail of the curlew in the flats, while my heart used to nearly burst with fright at the rustle of a mouse among the papers in the empty grate. I left here so thin and nervous I was kept at home for some time before I went to school again. Then I was sent to a good kind uncle – teacher at Yerong Creek, who took such pains with me that, when at sixteen I went up for examination as Pupil Teacher, I was said to have passed highest of all that year's candidates. I was given my choice of appointment in Sydney or any of half a dozen country towns. I chose Wagga as being near my own people, and because I had gone to school there. I was only a gawky country girl dressed in a home made frock when I entered the school to begin work, and when I went eagerly up to an old school-fellow (she wore a watch and her skirt was weighted down with pennies instead of shot, and who afterwards married a clergyman and wore glasses) she coldly gave me the tips of her fingers and turned away to another girl whose dress had six pearl buttons where mine had one. But deep inside the chill that came over me was the germ of a hot feeling of hate and determination to some day make her repent of her snub. Perhaps I did, perhaps I didn't, but when for months she came to me to help her with her hardest sums, unravel the difficulties of her analysis, and give her the punctuation in the punctuation lessons, when indeed she, who previous to my coming had been the bright one, looked up to me as the bright one, then I was satisfied. My pride was soothed, I had had my revenge – and she never knew. No one who ever injured me to a deep hurting can say I ever injured them. Indeed I sometimes feel I hate so hard I *have* to be kind. Well the mistress of the Girls' School at Wagga was Miss Everitt who for so long was Principal of the Hurlstone Training College. A girl from the University told me years afterwards in Sydney that Miss Everitt had told her I was the brightest Pupil Teacher she had ever had. After Miss Everitt left Wagga for Hurlstone other Mistresses used to tell me that my 'prose order' was more poetical than the poetry to *be* prose ordered. At this time I devoured Carlyle and Victor Hugo, and one or two Headmasters used to make fun of me by asking if various compositions were Carlyle or Miss Cameron. Also at the time I used to often read novels till midnight and then study till daylight. I *couldn't help* reading – I read everything, Jack Harkaways, Proctor's Astronom. works, Jevons's Logic, Family Heralds, Gordon's Poems, Kendall, The Koran, fragments of newspaper stories, even if only a few inches long – anything and everything I could get. And at this time I got my best reports as a teacher. It often seems strange to me how it should be so. But I expect it was sheer hard work and an unconscious vitality. I fell into such a condition of anaemia, that I was told that, unless I had a change, I would not live three months. Yet I never thought of either leaving school or of going home. Later, my landlady told my mother she often feared to call me to breakfast lest she should find me dead. Fortunately my mother came to live in town. She fed me up and pulled me round, but I doubt if I ever really got over the strain of that time.

I have so often been told that I have a strong personal influence over people that I begin to believe it especially as, when I look back over my life at school and as Pupil Teacher, I remember that I was either 'leader' or 'ringleader' (amongst my own partic-ular factions or schools) – according to whether I was good or bad. I resigned my pupil teachership and took a small school in order to speedily go up for examination as a classified teacher and to avoid the training school, of which somehow I had a dread. As soon as possible I sat for examination. Feeling sure of III C. and hoping for III B. to my surprise I came out with III A. Then I went as Assistant to Silverton in the palmy days of Broken Hill.

I had 2 years and three months there when I was appointed to Neutral Bay as Assistant, and three years from the previous examination I went up for Class II (this being the earliest opportunity) hoping for II B. I got II A. I was even more astonished over this than over the III A. and to make sure there was no mistake I wrote for the marks I had been awarded in each subject. They convinced me I had gone through alright. Then I went to Stanmore; was there about five years and when I left the streets were lined with weeping children. I left for South America a few days later . . . William Lane once said in some surprise, like a man who is convinced against preconceived conviction – 'You reason like a man! I have never met any woman who could reason. I speak of pure reason, reason going logically from point to point – indeed I have met few men who can reason like you.' Also 'You have the gift of intuitive perception in an unusually high degree. No matter how one talks to you, you can follow, and though you may not understand *exactly* as the other mind sees, yet there is always perception of the actual behind the seeming and you can always follow.' Another time he told me he never met anyone who knew English as I did – i.e. the language – I wish I knew it now.

Mrs Lane used to say 'I never saw anyone so quick and impulsive over big things, and so deliberate over little things as you' – but that is a question of issues, and in magnitudes, for and against are easily decided on.

One of the kindliest things I remember was when I wrote 'The crows kep' flyin' up, boys' – Henry Lawson came up to me in the little old New Aust. Office 'I must congratulate you' he said kindly. I looked at him – 'I saw those verses of yours about Larry Petrie' he said in answer to my look, then after a pause he added 'You have beaten me on my own ground, I haven't seen anything better.' It was so kind and so unexpected, and I never forgot it. And you, if you recollect, have often said you never saw anyone 'so doubtful of the worth of your own work' &c. – Farrell has often spoken kindly of my work, but he is too true a friend to ever say it was any better than he thought it, only, when I shewed him those love verses I wrote in December and January he said in a sort of an understanding, half-puzzled surprise 'I didn't think you had it in you!' – and that pleased me more than any compliment, for the only John is too kind a man to overpraise – later he wrote in rather flattering terms of stuff I had sent him for criticism, but the 'I didn't think you had it in you' pleased me most.

My mother once repeated to me a saying of an old cousin whom I had visited – 'Of all the cousins who come to stay with me, she is the only one who never talks ill of others. She will talk of books, or what she sees or reads, but I have never heard a word of scandal from her.' That also sank in as a pleasant thing to remember. I didn't talk scandal simply because I never thought of it, and later when I did think of it the remembrance of old Cousin Annie kept me from it. So grows the seed of a kindly word.

A woman with a tongue remarked to another that she would rather fall out with the whole neighbourhood than with me, meaning she was afraid of me – yet I never quarrelled with a woman in my life; I only feel that my back gets too stiffly straight to allow of anything but the most dignified and accurate speech, and if that is not possible, there is nothing to be said. I *couldn't* quarrel, the words wouldn't come; a sort of dumb feeling takes possession of me when anything like that approaches me. On the other hand, if anything caused me to think I ought to go out and preach at street corners, nothing would stop me. Duty – or contract – must be obeyed – it is the one thing that lifts man above the brute.

Suppose I get me sister to call on Mr Stevens?[2] She could take some photos and tell him lots of things – for instance how I cried 'Go to ruin! Go to ruin, then' because she would persist (as a little girl) in talking to the servant as an equal. She reminded me of it only recently.

As to South America: I had a lot of fever in the Colony; also people said I worked too hard. I was married there, and my child was born in the neighbouring town. The nurse – an ex-colonist – was drunk from before his birth till a week after and I did not write to the Colony for help because I did not care to expose her thinking no one but I knew she drank. Only for the kindness of a chance visitor, Mrs J. Pinder [*sic*],[3] I would have died, and only for the nurse's little girl of eight, I would have often gone all day (while in bed) without food. A month before my child was born, I went into Villa Rica. Imagine, me, a delicate woman, who had been a weakly baby and a frail child, a woman whose heart was so weak my Sydney Doctor had said that I must always be careful – imagine me starting from home with my hus-

[2] A. G. Stephens.
[3] John Pindar's wife.

band at four a.m. in a spring cart and two horses, and an hour later having to get out and wade through water often over my knees, wading thus, with an occasional 'lift' in the cart where the water and mud were not too deep for the horses to struggle through with my additional weight, till about 11 a.m. when we came out on a plain where the keen June wind cut like a knife. I didn't dare ride then for fear of a chill, and I had to walk on to keep up the circulation till we reached the Railway Station just as the one o'clock train was heard to whistle in the distance. We had just time to change a note and get my ticket. I got into the train wet, cold and alone, for we did not feel justified in spending money on a ticket (1s. 8d.) for my husband. And there I travelled in a filthy third class carriage full of natives, of whose language I was quite ignorant – all smoking, men and women alike, with baskets of meat here and there on the floor – game-cocks perched on the backs of the seats, and young pigs in bags among our feet. I got into Villa Rica about six o'clock. God knows how I escaped fatal harm; yet somehow I got through alright. Vitality I suppose. I have been told more than once that I would have been dead only for my will.

When my child was two weeks old I returned to the Colony, and when he was sixteen days old I was at the wash-tub – this because I knew every woman in the Colony had as much work to do as ever she could manage without mine being added. I remember the longing I had when my child was born to send a wire to my husband, but I was afraid of the expense – it would have seemed like taking bread out of the children's mouths, and I only sent a letter. But I never think of that telegram without a feeling of sadness. I was away and the baby was come, and I had to wait for the chance of the mail being sent for from the Colony for my husband to know.

I remember how we made a cot for the child. Will split the timber – lapacho, a hardwood and a heavy – with maul and wedges, then he trimmed down the splintered sides with an adze, after which he split the pieces with an old saw. He was weeks over the work – the wood was so hard – then with a plane and a spoke shave he smoothed all the surfaces. It was a bit out of plumb in some of its legs, but it would take a beautiful polish. The idea of the polish was a joy to us, but we had neither the time nor the material to polish with, so the joy never had a foundation in fact. And though the cot was finished I never put the boy to bed in it except by day. It seemed so cold-hearted to put him away in the night – and we thought he might feel lonely – 'besides,' his father said, 'he is such a little fellow' – We made also a what-not – but it was sawn out with a cross-cut; I was the architect, Will was the Executive; it was a thing of beauty, actually had a bead on its front edges, and wouldn't go skew-wise if stood away from the wall. In fact, it could on occasion stand alone; but we kept it nailed to the wall for security and safety's sake.

Some time after we severed our connection with the Colony (Cosme) and while Will was in Patagonia, I went into Villa Rica to live, renting the same little house where my baby was born. The evenings were pleasant, for it was May, and I used to sit in the verandah at sundown and even till nearly dusk. After a week of this my landlord and his six daughters came one evening to see me and remonstrate. 'It wasn't safe' they gave me to understand; 'there were bandidos about'. 'And would I go indoors before sundown and fasten up the house'. And he hauled in the trunk of a small orange tree to add to the security of my door. The door, I may mention, opened in the middle, had a bolt top and bottom, and a double lock in the middle. He fastened the bolts, double locked the door, and then jammed the sapling against the middle of it. One of the daughters, to make things more secure, brought in a long board; this was propped in against the upper part of the door. Some weeks afterwards, finding the door rattle in a high wind, I examined the hinges. There were no screws in them, only nails, old rusty nails, about two to each hinge. I smiled. The thing was so like Paraguay. After that I ceased to barricade the door in the middle and did it at the sides – not that it mattered much, except as a precaution against it being blown in. To this house used poor Larry Petrie to come after his seventeen hours duty at the Railway Station. 'Larry, Larry, you foolish fellow' I used to say – 'Why don't you go to bed instead of coming up here?' 'Bed!' he would reply 'How can I sleep? The carpenters work beside me and the lampmen are in and out all the time, and so it's a case of get drunk, or come and talk to you,' and he would stay and talk till his nerves quietened and then tramp wearily back to his little lamp-room for an hour's sleep. Twice he prevented a collision; once he saved a train from fire, and died at last with his ribs through his lungs, his life given for that of the Station-master's child.

Will came up to Villa Rica from Patagonia, intending we should all go down as soon as the summer came. We went from Villa Rica to Sapucay (the Railway works) and lived there two or three months. Then to Buenos Aires for a few more months. Here Will went shearing in the Argentine – such an experience! In November nearly three years ago we left for Gallegos, in South Patagonia. From Gallegos the Falklands lie east 300 miles, so you may guess how cold it was. Magellan's Strait is two days' ride south. On the way south an epidemic of measles broke out; my little son took the complaint, inflammation of the lungs set in. There was no milk, water ran short; it was thick and purple, we were on a waterless coast in an old ship whose engines might blow up any time, whose condenser only condensed enough for the first class, and used to break out in leaks every second day. The Doctor suffered from melancholia and loss of memory; he was kindness itself, and used invariably to pray over my little one, but he dared not trust himself to do anything else beyond take his temperature. When I would beg of him 'Doctor, is there *anything* can be done?' he would say 'We can only wait, we can only pray' – and sometimes 'He is too weak for anyone to do anything' – we were 31 days on a voyage that should only have taken six or seven. The Pacific boats do it in two-and-a-half. *Yet* Billy lived.

In Patagonia I was for a time governess to, I think the most awful girl that ever lived. She was 16; looked 18, and called herself fourteen. She knew everything ever known, and what I told her one day, told me back in a day or two as entirely her own. Among the items of her own peculiar knowledge was that 'she knew the woman who made *all* the lace for Queen Victoria's wedding.' Her mother was a nice woman; her father a big man with a thin nose, a high voice, and a character and reputation to match. After three months' governessing I went from the Estancia to live in Gallegos. Here I was advised to take up English teaching. I demurred on the grounds that I could not speak Spanish. 'Oh, but you are such a good English scholar' was the reply, 'you should do well at it'. It seemed a queer reply and a queer reason for success, but there was a lot in it; so I took a house and began teaching. My first pupil was Don Vicente Cane, of the Bank of Argentina, nephew to a gentleman whose name I forget, but who was one time Plenipoa, for Argentina in London. A fine scholar and a brilliant writer. Don Vicente lent me his uncle's translation of

Henry V. which was *really* Shakespeare in another language. The first month of teaching was dreadful. I felt such a fraud, for I hadn't the use of twenty words of the language, though with a dictionary I could read fairly well. As the lesson hour came round my knees used to shake with apprehension lest Don Vicente wouldn't come, and my stomach grow sick in dread of the lesson should he come. Whichever way it was it was awful. Yet in a week Senor Cane brought me other pupils, and the Deputy Governor sent me more. Indeed, in a little while I had to take a more convenient house and had as many pupils as I could manage. And they were so kind, all of them. I got on splendidly with my Spanish, and they were kind enough to say they did well with the English – and indeed, after awhile, I think they did for I tried hard enough. Moreover they all expressed their sorrow and disappointment when I told them I was leaving.

Half the lessons I gave at my own house, the rest at the houses of pupils, and many and many a day the wind blew my little boy off his feet as we hurried along to a lesson, or dashed me against a telegraph post or a fence. The wind is incessant. Except in the dead of winter when all is frozen it never ceases. I have been half an hour going 100 yards, and holding on to fences all the way, and I have seen men – who wear no skirts – have to put their hands to the ground to maintain their balance. My little boy I couldn't leave at home as he was too young, and a servant was out of the question. Only soldiers' wives were available, and they would only stay till they had pilfered all they wanted, in addition to which none of them could cook, and all were dirty and immoral.

During the time I was in Gallegos war was threatened between Argentina and Chile. The disputed territory was only 60 miles away. It was a time of great excitement. Soldiers drilled daily back and front of my house beginning at 2 a.m. – the days were long and there was little darkness at night; the pigeons were taken out and trained, and the wildest rumours prevailed. Chilenos were openly arrested in the streets and locked up, and I was frankly told that unless we had our passports Will would be imprisoned. He was away and I was alone – away fifty miles off at Estancia Condor initiating machine shearing at the Station. There was no direct mail to him, and if I wanted to telephone or telegraph I would have to do so via Chile, as the lines ran to and from Punta Arenas, and when Chile chose that we should get news of the progress of negotiations she opened the lines, when she didn't choose she closed them. We had no Consul, but the English officials in the Chilean English Bank swore to defend the bank and the English women with their lives. There were a few robberies and I slept every night with an axe, two or three carving knives, and a siren whistle under my pillow, some of my pupils impressing upon me never to open my door at night should a knock come till I knew who was outside and indeed I was thought to be a phenomenal woman to live alone and not be afraid and indeed I wasn't afraid, but I was mightily excited, and terribly anxious for the future. We had weeks of this, every few days bringing news of mobilization of troops first on one side and then on the other. Our hope was that negotiations would go on till snow fell in the Andes, when the passes – there were only two – would be closed, and in the meantime we might get a man-of-war from the Falklands. Remember we were living amongst people only semi-civilized, and among whom three parts were of Indian extraction. I never kept a revolver in the town, though I had one offered me. It is an awful thing to kill a man, and down there unless you kill it is useless shooting, and I wouldn't dare to kill. My husband, too, was considered mad because he did not carry a knife, not even when over the machines at Condor, where he had all nationalities under him and not one but was armed. For many reasons I liked living in Patagonia, but the cold was too severe, not the degree of cold, but the cold combined with the wind. The wind gets in everywhere. I have been three days (on the edge of the Pampa) trying to get the irons hot enough to iron, and burning English coal all the time; and water dropped on the floor in my kitchen froze at once. In the poorer houses the breath formed frost on the blankets, and I have had ice one-eighth of an inch thick day and night on the inside of my bedroom window. As I sat governessing on the Estancia my breath formed frost flowers on the schoolroom window and the thermom. stood at 32 degrees and a shade under. This with a kerosine heater in the room.

After fourteen months of Patagonia we left for B. Aires and in March 1902 left B.A. for Australia via England. On the way over we fell in with a cold spell shortly after leaving Rio. It was perishing; whooping-cough and bronchitis broke out. Billy got bronchitis; the Doctor said it was whooping cough and made me have him on deck, result pleurisy and pneumonia. At the same time Will got whooping cough. I was weak after being in the B.A.

Hospital with an illness caused by the cold of Patagonia and had to nurse single-handed. The cold was intense, with rain, fog and sleet as we neared England. Two or three times every night I had to go from one end of the ship to the other for hot water, feeling my way over the wet dark slippery deck. The marvel is I didn't go overboard in the Bay of Biscay. A few hours before reaching Liverpool Billy passed the crisis. 'He will live – with care' the Doctor said. We came into Liverpool in a drizzling rain and biting wind – too late to draw up to the landing stage, and so had to go off in a tender. Wrapping Billy so that we could keep the air from him I took him out of bed and got a passenger to carry him from the ship to the tender as his father was too weak to hold him. The Doctor came and looked at him. Then he turned to another passenger saying 'He hasn't the ghost of a chance'. The passenger said something. 'He won't live,' reiterated the Doctor. Yet he did and I knew he would. Coming to Liverpool I had written to my brother, Mr J. A. Cameron, to Hy. Lawson and another friend. My brother who was then in London did not get my letter. Lawson got his and wrote for us to come from Liverpool to London as soon as we could saying 'Bed's made, and cot's ready for the little fellow. Come at once, am simply mad for the sight of an Australian face.' Three weeks later we came to London staying ten days. Leaving London we took in marble at, I think Genoa. At Suez we ran on a sandbank and the propellor was broken. It was partly fixed at Aden, but another blade dropping, the divers were set to work at Colombo. From Colombo we crossed the Equator, speed dropping to about seven knots when we turned and went back. Permission to land under the ordinary circumstances being refused to the third-class passengers, we went to Bombay to dry dock. The night we left Colombo the tail of a cyclone struck us. The marble shifted. We had been told we would only take two and a half days to Bombay. We were six. As the wind and the sea went down the rolling of the ship grew heavier and more alarming, indeed some of the passengers tied themselves in order not to be thrown from their seats. Over and over the vessel hung no one knowing which way she would go. One of the chief officers said, 'I believe that had she gone over not a soul would have been saved,' and another speaking to me of the propellor said that in over twenty years he had never seen one in such a condition, and the marvel was that any of us were left alive. On the return to Colombo Henry Lawson joined his family and we found that the first and second class passengers had gone on by a ship of the same line. Arriving in Sydney the first hand to grasp mine as we landed was John Farrell's and then Charlie White of the Bathurst Free Press. Since which it has been a case of going round renewing old friendships . . .

I don't think I'm mercenary, and I recollect that when I was leaving the Ed. Dept. the Bill cutting off the Superannuation was about to be passed, I was advised to apply for 12 months' leave instead of immediately resigning, so that I could claim my refund under the about-to-become-law Act, resigning after I got the money. It is a usual thing I believe from Judges down, that kind of thing, but it doesn't and didn't seem to me honest and I resigned right away – eight years ago come next November.

A girl I met in Sydney – an ex-pupil – told me that owing to my encouragement as a child (in composition) she kept on writing and is now writing a novel; a couple of others kept on writing verse for the same reason. I hope they may be successful and I can certainly say I have always encouraged where I could, both child and adult. And more than one child came to me abjectly untruthful and left me with a pride in himself that kept him from lying.

I write much about Billy and little about Will. But motherhood is the thing that is of the world and for the world, that says 'This have I done and this do I give', but wifehood is the little world apart where none may come in – and so I only write of the outside things. But of Will Lane said: 'He is the best man I ever knew', and Henry Lawson said 'The best mate; the best mate I ever had. No man ever had a better.' And so let me end.
Yours faithfully,

To Dowell O'Reilly

135 Bondi Rd, Bondi
22 October 1912

Dear Mr O'Reilly,
Your card just to hand. I'm not going to say anything, argue anything, think anything, or do anything. You & Mrs Griffiths can talk it out. I happen to have trouble with my heart again – a little hot weather & an extra flight of stairs & the old inflammation

starts newer than ever. Are there any stairs at Mockbells? And where is Angel Place? And can I ask Dr Rosamond Benham to come, too? Her husband's name is Taylor, but she prefers to remain Benham. Does that promise an interesting time for you? And will next Friday do?

By the way I can't afford not to say this: — Mrs Griffiths, Dr Benham & I are three women of some mental capacity. The first two never abated one fraction of their mental activity because of their motherhood. I gave everything up for the child. He was nearly or quite six years old before I allowed myself to write more than letters for fear of in some way robbing him by neglect or want of interest. If I had had a dozen children it wd. have been the same.

Yet my boy is no stronger, better, finer or more intelligent than Mrs Griffiths' children. He may be better balanced than Dr Benham's, but the difference of parentage accounts for that visibly. Dr Benham is the more mother-caring, Mrs Griffiths the more feminine, as women. John Lane coming back to Australia said to a connection who had never seen me 'A nice woman, but mad over the baby'. How does all that work out?

To Nettie Palmer[4]

The Hotel Imperial, Goulburn
29 July 1924

Dear Mrs Palmer,
You will think me anything and everything.

I have waited to write partly for glasses and partly because I had much to say. I have your husband's book[5] and your letters and your request for names to answer. I haven't read the book: for two reasons: one I wanted to get new glasses so that I cd. *really* read it i.e. not only with eyes but with mind; and the other because every time I open it I get stuck on The Hermit.[6] I begin it anywhere and go to the end with the same sense of surprise, the same flash of vision, the same feeling of reality, the same thrust of unknown memory, and the same cry of something familiar,

---

[4] For further information on Nettie Palmer see pages 599-600.
[5] Vance Palmer's, *The World of Men* (1915, London).
[6] 'The Hermit' is the first of the short stories the book contains.

lost and nostalgic, that the first reading gave me, and that Lawson gives me. That last picture comes so startlingly that *I* am *it*: the poised-for-flight: and I feel myself fall off the fence because there the story ends and there are no more words to carry me on in flight. I think it an astonishing thing. The art, and the suppression of any appearance of art, together make it remarkable. It wants for nothing; one can *hear* it; it tells itself with the sound of the things that echo and ache in it. I repeat that it wants for nothing. But if the others are like it, they or some of them will want for tears. Perhaps I should say 'want for falling tears' for tears lie behind this in an ache that cannot out, and yet is full of the bewilderment of life. It is the only thing I class with Lawson and I hope you will not mind me saying that. I put Lawson alone. There is in him the hot tears that no one else can give, that wash out weakness of construction and faults of execution.

I remember when I used to help Lawson in the young years, and long before he wrote sketches and stories. I urged him to write, I was only a girl but I used to say 'when you write, make the characters tell everything, not you.' And here it is. In 'The Hermit' is no author; the created is all. The stage nothing but the story. What a small, simple *little* story it is yet what concentrated years of history and of life lie in it!

There is something of the Russian in those stories – I have just turned two or three pages since I thought I had finished about the book. I think it is in dealing with the vast and forcing it to that which encompasses it, many a novel has in it less than this short story: most in fact.

Will you let me say I liked your husband and say it in my own way? I think I never met anyone more unconsciously sincere, and with so few subterfuges. Reticences, yes; but not the other thing. I would trust him with anything, knowing it would be treated with dignity and justice. And how sensitive!

Your Essay[7] has just been sent me by the 'Penny Post'. Not to notice it but to read, though I think they want my opinion. I have to thank you for putting me into it and in such a kind way. You are right about O'Dowd. Yet there is something in common between him and Vance Palmer, only where the one speaks in a small still voice the other shouts: comes trampling out of the forest, hair in his eyes shouting his discoveries. They both sweep

---

[7] 'Essay on Literature' published in 1924 as *Modern Australasian Literature, 1900-1923*.

a wide field, in your husband's case wider than appears on the surface.

I never told you with what feeling, what affection Henry Lawson spoke of do you mind if I say Vance? He saw in him the recognition of one who knew him as equals know each other: for what they were and are and not shallowly. The words were few and appreciative but the tone of the voice said so much. You know how the voice deepens and the eyes get that interior look, well, that is how Lawson felt. 'The *only one*' he said '*the only one who ever really saw*'. And he told me if ever I saw Vance to tell him what he had said. The years have taken away the words, that one sentence excepted, but not the meaning. He also spoke of his character as a being and as a man, and if I put it into conveying words it would be 'gentle folk'. (It was another instance of how we saw things in the same way.) The word he used was 'gentleman', but it is so abused that in writing it loses the meaning given by the speaker – the meaning of character and capacity as well as of usage . . .

Now I must end and say good bye, and my love to your children. What recollections they will have in years to come! Also remember me to all remembering friends, and believe me. Yours very truly,

The Hotel Imperial, Goulburn
7 November 1924

Dear Mrs Palmer,
I have just laid down Vance's book *The World of Men*.

Three weeks ago I began a chapter of recollections. It deals with people and happenings of over fifty years ago – and later. It cannot be published with real names because some of the children are still alive. I cannot put my name to it because my name would give too many clues. Yet the matter is, in justice to those dead or gone, necessary to be published. I thought, as I wrote it, might I ask Vance to act for me in the matter – there are so pitifully few one can trust; leakage is so usual.

I have just read 'Father and Son', and 'Under which King?'[8] and as soon as I can get the matter typed and in consecutive form,

---

8 Both short stories in *The World of Men*.

if you will, I shall send it to him. I know that it will be safe with both of you. Also I think of giving a m.s. copy with the real names (additional) for the children to keep till later years when it will have a greater value in our history.

I am reading *The World of Men* in miserly fashion. I think it an outstanding book altogether. The pain in it! and not one weak splash of the sentimental in it. I suffer as I read, for I too have seen what he has seen. The young eyes saw, and the old heart aches. Life's curious division! A sort of seedtime and harvest of which we know nothing till half the seed is lost.

I sent you the Goulburn notice of your Essay on Literature. I hope your hair did not stand on end that I quoted all you said about myself. But, for one thing, I wanted it in, and, for another, the people here know my name and because of that they will read what otherwise they wd. pass over, caught by it like a bit of wool on a burr.

If you *possibly can*, get *The House of the Ravens* by Hugo Wast. A translation of the Argentine, or did I tell you before? It is one of the books which an Australian can read, in wonder that another land is so like his own, and from which he can realize how his own land can be romantically written about. It is a book the writer of *The World of Men* should have – and his wife too.

All good wishes – and no need to write in a hurry. Yours sincerely,

The Hotel Imperial, Goulburn
23 December 1924

Dear Mrs Palmer,
If the book is *Cronulla*[9] I read it in serial, and cut out several chapters to send them away. This letter is not an answer to yours. That was written and got heaven only knows where. Some day it will turn up, probably when I am doing answers to corresp. or some such thing. No; this letter is for the purpose of asking Vance to do what I had planned for years to do and now never will do, – with the less regret that I think he can or will. Only keep quiet on the idea or some of the lesser fry will tangle it up with their *booted* (?) feet, or spoil it. The thing is to write an

[9] *Cronulla: A Story of a Station Life*, by Vance Palmer (1924).

Australian stalking chapter – stalking a kangaroo with only one slug in the gun and not too good a sight or none at all on the weapon. A thing in which shadows are real, a tree trunk almost a second sense – where the feet are bare, and a grass blade between the toes a reality. Where the intensity of the hunter is contrasted with the placidity of the sylvan and the sunset-safety of that which does not know it is hunted. The long toil for a gain of a few yards; the sky, the trees, the birds, the herbage; the patience of the wood craft; then the tempest of alarm, speed, flight and pursuit over logs and between trees; hearing still following when sight was lost and then sight again, and recognition of a grey thing still as a statue; and so on and so on. Ever since I was fourteen I have seen that and wanted to write it. But I couldn't and wouldn't touch it with the sacrilegious hands, I will not say of the incapable, but of want of technical knowledge of known things. It has never been done, not as a great thing. America has done it. Scotland has done it. But we haven't. I gave Henry Lawson *one* story of watching the snake ('The Drover's Wife').[10] People thought it *his* mother; it was us and my mother. I have never been *sorry* I gave it and I want Vance do this other, and without fear of making it too long. It is fear makes things short and meagre. All good wishes to you all.

Some one wrote on stalking of a deer in the Highlands. The cocks crowed and the wind blew, the twigs broke and the wind carried scent. I think it ran into three days, wh. is not needed in this one. But it was a noble piece of writing. I read it in Paraguay and never forgot it.

The Worker Newspaper, St Andrew's Place, Sydney
5 January 1926

Dear Mrs Palmer,
Thank you for your remembrance and letter. I had your copy of *The Tilted Cart* ready to send as soon as an errata slip needed was ready. I hope you will like it. I also came across a year-old letter I had written you in reply to one of yours. It reads like a thing without foundation now – an unrelated bubble that has no destination. I wonder do we go off at the end like that, or

---

[10] Part of the fascination of the literature of Mary Gilmore lies in such claims of influence.

face eternity as the unrelated? Bodies relate, touch, tingle, and mourn. But do souls? Our belief in eternity – in life after death – is rooted in our sense of justice. We may doubt revelation but surely justice is eternal and never to be doubted somehow, somewhere, somewhen! and what justice of reparation the world needs.

I hope you will like the notes at the end of the *Tilted Cart*. They are a new lot, no one has done early Church recollections, and these are fact. Some day I hope to do a whole lot of the same, but I must get among the old folk of Brucedale to revive and make them exact. *Daily Tel* got the book one day and within the turning of the press had a third of a col. notice next to the leading article. A most unusual thing! And wasn't I pleased. Although I thought the least important themes were chosen to praise the book. The old station melodrama *I* wd. have chosen, and the other tragic ones. But that's *me* and not *them*.

I was hoping my dear son would have had time to see you at Caloundra on his way back to Cloncurry, but I fear not. He went back on Sunday last and was pressed for time. Today is Tuesday and he will leave Brisbane as soon as he can.

While I think of it – if you have friends going to Detroit, Michigan, U.S.A. my brother is British Consul there, and is always glad to see anyone from Australia. He is regarded as rather a big man by other big men. He is the one who wrote *The Spell of the Bush*[11] (Bookstall series, and still a good seller – for *them* not for him.). . .

I see your two remarkable girls,[12] standing, sitting, walking about. They'll do foundation work for Australia yet. Recollections and biog. probably. Two people to inherit from, which is more than most get. When I get to my next book, I want to make an extract from one of Vance's short stories, when I have the thing in shape I will see you somewhere and talk over the matter.

My kindest wishes for the New Year. You know that Lawson told me that Vance was the only one who saw the inside of his (H's) work? Equality – of work in difference. That sense of pity so few have is in both.

Yours as ever (hoping to see Kathy[13] who is said to be in Sydney)

11 *The Spell of the Bush*, by John Cameron, 1909.
12 Aileen and Helen Palmer.
13 Katharine Susannah Prichard.

The Worker Newspaper, St Andrew's Place, Sydney
3 June 1926

Dear Nettie (my age writes it!)
I am a fool about papers, and if I say I do not know about where
a field of paying papers exists in Sydney do not look on that as
any guide! I sort of sit in my corner with my nose to my pen
and only now and then glance outside; also I promise to go to
see people and never go. So what *can* I know.

Mr Cockerill, the new editor of the 'T' is a live man and is going
to make something of the paper in time. He has a big leeway to
pull up and not yet much room to do it in but he knows what's
what and it might be worth your while to try him with something as a beginning. He asked me for verse, but it has bin
'squeezed out' for weeks and is not yet in. But that need not deter
you. He has re-established the Nature Notes and uses some
sketches and articles for Sat. Billy Moore[14] does work, but not
quite what he had before. Don't know the difference in it, though.
The *SMH* is taking special articles largely for the Sat. issue. Also
verse. The verse is an outrage, most of it. But it gave space to
two of Neilson's, so I have forgiven it. Then there are the weekly
and monthly Journals. The Triad is asking me for matter. But
you know the Triad anyhow. And of course there's the blasted
Bulletin – for it certainly is a blasted tree if ever there was one!
But you know all of this. So of what use am I as a guide to brains?
My use is for charwomen and the like. I forgot 'The Wentworth
Magazine', Miss FitzMaurice Gill is editor. It takes short stories,
articles or verse, but it must be of the 'happy' order. No moods.
I think it pays rather well. Miss Gill asked me for some verse
which I sent according to specification – short and not too
imposing.

I am returning you your Henry Lawson article as Vance may
want it for a reference. It reminds me that in a recent *Mercury*
(London) there was an article on Australia from someone in
Queensland and signed Dinning.[15] I think Vance might follow
that (or you) with something like your brochure on Aust. Literature. St. John Adcocks Anthol has included Angus & R. Aust.

---

[14] William Moore, 1868-1937, art and drama critic for the Melbourne *Herald* and
Sydney *Daily Telegraph*.
[15] 'A Letter from Australia' by Hector Dinning, *London Mercury*, April 1926, pp.
38-41.

writers, 'M' and Zora Cross among them. Today I get a letter from P. Serle asking permission to reprint as *he* is getting out an anthol. to be published by Collins & Co. so England may be waking up, and may take matter denied its place here. There's no doubt about it Australia is at the ice age for writers. I never knew it to be so hard and so much a patron of the worse than mediocre. It suggests to me either bankruptcy or the expectation of war – or a slump in all perceptive power and judgment: editorial I mean.

I like it that Aileen has thought of Swans.[16] The romance of the world is in the swan. It is the lotus among birds. My own mind has always gone out to it, on it, and with it 'Just as the sun like a fiery ball . . . such is the death of every day'. Two very definite pictures not niggard and yet in few words. I think her real work will be prose, though one can never tell what the loosening out of the mind in relation to language and its mastery will do. The instrument counts for quite a lot in poetry.

If you are writing to G. G. McCrae will you give him my best obedience and so make one letter do two pairs of eyes?

Curious how things happen! I have just had a letter from Gertie Lawson acknowledging that her mother intercepted Henry's letters to me. 'There was a letter for you', she said as a child, 'it was in Henry's writing'. 'There was *no* letter', said her mother, and ordered her out of the room. Now I have Gertie's letter of proof. Strange! Yours sincerely (all of you)

129 Phillip Street, Sydney
7 April 1928

Dear Nettie,
With this pen I wrote *Hound of the Road*[17] in the first draft, and I have only just found it again. (This to explain the difference, if any in the script.)

I am sending you by registered post my earliest *collected* writings, some written 41 years ago. Verse and thoughts – and all so young! and yet so much me of today. I did not read it all for somehow I couldn't. The book (MS.) has been packed and stored away for so many years unseen I have forgotten most of what

[16] *The Wild Swan*, Mary Gilmore, (1930).
[17] *Of Hound of the Road*, 1922.

is in it. It may give you the repayment of a paid article on beginnings and beginners.

I said 'Dear Nettie' when I saw your article in the *SMH*[18] this morning. I shall put you and Vance into the preface of my next book. Verse; and I think the typing will be done this month. When the typing is done I shall send the children the m.s. copy, as it is only on newsprint it won't be worth binding or keeping, but it will be of a day's interest, and you can make comparison on the change age and a fountain pen make in the hand-writing of youth and a steel pen.

I like your article very much especially that Monbulk part. The translation of names did not lie with the blacks but with us; and with us in the hard narrow meaning in English by which we branded the aboriginal. I hope you manage to collect a lot of odds and ends, and, however small in 'area', feed them out with generous and adequate English, so that even if you and I and V. should be regarded as a lot of harebrained fools, we shall still have fed the bread of life to the young literary schools that follow us. Monbulk – where the tribes meet in safety – for it is a place of peace! Some people when they see a telegraph pole only see a pole; some see the whole wonder of telegraphy and the land through which it goes. So most people only saw the telegraph pole in the aboriginal and his language. Who was that foolish person cavilled at what you wrote of Hardy?[19] It sounds blasphemous, but to me in his verse Hardy comes nearer to being God than any writer I know. His work however small is that of a Titan – is titanic. Struggle and strain and with it an implacable must and an equally implacable pity that suffers in all that it makes. His prose does not get me as his verse does. Perhaps his canvas is too large for me.

I have a dear delightful little flat that looks over Burdekin House to the North Head and even the ocean. But I am afraid the sea air coming straight at me out of the ocean is knocking me to pieces: I can't sleep. I am praying for cool weather and then I may be better. I should grieve to have to leave it. All good and best wishes to you all –

---

[18] 'Our Once Green Tree' (*Sydney Morning Herald*, 7 April 1928), which was an expression of concern for the preservation of Aboriginal lore.
[19] Thomas Hardy, English novelist.

15 April 1928

Dear Nettie,
There is no need to return any of these things enclosed. You may
have seen them or you may not. The summers increasingly tell
on me, so I have begun to 'divide up' before it is too late; but
all the same it is done with the very cheerful hope that I shall
continue to dodge the scythe in spite of its occasional nearness.
I don't know whether you will welcome being treated as my official assignee or biographer, or whatever it may be; but I am
pouring my other self out to you, because for one thing you have
the capacity of hitting straight what is essential, and of not exag-
gerating either praise or blame. Then, too, you may as I said out
of the forty years (or nearly) collection I lately registered to you
find something to give you a paid article knowing how well! that
it would mean more to me and do more to *make* me when I am
a wispy shade than it would mean, make, or do for you.
    Dorothy Cottrell's book[20] is to appear serially in the Sydney
Mail – in May or June.
    By the way I had a thundering letter in the Brisbane Worker,
4th of April, I was angry when I wrote it or it wd. have much
more bespoken a gentle manner, but the occasion justified me
as I had been accused by a member of my Board, speaking in
an A.W.U. Convention, as a conscriptionist. Me!!! The second
part for my next book (verse) is in the typist's hands, soon I hope
to have it all there.
    Best of wishes and boggins of thanks to you and yours.

29 August 1928

For them Palmers – and their children.
I meant to wire Hurroo! but my husband came down, and my
time had to be his. When he left – half an inch of rain reported
and he just flew, a possibility of grass and sheep being much more
important than a wife! I had such an arrears, and so many things
to see to for him that I am still meeting Apollyon in the way or
whatever is the equivalent of too much work. Dear Nettie, this
has to be an answer to your letter for the time being. I am *not*
Wynken de Worde. You must have forgotten or not received the

[20] *The Singing Gold*, 1928: for further information on Dorothy Cottrell see pages
    659-60.

letter in which I said that I thought it was P. O'Leary.

I have a hat that was Henry Lawson's, would them Palmers like to have it? I have had Vance in mind for it ever since it came into my possession because of what Henry thought of him.

My best love, trimmin's and all,

28 November 1928

Dear Nettie,

I'm nearly dead of MS novels since I wrote up Dorothy Cottrell, but I've got to send you a line somehow. In case you have not seen any of her story I am posting you two *Sydney Mails*, but *this* week's is the one – a bit about a lamb. I wept over the ms. and weep over the print each time I read it. It is so simple and so deep. Well, the Bulletin writes me that they are keeping my article (it is paid for) for Vance's 'Life'. I thought they meant Vance's own life, but at this moment wondered was it Henry Lawson's as I compared them a little.

I am devoured still by other people's affairs, and I am afraid I shall have to go out into the wilderness to escape them – and I starve in the wilderness for want of people. Only as I grow old do I realize how much I have been and am a hungerer for my kind. I swore I would not read another ms. this morning; and just now is gone a working man and his novel is written in an exercise book – script. Oaths seem to be no use to me. But I do so want to get at my own work; I do not grow younger. What a contrast this week between 'Singing Gold' and *Coonardoo*.[21] Get the Mail to see it. The gold so clear and warm, Coonardoo so cold and dirty – for it is dirty this week. And I am so disappointed, the first chapter was so good.

Well my dears, daughters and all, my love to you and a Happy Christmas.

Three parts dead and only one part alive – so tired – Did you see Sept. London Bookman? A good word for me in it – also Vance.

Am sending you Dorothy Cottrell's portrait for the children.

[21] Katharine Susannah Prichard's novel about black/white relationships: Mary Gilmore and Nettie Palmer differed in their appraisals of Dorothy Cottrell and Katharine Susannah Prichard.

16 April 1930

Dear Nettie,
I have just got the Bulletin with the story.²² What a fine man's
beginning, what a clearness of picture, and what values to Australia, inside and out, in the naming of things she possesses! *That*
is what gives individuality to a country. Trout, which they all
write about having read of it, belongs to all the world. So does
salmon (when it isn't in Ireland – and thank God for Ireland in
that individuality) and carp and pike. But who has the parrot-
fish and who the slugs that like 'Like black cucumbers' and who
the rainbow fish and the spotted sea bream but Australia – even
if they feed and live in other waters! Our fish should say 'Australia' as plainly as tarpon say Florida or America. And here they
•are. And what a boy in those 'Bright miraculous mornings' when
the Andes might possibly, as I remember, have poked up over
the horizon in the slow turning over of the world!
    There have been times, and not a few, when I have thought
you gave up too much to your family, and Vance as of, and not
of the group. Now I see your compensation, even if I do not see
your own fruition.
    'Even his loose-hung body seemed to be thinking about the job
in hand' – you see I go back to it! It has the observation which
has become part of the observer's own body and being, which
is so notable here. And it is that absence of being soaked through
with the accessories – the settings of the theme – that has hitherto
made Australian writing so thin. It has not eaten enough in the
subconscious to be able to trawl up a deep sea harvest from itself,
in season or out of season. It has been all on the surface – or too
much on the surface, and broken only by the emotions of the
appetites. The perceptions of the poet, which are the reciprocal
between nature and self, have been too much absent. We have
lived *on* nature and not *in* her. In this story we have the 'in', with
the 'on' as the subsidiary.
    Veronica Mills²³ came yesterday shy as a bird and as full of little
dartings. She is like what she writes, spurting up in unexpected
perceptions and summarizings just when one has begun to think
the field a little thin. What she wants is drilling as to the need
and the way to grasp impression and response and make it

²² *The Passage*, by Vance Palmer, serialised in the *Bulletin*.
²³ A literary protegée of Mary Gilmore's.

thought, and how is she to get that away in the bush, wanting a hand to guide her? . . . [letter incomplete]

8 May 1930

Dear Nettie,

I had nearly written you yesterday but hadn't a moment, and now your letter is here. What a last chapter in *Men are Human!*[24] *I felt stunned by it*, for the work was so quiet throughout that the end comes like the fall of a hillside, that *had* to fall, in a moment of quiet. The story has the relentlessness of *Coonardoo* without its mannerisms, flat passages, and sordidness. What a piece of work! Not an overstress in it, and yet what room for overstresses!

About yourself; not a martyr, of course, but the fictionist put out of sight. Possibly the fictionist might not have been greatly worthwhile – one never knows – but the door was closed; willingly, and with the eyes looking further afield.

Yes, the verse is good: very much like father's verse, not like mother's. Mother's verse puts out a hand, catches a warm little bird and holds it close; father's verse builds a house, and in it you can go from room to room. You might not like the rooms, they may even seem austere and bare, but they are there, and father's books are father's verse extended.

About Hugh McCrae, he thought of a lecture here, but has given up the idea. I suggested one on his contemporaries and showed him that, as he was going away what an opportunity he had for saying all the nasty things he liked! But Hugh has no remembrance of grouches, and also he didn't realize that I was only pretending. I doubt if he would have had a paying audience here – and certainly not on his own publicity work! He is still an infant when it comes to facing the world. I told him when in France to write verse, however bad as French, for the French papers. He said how could he, as French verse was so fixed in its forms. I said his aberrations, being a foreigner's, would be an attraction, for of course however bad his *French*, his poetry would still be there.

For myself, pain is more constant than it used to be. Still I may

---

[24] *Men are Human*, by Vance Palmer (1930).

again renew my youth. One never knows, and I have the first galleys of *The Wild Swan*.[25]

My love to all them Palmers –

I am afraid you are right about V.M.[26] yet with practice the capacity to shape could and perhaps would grow. She thinks you like a warm bird – Now that is funny! I just remembered writing that of your verse! She was afraid you ·vd. be 'haughty' and 'Oh how different she was'!

8 December 1931

Dear Nettie,

I know who Brent of Bin Bin[27] is, but may not tell. It is 'he'; that much I think I can say to you. But do not publish it without B's permission which you may get if he writes to you. I had thought him my brother Jack because of certain family matter in the book and the spelling of Cooma as Coomer, and which I at the time did not think anyone but Jack (or I) could tell in the words (*our words*) used. Then remembered telling a certain person the stories *in* those words, and of Coomer for Cooma. During the winter I was writing this man and called him B. of B – 'Dear B. of B.' I wrote. No denial has come. Equally no affirmation! But affirmation I did not expect. About Vance's books, and your H.B.H.[28] No, I do not want them just now. I am working on two books at once, prose and verse.[29] The verse now only needs final revision or selection; the other is going to the typist, as fast as my tired heart and eyes can get it into readable form. When these are off I am hoping to do no more at such speed. Then I shall see if I cannot do a few special articles on Vance and Nettie Palmer. And by that time, too, the papers may be in a better position to take articles from other than their staffs. But I want to put it on record here if I did not do it before, that I think Vance's 'The way of all men'[30] (? *was* that the name? my brain is like a

---

[25] *The Wild Swan*, Mary Gilmore, (1930).

[26] Veronica Mills.

[27] Another of Mary Gilmore's claims of influence: she was wrong in this instance as Brent of Bin Bin was Miles Franklin – as Nettie Palmer probably guessed.

[28] *Henry Bournes Higgins*, Nettie Palmer's biography of her uncle.

[29] *Old Days, Old Ways* – A Book of Recollections (1934) and *Under the Wilgas* (1932).

[30] *Men are Human*.

perforated sieve just now thanks to work and humidity) an outstanding study. It has all that *Coonardoo* has in it of the permanent, without its inhuman isolation of the main character (as a suffering unit) without its bald and arid areas (they *are* areas, not spots) and with a lovableness given to humanity that makes its men *all* men: they are not bounded by time, period, place or country, and they *are* men not effigies or shadows.

Some day I may ask you to requote this for me to give me my start. Till then I do not want to look at anything of yours or Vance's. I want it to come new and fresh, so that impressions will fountain and not merely flow or even just ooze.

I am to give a young girl, Joan Ryder, a letter to you. She has much in common poetically with Veronica Mills, but is steadier, and younger. She and her people have just gone to Melbourne to live. She and two or three others have been coming to me 'to talk' for the last couple of years. I trim their verse and it goes into the Herald. The whole group is promising – and each one different from the others. They are a very dear and interesting little hatching. So eager, so young, so ready to learn, and so fair, as youth, to look upon. I shall miss my Joan . . .

As to those books I sent – no thanks to me but all to Nettie Palmer. Affectionately and gratefully,

Am posting you a couple of *Tilted Carts* to do what you like with.

To Nettie Palmer

20 September 1932

Dear Nettie,
I am sending Nora Kelly a par from your letter about your Island[31] and Vance's books. The article I wrote on Vance over a year ago, and sent to the Bulletin is still there – somewhere. They promised to return, but it still is not returned.

It is curious to me how hard I worked for *Man Shy*[32] and could not get attention to it, till people used my words, forgetting they were mine. (Not you, of course!) To both you and Mackaness I wrote of it (then in short stories) and begged you

[31] Probably *The Enchanted Island*, Vance Palmer, 1923.
[32] Books of short stories by Frank Dalby Davison.

both to include one in your collections, as they were outstanding, non-localized, and yet Australian. But neither listened. At the F.A.W.[33], before he made a book of them, I declared them to be the beginnings of an era for Australian literature that would mean something to the world and not just the localized . . . Besides talking of it at the F.A.W. and to all sorts of people (for I never let up once I started, in, I think, about 1924) I wrote to Geo Robertson, and also talked to Mr Ritchie and Mr Cousins just as emphatically, and now A. & R. are bringing it out. And for that I thank the Lord that at last Davison and A. & R. have come together.

About my last book *Under the Wilgas*. I knew you were away on some distant horizon up north but did not know where. Good luck for today, and Long Life for tomorrow to Vance's books. But about my own: That *Black Bread of Night* ran away from me, and became before the middle of it, the black bread of night of the street. Themes do that with one sometimes. 'She dwelt Serene' was written at top speed to get another thing taken out of the galley proofs. Its date is 10.5.32. Most of the book was written '30 and '31 and '32. 'The Bull' was written practically at one sitting, and consequently I was never able to alter or reshape it. And the same with 'T.B.' except that in there is an addition (and one can feel it!) to the original stanza of reshaped extended lines, and that is in the first ten lines of the stanza about the 'thunderheads' – the ten were originally six. The first three and the last six had a paunch stuck in the middle of them, and I do not know that it adds to their dignity.

The misprint in the Sonnet 'The Fox Temptation Knoweth' does not worry me as the rhythm carries it, you notice it as an expert. And I have no Thesaurus and never had. My only one *is the crossword puzzle* as a distraction for a tired or spare moment. Once in about a million times it calls to memory a word known in younger years. Then I feel as if heaven opened and the Lord smiled on me. When I went to school at nine or ten the other girls used to say I used words they could not understand. I did! I used 'By my halidome' and 'Peradventure' and 'Verily, Verily' and 'Naithless' and 'scaith' and goodness knows what else.

You mention that re-reading some of the things leads to discovery. That was one of the things Frank Morton used to say.

'The more you read the more you find the work indefinably allusive'. I tell you I treasured that saying. For it is the unobviously allusive that is what I want. I do not *aim* at it. But it seems to come of itself.

That thing on Neilson: In all those on actual people there had to be the *interpretation of the person*, as well the verbal tribute. I think the verse on Parkes is *like* Parkes: neither delicate or feminine: and so on. The Lion Brereton one is I think *like* Lion in some way. Perhaps I am wrong, and merely imagine it. The subconscious is always the dictator in my writing, and I never know to what extent it is the impersonator or the subject to be treated, because (except for trimming afterwards) everything just comes!

A thousand good wish Hellos to you both and thank you for your letter, woman of wide sympathies.

The Labor Daily and also another paper said the Aboriginal verse was not poetry and then quoted 'Weenyah weenyah' in proof of the statement. My innermost soul said 'Gosh!' even if my lips withheld themselves from the utterance of such a word.

16 November 1932

Dear Nettie,
Your enclosed, Jessie Mackay's article on Hubert Church, and what you said, made me feel very sad – and also very glad, for I had written Hubert Church a tribute on some of his work to which he replied, 'Your very kind thoughts of the poem are such as I have never known. A few may like what I write – but they are silent. Fellow craftsmen are too busy to tell me their thoughts. Some are jealous – it is plain you are not.'

I am only allowed to use my eyes, again, a little so must be brief. About *Man Shy*. The actual first time I told you of the stories was in Melbourne when I went there from Goulburn and full of it because I had only that year read it. Then I wrote to you at Caloundra and I think in Melb. though both times may have been Caloundra. In one of the letters – the second? – I put forth a timid feeler about something of my own, and mentioned 'The Grove' in *Hound of the Road* but whether in the first or second letter I forget. One letter you replied to, am not sure about the other.

My eyes, and my general health, troubling me I went first to the Eye man. First examination he said 'Bring me all your wasted glasses and all your specialists' prescripts. so that I can study them.' I took five pairs of glasses I had never been able to use, and about ten prescripts. After a second examination he said 'No worry, no writing, no stooping, no leaning forward. And live all day in the open air.' The third time after examining he sat down in front of me: 'You are a woman and so do not swear; but I am a man and I tell you your eyes are in a *hell* of a condition!' So that's that. As there is still, after various half recoveries, the blasted facial paralysis (you see I *can* swear) I don't know whether to pray for a speedy recovery or a speedy death. Once I would have suffered visible agonies; now I am old and age suffers them in repression. But don't say anything to me about it lest repression 'bust'. Now I must put the pen away . . . All good wishes to you and Vance and the children, word-clothes and other –

19 December 1932

Dear Nettie,
Awhile ago, an hour, ten minutes, I don't know, a boy came. But he brought a book.[34] A book that is all alive, not some darned Professor talking slow, but a woman's quick mind flying from point to point, with a thousand wings fluttering at a time, and picking up that, this becauses it shines, that because it can *be* shined, and putting it all into the fit and living words that such things deserve and so seldom get. It is your book of Essays, and I don't know how I have put it down long enough to write this!

And the quotations! No quotation is drowned in itself; there is just the glittering point; no more, whether from a tear or a diamond, the tip of a gum-leaf or the glint from a bird's wing. What it is to have scholarship, *and what it is to have knowledge* – 'to observe' as you say, 'and be startled by what you see and hear'. My dear I can't tell you how delighted I am with your book. It is the expression of what I knew you had in you and which you had not, or rather had not had time to unloose.

Again and again I notice how important it is for a writer to be a poet – a singer poet, not a blankverser. In it lies that respon-

[34] *Talking It Over*, by Nettie Palmer, (1923).

siveness which enables one to flick with a needlepoint what others take a pitchfork to. (and I leave that 'to' like a stake in a plain to emphasize – more! – to 'specification' what I mean. It dimensions it.)

My dear girl I am rejoicing for my country. We have a background, now, a background is coming forward, we stand in line with the world's pride; we are one with the world – the world from which we have taken and which now can take from us. Funny thing ego, isn't it? Mine seems nailed to a mast.

To Miles Franklin

Kings Cross
15 October 1936

Dear Stella Franklin,
I have not read anything so wise & fine as your *All That Swagger*[35], I would not like to tell you how often it has wrung – not brought but wrung – the tears from my eyes. And tears again are all too scarcely produced in Australian writing. One of the things that has caught me in a whirl-wind is your astounding memory. I do not mean for facts, items, stories, and places, but the impressions of people singly, & in mass, of events. In this week's instalment. 'The Queen would be so pleased with the whelps. – She would invite them to Buckingham Palace' – things like that, for that is only one out of a thousand.

I must stop. There has just come in one of my last two Aunts (by marriage at that) and a girl she adopted, now here on furlough from a missionary station in Manchuria. But you don't know how I have felt about your work for Australia. All the flags in the world are but a circumstance compared with such a work as this. And the living style. 'Oh moi, Oh moi!' I haven't words to say what I would say.

Proud of you, proud for the country that brought you forth, yours very humbly by comparison.

---

[35] *All That Swagger*, by Miles Franklin, (1936): it won the S. H. Prior Memorial Prize.

To Nettie Palmer

20 June 1938

Dear Nettie,
I hope you are quite strong again. Miss Caton came here, and I met her again at Sra. de Baeza's reception. I find that the people who come here do not talk with *power*, they are too routine; so they do not make much stir. However, Sydney has a very able pair in the Consul Gen. for *China* and his wife, and the myriads of China loom larger than Fascism and the Spaniards. Moreover Sydney is very Anglican and that means Papal and Franco. One State Church buttresses another when both have political power. The Church of England as a parallel is Franco. The Church of Scotland, a state church without political power, is Catalonia – is Madrid. The C. of E. has come out for Franco, the C. of Scotland has not. One can fight politics, but politics and Church, where one buttresses another, is another matter. Senor de Baeza tells me he has better news from Paris than from papers here. But I can see that he is weighed down by uncertainty and anxiety. Such nice, such sincere, such high principled people! They have a boy and a girl. The boy is 17 and must go. 'We cannot keep him' his mother said 'when others over there of the same age are fighting!' – He is just a boy, young, and slender and small for his years. 'He is mad to go' said his father. 'We cannot keep him'. But when I last spoke to him of it, and was he still determined to go, his chin quivered as he said yes.

My letter must be short as my eyes do not now stand much. 'Wonderful sight for your age', 'Perfectly healthy eyes' say the specialists, but the glasses are badly made and badly set, and so I have had 10 pairs in two years, only one of which I have worn more than a day. Now I am back on my six years old ones – Love.

14 August 1938

Dear Nettie,
Just came across unposted enclosed. The exclamation on Vance will interest you. Yesterday, I think, or despairingly hope, that I have finished my next book of verse.[36] It is a mixed lot as it

---

[36] *Battlefields*, 1939.

will probably be my last book of verse *seriously* published. Some
of it was written many years ago, one bit yesterday. Not all of
it good, but all of it still a part of my sheaf. The less good wd.
seem better, if it were not for the actually better – or, shall I say,
totally different? I hope you are quite strong again and that Aileen
is still safe and sound. What a fool-governed Empire (unless
Chamberlain is moving secretly and underground) we belong to!
And what a man W. M. Hughes is! What a vision beyond today!

Louis Esson came to see me some weeks ago. He said his
wintering-in-Sydney flat was opposite mine, and, though I told
him to come over any time he liked, nary a sign have I seen of
him. Not even dangerous as it is at Kings Cross, to wave to him.
He told me an astounding thing: – About 1909 I went to Melb.,
and one day in the gardens near me (shabby and deadly poor)
two beautiful girls were standing talking books. Hungry for
intellectual converse, but too shy, three times I tried to muster
up courage to address these radiant beings. At last, as I feared
they were going, I nearly choked with dread of a snub, spoke.
They responded when I gave them my name. They were Hilda
Bull and K.S.P.[37] The result was we all had morning tea
together.

But, imagine my astonishment, when last month Louis spoke
of it, and said how excited the girls were, as I was *the first real
writer they had met*!!! It seems unbelievable. But I can still feel
the choke of blood in my heart as I tried to bring up courage
to speak to *them*. I was so shabby and poor; they were so fresh,
fashionable, and up-to-date. I was wearing what was still my best
dress – the one that had been my best when I went to South
America seven or eight years before.

To return to the world: I don't swear, but all the same what
a God-dam world we are living in. What a fertility of evil there
will be after all these wars! Wheat, rice, and wine will flourish
exceedingly. And we will eat and drink them.

Again I hope you are well and strong with the strength of ten.
My love to Vance and the girls and you –

[37] Katharine Susannah Prichard.

To Miles Franklin

8 July 1939

Dear Miles Franklin,
(With the Stella still shining), I want to congratulate you (&
Dymphna Cusack) on *Pioneers on Parade*.[38] There is not a dull
line in it, & there are some lovely terms of speech. I could only
gallop through it because of my eyes. But 'life' in a book is felt
and 'life' bubbles in it: the first written champagne we have had.
Except that Winifred Birkett's *Three Goats on a Bender*[39] is first,
and that is Sauterne. Some ass in today's 'Sun' vents spleen instead
of writing criticism. But what you will say is 'Let the galled jade
wince', and some of 'em will.

To Katharine Susannah Prichard

17 February 1953

My dear Katharine Prichard
I cannot say how glad I was to see you yesterday, but disturbed
that you looked so frail.
    I don't want to unsay your doctor, but seeing that your heart
could stand Sydney, after Perth, and then the altitude of Canberra, I should say the trouble was not structural (disease) but
a nervous or an exhausted heart – on your appearance the latter. You look bloodless, i.e. without red corpuscles, and want
feeding up. Good ripe tomatoes and oranges and milk by the gal-
lon, and cream from the dairy, if you can take it. Meat, of course,
and not much bread. I have weetbix and cheese and lettuce or
tomatoes, coffee half milk in the morning, no starch at mid-day,
bread, butter, salad or cooked fruit and cream, an egg at night.
The compartmenting gives *rest* to sections of the systems, I think.
But any time I feel like a change I make it. Also, I nearly boil
the spine or back of the neck with hot showers. It brings the blood
to the marrow and nerve centres. Now-a-days it is bi-carb, bis-
muth. Vitamins off and on, and tonics *ditto*. Nothing fixed or

38 *Pioneers on Parade* was written by Miles Franklin and Dymphna Cusack as a
    sesqui-centenary satire: for further information see pages 513-515.
39 *Three Goats on a Bender*, Winifred Birkett, (1934) an entertaining story about
    three women trying to breed goats.

constant to form habit. My trouble is want of sleep. But I just put up with it. I am writing this at 3 a.m. after over an hour of trying to sleep. No good trying. I am writing all this in case there is a hint of something useful to you. I have had 'a heart' all my life (as well as TB in spells since I was seven. Given up by doctors more than once.) I can't go to heights for 30 years and even the up-slope of our flat entrance is often too much of a strain and I have to *stop* or come up *backwards* pretending I am admiring the view – at your age I was nearly dead of TB with, of course the high pulse and worn out heart that went with it. My lesson came in an A. G. Stephens' Bookfellow article – 'Fight on damn it-all' being a sentence in it. I fought on and left the damning to others.

Well, as I said, this is all me. But it might give a hint somewhere that in time would make you look less like a bit of thistledown. You are too white and too thin.

And that is all the lecture for *this* time. Also don't sit writing continuously too long – the body (and the heart) needs movement – for circulation and the brain is too full of tired blood. May your shadow *increase*.

To Nettie Palmer

3 September 1960

Dear Nettie Palmer –
What a kind remembrance you sent me in your second letter. It brought back all the happy astonishment of when the quatrain was sent me.

My first card came from China, and two wonderful cables from Moscow. The first (timed to reach me *on the morning* of my birthday)[40] from the writers, and the other from a society I do not know, but in wh. after saying I had the 'warmest heart and youngest spirit' and my 'human words widely read in our country' they said they were 'celebrating the anniversary' in Moscow Friendship House. What an astonishing thing! If it were K.S.P.[41] it wd. seem natural. But me? I have done so little.

I gave your name and address to Mrs Hazel de Berg, who is

[40] 16 August, 1960: she was 95.
[41] Katharine Susannah Prichard.

doing tape records (now for storage at Canberra) of Australian writers. (She may have done you when she was last in Melbourne.) By great good luck and long search she found a Bernard O'Dowd record and was able to get it. I have had letters from one of Bernard's granddaughters – trying to be a writer, on a farm and with a large family. Trying to write orthodox verse she cripples herself, but now and again, in what she sends me, Bernard breaks through. I had told her to write Bernard not ordinary verse and so find herself. My love to you, Nettie.

Don't forget to see the next *Meanjin* with R.D.F.'s analysis of my verse.[42] I feel broken hearted over the possibility of *Meanjin* coming to an end – Our only magazine of international standing!

Can't Australia stand up on its own feet and save it? And all the years, life – money Christesen put into it, and then to have to give up. It is too cruel – and it is wicked to Australia.

[42] 'Mary Gilmore: Poet and Great Australian' Robert D. Fitzgerald, *Meanjin*, 4, 1960.

'HENRY HANDEL RICHARDSON' (ETHEL RICHARDSON), 1870-1946

Born Ethel Florence Lindesay Richardson, in Melbourne, she went to Leipzig in 1888 to further her musical education; in 1895 she married J. G. Robertson, an academic, and before taking up residence in London in 1903, they lived in Strasbourg where Henry Handel Richardson began to concentrate more on her literary than her musical studies. Although it took some time for her to achieve recognition she is now considered one of Australia's most talented writers (she was nominated for the Nobel Prize in 1932) and is generally best known for her three-volume chronicle, *The Fortunes of Richard Mahony* (1917, 1925, 1929), a perceptive psychological exploration which is characteristic of the author's style. Among the works which helped to establish her reputation are *Maurice Guest* (1908), *The Getting of Wisdom* (1910) and *The Young Cosima* (1939); Henry Handel Richardson wrote one autobiographical account – *Myself When Young* (1948).

A number of biographical and critical studies on her have been published including an early one by Nettie Palmer,[1] *Henry Handel Richardson; A Study*, (1950) and a most recent one by Dorothy Green, *Henry Handel Richardson and Her Fiction* (1986).

The following short story, which can only suggest

---

[1] For further discussion see Nettie Palmer, pp. 599-629.

the extent of Henry Handel Richardson's literary
skill, has been taken from *The End of a Childhood
and Other Stories*, (1934, Heinemann, London).

THE BATHE

A Grotesque

Stripped of her clothing, the child showed the lovely shape of
a six-year-old. Just past the dimpled roundnesses of babyhood,
the little body stood slim and straight, legs and knees closely met,
the skin white as the sand into which the small feet dug, pink
toe faultlessly matched to toe.

She was going to bathe.

The tide was out. The alarming, ferocious surf, which at flood
came hurtling over the reef, swallowing up the beach, had withdrawn, baring the flat brown coral rocks: far off against their
steep brown edges it sucked and gurgled lazily. In retreating, it
had left many lovely pools in the reef, all clear as glass, some
deep as rooms, grown round their sides with weeds that swam
like drowned hair, and hid strange sea-things.

Not to these pools might the child go; nor did she need to prick
her soles on the coral. Her bathing-place was a great sandy-
bottomed pool that ran out from the beach, and at its deepest
came no higher than her chin.

Naked to sun and air, she skipped and frolicked with the delight
of the very young, to whom clothes are still an encumbrance.
And one of her runs led her headlong into the sea. No toe-dipping
tests were necessary here; this water met the skin like a veil of
warm silk. In it she splashed and ducked and floated; her hair,
which had been screwed into a tight little knob, loosening and
floating with her like a nimbus. Tired of play, she came out,
trickling and glistening, and lay down in the sand, which was
hot to the touch, first on her stomach, then on her back, till she
was coated with sand like a fish bread-crumbed for frying. This,
for the sheer pleasure of plunging anew, and letting the silken
water wash her clean.

At the sight, the two middle-aged women who sat looking on
grew restless. And, the prank being repeated, the sand-caked little
body vanishing in the limpid water to bob up shining like ivory,
the tips of their tongues shot out and surreptitiously moistened

their lips. These were dry, their throats were dry, their skins itched; their seats burned from pressing the hot sand.

And suddenly eyes met and brows were lifted in a silent question. Shall we? Dare we risk it?

'Let's!'

For no living thing but themselves moved on the miles of desolate beach; not a neighbour was within cooee; their own shack lay hid behind a hill.

Straightway they fell to rolling up their work and stabbing it with their needles.

Then they, too, undressed.

Tight, high bodices of countless buttons went first, baring the massy arms and fat-creased necks of a plump maturity. Thereafter bunchy skirts were slid over hips and stepped out of. Several petticoats followed, the undermost of red flannel, with scalloped edges. Tight stiff corsets were next squeezed from their moorings and cast aside: the linen beneath lay hot and damply crushed. Long white drawers unbound and, leg by leg, disengaged, voluminous calico chemises appeared, draped in which the pair sat down to take off their boots – buttoned boots – and stockings, their feet emerging red and tired-looking, the toes misshapen, and horny with callosities. Erect again, they yet coyly hesitated before the casting of the last veil, once more sweeping the distance for a possible spy. Nothing stirring, however, up went their arms, dragging the balloon-like garments with them; and, inch by inch, calves, thighs, trunks and breasts were bared to view.

At the prospect of getting water playmates, the child had clapped her hands, hopping up and down where she stood. But this was the first time she had watched a real grown-up undress; she was always in bed and asleep when they did it. Now, in broad daylight, she looked on unrebuked, wildly curious; and surprise soon damped her joy. So this was what was underneath! Skirts and petticoats down, she saw that laps were really legs; while the soft and cosy place you put your head on, when you were tired . . .

And suddenly she turned tail and ran back to the pool. She didn't want to see.

But your face was the one bit of you you couldn't put under water. So she had to.

Two fat, stark-naked figures were coming down the beach. They had joined hands, as if to sustain each other in their nudity . . . or as if, in shedding their clothes, they had also shed a portion of their years. Gingerly, yet in haste to reach cover, they applied their soles to the tickly sand: a haste that caused unwieldy breasts to bob and swing, bellies and buttocks to wobble. Splay-legged they were, from the weight of these protuberances. Above their knees, garters had cut fierce red lines in the skin; their bodies were criss-crossed with red furrows, from the variety of strings and bones that had lashed them in. The calves of one showed purple-knotted with veins; across the other's abdomen ran a deep, longitudinal scar. One was patched with red hair, one with black.

In a kind of horrid fascination the child stood and stared . . . as at two wild outlandish beasts. But before they reached her she again turned, and, heedless of the prickles, ran seawards, out on the reef.

This was forbidden. There were shrill cries of: 'Naughty girl! Come back!'

Draggingly the child obeyed.

They were waiting for her, and, blind to her hurt, took her between them and waded into the water. When this was up to their knees, they stooped to damp napes and crowns, and sluice their arms. Then they played. They splashed water at each other's great backsides; they lay down and, propped on their elbows, let their legs float; or, forming a ring, moved heavily round to the tune of: *Ring-a-ring-a-rosy, pop down a posy!* And down the child went, till she all but sat on the sand. Not so they. Even with the support of the water they could bend but a few inches; and wider than ever did their legs splay, to permit of their corpulences being lowered.

But the sun was nearing meridian in a cloudless sky. Its rays burnt and stung. The child was sent running up the beach to the clothes-heaps, and returned, not unlike a depressed Amor, bearing in each hand a wide, flower-trimmed, dolly-varden hat, the ribbons of which trailed the sand.

These they perched on their heads, binding the ribbons under their chins; and thus attired waded out to the deep end of the pool. Here, where the water came a few inches above their waists, they stood to cool off, their breasts seeming to float on the surface like half-inflated toy balloons. And when the sand stirred up by their feet had subsided, their legs could be seen through the translucent water oddly foreshortened, with edges that frayed at each ripple.

But a line of foam had shown its teeth at the edge of the reef. The tide was on the turn; it was time to go.

Waddling up the beach they spread their petticoats, and on these stretched themselves out to dry. And as they lay there on their sides, with the supreme mass of hip and buttock arching in the air, their contours were those of seals – great mother-seals come lolloping out of the water to lie about on the sand.

The child had found a piece of dry cuttlefish, and sat pretending to play with it. But she wasn't really. Something had happened which made her not like any more to play. Something ugly. Oh, never . . . never . . . no, not ever now did she want to grow up. *She* would always stop a little girl.

ETHEL TURNER, 1872–1958

Known primarily as a children's author (and for her first published work of fiction, *Seven Little Australians*, 1894), she was born Ethel Burwell in Yorkshire, England, and settled in Australia with her widowed mother and two sisters in 1881. She attended Sydney Girls' High School – along with her sister Lilian, another author – and soon became immersed in editing and writing activities on the *Iris* and the *Parthenon* magazines. Later the children's editor of the *Illustrated Sydney News* and the author of more than thirty novels, Ethel Turner was an extraordinarily popular writer for generations of young Australian women.

The following extracts are taken from *The Diaries of Ethel Turner*, compiled by her granddaughter, Philippa Poole (1979, Ure Smith, Sydney) and reveal not just the early literary leanings of the diarist but also give a glimpse of the life of a middle class girl at the end of the nineteenth century in Sydney; there appear to have been more opportunities then than are generally recognised today.

*   *   *

Ethel, aged seventeen, has with her sister Lilian launched a new monthly magazine, the *Parthenon*, which carries commentary, poems, stories, book reviews, and runs competitions.

DIARIES

1889

3rd April   Practised 1 hour, sang 20 minutes. Cleared out boxes and drawers, cartloads of rubbish and old letters, etc. Addressed *Parthenon* wrappers and then in afternoon went to town – Lil bought a new dress, I am penniless. At night tried to write a poem and failed, so instead read and idled.

6th April   Went to Newington Sports. Took cab to the grounds. The Sports were very poor. I walked with Mr Curlewis a little and after with Mr Curnow. We left Annie, then Lil and I hurried off and caught the 5 o'clock train to Picton to stay with the Daintreys.

10th April   Mr Daintrey took us all in a buggy to Douglas Park for a picnic. It was a fearfully long drive but very pleasant there, we went mushroom hunting. Afternoon we went to the Show. It is the first country show I have been to. We had tea on the grounds with the Abbotsford Antills and a lot more people.

24th May   Mr Cope[1] took Lil and me to the opening of the Darlinghurst Skating Rink. It was too crowded to skate but we got our season ticket.

6th June   To-night Lily and I went up to the Christian's and wrote the invitations for our Parthenon Dance and we posted them coming home – we have asked about seventy-five people and have ordered the lemonade, programmes and pencils, etc.

18th June   Busy all day decorating the rooms, waxing the floors, setting the supper tables, making claret cup, etc. We went home to dress at 6 – Lil wore a crepe dress, Annie blue liberty and I my pink and silver dress. I enjoyed the night immensely.

---

[1] Mr Charles Cope – Ethel's step-father.

10th July   Went house-hunting with Mother – Woollahra, Double Bay and Darling Point. Walked quite 10 miles with usual result – loss of time and temper. Went to Annie's for dinner and evening. Mr Lawes and Mr Curlewis[2] came up – the latter would not be so bad if he was not conceited – he talks rather well which is more than most boys do.

20th July   We went to the Darlinghurst rink this afternoon – I skated with C. Osborne, M. Backhouse, and D. Benjamin – no one else there. We got invitations for Felix dance for 7th August. Wrote for *Parthenon* at night. I liked Maurice this afternoon very much and promised to keep him a dance or two.

24th July   Mother and I went to town to Anthony Horderns. I bought a pair of dancing shoes, a fan, a diary and some skates for a prize for *Parthenon* competition. Went to Fresh Food and Ice for lunch –

25th July   Made the drawing room pretty, wrote Aunt Elgitha; corrected proofs, etc. In afternoon Nina Church came up to see us – she is growing really lovely but she is frightfully conceited and drawls dreadfully. Went to dancing lessons, had 2nd and 3rd figures of the Minuet and the Quadrille, Polka and Lancers. Did *Parthenon* work till 12 o'clock. Kate left, I am so sorry. I never liked a servant so well.

26th July   The five of us went to distribute the toys at Prince Alfred Hospital and the Deaf and Dumb Institute. What a lot of dreadful things there are in the world, and how free from them we all are – we oughtn't to be discontented so often.

2nd August   Had a grand clearing out of boxes and drawers and the result is an abnormal state of tidiness exists in my bedroom. Sewed pearl beads on my evening dress, trimmed some

---

[2] H. R. Curlewis later became Ethel's husband.

pretty underclothing and stitched ribbons on my long gloves. Mr McKinney[3] and his little girl came; he said he was sure she had been very careless and took a list of words to see if they were invented. Rex[4] was very ill in the night, we were up with him for a long time. Went to Felix dance at night and came home after the twelfth dance. Lily wore her pink silk, I my white liberty and jonquils, Annie white liberty and hyacinths.

9th August   This morning I made myself a black lace hat. Idled in afternoon. At night went to Articled Clerks dance and wore my white liberty again, this time with crimson flowers and snowdrops. M. Backhouse asked me for a dance and then did not account for it. I shall never notice him again. He was a bit intoxicated last night I think, it is a pity, he might be such a very nice boy. I'm awfully sorry for him.

10th August   Lil, Annie and I slept till 9 am, talked and idled about all the morning. Went to Darlinghurst Rink and I got a spill, the first I've had this year. To-night I tried over a lot of songs, I do wish I could sing.

14th August   We all went to Bondi for a picnic. It was a lovely day but Lil and I had so much writing to do we really ought not to have gone. A second letter came from Mr McKinney requesting us to apologise and pay costs one guinea. Of course we refused to do either so I suppose they will take proceedings.

17th August   Went to University Sports in the afternoon saw and walked with Mr Belbridge, Drummond and Read – saw M. Backhouse and cut him, ditto K. McCrea.

[3] Mr McKinney – the father of one E.M. who had entered a *Parthenon* competition which sought the greatest number of words that could be compiled from the letters of the word 'regulation': E.M. submitted a list of 687 words and the editors, Ethel and Lilian, intimated that many of them were inventions.
[4] Rex, Ethel's stepbrother.

19th August   Lil and I went to town, we are thoroughly tired of the work of the *Parthenon* and quite ready to give it up. I should not at all mind being a governess on a station though I should not like it in Sydney. A third lawyer's letter on the McKinney case came, so we went to Mr William Cope[5] and asked him to defend our case – he is very nice indeed and said he will see to everything. We would rather the case went on; it would be so good for the *Parthenon*. Mother and I went to the editor of *The Bulletin* to see if he would take the *Parthenon* and retain us as writers. He is to let us know. At night wrote the Children's Page and several things till 11 o'clock.

26th August   Wrote hard all the morning at an article for the *Parthenon*, idled this afternoon. It strikes me I *idle* a great deal of time away – I really ought to practise and do lessons. To-night Cope Lethbridge and Sid Mack[6] came and we went to the hall for a rehearsal. Afterwards the boys came home for supper and stayed some time. I think Cope is one of the nicest boys I know.

27th August   This morning I wrote a little and read *Faithful and Unfaithful*. Did some cooking as it was too wet for tennis. Our new servant Phyllis came, thank goodness. To-night after a lot of fuss we got Mr Cope to take us to see *Pepita*, it was simply splendid. I never laughed so heartily in my life.

30th August   Practised a little and did my accounts. Charlie Button came and bought us two lovely bunches of flowers, roses and camellias. I arranged them all and went to Sydney to see solicitors Cope and King as we have had another letter re our libel case. I am afraid we shall be obliged to register the paper. Lil bought the score of *Pepita*, I of *Monte Christo*. At night tried over new music, then read a little French History and went to bed early.

---

[5] Solicitor and brother of Charles Cope, Ethel's stepfather.
[6] Brother of Louie and Amy Mack, two more sisters who were also writers.

2nd September   Copied out E. McKinney's words and went to Dr Rutledge's, he put us in a cab and took us first to the University, then to Professor Scott's. P. Scott said as far as he was concerned many of the words were absurd and he's going to write. He was very nice. Then we went to Cope and King. Mr William Cope came in and although I hated him at first he has such good true eyes that I felt I could trust him with anything and someway I could not help liking him exceedingly.

3rd September   Went for a run in the park before breakfast with Rose.[7] Helped the dressmaker with the Hospital Bazaar dresses. Read and tried to start a new tale but failed dismally. I can't get a single idea for one. To-night Cope Lethbridge came up alone and stayed all evening chatting in his free boyish fashion. He is just the kind of boy I should like for a brother.

4th September   Tried again to write a tale and again could not get in the vein. H. Curlewis wrote a very 'cranky' letter, – I suppose he has found out Socrates in *Stray Shots* is his beloved self and it has made him feel amiable to me. I don't know why he should like me, I always snub him unmercifully.

5th September   Lil and I went to town and bought collars at Farmers. Saw F. Parker and Maurice Backhouse and cut the latter again, – I'm afraid he'll never get over it. At night Lil, Annie and I went to Theatricals at Victoria Barracks – we went with Colonel Spalding's party – saw Arthur Barry who looked as grumpy as usual.

12th September   Went to Hospital Bazaar early this morning and worked hard till 1 o'clock. Flew home, put on uniform, blue serge dress, white apron, cap, etc. and went back. Lord Carrington opened the Exhibition and came and talked to Mother for some time. Business was not very brisk this afternoon. At night it was a little better, then the band played and we had sets of lancers. It looked very nice all the nurses dancing.

---

[7] Rose: Ethel's young sister, four years her junior.

27th September   Went with solicitor to the Supreme Court, it was all so strange; we had the paper registered. Then Lil and I went to see Mr William Cope and he said the same as he always does. I don't like him much now. Then Lil, Mother and I went shopping to David Jones. Bought Rex two suits, etc. a lovely little drawing-room chair, new door mats, stair cloth, liberty silk, etc. etc. At night I corrected proofs and did *Parthenon* work. Lottie our new servant came, she is a bright English girl.

4th October   Lil and I did some shopping at Farmers, I bought a brown parasol for myself and a red one for Rosie. Then we went to Lavender Bay and I had a bathe and Lil watched me but did not get in. I read this afternoon and sent the rest of the *Parthenons*. Played a practical joke on Mr Cope by sending him a letter containing a formal proposal for 'my own hand'.

5th October   Tidied my bedroom, put flowers in the drawing room, etc. Mr Cope came home at 10.30 am, funny about the letter – he thought it was real, I never saw him in such a state. I am sorry now I did it but it was only a joke. He declares he would rather bury me than see me married. It is extremely hot, I read life of Handel, Goethe, etc. this afternoon – did Geography, Latin and French at night.

7th October   Eleanor Addison came and stayed an hour or two, she is our new secretary and we were initiating her. Idled all night and drew up a programme of future lessons to do with Lil. We both have a happy knack of 'making little lists' like the *Mikado*. I think we would like to take pupils to make a little more money each, just three or four. A bad boating accident on the harbour, six or eight drowned.

16th October   Went to Church of England Depot to buy Sunday school prizes. We were there such a long time, from 11.15 am to 3.30 pm. We bought 68 books and spent £5 11 8 with discount off. Then I went down to Bondi for Rex's picnic – he got 16 beautiful presents, the best one was from Dr Barry, a splendidly fitted-up paint box, far too good for a child.

24th October   Went to Sunday School picnic by 9.30 am boat,
I did not like to go in the tram with all the children. Spent quite
a nice day at Chowder, I took my class up the rocks for their
dinner, and stood with Arthur Barry watching the races. They
made me go in the teacher's race and I came in second, about
1 foot behind the winner. I liked Arthur Barry to-day. To-night
Mr Cope, Lil and I went to hear Snazelle. He is very good. Nellie
and Marcia were sitting just behind us. Marcia looked at me and
bowed most sweetly, I looked her full in the face.

25th October   Decided to have the play on October 30th,
wrote out programmes, etc. Tonight Cope Lethbridge and Fred
Belbridge came up for rehearsal, the latter was very nice and took
the part willingly. After all was over we came home for supper
and a chat. I quite liked F. Belbridge, I generally hate him.

27th October   Church this morning. Sunday School – prize-
giving day and flower service. Read *Coming Thro' the Rye*.

29th October   Got a letter from Press Association asking me
to call. I went and the editor Mr Astley was very nice – he said
he liked my style of writing and offered me the position of fashion
writer and warehouse noter (about £60 a year). I refused for I
should not like to go to the places taking notes. He told me to
write him a specimen leader – Women's College Bill.

30th October   Busy cooking and preparing all day. The play
went off splendidly – *Sleeping Beauty*, *Uncle Tom's Cabin*, etc.
Waxworks with A. Barry as showman very good. Baby Show
noisy but fun. Everyone said we acted splendidly, but there was
a very poor attendance, the girls did not sell their tickets.

4th November   Started to make a new dress, a pale blue
zephyr, I'm going to save expense of dressmaker because I want
my money for singing lessons. Had eight replies to my advertisement, I shall learn from Madame Vera, she is an Italian and a

member of Schubert Society. At night played accompaniment for Mr Cope, read parts of *Hamlet*, did a little theory and a little German.

8th November Had my first singing lesson, scales and notes. Mother and Mr Cope went for a little picnic to themselves to Watsons Bay. I had a frightful headache after my lesson. In afternoon idled and read. At night young Charlie Button came up and bought with him a boy Alex Smith, who it seems was exceedingly anxious to be introduced to us. They were here an unconceivably long time.

15th November Singing lesson at 9 am. Had a letter from Gordon and Gotch saying they had been served with a *writ* for us, we shall have to go to court. Bought Boccherini's 'Minuet in A' and went to Edwards Dunlop for Review Books. At night practised a little and wrote a ballade about Xmas bells.

16th November Letter from Mr Astley asking me to go down to see him; he says if I will practise leader writing under his correction, I shall write leaders for him. Read to Rex at night, he has such a bad cough.

18th November Lil and I went to Sydney to Palings and School of Arts. Then to Free Library and looked out the *words* in Webster, unluckily most of them are given, though they are obsolete. I am afraid we are rather in a 'hole'.

23rd November Practised quarter of an hour. Went to Sydney to buy a flower for my new hat and strawberries for dinner. Mother and Mr Cope had a fearful row. He smashed her gold bangle to atoms to aggravate her and there was a terrible piece of work. Heigho – I wonder do all married people have rows. I wouldn't be married for *anything*. Mother and Rex have gone to Barry's for the night. Rex has whooping cough.

27th November   Lord Mayor's Ball. Annie and I went to town to buy flowers, we got maiden hair and roses. We went to the ball with the Caro's in a brougham. I wore my white silk with pink roses and maiden hair, did my hair very high and wore an aigrette in it. I didn't like the ball – I never liked any dance less and I thought I was going to enjoy it so much. I danced four times with H. Curlewis – also I liked fairly C. Lawes, W. Maitland, Mr Nelson, C. Osborne. Mr William Cope, our solicitor was there and looked so nice, he bowed and we bowed and a'that. The Thompsons were there and none of the boys asked us to dance 'cause it seems we've cut them, altogether accidentally as we've nothing to cut them for. Maurice Backhouse was there and put on such a peculiar look each time I saw him. Mrs Roberts introduced me to Miss Harris. She looked so terrified when she had to dance with Lord Carrington.

29th November   Mr Davis, editor of *Hermes* called and I was alone. He says he and Mr Brennan, the other editor, like the parody I wrote for *Hermes* and are going to put it in. In afternoon Mother, Annie and I went to Government House Reception. Lady Carrington had such a funny dress on, a dark silk with pale blue net-like sleeves.

4th December   Lil and I went to Bronte for a bathe. I think I shall take some lessons, I can't swim well and can't dive properly. In afternoon did some cooking. Mother went to a meeting to Naval Home Bazaar and had a long talk with Lady Scott, who she says is very nice and unaffected.

7th December   There was a good review of the *Parthenon* in the *Herald* to-day. The parody I wrote for *Hermes*, 'Altar of Examdomania' was put in this number. Lil and I went to town, did a little shopping. I went to Mr Astley, he is to give me a lot of writing to do. He has engaged me for certain to write the Ladies letter, at a guinea a letter, I am to write some political leaders too, and an Australian story. I'll be a Millionairess soon.

9th December   Mother and Lil went to town. M. paid Penfold for me the old *Iris*[8] debt, he said we had behaved very handsomely and honourably to him. In afternoon I read some Review books. After tea Mother and I went house hunting. At 10 Rex was taken very ill, we had to send for Dr Quaife, Mr Cope was so horrid and scolded poor little Rex. He is *intensely* selfish. I did not undress all night, but Rex got very quickly better.

13th December   Mother and I went to town to Edwards Dunlop to buy prizes; 2 years prizes were for B. Watkin, a handsome gold mounted glove case in red plush with companion; for B. Summerbelle, a nice floral album. Then to Mr Maclardy at *Daily Telegraph* and he has agreed to take the advertisements, subscribers, everything of *Parthenon* for 6 months, we are to do the whole of the writing and have half share of profits.

16th December   Practised one and a half hours. Sang half an hour. Tried to write but could not get 'in the vein'. Mother and Mr Cope's birthday. Mr C. gave her a lovely French bonnet, all lilies of the valley and rosebuds, and seven pairs of kid gloves. M. gave him a boudoir photograph of herself, Lil and I gave him a photo of our dog Rover and Rex, and Mother a parasol.

17th December   Got a letter from Mr Astley, he sent back my leader with a number of notes in the margin – he said it 'showed good capacity for high class leader work'. He didn't use it because it was on the fiscal policy but he asked me to write one for Xmas. I wrote at it all the morning and then *Bobbie* in the afternoon. Copied out leader and *Bobbie* at night till very late.

18th December   Went to Cope and King and saw our barrister Mr G. W. Reid – the brief is an immense one, about twenty huge closely written sheets. He asked us a good many questions. Then shopping, I bought a song, my first, *Only a Year Ago* by Claribel.

---

[8] *Iris*: this was the rival school newspaper edited by Ethel and Lilian while they were still attending Sydney Girls High School.

Afternoon we went house hunting to Glebe. Mother and Mr Cope are still rowing about moving. He is awfully selfish about it.

25th December   Went to church, all the six of us. It was beautifully decorated, it is the first year I have not helped decorate. Everyone wished everyone a Merry Xmas outside the church. In afternoon I read *All Sorts and Conditions of Men* and munched almonds, raisins, figs and biscuits.

31st December   Rose and I went to see a house at Newtown, it is such a nice one. It is in a terrace and the two terraces stand in a big piece of ground with good carriage drive and tennis courts and a lovely ball room. The house has drawing room, dining conservatory and six bedrooms, finished beautifully with tiled hearths, electric bells, etc. etc. In afternoon Mother, Mr Cope, Lil and I went out to see it, they like it very much.

1890

16th January   Lil and I went to town to Cope and King. Mr Gibson is our barrister now and the case will come off immediately.

19th January   Church. Sunday School in afternoon, gave all my girls a little keepsake each, they all seemed sorry I was going and I know I am awfully sorry to leave them all. Church at night, Mr Otley preached a splendid, helpful sermon and afterwards we all went into the Parsonage for an hour.

22nd January   Packing all day. Case did not come off thank goodness. Mother, Rex and I went to new house, it is all so beautifully fresh and well fitted. I put my bedroom in order, decorated the walls with new pictures, stacked *Parthenons* in a cellar, unpacked books, etc.

24th January   My birthday, Mr Cope gave me a nice pair of gloves and Rose a dear little butterfly handkerchief. Case came on, all morning we were waiting about Sydney killing time and at 2.30 pm we went to District Court with Mr Cornish. The upshot of the matter was we lost the case, Fitzhardinge the judge seemed prejudiced against our side the moment the other barrister spoke. The Judge gave a farthing damages against us and both of our costs to pay. I don't know how we shall pay them.

25th January   All the papers were full of the libel case, the *S M Herald* had a column in the law report, a leader and a piece in News of the Day. It is an awful shame that we have lost it, the child undoubtedly cheated. Cope and King sent us two letters, they are not satisfied with the verdict and want to see us . . .

'G. B. LANCASTER' (EDITH LYTTLETON), 1874–1945

Born in Tasmania but a keen and constant traveller, Edith Joan Lyttleton died in England. Her experience of people and places is drawn upon extensively in her thirteen novels, of which three – *A Spur to Smite* (1905), *Jim of the Ranges* (1910) and *Pageant* (1933) – have Australian settings. A contributor to the *Bulletin* and the *Lone Hand* she gained a reputation as a writer of distinction. Her novel *Pageant* (since republished by Penguin, 1985) is held to be her most substantive achievement; a saga of settlement in Tasmania (which drew upon her own family records), it won the Australian Literature Society's Gold Medal.

The following short story has been taken from the *Lone Hand*, June 1, 1909; it helps to suggest something of the independence of the early twentieth century Australian heroine.

WHY MOLLIE WOULDN'T

'If' – she said, very timidly, and looked at him.

'Please,' she said, louder, and still Terence did not hear.

He had pulled his cart in under the bunch of naked willows, where the bite of the air was less; and he was whistling, with his hands thrust deep in his ragged pockets and his feet hammering a tattoo on the cart bottom until the milkcans danced and rattled.

The day was raw with cold. The first touch of sun had drawn the frost from tea-tree and hawthorn hedge and winter-bitten earth, to set it loose in dripping mist on the tussock-spines and the willow-tendrils, and the backs of the shivering horses and the edges of the milkcans. A smell of damp blew up from the swamp across the half-stumped paddocks, and a sickly smell of milk blew out from the creamery door, where a cart was unloading.

Again the girl looked at Terence. Except old Michael Dalgliesh, dragging his cans along the platform, there was no one else in the whole landscape of grey downs and dead timber and lonely winding road. Her lips quivered, and she rubbed her numb hands against them, bringing no relief to either. Then the spirit that was in her small body plucked up courage, and she called:

'Terence!'

Terence ceased his whistling, pulled himself straighter in his seat, and looked at her.

'Was yer speakin'?' he said, distantly.

The girl met his eyes bravely, and there was nothing in either the blue or the grey pair to show that the two had met last as lovers and parted last as strangers.

'I've got my foot caught,' she said. 'I can't get it out, an' my hands are too cold to unlace my boots.'

Terence slid his long, strong body over the wheel easily, tramped across through the slush of the road that held icy roughness below it yet, and peered into the cart.

'Lift yer skirt a bit,' he said, unemotionally.

The girl pulled the poor stuff aside, and Terence's brows drew together. The rotten bottom of the cart had let her foot through to the ankle, and jagged edges were wedged round the soft flesh.

'Didn't I tell yer that there bottom' – he began, bit the words short and swung himself into the cart.

He brought with him a sense of warmth and vitality that called tears to the girl's eyes in a sudden rush. Then she felt his hands about her ankle – firm, quick and tender.

'Ah!' she cried, and caught at his collar with a sob of pain.

'Kip still,' said Terence, roughly.

He thrust his fingers down beside the ankle-bone, breaking away the wood in tiny splinters. The thin stocking was torn and there was blood on the white flesh. He could feel the shudders running through her, and he steeled his heart. She was half-frozen, half-clad, and half-fed; a day's work lay behind her, although the sun was not yet above the hilltops, and another day's work lay ahead of her. Terence knew. He had been on Mostyn's selection daily and nightly in the times when he had helped Mollie Mostyn milk the cows.

He broke away the last splinter and drew the foot out. A trickle of warm blood ran across his fingers. He dropped the foot, rubbed his hand on his trouser-leg, and said:

'Got anythin' ter tie around that there?'

Mollie shook her head. Her face was dead-white, and the pinched pain in it hurt Terence through all his big healthy body. He opened his lips; then pride caught the words before they were said, and twisted them.

'Well, *I* ain't got nothin'. Tear a strip outer yer petticut.'

'M-mother 'd be angry,' said Mollie, strangling a sob.

Terence stood up in the cart and regarded her. She was so soft and small, so young for the work that was bowing her slight body, and so utterly untouchable in the pride before which Terence's own pride was a poor thing.

'Terence!' yelled Michael Dalgliesh, and brought his pony past at a trot. 'Gordon's waiting on yer; back in.'

Terence turned, stooped to catch the trailing rein, and said shortly:

'I'll git yer cans in for yer.'

Mollie caught the reins from him.

'I can do it, thanks. Gordon 'll help me,' she said.

Terence dropped out of the cart without a word, and slouched back to the willows; and Mollie's arms shook as she backed up to the platform.

'He's hatin' me,' she said, under-breath. 'Let him! I'm hatin' him worse. I can allers do things harder 'n he can. I'm hatin' him – dead!'

She did not look at him again until she passed him, turning out to the barren length of road. And then he was hauling at his old mare with cheerful shouting and he did not see her go by; but he knew. And Mollie knew that he knew, and she shivered as she drew the old sack round her knees.

'He ain't the forgivin' sort,' she said. 'An' I ain't. I hate him.'

She beat the old spavined crock with her broken stick, and shook the dripping mist from her hair and eyelashes. But her eyes were dry as her heart and soul and she stared into the barren distance ahead that was no more barren than her life. Terence had once been the sun and the moon and the stars. Now, twilight and a chill wind were left to her only. She pulled round to an unmade, muddy road, bumped up it a half mile, and climbed out to open a couple of hurdles into the paddock. The pain of her ankle sickened her, and for a moment she clung by one lean arm to the gate.

'Terence, Terence!' she said, in half-prayer. Then she straightened. 'I can't give in,' she whispered. 'I won't. He's got to do it; an' I know as he won't – never.'

Far down on the made road she heard the strong trot of a hearted horse and the rattle of wheels. It was Terence going home to breakfast. Mollie set her face like flint, and went on across the rough paddocks to the dirty shanty which she never called 'home.'

Terence was silent at breakfast. The baby crowed at him and beat his hand with a sticky spoon in a playfulness that was the usual forerunner of a rollicking romp. But Terence moved his chair and shovelled up his porridge with no answering laugh in his eyes. The children were shouting for school-books, for slates, for lunches; and the busy mother, with pluck in her heart and tact at her finger-ends, found time to drop a kiss on the baby's head and to stoop to her eldest son.

'Would ye take yer plate near the fire, Terry?' she said. 'It must 'a' bin cold, shorely down to the creamery.'

'I'm all right,' said Terence; and the old man laughed, rubbing the crumbs from his beard.

'A poor peakin' lookin' chap, ain't he, mother? Couldn't make more'n about four o' thet gell o' Mostyn's. I seed her las' night. Gosh, there ain't much ter her but grit. Put her out in a blowin' wind an' yer'd never clap eyes on her agin.'

Carrie tossed her head, speaking with her mouth full.

'That Mrs. Mostyn has a cheek,' she said. 'Comed inter our dam paddick chasin' a hen yest'day. I never saw no hen. I telled her as she was after our hay, an' she called me all the names she could lay her tongue on. But I up an' give her some lip, I tell yer.'

'You hurry, children, or you'll be late,' her mother said. 'An' I won't hev yer talkin' ter Mrs. Mostyn, Carrie. She ain't a nice woman, an' it's the wonner ter me as Mollie Mostyn is the gell she is wi' the mother she's got.'

'I don't think sech great chalks o' Mollie Mostyn,' said Carrie. 'A stuck-up thing that won't never hev no fun wi' the boys. Thinks herself too mighty good, an' she ain't got a second dress, an' her boots jes' brown paper. Got 'em on tick, I s'pose.'

'Shut up!' said Terence, turning on her fiercely. 'You got a tongue like a hedge-knife, you little cat. Allers jaggin' at someb'dy.'

'Shut up yerself!' retorted Carrie, shaking back her red mop of hair. 'Bin givin' you the go, too, I s'pose. She's wantin' a hearl or the Pre-mire or —'

Terence pushed his chair back, sprang up, and went out, slamming the door. Carrie giggled shrilly, and the old man looked at the mother.

'She ain't got her tongue from me, mother,' he said, chuckled into his beard, and followed Terence out to the woodpile.

Terence was making the chips fly from a tough bit of blackbutt. The old man stood to windward, and spoke.

'I told Mollie Mostyn las' night as I'd ast yer ter go over an' give a hand wi' the milkin', times,' he said. 'She's milkin' twenty, an' bringin' 'em in, too. You useter go an' give a hand sometimes, didn't yer?'

Terence swung up his arms, and the red ran to his forehead. In the damp air his breath rose like smoke, and through it he saw dimly the feeding cows in the paddock, the roll of down, and, on horizon, the wizened line of gums that marked Mostyn's selection. Mollie's pinched face with the brave aloof eyes, Mollie's torn boot and stocking, and her bleeding ankle, were pulling the heart out of him. But the stubbornness of his nature would not give way.

'I told her I'd ast yer,' said the old man, scraping his pipe. 'An' she won't hev yer, Terry. Gosh, she can say a lot in a couple o' words. 'I'm not takin' help,' she says, wi' her head up, an' – blime, Terry, but she had me diddled all right. I was fur beggin' her pardon fur offerin' – ow!'

A fat chip caught him on the ear; and Terence flung down the axe, and laughed.

'All right,' he said. 'I'm not goin'. Will you be yokin' up while I'm carryin' this lot inside?'

He tramped by the plough through the length of the grey winter day. The crows calling in the windy trees and the occasional clank of the plough-chains made the only sounds in all the universe, until the children came home from school and brought the cows in, singing, squabbling, casting sticks and lumps of earth at each other as on other days. But just now the noise jagged Terence into unreasoning wrath. He flung down the lines and cursed them in a wide-sweeping condemnation. Carrie's shrill retaliation brought the mother out; and Terence answered sulkily, took the horses to feed, and turned his back on the milking-sheds. Dick went down to the creamery at night, and it was Terence's custom to grub stumps in the dam paddock until the light grew too dim. He gathered up his tools, and swung off down the cow-track with humped shoulders and a clear understanding that the world needed making over again from the beginning.

The dam paddock bounded Mostyn's selection. Terence walked to the fence and stared over. Mostyn's tumble-down shanty was some 500 yards off, and the cowshed was nearer. It had double bails, and in the off one many times Terence had milked eleven cows to Mollie's four. A couple of ducks were paddling in the slush before it, and the keen wind brought to him the dreary flap-flap of clothes drying on the line. That was Mollie's work. So was the bag cover over the broken dog-kennel, and the pitiful patch of garden, and the brown paper pasted squarely on the smashed windows. Terence knew. He drew a sharp breath and looked down the paddock.

The cows were coming slowly; gaunt, wild eyed brutes, halting now and again to drag up some tufty thing that held promise of chewing. There was no hay or winter feed on Mostyn's selection. They turned into the yard and crawled up to the bails. Mollie put up the slip-rails, went to the house for the buckets, and came out again to face Terence. She whitened, and put down the buckets as though the shock alone was too heavy for her to bear. But she did not speak. Terence looked at her – a little dull figure in the midst of a dull day and a duller life. The wind had bitten lips and hands and cheeks to livid blue, and the pain of her ankle had brought dark rims round the grey eyes. She limped badly, and the flutter of her skirt showed scantiness of clothing below. She was poverty and work put into the shape of a young girl: and she saw no future before her but poverty and work.

'Mollie,' said Terence awkwardly. 'I come over ter give yer a hand.'

There had been something of hope in her eyes. It died suddenly, leaving a blank.

'I can't let yer, Terence,' she said.

'There – there ain't nothin' fur yer ter objec' ter in that,' said Terence in swift sharpness.

Mollie pushed back the loose hair under her father's old cap.

'I can't give yer a little, Terence,' she said sadly. 'I made up me mind it'd hev ter be all or nothing'. An' you know why it isn't all.'

Terence kicked at the slush, frowning heavily.

'I ain't goin' to be jawed by no woman,' he said. 'I ain't no worse'n lots o' chaps.'

'You've got ter be better 'fore I'll take yer,' said Mollie Mostyn, standing up straight in her rags.

Terence shot a quick glance at her. There were other girls who would take him, unbargaining. He knew that. But he knew also that he wanted Mollie only.

'I – I was a bit on that night, Mollie, an' the fellers narked me. 'Sides, every feller cusses at folk sometimes; a woman gits used ter it.'

'Not me. I never gits used ter folk cussin' at me, an' I'm never goin' ter. A man what don't respec' a woman an' act civil to her ain't never goin' ter marry me.' She plucked up a fold of her thin patched dress. 'I got ter wear rags that shame me, an' I got ter hev a father an' mother that shame me, but I ain't goin' ter marry a man what'll shame me. I can choose there, an' – I *hev* choosed.'

Her voice fell on the last words, and the two stood, unmoving. A crow was cawing incessantly on one hoarse note by the manure heap, and at the bails a cow was lowing. Mollie stooped and picked up the buckets.

'I got ter git along,' she said. 'It'll be dark early. Good-bye!'

Terence watched her limp across to the shed. His hands were tight shut and his jaw was hard. In some vague fashion he felt that his manhood was being tampered with. What right had Mollie to say what he should or should not do? Who was she to demand that a man should always act civil to her? Would not all the district say that Terence honored her in taking her from a humpy like this, from a mother who was drunken and brutal, and a father who was doing five years in gaol? And Mollie? Mollie said that he had got to be better than the mates he went with in the township before she would take him. He drew a long breath, staring at her. Behind the cowshed a streak of red, like a weal on livid flesh, lay across the dulling sky. The line of wizened gums moaned in the wind. Night was coming – drearily, icily, dumbly, as all the nights had come since Mollie and he had parted.

Mollie locked the roan cow into the bail, drew up a candle-box and settled to the milking. He heard the first tinkle of the stream in the bucket. It was slow and uneven. Mollie's hands were too cold. Such little bits of hands. Something caught him like a grip on his throat. He crossed the yard swiftly, pulled Mollie's head away from the cow's side, and held it close against his shoulder.

'Mollie,' he said, half sternly, 'I love yer. I can't help it — I love yer.'

For a second Mollie clung to him, sobbing. Then she pushed him off.

'No,' she said, 'that won't do. You got ter give more 'n jes' love, Terence. That won't last by itself. You got ter give more.'

Her voice was broken by exhaustion, but she looked at him steadily, and her lips were firm. And Terence looked away towards the roan cow munching her scanty feed, and his face was thunder-black again.

'I ain't askin' too much,' said Mollie, quietly. 'A man what bullies his wife an' cusses at her in front o' folk ain't respectin' her an' he ain't respectin' hisself, neither. I'm goin' ter hev you respectin' us both if ever we git married, Terence.'

The quiver in the voice softened Terence's answer.

'What d' yer want me ter tell yer, then?'

'I told yer before. You got ter give me yer word as you'll think o' me always as somethin' yer loves an' respec's, an' not as one o' yer hosses workin' in the plough. I won't ast yer if yer'll kip yer word. You wouldn't fin' it so hard ter give if yer didn't mean keepin' it.'

Terence got up.

'Ef you're startin' out ter be the boss a'ready,' he said, 'I'm thinkin' I'm well shut on yer. Good-day.'

'Good-day,' said Mollie, steadily.

She bent again to her milking, and Terence crossed the yard and climbed the deadwood fence. Then he stood still, looking back. A sudden flare of angry light from the low sun struck over the old cart, drawn against the fence. The hole in the bottom quivered black through the bit of old sacking tacked over it. Mollie had neither saw nor wood for stouter mending.

In the cow-bail Mollie pressed her head to the rough cow-hair, milking blindly. Life was empty: empty, and dry, and cold, and she herself had thrust Terence, in his strong, vigorous, warm-blooded youth, away from her. And she was so cold . . . . so cold . . . .

And then Terence's arms came round her.

'Mollie,' he said. 'Tell me how yer wants me ter say it. Gosh, old girl, I think you've learned me ter do it, anyways.'

MOLLIE SKINNER, 1876–1955

Born Mary Louisa Skinner in Perth, Western
Australia, she was educated in England and initially
took up journalism on her return to Perth. Later she
trained and worked as a nurse, serving in India in
World War One. Her nursing and literary skills were
combined when in 1918 she published *The Letters of
a V.A.D.*: this work was read by D. H. Lawrence
when he met her in 1922 and, impressed by her
literary ability, he collaborated with Mollie Skinner
in her novel, *A Boy in the Bush* (1924). Their joint
effort enjoyed considerable success although Mollie
Skinner has not always been accorded due credit for
her contribution. Nor has the rest of her writing
received the recognition it deserves. The author of
seven published works of fiction, a book on
midwifery, an autobiography (*The Fifth Sparrow*,
1972), and numerous short stories, much of her
writing remains – regrettably – in manuscript form.

The following short story has been selected from
*West Coast Stories; An anthology edited for the
Western Australian Section of the Fellowship of
Australian Writers* by Henrietta Drake-Brockman
(1959, Angus & Robertson, Sydney). It reveals some
of the interests and aptitudes of the author.

THE WITCH OF WELLAWAY

Sent to take charge of an outback hospital when I was young,
I met the woman Isabella Abdul. She did not in the least look

like a witch, but the little community called her one. Tall and fair, very handsome, with mocking green eyes and an easy carriage, she lived in a little white house on top of the bush-covered hill across the highway from the hospital.

As we were a mile from the township, it was a very lonely place – appallingly lonely for me, for my only companions were a cook and an aged orderly, the only patients, as a rule, old pensioners in the men's ward.

When I had been there a week this Mrs Abdul, dressed up like a doll with cotton gloves and everything, came down to call; and when she knocked on the door, not knowing in the least who she was, I naturally asked her to come in, then found myself staring at a couple of magnificent cockatoos perched on her shoulders.

She appeared to read my thoughts, whistled to the birds and they hopped onto the veranda-rail, eyeing me with malice like little boys deprived of expected afternoon-tea and cake.

It would be a bore to get tea for anyone, I thought – there was no electricity or gas – so I put out the sherry.

'You don't drink wine,' said my visitor. 'Neither do I. Let's put the kettle on and make tea. I can tell you your fortune in the tea-cup.'

What cheek, I thought, lighting the primus, very much annoyed, for it always flared and made me sooty.

'It's you,' she said, as I stood back grasping the pricker ready for emergencies. 'You carry little flames in you that upset it.'

What did she mean? She was turning me into the one to be entertained instead of entertaining, and I resented it. I positively didn't like her. She smelt like a goat and put my clean white uniform in jeopardy.

'I can see you are not interested in having your fortune told,' she was saying, lounging in a chair. 'Perhaps if I give you a dead cert. at long odds for the Cup next Saturday you will be.'

'How can you know of a dead cert. when we are hundreds of miles from the stables?' I inquired, struggling with the pricker and the pump.

'A little bird told me.'

Did she think me a fool? I flounced away to get the tray, passing the birds on the veranda. They were lovely birds, but seemed to mock me, chuckling, 'Pretty Cocky! Cast a spell! Pretty Cocky!'

My dander up, I returned with the tray and made tea, knowing

I must show my visitor that I held pride in my position as next-in-charge to the doctor.

'Damn and blast!' shrieked the cockatoos, till their owner bade them shut up.

'What lovely birds,' I said. 'Corellas, aren't they?'

'Wee jugglers, to me,' she answered laughing, pleased. 'They're more than lovely – they're clever. They fly down and bring me news about the horses, and also herd my Angora goats.'

'So those goats that roam in the bush around the hospital are yours? Are the camels yours too?'

'The camels are my husband's. He runs one of the last teams left in Australia to bring in the wool-clips from far-out stations. He's usually away, as he is now.'

There were some moth-eaten camels wandering in the bush around us, and I answered sarcastically, 'Do your birds herd the camels too?'

She laughed good-naturedly. 'They look after themselves. It's my valuable Angora goats they herd. I milk them and make cheese to send to market, but I also clip them in season and get a splendid price for the hair.'

'That's unusual and interesting. It must keep you busy doing it on your own.'

'I'm not alone. I have the birds to help me.'

'How can birds help you?'

'I see you are sceptical. When we've finished tea it might amuse you to see.'

When we went outside it was such a heavenly afternoon, serene and blue, the sun in the west tipping the wide open space with gold, that I forgot her nonsense. The birds came again to her, kissing and caressing her. I had never seen corellas so near, or so tame. Their upper wings were satiny-white, the lower feathers primrose and under the tail brilliant yellow, the forehead scarlet, neck and breast tipped with red.

Against all this colour the eyes looked out from a ring of the palest blue crinkled skin like the blossom of a wildflower. Every movement they made was graceful and charming; only their dark-blue beaks and claws showed how cruel they could be. They gave no signs of anything but love, however, towards Isabella Abdul, rubbing their cheeks against hers, perkily lifting their crests and nodding as they chattered and cursed amusingly.

Presently she stopped and whistled a tune. They became

agitated, fanned a wing open and shut, cocked their heads at her and stretched their claws, leant towards one another as if in consultation, and flew off. Watching them, their shining white wings beating against the blue, circling and flying higher till lost to sight, I sighed with delight.

'Look on the right,' said Mrs Abdul, 'and you'll see them come down.'

As soon as they came into view I heard the bellwether goat's bell clanking, and presently the mob came tearing along as if the devil were on their heels.

It wasn't the devil; it was the cockatoos on the backs of the leaders. The birds clutched the hair of the goats' heads in those cruel beaks, using claws for stirrups and wings for whips, and rode them up to the little white house on the hill. Then all was still.

My eyes felt as big as saucers as they met those of the woman who had trained these cockatoos, but she merely returned my amazed look with one of triumph, waved good-bye and, saying 'Come up and see me some evening when neither of us is busy,' went after them.

When I spoke of this marvellous sight to the old orderly he shook his head, saying, 'Have naught to do with Isabella Abdul. She's a witch. She knows things she didn't ought ter. There's not a bloke around wouldn't dip her in the trough if their wives'd stand for it. She spells our women, tells 'em tales you wouldn't believe, and skins the cash off 'em.'

'Does she give them tips for the races?'

'She could, but she don't. She gives no one no tips worth nothing. She wins, all right. Our bookie lays off her – or he'd be ruined. How she gets the dope no one knows, for she's got no phone nor nothing, but she never makes a blue.'

'She offered me a tip, but I didn't take it.'

'You was cranky. Did she curse yer 'cos ye wouldn't?'

'She only showed me the birds bringing in the goats.'

One night I asked the old orderly to keep an eye on things as I was going up the hill to return Mrs Abdul's call.

'Gawd!' he exploded. 'It's full moon. She's quite barmy when the moon's up. Better stay home by the fire in the sitting-room and say yer prayers.'

When young and impressionable, such advice from an old wise man has its repercussions. I felt nervous as I plunged into the bush and up the hill, the moonlight casting eerie shadows. Besides,

I didn't like the goats skipping around, or the camels solemnly chewing the cud and looking at me over the shrubs as if they were from another world.

With a sigh of relief I approached the little white house, though the place was lit only by the firelight seen through the uncurtained window. I heard women's voices, but when Mrs Abdul answered the door there was silence and she seemed embarrassed.

However, she said, 'Come in. Come in, but take no notice. I have to go on. Just sit by the fire till it's done.' She drew me to the far side of the room and shoved me in a chair.

Half a dozen women of varying ages, their faces shrouded, sat around while their hostess continued what I had apparently interrupted – an incantation in a queer hoarse voice. The atmosphere grew tense. In my mind a door slammed and I was impotently beating against it, battering, trying to call 'Let me out!' It seemed as if the ceiling were slowly coming down, leaving us all on a quicksand bottom.

Then Isabella pranced from woman to woman and gave each a charm or token – I didn't see what – and finally waved her arms over the table. Finishing her weird performance, she then said a name and one of the women answered, her voice trembling, 'I want to know where my old man hides his cash.'

'I'll tell you, but you must give me one-third of it when you find it. Dip your finger in the blood of the goat on the table.'

The woman who had asked her favour moved to the table where the carcass of a goat, bloody and obscene, was dimly visible in grotesque shadows cast by the flickering fire.

I felt sick and wanted to bolt, but couldn't, and in a mist heard this woman Isabella speak again. 'It's behind the third brick back of the right of the dresser.'

Then she called another name.

Clenched as it were in the throes of some evil power, I sweated, hot and cold in turns, for fear is contagious and these women were filled with fear – an exciting, dreadful, superstitious fear that wiped out reason and decency.

One husband was courting the barmaid, another the hotel cook; Dick was thieving cattle, Harry drinking metho., Tom seducing Ada, Sam writing to a chemist for advice on behalf of Aggie. . . .

No wonder the blokes wanted to dip Isabella Abdul in the trough! I knew a lot as the doctor's confidante, but he didn't know as much as Mrs Abdul, of that I was sure.

Her voice, harsh now and malicious, went on and on. . . . Oh Lord, if only I could get away!

At last the chairs scraped back and weatherbeaten hands passed over money and had a joint of meat put in them – bloody meat, bloody – and then the women went away.

How to get out without an explosion of temper on my part and cackling mockery on the part of Isabella Abdul? I didn't even bother to think, but simply fled into the clear moonlight and clean bush. The cockatoos flew over my head screeching – they must have been released to do it. I didn't care, I only wanted to be free of that witch's kitchen.

Isabella Abdul knew I would say nothing of these happenings. She knew I hadn't the temerity to stir up the hornet's nest since no good could come of it and all be stung. She merely smirked when I met her on the road, but I knew in a strange way she felt respect for my uniform, if none for my person, and she knew I – well, we'll say believed in God.

It may have been this that brought her one dark and stormy night to the hospital when she was in dire trouble.

By some chance I had been reading – by no means a prayer or tract, but that little poem with the strange, almost unfathomable, meaning that begins:

> *Have you heard*
> *That silence when the birds are dead? Yet,*
> *Something pipeth like a bird. . . .*

Did I hear the pipe of a bird? Startled, I looked at the window and there I saw a white face peering in. There is something distracting about a face peering in through a window from the darkness of the night, and I flung open the door without a thought.

The draught blew the lamp out and at the same time a figure pushed past me and shut the door. This naturally made my heart pound like fury, for I was alone in the separate building that contained the hospital sitting-room and kitchen. Then I knew who it was.

The smell of musk and goat and a bird piping, 'Pretty, pretty Cocky!' made me shout, 'What in the name of thunder are you doing down here so late at night, Mrs Abdul?'

'I brought a patient.'

'Where is the patient?'

'Here in my hand.'

The woman was mad! I relit the lamp and my hurricane too. You may be sure I lit them speedily, though I was trembling. Then I saw the little cockatoo lying in her hands, his scarlet head on his white wing.

'Is he hurt, Mrs Abdul?'

'Bella, please, Sister.' She spoke so gently, that I felt ashamed.

'Is his leg or wing broken? Do you want me to put on a splint?'

Her voice broke as she said, 'Nothing is any use. He's dying.'

Just then the gay little bird stood and raised his crest, looking at me with one bright eye. Then he sank down, muttering, 'Curse him, Bella.'

'He seems perky enough, Bella, but only one eye is opened. Open your eyes for me, Cocky. Pretty, pretty Cocky.'

'He has no eye under the closed lid. That half-caste son-of-a-bitch Dan shot him with a catapult.'

'Oh no!' I cried. 'What can we do? Is the poor little bird in pain? Shall we try some eye-drops?'

'It won't hurt him – he feels no pain.'

'Cast a spell,' the bird muttered, fluttering up, his head on one side, fanning his wing and looking lovely.

'His feathers aren't drooping, Bella. Are you sure he won't be all right? We'll give him some brandy-and-water in a spoon and I'll pour you a spot – you are all done in. There's brandy here for patients.'

The bird cackled over the brandy, but fought against the eye-drops. Isabella drained her glass and took another stiff shot. Then she became argumentative. 'He *is* dying. Can't you feel how limp he is? Before his spirit leaves him I must cast the spell. I know he's dying.'

'How do you know?'

'His mate told me. She said "Take him away." She would follow him if she watched him go without her, and if I cast a spell on the murdering bastard in front of her, she'd die of fright.'

'What utter nonsense is running in your head!'

'You are a good woman with pure flames about you. Mediumistic, you are to Cocky, like me. I'll cast the spell here.'

'Mediumistic to a bird! Come off it, Bella. Wrap the little fellow up and take him home to his own nest. I'm sure you can save him with love and care.'

'You think I'm a witch, don't you?'

'I think you have a gift with birds.' She made me impatient, and I wanted to be done with this emotion of pity and helplessness, so I told her off. 'Chuck aside your traffic in spells and nonsense, Bella. Stick to training birds and keeping Angoras – you could make a small fortune with these two things and gain the respect of living men and women. You'll never gain it by this enacting of devilish tricks —'

She cackled with laughter, all her softness gone. Then, taking the bird from my hands again, petted and crooned over it. It raised its head from its snow-white wing and muttered, 'Cast a spell! Cast a spell!'

Looking over its red head as she raised it to her lips, her face went haggard, black circles came round her eyes and mouth, and raising her eyebrows she was like a picture of Satan.

'Look Bella, you'd better go home. It's very late. I can't do anything for you.'

But she wasn't heeding me, only gazing into the darkness beyond the window. Then I heard the sharp taps of hooves on the veranda and a rush of water and made an effort to rise and call the orderly, but I couldn't move. I felt as I had in the house on the hill.

Looking at the bird, I saw that it lay limp and was really dying, and Isabella was muttering, 'Get off those filthy sacks, Dan. . . . Go outside. . . . Now up the outcrop of rocks. . . . Find your catapult – it's where you threw it after you shot my bird . . .' and my mind began to beat the refrain of that poem:

> Our souls sit close and silently within,
> And their own web from their own entrails spin.

I struggled with myself. I declared, 'My soul is my own. Let me go. Let me go.' It was no use. I couldn't move.

Isabella's voice droned on: 'Run . . . Run down the rock. . . . Run. . . . The devil is after you.'

Oh, Lord, let me free, I prayed, and at last the power loosened and I clutched Isabella by the shoulders and shook her, but even when her teeth rattled she went on gargling in that horrible way:

'Fall. . . . Fall on your face. . . .' Then in a different voice she asked, 'Where am I?'

'At the hospital; and you ought to be ashamed of yourself.'

'You shook me! It was dangerous to shake me like that.'

The sounds of rain and the sharp little hooves tapping the veranda had ceased and the bird lay limp in Bella's cupped hands, its scarlet forehead tucked under its satin wing. It was dead.

'Oh, Bella.'

'I've scared you stiff. You *do* think I'm a witch!'

'I hope you don't think you've made an impression on me with this exhibition?' I countered.

'But I did. Sweat's pouring off your face.'

'The room is so close. . . .'

'Is that why you hold your arm over your eyes?'

I could stand no more. I was afraid of her, afraid of the dead bird.

> Have you heard
> That silence when the birds are dead?

The key of the kitchen door turned and a man's footsteps sounded on the stone floor. Then to my infinite relief the old orderly called out, 'I heard them infernal goats on the veranda and put the hose on them. Saw the light and came over, Sister. Is anything wrong?'

'Come round here, Orderly,' I called.

I heard him stamp round, but when he appeared, Isabella Abdul disappeared into the darkness, carrying her little dead bird with her.

Did all those things happen? I thought, when cook woke me with tea next morning.

Everything seemed so normal – the cat purring round her deplorable legs, the dog barking in the yard, the old orderly whistling, trucks passing along the highway; a bath and clean uniform, a run round the old-pensioners' ward and a good breakfast, then the doctor's daily visit, a minor operation and morning-tea with him.

The doctor was just going when a mob of natives appeared round the spur of the hill from their encampment. He called to them to hurry, but they made no haste, the old women giggling as usual, the younger lifting their babies more firmly on their hips.

We watched them with patience till at last a younger gin, not giggling, lugged a lad forward. The boy's thin black legs holding him back made me think of an obstinate foal. He had a cap pulled over half his face, held there with one hand. In his other hand he grasped a catapult.

He made to bolt, but the old orderly knew his man and caught him round the waist.

'What's up with your scamp this morning, Ellie?' the doctor asked the woman who had dragged him forward.

'Him hurtem eye, Doctor. Hurtem in night. Don't know nuffin.'

'Take that cap away from your face, Dan, and let's have a look at the eye.'

The boy remained obstinate and the orderly had to wrench the cap from him. Then, as the doctor raised the eyelid from the bruised socket, we saw that he had no eye.

MARY GRANT BRUCE, 1878–1958

Born in Sale, Victoria, Mary Grant Bruce began her
writing career almost by accident when she went to
Melbourne in 1898 to find work and was asked to
run the children's page of the *Leader*. In this way she
served her literary apprenticeship, graduating as a
fully fledged writer in 1910 with the publication of
her book *A Little Bush Maid*. Although known now
primarily as a children's writer, her fiction was often
considered appropriate for adults at the time and was
reviewed for general audiences overseas. A regular
contributor to the *Age, Lone Hand* and *Woman's
World*, in 1913 she went to England and from that
time continued to travel between Australia, England
and Ireland.

A prolific writer, author of almost forty novels, a
considerable amount of short fiction and countless
journalistic contributions, Mary Grant Bruce's major
claim to fame rested on her best-selling 'Billabong'
series which celebrated the virtues of Australian
pastoral life.

The following extracts have been taken from *The
Peculiar Honeymoon and Other Writings by Mary
Grant Bruce*, edited by Prue McKay (1986, McPhee
Gribble, Melbourne). 'How I Became a Writer' is
illuminating and self explanatory, while 'Overtime for
Wives' was written for the *Age* in 1912, and reveals
some of the values reflected in the author's creation
of the spirited and highly popular Norah of the
Billabong.

HOW I BECAME A WRITER

I was twenty when I left Gippsland to seek my fortune in Melbourne, much against my father's will. There were not many bachelor girls then, and he feared all kinds of disasters for me; but my mother begged that I should have my chance, and so, at last, I went – with a heart full of assorted ambitions, and £5 in my pocket. I had at that time no thought of earning my living by writing – daily teaching was what I sought to obtain, so that I might have my evenings for literary work. But a temporary secretaryship came my way, and, before it ended, the *Leader* asked me to run its Children's Page. The salary was not great – writers were poorly paid in those days – but I saw that I could live on it somehow, and the teaching project vanished for ever – leaving me one deathless memory of a lady who wished me to teach in her school, prepare her eldest daughter for the University o' nights, and 'share our highly-refined home' – and all for £12 a year!

Life became fairly strenuous then, and vastly entertaining. I had a bed-sitting-room in East Melbourne – later on it grew to two rooms and a balcony all of my own – and cooked for myself, after the fashion of women, scrappily; meals never meant much to me, and I have often pilgrimaged along Bridge Road to buy food, returning without any, but with a new pot-plant – the money rarely ran to both. I turned my balcony into a conservatory, and derived huge pleasure from it. I wrote many stories, only to burn them, studied hard in the Public Library (an excellent free club for the penniless writer), and had wonderful evenings at Dr Nield's house, where writers, artists, actors, and all manner of interesting men and women were wont to meet: where I sat meekly in a corner and listened to the talk, that was altogether marvellous to me. To branch out into different forms of writing did not occur to me until one day when I was horribly hard up. A new weekly paper, *The Outpost*, came my way, and, seeing in it that the editor desired paragraphs of local interest, I compounded three or four and took them to him, extremely shaky at the knees. He glanced through them, and remarked, 'We'll take a column like this every week if you can do them!' I emerged from his office feeling a bloated capitalist. That led to para-graphing for other papers, and then to special articles, and I believe I have written for most of the leading papers in Australia. *The*

Outpost and *Table Talk* used to send me to interview celebrities. My first experience was with Nellie Stewart at the Grand Hotel, and I was very nervous. I took a notebook and pencil, because it seemed to me the proper thing to do, and made occasional spasmodic efforts to use them. 'Sweet Nell' was as charming as though the most important paper in Australia were interviewing her, and we had a long talk – but when I began to write up my notes later, the one word I could decipher among my hurried hieroglyphics was 'cabbage', a vegetable to which I do not think either of us had made the slightest allusion. So the interview was written from memory, and I heard that its subject was delighted with it.

What days they were! Some of us founded the Writers' Club – which later merged in the Lyceum – and we had gatherings every Friday. Mrs Cross was our much-loved President, and we numbered most of the women-writers of Melbourne. None of us had much money, but we were a most cheerful band, and often we entertained really interesting visitors from overseas. We had a room near the sky in the Block Arcade, where we brewed our own tea: the lift-boy was always the recipient of the debris of the feast. He looked on us as angels, beneficent but mad, and confided to me once that Friday was the red-letter day of his week. They were merry tea-parties, where we discussed every subject under the sun, but always drifting back to the newspaper talk; that is the most interesting 'shop' talk of all. To think of them brings back many faces, some vanished for ever, some gone to other countries, but all with cheery memories of good-fellowship. I was one of the youngest, and they were all so good to me. They gave a party for me in 1913, when I was leaving for England: another when I came back in 1914: and a third soon after, the day before my marriage – at the close of which one of the cheeriest informed me firmly that 'this free-food business had got to cease!' Indeed, I did not deserve all their kindness.

My connection with the *Leader* led to increasing work in that office, thanks to the interest which the editor, Mr Henry Short, always took in my work . . . I wrote more and more stories that were not burned (possibly some of them deserved that fate), and articles for the *Age* and the *Leader* on every subject that I could handle – women's interests, baby welfare, education, agricultural matters, horse-racing, sea-fishing, sport in a dozen forms, theatrical matters – even politics, in which troubled sea I swam for some time while I edited *The Woman* for the Women's National League. I wrote on closer settlement for the *Pastoralists' Review*, and on cattle for *Dalgety's Review*, while I criticised theatres for one paper, reviewed books for another, wrote racing stories for the *Leader*, and special Saturday articles for women in the *Age*. I remember having a story returned to me by the editor of a Melbourne weekly with the remark that it was 'too depressing – people want to be amused, not saddened. I was young enough to send both the story and the letter to the *Bulletin*, asking was it a fair criticism. To my surprise, the editor answered me privately, in a delightfully caustic little letter, in which he said that he would have kept the story himself but that it was too long for the *Bulletin*, and begged me 'to write of life as I saw its truth, and not to listen to any old granny who wanted sugar-plums for his readers!' It heartened me wonderfully. Curiously enough, that very story was afterwards accepted by the daily paper belonging to the office whose weekly had rejected it.

Meanwhile, my work for children in the *Leader* had led me to write serial stories for their weekly page. Three or four of these had been published and forgotten, when one day Mr Short sent for me.

'I have been talking to the Australian manager of Ward, Lock and Co. about you,' he said. 'Why don't you offer him one of your stories?' He named two or three of my earlier ones.

'Not to publish as a book?' I gasped.

'Why not?' he asked.

It was an altogether new idea to me, and I acted upon it with trembling. But the manager proved to be by no means terrifying. He accepted the exercise-book into which I had pasted a couple of serials, and remarked that he would send them to England; and I regained the street, feeling that no more would be heard of the matter. But a few months brought me an offer from the London firm, with which I hastened to Mr Short.

'It isn't much,' he said, critically. 'But it is a beginning. I should advise you to accept it.' And I did so, still feeling that the whole thing was probably a dream. Print had become a common occurrence to me, but a truly-book was another matter. I did not realise it as a solid fact until I gave my advance-copy of *A Little Bush Maid* to my mother, and saw her face.

The success of my first book created a demand for a sequel, and so began the 'Billabong' series, from which I try to wriggle away, and to which the public and the publishers sternly draw me back. I followed the second one with *Glen Eyre*, of which the *Argus* said, 'It is a book that should be read by every man who wants to know his own country'; and since then it has no longer been necessary to choose between a meal and a pot-plant. The books go on, and people are kind enough to like them – at any rate, they demand new ones, and the old ones sell steadily. The Great War, following a wonder-year in England, interrupted freelance and journalistic work; and babies make writing by no means an easy matter. But still one hopes to go on 'becoming a writer'.

As I look back, it seems to me that I have been extraordinarily lucky. First, and always, in the help of a mother whose sympathy and perfect comprehension never failed; then in early training, and in the possession of good friends. There were hard times, seasons of acute financial stress, much loneliness, and many bitter disappointments; but always there has been the joy of the work – even although one never succeeds in satisfying oneself. And lastly there are the critics, good and bad, who teach one so much. I have had none sterner than my young nephews and neices, and now my sons are beginning to take a hand. One unsolicited testimonial from an unknown young reader ranks high in my collection. She wrote to tell me of her woe when a favourite pony in one of my books was killed. 'I don't know how you could kill Bobs,' she said. 'I cried so hard that the gold stopping in my front tooth fell out!'

OVERTIME FOR WIVES

There is a certain quaintness, from a woman's point of view, in the insistent modern demand for a shorter working day. The daily worker in the cities has long luxuriated in a toiling allowance of eight hours, and celebrates the fact yearly by making solemn procession and oblation, in which festal proceedings his wife takes a due and submissive part. Now that the march of the centuries is bringing still further enlightenment, a Labor conference has passed a resolution in favour of reducing the hours of prescribed work to six; while sundry members of the New South Wales

Legislature have expressed with some definiteness the opinion that four hours of work constitute as much as should be expected in any one day from any one man. While admitting that many Labor members can accomplish sufficient in four hours to keep their constituents ruminating for as many months, the question naturally arises as to where woman comes in.

> *Man works till set of sun,*
> *But woman's work is never done.*

sang some observant sage in days before man had agitated for a curtailment of his toll of labour. But it is not recorded that at any time has Woman seriously demanded a lessening of the impost laid upon her by nature and custom – task mistresses who insist to the full upon the handicap of sex. The progress of civilization brings no change to her position as bearer of the innumerable small burdens of life. Throughout the ages she has worked overtime, and so will probably continue to work; and not even the most excitable trade union worries about it.

The time table of a woman's daily occupations would probably surprise even her husband if she found leisure to record her operations in the domestic field for a week. Hers may be the life of little things; but it is none the less strenuous, and the demands it makes upon her energy and her organizing powers are often out of all proportion to her physical fitness. A mother of a family who is without household aid performs perpetually the task of Sisyphus – a task of which the constant monotony robs her of that sense of achievement which is the finest reward of labour. Moreover, she works with the knowledge that, toil she ever so strenuously, she will not accomplish more than a proportion of the duties that straitly beset her. There will always be things ahead to do, and many of them will always remain ahead, waiting for the day when the housemother shall have a little more time. The pride of work is some recompense. But its quality may be dulled by the incessant conviction of incomplete accomplishment.

It is not to be denied that the man of the house has troubles of his own. His is the constant responsibility for keeping things going, with the fear that untoward circumstance may rob him of his fitness or of his opportunities. But in the majority of cases the actual cares of his wage earning are limited to his hours of labour. He goes to his work in the morning well fed and cared for; he returns in the evening to comfort, rightfully entitled to his meal, his pipe and slippers, his easy chair and paper. He is apt to consider himself aggrieved should the baby be tactless enough to break across his calm with ill-considered wails. He has definitely put aside work until next day.

To the average housemother a restful evening is almost an unknown luxury. The work of her day culminates towards night, when the Man and the children come home to her, to be fed and tended. There are a hundred little services to be performed, a hundred things to remember and to watch for. There are babies of all ages, tired like herself, to be put to bed; nor must she neglect necessary preparations for next day, since she probably realizes the advantage of beginning each morning with a cash balance in hand of over-night achievement. If she be prudent, she realizes the importance of meeting the Man with a smiling face, and of lending an intelligent ear to his conversation – even though that ear be distracted by the sound of Tommy and Gertie in deadly conflict, or of the over-boiling of some cherished preparation on the stove. Should the latter calamity happen, she loses part of her dinner. She has the annoyance and disappointment of wasted work, and she has the consequent task of cleaning the stove. The Man merely loses part of his dinner. Yet it is on the Man's account, and not her own, that she grieves.

That a wife should work overtime is so ordinary a matter that so to phrase her habitual custom would probably excite ribald masculine mirth. Not at all unusual is the type of man who expresses more or less mild amazement at his wife's occupations. He is prone to recall with unction the prodigies performed by his grandmother, remarking, 'I can't think what on earth keeps you busy all day in a little house like this.' No more valuable lesson can be given him than the necessity of carrying on the household work himself, should his wife be suddenly disabled. Without managing to accomplish one-half of her daily routine, he will find himself kept extremely busy, and possibly suffering no small amount of fatigue and anxiety. He will learn how completely the comfort and well-being of the home depend upon the exertions of one pair of hands and one watchful mind, and how much contrivance is needed to make the money he earns cover the multitude of household requirements. Beyond these attainments, he will learn how rare and difficult a thing it is to preserve to the very end of the working day the serenity and cheerfulness that make a house into a home. For man takes the big things of

life, and lets the little, worrying ones go past him; but woman's
very existence is compact of details – none of tremendous import,
but each a thing that must be remembered. To comprehend her
point of view is a very healthful thing for the average man.

It is the lack of comprehension that is apt to make the wife's
overtime a labour of weariness. Work itself is largely a matter
of course to the house-mother, and she would be more than faintly
surprised if some beneficent fairy accomplished for her the multitude of daily chores that make up her existence. She knows that
in no case can she finish her day early. No branch of labour entails
heavier and longer hours than dairy farming, and the men who
make a living with the aid of the cow are loud in their self-pity.
It is 'a dog's life', say the men; and, without doubt, it leaves no
time for any of the softness of existence. But, despite the fact that
it is now almost impossible to obtain men for dairying, the burden
of it lies heaviest upon the women – since the men must be fed
before they begin work in the dawn, the day is never long enough
for its tasks, upon a farm, and long after the men come in at night,
and have settled peacefully to their pipes, the women are still at
work washing up after the evening meal and preparing for the
morning. It is overtime, of course, but a woman's overtime is
not a thing that really matters in the scheme of existence in
farming, or, indeed, in many walks of life. It is only when definite
payment is made for a thing that it assumes importance.

Not that women grumble at male misunderstanding. The
amount of their work and its value are not quantities that they
themselves are wont to estimate in words. They merely continue
to work, for home and children mean to them something that
no man can quite estimate, and sacrifices for home and children
do not count as loss. Nevertheless, the strain is not a little thing,
nor does it ever slacken. It is more wearing than man's work for
its keynote is monotony. Overtime is necessary – there are
branches of work that never begin until the husband has finished
his own day's work; much that cannot be attempted until the
children are out of the way, safely tucked into bed. Physical fitness
or unfitness are details that must to a great extent be disregarded.
Yet, being part of a woman's life contract, work and overtime
are ordinary matters, to be dealt with in a spirit of decent cheerfulness. The ability to maintain this depends largely upon her
wages – and more particularly upon the overtime wages.

The fact that wives are not paid in cash by no means infers

that as labourers they are not worthy of their hire. The payment that really counts with them is not cash, but kindness; the guerdon of unfailing appreciation of their efforts. Rewards more tangible – the little unexpected gift, the thoughtfully planned outing – may be out of the question in cases where income has all that it can do to keep pace with expenditure. But even poverty is no bar to the one thing that makes work worth while and takes the sting out of fatigue or failure. Recognition of what the daily struggle means to a woman, coming from the man for whose sake the struggle is undertaken, makes the hardest task easy; while the wife who works in the knowledge that her husband fails to notice the unselfish service that makes her life, toils under a handicap compared with which all others seem as nothing. The one is a partner – the other a servant; and only in partnership are work and overtime undertaken in the spirit that makes them mere details in the big scheme of existence.

MILES FRANKLIN, 1879-1954 AND DYMPHNA CUSACK, 1902-1981

MILES FRANKLIN ('Brent of Bin Bin')

Born Stella Maria Sarah Miles Franklin near Tumut, New South Wales, she grew up at Brindabella in the Monaro region and in the Goulburn area. From the outset she chose to write under ostensibly male names because she was aware that males enjoy a fairer hearing, an important consideration for an aspiring author. Best known for her first 'outrageous' novel, *My Brilliant Career* (1901) she ventured where earlier Australian women writers had not trod; although Ada Cambridge, 'Tasma', Rosa Praed and Catherine Helen Spence, for example, were all critical of the constraints imposed on women, Miles Franklin went further in the tradition they had shaped when she uncompromisingly demanded women's right to self fulfillment on women's terms. The Australian heroine as represented in *My Brilliant Career* embodies the much-admired qualities of creativity and independence.

Although there were those who were full of praise for the young author, there were critics and commentators who caustically condemned her contribution, and Miles Franklin was distressed at some of the reactions she received; she also had difficulty obtaining publication for the sequel - *All*

That Swagger – which did not appear until 1936 and
was the first publication to come out under her own
name after *My Brilliant Career*. Between the first
novel and the prize-winning *All That Swagger*, Miles
Franklin lived first in Sydney, where she became
involved in the feminist movement, before moving to
the United States in 1905; there she joined Alice
Henry and for nine years edited *Life and Labour*
jointly with her and played an active role in the
women's suffrage and labour movements. During
World War I she travelled to England, served a short
time as a nurse and then took to writing as 'Brent of
Bin Bin' at a desk in the British Museum. In 1932 she
returned to Australia and campaigned consistently for
greater awareness and appreciation of the national
literary heritage. In 1948 she established the Miles
Franklin Award for Australian fiction.

Among her lively literary contributions are *Up The
Country* (1928), *Ten Creeks Run* (1930), *Back to
Bool Bool* (1931), *Old Blastus of Bandicoot* (1932)
and *My Career Goes Bung* (1946). The author of
countless journal articles, reviews, critical pieces and
many plays, Miles Franklin collaborated with
Dymphna Cusack on *Pioneers on Parade* – a sesqui-
centenary satire published in 1939 – and on the
following play (previously unpublished), which
embodies Miles Franklin's commitment to the
acceptance of Australian authors, yet still reveals her
satirical streak.

DYMPHNA CUSACK

Born Ellen Dymphna Cusack in Wyalong, New
South Wales, she is another Australian woman of
politics and passion, whose work has been extraordinarily undervalued. Of working class origin,
disadvantaged by poor health, she nonetheless gained
entry to Sydney University (where she met Florence

James) and taught in New South Wales state schools
until forced to resign by ill health in 1944. From that
time she concentrated on writing (dictating most of
her work) and produced a steady stream of fiction
which skilfully dramatised many of her social and
political concerns – women's rights, workers' rights,
human rights and the peace movement were all
encompassed in her work. Her impressive novels
include *Jungfrau* (1936), a daring exploration of
women's sexuality and autonomy; *Come in Spinner*
(with Florence James), a brilliant chronicle of
women's lives in Sydney during the Second World
War, published in 1951; then *Say No to Death* (1951)
which deals with terminal illness; *The Sun in Exile*
(1955) which is an indictment of racism; *The Half
Burnt Tree* (1969) which raises the issue of the
Vietnam War, and *A Bough in Hell* (1971) which
addresses the problem of alcoholism. Her novels were
staggeringly successful outside Australia; they were
translated into fifteen languages and sold in the
millions in Russia.

Dymphna Cusack was also the author of many
plays: *Pacific Paradise* (published 1963), which deals
with nuclear war, has had many performances
internationally, and *Red Sky at Morning* (1942) was
produced as a film in 1944. The politics, priorities
and praiseworthy achievements of Dymphna Cusack
are reflected in the following play.

'CALL UP YOUR GHOSTS'

'Call Up Your Ghosts' was produced by William Griffiths at the
New Theatre, Melbourne during October, 1945. It was the winner
of the New Theatre's one-act play competition (Melbourne) along
with 'Sailor's Girl' by Ric Throssell. The judges were Nettie Palmer,
Hilda Essen and Keith Macartney.

Dymphna Cusack and Miles Franklin intended the play to
embody some of their experiences and ideas concerning the
situation of Australian writing and writers.

CHARACTERS (In the Order of Their Appearance)
MISS GUMBOOTLE   *Confidential Assistant to Publisher*
G.I. JOE   *An American Visitor*
JOSEPH HENRY   *An Author*
MR. FRIEND   *Head of the Firm*
PROF. EGBERT McCHAUCER   *Dr. of Letters, and distinguished Literary Critic.*
VENTRILOQUIAL GHOSTS   *Operate contrapuntally behind the scenes, preferably from a higher level.*

Time   *During the American occupation*
Place   *Any Australian Capital*
Scene   *A Prosperous book shop*

SCENE	*Section of a large book store. It is closing time. Miss Gumbootle is preparing to leave and is putting finishing touches to her facial make-up. [Enter an American soldier.]*
G.I. JOE	Good evening, Ma'am!
MISS G.	Good evening! Did you want something?
G.I. JOE	Sure! This is a book store isn't it?
MISS G.	Definitely, but we're just closing. Could you come in to-morrow?
G.I. JOE	To-morrow I'll be on my way, and I want to take some books with me.
MISS G.	If you could leave your name and address we could send them after you. [With paper and pencil.]
G.I. JOE	General Issue's the name – you'd better call me Joe.
MISS G.	[Genteelly] I'd rather call you General, thank you.
G.I. JOE	Please yourself, Ma'am, but I want some books . . .
MISS G.	It's frightfully late, but since you're one of our Allies . . .
G.I. JOE	Thought you didn't close till six?
MISS G.	We always close ten minutes in advance of other shops.
G.I. JOE	Is that an old pioneer custom?

MISS G. Not exactly, though of course we have done a
lot of pioneering. We're one of the most
successful publishing firms.
[A faint coo-ee comes from high up as MISS
GUMBOOTLE goes to shelves]

MISS G. [hastily, with frightened glance upwards] Did
you want something American?

G.I. JOE I just come from there.

MISS G. What a pity, when we have such a wonderful
American section: What about China? She's
our ally too.

G.I. JOE I wouldn't hold that against them; but I'm not
needing anything on China.

MISS G. What a pity! There's a glorious new translation
of 'Confucius Say', illustrated by Walt
Disney. So sophisticated!

G.I. JOE Send it to Tojo.

MISS G. [rattles on while indicating titles] We have an
absolutely superb section on Russia – another
gallant ally, you know.

G.I. JOE Sure, I know, but a lot of other guys don't seem
to.

MISS G. Everything from 'Ghengis Khan' to 'White
Russians on the Black Sea'.

G.I. JOE [emphatically] Nope! I'd like . . .

MISS G. Not even 'Revels with Rasputin?'

G.I. JOE Not my line. What I'm aiming to do . . .

MISS G. 'Censorship in the Irish Free State?'

G.I. JOE No go. Can't you gimme . . .

MISS G. [running finger along titles] 'Songs from
Sanskrit', 'Indian Vedas' – interested in India?

G.I. JOE Not at any price. Can't you . . .

MISS G. 'Butterfly Hunting in New Guinea'?

G.I. JOE Sister! The bugs up there are hunting us.
[A long sympathetic coo-ee from above]

MISS G. [increasingly uneasy, prattling on] 'War at any
Price', 'Houses for Heroes', 'Love is
Blind', . . .

G.I. JOE You're telling me!

MISS G. Limited Editions: 'Eskimos – their Diet and
Dentures', 'Icelandic Heat in Summer' . . .

G.I. JOE   I'd rather have a little central heating right here in winter. And say, Sister, I came in here to get . . .

MISS G.   [proudly] All this is the English Section: *'Peace in Someone Else's Time'* . . .

G.I. JOE   Chamberlain.

MISS G.   *'Blood Bone and de Beers'*

G.I. JOE   Churchill.

MISS G.   *'There'll always be a Bank of England'* . . .

GHOST   [MALE; moans] *'Robbery under Arms'* – a grand old classic.

G.I. JOE   [looking up] Who's the guy up there?

MISS G.   [With feigned indifference] Radio, I think . . . *'Post-war Housing in England'*?

G.I. JOE   Got anything on old castles?

MISS G.   [Relieved] Everything. Aren't they romantic!

G.I. JOE   I'm not romantically interested, myself. What I want . . .

GHOST   [a louder male coo-ee]

G.I. JOE   What kinder radio's that, anyway?

MISS G.   Oh, they're just testing . . . Pedigrees or architecture?

G.I. JOE   Ghosts.

GHOST   [MALE; Much louder coo-ee]

MISS G.   [beginning to be rattled] What did you say?

G.I. JOE   Ghosts.

MISS G.   [with mounting agitation] We don't stock ghosts . . . What – er – about fox hunting?

G.I. JOE   I bin living in fox holes . . . and Ma'am, if you could get off this global literary tour I could tell you what I really want . . . I want books about Australia.

MISS G.   What a pity! We can't really recommend them. Will nothing but Australian books do?

G.I. JOE   [firmly] Nothing!

GHOST   [MALE] *'Where is Australia, Singer, where is she?'*

G.I. JOE   Buddy, that's just what I'm asking.

GHOST   [FEMALE] *'Last sea-thing dredged by sailor Time from Space;*

Are you a drift Sargasso, where the West

In halcyon calm rebuilds her fatal nest?'

G.I. JOE   What do you think, Sister! I've bin sent ten thousand miles to fight for a place I never heard of, and now I'm here I can't find out where it is.

MISS G.   What a pity!

G.I. JOE   That's what I think too.

GHOST   [MALE; with excitement] Hooray! Whacko! Whoopee! Good Iron!

G.I. JOE   Say, would you mind putting me on to that guy up there? I kinder like his style.

MISS G.   I'm sorry, but . . . I can't.

G.I. JOE   Why not? Your time's limited. So's mine. Let me and him get together.

MISS G.   It's too incredible.

G.I. JOE   Say, your boss hasn't passed out with the liquor has he?

MISS G.   Oh no! He's not like that.

G.I. JOE   You can trust me, honey. Lots of big shots back home are nuts.

[Laughter from above.]

MISS G.   Oh, I've thought of an Australian book.

G.I. JOE   Honest to God!

MISS G.   Definitely. It was written bang here by one of our own professors, Prof. Egbert McChaucer. He's a Doctor of Literature. He has shares in our business. We've just published it.

G.I. JOE   Shucks! Why didn't you tell me about it before, without wasting my time?

GHOST   [MALE; Emits giant raspberry]

G.I. JOE   What's that?

MISS G.   I-I-I- think it's a vacuum cleaner.

[Enter JOSEPH HENRY, an author, in haste. He is a middle-aged man, respectably dressed, but shabby. He has a mild thoughtful face, now disturbed by worry.]

JOS. HEN.   Thank Heaven, you're still open.

MISS G.   We're not open.

JOS. HEN.   The door's open.

MISS G.   We're just not shut. [tartly] What are you pestering us for this time?

GHOST   [MALE; intones] 'Old Mate! In the gusty old
          weather,
          When our hopes and our troubles were new,
          In the years spent in wearing out leather,
          I found you unselfish and true – '
JOS. HEN. [looks up and raises his hat] Good night, Mate!
G.I. JOE Someone makes you welcome, anyway.
JOS. HEN. Merely ghosts.
G.I. JOE Did you mention ghosts, too?
MISS G.   [desperate to divert him] What do you really
          want at this late hour, Mr. Henry?
JOS. HEN. [distractedly] The Bank! The Bank! That bill
          you're always sending me for three
          presentation copies of 'Life's like That'!
MISS G.   What about it?
JOS. HEN. [Beginning to examine it] I've got it from the
          Bank – posted! I'm disgraced.
MISS G.   We had to do something . . . It's been years
          unpaid.
JOS. HEN. [with dignity] *Six* presentation copies were my
          right. I never got them, so I thought three
          could come out of the profits.
MISS G.   [sharply] There weren't any profits. You can't
          expect *us* to be out of pocket . . . business
          isn't run that way.
JOS. HEN. It was your own fault. You didn't advertise my
          book.
MISS G.   We never advertise Australian books. It's so
          selfconscious. We let people find out for
          themselves.
G.I. JOE I'll say you do! Just like it was nobody's
          business.
          [a lovely coo-ee from above]
MISS G.   Your second book was a dead loss too.
JOS. HEN. But I wrote it to your specifications . . . You
          said a ghost story would sell. You said
          authors would have to write as the publishers
          told them, to compete with America.
G.I. JOE Excuse me, Sir, but you said ghosts again.
JOS. HEN. What of it? 'Fisher's Ghost'.

G.I. JOE	[excited] Say! Are you the author of *Fisher's Ghost*?
JOS. HEN.	I am, but . . .
G.I. JOE	[eagerly] Say, a noospaper guy gave me that book at Leyte. It was blown clear out of my fist just as I got to where the ghost was sitting on the fence . . . Say, have you got another copy?
JOS. HEN.	I bought three for my own use.
MISS G.	You didn't pay for them either.
G.I. JOE	Ain't there any more?
MISS G.	Not now.
G.I. JOE	That sure was a limited edition.
MISS G.	Definitely, because it didn't pay either.
G.I. JOE	Say, how do you writing guys here live?
GHOST	[MALE] 'When you wear a cloudy collar and a shirt that isn't white,
	And you cannot sleep for thinking how you'll reach tomorrow night,
	You may be a man of sorrows and on speaking terms with care
	And as yet be unacquainted with the demon of despair,
	For I rather think that nothing heaps the trouble on your mind
	Like the knowledge that your trousers sadly need a patch behind.'
MISS G.	[almost hysterical] I can't bear it. My nerves won't stand any more. [to author] See what you've done . . . keeping me here till six o'clock!
GHOST	[MALE] Time Gentlemen, please. [books shower down]
G.I. JOE	What happens at six?
MISS G.	You can hear – the ghost.
G.I. JOE	You don't say that guy bawling you out up there's got something to do with a ghost?
MISS G.	[shattered] We b-believe it *is* a ghost.
	[enter MR. FRIEND and PROFESSOR EGBERT McCHAUCER from back of shop]

G.I. JOE   Good evening Sir.

MR. FRIEND   Good evening! . . . Miss Gumbootle, what is this gentleman doing here?

MISS G.   I'm sorry, but he's a customer – General Issue – er

MR. FRIEND   You shouldn't have customers at this hour – er – what did you say the name was – er – General . . .

G.I. JOE   Yes Sir, General Issue, and I hear you gotta ghost.

MR. FRIEND   Damn! Has it started already. My watch must be slow. Professor, your book has delayed us. [crossly, to MISS GUMBOOTLE] What have you been saying about a ghost, Miss Gumbootle?

MISS G.   The General came asking for an Australian book, and you know what that does to the ghost.

G.I. JOE   Primarily, I came for that, but I've heard about the ghost, and now nothing short of a Chicago Pianner gets me outer here.

MR. FRIEND   Dear me, are you interested in ghosts?

G.I. JOE   Listen Mister, they're my life work. I'm a graduate ghost-layer.

MR. FRIEND   [astounded] Have you really laid any ghosts?

G.I. JOE   Not yet. It was a correspondence course. I've bin waitin' an opportunity to demonstrate for donkey's years. Gimme the low-down on the situation here.

PROFESSOR   [myopically peering at volumes on the shelves] Impossible! Mr. Friend and I are due at the dinner for the overseas delegates to the Conference for Boosting Bigger Books.

G.I. JOE   I'm not quitting! No Siree! I haven't won the medal for Pacific Warriors – second class – and what have you, to retreat without what I came for. Where is this ghost located?

MR. FRIEND   This dinner for boosting bigger books is extremely important to the book trade.

G.I. JOE   Listen here! I was all fixed to study English ghosts in their natural habitat, but got

switched to Australia instead. Now I'm going
to study the Australian ghost in his habitat,
and believe you me, I'll lay him.

MR. FRIEND [calming down] That puts a different
complexion on things. I didn't know ghosts
could be laid.

G.I. JOE Sure they can! We laid them in the
correspondence course. I'm rarin' and tootin'
to demonstrate.

MR. FRIEND Right! Come in tomorrow morning.

G.I. JOE Sorry, mister, I only got today here.

MR. FRIEND Then we must consider it now. Sit down,
General.

G.I. JOE Thanks.

MR. FRIEND Miss Gumbootle, lock the door.

PROFESSOR But the dinner! If we don't cash-in on the big
overseas books – our shareholders –

MR. FRIEND This may be more important. [To G.I. JOE] You
don't know what this ghost has cost us . . .
can't work the staff back at night and help
the war effort . . . stock damaged . . . place
getting a peculiar name . . .

PROFESSOR A correspondence course – those minor
American colleges are deficient in
culture – provincial.

G.I. JOE See here, wise guy, it was a genowine registered
college. We studied all the works of Conan
Doyle and Sir Oliver Lodge. We've regular
Oxford guys with letters after their names on
our faculty.

MR. FRIEND If someone could really lay that ghost, Professor
McChaucer . . . and he's a general.

PROFESSOR *PERHAPS!* They're so covered in badges it's
hard to distinguish, and I never can
remember our own.

G.I. JOE Maybe we could make a deal.

MISS G. [cheering up and prattling] We think it's a
ventriloquist.

PROFESSOR [with nose in large volume] An hallucination.
[a book crashes beside the PROFESSOR]

G.I. JOE That's a mighty solid hallucination.

PROFESSOR	Poltergeist.
GHOST	[MALE; mutters] And boozing Bill is fighting D.T.'s in the township of sudden jerk – When they're wanted again in the Dingo Scrub, they'll be there to do the work.
MISS G.	It's so vulgar. It's often drunk. [A shower of books. A volume grazes MR. FRIEND]
MR. FRIEND	One night when I was here alone I was hit by a *Webster's Dictionary – unabridged*.
PROFESSOR	Must have been left on the top shelf.
MR. FRIEND	It came straight from the ceiling.
PROFESSOR	Levitation.
MR. FRIEND	Laid me out till I was found in the morning . . . In hospital for weeks with pleurisy and concussion. Bigger books may be all right for the shareholders, but I don't intend to risk my life again. If anyone could settle that ghost I'd give him shares in the business.
G.I. JOE	That's Oke by me.
MR. FRIEND	You guarantee . . .
G.I. JOE	I can't rightly guarantee. I guess there's gotta be morality and uplift in this ghost-laying proposition, or it don't work.
PROFESSOR	I expected a lack of ratiocination. No rationalist would . . .
MR. FRIEND	Ghosts aren't rational. Let the General explain.
G.I. JOE	Well, in this correspondence course it lays down that ghosts are in two classes – the evil and the good – but they both gotta work it outer their systems. If the poor devils are working out some crime they done, you can sometimes set 'em at rest by prayers, and by assuring them of Christian forgiveness. Jolly them along a bit with this 'love-thy-neighbour-as-thyself' stunt. Then there's the other kind that tries to turn us from our sins here. Like all religious uplifters they enjoy doing good to others. It ain't kind to restrain 'em. That kind better be left going right on clearing up one condition after the other.

	They come in the category of 'help from beyond the veil'. Now in what category is your supernatural visitor here?
MR. FRIEND	Hang it all, you're the one to find out. And now's the time.
G.I. JOE	Oke; [looking up] who are you? Tell us what's on your mind, Buddy.
GHOST	[MALE; declaims] This is Australia, this is the wide continent that holds the gate of the world for men and warmth against icy immensity of emptiness cold night and great darkness – of southern seas.
G.I. JOE	Sounds like a lay-out of facts . . . Go on, Buddy.
GHOST	[FEMALE] Only by heartbreak shall we hold her, by bloodshed's high unhappy fame, who've starved her spirit, wrecked and sold her beauty for wealth, and scorned her name.
	She must be bitterly won and cherished, The loved-too-lightly, exploited land, and the blameless hearts with the guilty perished a monument to our sin shall stand.
G.I. JOE	I can't figure it out. Sounds like they're denouncing sin, only they're kind of literrrary.
MISS G.	As far as we can make out, it seems to be the ghost of Australian literature, and it's *so* bad for business.
G.I. JOE	[with face up] Buddy, I'm sure aching to meet you.
MISS G.	You'd better not encourage him if you're going to lay him out: he can be very violent.
G.I. JOE	Wait a minute! He seems the guy I bin looking for. Laying him mightn't be the right technology.
GHOST	Out on the wastes of the Never Never – That's where the dead men lie! There where the heat waves dance for ever – That's where the dead men lie!

G.I. JOE	I know exactly how you feel . . . I know where they lie . . . but where the heck do the books about this country lie?
GHOST	Where the bleaching bones of a white man lie by his mouldering swag out back.
JOS. HEN.	That's right, ain't it? Sounds more like a dinkum Aussie.
MR. FRIEND	This doesn't sound like curing the trouble. How do I know you're not some Gestapo agent working a secret code, wearing a general's uniform as a disguise?
G.I. JOE	See here, Sir, am I demonstrating, or are you?
MR. FRIEND	[murmurs] You are, I suppose, but I don't understand.
G.I. JOE	Lemme explain. You gotta make your diagnosis. In some cases if you don't want to be given the run-around, you gotta begin with a jam session, specially if it's a dame . . . you can't give me Australian books, just let me consult this guy . . . I wasn't wantin' something for nothing . . . Don't you want any trade in indigenous books?
PROFESSOR	If an Australian book will end this ridiculous farce, I shall give him my advance copy that we have for the book boosting delegates.
MISS G.	Do you think you ought, Professor McChaucer? [PROFESSOR hands book to G.I. JOE]
G.I. JOE	Now you're talking!
PROFESSOR	[graciously] I'll autograph it for you.
G.I. JOE	[Shakes PROFFESSOR's hand enthusiastically] That's swell, Professor!
MR. FRIEND	That's the kind of publication to put Australia on the map. Universal subject.
GHOST	[MALE] If ever it were time for the dead to ride Then surely that time is now: From the Leeuwin's cliffs to the roar of Sydney-side, From Wyndham to the Howe. [PROFESSOR McCHAUCER and MISS GUMBOOTLE both rush in attempting to drown the ghost]
PROFESSOR	I – er – er –

MISS G.   [gushing] Bound in the duckiest blue morocco.

JOS. HEN.   [sourly] What about war-time restrictions?

MISS G.   We got a special licence for a world masterpiece like this.

[G.I. JOE has been turning the book over in growing bewilderment. He reads the title slowly.]

G.I. JOE   Professor Egbert McChaucer, D.Litt. *The Inflooence of Shakespeare's Second-best Bed on the Merry Wives of Windsor.* [whistling] Whew-w! Do I get that right?

PROFESSOR   [beams] Quite! I spent seventeen years in research on it.

G.I. JOE   Take in the Bahamas?

GHOST   [MALE] 'The world is narrow and ways are short
and our lives are dull and slow
for little is now where the crowds resort
and less where the wanderers go'

G.I. JOE   [shaking book at PROFESSOR] See here, wise guy. I'll pin your ears back if you put anything over me. I want Australian books about Australian guys and dames, like those riding on the trams in Brisbane and Melbourne. The folks that go to the beaches, and ride in the surf, and eat mutton in the joints around town, and go to the race tracks. I want to read about your sheep, and gum trees; and this *bush* I'm everlasting hearing about.

GHOST   [MALE] Did you see the bush below you,
sweeping darkly to the range;
All unchanged and all unchanging, yet so very old and strange,
Did you hear the bush a-calling when your heart was young and bold,
I'm the mother-bush that nursed you! Come to me when you are old.

MISS G.   [genteelly] We're trying to get the bush and the gum-trees out of our literature. So crude, don't you think, Professor McChaucer?

MR. FRIEND   And there isn't any Australian literature yet. It doesn't pay.

G.I. JOE   See here, how can you take the gum-tree out of it, if there's no literature to take it out of? Ghost, you tell me.

GHOST   [MALE; intoning] Gordon, Kendall, Lawson, Furphy.

GHOST   [FEMALE; intoning] Paterson, Steele Rudd, Louis Esson, G. B. Lancaster.

G.I. JOE   Who are those guys?

JOS. HEN.   Our dead writers: our Australian classics.

GHOST   [MALE; hiccoughing] Ned Kelly. Alcheringa. *Robbery Under Arms* – grandest old classic of 'em all.

PROFESSOR   The names are familiar to me of course, but I'm not really interested in anything later than the seventeenth century.

G.I. JOE   [looking up] Brother, you may be dead, but you're a durn sight liver than this college guy.

MISS G.   [propitiatingly] Oh, yes, when I was in your class at the Uni, Professor McChaucer, we were all thrilled to tatters when you read Burns and Villon. The tears used to stream down your cheeks, you felt them so deeply. We used to take a lot of hankies to be ready to cry with you . . . After that this Australian stuff always seems crude.

G.I. JOE   Madam, life's like that.

MR. FRIEND   Not a best-seller among that local lot either.

G.I. JOE   [turning to Joseph Henry] Where are your young writing guys, Buddy?

GHOST   [MALE] We have grown weary young. We have lost touch
With the old stories and the old delight.
The wine of life has cloyed our tongue too much
and water lost its sweetness though we break with swords
a great oppression and a greater wrong,
stumbling along uncertain paths towards
A time when laws are just and peace is strong –

Though we give freedom to the race of men,
Yet who shall give us back ourselves again?

G.I. JOE Buddy, you're asking.

PROFESSOR [peering at watch] It's very late, and I have to make the opening address at the dinner.

MR. FRIEND We must get away. You can work on your own. Miss Gumbootle and the watchman can take care of you.

MISS G. Really, Mr. Friend, I couldn't stay here . . .

G.I. JOE I ain't satisfied. Gimme a copy of this author guy's ghost book to begin with.

MR. FRIEND It was a failure. Waste of paper.

JOS. HEN. Remember I wrote it to your specifications, and I kept to the facts.

MR. FRIEND Facts – in a ghost yarn!

JOS. HEN. I have a reputation to uphold. My novel *'Life's like That'* . . .

MR. FRIEND You've been nagging about that novel for ten years. My father was in his dotage when he took it.

JOS. HEN. The London *Times* said . . .

MR. FRIEND The London *'Times'*!

JOS. HEN. [persisting] They called it a classic.

MR. FRIEND *Classic*! The wrong kind of boost . . . What did I make out of it?

JOS. HEN. I don't know.

MR. FRIEND What did you make out of it?

JOS. HEN. Nothing.

MR. FRIEND Exactly! Can't afford to waste paper on Australian classics – full of bullockies and bolshies.

JOS. HEN. Bolshevicks weren't invented then.

MR. FRIEND Never mind. They were always Leftists.

GHOST The large flat foot of privilege.

MR. FRIEND [shaking foot at ceiling] He's a Bolshie too . . . That book's no good to me or you.

JOS. HEN. I didn't write it for you, my friend, nor for myself. I wrote it for Australia.

GHOST For Australia! Australia or nothing!

PROFESSOR We must go.

G.I. JOE Not so fast! Boosting Bigger Books' no good to

	me, brother, not till I get what I want . . . step lively!
PROFESSOR	This is outrageous!
G.I. JOE	You're telling me! Say, ain't you guys ever heard of publicity? I come to an Australian book store in an Australian burg and there's not a goddamned Australian book in the whole dump.
MR. FRIEND	You listen to me for a minute . . . You've been swallowing a lot of red propaganda about Australian books. Let me tell you, my father nearly went broke on that kind of stuff. It cured me. I'm not a philanthropist.
GHOST	[FEMALE] I've had experience of many publishers in many lands. No hyphen could be stout enough to hold the words 'publisher' and 'philanthropist' together.
G.I. JOE	That ghost must be turning on a gramophone of records.
MR. FRIEND	[continuing] These good Australians you've been listening to fling up their hats and hooray as a catch-cry now [pointing up] but they never bought those books, and [pointing at JOSEPH HENRY] they won't buy his books now. They're left for the silverfish to eat. I can't afford the storage.
GHOST	[FEMALE] Not for any dividends to be paid tomorrow Is this my land most passionately praised: not from any fabled future need this pen borrow vigour and hope and any banners raised.
MR. FRIEND	[persisting] As a business man I have no obligation to Australian literature. It hasn't paid in the past. It's going to be less profitable in face of what modern machinery can turn out from overseas.
PROFESSOR	We haven't the population to make Australian books pay. [dismissingly] Australian literature will come in time. We must wait.
G.I. JOE	Guys like me have no time to wait.

JOS. HEN.   In waiting, guys like me have outworn hope
             and enthusiasm.

MR. FRIEND   [impatiently] I have no more time to waste. If
             you can't lay the damned ghost I must ask
             you to go – general or buck private.

G.I. JOE   [whips out gun] I'll quit this joint when I'm
             good and ready. I'm set to demonstrate three
             things before I go.

PROFESSOR   [superciliously] Could you give us some idea of
             how long this – *demonstration* – will occupy,
             so that we may be able to estimate with some
             accuracy the length of time we shall be
             delayed?

MR. FRIEND   What are the three things you're going to do?

G.I. JOE   1. Find some Australian books. 2. Get
             acquainted with that ghost. 3. Give this
             author guy a break . . . Get going on
             Number One.

MR. FRIEND   [impatiently] Surely you can find
             something – anything – for this fellow, Miss
             Gumbootle? [aside to PROFESSOR] I see now
             he's bomb happy.

MISS G.   Mr. Friend, I've offered him everything we
             have.

MR. FRIEND   Rubbish! There must be an Australian book
             somewhere.

MISS G.   The soldiers rushed everything we had, and
             then the paper shortage came.

JOS. HEN.   You sold only thirteen copies of *Life's like That.*

MR. FRIEND   What happened to the rest Miss Gumbootle?

MISS G.   They were in the cellar for years, but at the
             outbreak of war we used them instead of
             sandbags in the air raid shelter.

MR. FRIEND   They must be still there.

MISS G.   The shelter's been full of water for months.

G.I. JOE   Speed it up, sister. It's getting late.

GHOST   Time, Gentlemen, please! Time!

PROFESSOR   You're certain this won't satisfy you. I've
             autographed it.

G.I. JOE   Go can it!

MR. FRIEND   Isn't there anything in the place? You should be

MISS G. more helpful, Miss Gumbootle. My father
published dozens of local scribblers in his
day – came crying to him to print them.
Surely there must still be something lying
around.

MISS G. [pondering] There used to be a copy of the
Oxford Book of Australian Verse propping
up the leg of the couch in the ladies' retiring
room, but it's locked up for the night.

MR. FRIEND Where are those three copies of yours Mr.
Henry?

JOS. HEN. The Bailiffs took them.

G.I. JOE [warningly] I'm waiting, sister.

MISS G. We used to have a copy of *Fisher's Ghost*. Oh,
I know, we put it under the teapot to save
the table. I'll get it. [she rushes out]

GHOST [FEMALE] He crouches and buries his face in his
knees
And hides in the dark of his hair;
For he cannot look up to the storm-smitten
trees,
or think of the loneliness there –
of the loss and the loneliness there.
Is this the sequel of Westward Ho
of the days of whate'er betide.

GHOST [MALE] The heart of the rebel makes answer No!
We'll fight till the world grows wide'.
[MISS GUMBOOTLE returns triumphantly bearing a
stained and ragged volume, which she hands
to G.I. JOE]

MISS G. It's a little dilapidated, but it's all here but the
cover.
[G.I. JOE examines it carefully then puts his arm
about the author]

G.I. JOE Buddy, from now on we're partners. [calling up]
Say Ghost, if I take him with me and keep
him from starving, will it be O.K. by you?

GHOST [MALE] Buddy, it will. I don't believe in this
gory sentimentality about the dead,
monuments and such, at the expense of the

living. I believe in justice for the living and
the dead too, for that matter – but justice for
the living.

G.I. JOE   [to JOS. HENRY] Will you come?

JOS. HEN.   [staggered] I-I-don't know . . .

G.I. JOE   You'd better. Nobody wants you here.

JOS. HEN.   But you see . . .

G.I. JOE   I offer you half my fox hole. We'll lay all the
ghosts from Kokoda to Okinawa, and boy,
are there plenty.

JOS. HEN.   What a story I could write!

G.I. JOE   Sure! You can catalogue my demonstrations.

JOS. HEN.   You mean I can ghost for you?

G.I. JOE   [to the others, admiringly] Ain't he clever! It'll
be the Book of the Month for the
Correspondence Courses.

JOS. HEN.   Ah, but what of my real book, *Life's like That*?

G.I. JOE   We'll distribute it as a bonus to the members.
Where I come from they're rarin' to hear
about Australia. They'll eat it up.

MR. FRIEND   But with an Australian book there will be
limitations on royalties . . .
[books rain down]

G.I. JOE   Somepin's cookin' he don't like. He's getting
rough.

GHOST   [shouts] Whackho! Good show!

G.I. JOE   [looking up] What can I do for you, Buddy,
before I go.

GHOST   [FEMALE] Let our songs be sung and our stories
told.

G.I. JOE   I'm with you there. What you're after is
publicity. It'll satisfy me if I can buy your
books. Will it satisfy you if guys like this one
print them?

GHOST   [MALE] Liberty, Equality, Fraternity, Publication,
Payment. For the term of his natural life.

G.I. JOE   I get you. Five freedoms.

GHOST   [FEMALE] Freedom to sing our songs, to write
our tales, to paint our country's people true.

GHOST   [MALE] And let us hear no small witticisms to

	the effect that our stories are tales told by vulgarians, full of slang and blanky, signifying nothing.
G.I. JOE	I get you! You want a square deal and your share of the dough. O.K. [to Mr. Friend] What about it, Big Boy?
MR. FRIEND	It would mean a reversal of policy.
MISS G.	Wouldn't it be worth it to get rid of the ghost?
MR. FRIEND	Hum-m m. The Staff could work back at night again. Hum-m-m. But the booksellers would never consent.
PROFESSOR	Absolutely! And it must not be allowed to affect my project.
MR. FRIEND	That's right. It can't be done. [to G.I. JOE] We're bringing out the Australian National Library – quarter of a million books – all foreign classics. Professor McChaucer here is working on a Government subsidy.
G.I. JOE	Ghost, will that satisfy you? [mighty raspberry]
PROFESSOR	But we must have culture.
G.I. JOE	[looking up] He don't like it.
GHOST	[MALE] My cultured friends! You have come too late With your by-paths nicely graded; I've fought thus far on my track of fate, And I follow the rest unaided.
G.I. JOE	[waving gun at MR. FRIEND and PROFESSOR] You're stalling on me. I got a dooty to my profession, and I got an itchy finger on this gun.
MR. FRIEND	We've got a duty to our shareholders. We'd be ruined.
GHOST	[MALE with Irish accent] We'll all be rooned said Hanrahan before the year is out.
G.I. JOE	You won't co-operate. O.K. You can chew it over with the ghost yourselves. [taking JOS. HENRY's arm] Buddy let us get outer this.
MR. FRIEND	Wait, Mr. Henry, you can have 80% of the royalties.
G.I. JOE	Nerts! We're high, wide and careless. We're free,

we're democratic! [Throwing book to
PROFESSOR] Go give your second best bed to
the ghost. I'm on his side. Come, writing
guy, let's us get cracking!

MISS G. [clasping hands imploringly] Don't leave us with
the ghost.

MR. FRIEND [going down on his knees] We'll promise you
anything.

G.I. JOE [to GHOST] Promises any good to you?
[rain of books. PROFESSOR, MR. FRIEND and MISS
GUMBOOTLE take cover]

Exit G.I. JOE and JOSEPH HENRY, author. The stage
is blacked out. The sound of falling books
ceases. Out of the darkness come the voices of
the Ghosts, speaking with great dignity and
emphasis.

GHOSTS [MALE]
Call up your ghosts, Australia, and set them
riding far
to rouse a sleeping nation to its seven-pointed
star.
[FEMALE]
Call up your dead, Australians, and bid them
ride with you
to set your rivers brimming with Eureka's flood
anew.
[MALE]
Call up your hosts, Australia, to strive with
you amain,
to fight, to sing, to honor, your Flag of Stars
again.
[FEMALE]
And only those go on, in glory their story to
make,
who ever keep their dead alive, their songs and
heroes awake.
[MALE]
Now is the time for the nation's urgent dead to
ride,
so set them riding here and now –

From the Leeuwin's cliffs to the roar of
Sydney-side,
from Wyndham to the Howe.

KATHARINE SUSANNAH PRICHARD, 1883-1969

Born in Fiji, but moving to Australia when young,
Katharine Susannah Prichard spent her childhood in
Tasmania and Victoria; during her schooldays (at
South Melbourne College) she met Nettie Palmer and
the two remained firm friends throughout their lives.
Katharine Susannah Prichard spent a few
disillusioned years as a governess before beginning
her literary career – as a journalist; but she found the
demands difficult and distracting and in 1912 set sail
for England for the second time. Her literary
ambitions met with considerable success; she returned
to Australia in 1916 having won the Hodder &
Stoughton prize for colonial fiction.

After her marriage to Hugh Throssell she moved to
Perth, Western Australia, and continued to pursue
her literary and political interests: committed to
social and political reform, she was a founding
member of the Communist Party of Australia. Her
abhorrence of exploitation is reflected in her writing
which addresses some of the fundamental issues of
injustice in relation to class, race and sex.

Novelist, dramatist, essayist and poet, her work
was widely known outside Australia, and was
translated into fifteen languages. She was nominated
for a Nobel Prize, and one of her most impressive
achievements is her three-volume chronicle of
personal and political conditions on the Western
Australian gold fields (*The Roaring Nineties* (1946);

Golden Miles (1948); *Winged Seeds* (1950)). Her
novel *Intimate Strangers* (1937) is an astute analysis
of personal/political relations between the sexes.
Coonardoo (1929), with its documentation and
exposé of Aboriginal exploitation, caused controversy
on publication but nevertheless was awarded the
Bulletin prize. She continues to warrant recognition
as one of Australia's most talented writers.

Her poetry includes *Clovelly Verses* (1913) and *The
Earth Lover* (1932) and among her non-fiction
publications are *The Real Russia* (1934) and *Straight
Left* (1982 and edited by Ric Throssell).

A skilful dramatist, Katharine Susannah Prichard
wrote many plays, the majority of which remain
unpublished. *Brumby Innes* (included here) was first
published in 1940 and in its treatment of sex and race
exploitation provides a dramatic example of the
author's abilities and concerns. Her intention is not to
entertain but to promote doubt, discomfort and
reform.

The version printed here has been taken from the
edition *Brumby Innes and Bid Me to Love*, 1974,
Currency Press, Sydney, edited by K. Brisbane;
Katharine Susannah Prichard's preface to the 1940
edition has also been included.

The play is followed by a short story, 'The
Cooboo' (from *Happiness*, 1967, Angus & Robertson,
Sydney) which is a comparable expression of
Katharine Susannah Prichard's views and values in
prose form.

BRUMBY INNES
Author's Preface to 1940 Edition

The staging of the corroboree should not present too great
difficulties. Gramophone records of the airs sung are available,
and the mimodrame, gestures and dancing, although of a strange

wild grace, are simple enough. The corroboree in this play is used to give something of the dignity, beauty and mystery of a primitive people in their natural surroundings: against their appearance under the conditions of a vanquished race.

Polly is a Hecuba in bronze: the tragedy of the vanquished Trojans, the tragedy of the Aboriginals in the Nor'-west. Americans are depicting the Negroes in music and in the theatre, and it should not be impossible for players to give the natives of Australia, seriously, and with sympathy. All the men and women of the tribe in this play are studies from life. If, however, the corroboree makes for insuperable difficulties, Act I may be reduced to a suggestion of the blacks' camp and the women sitting and clicking sticks, about the fire.

Words sung to the corroboree are treasure really. The Aboriginals seem reluctant to tell them, superstitious of unravelling their mystery, perhaps. Often the words they sing are not words of their everyday language. Many of the corroboree songs, or tabee, are in a dead language, I think . . . hereditary legends and saga drifted down from remote ages; others are inspirational, sung by the yinerrie, inventor of corroborees, or poet of the tribe, and director of ceremonies, as the spirit moves him.

Only folk reared on isolated stations who have had lifelong associations with the blacks, or a native who has broken with his people and traditions, are able to gather some of these songs and to tell us their meaning. 'The Song of the Stranger' and 'The Song of the Mate' in Act I are both authentic fragments in an ancient language of the Gnulloonga tribe. Words of the narloo corroboree are in a local dialect. The gins seemed afraid to give me the ancient words. They would only say: 'Sing go away narloo . . . come dark,' waving to the hills. 'Narloo, eagle-hawk . . . like smoke . . . moon, maybe.'

One writes as one must: produces as one may. Which is to say, the language of a Nor'-westerner must be tempered to the ears of city-dwellers – so be it! The same applies to the song in Act II. Sung by a stockman under the stars you would not miss a word; but as little or as much may be used as the play will carry.

Characters

WONGANA　*Aboriginal men*
MICKINA
SPIDER
GINARRA
OLD JIMMY
MUNGA
TULLAMURRA　*Aboriginal women*
NARDADU
WARRARIE
WYLBA
POLLY
BRUMBY INNES
JACK CAREY　*An old stockman*
JOHN HALLINAN　*Owner of Nyedee Station*
MAY　*His niece*

ACT ONE
The blacks' camp.

ACT TWO
The kitchen of BRUMBY INNES' homestead on a wild and lonely cattle station of north-west Australia.

ACT THREE
The same, three months later.

ACT ONE

Under a wide stretch of starlit sky, native women and children are sitting in two rows at a little distance from the camp fire, burning low. Opposite, on the left, a sun-dried bullock's hide is stretched between a tall, spindling mulga and two or three low-growing bushes, to form a screen for the men who are painting themselves with white clay, making long curly lines on their legs, and circles, or squares with spots inside, on their breasts. A huge face, cut from the chalk-white bark of a river gum, is lying on the ground. The men are naked but for wandy cloths, three-quarter wise in front, a string between the buttocks. An old man,

very fat, has a tuft of emu feathers tied on like a tail behind.
MICKINA, *a handsome stalwart young black, wears parrot
feathers under an armlet on his left arm and swathed round his
head, showing red and green. Two or three kangaroo dogs prowl
about the fire and among the women and children. The plain is
bare to the far horizon where a line of low-growing scrub touches
the starlit sky.*

WONGANA, *in his everyday clothes and hat of a station stockman, comes from behind the screen where the men are getting
ready for the corroboree, and crosses to the women and children.
He is the man of authority and director of ceremonies, good-
looking and powerful; older, more mature than* MICKINA. *He sits
cross-legged at the end of the front row of women, picks up the
kylies, and clicking them rhythmically, begins to sing in a full,
melodious alto. The women sing with him in a slightly higher
key, beating small sticks together.*

WONGANA   Balgarilla mardoo mardourie yiendie warilla . . .

WOMEN   Balgarilla mardoo mardourie yiendie warilla . . .

[Then WONGANA, *the* WOMEN *and* CHILDREN *sing the line together,
repeating it many times, but varying the key each time. When
the singing dies away there is silence for a moment.* NARDADU,
*a grandmother of the tribe, in an old skirt, man's coat and hat,
stands up at the further end of the front row of women, a long
stick in her hand, and waves it towards the bullock hide where
the men going to corroboree are.]*

WONGANA   *[clicking and singing again]* Balgarilla
             mardoo . . .

*[*WOMEN *and* CHILDREN *join in; but the singing takes on a tone
of incitement, jeering, as if to say: 'Come along you fellows!'
'What's the matter?' 'Are you frightened?' 'Don't be shy!' 'Let's
have a look at you!'*

SPIDER *appears from behind the bullock hide, followed by the
rest of the men. Tall, agile, the most adept and experienced dancer,*
SPIDER *stands in the attitude of a man in a strange country,
looking about him, throwing out both arms in the native gesture
of surprise; begins to dance with little jiggling steps as if walking
or running quickly, then like a kangaroo scenting water, hops
forward, legs bowed, arms loose, prancing first on one leg, then
on the other, coming down on both together with the thud of
a kangaroo's tail. All with rhythm and stark wild grace to the*

women's singing. At the fire, though, as if the step were finished, no audience there, he turns and walks back to the bullock hide. Each of the men imitates closely every movement of the leader. MICKINA, *muscular and dandyish;* MUNGA, *boyish, undeveloped, watching anxiously what the others are doing;* GINARRA, *sturdy, well-formed;* OLD JIMMY, *pot-bellied, with slender legs, the emu's feathers bobbing behind him. Each of the men does the step singly; then in a row, and round the fire, walking back behind the bullock hide when it is finished, in everyday fashion.*

One of the dogs, springing out, goes for OLD JIMMY's *emu feathers, is driven off angrily by* NARDADU, *causing a drift of laughter among the women and children. But the occasion is one of high seriousness, dancers absorbed in their interpretation of these songs in a dead language which have come to them from bygone generations of their people. Singers are under the influence of the night and the secret, mysterious movins, or charms, in the songs they are singing.]*

WONGANA   *[clicking the kylies, giving the rhythm of the*
              next dance, to a slightly different melody]
              Narloo, narloo . . . gindoo bun abbie . . .

[The WOMEN *and* CHILDREN *join in, repeating the line as before. From the darkness beyond the firelight,* SPIDER *as the narloo comes hopping. He seems to come from the horizon, a crouched figure, hopping low, like a frog, all his bones outlined with white, a huge face of white bark over his head. A fearsome figure, he hops and crouches right up to the fire, peers at the women and children. Still singing, their voices quivering with fear and excitement, they watch him, beating their sticks.* NARDADU's *voice shrills out as she steps forward and threatens the narloo with her stick. Singing of the women vibrates to the charm they are trying to use against the narloo. The narloo wavers before the old woman's threatening figure and upheld stick. He retreats backwards, thwarted, intimidated, and hops off into darkness across the plains again while the singing of the women takes on a tone of derision and triumph. The singing dies away, voices wandering into silence, dropping out one by one, until* NARDADU's *are the last low notes.* NARDADU *puts more wood on the fire.]*

WONGANA   *[clicking and singing]* Narloo, narloo . . .
              gindoo bun abbie.

WOMEN   Narloo, narloo . . . gindoo bun abbie.
Warieda munga murnda bun abbie.
*[The first line is repeated as before. A flock of narloos, the rest
of the men from behind the bullock hide, their faces whitened
and white feathers in their hair, run up to the fire. They dance,
hovering and fluttering like white cockatoos. The women drive
them off and the singing dies away.*

*Before the next dance, the women turn their backs to the camp
fire, crouching against the earth.* WONGANA *spreads old grey
dirty blankets over them. No native woman must see this
corroboree. When* WONGANA *clicks and sings, the women join
him in muffled tones.]*
WONGANA   *[clicking and singing]* Ubi! Ubi! . . .
WOMEN   Ubi! Ubi! . . . hebina hawiah!
Wara lunghia bina hawiah!
*[*SPIDER, *a high white head-dress like a spider's web, erect from
his head and jutting over his forehead, comes from the bullock
hide, gestures and dances before the fire with gaiety and an
abandon which suggests the Dionysia, working himself into such
a frenzy that he stands shivering, overwrought. Men behind the
bullock hide join in the singing, rush to join* SPIDER *and dance
beside him, shivering, shaking themselves, stamping, shouting
and singing.]*
ALL   Ubi! Ubi! . . . hebina hawiah!
Wara lunghia bina hawiah!
[While the excitement is at its height, BRUMBY INNES *staggers in
from the left. He is drunk; a powerful man, handsome and
attractive in a rough and brutal way, wearing well-worn buff
trousers, loose cotton shirt, with leather belt, matchbox attached,
pipe stuck through, revolver in a leather case, widebrimmed felt
hat and elastic sided boots, the ends pulled over his trousers.]*
BRUMBY   *[swaggering into the firelight]* Wylba! Hi, there,
Wylba!
*[*SPIDER *retreats from the fire; the rest of the men surge forward.
Women throw back their blankets.]*
WONGANA   *[facing* BRUMBY *angrily]* Wiah! No, Brumby!
BRUMBY   Wylba? Where is she? Want . . . Wylba.
*[A girl among the native women, very slight and childish-looking,
draws attention to herself by shrieking and shrinking against*
NARDADU.]

MICKINA   *[striding over to stand beside* WONGANA, *the other men following him, defensive and aggressive]* Wylba stay camp.

BRUMBY   *[seeing the girl, without paying the least attention to the men]* There you are! *[Staggering over to her]* Wylba . . . you come with me, Wylba.

WYLBA   *[shrinking and clinging to the old woman]* Wiah! Wiah!

WONGANA   *[going to* BRUMBY, *humouring him, but with dignity]* You go back, Brumby. Boys, angry. Say Wylba stay camp . . . not go with you.

BRUMBY   *[roaring]* What?

WONGANA   *[repeating]* You go back. Boys badgee. Say Wylba stay here . . . not go . . . with you . . . .

BRUMBY   Not go with me?

WONGANA   Boys angry. Bita muna you, Brumby.

BRUMBY   Fed up with me, are they? Christ, what's this place comin' to, I'd like to know. Who's boss here? I'll show 'em.

[He goes over, tugs the girl from the women. MICKINA *bounds over and wrenches her from him.]*

WONGANA   *[coming between them]* Better go, Brum. Boys won't give up this girl.

BRUMBY   *[pulling the revolver from his belt]* Won't give her up, won't they? We'll see if they won't give her up . . .

[A spear whistles and plunges into the ground beside him.]

That's it, is it? Young bucks down this uloo think they . . . got everything their own way . . . Keep the women to themselves. Where do I come in? That's what I want to know. *[Covering* MICKINA *with his revolver]* Leave her go, or I'll shoot. *[As the native releases the girl]* What's she got to do with you, anyhow? *[To* WONGANA] Is she his woman?

*[*JACK CAREY *enters from left front, running and stumbling blindly. He is an old stockman and teamster, very tall, over eighty and nearly blind. He wears faded blue dungarees, a loose greyish*

white shirt, elastic sided boots and belt of a stockman, but has
come hatless in his hurry.]

WONGANA   No. Promised one.

JACK   Brumby!

BRUMBY   Well! *[Laughing hilariously]* I'll give her father
blankets, tobacco . . . See.

JACK   *[sharply]* Don't be a fool, Brum. *[As a kylie*
shies past BRUMBY*]* Tell the boys to let up,
Wongana. He's drunk, can't you see? Mad
drunk. They'll get the worst of it.

BRUMBY   *[shooting high and laughing]* Show 'em! Eh? *[As*
the women and children shrink together,
crying out and wailing] Show 'em who's boss,
here . . .

JACK   Humour him or he'll shoot the lot of you. Let
him have the girl, Wongana, for God's sake.

BRUMBY   *[pushing* WYLBA *out before him]* Come along
now.

WYLBA   Wiah! Wiah!

[She wails and moves off before him. The men surge after her
threateningly. A kylie hits BRUMBY. *He shoots before him. There*
is a scream of pain.]

JACK   Get out. Get out, Brum. They'll do for you.

BRUMBY   *[laughing boisterously]* Do for me?

[He goes off backwards, dragging and pushing WYLBA *with him.]*
Do for me, eh? *[Shooting over the camp]*
We'll see.

[He goes off, shooting. Cries of fear and pain, the yells, screams
and shouted imprecations of the blacks follow him.]

END OF ACT ONE

ACT TWO

The kitchen of BRUMBY INNES' *homestead, a long room of mud*
bricks with brushwood screen for a verandah. We see the
brushwood of the verandah, and its long sapling posts through
a wide-open door. Windows on either side, double the size of
ordinary windows and without glass, show level, sun-blasted

country stretching to a far horizon under the glimmer of dawn.
Stars are still in the sky; a butcher bird fluting. [Two notes on
the musical pipes and a short chromatic, give it.] The light grows
quickly to the full, clear radiance of early morning.

BRUMBY *is asleep, snoring heavily, in a bunk below the*
fireplace, left. A box against the end of the bunk serves as a seat.
A rifle leans to the wall near the hearth. There are shelves and
tins for flour, tea, sugar, jam, in the corner on the other side of
the fireplace; two smoke-blackened kerosene buckets for water
on the hearth, and a bench for dishes and cooking pots under
the window, left of the door. A table stands out from the window
on the right, a chair at either end; a bottle of whisky and a quart
pot are on the table. The door to the storeroom opens below the
table on the right. A case of whisky has been pushed against the
wall. JACK CAREY, *stirring the ashes of the fire, raises his head*
to listen, stands poised, his arm hung as he was going to throw
wood on the fire. WYLBA, *curled in a faded pale blue gina-gina,*
is sleeping like a dog on the floor beside the table.

WYLBA   *[wailing in her sleep]* Wiah! Wiah!
    JACK   *[cursing under his breath]* Be quiet, can't you?
[He throws a branch on the fire. As the flames leap up, he turns
quickly to face the door.]
           Who's there?
*[*POLLY, *a tall gin in a long straight dark blue gina-gina, standing*
against the doorpost, pressed close to it so as not to be seen in
the light of the doorway, edges herself into the room, left of the
door. She stares at WYLBA, *at* BRUMBY *asleep on the bunk; then*
her eyes go to JACK CAREY.*]*
           What is it, Polly?
    POLLY   *[in flat, steady tones]* Boys comin' . . . bump
           him.
     JACK   They are, are they?
    POLLY   Eeh-erm.
     JACK   What do they think they're goin' to do?
    POLLY   Beat'm.
     JACK   You wongie them not to be damn fools, Polly.
           You know Brumby . . . You know he doesn't
           care what he does when he's mad. He'll lay
           them all out soon as look at them.
    POLLY   *[morosely]* Bin talkin' all time.

JACK   No good?

POLLY   No good. Boys mad too.

JACK   Wylba's Mickina's woman, isn't she?

POLLY   Father give'm Wylba when she baby.

WYLBA   *[stirring sleepily]* Mickina!

[Waking, she looks about her.]

JACK   He's her noova – lover, eh?

POLLY   Wylba . . . weary-booger noova.

JACK   She's got plenty of lovers? All the men in the camp want her?

POLLY   *[with a backward glance]* Boys comin'.

WYLBA   *[jumping up and running to the door, peering out excitedly]* Plenty boys . . . plenty sticks . . .

JACK   *[trying to wake* BRUMBY*]* Shake y'rself, Brum! *[Shaking him roughly]* Wake up. *[As there is no response from the heavy sleeper]* Wake up, you blasted idiot! *[To* POLLY*]* John Hallinan campin' Sixty Mile?

POLLY   Eeh-erm.

JACK   Sent a boy along to say he'd be over when they was musterin' the Sixty Mile, didn't he?

POLLY   Munga.

BRUMBY   What . . . wa'sh that?

JACK   Wake up. There's a mob comin' up from the camp to lay you out.

BRUMBY   Mob . . . what? Aw, go to hell!

[He turns over to sleep again.]

POLLY   *[looking from the doorway]* Horse trough, Jack.

*[*WYLBA *withers away from her glance.]*

JACK   *[pulling* BRUMBY *from the bunk]* How many?

WYLBA   *[excitedly]* Uloo . . . all men in camp.

[She shrinks away under POLLY's *glance.]*

JACK   *[pitching* BRUMBY *to the floor]* Wake up, blast you! *[Kicking him]* I've a good mind to let you take what's comin' to you. *[Going to the table]* If we weren't the only two white men on the place . . .

[He pours whisky into the quart pot.]

BRUMBY   Wh'sh that? . . . What . . . Jack? What the bloody blazes . . .?

JACK   *[giving him the quart pot]* Here, put this into
       you.

*[He goes to the hearth, examines the rifle to see whether it is
loaded, takes cartridges from a box on the shelf beside the
fireplace, puts them in his pocket.]*

BRUMBY   *[drinking]* That's the stuff! Good old Jack! *[As
         JACK puts the cartridges in his pocket]* What's
         up? What are you doin'?

JACK   Camp's comin' to lay you out. Pull y'self
       together. Can't y'hear 'em?

[A distant murmur of voices is heard.]

BRUMBY   Comin' to . . . lay me out? *[Struggling to his
         feet]* That's a good one. *[Laughing and
         fingering the revolver in his belt]* Comin'
         to . . .? *[His eyes wandering from WYLBA to
         POLLY]* Wylba . . . I see. And old Polly.

*[JACK goes to the door with the rifle in his hands, stands it against
the doorpost and looks out. The natives are heard approaching
with a noisy, clamorous chatter.]*

JACK   They're comin' round the wood heap, Brum.

BRUMBY   It's off with the old love and on with the new,
         Polly. *[To WYLBA]* Come here.

WYLBA   *[going to him cringingly, whining]* Wiah! Wiah!

BRUMBY   Stop that row!

*[He pushes her away roughly and with a kick, as all the natives
from the camp swarm along the verandah, surge about the
doorway and windows, the men in faded blue and yellow trousers,
grey shirts, felt hats of station stockmen, with sticks and kylies
in their hands.]*

JACK   Look out! Brum!

BRUMBY   *[startled and realizing what he is up against,
         facing them harshly]* What the hell's got you,
         the lot of you? *[Roaring as he takes the
         revolver from his belt]* Take y'r carcases out
         of my daylight, or I'll shoot the whole damn
         lot of you.

[The blacks hesitate to push on into the room.]

JACK   *[in the doorway, using the butt of his rifle]*
       Keep back.

[BRUMBY takes aim, but his revolver clicks on an empty barrel.]

BRUMBY   *[snarling at WYLBA]* That's you, is it?

[Pushing WYLBA *before him, he springs back into the storeroom and bangs the door.]*

JACK   *[retreating as the blacks swarm forward]* Now's y'r chance! Clear out the rest of you. He's got powder and shot to blow you to blazes in there.

[A bullet cracks through a chink in the storeroom door. Most of the boys stampede for the open doorway. There is a howl of pain. All but MICKINA *retire to the verandah, frightened and cowed.]*

WYLBA   *[screaming]* Mickina! Mickina!

MICKINA   *[dashing at the storeroom door]* Wylba!

BRUMBY   *[throwing back the door]* It's you, is it? *[Jeeringly]* Come on, Wylba, give Mick his spears.

[The black springs at him.]

WYLBA   *[dancing and screaming fiercely]* Munyinbunna, nuki-nuki, chungee-chungee.

[As the black and BRUMBY *grapple and struggle,* JACK *holds the crowd in the doorway with his rifle, although they are more or less interested in the scrap.* BRUMBY *tries to use his revolver.]*

Walyinna, booketera, kundikundi spa!

*[*MICKINA *sets his teeth in the flesh of* BRUMBY's *arm to make him drop the revolver.]*

Belyee mari, chungee-chungee, belyee mari, koo.

*[*BRUMBY *throws the black off from him and shoots.* MICKINA *falls.]*

BRUMBY   *[gasping and blowing]* Have the police on to yer – the damn lot of yer, damn and blast yer. Clear out if yer don't want what Mick's got.

[The boys drift out of sight from the windows and door.]

WYLBA   *[wailing beside* MICKINA*]* Mickina! Mickina!

BRUMBY   *[running* WYLBA *into the store]* You stay where yer are put, blast yer!

[He slams the storeroom door. JACK *goes to* MICKINA *and bends over him, feels his heart, examines his wound.]*

JACK   He's all right. He'll come round. You've made a mess of this, Brum.

BRUMBY   *[sitting down and pouring himself some whisky]*

Swine. Why didn't yer do for him, Polly?
[Drinking] I gave yer the gun.

POLLY   *[in her slow, level tones]* Shoot'm . . . bin
kangarooin'. Bullet go through hat . . . not
hurt'm.

BRUMBY   *[surlily]* Got a charm against bullets, has he?
Well, we'll see.

[He takes pipe and the tobacco from belt.]

JACK   *[as the gin turns away]* Here, Polly, bring water.
*[She goes to the bench under the window, takes a tin dish and
puts water in it from the buckets by the hearth, gives the dish
to* JACK *and returns to bucket; goes out for more water.* JACK *goes
to the bunk, pulls a box from underneath and rummages in it
for a piece of clean rag.]*

BRUMBY   *[stuffing his pipe with tobacco]* I'll put the
police on to'm for this.

*[*JACK *tears a strip of rag from the tail of a shirt and returns to*
MICKINA.*]*

See if I don't. I'll damn well –

JACK   Y'll get more'n y'bargain for, if you do.

BRUMBY   What?

JACK   *[washing blood from the wound on the black's
forehead]* Y'll get more'n you bargain for if
you do.

BRUMBY   *[smoking]* How do yer make that out?

JACK   The boys'll talk about this girl – and you givin'
old Polly there a gun to shoot Mick, first
chance she got.

BRUMBY   They will, will they? Well, let'm, I say. Let'm.

JACK   *[having tied a bandage round* MICKINA's *head]*
With this damned Morrison chap
about – Protector of Aborigines, they call
him – it'll go hard with yer.

BRUMBY   *[slowly, derisively]* Hard with *me*?

JACK   And there's John Hallinan, don't forget.

BRUMBY   What are yer givin' us?

JACK   If Morrison got onto it – the girl bein' under
age.

BRUMBY   *[crowing hilariously]* A blasted nigger! What are
yer givin' us? Ever heard of a white man
doin' time for a black girl? Aw, go on . . .

JACK   But times is different, Brum. Times is changing.
        This Morrison chap –
BRUMBY Changin' 'em is he? Well, don't let him come
        pokin' his nose in, around here, that's all.
POLLY   [*in the doorway, a bucket of water on her head*]
        Bin comin'.
JACK   Who? Morrison?
[BRUMBY *goes to the door.*]
BRUMBY Looks like a couple of horses.
JACK   [*steering towards the door*] We don't want
        anybody around this mornin'. [*Peering under
        his hand*] John Hallinan's musterin' the Sixty
        Mile –
BRUMBY It'll be him for a monte. Sent a boy over to say
        he'd be along when they was on the Sixty
        Mile, didn't he? I clean forgot.
JACK   He did.
BRUMBY Eh, Polly. [*As she turns*] What the boys do with
        that bush mob we brought in yesterday?
POLLY   Yard'm.
JACK   You've been lucky, Brum, dead lucky. But you
        were bound to get caught one of these days.
        John Hallinan's stood a good deal from you,
        and he warned us, if the percentage of
        Nyedee calves went down this year, like it
        done last, along our boundary . . . he'd have
        to do something.
BRUMBY Dry up, can't yer, [*going towards the black on
        the floor*] and help clean up this mess. Here,
        you, Polly, take Mickina down camp. [*As
        she stands staring down at the unconscious
        native*] Carry him on your back. You can,
        easy . . .
POLLY   [*flatly, looking down at the native who to her
        has a charmed life*] No.
BRUMBY [*knowing her superstitions and that there is no
        time for argument*] Scared eh? [*To JACK*]
        Come on, then. We'll have to put him here.
[JACK *helps to lift* MICKINA *and throw him on the bunk.*]
        Get a rag and wipe up that blood on the
        floor.

[POLLY *goes to the bench under the window for rags while he throws water, from the dish on the floor, through the open door.* JACK *covers* MICKINA *with a grey blanket.*]

JACK   It's more'n likely the boys will tell him about this.

[POLLY *kneels with water and rags to clean the floor.*]

BRUMBY   Tell him? [*In the doorway, looking out*] Tell him? I'll tell him meself. Ask him to send out the police. Hallinan's comin' in the top gate be the yards. He'll see them clean skins, all right. Christ!

JACK   [*hobbling to the doorway*] What?

BRUMBY   He's got a woman with him.

JACK   A woman?

POLLY   [*looking up from the floor*] Bin campin' Sixty Mile.

BRUMBY   Been camping at the well with him, has she?

POLLY   [*finishing her job and going out with rags and bucket*] Eeh-erm.

JACK   His niece, May Hallinan, I suppose. Been stayin' on Nyedee for the winter.

[BRUMBY, *falling back, passes a hand over his beard, gives his pants a hitch, goes into the storeroom.* JACK *looks up.*]

Gee, they're hitchin' their horses at the stable and walkin' over.

[*He glances anxiously at the native on the bunk, and returns to pull the blanket over him.*]

JOHN
HALLINAN   [*calling*] Hullo! Anybody at home?

JACK   [*hurrying forward as* JOHN *and* MAY *appear in the doorway*] Mornin', John. Glad to see yer.

JOHN   [*coming into the room*] Morning, Jack. This is my niece, May Hallinan.

[*He is a man of middle age with greying hair, kind and sturdy, wearing well-washed white moleskins, pale blue shirt, wide-brimmed felt hat, leather belt with matchbox attached, pipe stuck through, stockwhip looped around his neck, and the elastic sided boots of a stockman.* MAY *is a pretty, shallow, city-bred girl, wearing riding breeches, a white blouse and stockman's wide-brimmed hat.*]

MAY   Good morning, Mr. Carey. We *are* early birds, aren't we.

JACK   *[shaking hands with her, but standing so that she does not see the native on the bunk]* Not too early for this part of the world, miss.

MAY   It's nice riding before the sun gets too hot, isn't it?

JOHN   *[seeing the blood on the floor, but appearing not to while* MAY *is there]* How's the eyes, Jack?

JACK   *[cracking hardy, as always]* Good, thanks, John. They're real good. Though I can't see to read much, these days.

JOHN   Brumby about?

JACK   He . . . he's in the store.

[BRUMBY comes out, his hat on.]

BRUMBY   Gord a'mighty, John Hallinan, is it?

MAY   *[jauntily]* Hullo, Mr. Innes!

BRUMBY   Mornin' Miss May. Well, John, how's things?

JOHN   Not too bad, thanks Brum.

MAY   *[hovering in the doorway, looking back over the plains]* Is that punti – that little yellow flower, on those bushes beside the verandah – Mr. Carey?

JACK   *[nervous and apologetic]* I don't know what yer call it.

BRUMBY   *[to JOHN]* Come on, sit down.

[He goes to the table. JOHN follows him.]

MAY   And that's desert pea, isn't it – the red out there?

JACK   The blacks call it murda-murda.

MAY   Oh, I *must* get some.

[She goes out.]

JOHN   *[before he sits down, staring at the native on the bunk]* Hullo? What's up?

JACK   Been havin' a dust-up with the boys, this mornin', John.

BRUMBY   Came to lay me out. So I let 'em have it.

JOHN   *[eyeing the stained floor]* Looks like it.

JACK   *[apologetically]* The natives is gettin' proper

cheeky up here, John. You got to let'm have
it now and again.

[At this stage, the tempo quickens. BRUMBY *is playing to keep*
HALLINAN's *attention off the native and avoid further*
explanation.]

BRUMBY   *[boisterously, holding up a nearly empty bottle*
of Black and White whisky] Any of that
whisky left, Jack? Got a case a couple of
days ago *[as* JACK *goes to the case beside the*
storeroom door] and old Jack's been boozin'
up a bit. Never touched a woman in all his
born days, he says, but he ain't so teetotal
about sting.

[He sits down.]

JACK   It's a lie.

BRUMBY   *[in good humour, making a butt of the old*
man] He said that the other day when Ted
Duffy was here. [As JACK *brings the bottle of*
whisky and puts it on the table] Where's the
tin opener? *[Finding a corkscrew on the table*
and going on to draw the cork] Ted's camel-
punching for Sparkes now, did yer know?

*[*JACK *brings another quart pot and a white enamelled mug from*
the bench to the table.]

Was through here with a load –

JOHN   *[as* BRUMBY *pours whisky into the enamelled*
mug] Whoa!

BRUMBY   *[pushing the mug towards him]* . . . for Karrara.
Havin' some Jack?

JACK   *[yielding to temptation]* Oh, well, just a drop.

BRUMBY   *[pouring and holding a pot out to* JACK*]* Been
sixteen weeks on the road.

[He pours for himself. JACK *takes his pot and sits on a box out*
from the bunk.]

JOHN   No wonder Sparkes says loadin' for Karrara
doesn't pay. He was just thirteen weeks late
with our stores.

BRUMBY   *[drinking]* Well, here's skin off yer nose!
[Pouring for himself again] Camels was stuck
in the river. *[Pulling out his pipe and stoking*

it] But Sparko, he didn't worry. Went back
to The Breakaway for a gutful. *[Holding the
bottle to* JOHN*]* Come on, fill up.

JOHN   No, thanks. How about some water?

BRUMBY   Spoilin' the good stuff. Eh, Polly? When he was
here, Ted was sayin', too, he had to chase
the bloomin' camels every morning after
they'd camped. And it takes him a day and a
half to git 'em again. *[Shouting]* Eh, Polly!

*[*POLLY *appears in the doorway.]*

Water.

*[*POLLY *moves in a leisurely, dignified fashion to the bench under
the window, takes an enamelled jug, dips it into a bucket on
the hearth.]*

Well, when Ted was here, couple of weeks
ago, Ted an me –

JOHN   *[as* POLLY *puts the jug of water beside him]*
Thank you, Polly.

[He pours water into his mug and she goes out again.]

BRUMBY   We got onto young Tommy, the half-caste
[winking at JOHN*]* to tell us who his father
was . . .

JACK   Aw . . . dry up.

BRUMBY   And who'd you think he said? *[Roaring with
laughter]* And who do yer think young
Tommy said was his father? Why, Jack . . .
old Jack Carey!

JACK   It's a lie, John. Him and Ted got drinkin'
together and put the kid up to it.

BRUMBY   *[mimicking* JACK*]* Never touched a native
woman in me life . . .

JOHN   There's not many men have knocked about the
Nor'-west as long as you have, can say that,
Jack.

JACK   But you know it's true?

JOHN   I believe you, Jack.

*[*MAY *comes in from the verandah with red and yellow flowers
in her hand.]*

BRUMBY   Thousands wouldn't.

MAY   Believe what?

JACK   *[in an agony]* Aw, dry up.

MAY   *[as the men move to give her a chair]* Don't move, I'll sit here.

[She perches herself on the bench before the window and looks curiously about her.]

BRUMBY   Why, that . . . . *[relishing the fear and discomfort of the other men that he will repeat what he has said]* It's going to rain, Miss May.

MAY   *[fanning herself vigorously with her hat]* Does it ever rain up here? Oh!

[She jumps down and goes to look at the boy on the bunk.]
    Somebody sick?

JACK   *[awkwardly]* One of the boys. An . . . accident, miss.

BRUMBY   *[drily]* He got hurt.

JACK   *[to divert* MAY's *attention]* She'd like some tea, perhaps, Brum?

MAY   *[in her affected, sprightly way]* I'd love it!

BRUMBY   *[shouting]* Polly!

MAY   *[returning to her seat on the bench]* I've got what you'd call a forty horse-power thirst, Mr. Innes.

BRUMBY   *[jocosely]* Hundred and forty's nearer my mark. *[as* POLLY *comes into the doorway]* Tea for the lady, Polly.

POLLY   *[stately and indifferent, eyeing the girl]* Eeh-ermm.

[She comes and goes from the bench to the fireplace, making tea.]

BRUMBY   *[returning to the table and whisky bottle]* Yer see . . .

JOHN   *[refusing whisky]* No. No, thank you, Brum. Fact of the matter, what I came to see you about –

*[*WYLBA, *off, screeches and wails.]*

BRUMBY   He . . . old Jack rules the roost here, Miss May. Head stockman and all of that. And if he says –

MAY   *[hearing* WYLBA *wailing]* What's that?

BRUMBY   If he says it's going to rain, well, it's going to rain.

JACK   *[growling]* Head stockman, be blowed.

BRUMBY   *[sitting on the end of the table]* Head stockman! *[Throwing off another whisky]* Gord a'mighty, what am I thinkin' of? And him a bleedin' landowner like the rest of us. Wanted to sell me his place: homestead, a rusty tank, bush shed and a hundred horses. Leastways, he thought there was a hundred horses.

JOHN   More like two hundred, I reck'n, Jack.

BRUMBY   For a hundred pounds . . . goin' . . . goin' . . .

MAY   *[as* POLLY *puts a cup of tea beside her]* Thank you.

BRUMBY   Gone! 'No thank you, Jack,' he says. 'I got all the horses I want: and if I want more – I can always *get em.*'

JACK   You mustered'm for me in 1915, remember John?

JOHN   I remember all right, Jack.

BRUMBY   Ten years ago.

JOHN   *[chuckling]* 'They're quiet,' he says. 'They're fairly quiet. I've mustered 'em meself.' He might've done, down a kind of gutter between the hills, there was, over at his place . . .

MAY   *[putting down her cup and coming forward to listen]* Nyedee hills, Unk, that range at the back of the run?

JOHN   *[nodding]* Steep as the back of your hand, all tussocky spinifex and wash-aways. Well we went after 'em. Got a hundred and twenty, wild as hawks; eight and ten year old, not branded. 'Not branded, Jack,' I says. 'Oh yes, they're branded,' he says. 'Can't see the brand,' I says. 'Oh well, I branded 'em all right,' he says: 'through the fence, and the brand might've got cold.'

[Laughter.]

BRUMBY   *[when the laughter has subsided]* Thought he was all-in, the night he come ridin' up to the stockyards on his old blind horse.

JACK   *[gruffly]* Best night horse in the Nor'-west.

JOHN   Old Hero, Jack?

JACK   Yes.

JOHN   Flintlock, out of Reflection. He was a good
                horse all right, Jack.

BRUMBY   Well, y'r never see such a pair of scrags, the
                night they come in. Been livin' on salt emu,
                or somethin'. The old horse could jest about
                set one foot in front of the other and Jack
                here, was swayin' about and singin' . . .

JOHN   *[chuckling]* Same old song? 'So it's shift boys,
                shift. There isn't the slightest doubt . . .'

BRUMBY   That's right.

JACK   *[apologetically]* Touch of the sun . . . and the
                diarrhoea or somethin'.

JOHN   Why didn't you come to me, Jack?

JACK   Oh, well, you're a family man now, John. The
                women don't like an old moocher knockin'
                about.

JOHN   Women be damned. We were real sore on
                Nyedee when we found you'd come here.

MAY   *[prowling round and posing for* BRUMBY, *who is
                watching her]* What a lovely big kitchen.

*[*POLLY *goes to the bench for a cup and saucer.]*

JOHN   Funny thing, too. I got a feeling something was
                wrong with you.

BRUMBY   Eeh-erm?

JOHN   Went out to bring you in, and found your
                tracks comin' here.

JACK   *[apologetically]* Must've been pretty crook,
                John. Don't know rightly what happened. It
                was thirty miles against sixty, I suppose, and
                the old horse just took the nearest track.

JOHN   Oh well, there's always a home for you on
                Nyedee, Jack.

BRUMBY   *[boisterously]* Here, what are you up to, John
                Hallinan? Not takin' me right-hand man from
                me, are yer?

JACK   I can be a bit of use here, John . . . look after
                things when Brum's out musterin' . . . or on
                the skoot.

BRUMBY   *[uproariously]* My oath, he can. Hides the
                whisky and sees the gins don't pinch all the

	tea and sugar. Hear about that last mob we was takin' down?
JOHN	No.
BRUMBY	Gord, we had a time with them. Jack was comin' along to cook for us, and first night out, the mob broke. Dark? It was that dark, y'couldn't hear a dog bark; and away the blasted brutes went. We chased 'em for a couple of hours. Brought 'em back to camp. And away they went agen. Next night it was the same. Cock-eyed Bob, and a half-caste woman he had with him, was to do a go on night watch. They was changing horses with young Tommy and Mickina when the cattle made off. Bob waited for Tommy to go after'm and Tommy waited for Bob. The woman didn't know what to do and galloped after'm on her own.
JOHN	If the bullocks start breakin' like that, they make a habit of it.
BRUMBY	Third night, the boys fell off their horses and went to sleep where they fell. There was no gettin' a move out of any of 'em. I was dead to the world meself.
JOHN	But you got a bit of sleep during the day.
BRUMBY	We did, off and on, but the b--'s [*looking at* MAY] beasts was wild as flies. There they was, moochin' along, quiet enough, and there's me, havin' a bit of a snooze in the shade . . . and away they go.
JACK	Bad as that mob we brought down from Nyedee – an' lost about half. Remember John?
JOHN	Too right I remember, Jack.
BRUMBY	Third night, when I lay down, them bullocks could've broke to kingdom come. But Jack thought he was the on'y man to be trusted with'm. Went on, ridin' round'm all night – a blind man on a blind horse, singin' . . .
JOHN	[*singing*] 'For it's shift, boys, shift . . .'
BRUMBY	That's right. And he held'm on his own. Beasts

	must've knowed his voice.
JACK	They was dead-beat – like the rest of yer.
JOHN	Good old Jack!
BRUMBY	Best all round stockman in the Nor'-west.
JOHN	Haven't I always said so, Jack?
MAY	Oh, do sing that song, Mr. Carey! I'd love to hear you.
JACK	*[shaking his head]* Got no voice, now.
BRUMBY	Can't sing 'less he's well oiled, Miss May, *[pouring whisky into a quart pot]* or ridin' round the cattle.

[He hands the quart pot to JACK.*]*

| JOHN | Come on, Jack. Just one verse. There's no one can sing 'The Old Jig Jog' like you. *[Tuning up]* 'I'm travellin' along the Castlereagh, for I'm a station hand . . .' |
| BRUMBY | *[joining in]* 'I'm handy with the roping pole, I'm handy with the brand . . .' |

*[*JACK, *having drunk the whisky, puts down the pot and sings, diffidently at first, then with all the spirit of a stockman who thinks his game the finest on earth.]*

JACK	For I can ride a rowdy colt, or swing an axe all day,
	But there's no demand for station hands along the Castlereagh.
	So it's shift boys, shift, there isn't the slightest doubt

*[*JOHN *and* BRUMBY *join in the chorus:]*

	We've got to make a move for the stations further out.
	With the pack horse running after, for he follows like a dog,
	We get over lots of country at the old jig jog.
JOHN	Next verse. Come on, Jack, 'Now you see this old black horse . . .'
MAY	Go on, Mr. Carey, please!
JACK	*[singing]*
	Now, you see this old black horse I ride, if you notice what's his brand,
	He wears a crooked R, you see, no better in the land,

He takes a lot of beating, and the other day we
    tried,
For a bit of a joke, with a racing bloke, for
    twenty quid a side.
And it was shift, boys, shift, for there wasn't
    the slightest doubt.
I had to make him shift, for the money was
    nearly out.
But I cantered home a winner with the other at
    the flog,
He's a red-hot sort of pick-up with the old jig
    jog.
I asked a cove for shearin' once, along the
    Marthaga,
'We shear non-Union here,' says he. 'I call it
    scab,' says I.
I looked along the shearin' floor before I turned
    to go,
There was eight, or ten, damned Chinamen, a-
    shearin' in a row.
So it's shift, boys, shift, there isn't the slightest
    doubt,
I had to make a shift with the leprosy about.
So I saddled up me horses and I whistled to me
    dog,
And I left his scabby station at the old jig jog.
I went to Illawarra where the brother keeps a
    farm,
They have to ask the landlord's leave before
    they lift their arm.
The landlord owns the countryside, man,
    woman, dog and cat,
And they haven't the cheek to dare to speak
    without they touch their hat.

[The black on the bunk has been stirring during the singing and
WYLBA *is heard wailing in the store.]*

So it's shift, boys, shift, there isn't the slightest
    doubt,
Their little landlord god and I would soon have
    fallen out,
Was I to touch me hat to him? Was I his

bloomin' dog?

So I hooks-up for the country at the old jig jog.

WYLBA   *[crying in the storeroom, her voice rising above the singing]* Walygee booger! Walygee booger!

MAY   What's that?

WYLBA   *[her voice rising to a scream of imprecation as she bangs on the door]* Munyin-bunna, nunki-nunki. Chungee-chungee!

BRUMBY   *[pouring himself another drink]* Eh?

WYLBA   *[continuing her tune of rage and despair]* Walyina, booketera, kundi-kundi, spa!

BRUMBY   *[maliciously, as he drinks]* Oh that! That's one of old Polly's kids. *[Jerking his head towards POLLY, who is washing and putting away tea things at the bench under the window]* She shut her up in the store – for stealing the sugar, or something . . .

WYLBA   Chungee-chungee, belyee mari, koo!

POLLY   *[slowly and clearly, facing BRUMBY, her voice flat, without emotion]* Liar.

JOHN   *[uneasily, sensing domestic disturbances, and anxious for his niece not to discover them]* Well, we better get down to tin tacks, Brumby. Fact of the matter is, I didn't mean this to be . . . a polite morning call.

BRUMBY   *[derisively]* Go on? *[Tipping the bottle again]* Have another drink?

JOHN   *[firmly and sternly]* Fact of the matter is, we've got to come to some understanding about what's happening . . .

BRUMBY   *[guilelessly, as JOHN does not take the proffered pot, drinking himself]* Jesus. What's happening?

JOHN   The percentage of our calves, this end of the run is much less than anywhere else. The feed's good; there are more wells. And at the figure you're showin', your cows must be havin' two and three calves a year.

BRUMBY   *[crowing derisively]* I ain't responsible for the actions of my cows.

JOHN   There's the branded calf you had in your yards
the other day when Munga was over. And
the mother was one of our cows.

BRUMBY   *[laughing as though over a good joke]*
Cripes . . . and you should have heard him
go off!

[WYLBA wails more quietly now.]

JOHN   I did.

BRUMBY   Well, what are you goin' to do about it?

JOHN   *[amazed]* Do about it?

BRUMBY   *[flatly]* Do about it.

JOHN   You'll see what I'm goin' to do about it.

[MICKINA on the bunk lifts himself, listens to WYLBA still wailing in the store, lies looking warily round, then listens with closed eyes.]

It's over the fence, Brum, the way you been
carrying on. Way you been treating Nyedee.
I've shut my eyes to it, over and over again.
And I've warned you . . .

BRUMBY   *[jocosely]* He's warned me, Jack!

JOHN   So as not to make any bad feeling between us.
But it's come to this. Things can't go on the
way they're doing. The run won't stand it.
We lost 4,000 bullocks out of 12,000 in the
drought . . .

JACK   *[with grudging admiration]* Nyedee lost less than
most.

JOHN   Why? Wasn't it because I worked night and day
moving the cattle. Wherever there was a bit
of feed or water, we moved. Kept movin'
'em.

JACK   That's right. You did, John. I'm not sayin' you
don't deserve anything you got. You do. But
Brum – he jest can't run straight.

BRUMBY   *[watching MAY, who is trying the storeroom
door]* Speak for y'r self!

MICKINA   *[raising himself cautiously and making a dash
for the door]* All time . . . branding your
calves, John!

BRUMBY   *[starting to his feet, hand on his revolver]* God
damn and blast –

MICKINA   *[in the doorway]* Bring in cleanskin. He say
          brand'm B.1.4.

[MICKINA vanishes.]

BRUMBY   These bloody niggers is gettin' too bloody
          cheeky.

JOHN   He's about right, I reckon, Brum. It's only what
          I've heard before. Anyway, it's got to stop. I
          give you fair warning. I'm watching you from
          now on and if I find you running in any
          more Nyedee calves, I'll have the law on you.

BRUMBY   *[gazing at MAY]* Law? There ain't any law – out
          here.

MAY   *[provocatively]* Except for abos.

BRUMBY   What's that?

MAY   Didn't I hear you say you'd have the mounted
          police to your boys?

BRUMBY   That's right.

[There is a stir of movement: muffled laughter outside.]
          What's that?

JOHN   What?

JACK   *[going to the door]* Who's there?

*[Natives jump up behind the windows and run past the door,
laughing and hooting.]*

BRUMBY   Well, I'm damned.

WYLBA   *[springing into the doorway, flanked by MICKINA
          and other boys, yelling, hooting their anger
          and laughter]* Minyin bunna nunki-nunki,
          chungee-chungee, walyina, booketera, kundi-
          kundi, spa.

[JACK goes to the door.]
          Dirty dog . . . koo!

*[She, and all the blacks, disappear on this last note of mockery
and defiance.]*

BRUMBY   *[striding to the door]* By God, if I don't –

JOHN   *[harshly]* Hold on, Brumby. You might wait till
          we're gone.

JACK   *[from the door of the storeroom]* They've broke
          a hole in the wall, helped themselves to
          tobacco. There's flour and sugar all over the
          place.

BRUMBY   *[swinging to the storeroom]* Broken in, have
they? If I don't make some of 'm sweat for
this.

[He goes into the store.]

JACK   *[to* JOHN*]* Wylba must've been grubbin' a hole
through, and the boys was helping her from
the outside, all the time she was yellin'.

JOHN   Quite likely.

MAY   *[lightly]* An interesting morning, Unk!

JOHN   Glad you like it.

MAY   *[lightly]* I'd no idea life could be so exciting
outback, these days. What a good thing I
made you bring me with you this morning.
Mr. Innes is quite a thrill, isn't he?

JOHN   *[uneasily]* It's all very well, May, to trot out
your little airs and graces for men like Cecil
Grey or Arthur Leigh; but Brum's
different . . .

MAY   Different?

JOHN   He wouldn't understand . . . flirting.

MAY   *[laughing]* Not understand? Oh, Unk, you're
priceless! Why he took to it like a duck to
water when we met him over at Koodgieda,
last month.

JOHN   *[as* POLLY *stands beside him, erect and dignified]*
What's up, Polly?

POLLY   Go longa, Nyedee, John.

JOHN   Why? What's up, Polly?

POLLY   Go Nyedee, with you, John.

JOHN   *[puzzled]* Go to Nyedee with me, Polly?

POLLY   Good house-girl sweep, sew, make bread,
tea . . . wash'm *[with a gesture over herself]*
all time.

JOHN   Why? Had a row with Brumby, Polly?

POLLY   Bita muna, Brumby.

JOHN   Fed up with him, are you?

POLLY   Eeh-erm. Fed up.

JOHN   But you've been with Brumby, how many
years?

POLLY   Weary booger years. Tell me get out now.

Want young woman. Pretty young girl . . .
Wylba. *[Looking at* MAY*]* Two women,
maybe.

JOHN   Oh, that's it, is it? He wants a young and pretty
woman, now . . . two women, perhaps.

BRUMBY   *[coming from the storeroom with* JACK *behind
him]* Taken all they wanted: tobacco, pipes,
jam, sugar, flour, tea. Niggers on this station
need a lesson. That's what they need. I'll ride
into Yanigee with you, John, and get the
police on to this.

JACK   Aw . . . go on, Brum. There's not much damage
done. We got plenty of stuff till next loading.
Tell him not to be a fool, John.

BRUMBY   I'm goin' for the police, I tell yer. Think I'm
goin' to stand for niggers raidin' the store?

JOHN   You'll be making the mistake of your life, if you
go dragging the police into your affairs with
natives, Brum.

BRUMBY   *[propitiatingly]* Cut it out, John. Cut it out.
White men's got to stand together or there'll
be no livin' in the Nor'-west. I'm no bloody
angel – but you ain't, y'rself. And where
cattle's concerned it's fifty-fifty.

JOHN   *[harshly]* Speak for yourself.

BRUMBY   Oh, well, they're doin' a bit of brandin' all
round yer, and if y'don't do it, more fool
you. You can't tell me if Three Hills, or
Karrara, had a killer in the yards, and you
rode up, unexpected, you'd care to go down
to the stockyards.

JOHN   That's not the question.

BRUMBY   Oh, well, the long and the short of it is, John,
if there's been a mistake about any of your
calves . . .

JOHN   There's been mistakes about a good many of
our calves, Brum.

BRUMBY   *[amiably]* Oh, well, if there has, there has,
John. But cut it out . . . cut it out, for Gord's
sake . . . and I'll make 'em up to you. I want
to stand well with you. You been square with

me . . . dead square . . . and, by Christ . . .
I'll deal square with you.

JOHN   *[dryly]* Pleased to hear it.

BRUMBY   There's a bush mob in the yards now. You can
go and take y'r pick.

JACK   Or else *[glancing towards* BRUMBY *for
affirmation]* the boys'll be musterin' fats, next
moon, John, if y'cared to come over then . . .

BRUMBY   Anything in reason, so long as we cut out the
square talk and stop jawrin'. *[Cunningly, his
eyes following* MAY's *every movement]* But I'd
go while the goin's good, if I was you, John.
I might change me mind. Feelin' real good,
this mornin'. Lovin' me neighbour like meself.
But it mightn't last, might it, Jack?

JACK   Too right, it mightn't.

BRUMBY   You go along with him, Jack. See he don't skin
me while I fix up me tucker bags for goin'
into Yanigee.

JOHN   Right. *[Going to the door]* Coming, May?

MAY   *[hesitating, glancing back at* BRUMBY, *who is
busy folding and rolling his ground sheet and
blanket on the floor]* It'll be dusty up at the
yards – I may as well wait here.

JACK   *[standing in the doorway]* What?

[He looks anxiously at BRUMBY *who appears occupied with his
pack.]*

JOHN   We'll be back in two-two's.

*[*JACK *jams on his hat. He and* JOHN *turn away.]*

BRUMBY   *[genially, calling after them]* See you fix him all
right, Jack. Jack'll see you get a fair deal,
John. Thinks there's no one like you. And it'd
break me heart to see the way the brands on
some of them beasts has been mugged.

*[*MAY, *standing in the doorway, watches* JOHN *and* JACK *go to the
stockyards; then turns to look at* BRUMBY, *who goes up to the
bench under the window for his tucker bags of unbleached calico,
and spreads them out, apparently oblivious but intensely
conscious of her all the time.]*

MAY   *[flirtatiously]* Well, I came, didn't I?

BRUMBY   *[not looking at her, and going on with his*

preparations] Warned you not to.

MAY   *[gaily]* That's why I came, of course.

BRUMBY   *[taking tins down from the shelf beside the
            hearth]* I said . . . if you came to see me . . .
            you'd stay.

MAY   *[teasing him]* But I didn't come to see you, Mr.
            Innes. I came to see . . . Mr. Carey.

BRUMBY   *[as if talking to himself, and reaching for
            another tin]* White women are scarce. We got
            to get 'em as best we can.

*[MAY takes a powder box with mirror and lipstick, tied up in a
handkerchief, from her breeches pocket, powders her face daintily
and reddens her lips. BRUMBY watches her.]*

            Gord A'mighty!

MAY   Why . . .

[She laughs, pleased to have attracted his attention.]

BRUMBY   What are you doin' that for?

MAY   Oh . . . habit, I suppose. When in doubt,
            powder your nose.

*[BRUMBY, continuing his packing, rolls a huge piece of salt meat
in a bag, pours flour into a bag, throws them over to the pack.]*

BRUMBY   Where's the tea?

*[He finds it and pours tea into a bag, spilling some, takes a tin
of jam and goes to the pack, kneels down to arrange the bundles.]*

MAY   *[coming nearer and sitting on the end of the
            table to watch him]* I'm going down south on
            Saturday, you know. Uncle and Cecil Grant
            are taking me into Yanigee. We're camping
            two nights on the road. I adore camping,
            don't you?

[BRUMBY grunts.]

            And then I'm to be married next month, you
            know. Didn't you know? Oh . . . I thought
            everybody knew.

*[BRUMBY rises, goes to shelf for some cartridges and reloads his
revolver. MAY is alarmed.]*

            What are you doing that for?

BRUMBY   You never can tell when it may be useful.

MAY   But I thought the abos up here were all so
            quiet?

BRUMBY   They are. But sometimes one gets over the
fence; or a sulky fellow comes in from the
bush.

*[He thrusts the revolver into the leather case on his belt, and goes
to the bench again. Pouring sugar into a tucker bag, he spills a
good deal.]*

MAY   *[going towards him]* Here, you're spilling it all.
I'll hold the bag for you.

*[BRUMBY pours the sugar as she holds the bag, staring at her, with
glowering fascination.]*

BRUMBY   *[almost in a whisper]* I want you.

[He drops the sugar tin.]

MAY   *[startled]* What? What did you say?

BRUMBY   *[moving between her and the door]* You're like
water on a dry stretch to a thirsty man.

MAY   *[scared]* Oh –

BRUMBY   They call me the brumby.

MAY   *[frightened but fencing]* I've heard what a
wonderful bushman you are.

BRUMBY   You have, have you? *[With easy conceit]* Well,
that's right. I've knocked round with gins all
me days: gins and bullocks, blacks and
brumbies. Born in the Breakaway country.
Never been to school. But I want a white
woman. How about stayin' here?

MAY   *[coquettishly, thinking she has the reins again]*
It's awfully sweet of you to ask me, but –

BRUMBY   *[throwing an arm round her and holding her]*
You been foolin' all the men you've set eyes
on up here, for the last six months. You
aren't goin' to fool me.

MAY   Let me go.

BRUMBY   *[laughing]* Not on your life.

MAY   If you don't . . .

BRUMBY   Well?

MAY   I'll scream the place down.

BRUMBY   Scream away. They wouldn't hear you at the
yards . . . even if I let you.

MAY   *[struggling, but yielding]* Oh you . . .

BRUMBY   *[laughing triumphantly and embracing her*

roughly, as he pushes her towards the bunk]
I like 'em thoroughbred and buckin' a bit at
first.

END OF ACT TWO

ACT THREE

The kitchen of BRUMBY INNES' *homestead, four or five months
later. It looks the same as ACT TWO except that there is a gramophone on the table and a jar of yellow wildflowers. A few brightly
coloured magazines lie about; a girl's wide-leafed straw hat with
a ribbon hangs from the knob of a chair; and a chintz umbrella
and tennis racquet lean beside the door post; a scarlet kimono
dangles from a peg over the bunk. There is a bookcase beside
the storeroom door.*

MAY, *in a yellow frock, is leaning against the door post, right,
and gazing out over the plains.*

POLLY *passes the window on the left, a bucket of water on her
head; in the doorway she pauses, lifts the bucket down, and moves
with slow dignity to the fireplace, puts the bucket against the wall,
stirs the ashes of the fire, throws wood on.*

MAY   Does anything ever happen? Does anyone ever
      come, Polly?
POLLY   Eeh-erm.
MAY   Do they?
POLLY   Eeh-erm.
MAY   *[after a long silence in which* POLLY *washes
      some dishes at the bench under the window]*
      How long have I been here, watching the
      road . . . every dust? *[Bitterly]* Weary
      booger years? *[As* POLLY *does not answer,
      continuing very slowly to dip and dry cups
      and saucers]* Polly!
POLLY   *[mildly, with surprise at the sharpness of her
      voice]* Eeh-erm.
MAY   How long have I been here?
POLLY   Two moon, maybe.

MAY Two months . . . it's a dream, surely. Some queer sort of dream I'm in. It feels just like that Polly. You know how you can't move in a dream; the red dust blows into you – columns of it. Winning-arras, isn't it you call them, the whirlwinds?

POLLY Eeh-erm.

MAY It's got into my brain . . . the red dust. I've been eating it. It's suffocating me. *[Whirling away from the door and walking up and down]* If only I could do something. What can I do, Polly?

POLLY *[indifferently, glancing contemptuously and moving off with the two blackened kerosene buckets]* Murndoo.

MAY *[hysterically]* Murndoo. Don't know. You don't know. I don't know. And there's nobody else to know. *[Desperately]* Is Jack Carey back yet?

POLLY *[imperturbably]* Fetch'm killer.

MAY When will *he* be back?

POLLY Brumby?

MAY Yes.

POLLY *[flatly]* Murndoo.

MAY *[despairingly]* Don't know. You don't know anything I ask you. And the rest of the camp's gone pink-eye, till Brumby gets back. And the boys the police took. Will they come back? Mickina and the boys, I mean. Cock-eyed Bob, Bungarra and the rest of them?

POLLY *[staring away over the plains]* Murndoo.

MAY *[petulantly]* Murndoo! Murndoo! Don't say that to me again. You're not to say you don't know to me again. Do you hear?

[POLLY stalks off, a bucket on her head.]

Damn you.

[When POLLY has disappeared, a low wailing and groaning is heard.]

Who's there?

[The tall, stooping figure of an old native woman appears outside,

coming from the left. Her dark blue dungaree gina-gina is almost black with grease and dirt. A dust coloured rag, once white, is bound over her eyes and round her head. She walks with a stick, groping with one thin, scrawny arm before her, in the way of the blind.]

TULLAMURRA   *[hovering in the doorway]* Tullamurra.

MAY   Tullamurra. The blind one.

TULLAMURRA   *[wailing]* Ai-ey! Ai-ey!

MAY   *[going to her]* Poor old thing! How are the eyes, this afternoon?

TULLAMURRA   *[rocking herself in agony]* Ai-ey!

MAY   Poor old Tullamurra! Want some drops in them?

TULLAMURRA   *[hopefully]* Eeh-erm?

MAY   Very well.

[She goes to the bookcase near the storeroom door for a bottle of eye-lotion, while TULLAMURRA *sinks down on the floor and stretches flat on her back.]*

Gargoyle. That's it.

[Taking the bottle, she goes to the bench for a teaspoon.]

It's the black drops are the best, isn't it, Tullamurra?

TULLAMURRA   *[writhing and squirming]* Ai-ey!

*[*MAY*, kneeling down beside her, pours black lotion from the bottle into the teaspoon; the old woman pushes back her bandage.]*

MAY   Oh, they do look bad! Hold your eyelids apart.

[She drops the lotion from the spoon into the old woman's eyes.]

TULLAMURRA   Ai-ey!

MAY   *[rising, bottle and spoon in her hand]* There . . . it hurts! But it will do them good.

TULLAMURRA   *[writhing and squirming on the floor like a worm stabbed with a fork]* Ai-ey! Ai-ey!

*[*MAY*, after putting the bottle and spoon on the bench, takes the chair at the end of the table, sits down and watches as* TULLAMURRA *tries to sit up, holding her eyes and moaning with pain.]*

MAY   Stay where you are, Tullamurra.

TULLAMURRA   *[gratefully]* Eeh-erm.

*[*MAY *goes to the door and stares out, then returns to the chair as* TULLAMURRA *sits up.]*

MAY	That better?
TULLAMURRA	Eeh-erm.
MAY	What's this row between Brumby and the camp about, Tullamurra? Now don't you say, 'Murndoo'. You do know. And if you don't tell me, I won't do your eyes any more. *[As* TULLAMURRA *moves her head to listen whether* POLLY *is about]* No. Polly's over at the well.
TULLAMURRA	Brumby shoot over camp.
MAY	I know that. But why? Why did he shoot over the camp, Tullamurra?
TULLAMURRA	Blackfellow badgee.
MAY	Cross, eh? Angry with Brumby?
TULLAMURRA	Eeh-erm. Boys come up . . . plenty sticks . . . beat'm.
MAY	But they shouldn't have done that. Should they?
TULLAMURRA	*[firing up]* Brumby take'm Wylba. Bring Wylba *[gesturing about her]* yere.
MAY	What?
TULLAMURRA	*[emphatically]* Brumby shoot over camp. Take Wylba.
MAY	He had no right to shoot over the camp and take Wylba. That was it, was it?
TULLAMURRA	*[fearfully]* Eeh-erm. *[Listening for* POLLY*]* Yienda not telling Brumby?
MAY	No. I won't tell him. Wylba is very young, isn't she, Tullamurra?
TULLAMURRA	Eeh-erm. Mickina tell Morrison.
MAY	The Protector of Aborigines. That's why Wylba had to go down to Yanigee with him, and Uncle John . . . That's why they wouldn't let me go.
POLLY	*[coming in with water, one bucket on her head, the other in her hand, yelling furiously when she sees* TULLAMURRA*]* What you bin sayin'? *[Threatening her]* Get out!
TULLAMURRA	*[scrambling to her feet]* Wiah! Wiah!
MAY	What is it? What's the matter?
POLLY	*[marching to the fireplace]* Tell'm get the hell out of yere.

MAY   *[furiously]* Stay where you are, Tullamurra. I'll
        give orders in my own house, Polly. *[As*
        TULLAMURRA, *wailing and holding out her*
        hands blindly, moves towards the door]
        Wait a minute, Tullamurra. I'll get you
        some tobacco.

[She goes to the bookcase, takes a plug from a box while
TULLAMURRA *wavers deprecatingly and* POLLY *fixes her with a*
gaze of sombre will power.]

        There!

[She gives the tobacco, at which the old woman beams, and turns
to go, without thanks, as is the native fashion. She stumbles at
the door, groping her way with hands before her. POLLY *follows*
her out. They are heard jabbering outside, their voices shrill and
quarrelsome. Another native woman turns round the door post
on the right, with an eye cocked to be sure POLLY *has not seen*
her. She is of average height, fat and jolly looking, in a tawny,
dust-coloured skirt, man's hat and coat.]

        Oh, it's you, Warrarie! What do you want?

WARRARIE *[ingratiatingly]* Got'm t'read, missus?

MAY   What for . . . you want thread, Warrarie?

WARRARIE *[turning and showing brown limbs through a*
          very torn skirt] Weary booger, dress.

MAY   *[laughing]* I should think so.

WARRARIE Poor booger me. *[Wheedlingly]* Got'm gina-
          gina store miah, meetchie?

MAY   A new dress? What on earth do you want a
         new gina-gina for?

WARRARIE *[gurgling, coy and sly, hugging herself]* Got'm
          noova.

MAY   Noova . . . a lover?

WARRARIE Eeh-erm.

MAY   But your husband's only dead a few months.
         Isn't that his hat and coat you're wearing?

WARRARIE *[unabashed]* Eeh-erm.

MAY   Where you get'm lover?

WARRARIE *[giggling and cuddling herself delightedly]*
          Bullock muster . . . Nyedee . . . Young
          man . . . strong feller.

MAY   Munga?

WARRARIE *[gurgling happily]* Eeh-erm.

MAY   Poor booger me. Got no lover, Warrarie.

WARRARIE   Eeh? *[Chancing an upsquint and owl's eye, as if to say 'What are you giving us?']* Wiah?

MAY   Only Brumby.

WARRARIE   *[confidentially, leaning forward]* Yienda, kurrie . . . go bullock muster.

MAY   *[laughing]* A pretty young woman, am I? *[Thoughtfully]* Tell you what, Warrarie. We run away, you and I. We go bush . . . find lover for me?

WARRARIE   *[flatly and with emphasis]* No! . . . Brumby chase'm . . . beat'm . . . break'm back . . . kick'm be'ind.

POLLY   *[coming in, threateningly]* Go, woodheap, you!

MAY   *[jumping down from the table excitedly]* Mind your own business, Polly. Don't dare to chase her away while I'm talking to her.

POLLY   *[going to the fireplace, scowling and muttering]* Brumby tell'm.

MAY   Well, I won't have you interfering with me. Do you understand?

POLLY   *[waving her hand towards the horizon]* Bin comin' . . .

MAY   Coming? *[Going to the door]* Who?

WARRARIE   *[looking out beside her]* John Hallinan, may be.

MAY   Oh! *[With excitement]* There's Jack Carey! Who is it, Mr. Carey?

JACK   *[passing the window]* What?

MAY   There's someone coming, the gins say. That dust over there.

[POLLY comes to the door behind WARRARIE.*]*

JACK   *[his hand on his heart, walking crookedly, with a limp]* Who is it, Polly?

POLLY   John Hallinan's buggy.

MAY   Uncle John?

JACK   Brumby ridin'?

WARRARIE   Boys ridin'?

POLLY   Brumby in buggy, may be.

MAY   I'll go down to the gate to meet them.

WARRARIE   *[wheedlingly]* Got'm little feller new dress, meetchie?

MAY   Oh, I forgot. *[Coming back into the room]*
          Where are the keys, Polly? I see.

[She goes to the bookcase, takes the keys from the shelf, fits key in the storeroom door.]

          Just wait a minute, Warrarie.

[She goes into the storeroom.]

POLLY   *[to* JACK, *growling]* Give gina-gina.

JACK   *[letting himself down carefully on to the chair
          on the far side of the table]* Lazy old swob!
          Better not let Brumby catch you, hanging
          round cadgin' gina-ginas. You can go up
          and help them kill and skin that beast
          anyhow, Warrarie.

WARRARIE   *[watching* MAY *with eager delight as she comes
          from the storeroom, a piece of red print in
          her hands]* Yukk-eye!

*[*MAY, *after locking the door and hanging keys on their peg, gives the material to* WARRARIE.*]*

MAY   There you are.

*[*WARRARIE, *snatching it away, gurgles ecstatically, fondles the stuff.]*

WARRARIE   Pretty . . . pretty gina-gina.

[She slides out.]

JACK   *[calling after her]* See you don't let the
          stomach gas into that beast!

MAY   *[going to the door]* Are you sure it's Uncle
          John, Polly? I can't see anything but dust.

POLLY   Eeh-erm.

MAY   *[turning to* JACK CAREY*]* I begged Uncle to come
          and take me back with him, Mr. Carey—
          [As he sits, bowed with pain, over the table]
          Are you all right?

JACK   *[startled, and standing up stiffly]* I'm good,
          thank you, Mrs. Innes.

MAY   Polly says it's Uncle John.

JACK   *[with difficulty]* He'll be comin' back from
          Yanigee . . . I suppose Brum and the boys'll
          be with him.

MAY   You're knocked up.

JACK   *[sturdily]* Not a bit.

MAY   I shouldn't have let you go out after that killer.

JACK   *[gallantly]* Oh, the ridin's all right. Only I can't
see as well as I used to; and Brumby turned
out all the horses he wasn't takin'
himself – except old Hero.

MAY   *[quickly]* One of the gins went with you,
though?

JACK   Engi. Best gin on the place after cattle. She got
the beast, really, and you should've heard
her laugh when a white cockie, or
somethin', frightened Hero. He pitched me
off into a thorn bush –

MAY   There's the buggy. I can hear them pulling up.

BRUMBY   *[shouting]* Anybody at home?

JACK   *[as* MAY *turns to the door]* It's all right. It'll be
all right.

[Hearing BRUMBY's *voice,* POLLY *reaches for a bottle of whisky
on the shelf by the hearth and takes it with mug and quart pots
to the table.]*

MAY   How's the kettle, Polly? *[Looking round]*
Oh . . . well, Uncle John would like some
tea . . .

[She goes to the bench and POLLY *moves to help her.]*
No, I'll make it myself, thanks.

BRUMBY   *[swaggering in, boisterously]* Hullo Polly,
where's my woman? Oh, there you are,
May! *[As she stands off, staring at him]*
Well, aren't you going to give your husband
a kiss, like a respectable married woman? A
peck on the cheek'll do . . .

MAY   *[coldly]* I'd rather not, thank you.

BRUMBY   Right. I'll kiss old Polly instead. *[Going to and
kissing* POLLY*]* How's things, Polly?

[He swings to the table and the whisky. POLLY *goes out.]*

MAY   Uncle John! *[Clinging to him, and speaking
under her breath]* I can't stand it. Truly, I
can't. It's driving me out of my mind.

JOHN   That was over the fence, Brum.

BRUMBY   *[snarling and lifting his pot of whisky]* You
keep y'r mouth shut. *[Putting the pot down
and pouring again]* I've had enough of you
jawrin' me head off.

MAY   You meant it for the best, Unk. But let me
come home with you. Let me come home.

JACK   *[while* JOHN *is trying to soothe* MAY*]* How'd
things go, Brum?

JOHN   They nearly didn't go, and *[with anger]* I wish
to God, now, I'd let him stew in his own
juice.

BRUMBY   *[sitting on the edge of the table and exhilarated
by the whisky]* Lot you had to do with it.

JOHN   I had everything to do with it, that's all.

*[*MAY *moves away to the bench to make tea for him.]*

JACK   What?

JOHN   He'd've gone up for nine or ten years, for a
dead cert' . . .

JACK   On the age of the girl?

JOHN   Told the magistrate himself, she was thirteen
and three months.

JACK   You didn't do that, Brum?

JOHN   Got round the town before he went to court.
Did my best to get him there sober, Jack,
but it was no use.

BRUMBY   *[crowing and imitating the magistrate]* 'How
can you say the girl's age is sixteen, Mr.
Hallinan, when as a matter of fact, the
defendant states the age of the girl to be
thirteen years and three months? If he didn't
know – wasn't sure – why should he say
three months?'

JACK   Did you say she was sixteen, John?

JOHN   I did. That's what I reck'n her age is . . .

BRUMBY   *[continuing his recitation]* 'Oh,' says he, lyin'
like a tripe hound. 'I know she's sixteen
because I saw her. She was livin' with her
people on the Creek first time I come
through with cattle ten years ago. She was
six or seven then – couldn't be less. I been
on Nyedee ten years next January, and . . .'

JACK   That got him off, John.

*[*MAY *puts a cup of tea on the table beside* JOHN *and goes to the
doorway, looking out but listening too.]*

BRUMBY   *[enjoying his mimicry]* 'How do you account

for the fact that Mr. Innes says the girl is thirteen years and three months, Mr. Hallinan?' 'Oh, well, y'r worship,' says Mr. St. Anthony John Hallinan, 'he's been having a few drinks this mornin', and how much importance can you attach to anything a man says when he doesn't know what he's saying?' 'True, true.'

JACK He don't deserve it, John.

BRUMBY *[hilariously]* Discharged without a stain on me character!

JACK It's more'n most men would do for you, Brum.

BRUMBY Good old John. *[Pushing the bottle towards him]* Have a drink, John? But he's me uncle now, don't forget, Jack. We're relations be marriage.

JACK How did the boys get on?

JOHN Six months for assault.

BRUMBY And one month for burglary, and breakin'-in and stealin'.

MAY *[coming down to him]* Unk!

[JOHN rises from the table and she throws her arms round him.]
You will take me home with you, won't you?

BRUMBY *[savagely]* What are you crawlin' round him for?

JOHN You'd better let her come back with me, Brumby.

BRUMBY *[more sour and savage than he has been]* See here, John Hallinan, you can't have things both ways. You've got all you wanted out of me. You would have I'd got to marry the girl . . . hush up any scandal. Marry her I did, and she's my woman. I won't have no more tellin' me what I ought to do.

MAY *[distressfully]* Unkie!

BRUMBY See here, May. *[Walking over and twisting her by the shoulder away from JOHN]* You stay here.

JACK *[anxious to pacify everybody]* It's all right . . . It'll be all right.

BRUMBY You got them calves, John?

JOHN   Yes . . . I got a couple of dozen calves,
        Brumby.

BRUMBY Well, I reck'n, if you and me's not comin' to
        blows, you'd better get out – and quick
        feller.

JOHN   *[with indignation]* If that's the way you're
        talking' –

JACK   Don't be a fool, John.

BRUMBY *[pouring himself out another drink]* No. Don't
        be a fool, John. Y'r not a fighting man. You
        know y'r not.

JOHN   You know I'm not. And what's more, we've
        got to talk this thing out. Peaceably.

BRUMBY *[putting down his mug after having drunk]* We
        aren't going to talk no more.

JOHN   Then May's coming home with me.

BRUMBY *[bashing him across the face]* It's a lie.

JACK   Brum!

[JOHN pitches off his coat and shapes up.]

JOHN   Come on then, let's have it.

MAY   Unkie! Unkie!

BRUMBY *[to her]* You've asked for it.

[Game as JOHN is, BRUMBY pastes him unmercifully.]

JACK   For God's sake, Brum!

MAY   Make him stop. Oh . . .

BRUMBY Goin' back is she?

JACK   *[wrestling with BRUMBY]* Leave off. Y'll kill
        him, Brum.

BRUMBY *[as JOHN falls]* Goin' back, is she? Bloody fool!

*[Returning to the table, he sits down on it and reaches for the
whisky. MAY and JACK go to JOHN.]*

        Goin' back, is she?

MAY   Is he dead, Mr. Carey?

JACK   He's all right. He'll be all right.

[He goes to the table for whisky and pours some into a mug.]

        Polly!

*[Returning to JOHN, JACK puts the mug to JOHN's mouth. POLLY
appears in the doorway.]*

        Water.

*[POLLY stares silently at JOHN, goes to the hearth for a bucket of
water and puts it down beside JACK.]*

BRUMBY   *[slouching to the door and roaring]* Gingarra! Tommy! God damn and blast'm. No gettin' anything out of the bloody niggers on this place. Gingarra! Buck un-ma . . . quick feller . . . or I'll flay the hides off of you. *[As the natives appear]* John Hallinan wants to get a move on. Put his horses in and bring the buggy over.

[Slamming his hat over his head and with a contemptuous look at the man on the floor, he goes out.]

JACK   *[washing* JOHN's *face with his own handkerchief]* He'll be all right.

JOHN   *[moving and moaning]* May!

MAY   *[on her knees beside him]* I'm here, Unk.

JACK   *[as* JOHN *sits up]* Y'r all right, John?

JOHN   *[dazedly, passing his hand over his head]* I ought to have known better.

JACK   Course you should, John.

JOHN   What am I goin' to do about her, Jack? God, I could blow my brains out for ever having brought her here. And then marrying her to the brute. But I thought it was for the best. I thought I'd got to see he married her.

JACK   Look here, John. If yer take my advice y'll leave things alone. Brum ain't unkind to his women . . .

JOHN   Prides himself on that, doesn't he?

JACK   He's rough as bags; but he'll treat Mrs. Innes proper. He's well-in too. Can give her anything she wants if she only handles him right.

MAY   *[passionately]* I hate him.

JACK   *[shrewdly]* I'm not so sure of that. I think he gets you . . . like the rest of 'em.

MAY   *[flinging away impatiently]* Oh!

BRUMBY   *[in the doorway]* Kerridge, me lord.

JACK   *[helping* JOHN *to the door]* She'll be all right, John. Don't you worry.

JOHN   You'll do what you can, I know, Jack.

JACK   Course I will.

JOHN   *[kissing* MAY*]* I've made a mess of this, darling. I thought . . .

MAY   *[drearily]* I understand, Unk. It can't be helped now.

JOHN   *[uneasily]* Try to make the best of it.

MAY   *[desperately]* I don't know! I don't know what I'll do.

JOHN   It's true, what Jack says. Brumby's generous in his own way; and he prides himself on treating women better than most men.

MAY   Good-bye, Unkie!

JOHN   Good-bye. *[Kissing her again]* Jack'll keep me posted how you are. *[As he goes out]* I'll send a boy over with books and papers every week.

JACK   *[calling after him]* Good-bye, John. She's all right. She'll be all right.

[He comes back into the room, BRUMBY *behind him;* MAY *is standing at the window on the left looking out.]*

BRUMBY   Clear out, Jack.

*[*JACK *picks up his hat and steers his long creaking figure to the door again.* BRUMBY *turns to* POLLY *at the hearth.)*

   Scram! *[as she dawdles]* Get the hell out of this!

*[*POLLY *swings to the door, scowling.* MAY *moves to follow her, but he intercepts her.]*

   No, it's you I'm cuttin'-out.

*[*MAY *comes back into the room disconsolately, goes to the chair on the other side of the table and sits down.]*

MAY   Well, what is it?

BRUMBY   *[following and gazing at her cynically, savagely]* Think I'm shook on you, don't you? You damned silvertail. You poor, sickly, miserable-lookin' creature.

MAY   Then why don't you let me go back to Nyedee?

BRUMBY   I'll never let you go back to Nyedee. What you've got to understand is, you're one of Brumby's mares. You gallop with the mob.

MAY   *[jumping up]* It's outrageous.

BRUMBY   You'll get feed and water – the best. A brumby leads his mares to good grass. I won't bother you when y'r with foal. Like you are

now. You can go south, in a couple of
months, mooch off, and choose your own
place to lay down. There'll be money to do
what you like till it's a fair thing to come
back.

MAY   What if I don't come back?

BRUMBY   You'll come back, all right.

MAY   *[defiantly]* Will I? I'm not so sure of that. I
was engaged to a man who was really fond
of me when I came up here; and you –

BRUMBY   A brumby boss-horse don't allow his mare to
be took off . . .

MAY   Until another shows him he's not the boss he
thought he was?

BRUMBY   That's right.

MAY   *[desperately]* But if you're not keen on me –

BRUMBY   Got nothing to do with it.

MAY   Oh, how I hate men!

BRUMBY   And I hate women. Hate their silly, wimperin'
palaver about love. Dressin' themselves
up – plasterin' themselves with powder and
scent till they stink like an Afghan. For
why? To get men flutterin' round
them – like you had all the men up here.

MAY   You don't know the meaning of love.

BRUMBY   Don't I? Love! I don't want to. *[Spitting]* See. I
don't want to. Do y' know what love is?
[As she does not answer] It's the smoke you
blasted women put up to do men out of
being plain, ordinary, decent male animals.

MAY   *[with disgust]* You mean love gets between you
and . . .

BRUMBY   I mean what you call love's a god-damned
sham.

MAY   All you care about's your filthy lusts.

BRUMBY   Here *[taking her by the shoulder]* you keep
your tongue off of talking like that. My
lust's not filthy. It's natural. Makes me feel
good. Like the rain . . . and the rivers
runnin' when everything's dead and dry, up
here.

MAY   *[drearily]* I suppose so.

BRUMBY   But I want youngsters. And a good home. You can make it what you like. Now the station's grown, there's the question who's to get it when I'm gone. I want youngsters, and I want'm thoroughbred. It's a damned insult to a man not to see children about him.

MAY   Gins don't go in for child-bearing.

BRUMBY   The old men won't let 'em – if food's short. Look here, May, it's goin' to make a lot of difference to me, havin' the kid. Give me a chance, and we'll trot along well enough. I'll do anything to make things right for you and the young 'un.

MAY   *[passionately]* I loathe the sight of you, this blasted country, and everything in it.

BRUMBY   *[sardonically]* All right! Have it your own way.

WYLBA   *[prancing cheekily in the doorway]* Munyin bunna, nunki-nunki, chungee-chungee.

[She disappears.]

MAY   She's not coming back here, is she?

BRUMBY   *[recovering his good humour and pose]* Where else'd she go? She belongs here, doesn't she? Down at the camp.

WYLBA   *[putting her head in at the window, impishly]* Walyee Mari, booketerra, kundi-kundi, spa!

BRUMBY   *[exuberantly]* But Wylba isn't the only pebble on the plains. Not by long chalks – There's Melanie at Koodgieda. I've only got to send a rifle and couple of blankets to her old man, to get her when I want her. *[Putting on the gramophone]* How's it for a bit of music?

[A lively tune blares out. WYLBA comes sneaking back, looks in at the door, lisening.]

But Wylba don't mind lettin' bygones be bygones, do you Wylba? Come on, Wylba, give us a step.

[The little native girl dances forward. BRUMBY prances with her.

MAY *watches a moment, then with a gesture of defeat goes out. Across the plains the sun is setting.* BRUMBY's *laughter and* WYLBA's *shrill giggling mingle with the gay, harsh music of the gramophone.*]

CURTAIN

Glossary of Aboriginal words in Ngaala-warngga occurring in Brumby Innes

Compiled by Carl von Brandenstein and incorporating manuscript notes by Katharine Prichard in initial text.

Words in italics represent the modern spelling.
A: author's note

babba *(paba)*, water.
badgee *(padji)*, angry, wild.
balgarilla *(parlgarrala)*, on the plain.
belyee mari *(piljimarri)*, penis, puffy.
bina, hidden.
bita muna *(pidamanna)*, fed up with.
booger (purga), chap, fellow.
booketera *(pugatharra)*, stinker, one who stinks.
borki *(pu(y)unka(rr)ai)*, grey smoke, haze; australite.
buckunma *(pakanma)*, come here!
bun abbia *(pannabia)*, they have twisted, blurred, thrown at it.

chungee chungee *(tjandiji-tjandji)*, jagged (penis?).
cootharra, cotharra *(kudharra)*, two.

eeh-erm *(eh-eh)*, confirmation (A: 'Eeh-erm is like our Mmm!').

gina-gina *(tjina-tjina)*, dress.
Ginarra *(Tjinara)*, male name.
gindoo *(tjirndu)*, sun.

kala *(kalla)*, fire, firewood.
kalla miah *(kalla-maya)*, wood store, woodheap.
kinerra *(kinnara)*, full moon.
ko, koo *(ku)*, yes, derisively (A: 'a long hooting call of derision').
Koodgieda *(Kudjida)*, fictitious station.
Kulliwarigo *(Kuliwarrigu)*, meaning dubious.
kundi-kundi *(kurndai-kurndai?)*, shame!
kuningmarra *(kaningmarra)*, meaning dubious.
kurrie *(kurri)*, young girl, virgin.

mardoo mardourie *(mardumardurrii)*, it flattens, spreads out.
meetchie *(midjidji)*, Mrs.
meta warra *(midda-wara)*, pretty; white clothes.
miah *(maya)*, European house or hut.
Mickina *(Mirrgina)*, big one; male name.
movin *(maparn, mavarn)*, charm, witchcraft.
mulba *(marlba)*, man, mortal.
munda, murnda *(marnda)*, stone, rock, hill, metal, money.
Munga *(Manga)*, woman, or *(Munga)*, dark, female name.
munga *(munga)*, night, dark.
munyin bunna, minyin bunna *(manyinbana)*, a filthy swear word.
   (A: 'This defiance of Wylba's is in filthy language – quite
   untranslatable. So long as she hurls something at Brumby, it doesn't
   matter what she says.')
murda *(marda)*, blood.
murda-murda *(mardamarda)*, red, Sturt Pea.
murndoo *(murndo)*, could be, perhaps.

nabi *(nabai, from nuvalai)*, you fellows.
noova *(nuva, njuba)*, lover, spouse (A: 'a difficult word to translate.
   It means potential wife, and a woman with whom a man may have
   a sex relationship. The natives in this tribe actually use the word
   "lover", because the white people suggested it as nearest to lover, I
   think').
nuki-nuki *(nuggai)*, loathsome, dangerous.
nunki-nunki *(ngangai-ngangai)*, swearword.

piriyina *(pirriina)*, having become the end.
punti *(parndi)*, smell.

spa, an exclamation (A: ' "spa" is spat out').

tanbura, cliff(?).
taniwali *(taaniwalli)*, whither, (any)where to.
Tullamurra *(Tala-mara)*, Healthy-hand, a female name.

ubi, oobaya *(ubaya)*, mate.
uloo *(jurlu)*, camp.

walygee booger *(waldji-purga)*, false, bad chap.
walyinna *(waljina)*, bad one, false one.
wanarloo *(wanarralu)*, by a tall one; *(wanarra)*, tall.
wandy *(warndi)*, tail, penis; *wandy cloth*, a garment which covers the
    male pudenda.
wara lunghia bina *(warrala nga(rr)ibina)*, in the void lying.
warieda *(warrida)*, eagle-hawk.
warilla *(warri-la)*, on the ground.
wiah *(waya)*, no.
winning arra(s) *(win ingkarra)*, whirlwinds.
Wongana *(Wankana)*, Lively one, male name.
wongie *(warngkai)*, talk.
wudimaru *(wudimaru)*, run away, go home!

yaberoo *(yaburru)*, north.
Yanigee *(Yannidji)*, a fictitious town.
yienda *(njinda)*, you (singular).
yiendie *(yindii)*, goes down, slopes.
yinerrie *(njinirri)*, musician, composer.
yukk-eye *(yaggarri, yaggai)*, exclamation of surprise or sudden pain.

THE COOBOO

They had been mustering all day on the wide plains of Murndoo station. Over the red earth, black with ironstone pebbles, through mulga and curari bush, across the ridges which make a blue wall along the horizon. The rosy, garish light of sunset was on plains, hills, moving cattle, men and horses.

Through red dust the bullocks mooched, restless and scary still, a wild mob from the hills: John Gray, in the rear with Arra, the boy who was his shadow: Wongana, on the right with his gin, Rose: Frank, the half-caste, on the left with Minni.

A steer breaking from the mob before Rose, she wheeled and went after him. Faint and wailing, a cry followed her, as though her horse had stepped on and crushed some small creature. But the steer was getting away. Arra went after him, stretched along his horse's neck, rounded the beast and rode him back to the mob, sulky and blethering. The mob swayed. It had broken three times that day.

John Gray called: 'You damn fool, Rosey. Finish!'

The gin, on her slight, rough-haired horse, pulled up scowling.

'Tell Meetchie, Thirty Mile, to-morrow,' John Gray said. 'Miah, new moon.'

Rose slewed her horse away from the mob of men and cattle. That wailing, thin and hard as hair-string, moved with her.

'Minni!'

John Gray jerked his head towards Rose. Minni's bare heels struck her horse's belly. With a turn of the wrist she swung her horse off from the mob, turned, leaned forward, rising in her stirrups, and came up with Rose. But the glitter and tumult of Rose's eyes, Minni looked away from them.

Thin, dark figures on their wiry station-bred horses, the gins rode into the haze of sunset towards the hills. The dull, dirty blue of the trousers wrapped round their legs was torn; their short, fairish hair tousled by the wind.

At a little distance, when men and cattle were a moving cloud of red dust, Rose's anger gushed after them.

'Koo!'

Fierce as the cry of a hawk flew her last note of derision and defiance.

A far-away rattle of the men's laughter drifted back across country.

Alone the gins would have been afraid, as darkness coming up behind was hovering near them, secreting itself among the low, writhen trees and bushes: afraid of the evil spirits who wander over the plains and stony ridges when the light of day is withdrawn. But together they were not so afraid. Twenty miles away over there, below that dent in the hills where Nyedee Creek made a sandy bed for itself among white-bodied gums, was Murndoo homestead and the uloo of their people.

There was no track; and in the first darkness, thick as wool after the glow of sunset faded, only their instinct would keep them moving in the direction of the homestead and their own low, round huts of bagging, rusty tin and dead boughs.

Both were Wongana's women: Rose, tall, gaunt and masterful; Minni, younger, fat and jolly. Rose had been a good stockman in her day: one of the best. Minni did not ride or track nearly as well as Rose.

And yet, as they rode along, Minni pattered complacently of how well she had worked that day: of how she had flashed, this way and that, heading-off breakaways, dashing after them, turning them back to the mob so smartly that John had said: 'Good man, Minni!' There was the white bullock – he had rushed near the yards. Had Rose seen the chestnut mare stumble in a crab-hole and send Arra flying? Minni had chased the white bullock, chased him for a couple of miles, and brought him back to the yards. No doubt there would be nammery for her and a new gina-gina when the men came in from the muster.

She pulled a pipe from her belt, shook the ashes out, and with reins looped over one arm stuffed the bowl with tobacco from a tin tied to her belt. Stooping down, she struck a match on her stirrup-iron, guarded the flame to the pipe between her short, white teeth, and smoked contentedly.

The scowl on Rose's face deepened, darkened. That thin, fretted wailing came from her breast.

She unslung from her neck the rag rope by which the baby had been held against her body, and gave him a sagging breast to suck. Holding him with one arm, she rode slowly, her horse picking his way over the rough, stony earth.

It had been a hard day. The gins were mustering with the men at sunrise. Camped at Nyedee Well the night before, in order to get a good start, they had been riding through the timbered ridges all the morning, rounding up wild cows, calves and young

bullocks, and driving them down to the yards at Nyedee, where
John Gray cut out the fats, left old Jimmy and a couple of boys
to brand calves, turn the cows and calves back to the ridge again
while he took on the mob for trucking at Meekatharra. The
bullocks were as wild as birds: needed watching all day. And all
the time that small, whimpering bundle against her breast had
hampered Rose's movements.

There was nothing the gins liked better than a muster, riding
after cattle. They were quicker in their movements, more alert
than the men, sharper at picking up tracks, but they did not go
mustering very often nowadays.

Since John Gray had married, and there was a woman on
Murndoo, she found plenty of washing, scrubbing and sweeping
for the gins to do: would not spare them often to go after cattle.
But John was short-handed. He had said he must have Rose and
Minni to muster Nyedee. And all day her baby's crying had
irritated Rose. The cooboo had wailed and wailed as she rode
with him tied to her body.

The cooboo was responsible for the wrong things she had done
all day. Stupid things. Rose was furious. The men had yelled at
her. Wongana, her man, blackguarding her before everybody,
had called her 'a hen who did not know where she laid her eggs.'
And John Gray, with his 'You damn fool, Rosey. Finish!' had sent
her home like a naughty child.

Now there was Minni jabbering of the tobacco she would get
and the new gina-gina. How pleased Wongana would be with
her! And the cooboo, wailing, wailing. He wailed as he chewed
Rose's empty breast, squirming against her: wailed and gnawed.

She cried out with hurt and impatience. Rage, irritated to madness, rushed like waters coming down the dry creekbeds after
heavy rain. Rose wrenched the cooboo from her breast and flung
him from her to the ground. There was a crack as of twigs
breaking.

Minni glanced aside. 'Wiah!' she gasped, with widening eyes.
But Rose rode on, gazing ahead over the rosy, garish plains and
wall of the hills, darkening from blue to purple and indigo.

When the women came into the station kitchen, earth, hills
and trees were dark: the sky heavy with stars. Minni gave John's
wife his message: that he would be home with the new moon,
in about a fortnight.

Meetchie, as the blacks called Mrs John Gray, could not make out why the gins were so stiff and quiet: why Rose stalked, scowling and sulky-fellow, sombre eyes just meeting hers, and moving away again. Meetchie wanted to ask about the muster: what sort of condition the bullocks had been in; how many were on the road; if many calves had been branded at Nyedee. But she knew the women too well to ask questions when they looked like that.

Only when she had given them bread and a tin of jam, cut off hunks of corned beef for them, filled their billies with strong black tea, put sugar in their empty tins, and the gins were going off to the uloo, she realized that Rose was not carrying her baby as usual.

'Why, Rose,' she exclaimed, 'where's the cooboo?'

Rose stalked off into the night. Minni glanced back with scared eyes and followed Rose.

In the dawn, when a cry, remote and anguished flew through the clear air, Meetchie wondered who was dead in the camp by the creek. She remembered how Rose had looked the night before, when she asked about the cooboo.

Now, she knew the cooboo had died; Rose was wailing for him in the dawn, cutting herself with stones until her body bled, and screaming in the fury of her grief.

NETTIE PALMER, 1885-1964

Born Janet Gertrude Higgins, Bendigo, Victoria, she
was educated at Presbyterian Ladies' College and the
University of Melbourne. After graduation she
travelled, continued her studies, and married Vance
Palmer. Choice was responsible for her interest in
legitimation and promotion of a national literature,
and necessity was the prompt for her creation of a
network of Australian women writers; because of
domestic duties she was unable to lead an
independent literary life but she was able to write
letters of encouragement and criticism to other often
isolated and hard pressed writers. Critic and
reviewer, literary journalist, diarist, letter writer and
poet, Nettie Palmer helped to shape and substantiate
the Australian literary tradition and to insist on the
significance of women within it. She was an early
champion of Henry Handel Richardson and her work
(see *Henry Handel Richardson: A Study*, 1950,
Angus & Robertson, Sydney); she provided feedback
and support for a steady stream of writers from
Miles Franklin and Katharine Susannah Prichard to
Marjorie Barnard, Flora Eldershaw, and Barbara
Baynton, and a great deal of respect for Mary
Gilmore. A person of perspicacity and political
commitment, she also put considerable energy into
furthering her husband's literary career.

Her publications include the volumes of poetry,
The South Wind (1914) and *Shadowy Paths* (1915) as
well as the non-fictional titles, *Modern Australian*

Literature, 1900-1923 (1924), *Henry Bournes Higgins;
A Memoir* (1931), *Talking it Over* (1932) and
Australians in Spain (1937).

The following is an abridged version of Nettie
Palmer's diary, published in 1948 by Meanjin Press,
Melbourne, (also forthcoming UQP, 1988) and
entitled *Fourteen Years: Extracts from a Private
Journal*, 1925-1939. It reveals her commitment to the
development of Australian literature and the role of
women.

FOURTEEN YEARS: EXTRACTS FROM
A PRIVATE JOURNAL
Caloundra 1925-1929

February 9th, 1927   Lately the idea of editing an 'Australian
Storybook' has set me reading the short stories of the 'nineties.
Not that I intend to use any of them; the new anthology must
begin where A. G. Stephens left off when he made his collection
at the end of the century; but I wanted to refresh my memory
of what had already been written.

It certainly hasn't been a voyage of exciting discoveries. Who
invented the legend that a band of brilliant short story writers
existed in the 'nineties, and that in examining the early files of
the *Bulletin* one would stumble upon masterpieces? There wasn't
much basis for it. The names are quickening – Alec Montgomery,
Louis Becke, Dorrington, Barbara Baynton, Price Warung,
Edward Dyson – but the stories above the names are disappointing. Ironic fragments, brisk little dramas separated into scenes
by rows of asterisks, sketches of eccentric character, farcical
incidents and that's all. Not much evidence of the subtle, delicate
art that can seize upon some episode and give it shape and
significance, so that it remains in the mind like a poem.

A page of Lawson's pulls you up with a delicious shock. This
is what you've been looking for. Without apparent effort, Lawson
takes you straight into his own intimate world and makes you
free of it; his easy, colloquial voice has the incantation of rhythm;
even his humorous stories stand out from Edward Dyson's in the
same way that poetry differs from verse. Until this re-reading,

I had accepted Dyson's 'The Golden Shanty' as a sort of classic, but how crude and insensitive it seems beside one of Lawson's comedies! Quite plainly Lawson's short stories have a quality that makes the current grouping of his stories with the others' absurd.

Yet there must have been something about these writers of the 'nineties that gave their readers the sense of a new world being revealed. You can feel it when you place them against the conventional writers of that time – the three-decker novelists and the people who supplied glossy short stories to the American magazines. Whatever else might be said of it, the work of our short-story writers was not marked by a slick emptiness. They were robust; they did not accept circulating-library values; they tried to get near the core of life. This was particularly true of Barbara Baynton and Price Warung. I remember how R. B. Cunninghame Graham, that very eclectic critic, was attracted by Barbara Baynton's writing and compared it with Gorky's – this was somewhere about 1906, when only Gorky's bitter early sketches had come into English. As for Price Warung, he was limited by some conceived necessity to tie his stories to verifiable fact. He could not free himself from the historical convict records. What a masterpiece of pity and terror 'The Secret History of the Ring' might have been if he had been able to lift it from that world into one more definitely his own!

What might have been, though, is not much use to the anthologist. A short story must have its own perfection, or it is nothing. The element of completeness, of art, must enter into it so that it lives as a whole in the mind. Apart from Lawson's work, there is very little use in looking for this kind of perfection in the stories of the 'nineties. If they have left a tradition, it lies in their habit of seeking their subjects directly from life instead of fabricating plots and situations. But there is a greater mastery in Katharine Prichard's story, 'The Cooboo', published recently in the *Bulletin*, than in the lot of them. What a world of tragedy and strange beauty she has compressed into a couple of thousand words! It is a marvel of economy as well as of feeling – so little stated directly, so much implied. (How is it that in giving the merest necessary background to her story of the remote cattle country, her phrase 'the tumbled hills' is enough, where it occurs, to make the heart turn over?)

April 9th, 1927   At last Katharine Prichard's new novel, *Working Bullocks*, is here, and it was worth waiting for. It is as fresh and inspiriting as Louis Esson said it was when he read the manuscript, and it's good to see how he sustains his conviction in a fine Red Page review this week. What strikes me is the confidence Katharine has gained in recent years. She has now set any diffidence aside and writes out of her full self. Confidence is surely one of the main things lacking in our writers up till now, particularly our novelists. They never seemed quite sure of themselves or their public, never were fully convinced of the validity of their own point-of-view, or that there were people to communicate with whose minds were as adult as their own. Katharine's early work was hampered by this. *The Pioneers* carried a surprising weight of goodness, considering that it had to win the race of an overseas competition; *Black Opal* had still more. Yet in both books you were only dimly aware of the really original talent hidden behind the conventional cover.

Working Bullocks seems to me different not only in quality but in kind. No one else has written with quite that rhythm, or seen the world in quite that way. The creative lyricism of the style impresses me more than either the theme or the characters. From slang, from place names, from colloquial turns of speech, from descriptions of landscape and people at work, she has woven a texture that covers the whole surface of the book with a shimmer of poetry. As you read, you are filled with excitement by the sheer beauty of the sounds and the images.

And there is the assurance, the confidence, with which it is all done. To gain that is in itself an achievement. It is a break-through that will be as important for other writers as for K.S.P. herself.

August 31st, 1927   A note from S. H. Prior asking me to write an article for the Red Page on the *Bulletin* Novel Competition. Don't bother to pay us compliments, he says in effect, but let us have exactly what you think of the idea's value. This leaves me in rather a quandary. The first thing to say about such a competition is that its value depends entirely on the nature of the selectors and the amount of freedom they are given.

There is no doubt whatever about Prior's good intentions, but the fact that the chosen novels are to be printed as serials makes one a little uneasy. How would *Jude the Obscure* go as a serial or, to come nearer home, *The Fortunes of Richard Mahony*? It is not easy to think of either providing curtains for each week's instalment that would whet their readers' appetite for the next act.

Other doubts arise. The plain truth is that our promiscuous reading public is not used to the deepest kind of reality in books about the background it knows. Since the 'nineties, it has been trained to accept short stories that have a personal view of life – Lawson, Price Warung, Dowell O'Reilly – but as yet it expects our novels to mould themselves on a conventional and accustomed pattern, the pattern of second rate fiction in all countries – obvious drama and ultimate sunshine. To this public, the man who sets out to be a novelist must be essentially an entertainer, and it does not ask him to be penetrating, or to trouble his head about style, or to have a view of life. It will expect a slick story, using the familiar ingredients expertly in a local setting; and maybe this expectation will put an unconscious compulsion on the judges.

I am tempted to quote, for the benefit of all concerned, part of a letter Conrad wrote to a young Australian author who had sent him a manuscript:

'The principal thing is to write out of the best that is in one. And that one can't do every day. The trouble is not getting paid the uttermost penny; the trouble is in giving good value, in giving stuff with the truth at the back of it; in finding the word, the sentence, the page that satisfies one's conscience, concretes one's vision, expresses the state of one's soul and, at the same time veils the torment and pain of one's thought.

'If fiction is not approached in a spirit of serious devotion, then the writing of it is a fool's business. There must be purpose in such work. Not in the tale, but in the writing. A "story with a purpose" is, from my point of view, valueless artistically, and therefore it is rubbish. But he who undertakes fiction with no other purpose than earning a living has undertaken a contemptible task. He will never do good work because he will never think it worth his while to look beneath the surface of things. . .'

March 3rd, 1928   Today arrived a letter from Henry Handel Richardson, together with a signed copy of *The Way Home*. The copy sent by the publishers two years ago is always being lent, and now I needn't be so anxious about losing it.

A re-reading of *The Way Home* has sent me back to the first volume, and I'm surprised at the way I missed so many of its implications when I came upon it eight years ago. I don't think I was so mistaken about it as Arthur Adams, who passed it by contemptuously as a dull chronicle written by a 'retired grocer', but though I was impressed at the time by the book's reality and depth, I certainly didn't see its significance for this country. It ended so definitely with Mahony shaking the Australian dust from his feet, and Mahony was the core of the book – the other characters, except Mary, were seen from the outside and didn't seem to matter much. My impression at the end of the volume was that Mahony's life on Ballarat would be a mere 'colonial' episode in a long saga.

And then there came Mrs. K.'s quiet protest about my omission of her friend's name from my essay on modern Australian writing. When I went to see her, out came all the books, papers, letters, photographs, from special cupboards. *Maurice Guest* in English and German; articles on it from Danish and Swiss encyclopaedias; copies of *The Getting of Wisdom*; even a surviving group photograph, showing H.H.R. and half-a-dozen other 'young ladies' at the P.L.C., including Mrs. K. So H.H.R. was a woman, and had gone to my own school, where I had never even heard her name . . . I imagine the girls going there now are still in the same state of ignorance – in spite of *The Getting of Wisdom*.

It's fantastic that with all the newspapers and their gossip columns you can remain completely uninformed about the people and things that matter. Probably the story of Richard Mahony, if they knew about it, would not be regarded as a good advertisement for the country. It is plain from the second volume that Richard, for all his reactions, is definitely tied to this soil. *The Way Home* is a bitterly ironic title, surely; where is home to Richard? Not here; not in that England he dreamed about sentimentally in his grocery store at Ballarat, but hated when he savoured it again. The third volume, due this year, may provide a home for his proud spirit somewhere.

I remember that some time ago, Louis Esson said to me dogmatically, and not troubling about evidence, that the next ten years would see a great development in our writing, especially in the novel. He had no inkling of H.H.R., who was there and fully grown all the time. It seems as if his prophecy may come true . . .

July 8th, 1928   At last something is happening in the theatre, according to Louis. He writes about the organization of a new professional company that will make a point of including some original plays in its repertoire, and the first two mentioned are Katharine Prichard's *Brumby Innes* and Harrison Owen's *A Happy Husband*.

What a curious pair! Can the choice have been made to confuse those who say that Australian dramatists have a sameness about them? Katherine's [*sic*] Brumby is surely as raw and ravening a figure as has ever been allowed on the boards. And the background of the play – with its corroborees, brutalities, and wild poetry – if its atmosphere can be captured it will certainly send a cold shiver through the stalls.

As for Harrison Owen's play, I don't know anything about it except what I've read in a copy of the *Neue Freie Presse* someone sent me, but it seems the kind of comedy he set out to write when he went to London. There was always a curious modesty about Harrison Owen. He never made any pretensions to creative ability, or even to a knowledge of the life around him. 'I'm just a young man from Geelong,' he used to say. But he had a distinct passion for the theatre, and could spend endless time taking plays by Scribe to pieces to see how they were fitted together. 'A Happy Husband', his second play, is an international success of an artificial sort. The Viennese critic, after saying that it is a delightful comedy, providing excellent opportunities for fine ensemble work, goes on:

'An English comedy? It is more exactly in the French style of comedy – only with English society figures and a shimmer of Wilde paradox over the whole. It turns on the entrance of a conventional gentleman-burglar (who has studied at Oxford and learnt Latin and a little Greek, and who can smoke or offer a cigarette in the most elegant way) into a conventional triangle scene. The lover, who is where he ought not to be, refuses, for his own sake, to denounce the burglar. The plot gets thicker and thicker, but seems to clear by sheer convolutions and wit in the third act.'

I have been wondering if the new company will have a leading actor capable of playing this elegant gentleman burglar in one production and Brumby Innes in the next . . .

January 19th, 1929   Find that with half of me I'm bitterly regretting our decision to go back to Melbourne. It's necessary because of the children's schooling and other personal matters, but will we ever again find a place so rich in all that makes for happy living? Quiet days of work, with odd hours on the beaches or the flower-plain; and then the breaks at the week-end – tramping up barefooted over the wet sand to picnic at Curramundi, or rowing over to the lee side of Bribie Island. There's been time to read and think, even to enjoy the company of the casual visitors who've wandered in. People don't unbutton themselves so easily in town. What long talks we've had on this old veranda, looking down at Maloney's boat coming in or watching the swans flying up the Passage about sunset!

Strange to remember that we only intended to stay a few weeks when we came here. We've stayed nearly four years, and the place has become part of us . . .

Melbourne 1929–1932

May 30th, 1929   The newspapers announce the death of Barbara Baynton, or rather it is a Lady Headley they are concerned with, the wife of an eccentric English peer and a woman of fashion. There is hardly a word spent on the writer – perhaps they aren't really aware of her.

In truth there do seem to have been two distinct Barbara Bayntons – one a follower of fashion and current values, and the other a gusty, original personality, who nourished her talent on Scandinavian writers and spoke with a forthrightness that had the effect of a strong bush wind on London gatherings. How brilliantly apt was her *Dingo Dell* for that rather hybrid meeting place of Anglo Australians known as the Austral Club!

A pity her work isn't better known; it had real power behind it. As the young wife of a country doctor she had gone through certain experiences that left a vivid imprint on her mind, and instead of sentimentalising them she recreated them with a harsh and relentless irony. The bush woman alone in the hut with her baby, cowering from the madman who prowls outside; the old shepherd apologising subtly to his dog for letting the ewe and lamb into his hut; the pregnant girl tracking home through flooded country and night fears to her mother and finding her dead. There is a feeling of cold objectivity in these stories. The writer doesn't go out of her way to win your sympathy for her characters. Her words fall as mercilessly as clods on a coffin.

And yet isn't there, perhaps, sentimentality of a kind, in this detached pose, after all? What is sentimentality but an effort to squeeze more feeling out of a situation than is warranted? and there doesn't seem much difference between doing it with brutal methods or tearful ones. Barbara Baynton's stories belong to a day when the best of the young writers were reacting against rosewater romance. She herself reacted with vigour and emphasis – too much emphasis. Sometimes she leant over backwards in her attempts to strip the idyllic cover from the appearance of things. Going over 'Bush Studies' just now, I came across this description of a railway engine in plain country:

'Suddenly the engine cleared its throat in shrill welcome to two iron tanks, hoisted twenty feet, and blazing like evil eyes in a vanished face. Beside them it squatted on its hunkers, placed a blackened thumb on its pipe and hissed through its closed teeth like a snared wild cat, while gulping yards of water.'

It reads like a feminine straining after power at all costs. And the images destroy one another. The old man squatting on his hunkers, placing a blackened thumb on his pipe, is wiped out by the wild cat. So with a good deal of her writing.

Yet one is always conscious of a strong and original mind behind her stories. Was it because of a false theory of writing that they failed? Plainly the people she wrote about mattered a good deal to her as human beings. She was once half amused and half indignant because a critic compared them – characters like Scrammy 'And and Squeaker's Mate – to denizens of the London slums: she couldn't understand it at all. For her those bush types weren't the remote rather sub-human people that actually emerge from her pages . . .

October 5th, 1929   Yesterday Katharine Prichard arrived on her round trip from Perth, a trip that included Singapore. There was some uncertainty about her train. After lunch V. went in to meet her, chasing Louis, who in the meantime, had come out to Hawthorn to invite us to dinner. Finally we all met at the Essons' over a sumptuous lobster meal, the sort of festival Hilda knows how to produce with miraculous speed and gaiety. Stewart Macky managed to come in for an hour in the middle of his medical engagements.

Katharine talked of her journey up the West Australian coast, stopping every day at a port, pausing for a wonderful fortnight at Broome. A crowded month at Singapore and inland. In spite of her long days of travel she looked radiantly alive, physically even more graceful than in the past, her mind teeming with impressions of odd characters, remembered bits of dialogue, her humour and understanding playing about everything like a soft light. She seems to be moving along very buoyantly on a full tide of assurance. In a way she's found herself. Even in those old days in London she knew the kind of books she wanted to write, but she was wavery in her approach to life and unsure of her powers. Now without having lost any of the sensitiveness which made her pace the floor of her Chelsea flat all night after finishing the newly-published *Sons and Lovers*, she's gained a sort of toughness. She can be deeply moved by the treatment of natives on the stations behind Broome, yet can look at the whole question with clear unsentimental eyes . . .

August 18th, 1931   From Marjorie Barnard, discussing the biography of H.B.H. I've been working on:
You class your work as not creative: but isn't biography at least a quasi-creative art? The author supplies form and manner. The raw material of a novel is 'given'; the author pieces it together, arranges, edits and synthesises it; only in doing this has he more scope than the biographer whose first duty is to interpret and analyse. I have always looked on history as one of the creative arts, and in my youth acted on this assumption, not without success. Of course one's classification of creative work depends upon whether one places the emphasis on form or content. My natural tendency is to attach much more value to form than to content, and I think I'm right, too, but that it's a mistake to think so – on the analogy of watching pots and loving life . . .

Green Island 1932

July 2nd, 1932   Coming back to Cairns after a week down in the cane country, we found that the *Gullmarn* had arrived after a slow passage up from Sydney. She lay tied up at the waterfront, looking very small, squat, and dingy with her peeling green paint beside the *Manunda* and the other ships. Somehow smaller and less fit to stand an ocean voyage than when we made that trial trip on her in the Bay at Melbourne. Yet she's rich in experience, having spent most of her previous life as a pilot boat in the North Sea.

The crew were in great heart – Hedley and Joyce Metcalf, Dora Birtles, Irene Saxby and a professional sailor called Nick, who is going with them on the chance of picking up a real boat at Singapore. Last week on their way to Cairns they had sailed round the island making signals to us, but couldn't pick up the entrance to the channel. All the better since we were away. And they have a week's extension in which to reach Thursday Island, so can spend the next few days with us at the camp.

This morning we all sailed over from Cairns to the island. A beautiful fresh morning, calm in the sheltered port, but with a stiffish south-easterly blowing outside. The *Gullmarn* has an engine stowed away somewhere in the hold, but it's only for emergency: they have no room to carry oil for it, so they're trusting to the sails. She moved with a long, rolling motion, riding the waves, so different from the launch that butts its way through, quivering in all its tiny bulk.

I lay on the deck, with a mackintosh over me, talking to Dora Birtles. She is using her experience on the *Gullmarn* to do a thesis on Cook's navigation of the Barrier waters. And what experiences they've already had, days of learning to live neatly in a space not big enough to swing a cat o'nine tails, shortage of supplies that made them glad of the goat Hedley shot on one of the Whitsundays. The girls are all standing up to it well. There's a professional casualness about them in their shorts and sunburn: they all take their trick at the wheel and are rostered for other duties.

To-night, after a week away, the island seems very snug and comfortable. Through the trees flickers the light of the *Gullmarn*, riding gently in the lagoon, its crew mostly camping ashore . . .

Kalorama 1932–1935

December 23rd, 1933   Yesterday Flora Eldershaw came up on the bus, having a day to spare while her boat was in port. She's on her way to Europe – her sabbatical year.

Until I met her, I'd thought of Marjorie Barnard as the directive part of that composite, the Barnard Eldershaw. Chiefly, I suppose, because I'd come into contact with Marjorie first and found she had so definite a personality, in letters and then in talk. There was that day last March, after years of correspondence, when she rang up to say she was in Melbourne on her way to Europe, and would I meet her in town. How musical her voice sounded on the phone, and how it lifted at the end of every phrase: 'You'll easily know me . . . I'm middle-aged . . . I wear brown . . . I wear glasses . . . I'll be watching for you.' (Middle-aged meant precisely thirty-five, or half way.]

Next evening, when she came to dinner, I remember being still conscious of that musical lift in her voice. With it was a sort of demureness that, at every fifth movement, was swept away by a most unusual frankness, often a spontaneous brilliance of expression that made you catch your breath. In her reading (mostly modern cultivated English writers and some Scandinavian) she struck me as being more like an English novelist than an Australian – more English in her literary ideas and range of values, for instance, than H.H.R. Yet there was her personal spontaneity and freshness, her sense of comradeship with other writers here. I knew from her letters that she had all the significant virtues – loyalty, selflessness, industry and, of course, sincerity.

Flora Eldershaw was a vaguer figure in my mind. Yet as soon as she got down from the bus yesterday it was plain that she couldn't be disposed of as part of a composite. A fine head, a broad, generous brow, she's physically powerful, though much too fatigued for her years. She must have called up her reserves and resources continually. Yet it's the extent of these that impresses you. A thinker, a personality in her own right, a robust woman of action, she seems to include the goodness of all her experiences, and her talk, though sometimes using inexpressive words, seems always to suggest the richness beneath.

Having the good inside of a quiet day (the girls were out picking raspberries dawn till dusk for a grower down in the valley) she told me something of her past. One of a long family, she grew up on a Riverina station and still knows what country life means, though not with indignant feminist rage, like Miles Franklin. When she reached boarding school late, she must have shown hunger and tenacity, for she got to the University as soon as Marjorie did. They were history students together under Arnold Wood, English students under the veteran 'little Prof' McCallum – though Flora remembers cutting even one of his vital hours to go to a lecture of Chris Brennan's. French literature wasn't her subject, but she knew what she wanted, knew she was fortunate to hear Chris Brennan once.

It isn't easy for an outsider to understand how a literary partnership is carried on, but in this case it seems to work well. At any rate it has so far, for there are no visible gaps or joins in *A House is Built*. Any difference in the characters of the two women doesn't make for a difference in their point-of-view or values. They both look at *A House is Built* itself in much the same way – a solid piece of work made to a standard design, something they rather hope to forget later when they've written a book that's 'all out'.

March 15th, 1934   The papers this morning bring tragic news of the cyclone that has just struck the Queensland coast, north of Green Island. Many luggers and fishing-boats have been sunk and nearly eighty coloured boys drowned, yet one of the correspondents says that it was not so serious as the 1927 cyclone since, though no lives were lost then, there was immense damage to property, amounting to nearly half a million.

Immense damage to property! And property is wood, bricks, iron! McDonald, the Cairns airman, reports that on a flight up the Reef he found the wreck of the *Mosman*, but no trace of Millard or any of the crew. The cyclone must have struck her somewhere near Batt Reef and there is no hope of survivors.

All day we have been talking of Bill Millard – his courage, his camaraderie, his love of independence, and his enthusiasm for that lean rich life of picking up a pittance with a small boat. There was that long, lovely trip we had with him down the Reef two years ago – lying off Fitzroy Island at night and listening to the broken coral fragments fall back tinkling like tiny bells as each wave receded, basking in the sun on the deck as the wind freshened between High Island and Dunk, creeping under the lee of Hinchinbrook looking up at the cascades of greenery that poured down from a height of two thousand feet. The beauty and timelessness of it all! And Bill – good comrade, good seaman – rigging up awning sails to make a patch of shade in the hot afternoons, laughing and telling stories during our picnic lunches on deck, growing serious-eyed as the land neared and it was a matter of making safe entrance through the channel or picking up an anchorage.

Among the casualties of the cyclone, too, has been the battered old boat of Tinos, the Greek. I can still see her clattering out to sea, with her blistered planks and noisy engine – see Tinos standing on the sand below our camp, rolling a cigarette and explaining just why the white man was superior to all coloured people. Fate has played one last ironic joke on him. In the paper he is listed among the casualties as 'Tinos, a Malay'.

March 28th, 1934   From Marjorie Barnard, writing of the Davisons who are making a motor trip up North:
I envy them passionately. The mind should be well-stocked and driven out into the wilderness every now and then. It is an absolute necessity. But there are so few wildernesses available. Virginia Woolf's £500 a year and a room of one's own is probably the best of them; you could make your own wildernesses anywhere you liked under these conditions, and a flowering one at that. God is sometimes kind enough to intervene, as when Eugene O'Neill developed a tubercular lung, or (more obviously God) when St. Francis was smitten with illness and changed his spots. To be thrown clear of life – like Lewis in the fortress, as anyone may be in a small ship – is the greatest of all blessings.

May 4th, 1934   This morning Eleanor Dark's novel, *Prelude to Christopher*, arrived – the first important book published by Stephensen since he left the Endeavour Press. It is also her first legitimate brainchild (for one gathers that a serial, 'Slow Dawning', is not acknowledged, and is clouded by some family ribaldry about a 'Fast Dark'). Read *Prelude* to-night. Its literary power gives it a unity, in spite of some unreality in the theme and a good many gaps. How hard a writer makes it for herself in choosing such a tangled, elaborate theme for her first novel! But perhaps that's a foolish way of looking at it. The theme's simple enough; it's the method that's tangled and elaborate. And the method's directed, in the modern way, at squeezing all the inwardness out of the subject.

Eleanor Dark's literary power, besides being what holds the book together, peers in through a few phrases with a hint of the poignancy and glow that were her father's peculiar gift. But how different they are in their stance; she so restrained and withdrawn, and he always ready to give himself away in handfuls. Yet Dowell O'Reilly was one of the most laborious of writers; a story or an essay took him months of work. That dancing light style of his wasn't achieved easily. Even his letters – there's evidence that he would carry a letter around in his head for days, whittling at it in odd moments and half-arguing with the person who was to receive it.

I've often wished there could be a companion volume to the *Dowell O'Reilly from his Letters* that contained those written to the woman who was to become his wife. An edited book of his general correspondence and few essays might show all his qualities, or might suggest what he would have done in an ordered world that let him exercise his full talents. His gift was in the direction of 'natural' confession: a Sterne in England, here a Tom Collins. Even in those few letters I had from him in the last year of his life there was a spilling-out of a great range of ideas – humour of an original kind, playful intimacy, fury that, without explaining, he let you feel and share. He ought to have left a fuller record of his difficult, personal, sentimental journey through life . . .

November 6th, 1934　　　　From Hugh McCrae, after talking about William Moore:

I haven't seen my other William (the Bede Dalley one) for months. I had asked him for a preface to 'Georgiana', suggesting a page and a half, but instead he wrote eighteen . . . all about pies and sausages. Nancy was so horrified that I was driven to protest; however, William agreed, and smilingly stroked out some potatoes. Then, when it came to Mr. Cousins' turn, there was a rumpus and W. jettisoned several bowls of soup and a leg of beef, but refused to sacrifice anything else. Meanwhile he had been going the rounds of the super-highbrows, reading rarebits to Mary Gilmore, Dr. Semple Jones, and others. 'By God, Hughie,' he said, 'this foreword's a corker: Semple blew his nose three times when I went through it last night'; and it happens to be true that the thing has been beautifully written, so I admitted the fact. William, wishing to return the compliment, answered that, since Georgiana could write well, it behoved him to run level with her at the tape. 'One mustn't stand before the Pope with holes in one's trousers!' . . .

December 13th, 1934　　　　To-day *Georgiana's Journal* with an inscription from Hugh:

> *Praise Georgiana, V. and N.*
> 　*For courage, virtue, wit . . . And then*
> *Count every grafted fault you find*
> *Well paid with stripes on my behind!*

In this year of the Victorian Centenary it's astonishing how few family diaries and records have been brought to light: people have used them to light the fire in bygone times of spring cleaning, or just plain lost them. It took a family like the McCraes to guarantee this Journal's preservation: a family affectionately conscious of its character and succession, and frugally preserving a firm roof, fixed shelves and cupboards, through the generations. And even so this preservation needed a certain amount of care. Georgiana herself, keeping the diary from her arrival in 1839 until 1851 when, with Victoria's stability, her own in the colony seemed assured, or inevitable, must have then laid the diary aside as something no longer crucial in her life: perhaps because she had given up hope of returning to Scotland and showing her diary to the folks. In her old age she came across the papers, dim and dilapidated; and she copied out the whole thing; so it's this copy, on firmer sheets, that turned up in the McCrae house after George Gordon died about 1926. And now it's published, with a sheaf of Georgiana's own sketches in black and white, pencil and wash. She regarded these as notes of their way of living in houses that would certainly not last long, in Batman's Town or Arthur's Seat, as well as notes of a landscape that she was probably the first artist to grasp so naturally.

Praise Georgiana! And praise her descendants for preserving her words and her art. As for Hugh's footnotes and insets threaded through the text, they aren't at all the perfunctory pedantic work of a mere editor. They're the exuberant comments of a grandson always devoid of a sense of time who feels himself contemporary with his grandmother in her best days. He chucks her under the chin as he explains to the reader who the gentleman was who sang after dinner at Georgiana's home in 1843. He is proud as she travels with her children from Arthur's Seat to Melbourne in a royal dray, 'and all the time as merry as a grig,' as I've heard him say of her, using a Scottish word in her honour. Indeed the task of inter-writing this ms. must have been after his own heart; one could wish he had several Georgianas in his past . . .

March 19th, 1935   Waiting in Sydney Harbour on the M.M. *Fridan*. This evening, when we were all on board but not sailing until tomorrow, there was a pocket of clear time, and into it stepped, very neatly, Miles Franklin. There she stood on the deck of this little French tub, her deep witty voice roaming in the half

lights; and when she sat down I saw she was bearing gifts, as
if we were going out into the desert. A pot of pineapple jam,
certainly home-made, and very good: flowers from her own
garden, a cake.

In fact, her impulses were those of a generous country-woman;
yet she lives in a Sydney suburb. Now I can see why she says,
so often, that the life expected here of a woman is too hard for
a writer. Living with her mother in the family house, too big for
them, she keeps a hospitable homestead – always beds and meals
for kinsfolk from the country; fowls laying at the back, flowers
blooming in the front, and besides, 'she not know der way to
der delikatessen shop at der corner.' An intact country homestead,
and therein Miles writes novels about the crowded scenes in such
a setting through the generations. In her atavistic devoutness, she
goes short of the freedom to write that she believes men writers
all enjoy, their good wives undertaking home chores and settling
all interruptions . . .

Her talk was rich and energetic, very much her own. I remember
Stephensen last year described a train journey to Norman
Lindsay's with her: 'all the way, that woman dropping ideas and
images like ripe fruit.' Ripe fruit – some polished, some velvety,
some prickly. This evening she mentioned an excellent staff
journalist who had first resigned, then died; why? 'He got better
every year at his job, but he couldn't stand it when all the
proprietors used to come and breathe down his neck' . . . We
asked her about the old days in the States, when she worked with
Alice Henry on the Women's Trade Union magazine. She has
never published anything about that, yet she has kept characters
in mind; like that young girl leader in a garment-workers' strike,
beginning her speeches to her mates, 'You're *plum* crazy,' and
carrying them all with her.

Some passengers came up a gangway from a launch, the French
liner always anchoring some distance from the usual pier. Miles
remarked suddenly, 'Oh, can you get here by launch? That's
handy.' And we found she had come by a sort of long back way,
walking miles through dark docks carrying her beneficent
parcels – and not saying anything at all about it to us nor making
us pay the penalty for her trouble in getting here, as some visitors
would.

We are making for Europe, and in a way it would have seemed
natural to ask for her view of the international scene which at

times she has known so well. Yet the evening has passed and she has gone, without any of the talk [of] leaving her Australia – the country where she has known both tradition and character and where she has been so angry about the downfall of young women's careers and yet so furious with visitors who don't see what a fine and peculiar life is arising here . . .

Paris 1935

April 25th, 1935   Spent most of yesterday looking at bookshops. One at the Odéon is marked Larousse, as a watchmaker's might be marked Greenwich, where time is made. Poking into its shelves, rich not only with dictionaries, I said to the young salesman, without first noticing his languid eyes, that it must be wonderful to be where knowledge comes from Larousse! He wasn't pleased by my bungling enthusiasm.

But how many ways there are of bungling in a foreign city! It's a long while since I shopped in Paris, and I'd forgotten about the business siesta from twelve till two. Walking from that Larousse down the narrow, neat, quiet Rue de l'Odéon, I came on Sylvia Beach's bookshop and library – Shakespeare and Company, in distinguished lettering. An impressive shopfront showing American and English classics and moderns in good editions; Shakespeare, Hemingway, Gertrude Stein, Whitman, Quixote (English), Christina Stead, Thackeray. In a frame, a striking piece of embroidery, showing a ship, a sunset . . .

I made to enter the shop and found myself banging at a shut door, my bump sounding like a knock. The door was opened by a dark-eyed American woman, with a forgiving voice: 'Did you *specially* want anything?' Of course not: I wanted everything in time and nothing now: I'd come later.

In the afternoon I found that the gentle dark woman was Sylvia Beach herself. The photograph I'd seen of her discussing proofs with Joyce had made her springy hair look fair, her eyes blue. (These preconceptions!) As she told me the story of Shakespeare and Company from its beginning in the twenties when American and other English-speaking people came in droves to Paris, I soon understood that from the first it was no perfunctory library and bookstore, but a workshop and a treasure-house. A leaflet she gave me, explaining library subscription terms, carried a brief testimonial, signed 'A.M.' Who? It was cautiously translated, its French bones showing through:

'. . . Is the student eager to pore over the great Elizabethans? He need not cross the Channel; in the rue de l'Odéon he will find them all . . . English novels from the earliest to *Ulysses*, writers of the Victorian Age and the Irish Renaissance. Those who follow the latest literary events know that the book that London and New York is discussing is always to be found at the same moment at Shakespeare and Company.'

So it seems that from being an English library for the foreign colony, it has become an institution for French readers, its value recognized by the French Government, which gives it a small subsidy now that bad times have come and the American invasion has receded like a tide.

Sylvia Beach's biggest single exploit has been the publication of *Ulysses* a dozen years ago, when both American and English publishers were afraid to touch the book. She has done other publishing, issuing novels (not only Lawrence's), and then, the tiniest exploit, that perfect book with a dozen poems by Joyce, 'pomes penyeach'. I remember ordering half-a-dozen copies of this shilling book when we were at Caloundra, seeing it mentioned in the *Times*. Sylvia Beach agreed that, of course, the title as spelt was taken from some kerbside barrow in Dublin, laden with perhaps penny broadside ballads. It was all part of Joyce's memory – Dublin photographed in his eyes, echoing in his ears, till he's made the whole world aware of this old shabby city on the Liffey.

Sylvia Beach has a good many of Joyce's papers – transcripts, corrected proofs, letters about details of production – the kind of thing that would gather in the course of publishing such an extraordinarily complex work as *Ulysses*. At the present crisis she'd be willing to sell them in England for the sake of Shakespeare and Company, taking them to Christie's herself, but a very high authority has assured her this wouldn't be possible; any Joyce papers would be seized by the Customs and burnt! So Shakespeare and Company limps along gloriously, providing not only the most stimulating books in the English speaking world but a rendezvous for writers. Not only for foreign ones. As a dark black-hatted, heavy shouldered man enters the shop and begins moving round the shelves she whispers: 'Excuse me a moment; there's Paul Valéry. I must see if there's something he specially wants.'

As a library and a place for the interchange of ideas the shop has its definite functions. Sylvia Beach said she didn't pretend to handle French books much; she's going to show me why to-morrow . . .

June 21st, 1935 Talks at odd intervals with Christina Stead. I feel rather ashamed of having brought her, with some others, to this Hotel des Grands Hommes, just because I knew it and they asked for a suggestion. It's suddenly burning midsummer, and the Panthéon makes this the hottest square in Paris. Christina, who knows her way everywhere, would have chosen better. But it has meant that we've seen a good deal of one another, going out for meals and walks, as well as sitting together in conference sessions. Her voice is easy to remember:

'My father wanted me to be a scientist like himself. When I was very tiny he used to tell me the names of what interested him most – fishes with frightening faces. It was all right, but when he saw I learnt easily he took me to science meetings. I suppose I was about ten by them. I wasn't frightened of fish with ugly faces, but those science women who didn't know how to do their hair or put their clothes on! I ran away from science forever.'

Or on Sunday morning, as we set out on a walk from our hotel, which is near an important police headquarters:

'Now *why* are all these gendarmes being sent out in lorries from the barracks to-day? What meeting of the people are they going to break up? Would it be that big communal picnic at St. Cloud? Look, there's another lorry being loaded with them. Who's going to be crushed?'

And later, in the Luxembourg Gardens, coming back to the dread science women:

' . . . I was determined to make enough money some day to have the right clothes. I must admit that I've got rather a weakness for shoes. And gloves. Yes, and hats. I buy my hats in London, but it does seem a pity not to be able to take one back from Paris now. It's not the best part of the season, though; it's too late. You see, in Paris when hats come in at the beginning of the season you don't think of buying those. Hats in the first wave are bound to be exaggerated, put out to attract people who are bound to be caught by anything showy. You just wait till that short wave's over and then the good hats appear – the serious ones; you simply must have one of those. Yes, of course there's a third wave later

in the season, as now; it consists partly of failures, rather cheap.
It's not safe to buy one of them, but it's not at all safe to buy
from the first wave, either.'

All this carefully adjusted wisdom uttered by this lightly-elegant
young woman in a voice of homely realism; a voice without
accent, but slightly coloured by her recent pan-European
years . . .

London 1935–1936

July 4th, 1935　　　Settling down to life in Bloomsbury, and picking up some of the threads dropped twenty years ago. In a way
Bloomsbury has the atmosphere of a small town, with the advantages of a metropolis. You can walk home from the theatre
or concert hall; most of your marketing can be done on the kerb
or just round the corner; you find people you know popping up
at every turn, though they're mostly birds of passage like yourselves. There is a homely feeling about those greyish streets and
green, enclosed squares. English? Yes, in every stone and railing,
yet with none of the English stiffness towards outsiders. Already
I feel more at home than I ever did out at Muswell Hill, where
we spent the first years of the war.

At Edith Young's flat to-day we were talking of the gibes flung
at Bloomsbury in recent plays and novels and trying to find out
what the word conveyed to most readers. Long-haired men and
short-haired women? An 'arty' approach to life? An un-English
cosmopolitanism? Is it true that Bloomsbury has become a refuge
for rather hard-up writers and painters? Edith's own circle has
a fairly large sprinkling of Indians – Mulk Raj Anand, Iqbal Singh
and others – and she herself still slaps vivid colours on her
casement frames and skirtings as soon as she moves into her latest
hospitable attic. A malicious satirist could picture Edith as typical
Bloomsbury. Yet what freshness she has, what eager absorption
in life! As much now as when, years ago, she used to try to adapt
herself to Australian ways of thought and feeling, flinging herself
into our dramatic movements, learning whole pages of O'Dowd's
The Bush by heart, wandering absorbed as a child through the
fern gullies of the Dandenongs . . .

July 12th, 1935　　　Another hot July afternoon. London people, plunging into shorts, seem to feel the pressure of it. I had to go up to see Christina Stead with a message. Up. I remember, when we arrived in London from Paris, and people were sharing a taxi to Hampstead, Christina was emphatic that it would take in her place in Baker St. A huge building of flats, and hers on the seventh storey – a long corridor from the lift. Lightness, modernity. One room given up to a gramophone with masses of records on shelves, and to a typewriter, with masses of files in pigeon-holes. (File of *Humanité*, for instance, on account of its *faits divers*, Christina surprisingly said.)

She looked flushed, emaciated, romantic. She had been writing a long, elaborate account of the Paris Writers' Congress, as well as her usual work, and taking it out of herself. Her husband, William Blake, came in, a powerful, rather nuggety dark man, and his mother, a little lonely expatriate from Germany. He speaks English with a cosmopolitan accent, rather bent by the U.S.A. Christina would make tea for me, gracefully whisking out pink serviettes, but adventurously, as if making maté in honour of a Uruguayan; and offering me some wine as if for relief.

From one window there was a view of Westminster, not only the spires but the parks. A sense of rolling carriages in golden afternoon dust (motors, I suppose). The London season in flower. Much accumulated glory. I said, 'And he called this city The Wen.' W.B. quirked, 'I haven't read Cobbett for a long while,' pronouncing it Cubbitt, as Christina would say, 'It's hut to-day.' They were speaking of Ralph Fox, who comes regularly to read economics with W.B., and what a serious, versatile fellow Fox is. And what a linguist; they declare he can talk Russian with peasants in their villages, and of course he's in Paris every few months making speeches at workers' meetings in the suburbs.

W.B. had a bit of a hangover from too many cocktails somewhere yesterday evening. I happened to mention being to dinner at the fantastic-serious Boulestin's, where R.D.W. took us last night before the ballet. 'Boulestin,' said Blake with heavy caution, 'Boulestin's not entirely trustworthy with his *plat du jour*; that can be commonplace. But with someone who knows how to order, as I gather your host did . . .'

He's like that – a connoisseur in all the arts, an epicure to whom even Boulestin's is not the last word in cookery. When we moved back to the next room, Christina put on a special recording of 'The Sunken Cathedral' . . .

July 26th, 1935   Yesterday and to-day I was at 'Green Ridges';
my first time of meeting with Henry Handel Richardson, except
by telephone a month ago (a firm voice, recognizably Australian
still) and by letters for the past ten years. And by her books.

All was accurately arranged. Miss Olga Roncoroni ('my friend
and secretary') drove me out from Hastings along the high road;
we passed through a tight little village, then along the road to
this lane near Fairlight. Miss R. sounded the horn as we drew
up near the gate. As we entered the front door, the staircase was
on the left; H.H.R. was standing on the bottom step to receive.
Formal, yet making her own rules; a slight and perhaps – as the
press says – 'diminutive' figure, yet commanding. She wore a
velvet house coat and dark slacks, wore her clothes as if she meant
them.

Tea in the big room downstairs: grand piano: Böcklin prints –
Maurice Guest period. The french window opened on the rather
formal garden; beyond that, there were miles of empty green
ridges to the Channel cliffs. (Hastings was further to the right.)
Summer haze; timeless summertime, 'all the long, blest, eventless
day.'

Long talk with H.H.R. after dinner in her study upstairs. Here
was another piano, a radio ('it's the only way you can hear modern
music without making the journey to London'), a stylized bust
of H.H.R. by the Roumanian, Sava Botzaris. The huge windows
gave a wide view over the ridges, the bay, the Channel. But I
sat with my back to the window, by some shelves nearly filled
with books by Australians. H.H.R. on another sofa across the
room.

The talk wandered like a quiet river around themes raised in
our letters during the years. H.H.R. said she was glad I had never
hesitated in the use of her pen-name, her name. There was that
time in 1929 when the press at home had sudden headlines about
Ultima Thule: 'Australian Woman Writer Leaps to Fame.' (Leap
in slow motion; it was 21 years since *Maurice Guest* had first
appeared.) Two editors, knowing I had written about her books
for years, now wired me: 'Who is Henry Handel Richardson?'
I said she was H.H.R. and a great writer: I gave literary
particulars. It wasn't my fault that, after all, sundry relatives and
friends had come to light with personal information the editors
wanted, her looks, her likings, and that she was Mrs. J. G.
Robertson, her husband being Professor of German Language and

Literature and director of Scandinavian Studies at University College, London.

'But I've worked more than twenty years to establish my own name,' she said. 'Why shouldn't I have it? After all, Richardson was the name I was born with – and perhaps I place an almost oriental valuation on a personal name; any way, why should a woman lose her name on marriage? As for Henry, well, *Maurice Guest* appeared at the time of feminist agitation, and I wanted the book to be a test. No one, positively no reviewer, spotted it as "just a woman's work". Handel – an uncle in Ireland, rather musical, adopted it, and I took it over. My husband rejoiced that I wasn't merely Mrs. J. G. Robertson.

'Those who begrudge me my H.H.R. are all of a piece with the journalists and librarians greedy for identifications. I insist that *Maurice Guest* and *Mahony* are works of fiction, not just essays in autobiography. There's that German baron, botanist and musician, in *Ultima Thule*. Of course I had Baron von Müller somewhat in mind; but all I knew of him was gathered from an old photograph, found in a family album. The rest was imaginary. I believe my father knew the Baron in earlier life, and his botanical studies were common property, of course. As for the music, well, all Germans of that date had it in them. His face, with its brown beard, might have been that of my counterpoint teacher in Leipzig . . . So much you see' (she spoke very firmly), 'for the "facts" in *Richard Mahony*.'

Some time during the long evening the blinds were drawn, the lingering light shut out. All I remember is that H.H.R.'s face across the room was first shadowed, though still firm, then clear again. Her alert talk is what stays in the mind, its vigorous questions, its firm outlines.

I didn't expect to see her this morning, as she usually sits down at her study desk at 9.30, takes up a well-sharpened pencil from a dozen on her tray, and works till lunchtime, when she hands the result, whether pages or sentences, to Miss R. for typing out. To-day, though, there was a walk for three, further up Tilekiln Lane and out of it, climbing to the old Coastguard station on the rise, and looking over towards Romney Marsh and, again, the sea. H.H.R. walks lightly and strongly. It's hard to remember how uncertain her health is: easier to grasp that lately she played tennis nearly every afternoon; that was, I think, till her husband died two years ago. Then she left their house in Regent's Park, placed her husband's collection of books in the University as he wished, found this house and made a few alterations, and built up a way of life here – so that she could write steadily, as before.

Here is her house, alone and self-contained, with Miss R. to keep visitors and inquirers away, in person or on the telephone. Visitors, if they must come, can be received in the drawing-room, which looks intimate and hospitable enough, being within the shell that H.H.R. keeps round her. But the drawing-room, for her, is almost a public room, and on the ground floor. She needs to retreat and retreat into perfect solitude for work. It's only by passing through her bedroom, and then through a muffled baize-door beside her bed, that you reach her own study.

People call this secretiveness, but it's rather economy of effort, all for the sake of her writing; she finds it exhausting to meet more than one or two people at the same time, and she can't afford exhaustion, so she keeps withdrawn. She knows where she's going; she has known it ever since she was a child. When they flattered her about her music, and sat her at the piano, a child of eight or so, to play at country concerts, she wanted to play with her pencil, too; wanted to write poetry. When she went to study music at Leipzig, she worked at it hard enough – six hours' practice a day – but while she practised her scales she'd prop a book before her, one of the classic novels of Europe. At last her ambitious, energetic mother gave in and admitted that, for all her marked inborn talent, her training had come too late to make her a concert performer, and H.H.R. was overjoyed: it left her free to write. Married and in London, she settled down to write; her husband took this utterly for granted. 'But then,' she says, 'when I actually read him the first twenty pages of *Maurice Guest*, no one was more amazed than he was. He hadn't guessed I could do so well. I'll never forget that day.' Ever since, except in illness or when taking a holiday for health's sake, she has regarded every day as a working day. To live is to write.

After lunch there was still some time, and we went for a dazzling drive. Up and then past Romney Marsh, yellow and luminous with summer, inland to the old sea-cliffs of Rye. We didn't stop there for any of the 'olde' places, nor for Henry James' house, and when we drove back through little white Winchelsea, we didn't look for Beverley Nichols' thatched roof; we went into the old church, but H.H.R. felt it cold and went outside in the sun. 'We're walking on the graves of infants,' she said in a tone of fatality when we joined her across the grass.

A swift drive back to Green Ridges, swift enough even for H.H.R., who's curiously modern in some of her passions, and then indoors for tea, looking out on the brilliant summer garden. Miss R. drove me to the five o'clock train – a smooth train, its quietness filled for me with the last twenty four hours . . .

November 13th, 1935   To Rebecca West's for lunch in her flat somewhere behind Selfridge's. I'd been looking forward to meeting her since her friendly letter of some years ago, in response to a review I'd written of *This Strange Necessity*. No, long before that. How well I remember Rowland Kenney talking, in 1912, about this Hampstead girl, fabulously young and clever, who wrote under a pen-name she'd taken from one of Ibsen's heroines; from then on, I'd followed her essays in *The Feminist* and then in *The New Republic*, marvelling at her growing power and assurance. There was her little book on Henry James, about 1917, as notable for its penetration as its wit.

She came in, a little late, to the drawing-room where the butler had asked me to wait – breezy, and with the brilliant dark eyes I'd expected.

'Excuse me, I couldn't get away sooner: I've been working.'

And as we went in to lunch through the folding doors she lightly gave me an inkling of the extent and variety of her work. There were not only her regular assignments – book reviews and causeries for this country and America – but her short stories and her occasional novels. Then much of this year has been spent in travel, giving literary lectures for the Foreign Office in North European countries.

'Lately I lectured in Finland, Lithuania, Latvia, and Germany – in that order. Not the most convenient order for travel-arrangements. The worst of the F.O. is that it knows nothing about geography.'

She was responsive and forthcoming, but when we came to literary matters several dark little snags cropped up in the current of our talk. We disagreed about Henry Handel Richardson, about the achievements of Orage as an editor. When I spoke of the young writers he'd helped to find their feet and direction, she challenged me abruptly:

'Tell me one writer of any quality he helped – tell me one.'

A dozen names were on the tip of my tongue – from St. John

Ervine and W. L. George to Ruth Pitter – but it's hard to give chapter and verse in such matters. And I suddenly remembered a long, seemingly malicious attack by Randolph Hughes on R.W.'s 'St. Augustine' that Orage had found space for in the *New English Weekly* before he died. Evidently there were antagonisms working that I knew nothing about. The difficulty of coming into this London literary world from outside is that one fails to remember it consists of fallible men and women, with their accumulation of likings, antipathies, imperfect sympathies. Judgments always look so impartial when committed to cold print and read in, say, Green Island . . .

December 19th, 1935   Just back from another couple of days at 'Green Ridges'. H.H.R. is perhaps more revealing, because more concentrated, in midwinter. The chunky house, with its central heating, cut off from the creeping cold of the Downs and the sea mist, seems a little dynamo, humming with long-stored energy, carefully husbanded. We went out, drove along the foreshore, then inland to the glorious town of Battle, returning through countless other little country places they had visited before H.H.R. decided on 'Green Ridges'. We walked to the highest ridge above the Lane, heard the fog siren on Beachy Head a dozen miles away, saw the nothingness of distance over the Channel. Always I felt her tautness, like a coiled spring.

She is working now on another book, highly documented. Nothing to do with Australia this time. Her general ideas on writing have never changed. More than ever she is determined, for her part, not to interfere with her characters but to let them work out their own destinies; to keep the author out of it. It was the same when she began, in *Maurice Guest*; to the confounding of the critics who wanted, for instance, to represent the controversial passage on Mendelssohn as her own opinion. Later on, people quoted Richard Mahony's view of Australian life, people, and landscape as her own; this in spite of the brief aside at the opening of *Ultima Thule* where she speaks as a 'native born'.

I listen to her out of doors, where she shows me, on the misty Downs, some grand stuggy horses, Suffolk Punches, actual importations of a farmer who had once travelled abroad to Suffolk; or indoors, in the study all the evening, the mild central heating quickened by a fire, the mental atmosphere warm and fluid. She asks me about some Australians on her shelves. What is this novelist likely to do next? Hasn't that one rather the over-emphasis of a journalist? What poems are to be expected from So-and-so?

So much of my own life has been spent watching writers at work, reading in manuscript their poems, stories, novels, listening to their ideas – or guessing at them; trying to come to some conclusions about the special nature of each. But what makes up the special nature of this writer, H.H.R.?

First of all, concentration: her life planned to fertilize those hours of creative work. But concentration to what end? Economically free, she has never thought of writing for money, never been tempted to please a publisher by writing a novel for the new season. Her impulse to create has all along come from a passionate interest in human relationships and character; perhaps a lifelong absorption in a few figures that have touched her feeling and imagination. Her need for human contacts is mainly satisfied by the people in the world she builds up. She seems to have few close friends, and has no love at all for large groups.

To write is her joy. Suggest to her that a writer's life is a hard one, an agonizing struggle with intractable material, and she will deny it. 'But I love every moment at my desk. How else could I have kept on writing all these years, getting nothing for it but starvation-fees and obscurity?'

Success, immediate and retrospective, came, ironically, with *Ultima Thule*, her most intransigent book (one that had to be published privately). It might never have come in her life-time. She would have kept on without it. She is a writer.

December 27th, 1935   A small, interesting party at Rebecca West's flat, very cosy and Christmasy. Central heating for warmth and a log fire to provide a centre, with Christmas cards spread round in their hundreds and everyone conscious of the timeless-ness that is part of this season.

We rather expected a crowd, but there were only Vera Brittain and her husband Prof. Catlin – he gently ex-cathedra and professorial, with that falsely-youthful exterior of Harrison Moore and Keith Hancock – John Beevers and his wife, a young, fair-haired Mlle. de la Tremblaye from Switzerland, and Mr. Henry Andrews. ('I am the husband,' he said with a twinkle, as he met us on the landing) . . .

April 5th, 1936   Yesterday met Jean Young in Cambridge, and she took me to see her old friends, the Leavises. Mrs. Leavis, a friendly, dark, young spectacled woman, welcomed us and, after we had dropped our cloaks, ushered us in to the sitting-room where Dr. Leavis was handy-man, watching the tea kettle on the fire. He was tallish, baldish, with brown hair and side whiskers; brown, sensitive humorous eyes, with a droop at the corners. Mrs. L., with her high, very rapid utterance, and Dr. L. with his slight drawl broadening his vowels, were both of them fatigued, and utterly aware of it all the time – admitting it in words.

Coming along, I had asked Jean Young about their position, which is known to be unfortunate. She explained that Mrs. L. had been L.'s most brilliant student while he held a University post as English lecturer for six years. Then they had married. At the end of the six years the post came up for revision: L. had expected re-appointment for another period, thereafter permanently. Nothing of the kind. Through some hostility of the academic authorities he lost the post and has now to live on giving lessons, though he has also a tiny post as lecturer in a specially hard-up college. Yet he published *Scrutiny*, which is eagerly read by his old students all over the world, and he is overwhelmed by students who make their way to him for advice and training. As for his wife, she wrote her brilliant, searching book, *Fiction and the Reading Public*, as a thesis years ago, but has not had leisure to do anything else except articles for *Scrutiny*.

Dr. L. has fluency and pungency in talk, though he finds writing a slow, difficult matter. 'My wife's the making of *Scrutiny*, you know. She's a born journalist, and comes to the rescue, especially when a promised article fails to turn up at the last moment. Incredible to me how she can write straight off like that. With me, writing's a long struggle . . .'

Again and again he confessed: 'But I'm so tired. I'm undertaking too much. Even now I can't speak as I should because I've got my eyes on that boy over there. There's no need, as his mother's here and at leisure. But we're so used to the need for watching him.'

The boy was little Ralph, terribly nervy and delicate, physically unable to 'tolerate fats' and mentally alert enough for the age of six instead of two. He didn't sleep, his father said, and he had been very ill.

While Jean and Mrs. L. talked on the sofa about their common friends, I asked about *Scrutiny*, in which (March) I had just been reading his grand revaluation of Keats. What relation was *Scrutiny* to the two volumes called *Scrutinies*, collected from files of the *Calendar of Letters*? He said it was in direct descent. He had immensely valued the *Calendar* while it lasted, and had admired the critical intelligence of the young men – Edgell Rickword, Garman, and Bertram Higgins – who had run it:

'The *Calendar* was an important review, and I couldn't help regretting it should be forgotten and unused. It was very little known or circulated at the time, and complete sets are now unobtainable. I had my set bound and kept it safely; but I thought something could be done about it and, two years ago, I got Wishart to publish a volume compiled from the *Calendar* – *Towards Standards of Criticism.*'

He showed me a copy, with an essay by Bertram Higgins in it, which he much admired; said Bertram was a wonderfully sound and shrewd critic and wondered how that little *Calendar* group had got themselves 'educated' – had they educated one another by good conversation? He asked me how old Bertram was, and when I told him thirty-five said that made him think all the more of him – he must have been under twenty-five in the days when he had followed him and found him so sound.

'As for Rickword and Garman, it seems they've gone all to pieces. Call themselves marxists, but are really just Bloomsbury, knocking round at cocktail parties and not doing any thinking.'

I told him I thought he was misinformed – that Garman was in poor health, lived in the country and came to town every week to deliver a careful literary lecture, while Edgell Rickword had just taken over the managership of an important publishing business. But L.'s apt to suspect a young writer of turning Bloomsbury, which means for him – I asked for his definition – 'an acceptance and bandying about of current fashionable notions on literature.' He complained that the Indians he had seen lately were hopelessly Bloomsbury, and I found he meant Iqbal Singh and Anand.

'I've known Singh for years and have been disappointed in him. After a term at Cambridge he decided to leave. He was to be a genius; the University could give him nothing. Then lately he brought me his long story, "When One is In It" – you've seen it?'

I certainly had: a tense, imaginative story of life among the cotton-spinners of Bombay.

'Well,' said Dr. L., 'that, of course, was so hopeless I hardly knew how to tell him. He has no sense of writing at all. It's not as if he were a beginner. He's quite twenty-five and doesn't know more than that.'

(Leavis's tha-at has a dying fall; he never bites his words off with a snap. He is tired, neurotic, never indecisive, though; the dying fall finds its angle of repose.)

I demurred about Singh, admitting some turgid passages in the story but insisting on the strength and pattern and sincerity; L. said he would read it again, but I'm afraid he knows the answer. From Anand he seemed to hope for nothing, though he knew that E. M. Forster had prefaced his 'Untouchable'. When it comes to new material, entirely new material, I feel, L. is just as academic as the other academicians. He told me, innocently, that when he found a New Zealand student of his, named McCormick, doing a thesis on Tudor literature that bored him, he proposed that he should investigate something nearer home – 'The Reason Why There is No Literature in New Zealand'. An investigation with the answer known beforehand, x – o! The little modern continuity he admits in literature is nearly all very safe – Eliot, Forster, Virginia Woolf, Lawrence, Joyce and (I hear incredibly) Charles Morgan!

But time was going; Ralph was being put to bed; day was closing. Dr. L. sauntered down to the bus with us, hatless and without overcoat. 'I'm Cambridge born, but my wife's Mediterranean and never gets used to this cold.' Jean was advising holidays in the Scilly Islands if they couldn't get as far as Greece or the South Seas. He shook his head. The child needed his regime, his doctor; he himself needed his books. The vacation was the only time he could do his own work, and if he didn't produce a new book regularly his reputation would drop; he couldn't afford that.

We missed a bus or so; at last caught one. A short ride. We hopped out, in the middle of Cambridge, near the Market. Can you run like a hare? Jean asked. Not very. Dodging evening shoppers and promenaders, still possible in a town of narrow streets and few cars, we passed the Market, reached King's Parade, and raced down to the Bull Hotel . . .

MARJORIE BARNARD, 1897–1987

Novelist and historian, Marjorie Barnard was born in
Sydney, attended Sydney University, and graduated
with the University Medal for History in 1918. Her
life was constrained by some of the customary
restrictions placed upon 'young ladies' at the time;
convention required her to be available to her
parents and despite the fact that she won a
scholarship to Oxford, her father would not allow
her to go. She did become a librarian at the Sydney
Technical College but the demands of work (and
home) were too great to allow her sufficient
opportunity for her writing; in 1935 she left the
library and devoted herself, full time, to a literary
life.

Part of Nettie Palmer's network, and a member of
the literary circles of her day, Marjorie Barnard
embarked on a highly successful literary partnership
with Flora Eldershaw whom she had met at Sydney
University. As 'M. Barnard Eldershaw' they published
the historical novel *A House is Built* (1929) as well as
Green Memory (1931), *The Glasshouse* (1936),
Plaque with Laurel (1927) and their most ambitious
novel, *Tomorrow and Tomorrow* (1947) which was
published in unabridged form in 1983 by Virago as
Tomorrow and Tomorrow and Tomorrow.

When their literary collaboration ended (partly
because Flora Eldershaw moved to Canberra in 1940)
Marjorie Barnard continued to write. She produced
an impressive list of non-fiction works including

Macquarie's World (1941), *Australian Outline; A
Brief History of Australia* (1943), *The Sydney Book*
(1947), *Australia's First Architect: Francis Greenway*
(1961) and *Miles Franklin* (1967). She also wrote a
work of fiction, *The Persimmon Tree and Other
Stories*, first published in 1943 and reprinted by
Virago in 1985; 'Habit', reprinted here, has been
taken from the later edition of the work.

HABIT

Miss Jessie Biden was singing in a high plangent voice as she made
the beds. It was a form of self-expression she allowed herself only
when there were no guests in the house, and she mingled the
hymns and sentimental songs of her girlhood with a fine
impartiality. She made the beds with precision, drawing the much
washed marcella quilts, with spikey fringes, up over the pillows
so that the black iron bedsteads had an air of humility and self-
respect. The sheets, though not fine, smelt amiably of grass, and
the blankets were honest, if a little hard with much laundering.
With the mosquito nets hanging from a hoop which in its turn,
was suspended from a cup hook screwed into the wooden ceiling,
the beds looked like virtuous but homely brides.

Jessie stopped singing for a minute as she pulled the green
holland blind to the exact middle of the window, and surveyed
the room to see if all were in order. She had very strict notions
about the exact degree of circumspection to which paying guests
were entitled. Yesterday everything washable in the room had
been washed, the floor, the woodwork, the heavy florid china
on the rather frail, varnished wooden washstands. The rooms
smelled of soap, linoleum polish and wood. The lace curtains were
stiff with starch. Indeed, there was more starch than curtain, and
without it they would have been draggled and pitiful wisps.

As every door in the house was open and it was a light wooden
shell of a place, old as Australian houses go, and dried by many
summers, Jessie could quite comfortably talk to Catherine, who
was cooking in the kitchen, from wherever she happened to be
working. But presently, the rooms finished, she came to stand
in the kitchen doorway with a list of the guests they were expecting
for Easter, in her hand.

The kitchen was a pleasant room looking on to the old orchard, a row of persimmon trees heavy with pointed fruit turning golden in the early autumn, squat, round, guava bushes, their plump, red-coronetted fruit hidden in their glossy dark leaves, several plum and peach trees, one old wide-spreading apple tree and a breakwind of loquats and quinces. Beyond again was the bush, blue-green, shimmering a little in the morning sunshine.

Catherine Biden, too, was pleasant, and in keeping with the warm autumn landscape. Her red-gold hair, fine, heavy and straight, made a big bun on her plump white neck, her milky skin was impervious to the sun and her arms, on which her blue print sleeves were rolled up, were really beautiful. In the parlance of the neighbours, neither of the sisters would see forty again, which somehow sounded duller and more depressing than to say that Catherine was forty-two and Jessie forty-six.

'I'm putting the Adamses in the best room,' Jessie was saying, 'because they don't mind sharing a bed. And Miss Dickens and her friend in the room with the chest of drawers. Mrs. Holles says she must have a room to herself, so it will have to be the little one. The Thompsons and Miss George'll sleep on the verandah and dress together in the other room. The old lady and her niece next to the dining room. That leaves only the verandah room this side, for Mr. Campbell.'

'It's quite all right while the weather is cool,' said Catherine, in her placid way, rolling dough.

Jessie looked at her list with disfavour. 'We know everyone but Mr. Campbell. It's rather awkward having just one man and so many women.'

'Perhaps he'll like it,' Catherine suggested.

'I don't think so. His name's Angus. He's probably a man's man.'

'Oh, if he's as Scotch as all that he won't mind. He'll fish all the time.'

'Well, all I hope is he doesn't take fright and leave us with an empty room.' The Easter season was so short, they couldn't afford an empty room.

'I hope,' said Catherine, 'we don't get a name for having only women. We do get more teachers every year and fewer men, don't we?'

'Yes, we do. I think we'd better word the advertisement differently.'

She sighed. Jessie, growing stout, with high cheek bones and a red skin, was the romantic one. She had always taken more kindly to this boarding house business than Catherine, because of its infinite possibilities – new people, new chances of excitement and romance. Although perhaps she no longer thought of romance, the habit of expecting something to happen remained with her.

Their father had married late. This house beside the lagoon had come to him with his wife and he had spent his long retirement in it, ministered to by his daughters. When he and his pension had died together, he had not, somehow, been able to leave them anything but the house, the small orchard and the lovely raggedy slope of wild garden running down to the water. Jessie, in a mood of tragic daring, advertised accommodation for holiday guests, carefully copying other advertisements she found in the paper. This expedient would, they hoped, tide them over. That was twelve years ago. A makeshift had become a permanency. In time, with the instrumentality of the local carpenter, they had added a couple of rooms and put up some almost paper-thin partitions. It looked as if they had developed the thing as far as they could.

They both still looked on their home as something different from their guest house. It was vested in that company of lares and penates now in bondage to mammon, but some day to be released. 'Our good things,' the sisters called them, the original furniture of the house, the bits and pieces that their mother had cherished. The big brass bed that had been their parents' was still in the best bedroom, though the cedar chest of drawers with pearl buttons sunk in its knobs and the marble topped washstand had gone to raise the tone of other rooms. The dining room was very much as it had always been. The sideboard with the mirrors and carved doors took up the best part of one wall, and set out on it was the old lady's brightly polished but now unused silver coffee service. The harmonium, with its faded puce silk, filled an inconvenient amount of room by the window. The old people's enlarged portraits, an ancient, elaborate worktable with dozens of little compartments, and other intimate treasures not meant for paying guests, but impossible to move out of their way, gave the room a genteel but overcrowded appearance. In the dining room in the off season it was almost as if nothing had ever happened.

In twelve years Jessie's hopefulness had worn a little thin and

Catherine's gentle placid nature had become streaked with discontent, as marble is veined with black. Sometimes she asked herself where it was all leading, what would happen to them by and by and if this was all life had in store? She began in a slow blind way to feel cheated, and to realise how meaningless was the pattern of the years with their alternations of rush and stagnation, of too much work and too little money. Of their darker pre-occupations the sisters did not speak to one another. In self defence they looked back rather than forward.

The guests began to arrive at lunch time. Angus Campbell was the last to come, by the late train, long after dark. Catherine went up to the bus stop with a lantern to meet him. He saw her for the first time with the light thrown upward on her broad fair face, and he thought how kind and simple and good she looked. His tired heart lifted, and he felt reassured.

Undressing in the small stuffy room they shared, next to the kitchen, Jessie asked her sister, 'Do you think he'll fit in all right?'

'I think so,' Catherine answered. 'He seems a nice, quiet man.'

'Young?' asked Jessie with the last flicker of interest in her tired body.

'About our age.'

'Oh well . . .'

They kissed one another good-night as they had every night since they were children, and lay down side by side to sleep.

The shell of a house was packed with sleeping people, all known and all strangers.

Angus Campbell evidently did not find his position of solitary man very trying, for on Easter Monday he asked, rather diffidently, if he might stay another week. He was taking his annual holidays. When the other guests departed, he remained. One week grew into two, then he had to return to Sydney.

He was a tall, gaunt, slightly stooped man with a weather-beaten complexion – the kind of Scots complexion that manages to look weather beaten even in a city office – and a pair of clear, understanding, friendly, hazel eyes. His manner was very quiet and at first he seemed rather a negligible and uninteresting man. But presently you discovered in him a steadfast quality that was very likeable. You missed him when he went away.

When he was alone with the sisters, life settled inevitably into a more intimate rhythm. They ate their meals together on a rickety table on the verandah, where they could look over the garden to the lagoon. He would not let the sisters chop wood or do the heavy outdoor work that they were accustomed to, and he even came into the kitchen and helped Jessie wash up while Catherine put away. He did it so simply and naturally that it seemed right and natural to them.

One day he began digging in the garden, and, from taking up the potatoes they wanted, went on to other things. 'You oughtn't to be doing this,' Jessie said. 'It's your holiday.'

'You don't know how I enjoy it,' he answered, and his eyes, travelling over the upturned loamy earth to the blazing persimmon trees and the bush beyond, had in them a look of love and longing. She knew that he spoke the truth.

He went out fishing and brought back strings of fish for their supper with pride and gusto, and then had to watch Catherine cook them. There seemed to be something special about Catherine cooking the fish he caught.

He helped Catherine pick fruit for jam and she was aware that for all he was thin and stooped he was much stronger than she, and it gave her a curious, pleased feeling. Jessie, alone in the house, could hear their voices in the orchard, a little rarefied and idealised, in the still warm air.

One day it rained, great gusts of thick fine rain that blotted out the lagoon, and Angus, kept in, took his book on to the verandah. Passing to and fro doing the work, Catherine saw that he was not reading, but looking out into the rain. Then he went and stood by the verandah rail for a long time. She came and stood beside him.

He said, 'If you listen you can just hear the rain on the grass and among the leaves – and smell the earth. It's good, isn't it? The trees are more beautiful looming through the mist – the shape of them.' Marvelling, she saw that he was half in love with the beauty that she had lived with all her life.

A magpie flew through the rain, calling. He laid his hand on her shoulder and she was a little shaken by that warm and friendly touch. The eyes he turned on her still held the reflection of a mystery she had not seen.

Angus Campbell told them about himself. He was a clerk in a secure job and for years he had looked after his invalid mother, coming home from the office to sit with her, getting up in the night to tend her, his money going in doctor's bills. She had often been querulous and exacting. The pain and the tedium were so hard for her to bear, and there was so little I could do for her. Of course I remember her very different. No one could have had a better mother. She was very ambitious for me, and made great sacrifices when I was a boy, so that I should have a good education and get on. But I never did – not very far.' It was evident that he thought he owed her something for that disappointment. Two months ago she had died and he missed her bitterly. 'She had become my child,' he said. He felt, too, the cruelty of her life that had been hard and unsatisfied, and had ended in pain. Now there was no hope of ever retrieving it.

'He is very good,' said Jessie to her sister when they were alone that night.

'And kind,' said Catherine. 'The kindest man I've ever known.' Neither of them thought how few men they'd known.

Jessie raised herself on her elbow to look at Catherine as she slept in the faint moonlight, and thought how comely she was, sweet and wholesome.

When Angus had, at last, to go, he said he would be back for the week-end. They kissed him. He was to arrive on the Friday by the late train again, and Catherine prepared supper for him before the fire, for it was getting cold now. She took the silver coffee pot, the sacred silver coffee pot that had been their mother's, and put it to warm above the kitchen stove. She cast a half defiant glance at Jessie as she did so, but Jessie went and took the silver sugar bowl too, and the cream jug, filled them, and set them on the table.

Angus asked Catherine to go out in the boat with him or to go walking, and then he paid Jessie some little attention. But they both knew. One Sunday, perhaps it was the fourth week-end he had come, the autumn was now far advanced, he and Catherine went for a long walk and he asked her to marry him. He took her in his arms and kissed her. She felt very strange, for she had never been kissed before, not by a man who was in love with her. They walked home hand in hand as if they were still very young, and when Catherine saw Jessie waving to them from the verandah she stood still and the unaccountable tears began to flow down her cheeks.

They said, everybody said, that there was no reason why they should wait, meaning they had better hurry up. The wedding was fixed for three months ahead.

It was a curious three months for Catherine. When Angus came for the week-end they would not let him pay his board, and that made a little awkwardness. Even calling him Angus seemed a trifle strange. He did not come every week-end now. Once he said, 'It seems wrong to take you away from all this beauty and freedom and shut you up in a little suburban house among a lot of other little houses just the same. Do you think you'll fret, my darling?'

Catherine had never thought very much about the beauties of nature. So she just shook her head where it rested against his shoulder. Still, her heart sank a little when she saw his house with its small windows, dark stuff hangings and many souvenirs of the late Mrs. Campbell. It seemed as if sickness and death had not yet been exorcised from it.

Catherine and Jessie sewed the trousseau. 'We must be sensible,' they said to one another, and bought good stout cambric and flannelettes, though each secretly hankered after the pretty and the foolish. Catherine could not quite forget that she was going to be a middle aged bride, and that that was just a little ridiculous. Neighbours, meaning to be kind, teased her about her wedding and were coy, sly and romantic in a heavy way, so that she felt abashed.

A subtle difference had taken place in the relationship of the sisters. Jessie felt a new tenderness for Catherine. She was the younger sister who was going to be married. Jessie's heart burned with love and protectiveness. She longed, she didn't know why, to protect Catherine, to do things for her. 'Leave that to me,' she would say when she saw Catherine go to clean the stove or perform some other dirty job. 'You must take care of your hands now.'

But Catherine always insisted on doing the roughest work. 'He's not marrying me for my beauty,' she laughed.

Catherine too thought more of her sister and of how good and unselfish she was, and her little peculiarities that once rather irritated her, now almost brought the tears to her eyes. One night she broached what was always on her mind.

'What will you do when I've gone?' she asked in a low voice. 'I'll get Ivy Thomas to help me in the busy times,' Jessie answered in a matter of fact voice, 'and in between, I'll manage.'

'But it will be lonely,' said Catherine weakly.

Jessie cast a reproachful glance at her. 'I'll manage,' she said.

Catherine was no longer discontented and weighed down with

a sense of futility. Another emotion had taken its place, something very like homesickness.

As she did her jobs about the place she thought now, 'It is for the last time,' and there was a little pain about her heart. She looked at her world with new eyes. Angus's eyes perhaps. Going down to the fowlyard in the early morning with the bucket of steaming bran and pollard mash, she would look at the misty trees and the water like blue silk under the milk-pale sky; at the burning autumn colours of the persimmon trees, and the delicate frosty grass, and her heart would tremble with its loveliness.

One evening, coming in with the last basket of plums – ripe damsons with a thick blue bloom upon them – she stopped to rest, her back to the stormy sunset, and she saw thin, blue smoke like tulle winding among the quiet trees where a neighbour was burning leaves. She thought that she would remember this all her life. Picking nasturtiums under the old apple tree she laid her cheek for a moment against the rough silvery bark, and closed her eyes. 'My beloved old friend,' she thought but without words, 'I am leaving you for a man I scarcely know.'

It would seem as if the exaltation of being loved, of that one ripe and golden Sunday when she thought she could love too, had become detached from its object and centred now about her home. She even became aware of a rhythm in her daily work. Objects were dear because her hands were accustomed to them from childhood. And now life had to be imagined without them.

'Wherever I am, I shall have to grow old,' she thought, 'and it would be better to grow old here where everything is kind and open, than in a strange place.' It was as if the bogey she had feared, meaningless old age, had revealed itself a friend at the last moment, too late.

Jessie lit the porcelain lamp with the green shade and set it in the middle of the table among the litter of the sewing. She stood adjusting the wick, her face in shadow, and said:

'We'll have to have a serious talk about the silver and things, Cathy. We'd better settle it to-night before we get too busy.'

'What about them?' Catherine asked, biting off a thread.

'You must have your share. We'll have to divide them between us.' Jessie's voice was quite steady and her tone matter of fact.

'Oh, no,' cried Catherine, with a sharp note of passion in her voice. 'I don't want to take anything away.'

'They are as much yours as mine.'

'They belong here.'

'They belong to both of us, and I'm not going to have you go away empty handed.'

'But, Jessie, I'll come back often. The house wouldn't seem the same without mother's things. Don't talk as if I were going away for ever.'

'Of course you'll come back, but it won't be the same. You'll have a house of your own.'

'It won't be the same,' echoed Catherine very low.

'I specially want you to have mother's rings. I've always wanted you to wear them. You've got such pretty hands and now you won't have to work so hard. . . . and the pendant. Father gave that to mother for a wedding present so as you're the one getting married it is only fit you should wear it on your wedding day too. I'll have the cameos. I'm sort of used to them. And the cat's eye brooch that I always thought we ought to have given Cousin Ella when mother died.' Jessie drew a rather difficult breath.

'You're robbing yourself,' said Catherine, 'giving me all the best. You're the eldest daughter.'

'That has nothing to do with it. We must think of what is suitable. I think you ought to have the silver coffee things. They've seemed specially yours since that night – you remember – when Angus came. Perhaps they helped . . . .'

Catherine made a funny little noise.

'I don't want the silver coffee set.'

'Yes, you do. They're heaps too fine for guests. They're good. What fair puzzles me is the work table. You ought to have it because after all I suppose I'll be keeping all the big furniture, but this room wouldn't be the same without it.'

'No,' cried Catherine. 'Oh, Jessie, no. Not the work table. I couldn't bear it.' And she put her head down among the white madapolam and began to cry, a wild, desperate weeping.

'Cathy, darling, what is it? Hush, Petie, hush. We'll do everything just as you want.'

'I won't strip our home. I won't.'

'No, darling, no, but you'll want some of your own friendly things with you.'

Jessie was crying a little too, but not wildly. 'You're over-wrought and tired. I've let you do too much.' Her heart was painfully full of tenderness for her sister.

Catherine's sobs grew less at last, and she said in a little gasping, exhausted voice. 'I can't do it.'

'I won't make you. It can stay here in its old place and you can see it when you come on a visit.'

'I mean I can't get married and go away. It's harder than anything is worth.'

Jessie was agast. They argued long and confusedly. Once Catherine said: 'I wish it had been you, Jessie.'

Jessie drew away. 'You don't think that I . . . .'

'No, dear, only on general grounds. You'd have made such a good wife and,' with a painful little smile, 'you were always the romantic one.'

'Not now,' said Jessie staunchly.

'I'll write to Angus now, tonight,' Catherine declared.

She wanted to be rid of this intolerable burden at once, although Jessie begged her to sleep on it. Neither of them had considered Angus, nor did they now. She got out the bottle of ink, and the pen with the cherry wood handle, which they shared, and began the letter. She was stiff and inarticulate on paper, and couldn't hope to make him understand. It was a miserable, hopeless task but she had to go through with it.

While she bent over the letter, Jessie went out into the kitchen and relit the fire. She took the silver coffee pot, the sugar basin and the cream jug, and set them out on the tray with the best worked traycloth. From the cake tin she selected the fairest of the little cakes that had been made for the afternoon tea of guests arriving tomorrow. Stinting nothing, she prepared their supper. When she heard Catherine sealing the letter, thumping the flap down with her fist to make the cheap gum stick, she carried in the tray.

Although she felt sick with crying, Catherine drank her coffee and ate a cake. The sisters smiled at one another with shaking lips and stiff reddened eyelids.

'He won't come again now,' said Jessie regretfully, but each added in her heart, 'He was a stranger, after all.'

ELEANOR DARK, 1901-1985

Born Eleanor O'Reilly, in Sydney, she adopted the
pseudonym Patricia O'Rane (and retained it, and
others, for a few years) when she had her first poems
published in 1920. In 1922 she married, and moved
to the Blue Mountains in New South Wales, where
she remained for most of her life.

Despite 'interruptions' she turned to serious writing
and in 1932 her first novel, *Slow Dawning*, was
published. *Prelude to Christopher* (1934), *Return to
Coolami* (1936) and *Waterway* (1938) which
followed, helped to establish her literary reputation;
her historical trilogy, *The Timeless Land* (1941),
Storm of Time (1948), *No Barrier* (1957) must stand
as a classic interpretation of people and place on the
Australian continent. *The Little Company* (1945)
explores some of the issues about the role of writing
and the place of the writer in social and political
reform, and throughout much of Eleanor Dark's
fiction run the themes of justice, harmony,
equity – and peace and war.

The following short story, 'Sweet and Low' (from
Lantana Lane, 1957; 1986 Virago), represents her
mature achievement, and marks her as one of
Australia's most distinguished authors.

SWEET AND LOW

Tony Griffith is just eleven. He is one of those lean, light little boys whose movements are nostalgically observed by persons of middle age and increasing weight. Was there ever a time, they ask themselves wonderingly, when *I* had so small a burden of flesh to carry about with me, and carried it like that? . . .

For Tony hardly ever walks, and when he comes running, skipping or hopping down the Lane, or proceeds with a kind of dancing step – as if he were trying to keep his feet in order, and not succeeding very well – he has an air of being only temporarily and accidentally in contact with the earth, like a head of dandelion seed blowing along the ground.

It was probably the sight of some such little boy which first brought to a poet's mind the words: '*There was a time* . . .'; words to which, as we all know, he added many others about celestial light, bounding lambs, and trailing clouds of glory. He cannot have been ignorant of the fact that little boys are devils, and that lean, light little boys are the most diabolical of all, since a minimum of their horrifying energy is required for the business of moving them from spot to spot, and a maximum thus remains for the conception and execution of various devilishnesses. But he evidently decided (and we believe quite rightly) that their fiendish habits are abundantly redeemed by the intimations of immortality which they evoke in the minds of those about whom shades of the prison house have closed; and no little boy ever more poignantly evoked them than Tony Griffith.

His face is as brown as a dead leaf, but as smooth and blooming as a peach. His nose is endearingly snubby and babyish, but the angle at which he holds it proclaims self-confidence, goodwill and indefatigable enquiry. His eyes – light-grey, and clear as water – stare at the world with an expression so genially and candidly searching that the world, if it had any shame left, might well blush and shuffle its feet. But the most noticeable thing about him is that he is never, never, never tired.

In any farming community the manifestations of fatigue are, of course, too obvious to be overlooked, and Tony is accustomed to the sight of his parents, his great-aunt Isabelle and his neighbours slumping into chairs at the end of the day, and exhibiting every symptom of exhaustion; but he is quite unable to comprehend what can be the matter with them. The opening of his eyes at five o'clock every morning brings into instant operation a powerful dynamo, incredibly concealed somewhere in his slip of a body, and this continues throughout the day to drive him at a furious and unfaltering pace. If he comes upon anything climbable, he immediately climbs it; if he chances upon anything that can be thrown, he immediately throws it; if a log, a wheel-barrow or a packing-case lies in his path, he not only jumps it, but returns several times to jump it again before proceeding on his way. He passes a great deal of time in hitting things – sometimes (as when he smites tennis or cricket balls with racquet or bat, or nails with a hammer, or tobacco-weed with a brush-hook) for some definite purpose; but sometimes (as when he puts in half an hour swiping at tufts of blady-grass with a stick, or belting stones along the Lane with a bit of board), merely because he feels like it. In either case, the vigour and impetuosity of his hitting are attributable to the fact that his dynamo produces so much surplus power that he must expend it rapidly, lest it burst his slender frame to smithereens.

This power is not only supplied to his muscles; it also floods his mind, sending forth, like a stream of crackling sparks, questions, comments, protests, petitions and conjectures. He says: 'How?', 'Why?', 'What?', 'When?' and 'Where?'; he says: 'Look!' and 'Watch!'; he says: 'Can I?' (and, when corrected, 'May I?'); this last frequently leads him to 'Why not?', and thence to a last ditch where he can always be depended upon to make a heroic stand, firing the word: 'but,' *'but'*, 'BUT', into the ranks of inimical adulthood until he goes down at last, with his colours still flying.

He does not lack companionship in the Lane. The Bell twins are his constant associates (though some might prefer the word accomplices), and there is also Daphne Arnold, who is twelve. She is unfortunate in that the Lane yields her no playmate of her own age and sex, so it is natural enough that she should turn to Tony; but for a long time no one could understand why Tony welcomed her with such consistent cordiality, for not only did she always have her five-year-old sister, Joy, at her heels, but she is herself a very polite, ladylike and motherly little girl who is apt – like mothers – to be easily shocked. She almost invariably disapproves of everything Tony proposes to do, and reprimands him at length when he does it all the same. So it seemed rather a bewildering friendship, and even Sue Griffith took a long time to realise that it was not really Daphne whom Tony liked to have

646 Eleanor Dark

around, but Joy. This may appear stranger still until you know
Joy; but when you do know her, you cannot fail to see that she
and Tony, out of all the children in the Lane, come nearest to
being soul-mates.

Joy does not share Tony's physical characteristics, for she is
a plump little person, and though she is untiringly active, she
creates no illusion that her feet are winged; on the contrary, one
might imagine them to be equipped, like those of flies, with some
kind of suction-grip, so firmly does she keep them on the ground.
Her pastimes and Tony's are, of course, the poles apart, but the
manner in which they pursue them is also subtly different. Tony
is volatile; Joy is constant. Tony is energetic; Joy is busy. The
activity of Tony's body frequently has nothing to do with the
activity of his mind; but Joy's doing is always strictly directed
and controlled by a fertile imagination, and her life is, consequently, one long, rich and coherent drama. Its theme (which
is that of a lady burdened by many cares) never changes, though
she improvises endless variations upon it. The more cares and
responsibilities she can conceive for herself, the busier she can
become, and her experience of life seems to have persuaded her
that the most fruitful sources of care are maternity, illness and
shops.

Tony is aware of himself only as we might suppose a plant
or an animal to be, and if it is difficult for others to remain
unaware of him, this is simply because any tremendous natural
force is apt to be conspicuous. When he is present, the throb and
pulse of his dynamo are almost audible, and the very ground
seems to vibrate; but he does not court attention. Joy, on the
other hand, is, in her own view, the absorbing and always vividly
apprehended centre of the universe, and she finds it intolerable
that the phenomenon of her existence should ever be, for one
instant, disregarded by anyone.

From these traits arises, perhaps, the further difference that
while she is extremely sensitive to criticism, Tony couldn't care
less. If his mother, in a moment of desperation, tells him that
he is, without exception, the most maddening and abominable
child it has ever been her misfortune to meet, he merely gives
her a blank stare from his limpid, grey eyes, and remains perfectly
unruffled. But a hint of reproof, or even the shadow of a
censorious expression, will cause Joy's rosebud mouth to droop,
and her round eyes to fill with tears as she demands piteously:

'Am I a *good* girl?'

This is obviously a point of vital importance – for what would become of us all if the centre of the universe were less than perfect? Cracks in its virtue are unthinkable, and therefore, upon learning that her perfection is, for the moment, slightly impaired, but that it may be speedily restored if she will do such and such, Joy hastens off to set things right, and returns for reassurance.

'Am I a good girl *now*?'

'Oh yes, you're a good girl *now*.'

'Am I a wery good girl?'

'Very good.'

'Am I a werry, *werry* good girl?'

'Very, very.'

'Am I a werry, werry *indeed* good girl?

'You're the best girl in the world.'

The mouth no longer droops, and the tears have vanished. The peril has been averted. Joy is once more at her station, and all's right with the world. It may safely begin to revolve again, and she forthwith sets it in motion.

'Now,' she says briskly, 'we'll play shops, and you must be the lady, and I'll be the shop-lady, and these must be the money, and my Uncle Mont must be in hostable because he's werry sick, and you must ask me how he is.'

All this being accomplished, Joy assumes an expression of quite heartrending anxiety, and distractedly waves her hands as she describes the predicament in which she finds herself. For it now appears, as the plot thickens, that no only Uncle Mont, but Auntie Flo and another character (of whom we learn nothing save that her name is Mary) are also in hostable, all suffering from fever, and all getting to be nearly quite dead. Thus Joy has the shop to mind, the housework to do, a large family of children to scold, and a heavy programme of sick-bed visiting as well. Here, becoming momentarily confused as to her identity, she thinks she will buy something to take to poor Uncle Mont; but, observing her mistake, she deftly switches parts.

'*I* must be the lady, and *you* must be the shop-lady, but you mustn't have Uncle Mont and Auntie Flo, see, because I must have them.' She pauses, considers, and adds magnanimously: 'But you can have Mary.'

With these alterations in the script duly understood, the drama is re-enacted, though by now Uncle Mont's condition has worsened, and the doctor has prescribed pills. In the confusion occasioned by hurriedly transforming the shop from a general store into a pharmacy, another switch of parts accidentally occurs; but the situation is so tense that this passes unnoticed. The pills having been wrapped up, and their cost fixed at one shilling and six pennies, this amount is handed over by the lady who receives, to her gratified astonishment, one shilling and eight pennies in change.

Now imbecilities of this kind are naturally beneath Tony's notice, and it must not be supposed that when Joy visited him he took any part in such nonsense. They were not playmates at all. What they recognised and valued in each other (until a regrettable occurrence which we shall presently recount put an end to their association) was the superb quality of their respective dynamos. They were like two great artists working in different media, who have no dealings with each other's arts, but still salute each other's genius. When the four older children played a game, Joy was neither invited nor forbidden to join in, but she was quite content to disport herself on its outskirts, turning it to her own purposes, and transforming it into something more her own. Nevertheless, she was, in a sense, more emphatically a participant than Daphne or the twins, for even her semi-detached gambollings at the periphery contributed to it a zest which was equalled only by Tony's. They were both very conscious of this. Like two royal personages in a crowd of commoners, or two millionaires in a suburban cottage, or two gangsters at a church social, they were always sharply aware of each other. But whereas Joy knew that Tony was aware of her, he did not know that she was aware of him; whereas he merely felt her gusto, and enjoyed it, she not only felt his and enjoyed it, but enjoyed even more the knowledge that he was feeling hers. And this was why, on the fateful evening which we are about to describe, she ran away and hid in the dumpty.

The subject of sanitation is not one which is commonly introduced into simple, family tales, but since it is germane to this one, it must be briefly discussed. There are few houses in our neighbourhood which boast septic tanks, and in the Lane we are all resigned to, if not content with, a less elaborate arrangement. This consists of a hole dug in the ground – a good, capacious hole, some four feet square and six deep – over which a suitable building is erected and furnished with the kind of seat appropriate to its function.

On the evening in question, Ding, Dong, Daphne and Joy were all at Tony's place, and Tony was practising on his fife. This had been given to him by Aunt Isabelle who – though not herself a performer on any instrument – comes of a musical family, and had often deplored the fact that Tony was prevented by his residence in this remote spot from developing the musical gifts which he must undoubtedly possess. She had accordingly presented him, on his birthday, with the fife, shrugging her shoulders the while, and protesting that – *faute de mieux* – it might serve to allay the hunger for melody from which the poor child was suffering.

Tony had no idea that he was suffering from anything, but he was delighted with the fife, and immediately began to experiment with it. After only a few hours he accidentally blew three notes in succession which formed part of a recognisable tune. After another hour he had thoroughly mastered these three notes, and could repeat them any time he liked; but more than this, he had identified them as belonging to the well-known hymn *Once in Royal David's City*, and was tirelessly in search of the fourth note to put after them. This he discovered in due course, and followed it with the fifth, the sixth, and the seventh; by this time he was so elated that only with the greatest difficulty could Sue persuade him to lay down his instrument for long enough to eat. She was clutching her head, and Henry was nearly frantic, but Aunt Isabelle was enraptured. Bless the little cabbage, she cried fondly, he executed the tune to a marvel, was it not? Within a fortnight he could play the whole thing from beginning to end; Aunt Isabelle, with proud tears in her eyes, said it was formidable, and Henry agreed that it damn well was.

Whatever his parents may have endured, the rest of the Lane (with one exception) quite enjoyed Tony's fife, and took a benevolent interest in his progress. Since distance lends enchantment to a view, it may, in like manner, soften the impact of sounds upon the ear; at all events, the intimations of immortality which Tony had always exuded were, if anything, enhanced by the sweet and plaintive notes of his fife. Those who dimly recalled their poetry lessons at school found themselves thinking vaguely and sentimentally about Pan, and shepherd lads, and some boy or other who came piping down a valley wild.

Joy, however, did not like the fife. It provided her first
experience of that terrible obsession known as Art, which causes
otherwise normal people to become queer and distrait, and to
go away into a world of their own, and cease to be conscious
of anything outside it. All these symptoms Tony was now exhibiting. Daphne and the twins were rather taken aback when they
found that he no longer wanted to play with them, but they just
played together and – if the truth must be told – sometimes felt
that things were simpler and cosier without him, if less exciting.

Joy, however, was in a terrible state. Tony was not aware of
her any longer; he was aware of nothing but his fife.

A woman scorned is popularly supposed to be fury personified,
but she is a dove compared with a woman ignored, and on this
memorable evening Joy had reached a stage where she would have
stopped at nothing to detach Tony's attention from the fife, and
transfer it to herself. There he was, sitting under the mulberry
tree, tootling away at some notes which did not, as yet, seem
to have any idea of co-operation, and looking rapt. She simply
could not bear it. She tried singing a song at the top of her voice
to drown his music, but he didn't seem to hear. She tried throwing
pebbles at him, but he didn't seem to feel. Then she tried falling
down and pretending she had hurt herself so werry, werry indeed
badly that she couldn't get up again, but he didn't seem to see.
This was so dreadful that she was just wondering if she could
find his football and hammer a nail into it, when Ding happened
to hit what would have been a sixer if Tony had not been in the
way. The ball caught him on the wrist, knocking the fife out of
his hand, and he sprang up wrathfully, yelling: 'Hey! Cut it out!'

Joy went into action so fast that only a blur on the landscape
betrayed her strategic move to a position behind him. While he
was still stamping about, shouting revilements at Ding, and
clutching his bruised wrist, she pounced, seized the fife, and ran.

She got away to a good start because for a few seconds Tony
remained unaware of his loss. Then, with a vengeful cry, he gave
chase. But she had disappeared round the back of the house, and
when he turned the corner he could not see her anywhere. He
looked behind the mango tree, he ran up and down the pineapple
rows, he poked about in the lantana; he summoned Daphne and
the twins, and they all searched too. The sun went down. Daphne
called, scolded and threatened. At last, addressing the empty air,
she announced loudly:

'All right, I can't wait any longer – I'm going without you, and you'll have to come home by yourself in the dark.'

Whereupon the door of the dumpty flew open and Joy shot out, bawling; but, alas, without the fife.

The full truth of this deplorable affair is so securely hidden in the centre of the universe that we doubt if it will ever become known. To the question: 'Did it fall, or was it dropped?' we shall never really know the answer. But we have it on Heather Arnold's authority that Joy reached home still bawling, continued to bawl until bedtime, and refused to compose herself for sleep until she had been assured – not once, but twenty times – that she was a werry, werry indeed good girl. From this we may draw our own conclusions.

But there is no doubt at all that Tony's dynamo, stimulated by crisis, went into operation so powerfully that his parents, to this day, remember the occasion as one when they felt themselves driven and dominated by an irresistible force. They were reclining in their chairs, exhausted by a particularly tough day's work, when he presented himself before them wearing an expression compounded of outrage and invincible determination. He said bitterly:

'That beastly damn kid, Joy, dropped my fife down the dumpty.'

'Tony,' yawned Sue mechanically, 'don't say . . .' She blinked, sat up, looked at him, and asked: 'What?'

'Joy,' repeated Tony with terrible restraint. 'My fife. Down the dumpty. And I want to practise, so come on.' And then he burst out with sudden ferocity: 'What's so funny?'

For his parents – revealing a callous lack of sympathy which shocked him to his soul – had actually begun to laugh. Aunt Isabelle, however, had greeted his news with exclamations of dismay, and was now giving a rapid sketch of her views on the matter, which were that this instrument, though of an inferior kind not hitherto used, or even recognised, in her family, had nevertheless cost money, and was not to be flung away – and into such a place, *pfui!* – by a naughty and undisciplined child, for that little Joy there was, and had always been of the most mischievous, and could with advantage undergo chastisement which she herself would willingly administer, though it must be understood that she did not, as a question of principle, favour the punishment corporal, and had so repeatedly informed Henry when he had lifted his hand against *ce pauvre* Tony, who had now been so maliciously deprived of his instrument which, though of an inferior kind not hitherto used or even . . .

Tony, glad as he was to find himself with at least one ally, felt that this had gone on long enough, and could not be allowed to begin all over again, particularly as it seemed to be increasing his parents' scandalous mirth, rather than arousing them to a proper sense of the urgency of the situation. So he interrupted hotly:

'Mum, I never gave it to her! It just fell out of my hand, and she sneaked up and grabbed it and ran away with it! You're always telling me I mustn't meddle with other people's things, but when she does it, you only *laugh!* . . .'

Sue, smitten by the justice of this, remembered her maternal duty, wiped her eyes, and said soothingly:

'No, darling. I mean, yes, darling. I mean it was very naughty of her, and we're all very, very sorry.'

Henry, belatedly contrite, reached behind his chair and patted Tony's leg.

'Yes – bad luck, old chap. But she's only a little girl, and I expect she didn't mean . . .'

'Didn't *mean* . . .!' snorted Tony fiercely. 'She meant it all right! And I was just beginning to learn *Sweet and Low!*'

At this, Henry, for some inexplicable reason, suffered another paroxysm of misplaced hilarity, and Sue went off into a veritable fit of hysterics. Aunt Isabelle, eyeing them with astonished indignation, bade Tony rest tranquil, for although his parents appeared insensible of the anguish which such a loss must occasion to one of the artistic temperament, she was of a nature more *sympathique*, and would, at the first opportunity, buy him a new fife. . . .

'I don't WANT a new fife!' roared Tony. 'There's nothing wrong with my old one, and I want to do some practice, so come *on!*'

Henry turned slowly in his chair, stared hard at his son, and enquired cautiously: 'Come on . . . where?'

'To get it, of course,' said Tony.

There was a long, hushed pause. Then Sue said briskly:
'Oh, come, darling, don't be silly!'

Henry was heard to chuckle indulgently; but from the way he settled himself on his shoulders and propped his slippered feet on another chair, it was plain that he had no intention of coming on anywhere. Tony stood looking at them in silence for a moment, drawing deep breaths and gathering his forces for battle. Within him the throb of his dynamo grew faster and stronger until the whole room seemed so charged with power that his parents exchanged glances of alarm, and shifted uneasily in their chairs. Sue – though she has described the later events of the evening with precision – has never been able to recall very clearly the exact details of the awe-inspiring struggle which now ensued. She knows that Aunt Isabelle vaccillated, sometimes declaring that the child's resolution was *magnifique*, and repeating (with that air of triumphantly settling a matter which proverbs lend to those who quote them) '*Qui ne risque rien, n' a rien*'; but sometimes, when her imagination got the better of her, protesting, imploring, expressing profound repugnance, and recklessly promising not only a new fife, but also a bugle, a concertina, a ukelele and even a drum. She knows that Henry, eschewing argument altogether, performed a swift and masterly retirement to that impregnable position which parents always keep prepared, and thundered: 'No! No! NO!' at frequent intervals. She is not sure what part she herself played in the scene, except that her lines all seemed to be short and unfinished. 'Henry, dear, *please*! . . .' 'Tony, you must not! . . .' 'Isabelle, I wish you wouldn't encourage . . .'

But she is quite sure that throughout the engagement Tony was the attacker, and that they really knew they were beaten before they began. To every objection he unhesitatingly produced an answer beginning with 'But . . .' To every bellowed 'No!' he replied indomitably with 'Why not?', and gained strength, as his adversaries weakened, from the obvious fact that they could put forward absolutely no valid reason why not. They could do nothing but shout, shudder, exclaim, wave their hands, make faces, and declare that he must be mad, it was out of the question, it was impossible, it was not to be thought of. And at last, when Henry, desperate and demoralised, unwisely exposed his flank by shifting ground and asking 'How?', Tony knew that he had them where he wanted them. He told them how.

To his astonishment and disgust, he found that his admirably simple plan of action, far from being greeted with applause, provoked a fresh outbreak of protestations. Even Aunt Isabelle finally went over to the enemy, asserting that she was a realist, she, and had never demanded that life be presented to her *couleur de rose*, but there were undoubtedly certain aspects of it from which all civilised persons agreed to avert the eyes, and the proposal of Tony, though made in all innocence, could not for one instant be entertained. Tony was annoyed by all this time-wasting chatter, but not seriously disturbed by the renewed opposition; he recognised it as being merely the sudden flare of a dying fire. And, true enough, there were only a few more flickers – a few weak, craven attempts at procrastination.

'But look, Tony,' Sue urged despairingly, 'not to-night. Not to-night, darling, *please*! Dad's worn out, and so am I. It'll be . . . easier by daylight, anyhow. Just wait till to-morrow . . .'

Tony stood his ground, immovable.

'To-morrow you've got to start picking and packing early – you'll say you haven't time. *I* know!'

'We-e-ll, yes, we *will* be busy in the morning – but in the afternoon we could . . .'

'Have some sense, Mum, can't you?' Tony cut in scornfully, 'It'll be worse then.'

'Worse? . . .' She stared at him. Henry gave a hollow laugh, and said:

'Wake up, old girl! Worse is right. It's now or never.'

Light broke on Sue. 'Oh, *dear*!' she cried. 'Why do things always happen to us? Well, if we must . . . I suppose we must. After supper, then – yes, Tony, I promise. Oh, *dear*!'

Henry stood up suddenly, swept Tony out the of way, and fetched from the cupboard the bottle of brandy they kept for emergencies. True, they had never envisaged just such an emergency as this, but the three adults immediately recognised it as one calling for the Dutch courage which alcohol supplies. Sue tossed off a stiff drink, and demanded another. Aunt Isabelle (who is practically teetotal) downed hers with an air of martyrdom, as if it were hemlock. Henry, with his glass half-way to his lips, paused and looked with disfavour at his son. 'You,' he said coldly, 'may have a glass of lemonade.'

But what need should Tony have of artificial stimulants? His dynamo was pounding away as strongly and steadily as ever; he had expended fabulous amounts of energy, but he still had plenty in reserve. Erect and inflexible, contemptuously observing their abject and lily-livered behaviour, he replied with dignity:

'I don't want lemonade. I only want my fife.'

It was quite dark when the little procession emerged from the back door and passed in single file along the narrow, foot-worn path. No one except Tony had felt like eating much after all, and Sue, remembering what was in store for him, had queried the wisdom of his third helping of pudding; but he had only stared, and said impatiently, 'Why not? I'm hungry.' Now he strode ahead, marching fast and resolutely like a good officer who must instil confidence into his wavering ranks. Behind him – muttering that this was a nice, peaceful sort of evening for a man who had been working since dawn – came Henry with a torch. Sue followed, trying hard, now that the moment was at hand, to behave like a mother of Sparta, and not let poor darling Tony down. Aunt Isabelle (in whom the brandy seemed to have induced a mood of rather tearful sentimentality) brought up the rear, lamenting that Sue's late and so talented mother had not lived to see the incomparable resource and fortitude of this grandson, whose devotion to his art should be rewarded by the gift of a grand piano, and a musical education under the best masters of Europe.

When they reached the door, and Tony, without hesitation, entered, Sue's nerve wobbled, and she began to cry out: 'Oh, no! Oh, Henry! Oh, Tony, darling! Oh, no!' Tony said sharply: 'What's biting you? Here, Dad, give us the torch a sec. I've just got to see exactly where . . .'

'Oh, no!' babbled Sue. 'Tony, you really can't . . .!'

Aunt Isabelle now caught the infection of panic and, entirely deserted by her English, began a long and impassioned plea in French, the gist of which was that Tony must render himself more philosophical, and recognise that life was full of losses, ah, *Ciel*, did she not know of what she spoke, she who had lost her country, and her home, and her Sèvres dinner service the most elegant, and her silver spoons of the period *Louis Quinze*? From such trials was character formed, and here was an opportunity – unlikely to be repeated in this land where all were apt to be *sans gêne*, and few encouraged the young to treat life *au sérieux* – for Tony to practice a mature self-discipline. He must therefore resign himself; he must renounce his life. She reached into the dim illumination of the torchlight, laid hold of his shorts, and urged desperately: '*Il faut t'en passer, mon pauvre, il faut . . .*'

But Tony (who does not normally admit to knowing any French at all) jerked himself from her gasp and yelled in exasperation: 'I will NOT! Why should I? I can see it as plain as anything!' At this Aunt Isabelle was seized with a fearful spasm of shuddering, Sue moaned faintly, and Henry burst out:

'All *right*, then, blast it! What the Hell are we waiting for? Here, Sue, you take the torch. Come on, Tony, lean over and I'll grab your ankles.' Tony eagerly complied, and was presently suspended, head downward, over a black void.

'*Prenez garde!*' shrieked Aunt Isabelle in agony. '*Prenez garde de tomber!*'

'He can't, snarled Henry. 'I'm holding him, aren't I?'

Sue remained dumb. She was watching, with fascinated horror, a fair head and a rosy, upside-down face disappearing slowly into unspeakable depths; but before it vanished, it opened its mouth to reproach her. 'Stiffen the lizards, Mum, how d'you think I'm going to see? Give us some light down here, can't you?'

She gulped and obeyed, reaching round Henry and holding the torch at arm's length. Now she could see only that portion of her child which would usually be described as from the neck down, but which had become, in this nightmare, from the neck up. Slowly he sank from her view until nothing remained visible but his knobby knees, his lean, brown calves, his ankles – gripped in the vice of his father's hands – and his dear, darling, dirty feet. She turned her head away, and held her breath. Henry, his arms rigid and quivering, muttered that the damn kid was heavier than he thought.

Tony's voice, muffled, but gallantly cheerful, came up from the pit.

'A bit more, Dad . . . a bit more still . . . Hi' That's *enough*! Oh, gee, Dad, pull me up a bit, quick!'

Aunt Isabelle whispered: 'I can bear no more!' and melted into the darkness outside. Sue clenched her teeth, and thrust the torch lower. 'Oh, darling, *do* hurry up!' she besought. 'Henry, *do* hold him tight!'

But now, from the abyss, came a shout of triumph.

'GOT IT! Okay, Dad, you can haul me up now.'

Aunt Isabelle met them at the kitchen door. She informed them that she was filling the copper with water, and lighting a fire beneath it. When the water was hot, Tony would kindly take a bath, to which she would add some disinfectant. Before entering the bath, however, he would be so good as to place the instrument (no, no, she did not want to see it, God forbid!) in the copper, where she would boil it for an hour. Better, for two hours. She rejoiced that he had once more his fife, and would thus be enabled to pursue his musical studies; but for herself, she was no longer young enough to support such incidents, and she would recommend that, in order to foil any further wickedness on the part of that Joy there, a strong catch be affixed high on the door of the *cabinet*. She then returned to the copper, and as Tony entered the house behind his parents, Henry barked at him:

'Don't you bring that revolting thing inside! Leave it on the step.'

'Yes, Dad,' said Tony, a model of docility.

In the living-room the brandy was still on the table. Without a word, Sue brought their glasses, and Henry poured it – straight. Tony was offered lemonade again, and this time affably accepted. He beamed at them over its rising bubbles.

'Gee, Dad, it worked well, didn't it?'

'It worked,' said Henry.

'Thanks for helping me get it back, Dad. Thanks, Mum.'

'Don't mention it, darling,' said Sue, sprawled in her chair, and half raising her glass to him. 'A ple-easure.'

It was almost a hiccup, and she began to giggle weakly. Henry gave her a stern look, and said: 'You're drunk, old girl.'

Tony, advancing eagerly to stare, demanded with interest: 'Is she, Dad? Is she really dr . . .?'

'No!' wailed Sue. 'I'm only te-erribly tired! . . .'

'Tony,' commanded Henry, 'go to your bath.'

'Okay, Dad,' said Tony, and went, with wondering backward glances.

So when faint, sweet sounds of distant piping are heard, we are all thankful to know that the music so nearly lost to us was saved, and that presently we shall see Tony coming buoyantly down the Lane, treading on air, his fife (two hours boiled) at his lips, and his clouds of glory trailing behind him. He has *Sweet and Low* to perfection now, and he is learning, at Henry's suggestion, *Safely, Safely Gathered In*.

Dorothy Cottrell, 1902–1957

Born Iola Dorothy Wilkinson in Picton, New South Wales, she had an eventful and difficult short life. As a child she contracted infantile paralysis and from that time was confined to a wheel chair, although this did not prevent her from leading a full life; she studied at the Royal Art Society of New South Wales becoming a competent artist; and she became an original writer who portrayed disability with a new sensitivity. Partly because of domestic difficulties she spent a considerable amount of time in her youth on a station in Queensland until, in 1922, she married Walter Mackenzie Cottrell and they moved to the United States of America where she embarked on a career as a professional writer and journalist. A prolific short story writer and the author of a number of novels (not all of which have been published), her first, *The Singing Gold*, was published in the *Ladies Home Journal* before appearing in book form in the United States (1928). *Earth Battle* (1930) also enjoyed some success and *The Silent Reef* (1954) was made into a film in 1959.

Dorothy Cottrell and her art were a point of contention between Mary Gilmore and Nettie Palmer, with the latter being prepared to criticise Australian writers who did not try to further the growth and development of Australian literature. But in the United States, Dorothy Cottrell enjoyed a considerable reputation and was a regular contributor to the *Saturday Evening Post*.

The following short story which suggests the
author's views and values on the treatment of
members of her own sex was published in 1933 in the
Winchester Storyteller.

CABBAGE ROSES

Old Gustav placed the handles of his knife and fork on the table,
and his hands shut about them in fists. He smiled as he munched
his liverwurst and moist potato-bread.

'This English Reverend, you are not to take notice if he makes
love to you,' he said in German. He had lived for thirty years
in Australia and had prospered there, but he seldom spoke English
unless he was forced to, after which he usually spat to get the
taste of it from his mouth.

'What nonsense you talk, father,' said Emma, serenely, but her
heart felt wildly warm with happiness and beat to a little tune
because anyone thought that the Reverend might do anything
like that. As she brushed a crumb from the blue and white cloth
she bent her head to hide the blue shining of happiness in her
grey eyes; her cheeks deepened like velvety rose petals; even the
firm curve of her chin, drawn back into the column of her throat,
grew pink and quivered with the effort of suppressing a smile
of happiness.

Old Gustav took in a big sour pickle, and his face looked red
and pleased, and his keen-pointed little grey moustache moved
knowingly and complacently.

'This is not the time to think of love! This is no time for Gustav
Hedwig's daughter to think of an Englishman, eh?'

Emma moved largely to bring more potato salad. 'No, Father.'

He flourished his beer mug and drank pompously. 'Der Tag!'
he said, as the old men of the colony had said over their beer
for many years.

'And she has come!' he added in English, banging down the
emptied stein and confusing his genders as he always did in the
unfamiliar tongue, with which he struggled at the moment in a
seeming hope that the English might learn what he thought of
them. He looked at Emma under his grey brows. 'This is 1915!'
he said in a way which made Emma know that he was practising
for the talk when Old Herman and Otto and Herr Braun and Herr
Hilverkus would come in after supper. 'For fifteen months the

Fatherland has been at war. She calls to her sons and daughters – and they answer her! Shall Gustav Hedwig's blood fail that call?'

She knew that he did not doubt her. He just liked the sound of the good words, as all proper men did. German men were proper men. All her life she had heard the old men say it. Her mind accepted it without question. One part of her knew that it was fitting that men should dominate and arrange and take, and that women should give and submit, and accept the world as arranged by the old men for their own glory and the slightly subsidiary glory of the young men – who would one day be old men.

While she was still a child she had bent her strong young back at the plough so that her brothers might go home to Germany to study for the army. Most of the German girls about Toowoomba worked like oxen and ate cabbage soup and existed miraculously on a few shillings a week, so that their brothers might go through German colleges. They were women. The men were men. It was as it had always been and as it should be. 'The sons of Gustav Hedwig shall not be plough animals!' Old Gustav often boasted. 'They will be officers with swords!'

After Emma had taken service with the English Reverend at the Children's Home, she had regularly and uncomplainingly paid over 'to the brothers' eleven shillings of her weekly sixteen shillings, and somehow remained plump and sweet as a great, full, pink flower, and modest and clothed, on the five shilling balance. At seventeen she was very definitely a woman. She could manage a house, cook heavy, wonderful food and make rich, dark blood soup.

'The mother is giving up the treatments', said Gustav, wiping his mouth complacently. 'I can then send more money to the Great Cause than any other man in the Lodge!' His cheeks blew in and out a little, his small grey military moustache rolled with the movement of his lip. Emma stopped clearing the table.

'Mother's treatments? But the Herr Doctor said that she must have them . . .'

Old Gustav looked noble.

'This is no time to think treatments,' he said. He rose, 'This is 1915! The Fatherland calls! Shall Gustav Hedwig's blood fail to answer? Never! There is no sacrifice too great – and none too small!'

Young Herman Blitz entered. Soon he was getting away to America and thence to Germany and the Front. Emma knew Freda, his young wife, and she hoped, with unembarrassed German thought, that he would manage to leave Freda a little baby before he went – Freda had always loved babies.

The men sat by the fire while Emma washed the dishes. Young Herman had once 'admired' her, but he did not offer to help her carry out the unwieldy tub when she had finished. Instead, in his grave young voice, he asked her to throw some hay to his horse while she was outside. Old Gustav was telling him of how nobly he had given up his wife's treatments, and Herman was obviously impressed. Even Emma, racking her brain for a way to pay for the continuance of the treatments, did not question the legitimacy of Old Gustav's giving them up while he had not given up his beer, which cost a like amount.

It was with an entirely different department of her heart that she so sweetly and utterly loved the Reverend because he was the opposite of the Australian-German manly virtues.

By the time she was ready to leave, after having cared for her invalid mother and finished the week's baking, there was quite a gathering of old men by the fire, drinking her father's health for his noble sacrifice, and drinking to the Fatherland and 'to the Victory to Come!'

She kissed her father and he told the group that she was a good daughter. 'No fly-away girls for Gustav Hedwig! This girl, before she was ten she could bake and plough and cut wood! Emma blushed deeply with pleasure at the compliment. The men returned to their drinking to Der Tag – which had come!

There was something naive in their attitude, although Emma did not see this. They did not regard their hate of England as any disloyalty to the adopted country of their prospering. Nor, in a sense, was it disloyalty. It was rather premature patriotism: they were so sure that the British Empire would presently be the German Empire. The fact that it was British for the time, was a thing so slight as to be ignored.

Apart from their patriotism they were excellent neighbours; fine farmers of the rich black, volcanic soil.

Emma stepped out into the fragrance of late afternoon. She had been working since four o'clock that morning – there was always so much to do on her 'day off': so many things for the mother: cooking: washing: baking.

Now there was a six-mile walk ahead of her, but she didn't mind. Her physical weariness simply stilled the questionings of her heart – which came of looking too far ahead – and it beat warmly and steadily to the poem of a simple hour. The world smelled utterly lovely, fresh and near the sky, and moist: she was walking towards the Reverend. The Reverend never would do what her father thought. But her heart sang the words over and over.

She moved with a firm, modest step, her face flushing beautifully beneath her hideous, small, straw hat, her calm grey eyes starry with happiness. She passed fields all glittering with young corn. To her left lay the tree-set bowl of the town. To her right the mighty valley plunged away; deep blue and lilac, and the thin green of crops seen across miles of air. Blue hill-waves; thinner blue; blue like air: blue so transparent that it only showed itself as mountains where it touched the sky.

She smiled at it, and smiled because the Reverend was so kind to the little children and to all.

If Emma had been asked what land she loved, she would have promptly answered 'The Fatherland', and yet it was merely a reiterated name to her, while she so loved these soft, rich mountain farm lands and the little town that she never looked at them without smiling.

It was all so nice. The town, with the spicy miles of the camphor-laurel avenues; the gardens, purple and maroon, with tall sweet-peas like arrested flights of velvet-sheening butterflies; heaven-blue with delphinium; splashed with blazing marigolds. It was her little town – and yet since the war it was not her town. Her eyes filled with angry tears at certain memories of cruelty and change. She tossed her head scornfully.

Then, having left the fields, she diverted from the direct way to the Rectory. For by going round a few blocks she could pass the Sunday School as the children came pouring out. In her pocket were many cookies made during her day's baking. They were glazed with brown sugar and she had arranged half peanuts upon them in the pattern of flowers. So clever – the children would be pleased!

She entered the playground, walking rather more quickly, her face lit by its deep smile of pleasure-to-come. But instead of the children running towards her pell-mell for their cakes, they huddled back with a strange expression on their little faces.

Emma's hand was already in her pocket.

'Come', she said.

The children whispered together. Suddenly they darted towards her with excited, cruel expressions, and dancing about her, they began to sing: 'Emma is a *German*! Emma is a *German*!'

Emma stood still amongst them, the blood mantling her face in poppy red. Then she turned to go, but somehow her hand jerked the foolish cookies from her pocket. The children hesitated, then pounced upon them, and with shrieks of excitement, they flung them back at her. One of the brittle peanut flowers cut her cheek so that a drop of blood came.

She walked on as though she had not felt.

Well, she would never go that way again! She tossed her head: breathing deep to stop the tears. But the hurt burned on in savage hatred against the English. Hate hurt her breast: hurt her throat. She did not speculate as to who was to blame for it all. She was simply hurt, and hated the English people who had hurt her. She was quite sick and weak with hate.

Then she turned down over the very lip of the great valley that seemed to pull things into its cool purple tide of shadow, and there was the Reverend's house where he cared for the little, homeless or delicate children who needed so much more than the State could give them. Camphor-laurels towered over the little house and garden and through the delicate green of their foliage showed the Range, dark blue and purple like the great waves of a halted sea.

Emma knelt largely by 'the adopteds' playing on the grass. *They* were too little to know anything but love! She rolled them over and kissed their faces with generous German kisses. *They* loved her!

'Emma must go now – hurry with the Reverend's supper!' She carried in the children. Then went quickly out to the garden again. The cabbage rosebush by the steps had come from England, from the garden of the Reverend's mother. Emma loved the big, full, sweet pink roses, wide-faced and heavy in your hands.

Soon, she stood at the study door, holding a bunch of the sweet, heavily crinkled blooms in one of her large, somewhat work-reddened, young hands. She did not know it, but the wide, full, sweet and homely roses were rather like her own full-bosomed, sweet and serviceable, young German womanhood. She was broad and big, her face was smooth and warmly pink all over with a deepening of the pink in the wide cheeks and on the firm chin. Her lips were softly, pinkly rosy, and widely full, with a fine, virginal crinkling across their beautiful curves something like the crinkling of the unfolding cabbage rose petals. Her eyes were grey and steady and looked out under rather thick, light brown brows. Her light brown hair had a wave in it from the rigor of its nightly braiding, and it was drawn back into a firm, heavy knot low on her strong pink and cream column of a neck. If the hair was ever allowed to hang free, it fell far below her waist in a soft brown, rippling cloud that smelled slightly of vigorous washings with yellow soap.

Her dress was of faded blue gingham, immaculately laundered. Her apron could have stood by itself – and when her more intimate underthings hung on the clothes lines, they rattled as they dried. One knew that her body must be broad-curved and beautifully dimpled.

There was upon her the velvet bloom and firmness and wonder of triumphantly fulfilled, exuberant life peculiar to heifers, sunflowers, cabbage roses and seventeen-year-old Australian-German girls.

She read her Bible for a precise half hour each night, never more, never less. Sometimes this left the dear Christ in the middle of being born, or something quite dreadful just happening in Revelations. But when the half hour was up, Emma stopped reading.

She had very definite views on Heaven, Hell, Martin Luther, and the morality of her British-Australian female compatriots. She knew that the German people were the modern chosen people of God, and that there were no people quite so stupid and ignorant and immoral and detestable as the English people. And yet she stood at the study door for a long moment each evening, for the singing pleasure of seeing, unseen, the young British clergyman sitting at the writing table.

'He is a minister!' said Emma, in justification of this attitude. 'That is different. He is also very kind to the little children and to all.'

She knocked, and the fair-haired young man looked up from beyond the writing table. He looked very young, and rather tired, and very shyly pleased at seeing her. If she had been carrying a tray, he would have hurried to open the door for her. He was so kind to all.

'Good evening, Emma,' he said in his friendly tone, taking up his pipe in his brown, hard-working-looking hand. The lamplight glinted on the short, golden hair-waves at the back of his brown neck and on the short, tossed curls above his forehead. Then the flare of the match lit his grey-blue eyes and his young face with the worry lines across the brow.

'Good evening to you, Reverend,' her voice had a little tuneful note of tender happiness – because of the poem in her heart.

'Did you have a good day at home, Emma?'

'Very!' It suddenly seemed to her to have been a perfect day. Everything was perfect. She began to arrange the roses; their scent made the poor room beautiful.

Lifting her grave eyes, she said pleasantly:

'We have some chicken for supper and then the little pear tarts with cloves.' He loved chicken and pear tarts. He looked pleased. They had not had so many presents of chicken lately: not since the outbreak of war, and subscriptions had fallen off too, so that it was harder and harder to make ends meet and to care for the children.

The young man took his pipe from his mouth and held it in his hand on the desk. The hand clenched and the frown deepened on his forehead.

'I suppose we could not manage another little chap, Emma?'

Emma put down the shining silver, with which she had begun 'setting', and considered.

'If we used cabbage soup more often and fed them more porridge and fewer eggs – yes, we could, I think'.

He ran his hands up through the fair curls.

'I don't like doing that – and yet we should take him. Such a poor little thing . . . illegitimate. Left in that Nurse Porter's Home and half-drugged most of the time.'

Emma's eyes clouded with ready German tears. 'Ach, Reverend! We must manage him, somehow!'

'I'm cutting my smoking,' he said, flushing. 'This is the last tin.'

'You should not do that,' said Emma, slowly. 'You have nothing for yourself. You are very good.'

He flushed more deeply. 'You're pretty good yourself', he said. 'Sweet and good'.

Emma laughed and dimpled and shook her head.

'Ach! Nonsense. Are you ready for dinner now?' But her heart beat in a strange confusion under her stiff white apron. She wanted to sing as she served the chicken. A good meal such as a good man deserved! Not the skimped meals she so often had to serve him. Her thoughts ran in a pleasant, singing litany which drowned even the sounds of war. He is so good. He is so kind to the little children. He is so kind to all. He is as the saints. He will enjoy so the chicken. (She would never tell him that she had bought it.)

Then she thought of the nightly details of caring for the children. And after she had finished serving, she ran out to the nursery to see that they were all in bed. Gresha, the musical one, with his mouth-organ under his pillow; little Peter whose crippled spine they were trying to straighten, so patient with his leather harness.

Her hands slipped smoothly, tucking sheets; she moved quickly, filling drinking cups. As she moved, her mind was busy with the thought of how they could manage the other child that the Reverend had found today. Somehow they must! And all the while her heart continued to beat its exultant rhythm beneath her stiff apron. He had said that she was good and sweet! At times she had to stop her work and put her clasped hands up to her breast to keep the joy still.

She chided herself. What was she thinking? Where was her sense? The Reverend never would . . . But he *had* said that she was good and sweet! Wings of Heaven beat about her: faded through impossibility.

She went in to clear away. He said:

'What cut your cheek, Emma?'

She bent her head and flushed.

'The children at the Sunday School threw cookies at me'.

'Not meaning to hurt you?'

Her mouth closed tightly for a moment. 'They said I was a German.'

His face went scarlet with anger. 'That's an outrage!'

She looked stubborn: because, reminded of her clever little cakes, she was holding back the tears.

'Well, it's true. I am a German! I'm proud of it!' But her lips trembled.

'Oh, this war is a mess!' he said. He came forward and took her hands into his while he looked at the cut. It lay like a little string of dark beads across rosy satin.

'What a damn shame!' he said, and then suddenly, as one might comfort a child, he kissed the hurt.

Emma trembled and they both stood still in sweet surprise.

'Oh, Emma!' he said. She drowned in the rush of wings. She looked up into his face.

'Oh, Reverend!' she said.

Thinking about it, Emma thought: 'That was the sound of angel's wings in Heaven, but I could not see them because the gate was not quite open. It will be opened when he speaks me for his wife with the date'.

She thought also: 'I need not tell the father until I am spoken with a date. It is not wrong to love this Englishman. He is not an enemy of the Fatherland – he is a saint, so good to the little children and to all.'

The war must end soon. She would be happy and have no fears. 'I will take much care of the Reverend's house,' she thought. 'I will cost him little money as his wife.' This thought made her so happy that she sang deep, Lutheran hymns about damnation.

And in the weeks that followed they both needed the inward song they had found, because it was harder and harder to manage on the money that came in. The adopteds had 'meat substitutes' and 'milk substitutes' and 'egg substitutes'. 'Pretending things', Emma called them, and for a while the adopteds were very sporting about it but at last their chubby lips shook and the little Peter asked: 'Will we have to play this game much longer, please?'

'But a little now.'

In the town the people stopped the little orchestra playing the music of Beethoven, and burned the scores of Wagner's operas so that the students could not study them. It was, they said, a time to prove that they were Englishmen.

Emma saw trouble deepening on the Reverend's brow. His face lost its saintly shining of happiness in helping the little children: when it did not shine for her, he seemed half-guilty, wholly perplexed. It was some time before Emma realised just what was happening to him.

She had continued her church attendance with stubborn pride: she was not going to be driven from God's house by this foolish British people who were soon to be conquered. But because of her isolation, she did not hear the church-gossip for a long time. Then she learned that they were saying that he should be at the Front because he was 'a young, able-bodied man without dependents' and that he was 'hiding behind his cloth'. Her breast grew hot with the absurdity of it!

He who was so good, working with the little, homeless children and building new life and hope for them – this cruel people were trying to drive him out to kill and be killed! His own congregation was shunning him: his own people talking against him. A woman, to Emma's right in church, had said audibly: 'He should be using guns instead of baby bottles!' And she had looked at the young Rector with cunning, hostile eyes.

'Slackers may find themselves without a cloth to hide behind', her companion answered significantly.

Emma had hated them with increased passion of hatred. Instead of turning upon War, she turned upon the British people about her. Cruel, stupid, wicked they were! She had been so angry she could hardly keep her seat. Her face and her neck had grown all red with anger. Her hands were so hot inside her gloves that she had wished that she could take her gloves off – but that was not proper in church.

Outside the church the old men stood together in the scented sun, and stroked their red throats where the white bristles lay like hoar frost on the necks of turkey gobblers hung out to chill.

'This is a time,' they said, 'to remember that we are Englishmen first and last.'

'This is 1915, and actions speak louder than words!' People murmured approval.

Didn't they think that caring for the little children, and struggling and struggling to manage, was action? Emma would have liked to see the red-faced old gentlemen try it!

As Emma passed through the gate, she heard an old gentleman, who was more kindly than the rest, explaining his method of encouraging slackers.

'I say to the boys who aren't sure,' said the old gentleman, 'I say "Wait until we have you in uniform with a forty-inch chest measurement and all the girls running after you." '

Emma fastened the gate with both hands.

'I will not come here again,' she said, as she had said about the Sunday school.

During the evenings Emma and the young Reverend sat upon the steps by the rose bush and talked. One night he said hotly:

'They needn't suppose I don't know that they want to be rid of me. I know they think I'm a coward . . .'

'Ach! They would never think that.'

'They don't only think it – they say it,' he said. 'I never meet one of the committee but they throw out hints as plain as my hand. Old Mr. Foster's done his bit – 'given' three sons! Or have I heard of the last advance? They *suppose* I read the war news!' He pressed the troubled place in his forehead with his hands. 'I went to the elders and told them that if they would pledge themselves to carry on the work with the children, I'd go tomorrow. But they wouldn't do it. Said that at a time like this all their 'little sacrifices' must go in the War Loans – at five per cent!'

Emma's heart pitched with narrowly averted and frightful disaster. The Reverend enlist? A thousand things stopped her thinking of that. It was like death. No, no that could not be! She shut her mind to it.

'I can't just throw down all the children – I haven't been able to give them much, but they need it so badly!' he said, and pressed his palms over his face. 'They talk about this place as their house', he said, speaking of the little children. 'They are like little puppies at play . . . and they are so sure that they won't have to go back.'

'Yes – Yes!'

'But I can't stand this much longer'.

Then his hand moved over hers on the step and they forgot the war for a little while, and began to talk of the future. With the shy thrill of great and secret happiness, they spoke of plumbing fixtures: even of sun-rooms for 'the adopteds'; of running hot water, and better devices for straightening crippled limbs. Then through the happiness would run the current of fear that these wild dreams might not be, and they would reassure themselves.

'It *must* end soon!'

'Yes, *soon* now!'

Then one evening she got back to the Rectory a little late after a 'day off'. It was almost dark in the study. Before the fire the Reverend was sitting with his face upon his hands. When she came in he looked up.

'*I have enlisted, Emma,*' he said.

She put up both her hands to her heart. Such pain filled her that she felt weak.

He rose and leaned his head on the mantelpiece.

'Today they called a meeting,' his voice broke. 'Today they told me they were getting a new minister. This is what they gave me for a going away present. I opened it there in the hall', the blood burned up his neck. He took a little cardboard box into his clenched fist: then he opened his hand and white feathers fell out onto the carpet. '*Lies!*' he said.

Emma said: 'But the little children?' She supported herself on the table. 'But the little children – and all?'

'They can go back to the State and the dope nurses. That doesn't matter – who cares about little children now?'

Emma's face went red with pain and anger.

'You should not have left the little children,' she said. She could not speak of what he had done to her: of what this meant.

'I couldn't keep them without a salary,' he said. 'And there would be no more donations!'

'But little Peter with the bad back?' she said. Then she began to weep deeply. He stood up and put his hand on her shoulder.

'Little children don't count in war, Emma,' he said.

They looked at each other, trembling, young and beaten about by war, and alone. Suddenly he put his arms round her and kissed her.

'I love you so, Emma! Marry me before I go away!'

'I cannot now! *I cannot!*'

He stood back from her in bewilderment, as if she had struck him.

'You are a soldier! My father – what would he say?'

The sweetness of his kiss upon her lips, the sweetness of his cheek against hers, made her faint and weak with bliss, and yet she pushed him away. The hardness of doing it made her strong. But it scarcely seemed to her that it could be she who spoke, but rather the old men about her father's fire.

'I am a German,' she said with difficulty. 'I would not marry a man who was going to kill my own brothers, perhaps! I hate you! I hate all your people!' Then she ran heavily out of the room, expecting her heart to break with pain.

Heaven had opened to her – but in such a way that she must close the gates again.

That week the little children were sent away, weeping. The furnishings were sold. The house turned over to the new minister. The Reverend went into camp: the uniform setting badly over his stooped young shoulders. Emma went home. But she took with her the cabbage rosebush from beside the steps of the Reverend's cottage. She planted it at the corner of the vegetable patch.

At nights she heard the old men boasting as they sat about the fire, and planning to send more money to Germany to help the Great Cause. Because her father said it was no time for personal indulgence, Emma worked in the fields like a man, stooping her broad body to the plough, and her heart hurt her all day long because of the look on the Reverend's face when she would not marry him.

He came once to try and see her, but Old Gustav sent him away, and laughed to the old men about it.

'I said "My girl, she laugh at you, English soldier!" ' said Old Gustav, triumphantly.

'Gustav Hedwig's daughter is a true daughter of the Fatherland,' they said. 'This is no time for Englishmen to bespeak German girls.'

Emma thought: 'I would like to die soon.' But one could not die.

At night she watered the rosebush. All that she would ever have of him. All that there might ever be of him. With his puzzled brow and his kind hands and stooped young shoulders and nearsighted eyes. All – *all*.

All night, she saw him looking at her as if the last person in his whole world had struck him. By day, she worked harder.

Then she came home one evening and found that her father had been altering the garden. He had thrown out the rosebush to make room for more turnips – to be sold later to help buy guns. The rosebush was shrivelled by the sun: its brave new shoot collapsed.

'This is no time for sentiment,' he said. 'This is not the day of roses but of blood and iron! No time for growing kohlrosen this! A time for putting our shoulders to the plough. For self-forgetfulness!'

Emma stood quite still. Her large face turned redder than the red roses then paler than the white. Her eyes looked blue and the pupils dilated. Suddenly words began to pour from her. She did not seem to be thinking them and speaking them, but rather to be listening to them, frightened and amazed and exultant.

'When has it not been a time for self-forgetfulness for German women?' she said in her big, deep voice. 'When have we not been putting our shoulders to the ploughs? What have I ever had for myself? Just enough food and clothes to work and work and work for the brothers that they might wear bright uniforms and go to fight so that you old men could boast of it?' Her voice poured on, deep and angry as a flood. She trembled in its grip and clasped her large work-reddened hands. ' "Do not marry him", you say to me, so that you can boast you have a German daughter. He, who was so good to the little children and to all! Send him away with the hurt in his eyes and never see him again, never have one little happy hour to remember to him down the years! Never mind the pain that kills the heart . . .'

Old Gustav had turned red. His hair bristled directly upright. His moustache stood out like a terrier's whiskers.

'Never mind if the mother have the treatments,' cried Emma, stamping her large foot before him. 'She is only a woman! Let you be able to boast that you send most money home to the Fatherland.' She stepped closer still and shook his shoulders, realizing with a shock that he was a very insignificant little man. 'You hear? I am sick of the Fatherland! Sick of the boasting of the old men! I had sent him away with the hurt look in his eyes – with nothing of him for all my life but the kohlrose – and you have killed it! Now I have nothing. But you have not me! You hear? Someone else may send the money to the brothers. I will pay for the treatments for the mother – but I will go to the Herr Doctor and pay, so you cannot rob her. You hear?'

'Traitor,' shouted old Gustav. 'English swine!'

Emma lifted the withered rosebush in large arms, against her large breast. 'No!' she said, sobbing now, 'No!' She did not know what she was, but she was not English. She had seen what the boasting of *their* old men did to him who was so good to the little children and to all; had seen what it did to the little children.

'I hate you all,' she cried. 'English and German! You have killed the kohlrose! All I had left of him!' She stood clasping the bush, her great breast shaking with her sobs, her hair dishevelled. Suddenly her eyes shone.

'I will go back to him, to the Reverend, and say I love him for he is so kind to all! You hear me? I go to tell the Reverend that I love him!'

Packing her armor-plated-underwear in her attic room, she sobbed, forcing her trembling fingers to greater and greater haste.

'Oh, let me not be too late. God, my father, let him not have gone!'

She walked into the training camp, a large young woman in rather severe, worn clothes and a little straw hat.

After a search, she found him peeling potatoes with a blunt knife and a furrowed brow.

She stood before him with her gloved hands clasped. He jumped to his feet, spilling the potatoes. Their faces were both trans-figured: hers growing satin pink like the petals of the cabbage roses.

'I will marry you today, Reverend, if you wish it,' she said.

He took her large young body in his rather thin arms and drew her large, beautiful head down to his rather stooped shoulders. They stood in heaven, amongst the potatoes.

They took a cheap room with a gas burner and a shower that worked sometimes. In the evenings they walked hand in hand along the dusty roads. They went to one piano recital and thought it unspeakably wonderful. They went once to church – not the Reverend's church. Emma cooked rich, heavy things on the gas burner, and knitted after supper. Whenever their eyes met they smiled, because they loved each other so.

Then it was ended.

'I will take a tiny cottage,' Emma said, 'where I can grow things, and I will get the little Peter back from the Home and care for his back – and soon you will be returned.'

He smiled, holding his pipe in one young hand.

'Soon!' he said, confidently. Then his forehead puckered. 'Emma I can't bear to think of you alone. Of leaving you just when we've found each other. Oh, Emma!'

She wanted to tell him of her desperate hope that she might not be quite alone, but she could not manage it. Instead she put her hand on his hair:

'It will not be long, and the dumpling soup is ready,' she said. He took the large hand down in both of his and kissed each finger and then the palm. It gave her such pain and joy that she had to shut her eyes.

The search for the cottage and the over-optimistic replanting of the withered rosebush – which she had gravely carried with her, set temporarily in Old Gustav's best bucket – gave them a last day's delight.

Then his train was leaving to take him to his troop ship. They had been very cheerful about all the preparations for departure. The packing of his train-lunch. The brushing of his badly fitting uniform. They joked about the crowding people on the platform. Then the bell rang. Suddenly they could not joke any more, they held each other's hands and looked at each other with a betraying look which admitted that it might not merely not be 'soon' but might be 'never'. They could not speak. He blinked behind his glasses. Tears ran in two steady rivers down her large, smooth cheeks.

'This is goodbye, Emma.'

Terror filled her large face. Her eyes tried to realize his fair, curly, thick hair, his furrowed brow, his blue eyes behind his glasses. She tried to see him so plainly that it could last forever, if need be, but she could not. She could hardly see at all. Her lips moved almost soundlessly.

'Oh, Gott in Himmel! Not so soon!'

'I can't leave you alone, Emma! Not to come home to you in the evenings . . . not to be with you!' She breathed desperately and from somewhere summoned a smile. Looking full into his eyes, she said clearly and tenderly.

'Maybe it will not be alone. We will hope.'

He flushed scarlet, regarded her with tender rapture, stammered: kissed her face and her large firm neck and her wet eyes. Then he had to run. They repeated their lie as the train moved out.

'Soon back!'

'Soon back!'

'Goodbye, love!'

'Auf wiedersehen!'

Then the train was gone and the black smoke drifted up through the station and out into the foggy morning. Gone. Perhaps to be cruelly hurt. Perhaps to be killed, and never come again.

She was very large and capable, but she was only seventeen. She began to sob with large German sobbings.

'Auf wiedersehen! Oh my heart will break!' She had forgotten the people, but they looked at her. They knew she was a German and their eyes were resentful. Seeing them, for a moment she was puzzled by this. She heard someone mutter: 'Most likely a spy!' Someone else said that she should be interned.

She folded her handkerchief back into her bag and arranged her much-mended gloves over her large young hands. Then she walked with her composed, firm step down the long platform, amongst the hostile people. She felt no resentment towards them: only terrible pity. They had been deceived by the old men. They too were being robbed.

As she left the platform, she heard someone declaring excitedly that the war might last five years – but that they would 'lick 'em in the end.'

She went back to the silent little house. There was no need to hurry and get supper. No need to see if the fire was burning. For him, there might never be need again.

Tomorrow, she would get little Peter and be sensible. But tonight the house hurt her too much. She went out into the dark little garden across which the wet, white skirts of the mist were already driving.

The pain weakened her so that she could not stand. She lay with her large breasts pressed into the moist earth by the dead rosebush. He might come back. But they spoke now of years for the war to last. Three years? Five years? Nothing could pay those years back! They were stolen from youth and love and happiness and cooking and sweet serviceable things. Nothing could pay back for the pain in her breast.

Nothing could give the little children back the lost years of timid happiness. Nothing in life could fill the loss if her hope was not fulfilled . . . But she dared not think of that. She must believe.

Nothing could give the dead rosebush back its bloom – the poor, sweet, kohlrose bush that the war had killed.

'Oh God,' she prayed fiercely. 'Do not let women and the little children have to bear any more the boasting of the old men. Do not let any more little babies not be born because of it! Oh God, do not let it happen in the world any more!'

CHRISTINA STEAD, 1902–1983

Born in Sydney, Christina Stead grew up at Watson's
Bay and later made extensive use of her local
experiences in her many fictions. She set sail for
London in 1928 and despite pecuniary difficulties in
Europe, persevered with her pursuit of a literary
career. Her first work of fiction, *The Salzburg Tales*,
was published in 1934 as was *Seven Poor Men of
Sydney* and these were soon followed by *The
Beauties and the Furies* (1936), *House of All Nations*
(1938) and *The Man Who Loved Children* (1940).
After marrying William Blech she spent a
considerable amount of time in the United States
where her work was well received; in 1943–44 she
taught at New York University and she was an
established writer at MGM Film Studios in
Hollywood. Although she was accorded widespread
international acclaim, she was not given the credit
that her work deserved in the land of her birth. Her
books were largely unavailable in Australia until the
1960s.

In 1969, however, she was created a Fellow of the
Australian National University, Canberra, and in
1974, the year she returned to settle in Australia, she
received the Patrick White Award. After many years
of neglect she has more recently been appraised as
perhaps Australia's greatest novelist.

Among her later publications were *Cotter's
England* (1967), *The Puzzle-headed Girl* (1967), *The
Little Hotel* (1973) and *Miss Herbert, The Suburban*

Wife (1976); the following story, which cannot begin
to indicate the distinctive and distinguished qualities
of such a great writer, has been taken from *Ocean of
Story: The Uncollected Stories of Christina Stead,*
(1986, Penguin) and gives some insight into her life
as a writer.

A WRITER'S FRIENDS

Such a poor fist! But as soon as I fisted cat before mat, they
recognised at school that I was a word-stringer (as my medical
friend says, he a pill-doler). The teachers were friendly to me.
At home, in a mass of children and potage there was no time
for vanity. So although I was not good at lessons, I was quite
happy in the classroom – except in that hour from two to three,
the siesta hour, when we could not keep our eyes open in the
pollen-yellow dust-cloud of sun that poured over our heads from
the high windows, built in brick walls, in courtroom and
penitentiary style, and good for discipline; so that we could not
turn our eyes to the interesting yellow dust playground divided
by pepper-trees and coprosma and privet from the enthralling
yellow dust street, on which were steel rails blinding in the light;
and sometimes dusty men working at them. Then, in the heat,
my leaden head!

But in the mornings, fresh and blue (the mornings), I was all
right. I first made my mark with a poem written suddenly in
arithmetic class, at the age of eight, of which all is now forgotten
but the line 'And elephants develop must'. Mr Roberts, a fatherly
and serious teacher, confiscated whatever it was, was making the
second backbench giggle and asked suspiciously, 'Who wrote this?'
and 'What is must?' I explained, but he did not return the paper.
This animal learning, though shallow, has been a pleasant solace.

My next achievement, my first novel, was an essay, at the age
of ten, on the life-cycle of the frog. I was content with it, it could
not have been better; the style was good, I defended some
irregularities and the teacher stood by me. I remember the feeling
of certainty accompanying both these productions. You are lucky
to feel it: it is rare.

Later than that, at the age of fourteen, I found ideas in my rather
addled head, wrote a malicious poem called 'Green Apricots' about

a teacher who had never done me any harm. (She was almost driven from the school by the dislike of the pupils and no one knew why – she simply told the first year girls not to eat the apricots.) This school was an old house just turned into a school and with garden beds, fields and part of an orchard still growing. After that, a mnemonic poem intended for examination girls, incorporating the rules for the bodice basic draft. (No doubt it was easier to remember the rules than my verse.) About this time began the first great project of my career, celebrating a teacher of English I had fallen in love with (in schoolgirl innocence) and called the 'Heaven Cycle' – I am mildly concealing her name. It was supposed to be hundreds of poems; it reached thirty-four. She was grateful I think. The other teachers were accustomed to adolescent eccentricity, all except one, a teacher of French, who was heard to say that she thought it disgraceful to take the name of a teacher in vain. This view of literature astonished me and did not move me. (It is common enough – 'How can you write about real people?')

It was accepted by this time at school that I was a writer; and I accepted it simply, too, without thinking about it. I had never considered what a writer could do. I had no ambitions of that sort. Later on, at Sydney Girls' High School, I had my first serious project, based on a footnote in the textbook of European history we used. The footnote referred to the *Lives of Obscure Men* and this appealed to me markedly. I planned to do that. (But I still did not think of being a writer.) It came back to me later, when I returned to England, after the war and felt I did not understand the people. I began to collect notes for an Encyclopedia (of Obscure People), to have another title; a sort of counter Who's Who. By this time I knew something about official reference books and I knew some very able people who would never appear there, because of their beliefs. Anyone I approached was willing to help with his life-story; but I had to do other things; and the Encyclopedia was a time-taking idea.

At teacher's college in my second year, there was a young art teacher, engaged to be married, who was sensitive to the charm of girlhood, young womanhood and all that was interesting in her own position. She had soft brown hair, brown eyes; she was lively, romantic and severe to her fiancé, la Belle Dame Sans Merci, she thought perhaps. He was in the navy and had to pass such and such examinations before she would marry; in fact, another two years. I thought it cruel and wondered at her. She took us out on a sketching expedition and we stayed the night in some country boarding-house in a pretty place. It was full moon, fair weather. She called the girls to come out in the moonlight, take off their shoes, loose their hair and dance in the moonlight, on the grass. She did grass-dancing nicely and some danced with her. Others felt embarrassed or amused. She said she could read destiny in our hands. She took mine, thrust it back at me with a hard look – thinking it over, I supposed it was my calloused hands. Before that, I had had to carry a heavy valise full of schoolbooks several miles each day, up and down dry and streeted gullies; and this had caused the callouses.

I was surprised, then, when she said that if I did a book of short stories she would do the illustrations. I did the stories, she did the illustrations, four or six; and offered it to a well known publishing house in Sydney, which in the spirit of colonial enterprise said they would take some if a British firm did it first. (It is now quite common here for a British firm to say they will 'take some' if an American firm takes it first.)

I made no attempt beyond that. I never had any idea of publishing and in a way I do not care about publishing now; I only do it because it is something that is done and if you do not, others think that you are writing for yourself. That is thought to be shameful. (I don't think so. If I were on a desert island, say like Australia or even smaller, what would I do? Classify the birds and fish, write poems and ideas in the sand: just as good as anywhere else.)

With regard to the 'obscure men', I did eventually do something of that sort. My first novel was called *Seven Poor Men of Sydney* (title taken from Dickens's *Seven Poor Travellers*) and one of my most recent, *Cotters' England* (the workingclass north of England) has this subject.

The MS. of the first book of stories (offered in Sydney) was lost in a Paris hotel. I paid the rent all right but had not the space in the small room I then took for two large valises, which I left at the hotel. When I went back for them two months later, the voracious Swiss hotel-keeper asked for 400 francs for keeping the two cases; so he said. I had not 400 francs. My belief is that he had already opened them and sold the contents, some of which (my presents from Australia and some beautiful art-books I had been given later) were valuable enough. The MSS. – I often wondered where they were – nowhere no doubt. However, I remembered three of the stories and put them into *The Salzburg Tales (On the Road, Morpeth Tower* and *The Triskelion).*

I wrote my first novel, *Seven Poor Men,* in a London winter, when I got home from work and was in poor health: something I had to do 'before I died', but this was only an instinct. I must have mentioned it to William J. Blake for whom I was working (in the City of London in St Mary Axe, opposite the Produce Exchange in a new white-tile building which was famous then as a novelty). He read it over a weekend and returned it, rather surprised. 'It has mountain peaks,' he said. When I went to Paris to work in the bank in the rue de la Paix, I took it along.

As a hobby I took up bookbinding, popular then with foreign girls in Paris as it always has been with French people. There was an atelier in the rue des Grands-Augustins, near the Pont Neuf, an old quarter. This atelier was run by Fru Ingeborg, a lively goodhearted yellow-haired Danish woman, who used to call out when she saw me come in, 'Oh, Mrs Stead' (as she said), 'tell us some more about Eric's wonderful stories!' and turning to the young girls, mostly handsome Scandinavians, in the workshop, she would say enthusiastically in a loud lilting voice, 'Oh Mrs Stead has a wonderful friend, he sits all day at the *Deux Magots* and tells the most marvellous stories,' when she would proceed to tell some of the stories herself, saying, 'Oh, tell us the one about the thunderstorm' and tell it herself. This true story related that Eric and a friend were out in a car somewhere around Baltimore (Eric's hometown) when they saw a thunderstorm coming up behind. They raced it, beating it home; but the dog which followed them, reached its kennel wet to the bone. There was also the story (which she told) about the frightful wind which blew all the water out of the river, leaving the fish gasping in the mud. (Which river? The Susquehanna?)

Eric did tell me stories, but not these. He was the eldest son of a thriving Baltimore business family which sent him an allowance. He was tall, quite deaf, something like Robert Louis Stevenson, if R.L.S. could have lain under leaf-mould all the winter, that is pale as fungus, tall, graceful when not toppling, with long moustaches hanging over his long teeth, which he bathed all day in Pernod, drinking his Pernod at ease, consummately (to get your notice) balancing the pretty perforated spoon with the sugar lump, over the delicately coloured drink until, with the addition of water, it turned blue opal. Meanwhile, if you listened (and I am a listener), in his low deafman's voice, he told tales!

He had studied chemistry in Munich, retired to run a press for rare and obscene books, run a press in Paris with a few choice nonchalant friends; and did not work at all, not even to the extent of opening his family letters. Some friend or other would slit open the envelopes with the monthly remittances, make him sign, take them to the bank. He told tales of Corsica, Italy, Sicily, North Africa, where he had been – all his tales had an improper idea to them; I often missed the point. He retold Terence, Ovid, Petronius, shortly and to suit himself. He was never amorous, though he had a son (so he said) in Denmark (not Ingeborg's, no connection here); and he had left a pretty little wife, whose picture he had, at home. 'I don't know whether I am divorced or not.' He remained there till the Germans walked into Paris, then employed a Jewish scientist in hiding to write articles for him for the occupant and this was how he got his Pernod. (I found this out later, when he came to New York on a Red Cross boat. He had meantime married two women and deserted them.) He was a friend to me. He named all kinds of books, novels, I had not read, every one of them a masterpiece. When I was sick and alone in a small hotel room, he came and nursed me, brought me food and talked to me, not now his erotica; and he knew, from chemistry, a great many household hints: 'a glass of milk will kill garlic'. (I still do carrots à la Eric.)

At this workshop where he was the unseen hero, I bound the manuscript of *Seven Poor Men*, and once it was bound, William J. Blake took it, unknown to me, to Sylvia Beach, of Shakespeare & Co., 12, rue de L'Odéon, a very famous person and address to all literary Paris, an American woman who had lived all her life in Paris. She had helped many writers by finding them. With her commendation, we had the courage to send the MS. to England and after a roundabout run (which brought in another friend always devoted not only to me but to any wanderer and to letters), I had a letter at the Bank from Peter Davies of London who said he would meet me at *Philippe*, a famous restaurant in the rue des Petits-Champs. (That part of the street is now called rue Danielle Casanova, after the resistance heroine.) This restaurant I knew because it was just around the corner from the Bank where I worked (I lived in a little hotel in St Germain des Prés and took a bus to the Opera to work in the rue de la Paix).

When we went into Philippe's, we saw at the back on a little table, my MS. bound in one of Ingeborg's homemade dazzle papers. This was the beginning of a friendship. Peter Davies (a famous man, godson of Sir James Barrie and the original Peter Pan), was a friend to many writers; he admired Australian writers. He said he would publish *Seven Poor Men*, but for me first to give him another book. I went home and began the *Salzburg Tales*. I had been to Salzburg in the meantime. I wrote a story every first day of a pair, finishing it and putting in the connective tissue the second day; the third day starting another story. They let me do this at the Bank, where really they only wanted me to write private letters at times, for private clients. (Sometimes I filled in at the cable switchboard, telegraphing from the code book to New York, spelling out the code; and I still tend to spell A, B, F – Alice, Berthe, Fernand, etc. in French.) I wrote the *S.T.* very fast and it gave me the same satisfaction I had with the History of the Frog; simple, complete, no questions asked. It doesn't often happen.

This book was well received in London and I was out of it all in Paris, and so I have remained. It was good for me. I think I have remained out of it to have a quiet life. I know the literary life is just what some people need, it helps many; but my life has been spent in different places, in touch with businessmen and people interested in economics – and even medicine.

How many other people have helped me! In the first place, those businessmen – they are good raconteurs; for some reason they will tell a writer anything, even business secrets. I have some close friends: one, the American poet, Stanley Burnshaw, who when able to, saw to the revival of several works he had admired, one was Henry Roth's *Call It Sleep* and one was *The Man Who Loved Children*, which became a success commercially. There was, in the beginning my father, who told me endless tales, night after night, when I was a little child; and gave me a strong feeling of affection for Australia and an understanding of the country. Then, of course, a great friend, devoted and true, my husband William J. Blake. But there is too much to say about that: not here; and indeed, a whole book, the others, the writer's friends. Who are they? And wonderful this devotion to a writer.

SARAH CAMPION, 1906–

Born Mary Rose Coulton in Eastbourne, England, she
worked as a teacher before travelling to Canada,
Germany, South Africa and New Zealand. In
1938–40 she lived in Australia before moving to New
Zealand on her marriage to Antony Alpers. Her
impressively detailed and perceptive account of
Australian northern life is even more remarkable
given the relative shortness of her stay; the power of
the continent, and the puny and painful nature of
human existence, are starkly portrayed in her
Australian novels and leave an indelible imprint.

Among her many works of fiction are *If She is
Wise* (1935), *Duet for Female Voices* (1936),
Cambridge Blue (1937), *Thirty Million Gas Masks*
(1937), *Unhandsome Corpse* (1938), *Makeshift* (1940)
and *Come Again* (1951). Her trilogy, *Mo Burdekin*
(1941), *Bonanza* (1942), and *The Pommy Cow* (1944)
is a tragi-comical account of life in North
Queensland and represents an outstanding
achievement.

The following extract has been taken from *Mo
Burdekin*; it contains the author's prologue which
describes the great flood that was responsible for the
baby floating in the basket on the Burdekin river.
When the baby is rescued, the choice of the name
Moses Burdekin ('Mo') becomes virtually inevitable.

To reveal the strength and diversity of Sarah
Campion's literary range, a chapter from *Mo*

Burdekin has also been included. Having reached
relative maturity, Mo has joined the runaway Lucy
in an itinerant life in North Queensland where, in
return for Lucy's domestic services, the two have
moved into 'The Royal Rose', run by Mrs Daisy
Sweeney.

MO BURDEKIN

Prologue

The Wet came in that year with a cock-eye bob; loud thunder,
ragged streams of lightning, and a wind of awful fury which
hurtled out of the north-west, smote the new settlement till it
rocked like a fleet at anchor, and was gone towards the coast
leaving a swathe of ruin. Bob McMahon lost the roof he had put
on only the week before in readiness for the deluge; the storm
had scarce begun when the roof whined, tipped, slowly lifted,
and sailed all of a piece into the bush, leaving Bob saucer-eyed,
and his wife screaming from a house now defenceless to the rain.
The wind went on past Frenchy's vineyard and laid the young
stocks flat to the streaming earth, while Frenchy danced and yelled
with rage on his veranda.

As if it had not yet finished with him the wind then took two
lean cows out of his paddock, lifting them unto itself and dropping
them on the vegetable garden of Cho Ling, where the poor
creatures, half starved through the long dry winter and the grilling
summer, at once fell to with fury on Cho Ling's green-stuffs and
mowed them down, while the Chinaman, hanging to the stringy
bark roof of his humpy lest it follow Bob's into the bush, yelped
at them in vain. The wind now blew in the door of the new telegraph office and flattened the operator against his own back wall
even as he grabbed the wires to get through to Jabiru: he fell
against an old iron saucepan his wife had vainly given him for
a cuspidor, and the saucepan and the cock-eye bob between them
stove in three of his ribs, which no one discovered till ten years
later when he was run over by Cobb's coach while returning blind
drunk from Jabiru, and had (his spirit then being fled) to submit
his body to an autopsy.

So, after dealing with the telegraph, the wind went on towards

Innisfail, and the rain which began with it came down in buckets-ful. The rain came down straight as piston-rods, heavy as hail, rattling and drumming on the tin roofs, steadily pounding the dry ground, turning the road into a foaming yellow gush, beating the bush, that had been so dry, so bright, so brittle with long heat, into a steamy jungle in which the grass sprang up to a two-foot mat of juicily brilliant new growth. Down came the rain remorseless as jealousy, awful as deserved doom: from a purple black sky it streamed for three days, then let up a little to draw breath, then streamed again. The creek, earlier a sluggish tired rivulet between baked sandbanks, now rose as fast as the grass, but yellow instead of green. Soon, seeping relentless over its banks, it oozed into the Chinaman's garden to finish the ruin that the flying cows began. The vegetables they had left now sank despairing into the tide, dropping from sight in a yellow soup which rose every second higher, higher, a little higher. Soon the swamp by the Chinaman's fence was two feet, three feet, four feet deep in water: then it was gone: then the ladder bridge which the Chinaman had laid with such precise care over the lead from the tin-workings was sucked free from its moorings, borne up by the rising water, hurled in triumph down the river that was now a river no longer but a surging flood fifty feet wide ripping and roaring past the sandbanks at whose feet it had whispered timidly all winter. Bit by bit the sandbanks sank into the tide: crumbling, dropping, gnawed at, devoured, the sandbanks too were gone, and the river flung on against the paddock fences, half-way up the trunks of the dark-needled shea oaks, the delicate black wattles. Soon the river roared in the lower branches of the trees, and retreating only for a moment as some bursting of banks downstream lowered its level, left hanging for a moment in the sodden trees the flotsam of a days' flood. Small uprooted trees, fence posts, old barrels, strange mats of ravished grass, hung dripping ten feet up in branches till the river, rising again, fed still by the streaming rain, picked them out and took them downstream to abandon them for good, days later, twenty foot high in some stubborn flood-resisting grove down the valley.

On the second day of the flood when the river was no longer a meandering landmark but a stretch of dirty water paddocks wide and still rising, the Irishman fossicking in the abandoned workings of the Old Glory struck camp. His family had gone hours before, knowing their parent too well to wait on his sense of caution. Gathering together a meagre heap of household goods, they had pattered sturdily off, across the narrow arm of the creek that still had a blue gum laid across it for bridge, off and away and up into the streaming bush. The rain had ceased for a few hours, though the sky was still heavy with it: there was time before the next storm to cross the far river to Red Pinch and shelter. So they went on, silent. Remembering that she had left her only needle sticking in the canvas of the tent-flap, that her mother lay dead on the stretcher beside it, that the baby was not a year old, Janey the eldest groaned in spirit, squared her narrow shoulders, and urged the little troupe upwards with a flood of oaths violent even for her. Pa couldn't be trusted to see to anything, not even the burying: seeing him, as they had left him, staggering drunkenly about the disused workings and picking feebly first at this heap of tailings, then at that, her shrewd soul despised him. But she would not go back to see that a body got its last rites: she drove her living flock relentlessly on, cursing them, cursing the weight of the sagging baby.

In the camp the Irishman fossicked aimlessly all afternoon while the creek rose foot by foot, ruddy with the soil of its ravaged banks, foaming and scummy as it swept past. He looked in twice at his woman, lying all in a heap as she had died on the stretcher, and now heedless of the delighted flies: he looked in, felt on his temples the heat of the tent, muttered to himself the need to bury her quickly, swept a few blowflies off her lips, killed a score or so of ants, and went out once more to kick at the tailings, the wretched leavings of other miners who had come, as he had, in the vain but potent hope of finding what other men had missed.

The water, sucking now at the foot of the great reddish yellow cliff whose floor was scored with sluicings, gnawed away foot by foot a great block which crashed at last into the flood and sent it inches higher. Now the water washed into the tent and swirled about the legs of the stretcher, floated the pans, the rags, the sordid remnants of this feckless family. The miner watched the soil fall, the water rise, waded to the tent flap to see that the body still swam dry in its dirty blanket, and cursing went out again. He must bury her, but could not bring his mind to it. He could bring his mind to nothing. He sat there on a kerosene can with his feet in the rising water, chewing on an empty pipe. The afternoon wore on. Its only incident was the death of a kangaroo which, leaping in terror out of the bush, landed with a sucking

splash in the red mud beside him and, floundering madly, slowly
sank and died. With a flicker of delicate dark paws it was gone,
and he had seen nothing of it.

At last he rose, in that insane flurry of energy which makes
a man long for a drink when every shebeen is closed, and
scrambled up the red slope to the bluff now ringed on three sides
by flood. Here the flood would never reach. He dug fiercely with
his mining shovel at ground that the rain had made soft for nine
inches, and the summer had left iron hard for foot after weary
foot after that. It took him an hour of sweating strain to hollow
at last a grave for a small woman. Thankful that she was so bony,
so bird-light, he staggered up the slope once more with the body
in his arms, drawing his breath in sobbing gasps and wheezes.
Now in with her, wrapped still in the bluey that the children's
odd piety had left her: in with the whole bundle, push it down
with one hand while the other shovels hard earth upon it, rake
the soil over at last, try to plant once again the tussocky grass,
the few brittle plants, as if to deceive the dingoes into thinking
nothing has been laid here. Busy thus, kneeling beside the patch
to smooth it over, he was suddenly forgetful of time, season,
circumstance: he was caught Elijan-like into some realm beyond
rising floods, hard earth, dead women; and floating there awhile
hummed happily through his few teeth *The Snowy Breasted Pearl*.
A sweet song, a rare song, he thought as he hummed and patted:
he had sung it himself, in the old days, when there was still a
song left in him.

Meanwhile, the flood stayed not for pearls or miners. Rising
inexorable, sucking greedily at the reddish bluff above the workings, flowing into the sluiced channels to make them deeper,
treacherously undercutting the steep clefts, this water ate and
passed on, followed by other gnawing waters dropping at flood-
speed from the Range. The Irishman, lulled into soft melancholy
by his tune, the sight of his bleeding hands, the thought that
women were rare in North Queensland and this on the whole
had been a good one, rose weeping to his feet to see how far the
flood had come, which way out still lay open. Below in the red
crater he saw his tent floating like a dingy swan, and the stretcher
sailing, tossing down the tide: then the whole pillow of earth
beneath him quivered like a wounded beast, he saw the grave
at his feet crack open, as the cliff swayed, rocked, toppled with
a roar and a hiss. In awful astonishment he saw his world of un-

ending grey-green bush, red earth, bruised sky, and muddy water swing past his ears: then he was struggling in the flood with his lungs full, seeing every second the shore ebb from him. The shore had been ebbing all afternoon, but he had taken no thought for it: now with the debris of the fallen cliff still dropping about his head, with trees and bushes and uprooted grass winding about him, with the flood water bubbling in his lungs, he could hardly struggle long. The flood abandoned as suddenly as it had claimed him, dropped him face downwards on the slimy mudbank: sucking in red mud with his latest breath, he cried and sank, vanishing a few feet from the choked kangaroo, and with as little trace.

The children streamed upwards through the bush, clutching things they cared nothing about but had snatched up at the last moment with the predatory instinct of the bush-bred young. Janey bore a camp oven as well as the baby, cursing both as she staggered: even the smallest sister, who had not as yet learnt to manage her own legs, held in a desperate clasp the tea-caddy, last relic of gentility to that shoddy crew, which had the Queen's bland cream-and-pink face, the blue satin riband, the Koh-i-nor, the pearls, brightly enamelled upon it. Sad, the things to which human paws cling in moments like these: these infants, the eldest not yet twelve, had disputed shrilly in the tent beside the dead woman about the things they should take, had fastened one and all upon the cradle as the one object without which they could not leave, and tugged it from each other with squeals and roars of rage. It was the family's trunk, pantechnicon and cradle too: a solid wooden square set thing made in the leisured old world of which they knew nothing, carved with acanthus leaves, odd beasts, bunches of grapes (and not one of them had ever seen any grapes but these, all grapedom for them was here in the bubbles of dark wood polished by a dozen mothers' hands): now; after the rude tug of war among the blowflies, it swung between the two elder boys, who sweated under it, grumbled at it, and would hardly have given it up to save their little lives.

So they forged on, Indian file, upwards through the hot steamy monotony of the bush, and came out at last on the ridge. Janey sat down on a boulder because the baby was heavy, the edge of the oven cut her arms: and thankfully the others flopped too, stared as she did across the valley to the Range. Fold upon fold of smoky blue, the endless, timeless Queensland bush spread out before them with no invitation, utterly indifferent as to whether they came or went.

A purple cloud was boiling slowly up from the north-west, heavy with rain: the leader rose, changed the baby from one hip to the other, and sighing set off down the path once more. Before she went the smallest sister put down the caddy and beseechingly lifted her arms.

'Who d'ja thinks goin' ter carry yer?' asked Janey without heat, without rancour, and plodded downwards.

The child sighed gustily, sniffed a little, then picked up the caddy, tightened her arms about the painted Queen, and trotted at the end of the line.

They came to more abandoned tin workings scarring the hillside, great wounds of earth gaping red in the dull green of the bush, the same canyons dug and rutted by sluicing, the same sluice-worn stream beds along which the boys walked instinctively with their eyes aground searching for the black speckle of tin. It was the landscape into which they had been born – the ruddy earth, the beds of the artificial rivers seamed and veined by a rush of water long since dried, the few rusting utensils cast down in the careless Australian way to rot and crumble when the fossickers wandered off somewhere else. Here under the eternal gums lay a shovel with a broken shaft, the metal fiery red with rust; and there a broken banjo-box half stuck in a muddy pool beside a drowned bandicoot with its stomach blown out by gas and its legs restlessly worried by the flies. The children went by with no more than a glance at scenes too familiar for comment: the boys with their eyes turned to see nothing but tin, the girls with worried frowns imitating Janey's. She hated going downhill, her instinct in flood time was all for safe heights: but on this island ridge they might be marooned for weeks, once across the second arm of the creek they were safe. So down they went, straggling as they tired, to the wide stream, the Burdekin in its young beginnings; and came at last to the fair grassy bed along which in normal days the river whispered.

Now instinct should have cried to Janey: 'Get across at once, find a place to cross, go up the other bank, get away from this pleasant green place where the lush grasses wave and the pandanus palms crackle overhead and the bright parrots dart from tree to tree – get across, get away, get up!' But Janey was tired, the baby grew heavier, the prehensile paws of the little sister clutching at her skirt dragged more and more. 'A bit of a breather won't do us any 'arm,' thought Janey, and let her children stop. There they flopped thankfully on the grassy space, into grasses so high and exuberant that they were at once lost in them, sat awed and exhausted peering at one another through a jungle of green stalks.

She set her brood down, the heedless Janey, and divided among them the sticky crusts of the tucker box, ramming the last impatiently into the baby's sagging mouth. Above them as they gnawed the day went on, sultry, threatening, purple-faced: the sky a mass of bellying mauve vapours which at any moment might void more rain, the sun hidden but still hotly potent, the air so heavy that raising a hand to brush off the stinging brindled flies was hardly worth the trouble. The children sat there sweating under the angry sky and chewed their meagre meal in silence: they finished it, they asked for more, were scornfully asked in their turn by Janey: Where did they think she was going to get it from? and fell to silence once again, and to staring, staring.

They had never been on the flood-bed of the Burdekin before: the strange wet heat of the heavy grasses, the strange horizon bounded for them by plumes of grass, the strange noise of the swollen river rising steadily as it roared past with the chuckling undertones of all rivers in flood – these were enough to keep the little ones still and fascinated, sitting there with their tired dirty legs stuck out in front of them, their thirsty mouths open. The baby, whimpering when Janey thrust the crust into his mouth, now whimpered no longer but chumbled at the dry bread, slobbered over it, wiped it down Janey's front, dropped it in the grass and at once forgot about it, sitting on her lap digging his sharp young heels in as he snatched at all he could. He leaned, he snatched, he dug, as if arms and legs were hung on a single string and could not move alone. He was an ill-favoured child with decided features, black silky hair, and the heartrending look of one whose light celtic eyes are set in thick dark upcurling lashes, beneath dark straight brows. The eyes were so blue, the lashes so black, that the child had a bruised and startled aspect, softened only when he slept, when the fringed eyelids, faintly blue as all babies' eyelids are, lay soft above his cheek. But now he would not sleep he sat and drooled and bubbled, his eyes as blank as sapphires, snatching at the grasses about him.

'Gertch!' groaned Janey wearily as he romped and pounded, 'stay still, carntcha!'

But he could not stay still, he bounced on her tired lap, dug his heels into her stomach, flopped a sticky fist into her mouth as he lunged at grass, and dealt a fusillade of small blows on her lean and aching thighs.

'Gimme that cradle.'

She plumped the baby into it and sighed with relief.

'Now jest you set 'ere 'n' watch 'im, all of yer, while I go 'ave a-looksee: then we'll be gittin' along.'

'Aw, whaffor?'

' 'Cos we gotta git acrorst th' creek some'ow, sillies!' she snapped, thinking, Poor lil cows, they're tired.

She rose, twitched her dirty sugar-bag garment, yawned, stretched, kicked at a darting lizard, and started upstream. Stared in horrow, gaped wider still. For there was a new roar above the voice of the Burdekin: now there was no getting across this creek nor any other, now it was too late. Now, swollen with the waters of a dozen rushing creeks, the new dam by Jabiru has burst its banks, the water comes roaring out in a solid curve to overwhelm the flimsy humpies of the workman's camp below it, sucking up a dozen gaping workmen in its first breath, taking them in as a tit-bit before pounding down the swollen creek, pounding, smashing, roaring downwards, onwards through Jabiru, lifting the bridge like a snapped match, engulfing thirty head of prize cattle in the yard by the depot, going on remorseless, its appetite merely whetted, down the valley past the tin-workings. Past the miners as they flee scrambling and shouting up the banks: past the tiny new settlement at Red Pinch where Bob McMahon, mending the roof torn away in the storm's first frenzy, lets go hammer and saw, falls on to the veranda roof which crumples beneath him, and yelling: 'Run, Ma! the dam's bust! Run, yer blunny cow!' subsides yelping and cursing among the ruins of his house: past the Chinaman's garden where Cho Ling stands mourning over the yellow rotten tips of his vegetables, then looks, then leaps for safety as the wave roars on: past Frenchy weeping over his ravaged stocks, and on with a mighty roar as Frenchy, weeping still, skips up the nearest gum tree and hangs there livid with fear and sorrow: past the abandoned tin mine, sucking out of red mud the bodies of the kangaroo and the Irishman, sucking out from the roots of a messmate into which it had been threshed the body of his woman still wrapped in shreds of bluey – past all these and on, on, on.

The wave had parted roaring at the junction of the creeks and raced down both, blood-red with the tin-rich soil, foaming, spuming, tossing, thundering, with a wild lacy pattern of up-rooted pandanus palms, sword grass, bottle-brush bushes and all the arboreal jetsam of any Queensland creek over its romping surface. On, on, to the children crouching like young quail in the deep grass, and gaping Janey looking for a way to cross. She saw first a dark casuarina cast sportively ten foot above the grass then dropping like a shot bird back into the flood: she saw the tree, she heard the roar, she saw the red tide of the wave heave up against the rainy sky, she leapt to the children, she caught her foot in the bright grass, she fell with her temple cracking against the cradle's edge, and lay senseless with a punctured skull.

Janey was quickly dead, the children were less lucky. Had they raced for the bush instead of staring at their dropped elder lying bleeding beside the cradle they might have been saved, for they were not in the line of wave but in a little hooked-out backwater up which the tide seeped more slowly. But leaderless, disorganised, frantic, they fell to crying and screaming, ran hither and yon in the thick grass as the wave went by, tripped in the lush, green, glorious grass, struggled up bemused and made off with one accord, like stampeding sheep, towards the rising tide. Up came the water in the wake of that towering wave: now their dusty little feet were ankle-deep, now their dirty little knees, scored and scratched by a hundred encounters with their mother the Bush, were wet and slimy with the flood: now, wrapping tepid and horrible round the waists, the armpits, the shoulders of these bush babies, the flood surged up. The smallest sister was first engulfed, tripped among the rampant grasses, gasping her little lungs full of flood-water as she dropped. Fiercely over her the water rose, one by one the cries died, the bobbing heads sank, soon even the grass had gone. Now there was nothing in the whole wide river but tossing water, uprooted trees, a few bandicoots and kangaroo rats feebly struggling still, and an old wooden cradle carved with grapes and acanthus leaves in which a dirty brown baby sat drooling with bubbles at his mouth, snatching at the twigs and floating grass-heads as he floated onwards, southwards, on the broad tossing breast of the Burdekin . . .

Chapter VI

Thus were Mo and Lucy established at the 'Royal Rose', and added to the menagerie of Mrs. Daisy Sweeney. Even at Mosman Towers, in an age when odd characters were two a penny, the 'Royal Rose' had more than its share. They ranged from Alfred Freckle, whom cruel gossip bedded with the fair proprietress every night, to her burden, bugbear and cupboard skeleton, the redoubtable Gramma, who haunted the place like an approaching Wet and was reputed to live solely on whisky and sheep's blood. This last was sheer libel: Mo saw her often enough with his own eyes tucking into the stringy goat, pale drowned cabbage and leaden plum-duff of the 'Royal Rose's' midday table: and as for the whisky, though she always smelt of it, no one had ever seen her imbibe.

Gramma was by now of an age to be quite sexless and beyond all normal standards, even the somewhat odd standards of a mining town in the 'eighties. Bearded like the pard, flat as a grenadier, quite bald, and fully six foot tall, she was the showpiece of the place, its rare card, its terror and delight. The miners loved to draw her past out of her: it needed little drawing. Mention Parramatta, prisons, uprisings, or the eighteen forties, and Gramma was off with the speed of a brumby leaving a bush fire. Transported for infanticide under William IV, locked for twenty years in that grim New South Wales town, released only to enter the tighter bonds of matrimony with a travelling tinker who cared not what his wife were like so long as she were stout enough to survive the bush, Hannah Wylie had seen Australia in its worst age, and lived in that age still, the relentless old ghoul, raking over the smelly past while Daisy moaned and miners snickered. One such, a stranger to the town, had, it was said, tackled Gramma when he had in him just enough beer and just too little caution, and approached her with hiccups, with the ribald question: 'What'd they sling *you* in the Calaboose for, Gramma?' To which Gramma, rising slowly to her full height, baring her yellow teeth at him, had stonily replied: 'Somethin' yer ma oughta done years ago, yer worthless piece o' crows'-meat!', and had so scared the wits out of him that he had stumbled to the nearest coach and was rumbled away to Hughenden, nor ever seen again in Mosman Towers.

Apart from Gramma, there were other oddities round Mrs.

Sweeney's table – not oddities to the town, perhaps, which was used to them; but definitely odd to the fresh eyes of Mo and Lucy. M. Delpard, the hairdresser, lemon-yellow and as bald as a coot: Miss Hymovitch, the dressmaker, with an ogle for anything that wore pants: a faded squatters' relict who hardly ever spoke and had been in Mosman Towers ten years already waiting for the lawyers in their tortuous wisdom to clear up the estate: and a stout wheezing officer lately cashiered from the service of Her Majesty, to exist as best he could on a mining agency or by humming for drinks from miners too drunk to know their own wives.

To this assembly, that hot evening in 1889, were added Mo and Lucy, she showing all the signs of an imminent bolt, but held firmly by Mo's tough young hand under the tablecloth. In truth, it was an ordeal for both, this entering of a strange room under a dozen or more strange eyes, to eat in public of cold mutton and pickles and slabs of bread and jam, when for weeks they had at this hour washed down roast game with hot tea, sitting on stump or boulder in the empty friendly bush. Both young savages were awkward now with knives and forks, apt to eat everything off the same plate, and to fill up their mouths with food before drinking, as you do when at any moment an emergency such as a bush fire or a bolting horse may send you from an unfinished meal at top speed. But the 'Royal Rose' was too stirred at their advent to notice these defects. The meal went on to a running fire of questions. Where had they come from? Why? How long would they stay? and so forth. Soon Ma and Dad and Auntie May and the twins had to be given an airing: the newcomers were now not only Strangers, but Orphans as well, it seemed; and the whole table listened in moist silence while Lucy gave a spirited account of Dad's last moments, delicately conveying as only Lucy could how much the bottle had had to do with it. All went very well, the two of them were pleased with themselves when they broke free at last to go upstairs. Here they were less pleased, for it now occurred to them that for the first time in months they would have to sleep in beds, under a roof.

'I'll take my bluey and sleep in the yard,' said Mo, leaning out of the window and seeing that for once Danger was not howling his heart out below.

'You'll do no sich thing – we're in a town now, and we gotta act classy. Dja think I wanna sleep in this mangy ole paddock?'

(turning down the cover to smell at the dingy calico sheets? 'O' course I don't, there's too many bin sleepin' in it already – but I'm gonna do it. Bring yer stretcher outa that 'ole and put it by the winder where yer can see the sky – c'mon, I'll give yer a 'and.'

Talking of gold, Mo fell asleep in no time, declaring as he did so that he was going to lie awake all night, but lulled by the familiar stars coming out over the 'Royal Rose's' washhouse and the hump of mines beyond. Lucy lay long awake, fighting off nightmare. She had not been in a bed since she shared one with the dead Alexander, and this alien stretch of dirty sheet was full of him. She groaned and grunted and cursed to herself, rolling hither and yon: sat up and had a long look at the stars: lay down and tried to count them all from where she lay: rolled over and put her face in the bolster, which smelt of human hair: took her face out again in a hurry: wondered what that cat had felt like, locked up in that closet and having three kittens in it: decided that motherhood was much over-rated: rolled round again and decided to wake up Mo and tell him how miserable she was: heard the clock in the town begin to strike and laid bets with herself as to whether it were striking eleven or twelve: was quite certain it had struck thirteen: and fell asleep feeling dimly that there was something wrong somewhere.

KYLIE TENNANT, 1912-1988

Born in Manly, New South Wales, Kylie Tennant
embarked on a variety of unusual expeditions and
temporary careers, more often than not to gather
material for her books which, be they fact or fiction,
were frequently a form of social documentary. A
woman of irreverence who used every opportunity to
literally expose injustice and hypocrisy, she
compassionately mapped the lives of many social
victims and revealed her own identification with
them. While not adhering to any particular party
political line, Kylie Tennant used her fiction to
promote an awareness of the need for reform as she
prsented moving portraits of outsiders, outcasts, the
dispossessed of society.

   A striking characteristic of her work is her sense of
humour which not only highlights the absurdity of
the human condition but helps to suggest the potential for improvement, and to sound a note of optimism
in a chaotic world. A thoroughly Australian writer,
she was one of the most underrated authors on
the contemporary scene; among her many well
crafted, consciousness-raising, and compelling
novels are *The Battlers* (1941) and *Ride on Stranger*
(1943). The realistic nature of her writing is explained
by the fact that so much of her fiction was based on
first hand experience – for *The Honey Flow*, (1956)
for example, she took to the road, (dressed generally
in protective male attire), and kept bees. Some of the
dramatic and deeply painful events of her own life

699

are recounted in her recent autobiography, *The Missing Heir*, (1986).

Journalist, novelist, historian, playwright and children's author, Kylie Tennant has more than twenty-five published books to her credit. *Speak You So Gently*, an account of the treatment of Aborigines and an appraisal of the role played by some missionaries, was published in 1959 and still marks the author as radical reformer. The first six chapters are printed here, along with an unpublished short story which suggests the author's sensitivities and concerns.

SPEAK YOU SO GENTLY
My Husband's Friend

It is a custom among the Eskimos for a man to lend his wife to a friend who is going on a long sled journey. The friend has no wife of his own and needs someone to see to his furs, carry the spare gun, and push the sled. In our society, the wife is apt to say that the children are too young, or just that she won't go.

'They send up a smoke signal,' Alf told my husband. 'You see the smoke signal going up from Rocky Point. That's to tell you that it's too rough for the lugger to get round Cape Direction.'

'She'll go,' my husband announced.

I gave a yelp of alarm. 'The children are too young,' I objected.

'Bring them too,' Alf suggested, rolling another cigarette. Alf is a bachelor. 'Bimbi John would like to come to the land of the wild Black Gollies and have an eight-foot spear with steel prongs?'

Bimbi John, who was three, nodded solemnly.

Bimbi John was sick in the plane for thousands of miles; he was sick in the lugger; he was sick in the blitz waggon. But he was upheld by the shining vision of that lethal, steel-tipped spear. Benison, age ten, refused to come. Benison, who cannot spell, has more sense than anyone in the family. She stayed with friends. People will mind a little girl with plaits, but not a little boy who has trouble with his buttons.

I had been lent to my husband's friend before, not to mind his furs, or to whip up the dog team, but to write articles or address meetings. The Reverend Alfred Clint once occupied a desolate rectory on the coalfields, a bachelor establishment furnished with camp beds, a crucifix, a table and some benches from the church hall. The other occupant of the rectory was a huge Irish terrier called Paddy, whose coat was impregnated with coal. He had an instinct that told him when someone was going to bath him. He retired under the house.

On one occasion Alf had arranged a series of lectures on co-operatives, and my husband had lent me to give those lectures. The female secretary of some co-operative society, the name of which I have mercifully forgotten, came with me. We arrived at the rectory on a blazing hot afternoon in time to see Alf hurrying in his cassock across to the church.

'I've got a funeral,' he called. 'Just go in and make yourselves at home.'

'I want a shower,' Nancy the secretary said. She was young and pretty, with curves. We had carried our suitcases from the station so I wanted a shower too.

While Nancy was having her shower, a knock came at the rectory door, and I answered it. Two men seemed puzzled to see me.

'The rector has a funeral,' I told them. 'Can I help you?'

'We came to fix the wireless aerial.' They pointed to a tall pole by the front gate. This they were to erect as a mast, and they began to hoist it. 'Hup, hup!' they encouraged each other.

Nancy appeared at the front door to see what the noise was about. She was wearing a play suit covered with a pattern of huge flowers which did justice to her hips.

'Oh Rector, half your luck,' one of the men said wistfully. The other stood with his mouth open in admiration.

The pole swerved, fell across the light wires in the street. There was a loud report and a flash, and the electricity for the whole town was cut off.

Next day Nancy and I were conducted over a co-operative store and bakery. We returned after dark to the rectory carrying fish and chips. We had tried to deal with the stove, a huge sullen relic left over from the days when rectors had thirteen children. It needed a hundredweight of fuel to cook a roast, and even then the mutton was raw on one side.

We waited for the return of the Reverend Alfred, and we continued to wait. We were extremely hungry. The enormous kitchen was empty, the chips were cold, so was the fish. Finally, radiant in the doorway, Alf appeared. In chorus, in the same tone of voice, two angry women spoke:

'This is a fine time to come home!'

The Reverend Alfred nearly fell off his doorstep. 'Now, comrades, comrades,' he remonstrated. 'I was just organizing a meeting. To-morrow' – he beamed at us – 'I've arranged for you to go down the coal-mine. Then we visit the vineyards.'

For going down the coal-mine Nancy wore a rainbow play suit of orange and red. In my old slacks nobody noticed me, but they were telephoning ahead about Nancy. In one black tunnel an old horse came plodding along dragging a truck on rails. From the edge of the truck protruded a pair of boots. As the horse drew level the owner of the boots raised his head and stared at us. He stared more wildly, then the boots and face disappeared as he fell backwards into the truck.

At the vineyards, an old man with a red nose showed us round the enormous casks, and the Rector delicately suggested that we wished to sample the vintage. The ancient nodded, produced three glasses and a rubber tube. He fixed the rubber tube to the barrel, sucked noisily until the wine came through into his mouth, and then held the tube over the glasses. Alf and I looked pale. Nancy, who had noticed nothing, cheerfully drank all three glasses.

My lecture on co-operatives that night in the church hall was followed by coffee and biscuits. Someone spilt a cup of coffee all over me, and I was rushing across the dark lawn to the rectory to sponge my skirt, when I overtook the rector sweeping along in his cassock.

'Want to see me organize a little co-operative of my own?' he asked, with a grin on his face. He went to the telephone, leant on it confidentially and called the local hotel-keeper. 'That you, Tom? This is Alf. George will be coming round to pick up a few bottles. O.K.?'

The elderly miners with hard, rocky faces sat round the rector's study, primly holding enamel mugs of beer, and capping each other's stories, about a Cornish character called Cousin Jack. It was a cheerful, decent and sober gathering, with the light falling on the crucifix and those gnarled faces.

From the coalfields, where his parishioners worshipped him, Alf found his way to New Guinea. On the coalfields his bishop had been distressed by reports that Father Clint was a rampant Communist, the leading spirit of the Labour League and the Unemployed Committee. The Bishop had also to deal with those who complained of the rector's High Church practices. New South Wales is dominantly Low Church, Queensland and New Guinea are High Church. In New South Wales, incense is an abomination of Rome. The natives of New Guinea like incense, also candles and copes.

In New Guinea, Father Clint worked with James Benson, who died during a visit to England where, at the age of seventy-six, he was learning boot-making. He wanted to teach boot-making to his students in the hook-worm area, people too poor to buy shoes.

Jim Benson and Alf were the curse of those planters who wanted cheap labour. They taught the tribes to form co-operatives and work their own plantations as they had done before the white men came, in village units. When the co-op. copra was left to rot on the beach because the white men's boats would not load it, and only loaded the white planters' cargo, the tribesmen built their own boat. They grew rice and fought rats for the crop that Alf and Jim had blessed with holy water.

During the war, Papuans of many tribes had been thrown together, and they talked around their camp-fires of what the white fathers said about staying in your own village and working your own land. After the war, men would make long and dangerous journeys through hostile territory to consult with the missionaries.

'We will go to Father and see what he says,' they would tell would-be buyers of their land. A few days' journey would find them squatting in the dust, rolling cigarettes with Father Clint.

'Do not sell the land,' he would advise them. 'Plant coconuts on it. If these men want that particular land, it will be the best.'

Alf would go tramping through the jungle with one loyal dark interpreter, and it stirred his sense of humour to see a government dignitary ride by in a wicker armchair with an armed guard. Then, just when the co-operatives were finding their feet, Alf was stricken down with some kind of Job's disease which caused the skin to peel from him like a mango. He was flown out to hospital in Port Moresby. Then they flew him south to Sydney. He sat up in bed writing letters about agricultural surveys, ploughs, and cotton and coffee crops. Nine months he was in hospital, most of the time planning and organizing a campaign to raise money for scholarships for Papuans, so that they could go back to their co-operatives trained to take skilled jobs, to keep accounts, to deal with correspondence, to manage their affairs themselves.

But Alf, for perhaps the first time in his life of certainty, saw, like a shadow of eclipse, a faint, smoky peripheral doubt.

'I have always tried to understand God's plan,' he told a bishop who came to see him in hospital. 'I have always tried to follow the blooming thing. But the Devil has got the upper hand. I was chucked out of New Guinea just when they needed me most.'

'The Devil is an over-simplification, Alf.'

'Call it what you like. Call it bad luck. Call it the subconscious, any flogging thing. I haven't got time to muck about, so I call it the Devil. Then I know where I am. The Devil – bang! like that. You can bust the Devil one. If you call it Fate or bad luck or a conjunction of stars, where will that get you? You only sit down under it.'

God, the bishop indicated, had moved Alf out of New Guinea for some good reason. I can imagine the look Alf gave him. He had been walking from the Mount Lamington area at Higaturi to Gona when he had been taken so ill. When he was flown out of New Guinea the area around Mount Lamington and the Sangara Mission was the most flourishing centre of the New Guinea co-operatives, plantations of sunlit green and thatched villages, self-respecting and fond of feasting.

'What a good time we are going to have at my welcome home,' Jim Benson wrote cheerfully. 'Pity the dear things have no good pigs for killing. Anyhow we will have a feast. I must get there before Lent begins. There should be good and glorious dances at the Harvest Festival. Two dances I would love them to dance for me: Kikiri and Gitara, and the Dance of the Flying Fishes.'

There was always a feast in prospect, always laughter. And then Mount Lamington blew up in a volcanic cataclysm so sudden that there was no time for flight! Ruin spread in roaring lava and evil smoke. The smiling mission buildings, the schools, the villages, the crops, were a shrivelled waste littered with dead bodies. The fish boiled in the stream, the birds fell on the scorched soil, the women with children in their arms died by their men. And the mission doctors, nurses, priests, died with their people.

'In one village,' Alf told me, 'there are only two men left alive. The other co-operatives have offered to take them in. "No," they say, "we will start again. We had our own co-op. and our sons will have it." '

'My dear Alf,' Bishop Hand wrote to Father Clint. 'It is very important that you get back here as soon as possible. The numbing blow of Lamington has halted everything. Now they are all trying to re-start and our uninformed efforts to help them are very pathetic. I've managed to keep the Sangara people up to persisting in the demand for the return of some of their Crown Land previously alienated. They're going to get back 2,000 acres so that they can get some lumbering of their own under way co-operatively. Had the chairman in this morning. I've got an excellent rice mill which is hulling rice. But I cannot always be here. I have New Guinea and New Britain to think about. Even if you come only for a short time with or without a suitable bloke to train in your ways YOU MUST COME.'

But no doctor would allow Alf to return to Papua. He was told he must never go to the tropics again. After seven years he still absentmindedly peels the skin off his hands after a trip North. His life and work lay in New Guinea. The men who understood him were there. They were fighting for the villagers' land, land that had once sold ninety acres for a few sticks of tobacco, but not now.

Tell me what a man believes and I will tell you what he is. Ideas are what people live by. A man's own idea of himself, false or true, is as important as his body because he will grow like it. Men will starve for ideas, starve their families for them, die for them, and there is precious little else they will do that for. All history is a history of ideas that have seized certain people at certain times and made them behave in a way abhorrent to contemporary society.

The early ideas of Alf Clint were formed watching his father, a great believer in co-operatives, a man of kindliness and intelligence, look in vain for work or food. Any child who sees its parents desperate will never lose that mark. The family came of a line of Irish actors, handsome and histrionic. Now young Clint, leaving school, identified himself with working-class people and their ideas.

He joined a Co-operative Society, and was one of the youngest members to hold a Labour Party ticket. The way was open for him to go to England on a scholarship and train in the co-operative movement there. But Alf was a stubborn young man of virtuous life. He taught in Sunday school though he studied Karl Marx. His family were solid churchgoers, and a fellow churchman persuaded him to visit Christ Church St. Laurence. This most famous of Sydney's Anglican churches had a ceremonial which young Clint regarded with disapproval. It also had a rector, Father John Hope, who could charm drunkards from their drink and old ladies from their interest in their ailments. After the service Alf decided he should remonstrate with the rector.

'I mean to say,' he began sternly. 'If you can see what I mean. . . .'

In the thirty odd years that John Hope has been known as the Archbishop of Railway Square, how many young men have challenged that great fair bull in his own arena, only to find themselves puzzled, disarmed, overthrown and tipped head over heels! All over Australia and New Guinea, in Bush Brotherhoods, isolated mission stations and outback parishes, you will find these spiritual toreadors, labouring as Father This and Father That, hard-working churchmen who were once gored by that great bull of the Lord.

Steeped in the traditions of Stanton and Dolling, those shepherds of the poor, John Hope knew exactly how to deal with Alf. 'The Church, my dear boy,' he smiled, pressing a bundle of Christian Socialist leaflets into Alf's hand, 'has need of men like you.' Yes, indeed, and down the drain went the career of a born trade union leader!

Alf's pulpit manner is woeful because he finds a pulpit as hampering as a clerical collar. But hear him address a pit-top meeting at dawn in the grey rain, and you will hear a speaker who can carry men away with the grandeur of simplicity.

'I saw Jim Benson once,' Alf said, speaking of some formal young cleric. 'Jim was so angry with one of the village elders – this chap had spoiled a piece of carpentry Jim had been working on – and Jim was so furious he called him a fool and – he hit him. That evening Jim went down to the village. In front of all the people he knelt down at the elder's feet and begged his pardon. The man lifted him up and they sat down side by side on a log and shared the evening meal. It's that sort of thing, I mean, that these chaps haven't got here.'

Out of hospital, Alf began addressing waterfront meetings, railway men, builders' labourers, raising funds for Papua. He took a brief holiday in a former parish out West, serving behind the bar counter for his friend, the publican. The prospect of parish respectability and the drone of the old ladies criticizing the organist – could he endure what he called the 'set-up'?

Then the Australian Board of Missions had one of those inspirations that ward off the Church of England's demise. The Rev. W. A. Clint was appointed Director of Native Co-operatives. His job was to found co-operatives where and how he could among the Australian aborigines and the Torres Strait Islanders.

The Australian aborigine, in his native state, was a natural born co-operator. He hunted for his group, not himself. What a man brought in did not necessarily belong to him. The catch was shared. Often a successful hunter was allowed, say, only the left hind toe, or, if his totem, his spirit brother, was roasting on the fire, he probably didn't get anything.

At Lockhart River Mission, way up the tip of Cape York Peninsula, Alf established his first registered co-operative in Australia, and the natives of the five tribes at Lockhart proudly nailed a shingle to the door of a bark and corrugated iron structure, the registered office of 'The Lockhart River Aborigines Christian Co-operative'. They elected their Board of Directors and began working three trochus boats.

When Alf proposed to borrow a useful wife from a friend, he was preparing to attend the Co-op.'s first annual meeting. He thought someone should write about it.

'They send up a smoke signal,' he repeated. 'You must come up and see the co-op. They'll put on a feast and they dance in carved devil masks.' Of course it wasn't Papua, but it had its consolations.

'We'll meet you at the plane,' I said resignedly.

Of the Pied Piper

'Got everything?' my husband enquired. 'Bim's toys, knapsack, the steel guitar?' He did not say, 'Come back safely,' because years of experience had taught him I would be on the doormat two days before I was expected home, and before he had a chance to do the washing up.

The steel guitar was my passport. I had found, when I lived in a small fishing village, that men hated to see me own a truck and drive it. They wanted to borrow my truck, but to do this they had to make friends with me. Lockhart River Mission abounded in guitar-players. The aborigines, lusting to borrow my steel guitar and play it, would have to make friends with me first. It is surprising how easily a means of communication is set up, and how friendly people can be when they want to borrow something.

At home, my clumsy attempts to pick out a tune caused a young Hawaiian teacher to resign in despair. You move a steel slug with one hand, while your other hand is clad in a set of tortoiseshell knuckledusters. For me this was like doing up a bootlace while fastening a button at the back of my neck.

'But, dammit, you don't *learn* to play the steel guitar,' an orchestra conductor had snarled at me contemptuously. 'You just *play* the thing – if you must.'

I never did. But the air hostesses all treated that guitar with great respect. They thought they ought to recognize me. I would tramp up the gangway with the guitar, in its blue canvas cover, whining a muffled protest as it swung from my shoulder, and they would pack it carefully with cushions on the luggage rack.

Bimbi John, holding my hand, was similarly girded. He had his leather satchel with his toys in it, a set of plastic blocks and model cars. Suspended in an adult vacuum, he refused to surrender to any tall incompetent this only link with home.

Brisbane smelt of yellow chrysanthemums and winter woollens. It had a taste of acid drops and its sunlight was an aunt's smile piercing gold-rimmed spectacles. Alf disappeared to stay at a friend's rectory, and Bim and his mother were left in a city hotel over Sunday. On the wall of our room a row of china ducks flew approximately in the direction we should be taking before daylight next morning. I sat cross-legged on the floor practising my guitar, and Bimbi held to my ankle in case I should leave him.

Through the shut windows that Sunday afternoon came the sound, far off, of brass bands bumping out 'Onward Christian Soldiers'. We burst open the long doors and emerged on a bird-cage above the corrugated iron roof. At the intersection, a policeman held up his hand against the trams and buses; a squad of motor-cycle cops slid forward with that interesting, stiff projection of their legs that suggests they may fall off at any moment. They were clearing the way for the procession, its banners tiny in the distance, and a glitter on the brass band.

I lifted my son to the rail and the tears began to gather in my eyes. I always cry at processions, just as I do at circuses. At first it looked like Corpus Christi, but as the bands came nearer the procession turned out to be the Reverend Alan Walker, looking cheerful and upright in the forefront of his Mission to the Nation.

Thousands of people marched in his wake, Sunday schools, their teachers vainly exhorting them to keep in step, young ladies in best clothes they had bought out of salaries earned in offices, clean young men from the Christian Fellowships, kilt-swinging Scots with bagpipes, Orangemen in huge velvet horse-collars, Methodists, Presbyterians, Baptists, stout women whose feet hurt them. They were no anonymous part of a mass. They marched like Protestants, all separately, the women's voices terrible against the band. Three stout women fell out and limped to the footpath, perspiration caking their face-powder. Another Sunday-school banner hove in sight like the desperate signal of shipwrecked mariners.

'What are you crying for?' Alf said behind me. He came out and held Bimbi John higher on the rail.

'Just pitying the poor damned. It's a kind of Pied Piper complex.' I blew my nose luxuriously. 'They pack after this beautiful idea like lemmings or mice. The Pied Piper can be disguised as nice Alan Walker or he can deck himself out with some other idea. And the procession will form up – the children will be taken to it. I cry, I think, because when they are in to the very last, the door in the mountainside shuts fast and the Pied Piper steals all their children.' The processions I had seen as an infant were those when men marched to the ships that would take them to a war on the other side of the world.

Bimbi John was bored and wriggled down. We went inside and I set about repairing my face.

'Alan does a good job,' Alf said with a professional appreciation. 'You've got to hand it to him.' He sat on the floor with Bimbi. 'How about coming for a walk, son?'

'Do I have to wear shoes?'

'Of course you do,' I snarled. 'And don't think I'm going to carry you.' He usually returns riding on my shoulders, saying his shoes hurt him.

We strolled between the great sandstone buildings along the river bank, where golden light was turning the grass unearthly green.

'You'd better see the Minister for Education on your way back,'

Alf said. 'The Mission children have got to have education, but where are we to get the trained teachers? The Department of Native Affairs is supposed to see to the teaching. They leave it to the bishop. The bishop hasn't a teacher, so he sends a girl who's been trained as a nurse and he hopes for the best. I'll drop a note to Joe saying I want you to see the Minister for Education as well as the Home Secretary.'

'Yes,' I said, wondering if I should ever get back. Months later, I did interview the Minister for Education. He was sitting behind an immense, dark-polished desk rather like a displaced railway platform. Bimbi John walked forward, took off his shoes, and put them on the desk. The Minister liked that. He thawed into a father of children, and the tone in which he assured me he couldn't possibly send teachers to mission stations, first because there was no legislation to provide for it, and secondly because the Department hadn't the teachers to spare, was quite friendly and confidential.

'Why do you want me to see all these people?' I asked Alf as we halted outside the Lands Department building. Inset in its wall is the stone which is Benchmark Number One. This is the stone from which all levels are measured in Queensland, all levels of land, levels of railways and roads. Brisbane, on the thick waistline of the continent, is the main belt button. Everything in Queensland depends on Brisbane, on what the politicians say in Parliament House under the mauve-coloured jacarandas, a pleasant building overlooking the Gardens, with ping-pong tables on the verandahs. The livelihood of everyone is affected by the decisions of the Trades Hall on the grim hill overlooking Central Railway Station. Every level is taken from Benchmark Number One. 'I thought you told me the Queensland Government treats its black people better than any other State?'

'It does,' Alf said grimly. 'Let me give you an instance. In a small town in Queensland a drunk went staggering down to a creek where some old black women were washing clothes. He broke the jaw of one of them, beat up a couple of others, and assaulted another. The police actually arrested him. What do you suppose he got?'

'Three months?'

'He was fined five pounds. The police are supposed to be the protectors of the aborigines and have to bank the money for full-bloods in the isolated places. They say, "Sign here" and point to a spot in the bank-book. The chap who is being protected signs or makes his mark and the policeman draws out a pound for the aborigine and two for himself. Of course I don't say *all* of them do it, but ask the missionaries. Ask Bill MacKenzie at Arakoon, ask . . .'

'All right, Alf, all right; you don't have to convince me.'

When the first white men landed in this country to found a colony of English thieves, they ran up the flag and declared that the whole country belonged to Great Britain, the land was the property of the Crown. The officers took care that the convicts, under penalty of flogging or hanging, stole not so much as a loaf of bread. They themselves stole a whole continent.

Australia was already occupied by a set of peaceable, naked, black citizens who had a prophecy that one day the land would be given over to demons in white skins and the black men would all be dead. The missionaries were horrified that these savages believed only in one great spiritual force and no gods whatever. The savages also believed that every place had a vibration or radiation of its own, and a man was part of the place in which he was born and shared its wavelength. This was called Alchuringa.

Their great works of art for religious ceremonies were destroyed the day the ceremonies were over. If they trespassed outside their own area, their neighbours killed them or they died of grief at being removed from their sacred territory. So thousands of them were killed by the white people driving them away from the place where they were born. The white settlers gave the starving tribesmen flour – there was arsenic in it. They organized shoots to put a bullet through the dark men and women as they ran with their children in their arms. This was pioneering, clearing the country, making it safe for cattle and sheep that a hungry aborigine might spear.

'My feet hurt,' announced Bimbi John. 'Someone could carry me.'

'I'll carry you, mate,' Alf offered.

'I want Mummy to carry me.' I bent down to hoist him to my shoulders.

'I shall be glad to get out of this place,' I said as we turned back to the hotel.

'They keep you messing about here,' Alf agreed. 'I'm kept tramping from Department to Department when I should have gone North a month ago.'

Queensland runs North for fifteen hundred miles to a large spear-point of land that looks as though it will prod New Guinea in the stomach. This spear-point is Cape York and, at the tip, a little down on the eastern side, we would see Lockhart River. It was still a day and a half of flying ahead of us.

Bimbi looked down condescendingly on Alf from the height of my shoulders.

'When do I meet the little black boys?' he demanded.

'Pretty soon now, mate,' Alf promised. He began talking to Bimbi John, explaining to him what would happen, where we would go. He did it gently and simply so that nothing should come as a shock to a little boy. He took as much trouble as he would have done had he been addressing an important meeting.

'It will be a smaller plane that we go on in the dark tomorrow morning, not a great big plane like the one we came in from home. This plane will fly all day, and in the evening we shall be in a big hot town, Cairns. We stay there all night. And in the morning,' he raised his voice and smiled as though this were the pink frosted cake, 'we take *another* even littler plane and that will bring us to Iron Range. And at Iron Range,' he sank his voice to a whisper, 'there will be black men waiting to take us in a boat with a *sail*. You'll like that, won't you?'

Bimbi considered this. He clutched my hair. 'Perhaps I'd better wait and *see*.'

Alf shook his head admiringly. 'Nothing gets past you, mate,' he said.

Along the Barrier

To an Australian airline, the rainy darkness before dawn is what moonlight is to a lover, the perfect time for meeting and parting. It gives a ceremonial gloom and indifference, the special surroundings of desolate tarmac, with a couple of mechanics doing something leisurely to a plane, while the passengers wait in forlorn groups under the artificial lights, forbidden to approach. In the funereal dimness of the terminal, breakfastless, uneasy, they have been weighed in, a scene reminiscent of Egyptian tomb murals showing Osiris judging the dead, the heart of the deceased balanced against a feather, while Thoth, the ibis-headed god, who bears a singular resemblance to an airline official, waits to throw the overweight soul to Amemet, who has the head of a crocodile, the mane of a lion, and the hindparts of a hippopotamus.

As Alf had slipped into my luggage some leather-bound account books and a pile of co-operative literature, my excess baggage charge had brought from me an outcry that was well up to the standard of a lost soul thrown to Amemet.

The air hostess gave the guitar a nervous pat. 'It's terrible flying weather,' she confided, 'and this is the worst run of the lot.' We were taking the slow plane to Cairns so that we could buy vegetables, meat, butter and pick up the radio set and clock for the mission.

Sometimes the rain cleared over a patched green of canefield. The commando mountains loped stealthily along the coast, disguising themselves in camouflage green and black shadows. Everywhere was water, mud, silt plains, forests and more curving deltas of rivers pouring into the sea with land drowned and rising again in a swirl of green bubbles and islands. This muddy field of combat between the inland rivers and the tide was the Great Barrier Reef, mecca of coral and coloured fish.

'What we keep circling out to sea for?' a man asked.

'Because, mate,' another explained, 'those clouds inland are stuffed with bloody rocks.'

Across the aisle, Alf wrote letters, a faint crease between his brows indicating that he was air-sick. He looked like a tough cherub with grey curls. Six times the plane circled down to land, and the hostess proffered us a dish of paper-wrapped toffee. At school we used to chant the names: Brisbane, Maryborough, Bundaberg, Rockhampton, Mackay, Proserpine, Townsville, Cairns. I had thought of them as a necklace of jewels over the dowager bust of Queensland, but they were small and far apart. You would look down and see a wharf, a breakwater and a toy boat, little scattered matchbox houses.

By late afternoon we trudged out of Cairns airport into a warm steam.

At the wharfside, liners towered over the town, almost in the main street. Tripper launches set out to show the wonders of the coral through the glass bottom of the boat; tripper trains wound off into the mountains to show waterfalls and tropical forests. I had an introduction to a man who milks deadly taipans, but reflecting that I was going into the heart of the taipan country myself, it seemed hardly worth while to ring him.

The hotel-keeper promised to mind the clothing we now discarded, Bimbi's woollens, my coat and skirt. We were frantically throwing out weight.

'The farther north you go, the tougher the airlines get,' the pub-keeper told us, leaning in at the door, or rather the curtain, for our rooms had no doors. 'The plane that goes into the Gulf – they wouldn't just weigh your luggage, they'd weigh you too.'

I threw out a lightweight coat.

'Come on, Alf,' I said, 'give.'

But Alf had no clothes to give. He had his sandals, the white cassock with the frayed yellow cord at the waist, of which he is very proud, as it is the mark of the co-operative priests of New Guinea: he had his prayer book, his razor and comb: he had shorts and shirt, and that was all. He wore a linen hat, and he would wear his clerical suiting on the plane.

Our brains were reverberating with the plane noises, and when we lay down we were giddy. Bimbi John was restless throughout the night, so it was a relief to be stealing quietly out of the hotel in the rainy darkness. At the airport the dawn was beginning to show, and the blue neons gave a ghastly hue to the faces of those waiting in the modern singularity of the lounge. Bimbi John picked up his satchel and waddled purposefully towards the plane.

'Not yet, old man,' Alf explained. 'See those two men out there? Well, when our baggage was brought, they found it made the plane so heavy that they're pumping petrol out to make it lighter.'

The rain began again as the plane took off. We thundered through the grey vapour, catching occasional glimpses of tree-tops in a dark fleece over the rolling muscles of hills. In Queensland, the North has resisted civilization longest because the tropical rain makes the tracks impassable for some months of the year, and prolonged drought, lack of water, lack of funds, lack of people, ring the land in a vicious circle, which does not seem so vicious but a blessing to a lover of bush country. Why does one feel so guilty for preferring land that is not choked up with food crops or eaten over by mouths of imported beasts?

The grey mists folded tastefully round the mountains as a model might drape a turban. The plane lurched and shuddered down between two walls of rock, zigzagging skilfully along a valley. We were coming to yet another airfield, a clearing in the scrub, with a tin-roofed bungalow for a waiting-room. A few miles away would be a scattering of matchbox houses and a long jetty with a toy steamer tied to it.

Beside the airstrip, two black girls were waiting shyly, in clean print dresses. They were there to see the plane come in. They giggled when Alf spoke to them, and only answered him in a whisper, tracing the dust with their toes. He was asking where they came from, how many of their people were working in these parts.

While we waited for the plane to refuel, the clouds were rent and rolled off, the ground glittered with a hard light. The leaves of the trees glittered. Despite the rain it was so dry that if you spat the earth would be grateful for the moisture. An aromatic pungency set me sniffing, taking deep breaths, with the sense of liberation, of coming home to my own kind of country, the monotonous scrub, the grey or yellow clay, the clear enormous sky, and the hard resistance of scales and horn and bark. Few care for such country. 'Give it back to the blacks,' people say of such places. But no one ever does give anything back to the blacks.

The plane lurched and zigzagged its way northward through the valleys. I clung grimly to my son. Alf leant across and tapped my knee, smiling.

'Cape Direction.' He stabbed his finger downwards. I caught the words, 'A few minutes to Iron Range.' There we should leave the plane.

Twisting sideways I bent my neck to look through the torn mist. The land was like a camel sinking to its knees in the sea, humps going down lower and lower, Cape Direction curving out and settling down as though it shed its load at the sea edge.

Suddenly the aspect of Cape Direction struck me as familiar. This was the landscape of a dream which had long remained in my mind. In my sleep I had been puzzled by the angle, the height. 'What a high mountain I must be standing on to see the hills going down lower and lower to the sea!' Now it was clear that I had not seen Cape Direction from a mountain but from a plane. That would account for the elevation. I had overtaken a point in time. But another puzzle remained: When I was asleep I had seen Cape Direction in full sunlight; now it was dark with rain.

Alf was talking in my ear. 'Pity you can't see Lockhart, but it's farther south. It's only a patch of jungle on the edge of the sea, a few thatched houses and the church. Sometimes the pilots fly over if you ask them.' He began to pack his papers in his brief-case. 'We get out here, old man,' he told the prostrate Bimbi.

During the Battle of the Coral Sea, Iron Range was the base for the planes that smashed the Japanese attempt to invade Australia. Iron Range had boiled like an ants' nest with equipment, fuel and maintenance staff, builders, canteen workers, concrete-mixers, jeeps, and all the foam of human activity in the slipstream of war planes.

When the Americans at Iron Range heard that the aborigines at Lockhart River Mission were dying of an epidemic, they sent down two doctors. The doctors reported that the natives were dying of malnutrition more than anything else. Lockhart River Mission had always been the most isolated, the most neglected, lost-and-forgotten place.

It was established in the nineteen-thirties, a period of dearth anyway. The remnants of five tribes on the east coast of the Peninsula were starving and begging round cattle camps and the few gold mines or fishing depots. They were a nuisance. They were riddled with diseases, mostly T.B. and V.D. The Government declared for these tribes a reserve of half a million acres stretching inland from the sea. Half a million acres is a small place in the North; most of the Gulf-side missions were one million acres.

Lockhart River was a place where the tribal land of the five tribes met at a point. This was important because every man could still feel he was on his own tribal territory. Aborigines hate nothing more than going from their own place. The savage little boy squats down with his father, while the man draws the circles that represent the boy's land, the water-holes around which he has the right to hunt. They are his and he memorizes them early.

The Government gathered in the natives and arranged with the Church of England for one of its missionaries to take charge of the settlement, distribute rations, keep the people alive and generally give them some standards of decency and hope. The government, of course, was doing this on the cheap. The mission would be half supported by voluntary contributions of the pious, and the Government would have to pay only half the cost of the settlement. Moreover, the missionaries would work for a fraction of what you would pay a government servant.

Bishop Stephen Davies, who toiled and travelled and wore himself out doing ten men's work, had no white chaplain to send to Lockhart. He sent a Torres Straits Islander, a copper-coloured missionary, who wrote the aborigines some sonorous hymns in their own language, which he took the trouble to learn, and taught them the Torres Straits Island dances and the High Church religious ceremonial.

The people had their rations of flour and tea and tobacco, and they caught crayfish and 'bush tucker' in the form of wallabies and bandicoots, but they were nearly tormented to death by sand-flies and mosquitoes which brought fever. It was a matter of urgency to move the mission, so they moved it from the mouth of the Lockhart River to the headland south of Cape Direction. Here there were few crayfish, the fishing was not good. Gradually the V.D. was cleared up, but the people were dying off.

There was a long stretch, best not remembered: a mission super-intendent who, as the aborigines said darkly, 'sit in his house in clean collar and white clothes while the people die', a man who never killed a beast for meat, no matter how hungry the people were, until he ran out himself. He made sure he did not run out. There was a parson who caught T.B.

The T.B. cases were packed off to the hospital at Thursday Island. Someone had collected a wonderful garden of hibiscus and frangipani and tropical plants around the mission house, but until John Warby came the church services were still held in a big corrugated iron shed, which also served as a school.

The able-bodied men went to Thursday Island, a hundred and fifty miles north, as indentured labourers diving for shell. They might not see Lockhart or their families from one year's end to the next. There were left at Lockhart a few old men and the women and children. It was all very depressing and worrying to the Church authorities.

Then came John Warby. John was born in Sydney. His father was a well-known political figure in New South Wales, and his mother an irresistible woman from whom he inherited a persuasive charm more dangerous than dynamite. When he was a boy he ran away from home. 'Everything,' he said, when he had to return, 'is too soft here.' In the war, he used his quick wits, his gift of improvising a tow-rope out of a shoe-string.

'You know, John,' I said once, 'you would never be among the top brass, but when they were having a staff conference, someone would say, "Well, sir, I suggest we just let Warby go out with a few of the men and do whatever he feels is called for by the situation." '

'Yes, indeed,' John's wife agreed. 'Carry on, Warby!' She said it in a tone of condescending encouragement.

After the war, John married Bunty and set up as a pearler at Thursday Island. He had four children and was building a new house, but he did not want to work only for money, especially since the death of his brother. What did a man get out of life? he asked himself.

In the long, hot nights he argued metaphysics with Archdeacon Peter Bennie of the Cathedral. This was fatal to an agnostic of John's shaky foundations. The general impression prevails that people are converted *from* the Church of England. But with John Hope booming joyously around, or Peter Bennie, with his subtle eighteenth-century mind, people like John Warby, who take on the theological heavyweights, are licked before the first round.

John became a communicant of the Church of England, and one of the trusted laymen of the Cathedral. The Diocese was desperate about the state of Lockhart. Would John go as super-intendent? He came sailing into Lockhart in his own boat, the *Sea-bird*, with his wife Bunty, a female Viking with an ironic sense of humour. They brought their four children, and John began planning how to build up Lockhart from an insanitary and poverty-stricken little pesthole, 'the worst mission of them all'.

He had to have labour, men who lived in the village and would make it a place fit to live in. If he brought them back from their indentured labour on the Island luggers, where they earned a poor wage but at least a wage, he had to find them a living. He began an audacious set of negotiations with the Diocese to take over a boat belonging to the Church and start pearling at Lockhart. There was plenty of trochus, from which pearl buttons are made, on the reef at the mission's front door. You only had to have boats, and men to do the diving.

His scheme was already in its early stages when Alf Clint, with his evangel of co-operatives, stepped ashore. John realized that this was what he wanted, not only as an economic way out, but a means of giving the aborigines new self-respect.

Alf Clint settled down at Lockhart and began teaching the people. He camped with them. He went walkabout with them in the bush. Only after months, during which the people were discussing things among themselves, did they come to John Warby and ask if they could start a co-operative at Lockhart. This was their own asking, not something imposed by the mission. Alf is scrupulous about democracy. It came of the confidence the people had in Alf Clint and John Warby. They would work with these white men for something that they themselves were convinced was worth while; but I suspect that John and Alf made a formidable propaganda team.

I had heard so much about John Warby from Alf that I was a little afraid John might be an enthusiast. Peter Bennie quotes with relish the bishop who refused to allow John Wesley to preach: 'Get you gone, sir. You are an enthusiast, sir. You get no licence from me.' Alf was an idealist, but he was not an enthusiast. Emotional high pressure was not for him. He plodded grimly from one fixed point to the next with a well-balanced goodwill, a politician's eye for an advantage, and a long-distance strategy that always surprised people who regarded him as a starry-eyed visionary.

'George is a good bloke,' Alf said as we tramped towards the groundsman's house at Iron Range. 'He'll see we don't have to walk the seven miles to the coast.'

Before the war, there were only a few old prospectors in the scrub between Iron Range and the one-wharf, one-store metropolis of Portland Roads. After the Americans left, and the surplus equipment was sold, there were just a few old prospectors in the scrub and, at the airstrip, George the Groundsman, with red hair and a matching disposition. George also had a wife and four children. At the sight of the children my son gave up his imitation of a corpse and hurried off to play.

On the verandah of George's house was an old peeled-away notice, obviously composed by George in a fit of petulance, a revulsion against his own generosity:

'Friends, Countrymen, Missionaries, Superiors, Workmates, Foreigners!
And all persons entering these portals!
Cast Your Glims This Way For Here is News!
This is not a Benevolent Society OR a Traveller's Rest Home.

'Over the past twelve months we have kept a record of all the folks staying at this residence. We welcome you all, but the cost of meals to all good visiting folk is five shillings a meal, amounting to £195 10s. 0d. We cannot afford this luxury, so henceforth, though we highly value your visit and company, our income will not allow us to cater freely to your appetite.

'We will provide you with meals at 5s. a time and should you require a bed we can also arrange that at a further 5s. each night. We regret that we are forced to do this. We trust you will not be offended.'

Alf, who understood George's touchiness in a way that I could not, would never have thought of paying George. Instead, he had provided sufficient food of a kind he knew George liked, furnishing our meal and the family's. His wife, as unruffled as a wife of George's would need to be, was cutting up wild pig in the kitchen.

'You shouldn't have bothered,' she said, smiling at Alf's thoughtfulness.

On George's verandah was a supervisor of the Presbyterian missions and his wife. They had come through in a Land Rover from the Gulf of Carpentaria, where the Presbyterian Church maintained three missions, Arakun, Mapoon and Weipa. The Anglican Church had two on the 'Gulf side', one at Mitchell River and the other at Edward River, both missions always desperately needing staff. The two visitors must have come a risky and often trackless way, more than a hundred miles across the wildest part of the Peninsula. But the supervisor and his anthropologist wife were as casual as if they were driving down a suburban street.

In the cool living-room at George's house there were two young engineers from Lockhart River Mission. They had come in a blitz 'thirty-forty miles' from Portland Roads, where they had taken delivery of the mission's new tractor. Every distance in the Peninsula is 'thirty-forty miles'. A meticulous man will tell you it is between thirty-five to forty-five miles.

When the young engineers parted from us to drive to Lockhart, we did not see them for nine days. In the 'thirty-forty miles' to Lockhart they had to ford rivers, dig themselves out of swamps – it was the middle of the dry season. At the end of nine days they abandoned the blitz fourteen miles from Lockhart, and walked, the new red tractor chugging majestically along in front. They went back later and built a bridge to get the blitz across the river. Why didn't they build one good road and be done with it? They do, but every year the wet comes down and the floods sweep the bridges away.

'We had a novelist staying here once,' George's wife told me amiably. 'You're *sure* to know her. I wasn't here at the time, but she dropped in, in a one-man plane all by herself and stayed overnight. They had to anchor the plane with rocks or it would have blown away in the gale. Oh, you're sure to know her if only I could remember the name. George, do you remember the name of the lady who drank those three mechanics under the table and then walked quietly out and was gone in the morning?'

'I don't drink myself,' said George stiffly. 'She was a very ladylike woman. Brought her own rum and asked if I objected to her taking a drink. 'Certainly not,' I said. The three men who were here doing a maintenance job kept her company. She just looked down at them where they finally lay, yawned and said, "Well, I must get some sleep," and off she went. She was a well-spoken woman. You're sure to know her.'

The two young engineers from Lockhart had waited to transport us seven miles to the sea before proceeding overland to Lockhart with the tractor. They were kind young men, but so excessively rugged and pioneering that they resembled heroes from Somerset Maugham's more sarcastic short stories. They would be ready to take us down to the coast just as soon as they had the blitz repaired. There was something wrong with the generator. They had a long technical discussion with George about the gearbox where it seemed likely all the teeth had chewed up again. Meantime in the cool living-room they rolled cigarettes and talked about the inefficiency of the 'boongs'.

Out in the sun, Frank O'Brien, dark-skinned, a director of the Aboriginal Co-operative, was lying under the blitz removing the sump. Occasionally one of the young pioneers would go out and speak sternly to Frank, then stroll inside again.

'The trouble with John Warby,' George the Groundsman was saying, 'is that he's got no discipline. He doesn't know how to get the work out of these abos. It's no use being friendly with them. You've got to show them who's boss. What they do to engines is a crime. It makes me want to cry when I see how they treat a truck. They'll never make good mechanics. They haven't got it in them.'

The young engineers spoke even more sternly to Frank before coming in out of the sun.

Father Clint's face was taking on a grim expression. He caught my eye and we left the admirers of discipline.

'The kind of man,' Alf said quietly, 'that they send to a mission like Lockhart! You see what I mean?'

He walked across to the hot shade where a group of aborigines were waiting patiently for something to happen. They had been waiting for several hours. Father Clint introduced me to each man by name and, as I shook hands, spoke as courteously to them as he did to people of any race or colour. They were quiet, dignified men, pleased to see 'Father' again. Their eyes lit up when he told them I had brought this guitar.

'Gee-tah! *We* play gee-tah!'

'I'm probably the worst player in the universe.'

'World,' Alf translated. He spoke in clear, simple diction, avoiding the atrocious and ludicrous 'Stockman's English'. When we walked away, he murmured, 'They don't know what the universe is. I was out camping with them once, and they asked me which part of Australia Jesus Christ came from. "You think Jesus Christ was a white man?" "Oh yes," they said. "Certainly he was a white man." "Well," I told them, "it may interest you to know that Jesus wasn't a white man at all. He was much more like your Old People when they came to this country." That rocked them. And yet, you know,' he went on, 'in New Guinea, in the church at Erero there's a reredos of the Crucifixion. John, the beloved disciple, is wearing the rami of the theological college, St. John's. The soldiers wear the rami of the Papuan Constabulary. Mary is a village woman, the people passing by are Papuans. That's the way it should be.'

I was given the seat of honour in front beside the driver, holding a waterproof over Bimbi John in my arms. Rain, leaves and boughs slashed into my face as there was no windscreen. Alf, in the back with the crew thoughtfully provided to push the blitz out of bogs, said that at least I could see what was going to hit me, and, even if I didn't have a hand free, I could shut my eyes. Alf was half stunned and nearly scalped by a swipe from a branch that caught him on the back of the skull.

The young engineer drove Lockhart style. When the petrol tank, which was suspended on two unbarked saplings in the roof, fell off, narrowly missing his head, he got a piece of bark in his eye and stopped the blitz. He tried to start again but the battery had fallen out. We recovered the battery to find we were bogged, but with some yelling from the rear and heaving at the wheels, the dark-skinned team pushed us to dry ground.

Lloyd's Bay, they assure me, can lie still as a green leaf. My fortune has always been to encounter this great stretch of water in howling movement, the wind blowing along the shore and human figures insignificant in the slap and scream of the bay's bad temper.

A young boy came slowly along the sand, as the dirty little sloop, see-sawing at anchor, sent its dinghy crawling to the shore. The boy hardly lifted his feet from the ground, contemplating the indignity of a woman's task, carrying luggage to the boat. He probably had hook-worm. He was incredibly beautiful in a dull blue lava-lava, his black skin taking a blue shadow against the violent green sea. He walked like an uprooted tree or a tree that dreamed it was walking. When he set his foot down, there was an intimate communication of sole and dust.

Those were the impressions that my mind would keep: Cape Direction lying below the plane as it had done in my dream; the blue-black boy dragging his feet along the sand with the sea screaming behind him.

Other men dragged themselves up by the roots, and we were then in a confused struggle of bucking boat, wet spray, wet seats, bailing tins, an oarsman dipping into the suck and boil of the surf. Slowly we crept towards the *Mary Lockhart*, that dreary, greasy, little maid-of-all-work with her disgracefully weedy bottom, and her sail stained with diesel smoke.

Alf carefully took out the clean handkerchief he keeps for his false teeth. He turned the engine pipe so that the smoke blew its foulness away from him. 'It's the smoke that does it,' he muttered.

Three-Nose, who had gained that name in some unhappy accident, put his large foot on the tiller, and steered with it gripped between his toes. The sail went swinging and the first wave slapped over us on the deck hatch. I braced my feet against the rail and held the bundle of seasick child. Poor Bimbi John! He just shut his eyes and lay heavy until this too should be past.

Alf, exhilarated that he miraculously was not seasick, gave me a shouted lecture on the profits of trochus diving. Trochus, he yelled, was bringing over three hundred pounds a ton, pearl-shell five hundred.

'But they know – I've told them so often – they mustn't depend on just one industry. They need to build up the cattle. They've got three councillors and a thousand head of cattle. They need a cattle manager, better breeding stock. Ah!' His eye had been ranging the triple zone of mangrove, cliff, mountain that burned against the sky. 'I knew we couldn't make it. They're sending up the smoke signal from Rocky. They're waiting there with the blitz.'

'But we left the blitz at Iron Range?'

'This,' Alf said carefully, 'is another blitz.'

Bimbi spoke, for he had been impressed by our ride. 'Belly-buster,' he said, and closed his eyes again. He always called one blitz the Bellybuster. His name for the other was The Rhino, and it did rather look like a rhinoceros. It had a horn on the radiator.

The *Mary Lockhart* anchored well out from the reef and, awkwardly clutching bread and the radio set and the guitar, we sat with water round our ankles being rowed to shore. There was a reception committee drawn up. A huge, imposing, coal-coloured person in an army uniform with some kinds of red braid, that was my dear friend Charlie Claremont; and the little dark boy in the red lava-lava was his son Sammy.

Among the hulking notables was a small-sized, compact white man with a neat black moustache, black eyes, a handkerchief tied round his head, which made him look like a French pirate. I approved most the way he was clean cut around the edges. Most people are blurred, but he always looked as though he could never leave ends trailing behind him or loose and indefinite promises. He was exact.

'John!' I yelled, leaping overboard in my joy, and wading ashore wet to the knees. I shook his hand vigorously. 'I thought you'd be one of these six-foot blond he-men!'

I carelessly forgot to mention that I detested blond he-men. He thought I was disappointed and it upset his speech of welcome, wondering about this. My son walked over to Sammy, held out his wooden engine, and they went off hand in hand to play, ignoring large people.

While the luggage was rowed ashore we ate roasted crab claws and scones.

'I hope they aren't too long with those bags,' John muttered, watching the last wine-coloured fading of light. 'Even in the daytime it isn't really a track. After dark . . .' He hesitated and decided to let us find out.

We took our seats, mine in front, holding the living burden, beside John who was driving.

'Why the head-kerchief, John?' I asked. 'Local colour?'

'It keeps the mosquitoes off my bald patch, old girl.'

The army dignitary ran ahead in the cautious advance of the headlights. The blitz twisted from tree to tree. It leapt at deep gullies and rocks. Suddenly John bent down and grabbed me by the ankle. Perhaps, I thought, he has mistaken it for a gear.

'That,' I said carefully, 'is my ankle, John.'

'Yes, I know, old girl. Just put your foot there.' He placed it down gently. 'On the low reduction gear, will you? That's right.'

We ground down a ravine with a terrifying roar and surged up the other side. Before this drive is over, I told myself, I shall be just a paid-up insurance policy. Inside, where laughter is really good for you, I began to laugh silently. John had learnt to drive on that blitz, after he came to Lockhart. He was a deep-water man by choice. The steering, he explained, had a hundred and eighty degrees play until they took some of it up. He spun the wheel frantically. Then the lights failed. There was only the misty rain and the shrilling of insects in the dark.

'I am willing to believe the mission is rugged, John. You're laying it on too thick. Don't *try* so hard.'

'Don't have to try, old girl. We haven't got a torch, so I can't find the break in the wiring.'

'I have a torch in the knapsack.'

Alf was sitting on it. The break was repaired, after John had checked over all the wiring, and the lights failed only once again. There was something wrong with the petrol feed, so we stopped for that. It took three hours to cover a little over seven miles.

Then the tribesmen in the back sent up a wild, musical yodel to let the people know we were coming, and lights were swinging ahead, lights racing to meet us. Giddily I looked up at a tree with yellow-striped leaves and red flowers. I gazed at flashing white teeth in splendid smiles and heard the cries of admiration as the little white boy was lifted out.

In my old boiler suit they thought I was only a man, and they craned in to see the important visitor, with vivid expressions of amusement and pleasure. Three hundred black people and ten whites, they were all there, with every lantern Lockhart could bring out. They had been waiting for us since six o'clock, and it was now nine.

Bimbi lay down on the floor and quietly went to sleep while we ate Chinese food at the rectory. Hazel Conn, the hospital sister, was staying at the mission house with the Warbys, because Bunty was sick. 'Oh, just the fever – everyone has it, but it goes away in a day or so.' We were to have Hazel's house on the hill-slope back from the sea. It was a simple large room divided by partitions into bedroom, bathroom and living room. In the bathroom was an enormous bunch of bananas, a present from Alice Hann, who lived next door and ruled the school.

The bathroom had a tin dipper and a tin tub. There was a kerosene refrigerator, convalescent and needing care, a wire-netted and padlocked store cupboard, full of fabulous delicacies such as potatoes and methylated spirits, which people might be tempted to drink. The house was gay with flowers, and a cot had been specially brought from the hospital for Bimbi.

'Now have you everything you want?' Hazel asked. She was a graceful, thin, dark girl with the Lockhart haircut, a bang above the eyes and at the back as short as hair can be.

'What is the spear for, Hazel? Mission furniture?'

'That's in case the snakes come into the house. Well, if you have everything – see you in the morning.'

When I looked out of the window in the morning I would recognize the slope, Alice Hann's pineapple plantations and banana groves. In all of us there are places that uncurl out of our deep selves, and are more real than great cities. Lockhart was my own place, familiar even if I never lived in it, if I never saw it again – mine.

Down by the seashore, under the coconuts, the drums had begun. When anything stirs the tribes of Lockhart, they dance. They would be squatting huddled up by the small fires, just enough to warm the drums or light a cigarette of black plug tobacco, the old men with the nine drums of Lockhart, under the great mango tree below the village. The women would have sleeping children in their arms. Dancers would drift out like moths. The shuffling and chanting would all be rather casual and informal, taking time from the drums. The white sign of the Lockhart River Co-op. would proudly show on the corrugated iron store.

Quite a Challenge

The first morning bell, insistent, from the thatched church on the edge of the sea, brought me to the window to see if Alice's pineapples and bananas were as familiar as I knew they would be. There was her dark-brown house standing high on the hill, with a tall flight of steps going dizzily up to the verandah. The house hung up among the bananas and paw-paws like a bird's nest. There was the dark-brown slope of earth planted with pine-apples in flower, a smoky purple flower in a sunburst of rubies, with blue-green thrusts defiant at all points. The bird of paradise flower was like a fire lit in the leaves, and the scarlet bouvardia made a hedge where Morris was sweeping up frangipani blossom under the tall windmill by the mission.

Two young men, one in a pink lava-lava, one in a mauve, went by blowing on mouth-organs, their arms about each other's necks. They had flowers in their hair – 'Island custom'.

Alice came, little and neat in her print frock, skimming purposefully through her garden, with her Greek Testament in her hand! Frightful swank, I thought, for Alice to have a Testament in Greek! Just showing off her Th.L. But it was really an economy. She had had to study Greek, so why not use the book.

It occurred to me that I might go to church. The rearguard actions I have fought against going to church! Commando raids as a child, when I sat on the roof and refused to come down; adroit flanking movements of adolescence, and treaties and diplomacy later. But I had fallen in love! Some solemn vowing-in was needed.

Of course, I did wrong to go to church, raising expectations in the breast of young Jim, the rector, who had two church services a day, an expectation that I dared not disappoint. You would see me belting off to church at the bell, reacting like one of Pavlov's dogs. This was no particular hardship, because the church was the most beautiful church, and it just suited me. I could sit in it contentedly, while Jim and his bare-footed, white-robed team went on reading out some serial about how Ahab was hewed in four pieces, or the dogs drank someone's blood in the streets of Jerusalem. While I was in Lockhart, I heard some of the blood-thirstiest bits of the Old Testament – Judges or Kings, I think – and I just sat through it placidly looking out through the great arches at the sea, stony blue with cloud shadows.

The hospital hung out its washing among the frangipani trees and the sea hung out its washing surging white on the reef; and Jim went on reading about battle, murder and sudden death in old Jerusalem.

The church was packed to the doors that first morning, and

I made a swift comparison of the congregation you would get at Christ Church St. Laurence for a weekday service. The hymns were a full-throated harmonious uproar in 'language' – which is what whites call any native tongue not their own. The women sat one side of the church, the men the other, all clean and devout.

Of course, I should have realized that most had come to see the strange white woman, and everything would be back to normal when their curiosity was satisfied; but there was a gay exhilaration about Lockhart. There was vitality, and hope and pride. Certainly, I was in love with them all. I never fell out of love. And they were in love with themselves, with their new village, their new co-op., their new church. They were so eager!

Never enough hands to do the work; always makeshift and patch because there was no money. The Christians who drove to church in shiny cars in the city never sent more than their spare threepence and some old clothes. Everyone at Lockhart was working for a wage that any trade unionist would despise. Margaret, the rector's wife, with a little daughter; Bunty with four children; both women transparent from fever, but working, always working. Bunty keeping accounts, superintending the store, Margaret running the Children's Centre, where meals were served every day to the tiny ones, the bigger ones. Hazel, the hospital sister ('up and down all night like the pump of the windmill', as John said), going down to the hospital to sleep with a little baby suspected of T.B. of the glands, so that it wouldn't be lonely. Jim Eley, the rector, going out to cut up a bullock for meat, washing the clothes of the children who must be got ready to go up to Thursday Island for T.B. checks, teaching in the school, unweariedly loyal, quiet, with a dry joke, doing ten men's work, and making his church beautiful as well.

Bill had his forty-acre irrigation patch supplying the settlement with fruit and vegetables; Garnet was bringing through a water supply, piping water to Lockhart from Cutta Creek three miles away. William Namuch, the Torres Strait Island preacher, was building houses.

They were all so young. They were all so thin from hard work, and their faces shone with pleasure, that you knew what they were trying to do.

'Yes, it's quite a challenge,' Jim Eley said. He was melted because I appreciated his church. *He* thought it was the most beautiful church in the world. But then he had helped build it with his own hands. They poured out the story of the church, Jim and John telling me alternately, interrupting each other, supplementing each other, blending in as they always did, so that you had two men who even told a story together, in the same way that they worked together.

'We were building the new village.'

'Because we wanted to get them away from the land that was infested with hookworm. It was the most urgent job at the time.'

'The Torres Strait Islanders used to swagger ashore from their luggers and boast of their fine churches. We *promised* to build a church. Then we looked at the calendar and found there was just six weeks before the Bishop arrived to bless a church that wasn't there!'

'So we held a meeting and asked the people. They voted to stop work on the houses and build the church. St. James's Church it was to be – by St. James's Day.'

'We had to blast the trees out of the ground with dynamite.'

'We had to level the site.'

'We had to cart two hundred tons of rock.'

'Then there was the concreting.'

'Jim was the only man on the mission then who could drive – we had one old truck.'

'John was learning so we drove shifts.'

'Then Jim dropped a rock on his foot and crushed it, but he still had to drive.'

'Pat the engineer – he owns a gold-mine now over at Wenlock – rigged lights from the generator and we worked till ten o'clock at night. The people would have worked all night if he hadn't stopped them.'

'And how they sang! Women weaving mats, cutting pandanus for the roof thatch; children from the school. Old people who hadn't done a hand's turn for years because they were crippled up, begging us to let them help.'

'Then the tyres of the truck began to go. We laced them with wire. We hadn't any money for new tyres. Three weeks left and two tyres split. We laced the tyres with greenhide and put a greenhide sleeve over them. We had three nine-inch tyres and George at the airstrip sent us a ten-inch tyre, so we managed with that.'

'We had to bring the messmate bark for the walls and the blood-wood for the pillars. Those bloodwoods were thirty feet long,

and we dragged them behind the blitz. The trouble was if you
lost the track – and you know there's no real track to Rocky – you
couldn't turn with thirty feet of bloodwood behind you. You had
to go straight on.'

'On the day the Bishop landed they're putting up the triumphal
arches of flowers, and you could still hear the hammering where
they were finishing the altar. John decided the church looked a
bit bare, so he dug up some full-grown banana palms and planted
them all around.'

Jim smiled.

'This'll tell you what kind of man John is. They grew.'

St. James's is sixty feet long by forty-five feet wide, walled with
messmate bark that is brown on the inside and black and grey
outside. The roof is palm thatch, and it makes me think of the
lines that say: 'Better is a temple made of bark and thong, than
a tall stone temple that may stand too long.'

The bloodwood pillars rise to the towering roof, and you can
see the flakings on the glossy dark wood where it has been adzed
by hand. Everyone sits on the cement floor on cushion strips.
Dusky and secret with its red sanctuary lamp, the altar is as richly
covered as any, and behind it is a great hanging of jade-coloured
matting. One mural, a Crucifixion, roughly painted on wood,
is on the East side, in colours of red, purple, white, yellow ochre.

I heard about the church-building also from William Namuch.
Torres Strait Islanders are a keen, energetic race, and William
had been brought to Lockhart, not because John needed a lay
preacher – William had been trained at St. Paul's Theological
College – but because he would have wooed a builder on his
bended knee. William had a carved, good-humoured face, and
the physique his ancestors had developed leaping in and out of
war canoes.

'You see those beams across and also those pillars,' William
said in his bass-drum voice. 'We had two little blocks of rattan
belonging to the cutter and we lift the pillars with those.' He shook
his head wonderingly. Two rattan blocks, a double block on top,
one below, and a little stick – twelve feet long – to keep that great
weight up. It *never* fell.

'On the twenty-fourth we put up the bell-tower. I am on the
roof making fast inside the tower. 'Nother man putting on chapel
and vestry roof. 'Nother mob on the walls and the last job is to
raise the bell.

'On the twenty-fifth day My Lord Bishop arrives and we decorate the church. He come at seven in the morning and we still working. We got a few hours before the Dedication. First he must bless the houses in the new village. All is ready in time.' He sank to his chest notes. 'Now I will tell you a miracle. You know the blitz?'

I fingered the scar over my eyebrow where I had hit the iron frame of the windscreen when we fell into Stranger's Creek.

'Well, all that time, carting those rocks, carting those trees – that blitz *never once break down!*'

William liked a miracle.

'I will tell you a miracle,' he would say at evening service, standing against the gold altar in his white robes. 'You, Ben, you Joseph, know the men to whom this happens. I will tell you about prayer. There were three men who went out to get turtle, and they were good way out.'

Naturally, this was in the Torres Strait, where men are more reckless on the sea than any men in the world. These men seemed to have been incredibly careless. They lost their boat and found themselves swimming in the sea far from the land. This puzzled me, but evidently the congregation, with nods and murmurs of agreement, knew the kind of circumstances where a man would find himself swimming with no boat.

'You know I say true. They swim in the sea, and now it is dark – only three men.'

Three bobbing black heads of exhausted swimmers, waiting for the sharks, seeing the sun sink like a stone into the sea and the darkness cover them.

'So they come together,' William continued. 'They swim together in the sea, and they pray: "Lord, save us, we perish." They swim on, and in the dark their foot touch coral.'

'They had come to an island with no one on it, but there was a fire. They rested by the fire, and in the morning there was a boat on the shore. They searched the island but there was no one there, so they took themselves safely home.'

A good sermon, I thought it. There is some dignity in 'Lord save us, we perish'. John Warby said that he had thought it an impressive sermon the first time he heard it, but about the sixth time it began to pall.

'These Christian natives,' one white man said to me, 'they're a curse, and so are the missionaries. Ding-dong goes the church

2 *Kylie Tennant*

bell, and they knock off to say their prayers. Then they have a smoke and a yarn. Cheeky, lazy set they are. The missionaries ruin them.'

'When are they going to build that air-strip at Lockhart?' an air pilot asked. 'What do they *do* over there? Just sit in the shade?'

I tried to explain that the floods had come down and swept away the silt flats on which the food supply for the whole settlement was grown, and the tractor was needed for the gardens.

'They must be a lazy lot,' he said contemptuously. 'Not even a lighting plant or an air-strip.'

Lighting plants cost money. You have to scheme for things like that, and beg from the Department of Native Affairs. You have to wangle as though you were in the army. Take the water supply.

The water supply at Lockhart had for years depended on one decrepit windmill pumping from a well. When there was no wind, the people on the hill got no water, and maybe the people on the flat had none. Scheming for a supply of pipes to bring water from Cutta Creek was no use because the whole project would cost more than a church mission could ever afford.

John had a brilliant idea. He persuaded the mission to buy the telegraph line from Portland Roads to Wenlock, the whole telegraph line left by the army. Then he cleared the five hundred pounds it cost by selling the porcelain insulators. A team of Lockhart men under Frank O'Brien, whom I had first seen lying under the truck at Iron Range, then went out to camp on the Portland Roads.

They sawed the steel telegraph posts off level with the ground. They were hollow and would make excellent piping, if they were joined by concrete sleeves. The lazy aborigines spent some months transporting the pipes to the coast over vile tracks in the Bellybuster. They were completely without white supervision. They were doing the job for themselves and their new village.

Then they built a barge to take the pipes out to the *Mary Lockhart* and whichever of the luggers could be spared from gathering trochus. The pipes were brought thirty or so sea miles and dumped overside at Lockhart at high tide. At low tide the blitz came down and they were loaded and taken out to the pipeline. The men were still working on the pipeline.

To get out of work in Lockhart, you need to have one foot in the grave or both. I had made the mistake of writing a friendly little note saying that I did not want to be treated just as a visitor.

If there was anything I could do while I was at Lockhart . . .

'When we got your letter, Kylie,' John told me, 'we held a special meeting to decide where you could be best *used*. So we decided to open the new kindergarten. But as you'd be teaching there only half a day, we moved the co-op. classes for adults from the night. We decided we'd have a real push on the educational front, and we're going to have adult classes every afternoon. They're all keen to learn.'

'There's the illiterates' class at five,' Jim struck in, fanning himself. They assured me the temperature never went above ninety-five. 'If this rain doesn't stop we'll have an epidemic,' he added casually.

'Boys,' I said, 'I have never taught kindergarten. I have never taught adult aboriginals. I have never taught illiterates.'

'Don't let that worry you. We're all doing things we never did before.'

I felt grateful I was not serving meals in the Children's Centre as well. Sometimes I did.

The kindergarten was fun. We made up our own songs:

Clap hands for Daddy comes home,
Daddy comes home in the boat,
Bring me a trochus, bring me a pearl,
Daddy comes home in the boat.

Daddy also came home in the blitz and brought a wild pig. We played 'Here we go round the paw-paw tree'. Bimbi John sulked under the school because he did not get the best toys, and on one occasion some wicked boys took his pants off to see if he was white all over. But as the owner of the only toy cars for several hundred miles he was 'Bin-Bin', the King of Lockhart.

In the adults' class, huge black men in shorts and singlets rolled cigarettes and spoke in such soft murmurs I could not hear them. So we had pronunciation exercises. Before I left you could hear them reciting 'The Fighting Temeraire' at the other end of the settlement. We had lessons on how to make fish-traps, on bee-keeping, on the man who cut a slice off the moon to make his wife a comb for her hair, on What to Do on a Train or an Aeroplane. We wrote compositions.

'Who is the most intelligent boy in the school?' John asked.

'Isaac Hobo,' I replied promptly.

'Isaac?' John was disappointed. 'He chases girls. I've never seen any signs of intelligence in Isaac.'

'The others watch me in class, but Isaac's eyes are glowing with joy, and he watches much more carefully because at night in the village he is going to do a splendid imitation of me teaching. I wish,' I said wistfully, 'I could see him do it.'

The Illiterates' Class, also known as 'The Illegitimates', was a pleasant social little gathering that met to smoke and drink tea in the co-op. office, and admiringly copy the strange little patterns called letters. The bright star of the Illiterates' Class was that big, stout man whose skin shone like a well-polished stove, Charlie Claremont. He was captain of the ketch *Yola* and a co-op. councillor. In his spell ashore he was doing his best to learn to read and write.

'And now Charlie will read what I have written on the blackboard,' I would say. 'Come on, Charlie. You can do it.'

At the end of the long table Charlie would rise to his feet and hitch his belt, taking a deep breath as though about to dive overboard for trochus.

'My pot,' he read slowly, 'is on my mat in my . . .' A pause of indecision while Bella opposite framed the words with her lips. 'In my house,' Charlie finished triumphantly, looking across at Barney the policeman as if to say, 'Beat that!'

Barney shook his head admiringly and congratulated Charlie in his own aboriginal dialect. Everyone would take a drink of tea after this exhausting effort before we attempted the word 'horse'.

One of Charlie's incentives was that his adopted son, Roy, was coming home from college. There were many adopted sons and daughters in a settlement where for so long people had died of T.B. Sometimes a family would say to friends, 'You have no children. You can have this one for yourselves.' It made no difference whose child he was. He would be treated with the greatest affection.

Charlie's love for Roy was more than paternal. Roy was coming home. He would be on the 'plane now; he would be stopping off at Iron Range. Then there would be shouting and dancing on the shore. The two boys would step out of the boat. Roy was a slim, shy youth in beautifully creased trousers, a college blazer, well-mannered, careful of speech. You never heard Roy say: 'He bin come.'

Charlie, with joy and emotion, flaunted Roy before his relatives.

In church on Sunday, Charlie wore a white starched shirt and tie and polished black boots. After church Roy held a little court under the big mango tree. He had to explain all over again to the men who had come in from the eight-mile camp at Umedjego what college was like. You did not sleep on a mat there or catch fish with a spear. There were not even coconuts. There were roads and a train. Roy changed out of his grey blazer and slacks and put on a lava-lava.

Charlie had been looking forward to his holiday with Roy, but unfortunately on Sunday night the *Yola* put in with a tale of woe. The mate was down with fever; two men had been badly gashed by coral and had to go to hospital for penicillin. They hadn't much trochus aboard either.

Charlie packed his belongings in an old sack – his swimming trunks, his underwater goggles. Trochus is only shallow diving, so you don't wear helmets. In an old flannel singlet and shorts he came to say goodbye.

'Well, Charlie.' I quoted from our last lesson, 'Put shell in my boat.'

Charlie smiled; then he looked stern. 'No more writin', readin',' he said. He turned to John Warby. 'I s'pose *Yola* no come back before Roy go?'

'It's up to you, Charlie,' John said. 'You're the captain.'

'She no come back,' Charlie said firmly. 'Plenty trochus, eh? Good few tons that stuff, eh?' He nodded cheerfully.

'And next time you come ashore,' I said, 'you'll really learn to read and write.'

'Ho, yus,' Charlie said, but without much conviction. 'Father say co-op. men must have education. But,' he looked apologetic, 'Roy writes good. He write for me.'

He turned to Roy, patting him on the back, speaking to him in their own language. Roy nodded expressionlessly and watched the stout figure of Charlie go off towards the waiting boat. I could see that till the last Roy hoped he might go with Charlie. But the *Yola* would be away perhaps six weeks. The boy would be gone to college long before that. Already he was growing into new ways. Every time he came home he would be a little farther away from Charlie. He would learn all the things Charlie wanted to know and tell him about them. But it was going to be very flat in the Illiterates' Class without Charlie.

Missionary – Old Style

Alice Hann is 'old-style' missionary. She learnt her anthropology
from the tribe instead of at the university. She has spent months
at a time camping in the scrub with the women of the tribe.

'What were you doing there, Al?'

'I was the chaperon,' Alice said primly. 'And of course one girl
fell and fractured her skull, and I had to organize a stretcher and
bearers and get her back somehow. I always went walkabout with
the women.'

Alice looks as though her red hair has been bleached a little
by exposure. Her eyes are intensely blue, startlingly blue, as
though you had come on an ambush. She would be *petite* if she
were a chorus-girl, but she is as tough as barbed wire from digging
the garden. If it were not for Alice's garden, the staff at Lockhart
would have only tinned food at times. They go round to Al's to
cadge a paw-paw, some bananas, tomatoes, radishes, lettuce or
pineapple. No one goes away empty-handed.

'When I was in training,' Alice said, 'I was taught that if you
were a missionary, you must look after your health.' She had
come to dinner, a return for all the magnificent meals we had
eaten at her house. Now she stood up and took a firmer purchase
on her knife and fork and began to cut her steak. The ancestors
of that beef had been driven from Mitchell River on the Gulf side.
I had just lost two fillings out of my teeth on Lockhart beef, but
Hazel had put in a temporary filling.

Margaret, who looked after our house and wore her hair tied
in a knot on her forehead, was not an expert cook. She spent
most of her time looking after her little grandchild, Shirley, who
rode to work on her shoulders. One morning I found Shirley
washing her chubby hands in our drinking water. I tried not to
think what went on in the kitchen, because I could not make bread
and Margaret could. I needed Margaret.

'Tell me about the time you nearly starved,' I said, my thoughts
following a natural association.

'We nearly starved plenty of times,' Alice said dryly. 'I've seen
the chaplain during the service suddenly snatch up a candlestick
and smack it down on a snake. We needed that snake. We ate it.'

Perhaps some of Alice's passion for growing magnificent
vegetables and fruit stems from those lean years. She had decided
to be a missionary, but when other girls had secrets and dreams,

Alice had a secret too. She was going to New Guinea. Her whole life was set towards New Guinea. And as soon as she left school she began her training. A woman missionary was needed at Forrest River, on the far north-western bulge of Australia. So the young girl who was Alice Hann was given a few weeks to get ready. 'They had to have a woman because of the tabu. Men couldn't take charge of women. For instance, Meg and I once decided to translate the Creed into language, so we called in some women to help with the words. I asked what the word for 'born' was. They were very upset. "We will whisper it to you," they said, "but the men must never know." '

So Alice had to give up her plan for translating the Creed.

'At Derby, where the Presbyterians had their church, the tabu was so strong that they had to have a partition down the church, men one side, women the other. Of course, during the war they made me leave Forrest River, but the military soon asked me to come back, because, of course, the women couldn't have anything to do with men, particularly the sick ones or pregnant ones. This made it very hard for the military. After that I didn't see a white woman for a couple of years.

'The reason they wanted me to leave was because of the air-raids. The boat had just called and left stores for six weeks. We made them do for six months. The boat was hit by a Jap plane after it left us, but the crew volunteered to take it into Wyndham. There was another raid while it was tied up at the wharf there and the boat turned over. Weren't they mad at Wyndham! They not only didn't get any stores, but there were a thousand cases of beer on board – sank like a stone!

'The Japs raided Wyndham only twice. They couldn't land because the rise of the tide was thirty-four feet, and, anyway, the boat sunk beside the wharf prevented any more ships getting in.

'The first time they raided Wyndham we were carrying on as usual, so as not to alarm the people. The 'planes went over the mission and then we heard them all shouting, 'Wyndham's being bombed!' They heard the explosion thirty miles away. That time,' Alice gave her small shy laugh, 'was the only time I've seen a full-blood turn *white*! We had twenty minutes before the planes came back. I grabbed all my girls and spread them over the countryside under grass. Then I had to run back – I had the medical work too, you see – to check up with the Superintendent who'd called – "You get the girls out. I'll see to the sick."

'I was just walking back after making the check when I heard him yell, "Run. The 'planes are coming!" I had to dive into a prickly bush and stay there too,' Alice said disgustedly.

'When the military let me come back, we lived on "bush tucker". The stores had to come eight hundred miles from Broome over a bush track. A couple of times the military had to fly food in when we were pinched. But, mostly, we got by on snakes, grass seeds, lily roots, lily stems. We minded the children, and the blacks brought enough food to the mission to keep us alive. There was great rejoicing when food came and they could come back and live at the mission. After five years the doctor said I was a bit worn-out and I wasn't to go back again.'

Alice laughed. 'I was thinking of it the other day when some girls were cutting palms on the swamp, and they killed a twenty-two-foot rock python with their cane-knife. I heard them coming along the road singing at the top of their voices. They took him down to the village to cook him. Talk about python steaks! I always say you'd like goanna if you didn't know what it was.

'Well, immediately after the war, the Bishop – that is, our Bishop of Carpentaria – wanted someone to go to St. Paul's on Moa Island. The civilians were just going back to Thursday Island. I would be the only white person on Moa, and, not knowing the language, I wondered how I would get along with the people. They were wonderful. Mary Bann – she was a South Sea Islander, I think – had kept the school running all through the war, so that the education of St. Paul's had not slipped back. Mary Bann,' Alice explained, as though I should know this already, 'was responsible for Dorothy Sevika, the first Torres Strait Islander to go through Brisbane Teachers' College. Dorothy lived with Mary Bann. Then she went on a scholarship to St. Gabriel's.

'I was ten months at Moa, superintending the medical work, teaching at the school. I was registrar of births and deaths. I'd show people how to fill in Child Endowment forms and distribute the cheques. They cashed the cheques at the store. It was a Government store, but the Church has taken it back again now.

'Then the Bishop asked me to come to Lockhart, and I've been here ten years. Of course,' Alice looked prim, 'Lockhart was in a very bad way. Boats hadn't been able to get through with the stores, and the people were not well fed.' Many had died, but Alice was too discreet to say so.

'It was much harder work then,' Alice said judiciously. 'I had the medical work, and one night just after midnight a knock came at the door. I called out, "Who's there?"

' "Me."

'I asked what was wrong. It was Reuben Hobo. His little girl had tetanus.

'I asked if the child had walked on a rusty nail. "Yes," he said; "three or four days ago." There was no wireless then, no anti-tetanus serum. The boat was away calling in for a load of coconuts – we were out of food. We had been eight and a half months waiting for a new superintendent, and he had only been here twelve months when he went down with T.B. This,' Alice explained carefully, 'was the one before John – the one with T.B.

'I had three expectant mothers I wanted to take to Thursday Island, and I had to get the child away. The *Mary Lockhart* got in at midday, and I wouldn't let them even stop to eat. There was just a chance for the child. The chaplain organized the men to rush out and unload. In half an hour the patients were going on board. All I had to take in the way of food was half a loaf of bread and a piece of cold roast beef.

'Just off Rocky Point the engine broke down, a squall blew up and the child had her first fit. It took the mother and father to hold her. The crew asked if they could anchor and have something to eat while they repaired the engine.

' "No," I said, "you can share what I have, but you have to keep going." We ate "tucker finish" more or less. Eventually we got the engine going. It would run for an hour and then stop. The child had several more fits. My first experience of tetanus. It's a cruel death! About two in the morning the natives raised their death wail and two hours later the child died. Oh! The wailing at that hour of the morning in the dark!

'I went to the skipper and said, "You can anchor when you like. There isn't any urgency now."

'Dawn had just broken so we anchored at a small island about fifty miles up the coast. The crew went ashore to dig the grave. They had only a bucket and a tomahawk to do it with. The three expectant mothers went ashore. I came last, after preparing the body for burial. I said the 1928 Prayer Book service, the Service for the Burial of a Child.

'It twisted my heart to see the mother and father walking hand in hand away from the child's grave in the sand. They found two pieces of driftwood and made a cross. They never had another little girl; only three boys.

'We decided to have breakfast, as one of the men has speared a fish, and we divided the rations, half for today, half for tomorrow. There was enough for one meal a day. The damper was cooked and shared out – "little piece each". I took a bite – and, oh dear! – if you could have seen the faces of dismay. Kerosene had been spilt on the flour. We had to eat it. This was Sunday, and our last meal had been Saturday afternoon.

'I decided to push on to T.I. I was a bit worried whether my mothers would get there or not.'

Alice's mothers, you see. They probably towered head and shoulders over Alice, but there would never be any question for all Alice's quietness as to who was directing the voyage.

'We were in and out of rainstorms all day,' Alice continued. 'The injectors kept blocking. Run for an hour; then clean them. Run for an hour; then fix the engine. That night we anchored for four hours to get some sleep. There were five women and Reuben Hobo, two children, a baby in arms, and a little boy of five, plus a crew of three men. It was a case of one turn, all turn. I think,' Alice said reflectively, 'that we were wet all the time. I know I was.

'Midday next day we landed to get water. It was just an empty coastline. We didn't call at Somerset, where there were two natives living. Let's see. We had one meal Saturday, one Sunday, one Monday. Anyway, Monday we had a wash. The great storm blew up, so we had to get back on board, otherwise they mightn't have found our bones. No radio then. I had my fingers still crossed that the women might hold out. So.' Again Alice laughed, as innocently as a child, the way aborigines laugh when things go awry.

'We couldn't cook in the storm. We had damper soaked in kerosene and it was half-raw. That night we anchored at the tip of Cape York, and next day we made Thursday Island. I've never been back to T.I. since. But was I glad to see it! One mother had kidney trouble. Another had to have blood transfusions. But there were three new babies.'

Alice never did get to New Guinea.

Missionary – New Style

John would tease Hazel for being so thin that she had to stand twice in the same place to cause a shadow.

'*He* should talk,' Hazel said. 'I've just taken the bloodcounts, and guess who has the lowest? John. There he goes. Down to start the refrigerator at the Centre, then out to the boat-slip, down to the store. He'll be racing back for the radio schedule. He ought to talk about me.'

Hazel was finishing her surgery at the hospital. I was watching her take small pieces of coral out of a diver's foot, while I nursed the baby Hazel was anxious about because it wouldn't sleep. However, it liked me, nuzzling in a suggestive manner, and saying, 'Mum. Mum.' I figured out that its mother smoked black plug tobacco, like most of the people at Lockhart. Hazel was a non-smoker, so she didn't smell right to the baby. It fell asleep contentedly in my arms while I sagged under the weight and decided to give up smoking.

'Hazel,' I said, 'it doesn't seem fair. Here you are – quite good-looking. You have a loving family, a good home. You could go to dances and meet young men. Instead, you spend your time at Lockhart persuading women to come to hospital so you can deliver the babies. You rush around seeing that mothers feed the babies properly instead of giving them half a green banana and a piece of damper. You dress sores. You watch temperatures. But what do you get out of it?'

'You sound like my sister,' she said. 'Or, rather, you sound like both of them. My elder sister says I'm a fool. My younger sister thinks I'm a heroine and makes me feel silly. I can't explain to either of them that I'm getting so *much* out of it. I have such a rich life that I wouldn't change with anyone on earth.'

So very carefully we put the baby in its cot and went off to inspect latrines in the Old Village.

With us went James Butcher, a huge, gentle black person, dressed as a town councillor in a navy suit and open collar and black polished shoes. Jimmy sat in the back desk of my class and was too terrified to reply when I spoke to him.

I like the Old Village, which the mission staff regard with disfavour because the ground is infected with hookworm. In the Old Village, the houses are scattered at the will of the occupiers. In the New Village, they are ranged elbow to elbow along a street that is lively with dogs and cats and children. The New Village lies between the steep jungle and the seashore. The Old Village is around the hill about half a mile inland. Gentle old people sun themselves there, conservatives who prefer peace to the tremendous pace and hustle of modern life in the New Village. Old ladies may weave a basket out of grass, but for preference they just sit. Old gentlemen may roll a cigarette, but they do it at leisure. They don't exert their strength.

'I think that lavatory should be condemned,' Hazel suggested. 'No proper roofing. How would you like to walk all that distance and sit in the wet without an umbrella?'

We strolled through the village, Hazel occasionally stopping to enquire about some ancient's ailment, suggesting a visit to the hospital for a check-up. 'Yah-wo!' she would say, as we bid farewell, and 'Yah-wo' the villager replied. This is a Torres Strait Islander word for goodbye. The Islanders have been foraging down the coast for centuries. When I am told that the Five Tribes of Lockhart are full-blooded aboriginal, I have some mental reservations. Of course, the Islanders despise the aborigines as a lazy and backward race, but when an Islander was a long way from home he probably acted like any other man away from home.

Latrines at Lockhart was one of those subjects that cropped up whenever two or three gathered together for a cup of tea. Alf brought the subject up again by asking where I had been all the morning.

'I am in favour of deep pits,' he asserted, taking a hearty bite of scone. 'This method of sluicing the cans in the sea is unhygienic. Yesterday afternoon I go for a swim. I dive in and come up and there's Andy out behind me emptying sanitary cans. I mean to say, a man ought to be able to have a swim without striking him.'

'But in a hookworm area, Alf, salt water is about the best disinfectant you can get.'

'Deep pits,' Alf repeated stubbornly. 'Yes, I know you haven't got a sanitary truck or a depot, but when I say deep pits, I mean *deep*.'

Hookworm burrows up through the sole of the feet and the victim becomes lethargic and droops like a wilted lily. As the cure is nearly as severe as the disease, prevention is indicated. It is doubtful if the population would wear shoes except on occasions of ceremony. Perhaps they would if they could afford them. Educating Lockhart children to use lavatories was one means of prevention, and another was the vigorous dietetic campaign.

Hookworm does not affect well-fed people as much as under-fed ones, so that feeding was doubly important. After morning tea, Hazel, Bunty and I joined the staff at the Children's Centre. In the dining-room, with its graduated tables in three sizes, and its files of neat children lining up with their plastic plates and mugs, I was ordered to dole out spaghetti. Next to me, spooning out meat and gravy, was the Delilah of Lockhart, a coal-black, heavy-bosomed, middle-aged woman, built, I thought, rather like a tank. What could there be about Nina, I asked myself as I walloped spaghetti on to plates, that made her so desirable?

I asked Bunty about this later, and she said it was a very strange thing, but every time there was a scandal about Nina, or Nina was caught out with somebody other than her husband, Nina's husband moved up one into the place of the man the scandal was about. But scandals in Lockhart were not big news, and Nina and I smiled amiably at each other and wiped the perspiration off our brows and said it was hot, wasn't it? With the bread-oven practically glowing behind us, and the iron roof nearly as bad above us, we had cause for perspiration.

When Bunty first came to Lockhart, she fed the children who were obviously undernourished. There were so many that she and Hazel decided they might as well feed all the children. The mothers at first were rostered as voluntary aid, but it was always a faithful few who did the work. You find the same trouble in white communities. So at the Community Centre there was now a staff of six capable women under Nancy Paloo, who had studied dietetics at the hospital at Thursday Island.

Hazel, at mealtimes, Bunty when she was free, and any other woman on the staff who could come, would be down helping with such jobs as sieving vegetables for the babies, doling out iron tonic and powdered milk, spooning ice-cream or custard and jelly and tinned fruit.

Hazel and Bunty had their greatest triumph when a dentist who made a survey reported that he had found cases of arrested caries resulting from the improved diet. The children had been weighed and checked and definitely there were no underfed children at Lockhart. 'And not one positive case of T.B.,' the staff told each other jubilantly. 'We've licked the T.B. and we'll lick the hookworm.' Hazel received a hundred pounds from the church in her home-town and she immediately ordered a microscope and prepared for a series of tests.

When we trudged hungrily away for our own lunch, Bunty was leading by the hand a small black child clad only in a brief cotton singlet. She spoke quietly to the mother who could never be bothered to bring the baby in for a meal, then joined us in a rather grim mood.

'Ho-ho!' Bunty said, in imitation of the local accent. 'That Emma, she run up mountain one time too much. She no gammon me this time. Every time Emma bin tellem me, "This man wrong totem. No no can marry 'im?" ' She lapsed into her own speech. 'But this time, by gum, she'll have a husband and look after those children whether she likes it or not. She's goanna-totem and the old men say there's no impediment. Always before, the man's been married or he's the wrong totem.'

Alice, who had been issuing stores for the next meal, smiled. 'A goanna is not really supposed to marry a sting-ray,' she said, 'but I have known it happen.' She hesitated, and then decided to tell her story.

'A former chaplain,' she said discreetly, 'was most anxious to see more permanent unions before he returned to the city.' Making a list of all the marriageables and their totems, he had paired them off in correct tribal alignment. The last half-dozen or so he announced had either to marry out of their totem or remain permanently single. Then before he shook the dust of the place off his shoes, and went off, leaving Alice alone in charge, he married off every marriageable couple.

'Thirty couples in one day,' Alice said. 'You wouldn't believe it, would you?'

'Dat feller better come back one time,' Bunty declared fervently.

Alf was always restless when he heard the staff at Lockhart use 'Stockman's English' to the people. The trouble is that 'Stockman's English' is a gingery kind of slang, grammatically horrifying, but easy on the tongue. 'Tucker finish' means, in various contexts, that there is no more dinner left, there will be no further ration at present, or that it is extremely likely that everyone will die of starvation. 'All bugger-up' indicates that the engine does not function, the boat, house or crop is entirely destroyed.

It was Store Day, so after lunch I accompanied Bunty down to the bark-sided building under the great, scarlet-leaved almond tree. Bunty sat at a table just inside the door, and Barney, the policeman, in an orange singlet and blue pants, stood outside.

'You sing out these people I tell you,' Bunty commanded, and as Barney called the names, the women came up one by one, to put their thumb-print on a form for child endowment.

'Slack 'im,' Bunty told those who tried to press the ink through the wood of the table. To those who attempted to overstretch their credit she was curt. 'No, George, I can't give you a pound this time. You've only got your wages.'

In bundles near her were the savings bank books, the trochus books, the account books. 'Part of the child endowment money goes to pay for food at the Children's Centre,' she explained to me. 'The Department of Native Affairs gives us a grant for that, too. The costs of shipping that tinned stuff are fabulous, but we buy in bulk and that cuts it somewhat. This is the trochus book. The skipper puts in the total, each man is paid for what he brings in, and a bonus for whatever trochus he brings in over a certain quantity. The co-operative sets aside forty per cent to pay for the debt on the boats, fuel, gear, repairs, capital. Forty per cent goes to the divers, and twenty per cent is voted to the mission. For instance, we paid for the timber flooring for some of the houses in the New Village out of the last trochus cheque. We're hoping to spare some for a movie projector.'

'What about the plumber's fittings and the new windmills?'

'The Department of Native Affairs is going to give us those. Every time John goes to Thursday Island he has long talks with Con O'Leary, the Director of Native Affairs. Con O'Leary is all in favour of what is being done here. He's a great help.'

Bunty knew every man, woman and child in Lockhart; their private crimes, their secret ambitions, their relationships, their family feuds.

'That milkman of ours is a psycho,' she said with a chuckle, as we walked towards the mission house, when the store closed. 'He really is a case. Every time he decides to hate the white race, he lets the cows go bush. He has a holiday, the cows have a holiday, and we don't get any milk.'

'Why don't you get a new milkman?'

'Oh no!' Bunty was surprised. 'He snaps out of it in a day or so.'

One of Bunty's retainers has a job at the mission house because she has epileptic fits. Another is so old she can only totter about. Bunty's household reminded me of the feudal manor or an old Southern plantation. There was the mission house, perched like a castle on the hill, with the village nestling at its foot, and Bunty, with this living web at her fingertips, indispensable, and a hierarchy of people who knew each other, not superficially, but in the daily judgment where you stood on your own worth and were valued for what you did and tolerated for what you failed to do.

In such a small community there was no disguise. You were not a unit of consumption, a number in a file, a notation in a department set of statistics. You were a person.

John and Alf were waiting for us on the verandah. They were discussing the aboriginal problem.

'Oh, blow the aboriginal problem,' Bunty told them. 'Isn't it bad enough to have Emma and Nina, the Ropeyarn family and the Hobos and the Warradoos, without the aboriginal problem as well?'

But when Bunty is sick, it is the people who are worried.

'She my *friend*,' Bella explained to me. Bella, a tall, thin black girl in my Illiterates' Class, was learning to read quite fluently. 'So she said I was her friend?' Bunty commented when I told her. 'Well that's better than being Missus, isn't it?'

THE FACE OF DESPAIR

When the waters of the first flood went down, the town of Narbethong emerged with a reputation for heroism. 'Brave but encircled Narbethong holds out,' a city paper announced, and a haze of self-conscious sacrifice like a spiritual rainbow shone over everyone. Women who would ordinarily have used harsh words if a husband came home late to his tea, were cooking for thirty on a spirit stove with the greatest cheerfulness. Families who made a fuss when a guest stayed for the weekend, walked unceremoniously across the bodies of complete strangers lying in rows on their upper landing. The most popular men in the town

747 The Face of Despair

were the policemen who, in an army duck, worked night and day evacuating grateful families. When they could safely descend into the mud, the residents swapped anecdotes and photographs while comparing the height of the watermarks on their wallpaper. There was a feeling abroad that Narbethong had defeated the flood single-handed.

The water receded only gradually. It lurked in backwaters and billabongs that had not been full since the great flood of '98. Below Paddy's Bend there was a new channel which led to lawsuits and trouble over fences. As the river retreated, it scattered its loot: tree-trunks, haystacks, buggy wheels, the carcasses of sheep. Neighbours returned any chattels found in their back yard if they were recognizable. The librarian moved down the thousands of books which had been moved up so hastily that they had to be catalogued all over again. Strong men grunted and cursed as they strove to shift a sideboard or bed which one small housewife in a panic had been able to drag up all by herself.

The farmers, ruined as usual, were trying to find corrugated iron, barbed wire, food for the surviving pigs. Somehow they felt they should live up to the high valour of the flood and hang on until the next cheque came in. Men who had put off painting the house decided they must do something about it. Wives demanded new covers and curtains. Furniture was hosed down; the awful decayed smell lessened a little. The piles of blackened and stinking water hyacinth were carted away. Where silt had formed a deep inlay in the woodwork, owners went over the carving with a clothesbrush. Refrigerators and radios were repaired.

'Look!' the town seemed to say. 'We've come through.' And the editor of the local paper closed his columns to any letter which mentioned silt, afforestation or erosion.

Presently, mile after mile unfolded the heart-lifting green of young oats, potatoes, lucerne. The river, like a silver snake, wriggled back into its bed coiling along deep below the level leafage so that strangers asked: 'But where is the river?' It twisted humbly past the town's backyards, collecting the old tins and bottles as usual, forgotten in its deep soil ditch.

The new paint was shining on the houses, most of the elderly people had recovered from their lumbago, the bronchitis epidemic was over; and then, out of all reason, the rain began again. The silver snake down below swelled, took on a new mottled brown skin. In the evenings there were people walking along the path just looking at the river. They said very little. When the rain stopped, even the trees seemed to sigh with relief; but the clerks in the Court House were already taking their records away in trucks.

Then the river was racing, powerful hideous. It was over the banks below South Narbethong; it had crept round and taken the town in the rear, cutting the main road so that the buses roared through a foot of water; it came slowly down the gutters of the back streets leaving the embankments still reassuringly dry, but joining puddle to puddle like a miser making an investment. The librarian at the city library set about stripping the shelves of books again, and cursed small unladylike curses.

'It won't come any higher,' old Doctor Riley announced, when his daughter wanted to move the furniture upstairs. He was always gruff and positive and, before he retired, the more a patient failed to respond to treatment, the more positive Doctor Riley became. 'I know what I'm talking about. Leave the furniture alone.'

At four in the afternoon the clouds parted, the sun shone over a landscape of mauve water with the delicate pale green of willows smudging the distance. Here and there what might otherwise have been a rather flat and monotonous expanse was lifted by a pleasing touch of scarlet where a house roof just showed above the waves. In the older part of the town, cars were being loaded, revved up, and raced to higher ground in the new town or the heights towards the gaol. The railway station was an island connected to the mainland by an overhead bridge. And the water began to pour over Dr. Riley's doorstep. In half an hour it was a foot deep in the front hall.

'Look at it!' his daughter shouted – she was usually a meek and forbearing woman. 'Not a thing saved.' And she spoke of her father in wrath and bitterness.

The doctor took no notice. He waded into his study and tucked under one arm a supply of cigars; under the other the stuffed trout in its glass case, a trout he had caught in Lake Neish on his trip home to Ireland.

'They say that the dam may break.' His daughter spoke as though this were a judgment on her father.

'Let it,' he grunted, and went upstairs to bed where he stayed smoking philosophically.

Down the main road came sailing a traffic of great clumps of water hyacinth. They swirled straight along the middle of the road importantly passing and re-passing each other. The road was now navigable and the current running strong. The police began to go round in their ducks rescuing the inhabitants, but a strong resistance movement was developing. They refused to be rescued. They had had one flood – that was enough.

'But there's a crack in the wall of the dam,' the constable in charge of the duck explained. 'You could have twenty feet of water down on top of you.'

'If the dam's going to bust,' one householder argued, 'it ain't much use ferryin' us up to the new town. If the dam goes, that'll go too.'

'You get in this boat,' his preserver snarled. 'Come on now.'

Nobody went to bed. In the minds of the townspeople was a picture of a huge grey wall slowly crumbling outwards over the treetops; but they all had a mutinous feeling that just by staying put they were defying the water to do its worst. They wouldn't shift, no, they wouldn't shift, even though they might be swept away. The rain came down as though it was being baled out of the clouds in large celestial buckets, and it looked as though the darkness and the rain were to be the death-watch of Narbethong. But in the face of this renewed malice there was no heroism, only a grim indignation and a kind of dignity.

At the little private maternity home, Annabelle, who did all the cooking and housekeeping for Nurse Aarons, went down into the kitchen to make a cup of tea.

'Never again,' Nurse was saying. 'All these years and the stairs so bad, up and down those stairs keeping the place open, taking up trays and sometimes bad cases, little babies – oh dear – and their mothers. And now we've had all the walls re-papered and new linoleum – no, Annabella, I can't stand it. I can't bear to think of it. The mud – it's too much work with my rheumatism. I'll shut the place. I can't start again. I won't. No, not again.'

Meanwhile she continued to tend four mothers and four newly born babies, while Annabelle, splashing about in a pair of fishermen's waterproof boots, cooked all she could until the water poured over the stove top.

When Nurse's two brothers came to rescue her in a rowing boat, they opened the front door, and the grandfather clock floated out to meet them like a large and elaborate coffin. They pushed the clock inside again, shut the door and went round the back.

Nurse and Annabelle leaned over the balcony rail like two princesses in a tower.

'No, indeed, Charlie,' Nurse said, 'I couldn't leave.'

'But the dam may go.'

'I can't help that. I'm not responsible for the dam. Last time,' Nurse said darkly, 'that linen bedspread floated away, and when I went to a bridge party at Mrs. Smith's, there it is as large as life made into a table cloth and serviettes. She said it was buried in the mud and not claimed.'

The police came and took the patients off. The police did not seem to realise that they were now identified with the flood, were part of it, and shared the feelings it aroused. One of them stood to lift down the patients and lower them, while he balanced in the rocking boat. He tried to make one lie down in the bottom of the boat. The woman glared at him.

'How perfectly ridiculous,' she said shortly. 'The idea!' She sat up straight and continued to snort and mutter. None of the patients was pleased about being rescued. They wanted to stay with Nurse. The last to descend, wrapped in a fur coat curiously distended, really threw the young constable into a state of panic.

'Be careful, madam,' he urged. 'Be very careful.'

From the front of the fur coat emerged the striving head of Nurse's cat. He too hated to be rescued.

In the old manse at the end of River Road, the wife of Harry Scott, the town's solicitor, was preparing for the siege. They had bought this dilapidated house because Peg Scott was an artist and could see its possibilities. They had done all the repairs themselves, and though there were still parts of the bannisters flapping like a rag, and a new set of leaks after every shower, the Scotts were proud of their home. Peg had moved up to the attics all the antique bits of furniture picked up cheap at sales, the walnut writing desk, the carved bed, the big mirror from the mantelpiece in the front room. She was plump and jolly and efficient; her husband and small daughter were safe with them upstairs playing rummy and eating sardines. They had plenty of food.

'I want you to remember everything about this, Winnie,' Peg ordered. 'You'll be able to tell your grandchildren. Dad used to tell me how in '98 the boat he was in was nearly shipwrecked in the awning over the chemist's shop.'

From farther up Bridge Road came a raucous shout of boatmen outside the house of a lady of no reputation. 'Come on, Rosie,' they yelled. 'There's eight of us out here waiting for you, Rosie.' But Rosie had already left.

'Mummy,' Winnie observed sedately, 'if the dam breaks I mightn't have any grandchildren.'

'There!' Peg raised her eyebrows dramatically at her husband. 'She takes after you. Always looking on the bright side.'

Their neighbour had seen the patrol boat approaching. 'Wait till I open the gate for you,' he cried hospitably, then gave a startled howl as he stepped into deep water. Peg hoped Winnie would not remember some of the things he was saying.

The boat approached the Scotts' lamplit window. Its own quite dazzling light shone over the dark water and disturbed the ducks sleeping in the wistaria on top of the pergola. The ducks had had a wonderful time eating all kinds of foods: frogs, insects and pieces of soaked pumpkin. Peg thought, it would be too fantastic to paint a picture entitled 'Ducks and Wistaria'. With those orange pumpkins floating in the foreground and the peculiar mauve shade of the water when the sunlight had struck it – but, no, no one would believe it.

'Come on, all out,' a dark figure ordered.

'Oh,' Peg groaned with disappointment, 'they can't *make* us go.'

'I think we had better, dear,' Harry Scott apologised. 'After all, the water is level with the verandah roof.' Peg wanted to argue about it. 'I heard they plunge hypodermics in people who refuse to go,' Harry urged. 'Besides, there's Winnie.'

'I won't go without Jessamine,' Winnie said stoutly. Jessamine was her baby doll, complete with bonnet and bootees.

Peg gave in. 'Here,' she said viciously, 'catch!' and flung Jessamine out the window. The policeman in charge, seeing what he took to be a baby whirling through the air, decided the woman had gone mad. With a yelp of horror he flung himself forward on his knees on the verandah roof and made the catch of a lifetime.

He had his revenge a minute later when the efficiently-clad Peg, in her plaid skirt, climbed out the window and found herself suspended from a stout nail. Delicately averting his face, the policeman set about freeing her while Harry carried Winnie down. The Scotts sat in dignified silence until their preservers set them ashore on the steps of the Town Hall.

'You'd better take Winnie round to your mother's,' Peg said coldly. 'I'll go to Jane's flat.'

In looks, Jane was as unlike her sister Peg as possible. She was frail, beautiful, and willowy, with a voice that rose to a delicate shriek, and long slim hands that she waved vaguely. But both of them were strong as barbed wire. When Peg burst in, Jane had just finished explaining to her husband how she carried all the furniture upstairs again single-handed, and she and Mervyn were arguing over the wall-to-wall carpet.

'No,' Mervyn said desperately, 'I won't do it. It's too hard to put down again. You know it shrank last time.' Their flat consisted of a kitchen, the back-stairs, and two servants' rooms, of what had been a great house.

'Too hard to put down!' Jane cried. '*You* never lifted a hand. Mother and I put it down.' She turned to her sister. 'He's only just come in. Never a word as to where he has been all day.'

'I walked over the railway bridge to the heights.'

'What on earth for?'

Mervyn looked confused. He glanced round his home which was furnished with one hard chair. A candle stood on top of a box. 'Had to go somewhere,' he muttered.

'But what did you do all day?'

'I was helping dig a grave,' Mervyn said angrily.

'Whose grave was it?'

'I don't know. For God's sake, Jane! I haven't had anything to eat either!'

Jane immediately became a ministering angel and flew upstairs to find food. While Peg told them her news, Mervyn sat morosely eating bread and hardboiled egg, and contemplating in his mind's eye that grave full of water, the red clay, the sucking noise as they pushed in their spades.

Harry Scott came in quietly from bestowing his daughter and reassuring his mother. 'Where do we sleep?' he asked.

'Oh anywhere, Harry,' Jane said. 'You might be able to dig out an armchair.

At least the water was no higher by breakfast time. 'You girls stay home,' Mervyn ordered, as he took Harry off to reconnoitre. But the girls could not stay home. Restlessness seized them. There was nowhere to sit, nothing to do. They prowled out, down the main street to the water's edge, meeting little groups who walked to and fro as uneasy as they.

'This is the finish,' one man said to another, looking at the brown lapping flood. His neighbour nodded almost without emotion. 'That's right,' he said. 'The stone finish.'

He looked across to where his farm had been, the crops which would have cleared his debts from the first flood, flattened and gulped down; the sodden pumpkins knocking against the back door where nobody was at home, the windows darkened by great piles of water hyacinth crowding its snaky flesh strands against the glass to blur out the light.

Then he looked down at his boots, solid boots for solid land. A froth of yellow soapy bubbles piled up about them, an unhealthy froth like that on the glasses of mineral water in the window of a refreshment room. This spume tossed ashore wherever there was a backwater. The farmer kicked at it; some of it flattened, some of it clung to his boot. He wiped it off on the grass, disgusted.

'Let's go across,' Peg said suddenly, 'to the heights.'

The rain was coming down again, beating on their eyelids, running down their necks. But over there, beyond the old town, the heights were carrying on a normal life. It would be better than standing like this on the edge of a nightmare unable to come or go, standing fascinated in the squalid foam. Occasionally a boat battled across from the new town on the heights, and presently a motorboat came by with two policemen, one of them the young man who had rescued Peg not so many hours before.

When they reached the heights, the passengers disembarked on the steps of a garage and went leaping and scrambling out with the help of their umbrella. There remained in the boat only Peg, Jane, the two policemen and a little wretched old woman with blue lips. Her feet were bare. She shivered continually, sitting huddled up.

'Oh, her poor feet,' Jane whispered. The boat headed towards the gaol. 'But you're not taking her *there!*' Jane cried. 'Oh no, what a shame! All she wants is a good cup of tea. You let her come home with me.'

'She'll be all right,' the policeman assured his indignant passenger. 'Vagrant, see? Got no place to sleep, doesn't belong to anyone.' The little old woman sat dumb. 'Come along, flower,' the young constable said gently, hooking his big hand under her elbow. He walked her ashore, considerately suiting his slow stride to her weak and tottering walk.

'But we're all vagrants,' Peg thought. 'We haven't anywhere to go.'

'Oh her poor feet,' Jane whispered again. She said no more.

Her husband had looked in the face of despair, and for him it had been a hole in the clay filling with muddy water. For the farmer in the thick boots it was the foam in which he had wiped his feet; but for the two women silently watching that little procession stumbling towards the gaol, the tall constable, the poor half-dazed old bit of humanity, the face of despair had blue lips. Despair does not cry out or behave itself unseemly, despair is humble. There is no pain left in it, because it is what the farmer said it was – 'the stone finish'.

The rain began again, and now they were over the other side of the flooded town, there was nothing to do, nowhere to go. 'We'd better be getting back, Peg suggested. But the difficulty was to find anyone going over.

'Mervyn and Harry are going to be so mad about this,' Jane sighed. It was getting dark, and the lights of the new town came over the waters in a comforting and reassuring way. There was a wonderful sunset.

Finally a boat took them off and carried them over to the Town Hall steps. The current seemed not quite so fierce. They hurried up the darkened street and clattered in the back door.

'Where have you been?' Mervyn was so angry that he swore at them. 'Quick! upstairs. Get upstairs.'

'But we couldn't help being late, Mervyn. We're sorry.'

'Sorry? Sorry! We've nearly gone mad. Word's come through that the dam's going any minute. Get upstairs. It's the *dam*, I tell you.'

'Oh dear,' Jane said wretchedly, 'the carpet! I knew we should have taken up the carpet.'

NANCY CATO, 1917–

Born in Adelaide, she was a journalist and critic for
the *Adelaide News* 1936–1958. For the past forty
years she has been primarily a writer of fiction with
her trilogy, *All the Rivers Run* (1978) being her most
popular work. Her historical novels are family sagas
which illuminate the relationship between individuals
and the environment and which are set in a
framework of social comment. Her concerns are
contemporary, often controversial; she deals with
issues from the treatment of Aborigines to the threat
of the bomb. The constant contradictions and conflicts
experienced by women through changing social patterns
form themes that run through much of her writing.

   Green Grows the Vine (1960) and *Brown Sugar*
(1974) are among some of the best known of her
works; the following short story was first published
in *Quadrant* (1970) and points to the quality of her
writing.

THE OLIVE STEALERS

Some people are born with trusting natures. Though I am one
of these, the first time my faith in human beings received a set-
back I must have been no more than four or five, for I was still
attending the local kindergarten.

   My current boy-friend was a thin little boy with snowy hair
and the name of Ronnie Grubb. We used to go home for lunch
together, in the company of a rather despised fat boy called Maxie.

   On our way we would pass a house with a large garden,

bordered by an unclipped olive hedge.

One day we noticed that the green olives had ripened, turning to glossy black fingers among the silvery leaves. Ronnie (whose mother kept him in a state of painful cleanliness, no doubt in an attempt to counteract his unfortunate name), was fascinated by the purplish-red ink the olives exuded when squeezed.

Maxie at once realised their value as ammunition. Hostilities were opened, Ronnie issued an ultimatum, and war was declared. I sat on my small case at a safe distance, a neutral observer.

After a while Ronnie was no longer painfully clean, most of the easily-reached ammunition was used up, and the boys grew tired of war. 'S'go!' called Maxie.

'C'mon!' cried Ronnie, calling me back from where I had wandered off in pursuit of a tiny blue butterfly with papery wings.

'Right-o,' I said, and we moved off as one, like a flock of sparrows.

Without giving it another thought – and establishing a pattern of behaviour which has since left a trail of lost property half across the world – I abandoned my school case and went home without it.

As I was passing on my way back from lunch, alone (for Ronnie and Maxie were still being scrubbed clean by their irate mothers) a tall grey figure rose behind the olive hedge, topped by a face with spectacles and a grey tweed cap. A long grey arm reached over the hedge, and a voice said, 'Is this your case, little girl?'

'Oh yes, thankyou!' I beamed gratefully. 'I must of left it behind, before. When we was playing here a bit.'

'Was – er, were you picking the olives?'

'Maxie and Ronnie was. I don't like them much.' What I meant was that I didn't like the stains they made on my fingers. Nobody could possibly *like* them, they were so obviously and horribly uneatable. Pickled black olives I had never heard of, and olive oil was something that came out of a bottle.

'Do Maxie and Ronnie go to school with you?'

'Yes. We go to Kindy. Over there.' I swung my retrieved case in circles and started to move off. 'Thankyou for minding my case,' I said politely. 'Goodbye.'

'Goodbye, little girl.'

The next morning a grave-faced kindergarten teacher called to us as soon as we arrived.

'You three, come over here, please. I want to talk to you!'

Wonderingly, and wearing expressions of bland innocence (for we had not chased sheep nor fired catapults nor hung by our legs from the dangerous high branches of the pine-tree; our consciences were clear) we went up to her.

'Mr Prisk, who lives down the road, has been to see me,' said Miss Ramsay, 'and he is very cross. He says you three have been stealing his olives.'

'STEALING!'

'His old olives!'

'We didn't.'

'He says that two little boys called Maxie and Ronnie, and a little girl whose name was written inside her case, pulled half the olives off his hedge. And when they saw him coming they ran away. And the little girl was in such a hurry to get away that she left her case behind.'

Afterwards, when we were kept in at recess-time to write a note of apology to Mr Prisk, the boys said it was all my fault. If I hadn't left the case behind, they said, we wouldn't have been 'caught'. And why had I told him their names?

'Because he didn't say anything, see? He's a mean old thing, and I thought he seemed such a nice man.'

Mr Prisk had got his version of what had occurred in first, and I had a glimpse of the erratic workings of justice in an imperfect world.

Mutinously, and with much-varied calligraphy we produced a joint effort on ruled paper, one line each:

Dear MR Prisk,

We are sor-ry we

took your o-lives

'And I hope the old beast gets as sick as sick when he eats the rest of them,' I said darkly.

I don't suppose Mr Prisk died of a surfeit of olives, but it was not many weeks after this when he was called to his Maker.

In those days I had a lively curiosity about dead people, and the trappings of funerals. Passing on my way from kindergarten in the afternoon I examined with interest the shiny hearse standing outside his house, the flowers piled on its roof and set inside in little silver vases.

Mr Prisk, or rather his earthly remains, would still be in the house; but his spirit, which I imagined vaguely to inhabit his chest and the upper part of his body, would already have gone up to Heaven.

I wondered intensely how a dead person looked after a part of him had been thus whisked away to the angels. Would there be a hollow shell, rather like the shed carapace of a crab, semi-transparent and empty? Or just a space, or what?

I turned in at the gate to make a last call on Mr Prisk. After all, I'd had a sort of bowing acquaintance with him in life. Grasping my small case firmly, I marched up to the open door. Some men in black clothes stood in the hall. They stared at me silently.

In the doorway of a room beyond stood two tearful matrons, plump ladies in flowered hats and damp handkerchiefs, who looked both surprised and shocked to see me. I went forward.

'What is it, dear?' asked one of them, putting out a hand to arrest my progress.

'I wants to see Mr Prisk.'

'I'm afraid you can't do that, dear.' She lowered her voice to a whisper. 'Mr Prisk is – '

'Mr Prisk has passed away,' said the second lady hollowly.

'Yes, I know, but not all of him,' I said reasonably. 'I only wants to see the part what's left.'

There was a peculiar silence at this. I saw their eyes meeting over my head. One matron made a limp gesture as if to say, You do something about her, it's beyond me.

'Listen dear,' said the first one, creaking in her stays as she bent down to my level and took my hand in her plump fingers, 'you want to say goodbye to Mr Prisk, is that it? He was a friend of yours? Now, I'll tell you what we'll do; we'll go into the garden and pick a dear little posy, and I'll put it in the coffin with him. You can't go in there now – '

She nodded at the room beyond, which was full of people looking solemn and somehow guilty for being still alive and healthy while Mr Prisk was dead. 'All his relatives are there, and besides, you're very young, and, er – '

She was propelling me out of doors during this flood of words, and I had no chance to say that the dead man was no friend of *mine*, or to explain the purely scientific interest of an inquiring mind.

I found myself unwillingly picking Cecile Brunner roses in the garden, while I imagined Mr Prisk looking down from Heaven (the top part of him, that is) and complaining to God, 'Look, she's stealing my roses now . . .'

FAITH BANDLER, 1918–

Aboriginal rights activist and writer, Faith Bandler
was born in Murwillumbah, New South Wales, the
daughter of a Pacific Islander who had been brought
to work in the Queensland canefields by slave traders
in the 1880s. Her father's narratives are contained in
her novels *Wacvie* (1977) and *Marani in Australia*,
(1980, with Len Fox). Co-founder of the Aboriginal
Australian Fellowship (1956), which challenged
discrimination against Aborigines, and the director of
the referendum campaign which established equal
citizenship rights for Aborigines under the Australian
constitution (1967), she is a powerful and perceptive
critic of exploitation, and a champion of justice. Her
fictional output includes *The Time was Ripe* (1983,
with Len Fox) and *Welou, My Brother* (1984).

The following extract is from *Wacvie* and helps to
reveal Faith Bandler's commitment to giving
expression to some of the slave stories that have been
suppressed and that until recently have gone untold.

WACVIE

Introduction

This is the story of my father, Wacvie Mussingkon who, in June
1883, was kidnapped from Craig Cove, a village on the coast
of Ambrym Island in the New Hebrides. He was sold as a slave
in Mackay, Queensland, and worked on the sugar plantations
until he escaped in 1897, finally settling at Tumbulgum in New
South Wales, where he died in July 1924.

Remembering the vivid stories my father told me about life in his village, I was bursting with curiosity; I wanted to see for myself the kind of people my father came from.

In May 1974 I went to the New Hebrides to find his village. Arriving in Vila, the capital of the New Hebridean islands, I asked around how I might get to Ambrym and the village of the Mussingkons. Finally the little boat which took me was captained by a man who came from that village – Biap. After sailing two days and two nights, we arrived. Although the captain had radioed the village to tell them I was coming, I was surprised to find that they had assembled on the beach to welcome us. I found the people thoughtful and kind, anxious to make me feel a part of the family circle. Special preparations of their foods – lap lap, roasted yams and taroes – were brought each day to the hut they had prepared for us. Many hours were spent sitting in circles with the women, battling to trace our kinship.

News had passed around that I was there looking for my father's people, and people came, walking many kilometres, to help with my search for my ancestors. One group from the hinterland and another from the coast both laid claim to a kinship with me. I left still in doubt as to my ancestry. When I returned twelve months later, the head man of Biap gathered the villagers together and said: 'Lessingkon' – calling me by my island name and pointing to a spot beneath a breadfruit tree – 'that is where your father's mother's house was'.

I came home determined that my father's story should be told.

There were other reasons why the book had to be written. The slave trade of Australia has never been included in school curricula. I have found that most Australians do not believe that slave labour was used to develop the sugar cane industry. Those who were enslaved did not have the opportunity to tell their story. The story has only been told by historians with a detachment from the thoughts and feelings of the people concerned.

This book is an attempt to convey those thoughts and feelings through the story of my father, who helped to break the chains that enslaved his people. He was a man of dignity, always telling his people: 'Don't take it!'

All other characters in this book are composites of real people but the main events are true.

Faith Bandler

Chapter One

Ambrym is only a small dot in the vast ocean of the Pacific and one of many islands that make up the New Hebrides. The mountains are covered with thick tropical forest and on the shores the Ambrymese wander among the coconut and breadfruit groves. Each house has a well-worn path connecting it to the others and the island is safely protected by a coral reef.

Islands of every shape – and one colour. Dark, jungle-green. Then the sea. Blue and pale blue. The coral reefs, beautiful and dangerous. One hundred islands.

There are no large animals but many lizards and snakes. Brightly coloured insects filter among the trees.

The jungle is strong and deep so the men have to work hard with their stone axes and shell scrapers, digging holes for the planting of the yams. The women come later, tending the plants with gentle care and carrying the little fresh water they can find in taro leaves, softly folded to form a deep vessel of green velvet. Diligently they minister to the pigs, feeding them with taro and coconuts they have cooked, because they know that pigs have purchasing power. Even they themselves may be bought with pigs.

The men do not fight others of the same village and do not marry women from it. All are related by marriage or ancestry and all relationships remembered by name. The men guard their rights to the land inherited from their fathers, carefully seeing that it does not fall into the hands of other groups. Each group within the village has its own feasting dances so many times they sit together and plan the great dancing.

The village of Biap is on the coast. It is the place of Wacvie's starting. The men are big and upright and the women too are strong and sturdy. Biap is the centre of the many villages around it. It was always there and for many, many moons the people have been coming and dancing, singing and fighting. Perhaps, in the beginning, the first person came from a succulent fruit . . .

At first there was no order in the layout of the houses. Now there is order. The houses are built in rows, some scattered away from the others, but the noise for all the houses is the same – the everlasting sound of waves washing the black rocks. The roofs of the houses are steeply sloped and the thatch is thick, like the hair of a pig. It takes two moons to build a house but it will stand to a storm or a hurricane. At one end is the door, low and small and by this the family come in and out. At the other end the fireplace breaks the clean, hard earth. Stone axe heads and bunches of bird feathers hang from the rafters.

A little to the centre of the others, is the men's house. The men meet there, but women never join them. There they talk of plans for the next day, or perhaps of the fight they may make with another village, or the festival they may hold with many villages.

When a man feels that death is coming, he tells his sons to make ready for it. So they prepare the feast and the dancing. The yams, coconuts and taros are gathered and brought together close to the club house, but they are not put inside the house that is only used by the men.

While night lasts they dance to music of the drums and pan-flutes and the old man remembers all the things that made his life. Gentle rain and cyclones. The sun and the moon. The women and men and children, the coolness and the heat. The richness of the deep green foliage; barren areas scorched by the white ash that poured down from the angry volcanoes. The ever-lasting-ness of the white waves, licking the unconquerable and indomitable black rocks; the ropes of sand, falling together and then apart – like the flimsy white ashes of the fires that have been burning all night, after the cinders and embers have given up.

The dying man remembers the rubbing to and fro of the hard sticks to make a groove in soft wood, slowly giving up heat until the gathering pile of dust at the end of the groove began to smoulder. Then the gentle blowing until the tiny flame came, to be fed by dry leaves and bark from the old trees.

The fathers had told him that long ago there had only been cooking by the sun's heat and this had not been good for during the moons of rain they had not been able to have warm bread-fruit or yams. So it was beneficial for all when a man walking in the forest had seen the branches of two trees rubbing against each other. He had stood and watched for he had only seen men and women in this movement. As he watched a gentle flow of redness had come from the rubbing. Although far from his home, in his excitement he had run all the way without resting, then he had rubbed two sticks together just as the boughs of the trees had rubbed together. He had rubbed and rubbed until the same redness had appeared.

The women pulped the yams and scraped the coconuts finely on the sharp edge of the sea shells until the rich, white milk came.

Then they poured it over the yam which they covered with young fish and young prawns, wrapping it thickly in banana leaves before putting it down into the hot stones below the surface ash of the fire.

So many tribes, only a few kilometres apart from each other; the continuous interchange of ideas and influences of faraway places, always passing from one group to the other. In the late afternoon, the gathering of many people bringing gifts to the dancing ground. Loaded with yams, taros, breadfruit, shellfish, fish and eels. The men retiring to the edge of the clearing. The women dressing themselves with scarlet hibiscus, plumes in their hair and pig tusk bangles on their arms. Bodies glistening with coconut oil; faces painted red and white. That dull sound of one drum in the distance at first, then coming closer and closer. The men now forming a firm column.

All are artists. Some more exquisite in their dance than others but all dancing as though they were one, their bodies blending with the complicated rhythms of the gong.

The old man remembers when he too had danced on the clearing ground. Sometimes the ground had moved from under his feet. The empty feeling, as though the earth were about to crumble! Earthquakes had been frequent occurrences in his life, like the tidal waves eating the shores of his land, threatening to swallow his people and take them into the sea.

And the making of canoes: the whole logs of the very hard wood. First the trees were cut and dressed, then the long labour for the men chiselling the canoe inside and out with the stone axes and firesticks; the painstaking task of making the outbooms, masts and outriggers. The women making the triangular sails of thousands of strips of pandanus. Then the great launching of the canoe, marking the end of many moons of hard work. Then the man may die . . .

The rainfall for Ambrym was predictable. For three moons there were heavy and frequent downpours in the morning, in the afternoon and most times at night. The villages were drenched and sometimes the people had to dry their soaked mats by the fires inside the houses. Torrents of water flowed rapidly around the cook houses and between the sleeping houses. If there was a sudden cloudburst the people were sometimes caught unprepared and so without dry wood. Then the making of the fires was troublesome.

The trees and foliage would appear weary from the constant weight of water falling on them. The flowers, though bright, were without their gayness. Too often they fell on the ground before their time, making soft and tender under-formed carpets. Before the heat of the day, brilliant yellows and reds and blues adorned the sides of the well-worn paths, but as the sun scorched their resplendence, they became misshapen and folded, and when the next downpour came they were only a graceless pile of brown mash.

Heavy rain took away some of the joys of the people's free existence. They did not swim as frequently because the sea became very angry, withholding its refreshing and sensual pleasures of gratification. It did not chill the people but neither did it warm them. The warmth and fervour for which their bodies longed was only present when the sun shone. Not broiling, nor hot enough to roast a pig, but just enough to melt its fat. Perhaps the sea needed the rain to assure it of neverness or infinite timelessness. The rain would always come. The sea would always embrace the pouring rain, even if it did become ill-tempered and impolite.

How many nights and days the coconuts stood the beating they were given by the heavy winds and rain in torrents was hard to tell, but they bravely fought back against the gushing, staying high and nesting together for protection from each other. Below, the irrigation was like a watercourse, waiting to take into the sea all the fallen fruit, to be broken by the black, pock-marked rocks.

Although the climate was hot and damp, it was not oppressive. There was fresh water in the mountain torrents and flowers and fruit grew everywhere. This island had a quality of lushness and beauty.

There were no ruins of a past civilisation but there was a culture rich in songs and dances. In almost every incident of daily life some art form was involved. Dances included dramatic performances and improvised pantomime, often very humorous. Dancing was never an independent ritual as music was almost always used. The fairy charm of the flute and the command of the gong were always interwoven with incessant physical action. Songs were a form of story-telling and told of many things, from human conception to cooking coconuts. The music was rich in social meaning. All art was performed co-operatively: a man did not carve the figure of a fish; he was one of the sculptors. Tradition dominated their art as it dominated all other things on their island.

The men were tall and well-proportioned with skin as fine as satin. The women were of a gentle, soft, endurable beauty, with uncreased skin and white teeth. Liquid eyes, black, like precious stones set in blue-white satin. They had little need to work. Food was all around them. Bananas with red flesh, yams with white flesh. Breadfruit and coconuts weighed down the branches heavily, almost on to their heads. Fish were everywhere, in the sea and in the lagoons.

In the main they knew no sickness. Childbirth was without pain. Their teeth did not decay. Their days were an endlessly repeated cycle only broken by their desire for food. They fished, cooked and ate; they danced, sang and made love.

A small community, cut off from the rest of the world by centuries of time and thousands of kilometres. Far from perfect, perhaps, but it had a natural balance and was without decadence. None was rich and none was poor, and there was enough for all.

This was Ambrym.

Wacvie only knew Ambrym after the boats with wings had been. The fathers told of how the ships had come up out of the sea, with creatures – whom they doubted at first to be men – with big noses, and ears that were partly hidden with reddish hair. The skin of their faces showed different shades of reds and pinks, and the rest of their bodies were covered with some woven stuff, finer than fishing nets. Their smell was sour, like the smell of over-ripe fruit. It was not wise to stand windward of them. Such a strange smell had never pervaded the village before. At first they were thought to be a whole family of lesevsev, but lesevsev were devils of stone and these things moved. They moved stiffly and it was a wonder that they did not fall over with so much heavy covering on their bodies.

The fathers remembered one in particular whose nose was very long and the skin very pink. He wore a tight, white thing around his neck and appeared to be a little feared by his companions. His voice was so gentle it made you afraid although you could not understand what he was saying. When he spoke in those somewhat monotonous tones even the children stopped laughing. He carried something they called a book, which was black on the outside and white inside. In the morning, after the sun was high in the sky, and in the evening, when it had gone to sleep, he would open the book and mumble, sounding like a trapped

fly. His own people would gather around and listen, while
Wacvie's people would only gaze in amazement.

One day he had called the village people to gather around him
and with his hands he had given signs that they should understand this new talk. This was no easy task, for the pink and red
people did not open their mouths very wide when they spoke.

The people of this peaceful island had only ever known security
because everything was always as it was. They knew nothing of
the persistent solicitous desires of the men of other lands. How
could they understand the workings of the white man's mind?
They had only ever prepared for the swift tribal battles, lasting
but a short time. The present invasion by those now in the cove
might be repeated many times over and they were faced with the
danger of their island losing many of its men.

Wacvie was tall and straight as a young tree reaching skyward
for the sun. His shoulders were very broad, his whole body was
without surplus flesh. Thick, black, woolly hair rested on the
topmost rim of a square forehead and a short, broad nose divided
his high-boned cheeks. The shape of his chin was like the
sharpened edge of a stone axe.

Wacvie had not slept soundly when, one morning, he went into
the cook house and found his mother, Lessing-Kon, stirring the
coals of the fire. She pushed them back from the warm ashes that
had grown during the night and were now ready to receive the
yams into their downy grey folds. He wondered at the deeper
bend of her shoulders and the perplexity of her mood.

She had been well trained to assume the burden of womanhood, her posture now permanently distorted from bending over
the fires in the earth, and from bearing children. She still retained
her good humour and was never at a loss for an opinion. Not
a chattering woman, but sensitive to the moods of those around
her, she moved soundlessly on her bare feet, her eyes digging to
know her daughter better.

In days gone by, as she had watched Tellie grating the white
yams and purple taros in preparation for the lap lap for the
evening meal, she had been reminded of cool running water and
tall ferns. It was by running water and ferns growing like trees
that she had given birth to her third-born, her only girl. Now,
when she watched the gentle and dextrous fingers expertly peeling
and slicing the bananas and vegetables, her joy was mixed with
sorrow. Her face, though calm and controlled, burned under the

skin. Would the men from the white-winged ships take Tellie as they had other young women of Biap?

People were born and they died, she was thinking, but they had never simply been taken away. Now Tellie and Wacvie were exposed to peril and harm. She sighed, hoping that life could go on as before. This weariness made her feel heavy; there seemed no relief from the tensions that made her muscles rigid. Although she readily responded to the slightest change, she had seldom been troubled by danger or apprehension. She had always thought of her village as impregnable; now she felt a sudden falling-in around her and sensed a current of uncertainty. At her clay pots she wondered that her hands felt warm and clammy when usually at this early hour in the morning she felt cool and refreshed.

The yams were over-roasted, although she had been sitting by the fire while they cooked. Her son was usually impetuous, often impatient, but this morning she knew that something was preying on his mind and his disquiet caused a pang in her chest. His gloom worried her.

This painfulness was unwelcome, distressing. If only the small children of the village would now come to her with their laughter and pranks, they might divert her mournful thoughts on the sombreness of her son. Remembering with horror the previous visit of the vessels that came with the white men, she was filled with blank despondency. If only the children's merriment and hilarity could be heard now, it might lift this depression.

Tellie shifted her weight from one thigh to the other, her eyes as restless as birds. This morning her brown skin had paled; her face was grey and heavy. She finished the preparation of the fruit and vegetables for the lap lap and after placing them into the clay bowl walked out of the house into the green clearing. Most mornings she would walk and remember the stories plaited into her childhood, feeling a confidence and closeness with the deep soft green under her feet. This day her childhood seemed like a legend. Her wandering thoughts caught onto a story, told around the fire one night, about the killing of one group of people by another. How the arrows flew through the air like angry birds and killed all the people of the village because it was thought they had not observed some of the tribal laws. She had many stories behind her, but this one now was foremost in her thoughts.

She was tall but not slim. Although her ankles were fine, her legs were thick and her arms appeared heavy. Most of the people had woolly hair, but Tellie's was thick and fine. It had a shine, sometimes looking as though it had been lightly oiled. With a wooden comb she treated it frequently, always putting a flower in it. One day the flower would be yellow and the next day red, but because her hair was fine, she would often lose it soon after arranging it carefully behind one ear. Then she would pick another and with extra care secure it more firmly in the black curls.

Like the other young women of Ambrym, she had mastered the art of bodily adornment, but this morning she was not thinking of the flower or her hair. Even while she felt the softness of the short cut grass under her feet, the muscles in her legs were taut. She had known that same feeling once before, when a great storm was building up. She remembered the storm-raped skies with the raving flames of lightning and how the unforgettable nightmare had clouded her mind for a long time. It was hard for her sometimes to recall the words of some of the songs that the women sang, because the lightning would come back into her thoughts.

Now the sun was shining and there was not a cloud in the sky. She must call the young children and talk to them about the black book given to her village by the man with the long nose and the white thing around his neck. There were also pictures telling the story of a man named Jesus who could walk on water. She was to tell the children about him and the supernatural acts he was said to have performed in some faraway country. The pictures too had been brought by the long-nosed man.

Tellie found it difficult to believe that this man named Jesus could walk on water. After all, her people belonged to the water, yet if they wanted to stay on the surface of the sea, they had to swim. The strange people who came to Ambrym to take the men and boys away had skin the same colour as this Jesus and they couldn't even swim. If they did not have their boats, they would go under the sea!

Her bewilderment deepened. Perplexed and confused, she hesitantly called the children. They came and gathered around as she sat on the grass. Firstly they must sing about Jesus because he was supposed to have liked little children and then she would tell them about him walking on the water. They would laugh at the idea of someone walking on water; even if he had done it, what was so courageous about the act that made it necessary for them to remember the story?

It was far more pleasurable to remember the stories of the flying spirits in the dancing lights, and soaring hawks. These stories were played out in their dances by the running waters, and among the tall taro leaves. If the water was not there, because the rain had not come for a long time, they would pick the bright yellow flowers and tie them with strips of fine pandanus leaves to long sticks and holding them high above their heads, they would dance the dance of the spirits with the lights. They would dance until they were exhausted and then they would lie under the thin foliage and young palms, watching the spiders spinning their webs between the branches of the trees. Before going to sleep at night they would draw the webs in the patches of sand outside their houses, remembering the spiders unwinding the soft silk rope from their bodies. With the same delicate movements, their long thin fingers would part the deep black sand.

Tellie carried out her task of teaching the children with a heavy heart. They listened, insensitive to her disquiet, and when the lesson ended, they swept away cheerfully to their merry-making in the trees. They must play in the trees today because their elders had told them not to go down to the sea.

The blueness of the sky folded into the sea and it was never-ending. It was always like this. Everything was eternal. The moons came and went and came again. The sun came every day. When the dark thick clouds which brought the rain covered the sun, there was no need to think about them, even to notice them, because the sun would come again.

Wacvie swam back to the rock. He was only there for a few moments when he saw something that made his heart thump in his chest like the beating of a drum. It was a boat. As it came from the south, it seemed at first like a white, thick wave, but it was a boat. Although he had seen other boats come into his cove, this one filled him with fear. He stood erect and still, remembering that boats with white wings brought the people with pink skins and yellowish hair, people who gave them knives and axes and beads.

The last time they had come, he had observed that the strangers had long lengths of rope. After they had lured one of his brothers and other men of Biap towards their boat, they had thrown the rope over their heads and pulling them roughly aboard, had taken them away. Some of the older people were saying it would be three moons and then his brother would come back. Now, three moons and more had come and gone, but his brother had not returned.

Wacvie had no wish to be taken from his island and now that he had grown taller and stronger than many of the other boys of the village, he felt he should shoulder some of the responsibility of protecting his fellows from the angry men with pink skins and hostile faces. From the rock he now stood on, he and his brothers and cousins had amused themselves spearing fish, diving or just swimming softly. This rock had always given pleasure, peace and safety.

The warm sun began to fade. Steadily the boat came nearer. Gently dipping in the swell, its white wings now touched with gold. Wacvie's heart beat faster. How could this boat, so gentle and serene, bring, as it had done before, such sorrow for his people. His bushy eyebrows, well-defined and clear cut, drew sharply together as he wrestled with fear and courage. His frown deepened as he watched sullenly.

With the people of Biap there was already a strong resentment of the white people. By now several boats had been and taken away the strong men and women of Ambrym. They were told they would be returned after three moons, but they had not been seen again.

Wacvie remembered how, at first, when he was a little younger, he had noticed a willingness of the strangers to be friendly, but it had not been the kind of friendliness that he understood, like that between the people of Ambrym and the people of Malo or Malakulla. His perceptiveness was subtle but clear: he recalled the tone in the strangers' voices and the look in their eyes, which were puzzling to him. Now he remembered that note in their voices and saw that the expression in their eyes had been impatience, hatred and anger. Perhaps his father should call a meeting in the club house, he thought, but what should be said to the men if they gathered to discuss how to deal with the invaders?

He stood up, turning his back on the sea and the ship with wings, and cast his eyes towards the winding shore that had forever given him comfort. What should the people be told? Only once before this time had his father spoken of the invaders and that was when he had recommended that all should try and be at peace. But the strangers had not been interested in the attempts of the men of Ambrym to have an agreeable friendship. They had set upon them and forcefully taken them to some unknown land. The problem presented by the ship which now lay in the cove appeared almost insoluble: the choice of meeting violence with violence or retreating to the mountains was not an easy one.

Wacvie's immediate reaction was to resist and drive the invaders from their island, but he had learned from his father to mistrust the counsels of wrath. The islanders had carefully watched the movements of the raiders' first visitation and had verbally recorded details of their accoutrements. Wacvie recalled an account of how some of the men of the winged boats carried heavy objects which made a sharp noise and smoke. Many of the people of Biap had been killed by them. These weapons were far more powerful than the spear; a man could continue to hold one in his hand while it killed a person a long way off.

The indecision was straining his nerves. He drew a deep breath, his anger and weariness turning to sadness. The boat lying there in the water and the terrible silence kept him painfully alert. The reflection of unfamiliar lights in the water around the boat brought a feeling of insecurity. Perhaps his belief in arresting time was only an illusion. Would there be a tomorrow?

He needed the comfort and assurance that the village houses would give him so he slipped down from the rock, his feet heavy as he trod through the water, onto the black sand, through the familiar coconut grove into the open grass space, then over the hill between the now dark vines and soft ferns, to the solace of the village.

Darkness was hiding his people and only the voices of the women and children broke the silence of the night. As he drew closer, he heard the low-pitched voices of the men in the club house. Moving in still nearer, he became aware that the men from the villages of Sissive and Fali had come to talk about the interlopers. The conclave had to make definite plans before the sun rose next morning and the decisions reached would affect all the people of the coast, so the opinions of those meeting together had to be carefully examined.

For the first time there was confusion in their hearts; they were conscious that such a situation had never before confronted them and their laws held no provision to deal with it . . .

NENE GARE, 1919–

Born in Adelaide and educated at Adelaide Art
School and Perth Technical College, Nene Gare is an
artist and fiction writer of renown. She is best
known for her work *The Fringe Dwellers*
(1961) – released as a film in 1986 – and her short
stories have appeared in a variety of anthologies.

Among her works are *Green Gold* (1963), *Bend to
the Wind* (1978), *A House with Verandahs* (1980)
and *Island Away* (1981). The following short story,
'A Good Job', appeared in *Bend to the Wind* and is
indicative of her identification with Aboriginal
experience.

A GOOD JOB

'Gunna work with white people, eh? Turn up ya nose at us fellers
now I spose.' Mrs Yorick's bright black eyes snapped at her
daughter and the smile that curved her mouth was almost
malicious.

But Belle sat with gaze turned inward, neither hearing nor
seeing, certainly unseeing of the letter she held in her fragile hand.
She swallowed after a while and turned fearing eyes on her
mother.

'I can't go mummy. Don't make me. Why did they have ta pick
on me?'

'Ya put ya name down dint ya?'

'You made me.' Belle was wailing now.

'Yes, n ya jus gotta go in there ta that shop an show em you
can work good as them,' Mrs Yorick ordered, snipping at the

words. Hard-eyed, she stood over her daughter daring Belle to disobey.

'What am I gunna wear?'

'Same dress ya wore when ya seen that boss feller.'

'It's dirty – an I tore it. Under the arm.'

'You go an find im then. Dresses can be mended I spose, can't they? An don't sit there cryin cos if ya like it or not ya gunna go in there ta that shop an do that job handin out change like they arst ya in the letter.'

Belle rose still holding the letter and went slowly in to the bedroom, rounded forehead crinkled. Emerging again with the dress trailing behind her she observed Mr Yorick, returned from his work.

'Daddy!' Here was one grownup she could manage. 'That shop wrote me a letter bout that cashier job an now mummy says I hafta take it.' Her voice rose. 'And I'm scared. I don't hafta daddy, do I?'

Mr Yorick looked torn. He loved pretty Belle with her cozening ways and big pleading eyes. He loved Mrs Yorick too, in a respectful sort of way. He was proud of his wife the way she stood up to people and didn't let anyone boss her. Not even him.

'I dunno,' he worried. 'Does ya mummy say ya hafta?'

'Course she hasta.' Mrs Yorick looked as fierce as she could. 'Don't wanta stay down ere in the dirt the rest of ya life, do ya? What ya think ya went ta school all these years for eh?'

Belle whimpered and widened her eyes on her father.

'So ya could get a bit a eddication, that's why.' Mrs Yorick informed.

'Susan Wells told me the girls where she works was horrible, slingin off an that all the time bout being dark. Like I am.' Belle looked at her raised arm and the tears overflowed.

'Nothin wrong with bein dark,' Mrs Yorick said stoutly. 'I'm dark too ain't I? An ya don't hear me screechin me head off bout it.'

'You're not a girl.'

'I am a girl.'

'Ya not. You're an ole woman,' Belle accused.

'What's that but a girl well,' Mrs Yorick said indignantly. 'Was one once wasn't I?'

'Nobody expected you ta go off an work some place there wasn't nobody but white fellers.'

'Hoh! Dint they? What you think I done all the time on that

mission? Sat bout playin cards? Hoh no! I hadda work awright. Dint I dad?'

Belle stamped. 'This is different.'

'None a that stampin now,' Mrs Yorick came on strong. 'I just about outa pachence with ya. No more cheeky talk, see? Men that dress where it need mendin an then you get some hot water out that kettle an wash it out an hang it up outside on the wattle ta dry. If it tint dry by morning we can iron the damn thing dry.'

Belle succumbed. But her sobbing and weeping did not go unheard as she mended and washed nor was this her intention.

'I dunno,' Mrs Yorick said moodily, 'These young ones – do ya best for em an what thanks?'

'Ya don't think we bein a bit hard on er, do ya?'

'You hush up ya foolish ole man. That one not gunna muck up er life like Anthony done, throwin up is job after a month. An what's e doin now, arst me that? Mrs Yorick's bottom lip shot out belligerently. Anthony was Mrs Yorick's first born, a gift she had brought with her to her marriage with Mr Yorick. Not that Mr Yorick had made any objections. He liked children and was perfectly prepared to father Anthony as well as any of his own that might turn up. But he could not be expected to feel the disappointment – humiliation even – that Mrs Yorick had felt when Anthony had run off. Her son had let her down as well as himself.

She answered her own question. 'Playin round with a loto silly young ones just like imself. Throwin up that good job in the post office.' Not for a minute did Mrs Yorick allow the sadness inside her to show on her face. Mr Yorick knew it was there however.

'I spose ya right mum,' he admitted. 'Bout Belle.'

'Course I'm right,' said she.

When Anthony's big chance had come he had gone from home to live in a hostel. Mrs Yorick decided to keep the next one at home under her careful eye. And so Belle was started on her way up, not without pain to her parents. Mrs Yorick in particular felt restless and frustrated because she could not take Belle's troubles on her own shoulders and deal with them herself. Her personal philosophy was crammed into a few words, 'Don't let them get ya down.' Even Mrs Yorick however was not up to the myriad ways in which Belle's workmates tried to get her down. For the first fortnight at least, it seemed to Belle's mother that they were at it from the time Belle got to her desk until she left in the late afternoon. 'The buggers,' Mr Yorick contumed and Mrs Yorick was at her wits' end to know what to advise that would not also bring Belle the sack. Obviously her own father's advice to give everyone a good belt over the ears would not serve here.

Then Belle received her first pay packet and instantly everything became worthwhile.

Round about her neighbours Mrs Yorick's stocks went up but she was easily able to deal with those who would have taunted her about setting herself up above others.

'Course I do,' she agreed. 'Look at my fambly an look at you an yours. Who done better, I arst ya. Eh?'

'Nother thing,' she threatened friend and relative as well. 'I don't want none a you lot goin worryin Belle fa money, see? An don't say ya wouldn't do it cos I know ya in there quick as a shot outa a gun the minute any a yous knows someone's got a bit a money in is pocket. I done it meself so I know. I ain't gunna have any a you mob doin it but. Keep away fum my Belle, understand?

There were grumbles and comments (out of sight and sound of Mrs Yorick) but there was understanding too. Whatever her opinion of them, theirs of her was high and they were as respectful of her abilities as Mr Yorick himself. If you were in trouble Mrs Yorick knew where to go and what to do. She knew her entitlements down to the last cent and the smallest free service and was ready to claim the lot on behalf of herself and her pals whenever it became necessary. She had a kind of pitying fondness for the partment officers. 'Poor bloody fools,' she would condemn them in her more tolerant moments. 'Turning theirselfs inside out fa us fellers. Ho no, Miz Yorick. Ho yes, Miz Yorick. How are ya to-day Miz Yorick. An us laughin at em behind their backs. They don't get me snivellin to em. I take all I an get then they can go ta hell. Them an their handouts. Then there are them other buggers, them do-good women. Give ya a pair a shoes one day an be lookin down at ya feet the next ta see are ya takin good care of em. Never forget they done ya a good turn. Pats themselves on the back. Thinks what good fellers they are ta help the poor bloody blacks.'

'Now mum,' Mr Yorick would pacify at times like these. 'Calm down. They ain't all bad, ya know.'

'Anyone's got a white skin e's bad,' Mrs Yorick laid down. 'Ya born white ya a bad bugger. Ya born black ya a poor creecher ony good ta spit on. Not for my childrens but. Nobody gunna look down on my childrens.'

Mrs Yorick never completely despaired of Anthony. One of these days she would catch him up and straighten him out again.

'My childrens.' was Mrs Yorick's war cry and if Mr Yorick substituted 'our' for 'my' he did it only inside his head where it wouldn't be noticed. Mr Yorick's job was to love his children, not raise them up. His children appreciated this.

When Belle had been at her job for over a month Mrs Yorick made up her mind to pay her daughter a visit at her place of work. Nobody else must visit but a mother had rights. The project was got under way most secretly, not even Mr Yorick allowed to know. Mrs Yorick's sister Edie had to know something because it was Edie who owned the coat and cap which Mrs Yorick had decided she needed in order to look respectable. Mrs Yorick did not want to shame Belle. The old purple raincoat would not do. Edie's coat was thick imitation fur. The cut was long and full and there were two big pockets. The cap matched the coat. Both articles together had cost Edie five dollars off the Town Hall stall but they had earned Edie more than that over the years she had possessed them. If you showed Edie a dollar she might let you have a wear.

Mrs Yorick visited her sister with the firm promise of a dollar from Belle's next pay packet.

'What ya wantim for?'

'Never mind.'

Edie didn't know if she would or she wouldn't. She wanted the money but she wasn't particular about doing Mrs Yorick a favour. Snubs smarted a long time in Edie's memory.

'Where you goin?'

'I'm goin – hout.'

'Hout where but? You gotta coat, ain't ya?'

'Somewhere special I'm goin. You gunna let me have them things or ain't ya? Make up ya mine.'

'The fur's gettin all rubbed,' Edie fussed. 'If I let ya have em ya gotta be careful.'

'Get the damn thing out an shut ya guts fa Gawd's sake,' Mrs Yorick said impatiently. 'Nobody gunna rub it where I'm goin.'

'An bring it back very nex day an don't forget ya owe me a

dollar,' Edie screeched after her as she made off with the coat and cap over her arm.

So that was that and at least the wardrobe part was all signed and sealed. Mrs Yorick had a good look at the bald patches on neck and cuffs and decided to wear the collar up and the cuffs down. She tried it on while Mr Yorick was out and was newly entranced with the cosiness of the cap over her grey curls. It was a wonderful outfit and those deep pockets were just the right size for holding money. Excitement rose in Mrs Yorick. She thought 'I look just about awright in this damn thing,' but was just as glad Mr Yorick was not there to pass remark. She wished for no attention to be paid to her doings until she had paid her visit and was back home again safe and sound. Any talk, any questions, any discussion of any kind might shatter her timorous resolve, make her project appear in some other light than reasonable and proper Also, if Mrs Yorick were in some manner prevented, say she got cold feet at the last moment or something, nobody was going to know but Mrs Yorick. There was a comforting lot of reassurance in that one single fact.

She undid the four furry buttons and hung the coat beneath her old purple one so nobody would notice it. To-morrow was the day.

'I'm gunna need the whole bucket full,' Mrs Yorick said next morning, bossily. 'I'm goin inta town to-day an I need a good washover.'

She had one. Everywhere. Clean as a flea when she had finished. Talcum too to be on the safe side. Clean bloomers and petticoat and shined shoes and her red dress. And over all the Coat and the Cap. She purposely took a long time to dress so that Mr Yorick would be out of the way when she was ready to go. Wasn't nobody else on the train going into town that she knew and nobody when she got out neither. And she was used to Forrest Place. The nerves began a bit of a tickle when she reached Murray Street. Every dark face was a friendly face and they were dotted about like the stations of the cross, to give her comfort. Mrs Yorick entered the department store without incident and tried her best to walk unobtrusively along the tight-packed corridors between the tables of goods. Once the skirt of the bunny rug coat caught a stand of material and set it to swaying and another time Mrs Yorick trod fair and square on somebody's foot but you couldn't be put in gaol for an accident like that so Mrs Yorick simply passed along and did not look back at her victim.

Up on the second floor, Belle had told her importantly. They had half the floor to themselves, the cashiers that were working on Accounts.

'Can I help you?' voices kept asking as Mrs Yorick went on her way but Mrs Yorick ignored them with ducked head and fierce murmurs. A staircase was what she was looking for and as soon as she found one she mounted it and the one leading on from it and she had arrived, slow and panting.

She had to raise her head to see over the counter.

'Yes?' the young woman enquired. Mrs Yorick had been hoping there need be no enquiries: that Belle would simply be there before her.

'Belle Yorick,' she said, louder than she had intended because of misjudging the push needed to get it out.

'Belle Yorick?' the woman repeated. 'Oh yes. Just a moment.' She called to a girl behind her. 'Betty, just run and get Belle for the lady, will you?' Mrs Yorick stood inside her voluminous coat and sweated. The damn thing was too hot for a day like this. Why hadn't she remembered it was summer – and that cap she could feel banding her head – did it really look so good?

Belle appeared looking different from how she looked at home and Mrs Yorick felt saved suddenly, as if Belle had been a light at the end of a dark tunnel. She gave her daughter a smile of thanks but there was no smile on Belle's face. Mrs Yorick had time to wonder at that before her arm was gripped and she found herself being hurried behind what looked like a great roll of floor covering.

'Mummy!' Belle said and there was no doubt about the expression on her face. It was not a welcoming look at all. Mrs Yorick was not going to be saved.

'Mummy!' Belle almost wept. 'You're the third person that's come in to see me with that coat and cap on. The third different person. What'll they all think?'

Mrs Yorick made a quick recovery. Ignored, the lead-heavy feeling in the upper part of her stomach. She was all fury and flashing eyes behind the sheltering roll of linoleum. 'Ya mean,' she belted out soft and savage, 'they been comin in ere ta see ya after what I tole em?'

'Auntie Edie an Millie,' Belle imparted.

'What they want? Money, I spose.' She might have laughed

if it had not been for Belle's long face. Them two buggers, only waiting until her back was turned before they got up to their tricks. She allowed herself the smallest smile. 'Us leopards can't change our spots an can't expeck ta. I'll get after them two leopards but,' she promised. 'You jus wait. Shoulda tole me before.'

'They said not to,' Belle said sulkily.

Outside the store Mrs Yorick retraced her steps unseeing. There was a terrible humility raging somewhere; it hurt and try as she would to swallow it away it refused to budge. Her mind showed her pictures of herself making her step-by-step plans and it was the hardest thing ever she had done, making herself see the funny side. 'Get back where ya belong, what you gotta do,' she told herself hardily. 'Give them two buggers a bit of hurry up an see how they like it.' One thing, she knew who was boss back home. She'd let a few other peoples know too. That Millie! That Edie!

Just let her get home.

It was in this confusing and humble state, hardly looking where she was going but just blundering along, that Mrs Yorick again bumped fair and square into a body. This one wore a black face above it. One of those Indian faces bound about with one of those turban things with a tail. Mrs Yorick was not up to staring. She just re-settled herself on her feet. One cautious upward flick of a look she allowed herself.

It was enough to banish her abasement. No room for such in the flood of wrath that instantly overcame her. Anthony! Got up all funny. Worse, not a sign of recognition on his face. Walking off up the street cool as you like thinking of course she wouldn't know him. Wouldn't know her own child just because he'd hidden himself away under a bit of a fancy-dress.

Mrs Yorick didn't let him get far. The good healthy cleansing fury was running hot through her veins. She had his arm in a second.

'Here!' she pulled him up with a jerk. 'Here, ya foreign-lookin bastard. Where do ya think ya going, eh?'

Anthony looked for a breath as if he would continue to deny her and he could not have chosen a worse moment. Twice in one day Mrs Yorick had been rejected by blood of her blood, flesh of her flesh and unlucky Anthony caught her combined fury.

One hand reached for his shoulder to swing him round and

the other gave him a great clout across the chops that sent his turban flying. The wounded look he gave her as he bent for his disguise would have melted Mr Yorick instantly but Mrs Yorick was not having any.

'An now,' she told him, 'ya can get on that train with me an come home where ya belong.'

OLGA MASTERS, 1919–1986

Born in Pambula, on the New South Wales coast,
she worked as a journalist and mother for many
years before turning to fiction writing in her late
fifties. Her literary reputation was established with
the publication of the prize-winning *The Home Girls*
in 1982 and this was followed by *Loving Daughters*
(1984), *A Long Time Dying* (1985) and the
posthumously published *Amy's Children* (1987); a
further volume of short stories has just been
published, *The Rose Fancier* (1988).

Her bitter-sweet accounts of female experience
make a significant contribution to the women's
literary tradition and warrant admiration: many of
the conflicts and dilemmas of women's lives are given
unresolved expression in her writing. The following
short story, 'The Home Girls' is taken from the
volume of the same name (1984, University of
Queensland Press) and is representative of the
author's work.

THE HOME GIRLS

'It's today,' the fat child said and rolled over in bed, landed on
her feet on the floor and held the window sill, looking back at
her sister, the thin one who had been jerked awake.

'Today!' the fat one said.

The thin one half raised herself on her elbows in bed. Her
straight hair fell over her face. The fat one had curly hair in
corkscrews over her head.

'Should be the other way round,' a visitor said once, looking at them with a stretched mouth and blank eyes.

The visitor meant that straight hair would have taken away from the fat one's rounded look and curls might have made the thin one look rounder.

The foster mother looked at them not bothering to stretch her mouth.

The fat one and the thin one looked away not knowing how to apologize for being the way they were.

'Go and play,' the foster mother said, but they were already going.

The fat one picked up a brush now and pressed it down her curls which sprang back in the wake of the bristles.

When she put the brush down she saw in the mirror her hair was the same as before.

The thin one screwed her body so that she could see the fat one's reflection. 'Are you?' she said.

'Am I what?' the fat one answered.

'You know.' The thin one moved a foot which need not have belonged to her body so flat were the bedclothes. 'Excited about it,' the thin one said.

'Yes!' said the fat one, too loud and too sudden.

Tears came into the thin one's eyes. 'Don't shout!' she said.

The fat one picked up the brush and began to drag at her curls again. The thin one's watery eyes met her sister's in the mirror. They looked like portraits on a mantlepiece, the subjects photographed while the tension was still in their expression.

The foster mother came into the room then. She made the third portrait on the mantlepiece.

The thin one started to get out of bed rather quickly. Her ears were ready for the orders so she began to pull blankets off for the bedmaking.

But the foster mother said, 'Leave that.'

The thin one didn't know what to do then. She thrust a finger up her nose and screwed it round.

The foster mother covered her face with both hands. After a while she took them away showing a stretched mouth.

'Now!' she said quite brightly looking between them.

Now what? thought the fat one and the thin one.

Their mouths hung a little open.

The foster mother squeezed her eyes shut.

When she opened them the fat one and the thin one were in the same pose.

She crossed to the window and raised the blind quite violently.

'Have you had your bath?' she said.

They knew she knew they hadn't because it was there on the back of her neck.

She turned abruptly and went out of the room.

They heard her angry heels on the stairs.

The fat one bent down and opened a drawer. It was empty.

'Our clothes?' she said.

The thin one stared at a suitcase fastened and strapped standing upright in a corner.

'They're all in there,' the fat one said, pointing.

'Take something out to wear,' the thin one said making a space on the bed for the case.

Inside the clothes were in perfect order, a line of dresses folded with the tops showing, a stack of pants, a corner filled with rolled up socks, nightgowns with the lace ironed, cardigans carefully buttoned.

The fat one's hands hovered over them.

'Which?' she said.

She touched the pants and they were soon screwed and tossed under her fingers.

'Stop!' said the thin one and slapped her sister's hand away.

She plucked up two pairs of pants and then put them back.

'Fold them the way she did!' the fat one said.

The thin one tried but couldn't.

'Let me!' said the fat one, but digging in she tossed a dress so that the folded one underneath came to the top.

They looked around at a noise and the foster mother was there.

'Look what you've done!' she screamed and the fat one and the thin one flung themselves together away from the case on the bed.

They blinked as if blows were descending on them.

The foster mother turned her head towards the stairs.

'Hilda!' she cried, squashing her face against the door jamb.

The body of Hilda the foster mother's sister who came to the house every day jerked into sight, coming from the bottom of the stairs like an open mouthed fish swimming to the surface.

The foster mother now had both hands pressed to her face.

Shutting the fat one and the thin one out of her vision, Hilda went to the case and began to lift little bundles of clothes onto the bed.

'You go down and pour yourself a cup of tea,' she said.

The foster mother's heels went down again, thudding dully this time.

'Go and have your bath,' Hilda said, her eyes on the folding and the packing.

They went into the bathroom off the landing.

There hanging on the shower rail were the clothes they were to wear. The dresses were on hangers, pants and vests and socks were folded over the rail.

Shoes polished to a high gloss were on a bathroom chair.

'She told us last night,' the thin one said.

The fat one's face remembered.

Very slow and deliberate she turned the water on.

She stared at it rushing away without the plug in.

The thin one sat on the toilet seat and began to pull on her socks.

The fat one too dressed slowly.

Before she put her pants on she turned around flicked up her skirt and urinated in the bath.

It trickled down to join the rushing water.

Thoughtfully she turned the tap off.

They stood in the silence staring about them.

The hard white shining walls stared back.

'Look!' said the thin one suddenly taking a lipstick from a little ceramic bowlful on a ledge below a cabinet. The foster mother kept them there sometimes using the bathroom to freshen up after housecleaning.

The thin one uncapped and screwed the metal holder sending the scarlet worm out like a living thing.

The fat one also took a lipstick out of the bowl.

She laughed when hers was longer and a shade more scarlet.

They looked in the mirror and saw not their own reflection but that of the foster mother bracing her jaws and pulling her lips back her cold watery eyes shutting out everything but her own image.

The fat one turned and leaned across the bath with the lipstick poised.

Her eyes flashing briefly on the thin one said what she would do.

Her pink tongue, shaped like the lipstick end, showed at the corner of her mouth.

She braced herself against the wall with a spread plump hand.

The lipstick cut deep into the wall sprinkling a few scarlet crumbs.

The fat one wrote her word.

Shithead.

The thin one made a little noise of breathing. She leaned over beside her sister. She was slower and her tongue was out further.

She wrote *cock.*

The fat one made a small noise of scorn.

She took a step level with a piece of virgin wall.

She wrote *fuck.*

The thin one wrote with the letters going downwards.

Piss.

She broke her lipstick when she dotted the *i.*

The piece fell into the bath. The fat one laughed and ground it into the porcelain wiping her shoe on the side of the tub.

Then she climbed onto the side of the bath. High above the words she began to draw.

It was a penis so big she wore the lipstick down to the metal holder when she finished.

The thin one climbed up beside her. She drew a cascade of little circles falling from the tip of the penis, the last unfinished because her lipstick stump gave out.

They jumped down together, the fat one light like a pillow and the thin one bending her knees and creaking when she landed.

They dropped the lipstick holders on the floor and watched them roll away.

The door opened then and Hilda was there.

All that moved was the hair sprouting from a mole at the corner of her mouth.

'Oh my God,' she said at last.

Then she breathed in raising her bosom and crossing both hands near her throat.

The fat one and the thin one jerked their smeared hands away from their stiffly ironed dresses.

'My God,' said Hilda, able to look at them now. 'I'd kill you if I had you.'

'Yes,' said the fat one and the thin one sounding as if they'd heard it before.

Hilda flashed open a cabinet and took out a cake of grey gritty soap and dropped it in the basin.

'Scrub your hands with that,' she said.

They did standing back with spread out legs to keep splashes off their clothes.

Hilda was ready with a soiled towel fished from the linen basket.

'She did everything in her power for you,' she said in a deep and trembling voice. 'Out of the goodness of her heart she did every single thing she could.'

The fat one and the thin one didn't know what to do with the towel when they had finished wiping, but Hilda seized it and flung it into the basket.

'Carry your case down,' she said going ahead of them.

Halfway down the stairs they came in view of the heads.

The foster mother and a man and a woman were standing around looking up.

The foster mother's mouth was stretched in one of her smiles.

'Your new mother and father have come to collect you. Isn't that nice!' she said in a gay voice.

'We're carrying you off before breakfast,' said the woman nearly as gay.

'Hilda, whip out into the kitchen and get some apples to chew on the way,' said the foster mother.

Hilda slipped past the group. The fat one and the thin one watched but the backs of her legs did not speak.

The woman took a hand of each. She rubbed a thumb on each palm wondering briefly at the cool and gritty feel.

'You'll have four brothers and sisters at the cottage,' she said.

'Cottage,' said the foster mother. 'Doesn't that sound cosy?'

Hilda returned putting the apples into a paper bag.

The man picked up the case and everyone moved to the car parked near the porch.

The fat one and the thin one got in quickly and each sat in a corner of the back seat wriggling until the leather clutched them.

The foster mother put her face to the half wound up window.

'Write us a little letter about how you're getting on,' she said.

When the car moved off she kissed the tips of her fingers to them.

Four brothers and sisters, the fat one and the thin one were thinking.

At that moment the foster mother being shown the bathroom by Hilda was clutching her sister and saying Oh my God, oh, my God oh my God, over and over.

The fat one and the thin one weren't remembering it at all.

We lived in this beautiful house with our own bathroom, the fat one said to herself seeing in her mind four pairs of entranced eyes.

The car swerved suddenly to miss an overtaking lorry.

The man swore and the woman put a hand on his arm to restrain him turning her head to see if the back had heard.

There was this terrible accident killing our father and mother, the thin one said silently to her imaginary audience.

Lapsed into their dream the fat one pulled at her corkscrew curls and the thin one twisted the ends of her hair and they watched for the cottage to come into view.

ORIEL GRAY, 1920–

Primarily a playwright, but fiction writer and
autobiographer too, Oriel Gray was born in Sydney
and now lives in Melbourne. Some of the details of
her unconventional and often controversial life are
contained in her scintillating and highly amusing
account, *Exit Left, Memoirs of a Scarlet Woman*
(1985, Penguin).

In many ways her work reveals a successful blend
of art and politics; she joined the Communist Party
of Australia and the Sydney New Theatre in 1937
and much of her drama gives substance to her
unequivocal and radical political views. A versatile
playwright, she has written radio and television
scripts – from soaps to serious dramas – as well as
for the stage. Regrettably, the majority of her plays
remain unpublished; 'The Torrents', included here, is
being printed for the first time.

Among her plays which did find their way into
print are *Drive a Hard Bargain* (1960), *The Golden
Touch* (1965), 'Lawson' (in *The Living Stage*, Book II,
1970, Rigby).

While 'The Torrents' shared the first prize with Ray
Lawler's *The Summer of the Seventeenth Doll*,
(Playwright Advisory Board Competition, 1956), it
enjoyed no share of the fame. Years before its time
with its account of an independent woman and
sexual harassment at the work place, it helps to set
the stage for the women's movement of the 1960s. It

stands now as a testimony to the excellence of
women's contribution to the theatre, and as an
indictment of their neglect.

THE TORRENTS

Characters

(In order of appearance)

CHRISTY
BERNIE
JOCK MacDONALD
GWYNNE THOMAS
KINGSLEY MYERS
RUFUS TORRENT
BEN TORRENT
JOHN MANSON
J. G. MILFORD
MR. TWIMPLE
MR. SQUIRES
MR. STUWELL *(Senior)*
MR. STUWELL *(Junior)*

The Scene: The office of the Koolgalla 'Argus'.

Time: The play is set in the late 1890's.

ACT ONE

SCENE 1

*The office of the Koolgalla 'Argus'. The larger part of the set is
occupied by an all-purpose room. It is a dreadful muddle – on
the small table downstage right, there are several green baize
boxes, bursting at their sides, spilling blocks on to the floor. There
is a scratched and bow-legged desk, with a typewriter of the
period, and a collection of newspaper files. There is also a filing
cabinet, and a branching Victorian-type hat-rack . . . empty at
the moment. A door marked* PRIVATE *leads into Rufus Torrent's*

office . . . a small area (preferably on a slightly higher level), furnished with an imposing desk and swivel chair . . . (all we can see of it).

Except for the dust and the untidiness, the impression of the set is warm and light – windows look down on the main street of Koolgalla.

On one wall is a dusty glass case carrying a plaster cast of a nugget – the first great find in the district. There is also a calendar, which displays – amid a quantity of scrollwork – a picture resembling the 'Stag at Bay', and the beginning of the year '189 – ' (the last digit torn off). There is also a picture of Queen Victoria – to which has been added a long, curly moustache.

As the curtain rises, CHRISTY *– old, gnomish, fantastic – is perched on the desk upstage, spinning a yarn to* BERNIE, *who is sixteen, gauche, with a puppy charm. The feeling of the scene is that of the schoolroom picture of the old sailor telling stories to young Raleigh and Frobisher . . .*

CHRISTY *[this is pure showmanship]* . . . O' course, we all knew there was goin' to be trouble – there had to be. 'By Grundy' says Jim Stephens to me . . . he was a mate of mine, little feller with a wall eye . . . 'nuther feller I knew had a piebald gelding with an eye the very spit of Jim's – Jim was hopping mad when this feller called his horse Stephens, but it won him a packet of money when it beat the favourite . . .

BERNIE *[anxious to get on with the story]* And then Jim Stephens said to you . . .

CHRISTY Eh? Oh, yes – 'By Grundy', he says, 'if the red coats take the Reform League lying down, we'll be able to use 'em for doormats!' O' course, we knew they wouldn't, but – *[swaggering]* 'Let 'em come,' we said!

BERNIE *[awed and believing]* And you really knew Peter Lalor, Christy?

CHRISTY *[with a light laugh]* Knew 'im . . .? Well as I know you, young Bernie! 'Christy,' he used to say, 'Christy, you're only the size of half a man, but by Grundy, you're worth ten!' He had a quaint way of expressing himself – Irish he was, y'know, like his Nibs. . . . *[thumbing a gesture towards the door marked* PRIVATE*]*

BERNIE And were you there when they took – the Oath?

CHRISTY Was I there? By Grundy, I . . . *[then slightly daunted]* well, I wasn't exactly there, because I was called away on business that day, but a mate of mine, Flush Saunders was there, and he had a wonderful way of telling things. You might just as well have been there yourself, and so saved yourself the trouble, so to speak. There was – oh, now, how many would it be . . . *[casting in the dark]* . . . a thousand say – or maybe eight hundred . . .

BERNIE Five hundred, Christy . . .

CHRISTY As I was saying – five hundred . . .

BERNIE *[softly: he knows it by heart and he lives it as he speaks]* Five hundred armed diggers then assembled, and Peter Lalor was on the stump, holding with his left hand the muzzle of his rifle, whose butt-end rested on his boot. A gesture of his right hand signified what he meant when he said, 'It is my duty now to swear you in, and to take with you the oath to be faithful to the Southern Cross. Hear me with attention. The man who, after this solemn oath, does not stand by our standards, is a coward at heart.'

Even CHRISTY *is caught by the boy's sincerity and by the picture he draws.*

BERNIE 'I order all persons who do not intend to take the oath to leave the meeting at once.'

JOCK MacDONALD *appears in the doorway – a man of fifty, very hard and stringy, a sharp voice, a Scots accent, a shrewd, competent, fairminded man. He watches and listens, half annoyed, half amused.* CHRISTY *and* BERNIE *are quite unaware of him.*

BERNIE 'Let all divisions under arms fall in in their order around the flagstaff.' Lalor now knelt, with head uncovered, and with the right hand pointing to the standard, exclaimed in a firm measured tone . . .

JOCK   Get those proofs pulled up!

CHRISTY *and* BERNIE *both jump.* CHRISTY *gets down from desk,* BERNIE *looks shamefaced.*

JOCK   When I tell you to do a job, Bernie, I trust you – I don't expect to have to be calling you every ten minutes, like a mother with a bairn in leading-strings. Now we're waiting for those proofs, and they're no' pulled yet, and the third page can't be locked up until they are.

BERNIE   I'm sorry, Mr. MacDonald, but Christy began to tell me. . . .

JOCK   *[sternly]* How old are you, Bernie?

BERNIE   Nearly sixteen.

JOCK   Old enough to be working – old enough to take responsibility. When I chide you again – if I should have to – don't let me hear you mention another man's name in blame or praise unless he ties you down to stop you doing your duty.

BERNIE   I've been hard at it since early this morning, Mr. MacDonald.

JOCK   If you don't like it, my lad, get your mother's washing up dish and start panning for gold like the rest of the town boys. But don't come back here when you're twenty, and needing a job that gives you bread and butter and a clean shirt. You wanted to be a journalist – you begged me to get you this position – I swore to Mr. Torrent that you'd justify me . . .

BERNIE   I'm going to, Mr. MacDonald, but . . . but . . .

JOCK   But what?

BERNIE   *[blurting it out]* Sorting type and greasing blocks and delivering proofs is an awful long way from being a proper journalist like Ben Torrent.

JOCK   *[bristling]* Indeed? And how do you think Ben Torrent – aye, and his father, too – learned to be 'proper' journalists except by sorting type, and greasing blocks and delivering

proofs . . . *and* waiting for them to be
marked and passed, instead of wandering
back to the office by way of the diggings
road and having to go back for them
immediately!

BERNIE   *[defensively]* Anyway, I thought you might be
holding the proofs until the new reader starts
work, so's he could check them, and . . .

JOCK   *[sweeping over him]* I tell you, Bernie, being a
journalist isna lounging in court with a
flower in your buttonhole and liquor on your
breath like some city fellows. If a man canna
get a story, write it, set it up, print it – aye,
and sell the paper if he has to – if he canna
do that, then he's not good enough for the
Koolgalla 'Argus' – or Rufus Torrent – or me!
Now away to those proofs!

Abashed, BERNIE *goes off at a fast slink.*

CHRISTY   By Grundy, you've got a powerful tongue when
you're roused. Jock – just the thing to put the
boy's nose back to the grindstone. These
youngsters don't stick to it like us old timers,
eh?

JOCK   *[turning his wrath on* CHRISTY*]* As for you,
Christy, you ought to be ashamed of
yourself, tempting the lad from his work with
your lying stories . . .

CHRISTY   *[indignant]* Now that's a libel if ever I heard
one! We was talking about the Eureka
Stockade.

JOCK   I suppose you were there, too . . . carrying the
banner, most like. . . .

CHRISTY   *[virtuously]* I never . . .

JOCK   If they had stood the flagstaff in a barrel of
beer, then you would never have left it, that's
certain! Fifty-four – wasn't that the year you
told me you were in Queensland as an officer
of the Native Police, holding the wild blacks
at bay, and sleeping across the doorway of
the Governor's lady's bedroom.

CHRISTY   *[unabashed]* So it was – and me wishing I was

on the other side. By Grundy, Jock, she was
a fine figure of a woman . . .

JOCK None of that talk in front of the lad – he's
drowsy enough already! Get to your work,
you old he-goat . . . and hurry!

JOCK *bellows this at* CHRISTY. CHRISTY *is unmoved, but* GWYNNE
THOMAS *is startled.* GWYNNE *is twenty-one, very pretty and
flowery. She wears a riding habit. Just now she is glancing
apprehensively over her shoulder, and* CHRISTY *takes advantage
of this to steady her, his little eyes gleaming as he grabs her slim
waist.*

CHRISTY Watch it now, Gwynne, or you'll be tail over
turkey . . .!

JOCK *glares, and* CHRISTY *vanishes from sight.*

JOCK That Christy . . .! I think Mr. Torrent keeps
him for the joke of him. Mind you, he can
work if he's got a mind to it – it's getting his
mind to it that baffles you!

KINGSLEY MYERS *comes in, as though he has run up the stairs. He
is a sturdy, good-humoured, pleasant-faced, downright young
man, and at the moment, he is annoyed.*

KINGSLEY Gwynne, why did you snub me just now?

GWYNNE I didn't see you – I mean – I did, but –

JOCK *coughs.* GWYNNE *indicates him.*

GWYNNE Mr. MacDonald's here, Kingsley . . .

KINGSLEY *shuts up, but he only postpones what he has to say.*

JOCK You'll be looking for Ben, Miss Thomas?

GWYNNE Oh, no . . . The city train's not in yet.

JOCK *[surprised]* Ben came back yesterday, with
everything arranged. The new man's
following on this morning's train . . .

GWYNNE *[surprised, hiding it]* Oh . . . oh, yes, of course,
how silly of me . . . He told me – last
night –

KINGSLEY *looking at her.*

GWYNNE *[hastily]* You'll be glad to see the new staff
member, Mr. MacDonald.

JOCK I will that. Bernie's a good lad, but Christy and
I've been fairly worked off our feet – I should
say Christy's been worked off *my* feet! Once
this new chap's settled in, Mr. Torrent'll take

on more staff. He's promised.

GWYNNE   Koolgalla's really expanding – that's what my
father says.

KINGSLEY   Oh, Koolgalla's bursting at the seams – wait for
the bang when the gold runs out!

JOCK *gives him a shrewd look.*

JOCK   That's a real hobby horse of yours, Mr. Myers.
A real queer one for an engineer.

KINGSLEY   I'm only an engineer by second choice . . . It's
the land and the saving of it that I love – *[he
looks to* GWYNNE*]* among other things.

JOCK *is aware of the tension.*

JOCK   I'll be away . . .

JOCK *goes out.* GWYNNE *starts to flutter after him.*

GWYNNE   Mr. MacDonald, I'll come back . . .

KINGSLEY *catches her by the wrist.*

KINGSLEY   I won't eat you, Gwynne.

GWYNNE *clutches at her dignity.*

GWYNNE   I have never considered that . . .

KINGSLEY   That I love you?

She shakes her head.

KINGSLEY   You're too honest to lie well, Gwynne.

GWYNNE   I don't lie!

KINGSLEY   No? Not even when you try to hide the fact
that Ben came back last night . . . and didn't
come to see you?

GWYNNE *pulls her hand away.*

GWYNNE   *[attacking him]* I thought you were his friend?

KINGSLEY   I am his friend – as much as Ben Torrent needs
a friend. But I'm tired of being 'mates'. There
are things I want – and not just for myself.
I've a right to fight for them.

GWYNNE   I'm to marry Ben – soon.

KINGSLEY *turns away . . . she follows him. She really doesn't
want to let him go.*

KINGSLEY   Because his father thinks it's a good
idea – because *your* father thinks it's a good
idea? Oh, I know how it's done – 'a marriage
has been arranged'. It's barbaric – one
Hottentot chief to another!

GWYNNE *touches his shoulder.*

GWYNNE   Please, King . . .

KINGSLEY   Don't think you're my only heart's desire! I
want to bring water from the river to the
paddocks out there! I want to hold the river
against drought and flood. I want to see fruit
trees, instead of mine shafts and pot-holes.
[savagely] I've got as much chance of that as
I have of you. But I haven't given up!

GWYNNE   This is gold country – Father says it's rich . . .

KINGSLEY   It *was* rich. Riches run out like the wrong kind
of love.

GWYNNE   You mustn't talk like this. I'm to marry Ben . . .

KINGSLEY   Different people love in different ways. Some
people love dangerously and carelessly –
living for themselves, as much as they live
for each other. That's their way, and I won't
quarrel with it. That's Ben's way,
Gwynne – but it's not yours.

KINGSLEY *takes* GWYNNE's *hands.*

KINGSLEY   For some people, love is a naked sword – for
others, it's a warm cloak.

She is very drawn to him.

KINGSLEY   I have a cloak for you, Gwynne, whenever you
need it.

CHRISTY *comes in with some proofs. His eyes pop from one to
the other as* GWYNNE *turns away sharply.*

CHRISTY   Didn't mean to make you jump – move like a
cat – can't help it. Trained myself to it, you
know, in Queensland . . . *[settling in for a
yarn]* . . . commanding a troop of native
police, I was. Oho, they were a wild lot,
too – kept 'em in order with the threat of a
flogging and the promise of rum . . .
[modestly] Terrible hard man I was then . . .
ashamed of meself when I look back on it.

JOCK's *voice is heard downstairs . . . sturdily respectful.*

JOCK   Good morning to ye, Mr. Torrent.

BERNIE's *voice chimes in on top of this, calling upstairs.*

BERNIE   Good morning, Mr. Torrent.

A heavy step on the stairs and RUFUS TORRENT *appears in the
doorway. He is a handsome, self-possessed man about forty-eight,*

with thick hair and a magnificent beard, well dressed, his back-flung coat displaying a rich, dark waistcoat, strung across with a heavy gold watch chain. In his deep-set eyes, curling nostril and deep-cut mouth there is pride, autocracy, exhibitionism (and withdrawal) and a big slice of charm. As he enters the room his quick glance takes in GWYNNE *and* KINGSLEY . . . there is no suspicion in it, just his usual observation. CHRISTY *greets him.*

CHRISTY   By God and by Grundy, it's a fine morning, Mr. Torrent.

RUFUS   *[jovially]* So good that God will forgive even the blasphemy, Christy. These proofs for me? *[he takes them]* Ah, Gwynne, my dear – and as pretty as the morning itself . . . *[in moments like these,* RUFUS' *brogue, usually carefully controlled, suggests itself]* Good morning, Kingsley. Christy, remind Mr. MacDonald to keep an extra half column open for the court stories, will you? Judge Shaw expects to adjourn early this morning, so Ben should be in at any moment.

CHRISTY *nods and shuffles off.* RUFUS *starts across room to hat stand on which he hangs his glossily dignified hat. He looks over his shoulder.*

RUFUS   Did Kingsley have to act as your escort, Gwynne?

GWYNNE *is embarrassed and that annoys* KINGSLEY.

RUFUS   I hope Ben hears of it . . . make him envious . . . keep him up to the mark.

GWYNNE   *[hastily]* King . . . Mr. Myers and I met here . . .

RUFUS   Do you want to see me – or Ben – Kingsley?

KINGSLEY   May I see you, sir . . .? *[the coolness intended for* GWYNNE *reacts on her – and on* RUFUS*]*

RUFUS   Well, that sounds serious. You don't want to see me, do you, Gwynne?

GWYNNE   Oh, no . . . I mean . . .

RUFUS   *[joking]* You mean, I'm not the right Torrent.

GWYNNE   How is Ben this morning, Mr. Torrent? *[she is wondering where* BEN *spent last night]*

RUFUS   I haven't seen him. For once, he had risen early, and had gone before I came down to

breakfast – so Mrs. Preston told me. I haven't
even had the opportunity to question him
about our new colleague, all he would say
was that I was completely justified in the
favourable impression I was given by his
application . . . clear, concise . . . *[to*
GWYNNE*]* Did Ben give you any information,
my dear?

GWYNNE　No, Mr. Torrent.

RUFUS　I thought he might have said something last
night – but then, young lovers who have
been separated have more things to talk
about, I imagine . . . don't you, Kingsley?

KINGSLEY　I've never given the matter any thought, sir.

RUFUS *shoots him a questioning glance . . .* RUFUS *is never so
intent on himself or his business that he loses his awareness of
small things.*

GWYNNE　Good morning, Mr. Torrent . . .

RUFUS　Goodbye, my dear. I'll tell Ben . . .

GWYNNE *shoots a troubled glance in* KINGSLEY's *direction and her
'Good morning . . .' trailing away is meant for* KINGSLEY. *He
knows it, but is still annoyed enough to ignore her. She goes.*
RUFUS *moves through into his private office. He is surprised when*
KINGSLEY *follows him in.*

KINGSLEY　Can I see you for a minute, sir . . .?

RUFUS　Close the door.

KINGSLEY *does so. He is rather bitter in his approach in this scene.*

KINGSLEY　Not that what I've got to say is very private – I
talk too much when I'm enthusiastic. Mr.
Manson often has a bit of fun at my expense.
We were having a drink in the Travellers'
Arms, and he got someone to go out and buy
a kid's tin bucket and he gave it to me full of
beer . . . 'Here you are, Kingsley,' he said.
'Feed this into your irrigation scheme.'

RUFUS *warms to* KINGSLEY, *because he loathes* MANSON *himself.*

KINGSLEY　Well – that's Mr. Manson . . . a wealthy man,
an influential man – but not one to look to
for understanding. Rufus, can I look to
you for it? You're a man of integrity – a man
of vision.

RUFUS   I'm also a man who runs a newspaper, my boy,
           and my directors, with good money sunk in
           those mines out there, will be screaming like
           banshees – *[apologetically]* – if you
           comprehend the term – if I come out in
           support of your scheme. [KINGSLEY's *mouth
           opens in further argument.* RUFUS *halts him]*
           Besides, I'm not – really – convinced,
           Kingsley . . . Koolgalla is a gold town. Oh, I
           know it isn't as prosperous as it has
           been – but all the interests here – big and
           small – are sunk in gold, and it's still paying
           off.

KINGSLEY   For the moment. The big interests . . .

RUFUS   I said big and small. And the small people will
           be against you, too, if you ask them to give
           up their dreams of Eldorado, their hope of
           swift and easy fortune. What can you give
           them in its place?

KINGSLEY   Real hope – not chance, and a blind stab in the
           dark. I tell you, Mr. Torrent, bring water to
           this land and it will grow anything – peaches
           this size, melons, grapes. With water, we
           can –

RUFUS   But we have water –

KINGSLEY   *[scornfully]* Yes – for the gold sluices – a muddy
           trickle in the dry spells and a roaring torrent
           in the floods. Look, sir, this isn't only for
           Koolgalla. If this scheme is successful, we can
           prove to the rest of the country – *[he pulls up
           short; stiffly]* I suppose you think I'm an
           egotist seeking applause –

RUFUS   *[his warmth and charm very apparent]* Worse,
           King – I think you're a self-sacrificer. People
           will follow an egotist sooner, because his
           sense of self-preservation gives them
           confidence. With a self-sacrificer, they're
           afraid that they may get caught up in his
           particular martyrdom.

KINGSLEY   *[brushing this aside]* And you won't help me?

RUFUS   I can make it possible for you to lay your

scheme before the town Council.

KINGSLEY   I've seen them . . .

RUFUS   You can talk to my directors at their next
meeting – try to win their support.

KINGSLEY   Thanks – I will. But you won't back me
personally – advocate the scheme
yourself . . .?

RUFUS   *[after a moment – understanding* KINGSLEY's
disappointment] No, Kingsley.

With a hopeless gesture, KINGSLEY *turns away and is about to
pick up his hat when* BEN TORRENT *comes in. Ben is young,
handsome, beguiling, a little spoilt, somewhat in awe of his father,
and certainly dominated by* RUFUS' *authority and leadership.
Despite the warm morning, he wears a dark overcoat buttoned
up to his throat and carries a soft dark felt hat which he tosses
on to the desk.*

RUFUS   *[glad of the interruption]* Good morning, Ben.

BEN   Good morning, Father . . . Hello, King.

KINGSLEY   How is crime in Koolgalla, Ben?

BEN   Prospering.

RUFUS   What's wrong with you, boy – wrapped round
in that heavy overcoat, with summer outside
the window. Take it off.

BEN *gathers the coat closer round his throat.*

BEN   I feel the cold, Father. I think I have a chill.

RUFUS   *[good humoured, but patronising]* I don't know
what's wrong with the young men today.
They're all becoming effete. Perhaps it's the
warm climate here that makes their blood run
thin. Now when I lived in Dublin – oh, those
winter mornings and the grey evenings,
standing on the street corners, clenching your
hands in the torn pockets of your overcoat,
watching the girls coming from the factories,
with their shawls folded over their beautiful
bright heads . . . *[he stops himself suddenly,
aware of the others' interest. Austerely]* It
made a man of me.

BEN   The weather, Father – or the girls?

RUFUS   Ben, you have a frivolous turn of mind. You
know, Kingsley, I wonder did I do right to

	trust Ben to engage our new colleague . . .
BEN	*[hastily]* May I remind you, Father – you had made your decision already.
RUFUS	Nonsense – I left it entirely to you. I did happen to remark that from the applications received . . . we had quite a number, Kingsley . . . Koolgalla must have become more than a fly-by-night village . . .
BEN	It will become much less, once the gold runs out.
RUFUS	*[testily]* As I say, I did remark that, judging from qualifications stated, J. G. Milford . . .
BEN	*[with a curious satisfaction]* Seemed by far the most suitable – yes, you did. And having interviewed the others we had considered, I was forced – *forced*, Father – to your point of view. And J. G. Milford arrives by today's train.
RUFUS	That should be in soon – we must meet it.
BEN	I'll attend to that.
RUFUS	Is he very fast?
BEN	Oh, I don't think – Oh, you mean the – the typing – and shorthand. Very, Father – and accurate – reads and marks proofs clearly . . .
RUFUS	*[pleased with himself]* I knew – there was a ring of truthfulness. And the letter, Kingsley – a really well-written business letter. Not too many men can write a good business letter. Yes, I think this Milford will be just what we need here.
BEN	That is your considered opinion, Father?
RUFUS	Certainly.
BEN	I'm glad of that.

BERNIE *comes in.*

BERNIE	Excuse me, Mr. Torrent, Mr. MacDonald asked had you checked that proof?
RUFUS	I've got it here – *[as* BERNIE *holds out his hand]* No, I'll come down for a moment. Don't forget that train, Ben – we don't want to seem unfriendly. *[jovially to* BERNIE *as he follows him out]* You'll have to be wide-

awake now, Bernie – mustn't let this city
gentleman think he's paddled his canoe into a
backwater, eh . . .

He has gone, in the sound of his own chuckle and BERNIE's
flattered 'No, Mr. Torrent.' KINGSLEY, *still glum, is lounging in
the window left, and* BEN *is standing at the desk, his back to the
audience.*

KINGSLEY   Ben, I talked to your father . . .

BEN *turns round to face him. Now his coat is open and thrown
back and under it, he is still in handsome but slightly rumpled
dress clothes.*

KINGSLEY   *[really laughing]* Ben – you fool! You haven't
been home all night!

BEN   Straight to court – and on the hottest morning
this year! Even the judge was looking at me,
as he sat with his gown thrown back as far
as decorum allowed . . .

KINGSLEY   But your father said you'd had breakfast . . .?

BEN   Mrs. Preston always hides me from the Wrath.
I have a way with housekeepers.

KINGSLEY   *[sighing]* You have a way with any female.
Gwynne – *[stumbling]* your fiancée – has
been here looking for you . . .

BEN   Oh, hell! Did she say anything to Father about
me not seeing her yesterday?

KINGSLEY   *[sternly]* No. She let him think you had.

BEN   I meant to – I met someone. Is Gwynne very
annoyed?

KINGSLEY   She is hurt.

BEN   *[groans]* Much worse. Dammit, King, why does
one have anything to do with nice women.
The not-nice ones are so much less expensive
in the long run. They do give something in
return for payment. Nice women take
everything from you, and still leave you
feeling you owe them something . . . it might
be your heart, or your brain, or your
soul – or your sins. And *they* are the hardest
things to give up!

KINGSLEY   *[who can be very Victorian]* Perhaps we men
forget what good women sacrifice for us.

BEN   *[lighting a cigarette –* KINGSLEY *refuses one with
           a head shake]* They never allow us to do
           that!

KINGSLEY   It's a pity you're so plagued with women,
           Ben – but you must turn to one kind or the
           other.

BEN   *[smiling]* Don't be too sure that there are only
           two kinds, King. You like Gwynne – very
           much – don't you?

KINGSLEY   *[stiffly]* I admire and venerate Miss Thomas . . .

BEN   You sound like the inscription on a tombstone!
           Gwynne is a perfect darling . . . *[meaning it]*
           You know, if you really care, King – I
           wouldn't stand in your way –

KINGSLEY   *[for whom the morning has been too much]* I
           wouldn't, Ben – stand in my way at this
           moment, or I'll punch your nose . . .

As BEN *is staring, and* KINGSLEY *glaring,* RUFUS *comes back in.* BEN
struggles to engulf himself in the coat, KINGSLEY *to hold* RUFUS's
attention.

RUFUS   Ben, you're still wrapped in that coat . . .

KINGSLEY   *[babbling, looking out of the window]* Big
           crowd in the streets, Mr. Torrent . . .
           wonderful view you've got from these
           windows . . .

RUFUS *is looking suspiciously from one young man to the other.
He knows they are hiding something.*

KINGSLEY   There's old Stuwell – and his son.

RUFUS *walks over behind him and looks out.*

KINGSLEY   I tell you, Mr. Torrent, if you want to try to
           talk sense to two stupid people . . .

RUFUS   My directors . . .

KINGSLEY, *turning his head and finding himself face to face with*
RUFUS , *decides to look out again.*

KINGSLEY   Now I know why there is such a crowd in the
           streets . . . the train's in early . . .

BEN   *[enshrouded in his coat again]* The train's in!
           Oh, damnation . . . I meant to meet –

RUFUS   Not much of a welcome for the new man, Ben.

JOHN MANSON *walks in. Physically, he is a worthy opponent for*
RUFUS – *an arrogant, forceful man, who can hide his ruthlessness*

in earthy good-fellowship, or display it when he chooses. He has no son – this increases his dislike for RUFUS. *His manner to* BEN *is indulgent, and even in disagreement, it is flattering. He would love to win* BEN *to some enterprise.*

MANSON *is not noticed at first.* BEN *is half-delighted, half apprehensive about what he has done.*

BEN Oh, I'll explain. The new employee will understand . . . very understanding, the new employee. I hope you'll feel the same way, Father.

RUFUS *[irritable]* Don't babble, Ben –

MANSON That's how a young man feels on a fine morning . . . like breakfasting on bubbly –

BEN *is thrown off balance.*

BEN Oh, hell! . . . you here!

MANSON Now what's wrong with me, Ben.

BEN I didn't know Mr. Manson would be here, Father. *[meaning I didn't mean to pull this in front of him]* You see – J. G. Milford may be something of a surprise.

CHRISTY *appears in the doorway, clutching the suitcases. He drops a suitcase, jerks a thumb over his shoulder.*

CHRISTY S'here . . .!

RUFUS Christy, you've been drinking!

CHRISTY By Grundy, I ain't – but by God, I'm goi' to . . . and I'll take a bet that I'm not the only one. J – G – MILFORD!

JENNY *comes through the doorway – neat, cool and pretty. She is aware of the odds against her, but she tries to carry it off – and it's a good try.*

Faces seen. JENNY *looks to* BEN.

RUFUS *looks murder at* BEN.

RUFUS J. G. Milford . . .

JENNY The 'J' is for Jenny – but I always use my initials. I do not wish to take any advantage from being a woman.

MANSON *roars with laughter.*

MANSON Ben, I congratulate you. Ben certainly took you there, Torrent.

JENNY *looks at him.*

MANSON John Manson, ma'am . . .

JENNY *ducks her head in acknowledgement. She looks to* RUFUS. *She is inwardly quaking.* CHRISTY, *at entrance, has been joined by* JOCK.

JENNY *has taken off her hat, puts handbag, gloves, etc. on desk. She is concentrating on the hat . . . she wants to make some move to establish herself.*

  JENNY May I . . .?

  RUFUS Please do . . .

JENNY *hangs her hat on the peg, below* RUFUS' *hat. It swings. She considers it. With a polite little smile to* RUFUS, *she moves his top-hat to lower peg, hangs hers above it.*

  BEN *inches towards exit.*

   BEN Remember, Father – your considered opinion.

As the curtain comes down, JENNY *is looking from one to the other.* RUFUS *is still glaring at* BEN.

Curtain is lowered to mark a time lapse.

 The office of the Koolgalla 'Argus'. Late afternoon (same day).

KINGSLEY *feels rather awkward, but also feels Victorian – protective about* GWYNNE. GWYNNE *shows more spark than she did in the morning – less the ideal of Victorian girlhood . . . in fact, she is angry with* BEN.

BEN, *dressed in a day suit now, his hat on the back of his head, is both non-committal and provoking (the way he often is when he knows he's been rather outrageous). He moves about the set a lot, sits on the edge of the desk, examines blocks, is impudent, cajoling, stubborn in turn.*

  GWYNNE Where is she now?

   BEN Settling into her room in Mrs. Crabtree's
      boarding house I suppose . . .

  GWYNNE Don't you know . . .?

BEN *gets enormously interested in a proof. Unconsciously,* GWYNNE *is relying on* KINGSLEY *as her supporter, so she looks at him.*

  GWYNNE Why did you do it, Ben?

  KINGSLEY You must have been out of your mind.

   BEN You're so keen on irrigation, King. I'm irrigating
      the intellectual stream. I'm tossing a stone
      into the pool of reflection. I've often said I
      wanted something to change in Koolgalla . . .

  GWYNNE How could you be taken in by someone like

	that – writing all those *lies!*
BEN	What lies? She has done everything she claimed in her letter.
GWYNNE	But she's a woman!
BEN	Her father was an editor of a paper in Tasmania – a paper very like the 'Argus'. He didn't have a son – and since he had liberal ideas . . . if either of you can understand that expression –
KINGSLEY	Steady on, Ben –
BEN	He wanted his daughter to be something more than a fashion-plate – or a queen bee!
GWYNNE	You mean that for me.
BEN	You always say I don't explain things to you . . . now, I'm explaining. Miss Milford acted in much the same capacity to her father as I do to mine.
KINGSLEY	Fair enough perhaps – in Tasmania. But it's rather much to expect Koolgalla to take.
BEN	So is your irrigation scheme. Gwynne, shall I see you home?
GWYNNE	No, thank you, Ben. If Rainbird hadn't thrown a shoe, I wouldn't have come back here today.
KINGSLEY	I could ride that way . . .
GWYNNE	Thank you, King . . .

She is quite angry.

| GWYNNE | *[to* BEN*]* I'm sure that will be suitable to you . . .? |

She looks at BEN. *She is still in love with him, would like to provoke him into making some claim on her.*

KINGSLEY *waits, too, then says:*

| KINGSLEY | I'll – get the horses from the livery stable – |

KINGSLEY *goes out. The light is dying, and there is a soft sunset light in the office.* BEN *turns to her with momentary remorse.*

BEN	Gwynne, I don't mean . . .
GWYNNE	What, Ben?
BEN	I don't mean to be – me, I suppose. *[he puts his arms around her]* But you know what I am.
GWYNNE	*[sadly]* No, I don't know what you are. I don't even know if you want to marry me.

BEN *is really very fond of* GWYNNE, *attracted to her sweetness and prettiness. They kiss – quite fervently – but* GWYNNE *draws away. To look at him.*

GWYNNE   You do want to marry me, Ben?

BEN *turns his head, to listen to a sound.*

BEN   Yes, pet, but it may not be possible. You may be a widow before you're a bride! Father has just come in.

GWYNNE   Oh, Ben, can't you give this woman some money and make her go away again?

BEN   Is that your solution? No – I can't.

RUFUS *walks in. He is still in a controlled fury. He unbends to* GWYNNE.

RUFUS   Gwynne, my dear . . . I didn't expect to see you in town still.

GWYNNE   Rainbird cast a shoe.

RUFUS *is longing to get at* BEN, *but ladies must come first.*

RUFUS   Well . . . I do want to see you, Ben, after you have taken Gwynne home.

GWYNNE   *[a touch of feline]* Ben thought you would want to talk to him. Nothing must stand in the way of that!

RUFUS *looks at* BEN. BEN *looks back, defiant.*

GWYNNE   Goodnight, Mr. Torrent.

RUFUS   Will you never learn to call me 'Papa' . . . That is what I will be when you and Ben are married.

GWYNNE   I think it would be very difficult to think of you as 'Papa' . . .

GWYNNE *goes out.*

RUFUS   *[a bit flattered]* Hmmmm. And now, Ben, have you any explanation?

BEN   Yes, sir – your considered opinion. J. G. Milford was your choice.

RUFUS   I left it to you . . .

BEN   You didn't leave it to me, Father. You had made your decision before I ever left Koolgalla. Had I come back with any other applicant, you would have considered my decision ill-advised. You'll just have to put up with it, Father – that the 'J' is for Jenny.

CURTAIN

ACT ONE

SCENE 2

The office. One week later, about lunch time. It looks much as before, but the desk with the typewriter is tidy, the blocks have been stacked neatly in the mended boxes, the files placed neatly inside them. On the hat rack, RUFUS' *hat sits square and determinedly over the very top of the rack itself.*

RUFUS is standing in the doorway of his inner office listening to CHRISTY, *who is holding the floor.* JOCK MacDONALD *leans up against the desk, and* BERNIE *is standing rather timidly near the doorway.*

CHRISTY *[on a full flow of oratory]* . . . By Grundy, I said to her . . . By Grundy, I been in the printing business for fifty years, I said! I have been, too! Started when I was as young as young Bernie here . . . used to work for a couple of brothers in Jindabyne; twins, they were – like a couple of peas. *[getting intrigued with his own story]* You know, a funny thing happened the time Jim got married to Elsie Wainwright. It was a pretty good wedding, and everyone had more than a drop of drink to wish them luck. Anyway, young Jim woke up the next morning in his own single bed at home – and no Elsie in sight! 'Hell,' he thinks, 'I've done it this time – she's gone back to her mother's, and I know that old faggot'll cook my goose for me.' He gets up – terrible agony he was in, too – and there, halfway through breakfast, is Elsie, fresh as a daisy. 'Elsie,' says Jim, 'Will you ever forgive me leaving you – and on our wedding night, too? Can you ever forgive your Jim?' And Elsie drops her marmalade and toast and shrieks, 'My Jim! Then who the hell's upstairs in the double bed!'

CHRISTY, *completely beguiled by his own story, slaps his leg and guffaws.* RUFUS *smiles slightly.*

JOCK *[with a reproving nod in the direction of wide-eyed* BERNIE*]* Stick to the subject, Christy.

	That has nothing to do with Miss Milford.
CHRISTY	Well, I was just telling *you* that I was telling *her* that I'd been in the printing game for fifty years . . .
JOCK	When you were not chasing outlaw blacks and fighting on the Eureka Stockade and . . .
CHRISTY	*[a quick glance at* BERNIE *. . .* CHRISTY *doesn't want to lose his audience there. Dignified]* Fifty years – on and off. And in that time I says to her, nobody has ever told me that my type needed cleaning – and nobody's ever going to make me clean it! Furthermore, I says to her, when I took the next proof up, furthermore, now that it has been cleaned, I defy you to tell me that you can spot any difference!
RUFUS	But you cleaned it?
CHRISTY	*[taken aback]* Just to prove my point though!
JOCK	*[who can't resist baiting* CHRISTY*]* He cleaned it all right, Mr. Torrent . . . the lassie tricked him into that finally!
CHRISTY	Taking her side, you old petticoat-chaser? 'Mister Christy' she calls me! Mister!
BERNIE	*[timidly]* She might mean to be polite, Christy.
CHRISTY	*[getting himself annoyed]* And who is she . . . her with her pink blouse and her sailor hat, to come being polite to Christy Blades? Furthermore, I said to her, by God, a woman's place is in the home!
JOCK	*[surprised by this phrase. Even* RUFUS *nods approval]* That's verra well put . . . oreaginal . . .
CHRISTY	*[basking in the approval]* Oh, I ain't been putting words together at a frame for fifty years without learning how to string a couple together in my head. I remember one time I was working on a newspaper –
RUFUS	*[deciding this has gone far enough]* So from all this, I gather that you men are not at all contented to continue working here with Miss Milford?

BERNIE *would love to speak out but just can't manage it.* JOCK *hesitates.*

> JOCK　We – ll, Mr. Torrent . . . It's not so much us.
> But you mind those new men you promised
> we'd be getting . . .

RUFUS *is amused . . . he knows this is blackmail.*

> RUFUS　I haven't forgotten, Jock. Just as soon as this
> matter is settled –
> JOCK　*We* might manage to rub along with the lass –
> BERNIE　Oh, yes . . .!

He gets quenching looks from the others.

> JOCK　– but if we've got the *new* men to
> consider – they might not care to work with
> a lady . . .
> RUFUS　We have all worked together here so
> harmoniously in the past that I would not
> like to see that harmony upset . . . If you
> wish it, when Miss Milford returns from her
> lunch, I will put your objections before her.

JENNY *has walked in. She takes the situation in – she has been waiting for something like this. She comes as a shock to them, even to* RUFUS.

> RUFUS　Oh – Miss Milford, Jock and Christy came to
> see me on this question of your continued
> employment here . . . you remember – a trial
> period . . .?
> JOCK　Well, Mr. Torrent, it was you that came and
> asked for our opinion.
> RUFUS　I felt it was my duty to discover the feelings of
> the rest of my staff. They – have an
> objection . . .
> JENNY　You mean you would like my resignation?
> BERNIE　Oh, no . . .!

He gets glared at by everybody.

> RUFUS　Thank you, Miss Milford . . .
> JENNY　I shan't give it!

General stupefaction!

> JENNY　Has my work been so unsatisfactory?
> RUFUS　On the contrary, you are very efficient. When
> you leave us, Miss Milford, I will be happy
> to give you the best of references. I shall

simply say that circumstances over which we
had no control necessitated your
resignation . . . and that any future employer
will be gaining an asset –

JENNY So long as he has more control over the
circumstances.

RUFUS Shall we be honest, Miss Milford –

JENNY I would prefer it.

RUFUS A printing office of a newspaper is no place for
a member of the female sex. It is a place for
men of the world – violent and terrible
happenings are its very life's blood. There is
no protection for natural womanly weakness.
Sometimes, the language – the language is not
fit for your ears.

JENNY Then you should all be ashamed! You are
worrying about the language heard by a well
travelled and experienced person of twenty-
eight, but you don't care what comes to the
ears of a sheltered fifteen year old –

JENNY *points dramatically at* BERNIE. BERNIE *blushes to the tips of
his ears.*

BERNIE Sixteen come January, Miss.

RUFUS *[sanctimoniously]* I hope you men do keep a
close watch on your tongues when the boy is
with you.

JENNY *seizes her advantage.*

JENNY So far as I am concerned, Mr. Torrent, I have
never heard anything said in my presence
that might not have been said by a
gentleman . . . a gentleman under stress,
sometimes . . . but always a gentleman.

RUFUS *has to turn away to hide his involuntary grin – she has
turned it neatly.*

JOCK Oh, lassie – lassie . . .

JENNY Mr. MacDonald – you've been kind. You're
good enough at your own work to know that
mine, too, is well enough in its way. Why do
you object to me?

JOCK Well – a fair question deserves a fair reply. I
don't object to you meself, lassie. You're a

good worker and a pleasant speaker, and I
suppose I could get used to the sight of a bit
of petticoat going up the stairs every day.
But if the others are unhappy about
you – and if Mr. Torrent's not easy in his
mind about getting those new men I need so
badly – *[lamely]* well, I've got to think of
what's best for everyone, don't I?

CHRISTY *looks at* JOCK *with scorn.* BERNIE *is looking at* JENNY.

CHRISTY   *[to* JOCK*]* A bit of petticoat –

JENNY   And you, Mr. Christy – why do you wish to
see me gone?

CHRISTY   Well, I – *[produces his masterpiece]* Because a
woman's place is in the home!

JENNY   So, when I am put out of my work here, Mr.
Christy, will you take me into your home?

CHRISTY   I'm a bachelor!

JENNY   A very good reason for employing me in your
home. I should manage it better than many
of your home-bred women. Teaching a
woman to do her work well in an office is
not going to stop her doing it well in the
house. On the contrary –

RUFUS   I think this discussion is becoming pointless –

Obviously RUFUS *wants to end it, because* JENNY *has made some
points.*

*He walks into his office. He sits at his desk, takes up proofs . . .
it is obvious from his attitude that the dismissal of* JENNY *hasn't
gone the way he thought it would.*

In the outer office, JOCK, CHRISTY, BERNIE *shuffle.*

JOCK   There's work waiting . . . *[they start out]* Look,
lass, I'm sorry, but it's not the proper station
of life to which the Lord's called you, see. It's
not your fault.

They go out, BERNIE *looking back.* JENNY *opens her desk and
begins to take out some personal belongings, including a lace
handkerchief.*

RUFUS *comes from his office.* JENNY *is over at the hat-stand
taking her hat off the hook, when* RUFUS *comes out of the inner
office.* JENNY *is near to tears, but defiant.* RUFUS *is a little
ashamed. They look at each other.* RUFUS *gets his hat from the*

hat-stand. He starts out, stops by the desk . . . he looks at the collection of JENNY's *personal belongings . . . without thinking he picks up a handkerchief . . . sniffs the perfume . . . realizes what he is doing and drops it back.* JENNY *seen, watching him.*

RUFUS   I am going out, Miss Milford – [he turns back] I am sorry, Miss Milford –

JENNY   When I began here, Mr. Torrent, they told me you were a hard man – hard but just. I see they were mistaken.

RUFUS   I suppose I do seem unjust to you. As for my hardness, I am sorry for it. But I set myself a task here – and hardness is unavoidable.

JENNY   Oh, I don't think you're hard, Mr. Torrent! I think you're rather soft. Well, it *is* soft to get rid of someone who can be an asset to your business . . . and you know I can be . . . because you haven't the strength to be different. It's rather sad.

RUFUS   [livid] I do as I see fit!

JENNY   They said that, too. 'There'll be women working everywhere in Koolgalla soon' – they said – 'now that Rufus Torrent has shown the way.' Oh, most of them didn't approve of the idea but they couldn't help – admiring. None of them would have had the courage to engage a woman to work for them. [comfortingly] I expect it will be quite a relief to them that you hadn't, either.

RUFUS *looks at her. He appraises her move. He is moved to unwilling admiration.*

RUFUS   Miss Milford, you may stay. I would refuse to accept your resignation if you offered it. I will be back in an hour. When I return, I expect to find the advertisements listed, the page make-ups ready for my initialling, and the Council Meeting notes typed up . . .

JENNY   [controlling her triumph she says obediently] Yes, Mr. Torrent.

RUFUS *picks up a type-written page from her desk.*

RUFUS   Miss Milford – you have an unfortunate tendency in otherwise excellent spelling to refuse to recognize that 'E I' generally follows 'C'. Watch that.

JENNY *nods obediently.*

    JENNY   Yes, Mr. Torrent.

At the door RUFUS *turns back.*

    RUFUS   I hope you realize that I saw the trap that you set for me. No doubt you feel you have achieved a victory. No doubt you have. But since you have chosen to un-sex yourself, do not expect any tolerance for feminine weaknesses. *[a warning]* One mistake, Miss Milford! . . . I will be back at two o'clock.

RUFUS *goes out.*

JENNY *expresses her delight by putting her belongings back in the desk drawer, hanging her hat back on its peg, dipping a curtsey to the hat stand.*

MANSON *comes in as* JENNY *is having her little triumphal play. He waits till she sweeps out of the courtesy.*

    MANSON   Does the King of Ireland make you bow to his hat-stand, Miss Milford?

JENNY *is angry at being caught.*

    MANSON   That was a very pretty gesture. What was it ˙for?

    JENNY   *[going to her typewriter]* Since there can be no reasonable explanation, Mr. Manson, I'll attempt none. Mr. Torrent has just gone out.

    MANSON   I heard him. I was in the printing room, looking at some proofs . . . something to do with a bit of a scheme of mine. I don't believe in putting all my eggs in one basket . . . Where's Ben?

    JENNY   *[always very terse with* MANSON*]* Mr. Ben Torrent has not come in yet.

    MANSON   Where can I find him?

    JENNY   I really don't know, Mr. Manson, he may be in Court or –

    MANSON   Anywhere . . . places a lady can't mention.

JENNY *looks at him coolly.*

    MANSON   I like Ben. I'd like a boy like Ben. *[a deep anger]* Hell, I *deserve* a boy like Ben . . .

JENNY *begins to type.*

MANSON   Do you like Ben, Miss Milford?

JENNY   I enjoy working here, Mr. Manson, with all the
                staff –

MANSON   Even Rufus Torrent, the King of Ireland.

JENNY *catches her nail in the keys. She sucks her finger briefly
and angrily.*

MANSON   A bit jumpy today, Miss Milford . . .? When
                Ben comes in, tell him I'll give him a good
                lunch at the Travellers' Arms . . . Bubbly in
                the middle of the day . . . Y'know something,
                Miss Milford . . .?

JENNY *looks up to him.*

MANSON   Twenty-five years ago, I couldn't've imagined
                bubbly at all . . . dirt poor I was . . . then it
                was pay dirt. All dirt, though –
                [MANSON *starts out, swings back]* I know you
                don't like me but I like you. I wouldn't allow
                a woman of mine to work like a man – but it
                must take guts. Don't forget to tell Ben I
                asked for him.

BERNIE *passes* MANSON *in the doorway.*

BERNIE *is carrying some proofs.*

MANSON *is aware of* BERNIE's *look at* JENNY. *A great deal of*
MANSON's *success has come from catching people off guard and
he never loses an opportunity – not even with* BERNIE.

MANSON   Don't go turning the boy's head now, Miss
                Milford –

He goes.

BERNIE   I suppose you think a man showed up in a very
                poor light, Miss Milford – not taking your
                part.

JENNY   [*glancing through proofs]* What man . . .?

BERNIE   Why – me, Miss Milford!

JENNY   You! [*she has an impulse to laugh. Then, with
                his eyes on her, her genuine kindliness
                prevents this.]* Of course – you.

BERNIE   I've been worrying about not speaking out.

JENNY   That's happened to most of us – not speaking
                out about something, and then being sorry
                for it. But there always comes another
                chance.

BERNIE   Not to speak out for – you.

JENNY   For something more than me next time. But thank you.

BEN *is heard downstairs, calling* 'JENNY' . . . *He comes in.*

BEN   What's all this nonsense about deputations and resignations? You're not to go away. I don't want you to go away!

JENNY *looks at him. She is aggravated by his peremptory manner. But she is charming to* BERNIE.

JENNY   I'll read this immediately, Bernie – it is all right to call you 'Bernie'.

BERNIE   *[overwhelmed]* Oh, yes, Miss Milford!

He exits, very happy.

JENNY *goes back to desk, starts skimming through proofs. She can't contain her annoyance with* BEN.

JENNY   I don't think you should call me by my Christian name, Mr. Torrent. It doesn't look well. I have had quite enough trouble in this office without being suspected of undue familiarity – with my employer's son!

BEN   *[laughing]* You sound like a subscription library . . . *[posturing]* 'Sir, I may be but a poor working girl, but my honour means as much to me as to the finest lady in the land!' *[*JENNY *has to laugh]* Anyway, you can be free with first names to Bernie.

JENNY   That is rather a different matter . . .

She continues to mark the proof. BEN *props against the filing cabinet, looks at her.*

BEN   Why don't you like me, Jenny?

JENNY   I don't dislike you, Ben –

BEN   First name at last!

JENNY   – *[crossly]* Oh, since you won't maintain a proper discipline, don't expect me to maintain it for you! I don't dislike you. Everybody likes you. But you're so very, very – *[hesitates for word]*

BEN   Is 'spoiled' the word you're looking for?

JENNY   I didn't mean to be rude –

BEN *begins to play with the blocks, building a house of them on top of the filing cabinet, as he talks.*

BEN   I'm Ben Torrent – good position, good
          prospects, tolerable looks – oh, don't prim up
          your mouth, Jenny! I inherited my looks
          from my father, as I inherited everything
          else – except my lack of private enterprise
          and public spirit. That's fortunate – Koolgalla
          couldn't stand *two* public-spirited Torrents.

As BEN *talks now, he is very moody, seemingly more intent on
the blocks.*

BEN   Now that's affectation if you like. That's the
          worst kind of pride . . . the kind that says 'I
          give the world away. I shall not speak – or
          move – or dream . . .'

JENNY *is really involved with this side of* BEN. *Proof in hand, she
gets up from her desk, as though responding to a challenge.*

BEN   Do you know why it's the worst kind of pride,
          Jenny? . . . The people who think like that
          believe in their deepest hearts that if they
          moved – or spoke – or dreamed – the world
          would change. By refusing to do any of these
          things, they believe they are teaching the
          world a lesson.

*With an abrupt gesture he knocks down the house of blocks. He
smiles at her – the dashing* BEN, *philosophy forgotten.*

BEN   [*positive*] You're not leaving. I won't have it.
JENNY   That has already been decided – between your
          father and me. Mr. Torrent saw my side of
          the situation.
BEN   Presented with a certain feminine subtlety?
JENNY   I hope you don't think I cried into my
          handkerchief – or fluttered my eyelashes?
BEN   Would I suspect you of such cheap tricks? But
          you're not such a fool that you wouldn't use
          all your capabilities. You're an independent
          woman – not an imitation man! . . . and
          clever women have the advantage, every
          time.

JENNY *has been sorting the blocks.*
BEN *comes close to her.*

BEN   You know that's true, don't you, Jenny?
JENNY   Well, Mister – Ben. If I wished to catch a

mouse, I wouldn't consider it a proof of
independence that I hit it on the head with a
hammer . . . not while there are mousetraps
and cheese for the purpose.

She goes out with the proof.
BEN *sits on her desk, laughing. He picks up the handkerchief she
has left behind, and smells the perfume.*

CURTAIN

ACT TWO

SCENE 1

*Three weeks later. A meeting of directors is in progress at the
office. A big table has been moved in for the occasion, jamming
the room.* RUFUS *sits easily at the head of it, with* JENNY *at her
desk behind him and to one side. The five other directors and
shareholders sit on either side.*

MANSON, *big and dominant;* SQUIRES, *a shrewd rather mean
little man;* TWIMPLE, *pleasant but ineffectual, very much in awe
of both* RUFUS *and* MANSON; *the* STUWELLS, *father and son, father
the leading storekeeper – rather pompous. With his bored son.
At the opposite end of the table to* RUFUS *sits* BEN, *coiled like a
spring, tense, watching* KINGSLEY MYERS *who has been addressing
the meeting.* KINGSLEY *hasn't much hope, but he's still trying.*

KINGSLEY   . . . and as you gentlemen can see from these
plans *[bending over plans laid out on table]* it
would be possible to pipe streams of water
from the main source and to divert them,
where necessary, over land in cultivation.
This portion here, which would flow across
Simmerton's Flat –

MANSON   Happens that's the richest gold bearing ground
on the fields, Kingsley – but then so's the rest
of the land you're after. *[Stands up and
moves over to* KINGSLEY, *stabbing with
forefinger on the plans]* Simmerton's
Flat – French's Gully – Coppleston Creek

	across to Kirby's Hollow – gold bearing land, every bit of it. *[Jerking his thumb towards the town outside the window]* Prospectors walking down that street at this moment with gold in their coats that they've taken out of it! And you want to plant – cabbages – on it!
TWIMPLE	It is unfortunate that the two schemes could not flourish side by side, Mr. Myers, but I understand from your explanations that that is impossible.
MANSON	Market gardens between the cradles?

They all laugh.

STUWELL SNR	One of the richest fields in that country, that was –
BEN	Was.
STUWELL SNR	Is. Plenty of it there still. Isn't that so, Charlie. Speak up, son.
STUWELL JNR	Loads. *[He resumes his covert studying of* JENNY, *to which she replies with a chilling look and tucks her ankles well under her skirt]*
TWIMPLE	Now if we could combine both enterprises satisfactorily . . . *[he looks hopefully at* KINGSLEY, *for* MR. TWIMPLE *likes things to go pleasantly]*
KINGSLEY	*[definitely]* Impossible, Mr. Twimple. Those same natural advantages that deposited the gold where it is would have to be used to carry the water where we want it to go.
TWIMPLE	Then, since we have taken out so much wealth from the fields here –
BEN	Yes, Mr. Twimple, taken it out!
RUFUS	That does seem to be a point – whether, having taken so much, we can count on taking more, or whether we should consider that our gold, though plentiful, does not replenish itself.
KINGSLEY	You can't plant gold, gentlemen. Once it's gone, the land lies dead and useless. But plant and water and harvest – put your work back into the land, and the land is grateful for it.

SQUIRES The land may be – er – grateful, Mr. Myers, but what about the people to work it.

MANSON *smacks his hand approvingly on the desk.*

SQUIRES There are farms all over the country crying out for men – and they can't get them! And it's not money – the wages being offered are higher than ever before – much too high, in my opinion, to maintain the economy. But still the men stay on the fields. Not only the farms going shorthanded, either – ships, stores – that is so, isn't it, Mr. Stuwell?

STUWELL SNR There's a notice in my left window at this moment – Man wanted! Been there for months. And what did we get in all that time . . .?

STUWELL JNR [unexpectedly animated] Little fellow in a lavender striped shirt – worked for us for a week, then took his pay out in tools, and joined up with Mike O'Brien in French's Gully.

STUWELL SNR That's right, son – speak up. And Charlie here's been doing every hands turn about the place ever since.

STUWELL JNR Damned dullish . . .

MANSON Then there's your point, Myers. I've got nothing against new ideas – I like to see things go ahead. There's always something in progress for the go-ahead man, and I like a fight of any kind – apart from the money to win. But Squires's got you – who's going to do the work? Some of Torrent's Irish pixies, maybe?

He laughs, followed by the others. RUFUS *looks at a portion of the wall through* MANSON's *head.*

KINGSLEY [after a swift and bitter glance at RUFUS] I see that Mr. Torrent has already discussed *his* objections with you gentlmen. He pointed out to me earlier that he did not believe that people will give up their chance of easy fortune for such a scheme as this.

RUFUS *looks up quickly about to deny this, for it has been pure chance. But seeing* BEN's *accusing look he stiffens and remains silent.*

KINGSLEY   I still think that people can see their way into the future better than you believe. But to do so, they would have to know the alternatives. I had hoped that the 'Argus' would support this scheme. It seems I was foolish. But can't you at least state the details – be absolutely impartial, you prepare the statement from my technical details . . . *[he looks at them all]* I believe I tell you the truth, gentlemen, when I say I am not being led by self interest in this . . . *[their stone wall faces halt him. Briefly, directly to* RUFUS] Shall I leave these? *[gestures to diagrams]*

RUFUS   *[looking in his turn at the others. Then, with an understanding of* KINGSLEY's *feelings]* Take them, Kingsley. We'll send for them – if we want them.

KINGSLEY *picks up the diagrams. Looks at* BEN *for a moment, turns on his heel and walks out.* BEN *half rises as though to follow him. Then he swings on* RUFUS.

BEN   You could have given him that at least! You could have abbreviated a church notice or cut out a social note and given him one day's space to speak. Or, since we're *[contemptuously]* business men here, let him buy it and have his say!

RUFUS   No. *[first to* BEN *then to the others]* No. The price of the 'Argus' is two pence. For that you get the whole paper. But outside of advertising – and Kingsley's scheme is not that – you can't buy one line of the 'Argus' – and never will, while I'm editor here.

STUWELL   You wouldn't call a newspaper a business
SNR   really – not like a store now. It's more of an interest – eh?

Looks at CHARLIE *who seems far from taking an interest in anything.* STUWELL *gives in, on a pensive* 'Yes . . .'.

RUFUS   Right, Ben – we're business men here. But it

happens that in our business we deal in peculiar commodities – events after they happen, and plans before they are realized. And people pay us to make for them the most honest collection we can of the news – and the hopes and plans of this town – this country. *[swinging on them]* Make no mistake, gentlemen – whether you think it right or wrong, the idea of this project must be faced by you sometime. Kingsley is not a single fanatic – whether or not the gold is running out in Koolgalla, it has run out in other places – and men are looking for new ways to live. Some time, I tell you, you will have to make up your minds – for or against. You can't just sit by and let him state his case – you – we – must either attack it bitterly as a dangerous and useless project, or give it our support as necessary life blood to a dying town!

TWIMPLE   *[worried]* But would you say a crisis was approaching, Mr. Torrent. I – I must say that I haven't noticed any falling off in my legal – er – commitments . . .

STUWELL SNR   Nothing wrong with my store – and my store was built on the diggings trade. *[heartening himself]* Oh, imagine the gold running out in Koolgalla!

BEN   Imagine it! Haven't you seen the empty stores in Cresswell, Mr. Stuwell? – shovels and billies and panning dishes still shiny under the dust on the wrappings . . . the broken office windows in Dalton's Crossing, Mr. Twimple, the courthouse falling down.

STUWELL *and* TWIMPLE *look a little aghast. Could there be anything in it?* STUWELL JNR. *bites a nail in vague worry.* MANSON *frowns.*

MANSON *rides in.*

MANSON   *[strong]* And what if it does happen here . . .? We're not tied hand and foot are we? The gold can run out in the ground, but gold is

where you find it. We found it before, didn't
we? Let it go then. We're not finished if it
does.

BEN   There'll be plenty of people in Koolgalla who
will be – if the gold goes, and there's nothing
else.

MANSON   You won't be one of 'em, Ben . . . your father's
seen to that.

BEN   Do you think that would be the only thing that
would count with me?

MANSON   No. But it's the first thing – it has to be. *[This is*
MANSON's *declaration]* You can't give anything
away, Ben, until you've got enough for
yourself – whether it's money, land or
dreams. *[Unawares* JENNY's *lip curls in
contempt]* Yes, Miss Jenny, I understand
dreams, too! *[to* BEN*]* I'm not so old that I've
forgotten what ideas a young man has. But
it's a hard world, Ben. When you're young,
you think you can make it a heaven on
earth – all for yourself and enough for
everyone else . . . but you get that knocked
out of you! Two hands and a brain, that's
what God gives to everyone, for himself.
And you've got to take what you can with
them! *[Suddenly he leans across and takes*
BEN's *hand, holding it flat, comparing it with
his own]* I've worked hard for what I've got.
I froze in Canada, got the yellow fever in
Brazil, dysentery in India – and I came to
Koolgalla, broke, Ben – hungry – broke.
Then I took a parcel out of Simmerton's
Flat . . . but I'd earned it already! You can't
make life easy – not for yourself or anyone
else, Ben. All you do that way is to breed a
race of weaklings, expecting to be saved.
There's plenty in the world to be taken for
the fighting – and any man who doesn't fight,
doesn't deserve it. *[challenging]* You've made
your way in the world, Torrent – have you
anything to add to that?

RUFUS   Nothing, Mr. Manson – you're so eloquent that you might be Irish! But I'll say this to Ben – if he's going to make his way by fighting, it's a good thing to be sure that his opponent is an enemy, and not merely a friend who calls his objectives by another name.

BEN *does not respond.* RUFUS *goes on, to* MANSON.

RUFUS   And, of course, it's always a wise procedure to look under a friend's cloak to see if he carries a dagger!

MANSON   I haven't got a son to advise, Torrent. If I had I'd say this. 'Australia's a big country,' I'd say, 'You look at it from here and what do you see – the diggings, a few green patches where the Chinks set their gardens, the plains beyond – but there's plenty more than that! And it's yours for the taking! When we're finished here, we've only emptied one barrel – so throw it away, Ben. Throw it away and open the next!'

His magnetism holds BEN, *who feels himself swayed though against his own convictions.*

MANSON   You're not the kind of boy who's meant to scratch the earth for cabbages!

BEN   I wish I could be as eloquent as my father. I wish I could put my arguments as well as Mr. Manson. I haven't that power – or the experience. But I do believe that we must go forward to the future.

MANSON   *[with friendly indulgence]* It'll come to us, Ben.

BEN   *[fiercely, by now he is angry, badgered, confused]* But then it's the present, and the harm's been done – and then it's the past and all too late. Gentlemen, I beg of you. Forget that I'm young – overlook that the mechanics of this plan are meaningless to me. But let me urge you to give this thing a chance. Don't pass up the future for the sake of the present that's nearly past. Don't pass up the glorious – impossible – realizable chance. *[His*

> *voice breaking with his conviction]* Oh, I
> know I'm right . . .! *[But now the words
> won't come]*

RUFUS   *[wanting to save him]* Ben . . .

BEN   *[wearily and emptily]* I know, Father. I sound
like a fool. Excuse me, gentlemen. *[At the
door he turns back, bitterly]* Oh, damn all
you old – cautious – safe men. You make the
world unsure!

BEN *starts out. Forgetting where she is,* JENNY *stands up, her
notebook falling to the floor.* BEN *looks at her, goes out.* MANSON
picks up JENNY's *notebook and restores it to her elaborately. He
looks over his shoulder at* RUFUS.

MANSON   *[baiting* RUFUS]* Be careful, Torrent – or you'll
lose him.

TWIMPLE   He has generous sympathies, Mr. Torrent.

MANSON *goes on wanting to irritate* RUFUS.

MANSON   I wouldn't let it worry you that he gets crazy
ideas about the world. All kids do. You
might even've had some yourself once – but
you've learned to knuckle down. Nothing like
going short of bread to make a man learn
what side it's buttered on when he gets it!

RUFUS   *[exploding]* I've learned many things myself, Mr.
Manson – but, by thunder, I've never learned
to lick the butter off my bread – and my son
will never learn it either. You're my directors,
your money is in my paper – and I bow to
that – a certain way. I've listened to
you – now you listen to me! I've told you
that one day you'll have to make up your
minds about this plan. Why not make them
up now – and favourably. *[back to* MANSON]*
For it's true – and you know it – that while
the gold supply *is* continuing, it *is* running
thinner. People who once made a good and
easy living are now scraping the earth for
their loaves of bread – and the men with gold
in their pockets from Simmerton's Flat get
fewer and fewer, Mr. Manson. There are no
more fortunes to be made – except by the

people who sell the loaves of bread and the God-given earth the people scrape. *[to* STUWELL*]* And not for long – think of that! For who makes money in a dead town?

MANSON   I've told you – move on.

RUFUS   *[he is concentrating on* STUWELL *and* TWIMPLE *knowing that* MANSON *will not come his way]* Somewhere you have to stay. And in that place you have to build as well as take. Shall this be our stopping place, gentlemen? Shall we harness the river, and make the town grow, and show them that the 'Argus' moves ahead of the times?

It is a good effort and TWIMPLE *and* STUWELL *are swaying.*

STUWELL   It'd take money . . .

TWIMPLE   You've shown logic there, Mr. Torrent . . .

SQUIRES   *[as* RUFUS *looks at him]* I would like to hear what Mr. Manson thinks about it.

MANSON   *[standing at window, looking down on town]* What do I think? I think Torrent makes up his mind very suddenly – unless it was made up already. Maybe he's got other interests he's not telling us.

SQUIRES   It is a rapid decision, Mr. Torrent. I don't want to pry, but if this scheme of Mr. Myers *might* be accepted by the Lands Department . . . I suppose it *could* be – certain property investments might become very valuable. *[shrewd]* Yours, perhaps . . .? So why not ours – if you have the information to share . . .

RUFUS   Mr. Squires, there is a rodent not yet registered in the catalogue of Australian animals – the lavatory rat –

He bows formally to JENNY.

RUFUS   – Excuse the term, Miss Milford.

JENNY *indicates 'pardon granted'.*

STUWELL   I hope no-one's calling no one a rat . . .
SNR

MANSON *picks up his hat.*

MANSON   Maybe Torrent wants to impress his son – *[he*

looks at JENNY] or someone – that he's still
young and adventurous. Nothing like youth
to wake up the last of a man's middle years.
Well, I don't fancy paying for it with my
money . . . *[the finger stabs at them all]* and
don't forget – that's what it'll come to in the
end . . . rates, taxes, levies,
loans – *money* . . . to pay for Torrent's
public spirit. Your money. Not mine.
Coming, Squires?

SQUIRES *joins him, bows to* JENNY.

   SQUIRES   Under the present circumstances, I think further
discussion would be quite out of order.

There's a stir among the STUWELLS, TWIMPLE . . . *they don't want
to be left alone with* RUFUS.

   TWIMPLE   *[edging his way out]* I do feel that we
might – at a later date, perhaps . . .

   MANSON   *[as he leaves with* SQUIRES] Remember,
Twimple . . . When a town changes its
nature, other things change. They bring in a
new parson, a new priest, a new solicitor . . .
and when a town is changing, they like 'em
young!

TWIMPLE *goes past him.*

   MANSON   Don't carry your head too high, Torrent . . .
easier to bring it down.

He and SQUIRES *go [after bowing to* JENNY].

   STUWELL   Well, everyone's got a right to their own
   SNR   opinion, haven't they? *[to* CHARLIE] That's
right, isn't it? Speak up, son . . .

   CHARLIE   Yes. My opinion is that you're all bloody silly
not to jump at Myers' idea. Of course it'll
work. Oh, come on, Dad – I want a drink!

CHARLIE *gives* JENNY *an outrageous wink – he gets a big smile.*
He goes. STUWELL SNR. *follows, saying feebly . . .*

   STUWELL   That's right, Charlie – speak up, son . . .
   SNR

JENNY, RUFUS *left alone.*

   RUFUS   Who could have expected that from Stuwell
Junior?

RUFUS *sits on the edge of the big table.*

RUFUS   God, I'm so tired . . .

JENNY *looks at him. Then she goes into his office, and begins to rummage through desk drawers.*

RUFUS   I thought I could sway them. But the moment Manson said 'money', they followed him like frightened sheep.

JENNY *speaks from the inner office.*

JENNY   I hate that man . . .

She has pulled a flask of whisky from a drawer in the desk.

RUFUS   At least he's worth hating . . . He wants my son.

JENNY *comes back wih the whisky, saying.*

JENNY   He won't get him.

RUFUS   Are you sure . . .? I lost that lot today. They're so stupid and narrow, but usually I can make them see.

JENNY *offers him whisky.*

RUFUS   And how did you know that was there?

JENNY   A good secretary knows where every essential is to be found.

RUFUS *drinks the stiff whisky she pours him.*

JENNY   You know that Kingsley's dream can come true . . .

RUFUS   *[savagely]* How do I know that? How do I know if a thing is right until I see it before my eyes? It's precious few of us, young lady, who can see the realities of dreams. No, it was no burning conviction – it was my destiny – my stupid Irish temper and my damned Irish pride. *[From this point on he forgets who she is, realizing only that he is tired, discouraged, desperately in need of an outlet for all the emotion he bottles up, and she is sympathetic]* I've worked for years to conquer them – to be cool and wise and responsible – an English gentleman in fact – and they trap me still! And suddenly there I am risking myself like a gambler on a chance card, fighting a fight that should be no fight of mine.

As though answering an unspoken need, JENNY *comes softly to the chair next to* RUFUS *and sits in it, her chin on her hands looking at him obliquely across the table.*

JENNY   Must your destiny be only pride and anger?

RUFUS   It's the destiny of any Dubliner – any poverty
stricken, broken footed, torn trousered,
Dubliner. Be proud and angry enough to cut
your way out – or else fumble and go
under – fumble with your person, fumble
with your girl, fumble with your God – and
so be trapped! I was not to be trapped!

JENNY   What did you do?

RUFUS   Denied my world – parents, friends, girls – even
my God. So I denied and defied all. And
where has it lead me . . .?

JENNY   Here, to Koolgalla – free of the past and with
your soul your own?

RUFUS   Is any Irishman free of his past? You don't
understand. Being Irish isn't a
nationality – it's a disease!

JENNY *gives him another whisky, and she laughs.*

RUFUS   That's nothing to laugh at, Jenny! The Irish
think they are fighting against Queen
Victoria. Actually, they are fighting for
Deidre, *[romantically]* that fair queen who
made sorrow so bright that it dazzled joy in
the Irish heart forever. *[practically]* They get
her all mixed up with the Blessed Virgin . . .
that's very Irish.

JENNY   And Deidre suits them very well. She's been
dead so long that they forget she was a great
nuisance when she was alive! They think
Helen was wicked to bring about the
downfall of Troy. But it was alright for
Deidre to ruin the sons of Barach – because
she was Irish!

RUFUS   *[lightly]* I can see you don't approve of us.

JENNY   Oh, you have charm – and the bright courage
on the brink of the grave that makes men
love you . . . Yes, and you've made your wit
part of this country, so that in all their
heroics there will always be a taste of
wryness, and the cream of their jest will

always be sour! But you hug your hurt pride
to your heart and pride yourself on your
ability to live alone. I tell you, to live alone
is nothing! Anybody can do it! But to live
with the world – not to perish, but to work
for it – not to weep for it, but to change
it – that makes a man – or a woman! And if
everything fails – love and religion, faith,
hope and charity are proven lies, there is still
something left that can make us go on! *[She
is almost hurling the words at him . . .
suddenly she breaks and her own doubts and
bewilderment catch up on her. She falters and
in a sudden collapse which is almost childish
says]* But I don't know what it is, or how to
find it.

RUFUS   *[tenderly]* You don't need to search, Jenny. You
have it in your heart. And what do *you*
know of battles?

JENNY   I am as much a soldier as any of your Irish
heroes. I fight for the things I believe in . . .
and it's a desolate thing sometimes to seem to
be the one woman alone on such a new
battle ground.

RUFUS   You chose it, you – NEW – woman!

JENNY   And proud of it! If you have to fight then
always choose your battleground! That is
only common sense!

RUFUS   And you know what you fight for?

JENNY   Yes.

*This is straight in the eye. They are very close. Slowly he puts
out a hand and touches her lightly on the shoulder, as though
acknowledging her equality.*

RUFUS   I believe you do – and will achieve it.

JENNY   *[eagerly]* That is why I felt so much for Ben
today . . .

REFUS *begins to chill.*

JENNY   That was his battleground . . . and you mustn't
let him feel he was driven from it in defeat.
He will be such a fine man. But he needs
encouragement, inspiration . . .

RUFUS *has turned away from her. Very deliberately he moves to the hat rack, takes down hat, puts it on.*

RUFUS   I think my son has reached the age when he must learn to make his own decisions, Miss Milford. If he does need – er – inspiration, I am confident that it can be supplied by his fiancée . . . the proper person, Miss Milford, to give solace and comfort . . .

It is dawning on JENNY *that this is a rebuke administered to her. She is hurt and angry.* RUFUS *turns at the door.*

RUFUS   When you have typed the editorial, Miss Milford, you may go. And please remember that 'E I' still follows 'C' as a general rule.

He goes out on the angry JENNY.
JENNY *tosses off the last of his whisky – and chokes on it.*

CURTAIN

ACT TWO

SCENE 2

An hour later, the same evening. JENNY *is sitting at the small table, a block in her hand that she has taken from the box, her thoughts far from pleasant.* CHRISTY *pops through the centre entrance.*

CHRISTY   Editorial ready?
Startled, the block flies out of JENNY's *hand on to the floor.*
JENNY   Oh – you startled me, Christy.
CHRISTY   Made you jump, did I? Made you drop the block . . . Now if that had 'a been a gun . . . *[he makes a decisive gesture]* One pounce and I've got you!
JENNY   Yes, you have, haven't you? *[despite her troubles she is very fond of* CHRISTY *and wouldn't offend him]*
CHRISTY   'Course, I move like a cat – learned it from the blacks, y'know . . . lived with 'em for years

when I . . . *[with a sudden apprehensive glance at the inner office door, he jerks an enquiring thumb]* In?

JENNY   Out.

CHRISTY   *[relieved, trots over to her]* Oh. Now where was I? Oh, yes, you were asking about me living with the blacks. Well, it was when I was shipwrecked when the Lustre Bell struck off the Cape. Would've died but for them blacks . . . *[chuckles]* Might've died because of 'em – they wouldn't't've said no to a meal of long pig, and I was a fine looking firm-fleshed young fella in those days. But I talked 'em out of it – jollied 'em along, chiacked 'em a bit – very light on me feet I was then, and I caught their fancy with a bit of a step dance . . . *[he whistles a tune and executes a shuffle . . .* JENNY *is smiling now]* When I caught up with the white men again and I left, they cried – the whole tribe just cried!

JENNY   I believe they would.

CHRISTY   And then there was this other time –

JOCK   *[bellowing from downstairs]* Christy!

CHRISTY   *[yelling from the stairs]* What?

JOCK   Have you got it?

CHRISTY   What?

JOCK   The editorial, you numbskull!

CHRISTY   Coming! *[chuckles, unregenerate]* Knew there was something on me mind. Have you got the editorial ready?

JENNY   Mr. Torrent's done it, Christy, but I haven't quite finished typing it. *[She stands up to move to typewriter]* I'll do it now.

CHRISTY   *[gleefully]* Don't worry yourself. You been busy this afternoon with the *[contemptuously]* Directors' Meeting?

JENNY   Rather busy . . .

CHRISTY   Newspapers never had 'directors' when I worked on 'em first. Just a damn nuisance! *[cunningly]* Did I hear the Old Man bellowing!

JENNY   *[demurely]* How could you, Christy – all the
    way downstairs.

CHRISTY   I happened to get up on me frame to knock a
    nail into the rafters – to hang me billy on.
    Who was he fighting with this time?

JENNY   Now, Christy, you know I can't tell anyone –

CHRISTY   No need to tell anyone, when his lordship lets
    his lungs out for an airing. Was it Manson
    got his goat?

JENNY   Christy, I must type –

CHRISTY   Manson and the Old Man'll come to blows one
    of these days – and I'll put me money on the
    Old Man. He's got the devil's own temper
    when it's up.

JENNY   *[determinedly]* Christy, you must go down now
    and tell Mr. MacDonald that I'll bring this
    editorial down in a few minutes . . . *[she
    gives Christy a gentle push in the direction of
    the door]*

CHRISTY   *[going slowly, still chuckling]* Feller beating a
    horse once – the Old Man took a
    stockwhip – took three men to get it away
    from him. Oh, he's got a fine temper alright!
    By God, if he finds out that young Ben is
    over at the Royal, filling himself up with
    whisky, there'll be such a –

He is almost out by this, but JENNY *pulls him back with such
force and abruptness that* CHRISTY *is left gasping.*

JENNY   What did you say?

CHRISTY   *[bemused]* What did I say?

JENNY   *[almost shaking him]* About Ben!

CHRISTY   Only that he's over at the Royal, filling himself
    up with whisky – *[a private grievance]* and us
    slaving here!

JENNY   Christy, what will I do? Should I go over there
    and get him out?

CHRISTY   *[appalled]* By Grundy, Jenny, you can't do that.
    Some of them drinkers are pretty far gone!

JENNY   *[contemptuously]* I won't be shocked.

CHRISTY   No . . . by, by God, they will be! You can't do
    that, Jenny . . .

JENNY *has moved across the window and is looking out.*

JENNY But we can't just leave him there – in that place!

CHRISTY Oh, the Royal's not a bad pub.

Looks around as BEN *comes in, rather drunk and defiant. He jerks his head at* CHRISTY *in direction of stairs and* CHRISTY, *glad to escape, goes.*

CHRISTY *[as he vanishes]* Ten minutes you said . . .

BEN Looking for someone, Jenny?

JENNY *[whirling around]* Ben! What have you been doing?

BEN Didn't anyone in Koolgalla find time to tell you – or were they all hurrying to tell Father? I've been drinking.

JENNY Oh, I know that. *[scornfully]* I can see it.

BEN Yes, I'm afraid I don't do it very well. But I'll improve with practice.

JENNY Stop talking like that. *[She brushes past him and goes to typewriter, sits down and begins to type on sheet in machine, banging through* BEN's *speeches]* It sounds so childish!

BEN Isn't that in keeping with my previous speech – the one I made today – or didn't make today – the stupid bumbling one I made, while they all sat round and grinned magnanimously. *[shouting]* Must you rattle that infernal machine?

JENNY *[still going]* I have two more paragraphs of the editorial –

BEN Oh, yes, my dear father's editorial! And what has my father to say to the public today?

JENNY Advocating better means of communication –

BEN *drags some crumpled sheets of copy paper out of his pocket, looks at it morosely, and stuffs it back.*

JENNY's *eyes follow the sheets.*

BEN Better means of communication. By all means – let us communicate with one another – freely and pleasantly, and without attempting to face vexatious problems which can only bring us discomfort and ridicule. *[sincerely]* Poor King, I told him I'd do my best and I failed him, didn't I?

JENNY   No, you didn't, Ben . . . and King would be the last to think that. You tried to say something. At least, you tried!

BEN   And with such wonderful effect. I suppose my father had everyone smoothed and smiling in five minutes!

JENNY   He didn't! He carried on where you left off. He was wonderful! He defended Kingsley's plans – he defended you . . .!

This is the wrong thing to say. The whisky in BEN *rises.*

BEN   I can defend myself. And when he defended Kingsley's plans – he did it better than I did, didn't he, Jenny?

JENNY   Ben, I was so proud of you when you spoke –

BEN   *[flatly]* But my father did it so much better.

JENNY   He's had so much more experience with these things –

BEN   He's so much cleverer, so much cooler, so much more dominating. Jenny, I have lived in my father's shadow all my life. Oh, don't think I haven't loved him, like everyone else, I've fallen under the spell. I think if you don't hate Rufus Torrent, you come close to adoring him. I tell you, Jenny, I have come to believe that if I ever truly loved a woman, my father – if it occurred to him – could win her from me like that! *[he snaps his finger]* Does that shock you, Jenny?

JENNY   *[slowly]* If you ever truly loved a woman . . . What about Gwynne?

BEN   *[arrested]* Gwynne . . . *[he turns away to stare out the window]* Gwynne. Oh, I know she's a sweet person and a good woman and –

JENNY   And she is to be your wife.

BEN   *[with a dignified candour which infuriates* JENNY*]* I know that, Jenny – and however weak you may think me, I am not weak enough to go back on the word I've given.

He looks for approbation and is shocked when JENNY *snarls at him.*

JENNY   That's a very generous gesture, Ben! Oh, why

does every man consider himself such a prize
that it becomes the highest pledge of
gentlemanly honour to marry the woman . . .
yes, marry her, and patronise and belittle her
for the rest of your lives together,
complimenting yourselves for your divine
condescension.

BEN *opens his mouth to speak.*

JENNY   No, don't deny it! Do you wonder, then, that
we – the ones you call in your contempt, the
New Women – that we fight for our right to
an independent wage, and independent mind,
an independent life . . . *[advancing on* BEN*]*
and, one day, my fine friend, we will be
condescending if we marry YOU!

BEN   *[laughing but sobered by her vehemence]* Jenny
for Governor!

JENNY   *[rather flattened]* You can laugh, Ben. But you
have no right to speak of Gwynne like that.

BEN   You know I wouldn't speak so to anyone but
you. You can understand. This marriage of
ours was always contemplated. My mother
and Gwynne's were schoolfriends. Gwynne's
father admires mine –

JENNY   Could you make her happy, Ben?

BEN   Well – I'd –

JENNY   You know you couldn't. You are much too
young – no, not in years – much too young
to sacrifice yourself and hide from her that
though you respect her, and like her, you
don't love her. And Gwynne needs love.

BEN   *[haughtily]* When I marry her, I will consider it
my duty to devote myself to her happiness.

JENNY   Duty . . . you, who cannot take this afternoon's
set-back without flying to alcohol! You, who
are much too self-indulgent, not to gratify
your own desires. If you – *[she hesitates]* If
you should meet a woman who meant more
to you, would you deny yourself – for
Gwynne!

After a moment, BEN *turns away from her eyes.*

JENNY   What would she suffer then? No – better to be
           brave now and let her turn to somewho does
           love her – someone like Kingsley –

BEN   Kingsley appears to have the knack of
           inspiring – confidence.

JENNY   *[flushing with fury]* Oh, you men – you talk
           glibly of women's preoccupation with love-
           making, and yet you cannot bear another
           man praised without accusing her in your
           thoughts! Oh, I'm so tired of men! *[flounces
           back to her desk, gives typescript to* BEN*]* If
           you will take this down to Mr. MacDonald, I
           can go home.

BEN *takes the papers . . . then he turns back.*

BEN   *[sincerely]* I'm sorry, Jenny. I'm weak and I hate
           it.

JENNY   You are weak Ben. And you're denying your
           own talent because you're afraid of it, just as
           your father denies the rebellion of his heart.
           You're a journalist, Ben – you could
           write – you could explain to everyone in
           Koolgalla just what Kingsley's dream can
           mean. You could do it, Ben.

BEN *turns his back on her, walks slowly to her desk, drops
typescript on it, deep in his sense of defeat.*

BEN   I can't. I tried today. There it is. But it isn't any
           use.

*She comes quickly across the room, picks up typescript and begins
to read it.* BEN *can't help watching her reaction as she flicks over
the first page.*

JENNY   *[delighted]* It's good, Ben – it's good!

BEN   I didn't think it was too bad, myself. *[she is
           reading on]* Sometimes, I think I can be a
           good journalist, Jenny. Maybe if I got out of
           this town – got right away, saw new things
           and new people and learned to understand
           more – then I think I could do it! *[then
           quietening]* Of course, most of that *[indicates
           pages]* is Kingsley talking.

JENNY   But it isn't. Kingsley talks for himself – and
           while he understands it, others may not. But

this, this is written so that everyone will be able to understand. Everyone will see why it's so important that we should beat our picks into ploughshares.

BEN   Good, Jenny, that's good – we ought to put that in . . . before we throw it in the wastepaper basket.

JENNY *[horrified]* You don't mean you're not going to do anything with this?

BEN   What can I do?

JENNY Print it! The space is waiting . . .

BEN   Print something in Rufus Torrent's paper without his permission, and something with which he disagrees? Father would go stark raving mad if I did!

JENNY *[shortly]* Let him! Anyway, he doesn't disagree, he said as much as this himself, this afternoon.

BEN   Then for the sake of all our necks, let us leave him to write it himself, too. Toss it in the wastepaper basket, Jenny – or keep it as a souvenir of Ben Torrent's first and last rebellion. *[he starts for door]* And now I'm going to resume my practice – at the private bar of the Royal. *[turns back]* Don't leave that stuff lying around.

JENNY Oh, Ben! *[fiercely]* Ben – are you afraid of your father?

BEN   *[as he exits]* Yes. *[he goes]*

JENNY *[forgetting her dignity and yelling after him]* And when they carry you out, I'll tell them to deliver you to Gwynne. It's the gentlemanly thing, isn't it, to allow the lady to unlace your boots and be sick in her lap?

She is screwing up the pages nervously when BERNIE *comes in.*

BERNIE Did you call, Miss Milford? Is it ready?

JENNY *[snapping]* What . . .? I'm sorry, Bernie. I'm . . . I'm out of sorts.

BERNIE Gee, could I do anything . . .?

JENNY No, thanks, Bernie. I suppose you want the editorial. *[goes to desk and picks it up, she is*

> *rather close to tears]* Here you are,
> Bernie – guaranteed not to set the town on
> fire . . . *[she stops . . . she looks at both sets
> of papers. She gives* BERNIE BEN's *article]* Take
> this to Mr. MacDonald, Bernie – tell him I'm
> sorry I kept him waiting but there was a – a
> last minute change of policy.

Left alone, JENNY *wanders from window to window then goes
to typewriter and begins to type very meticulously, pausing for
a word from time to time.* JOCK MacDONALD *comes in.*

JOCK   What's goin' on here?

JENNY   Oh – uh – wh – what, Mr. MacDonald?

JOCK   *[fixing her with a hard highland eye – he has
        the editorial in his hand. He gestures to it]* Is
        this right?

JENNY   I gave it to you, Mr. MacDonald. *[her tone and
        look beseech co-operation]*

JOCK   *[after a pause]* If *you* gave it to me, lassie – it's
        reeght!

JENNY   *[weakly]* Set it double face, Mr. MacDonald,
        and bold!

JOCK   Reeght! *[he goes]*

JENNY *relaxes. She takes the page out of her typewriter, signs it,
she goes into* RUFUS' *office. She stands, looking down at the
desk – touches it gently. She puts the envelope on it. She comes
back to outer office, takes her coat and hat from stand – looks
for a moment at the top of it. She is very near to tears again,
but her chin goes up, and she drives the hat pin venomously
through her hat and goes out.*

CURTAIN

ACT THREE

SCENE 1

*The 'Argus' office, the following morning. Bright morning light
is coming through the windows, and as the curtain goes up,
RUFUS comes out of the inner office with* JENNY's *letter in one
hand, a copy of the 'Argus' in the other. He is standing in the*

middle of the stage, bellowing . . .

RUFUS   MacDonald! MacDonald! *[then]* Christy! Where
the blazing hell is everybody? CHRISTY!!

A started CHRISTY *appears round the door.*

RUFUS   So you're here at last! Where is MacDonald?
More to the point – where is – where is
that – *[he struggles for words]* Where is Miss
Milford?

CHRISTY   's only half past eight, Mr. Torrent. She don't
start work till nine o'clock.

RUFUS   Nine . . .! D'you think I'm going to wait for her
till nine? Eh?

CHRISTY *is considering the diplomatic answer.*

RUFUS   Do you know where she lives?

CHRISTY   *[all knowledgeable]* Yes . . .

RUFUS   Then get her here . . . immediately!

CHRISTY   But – she might still be in bed!

RUFUS   *[meaning it]* Then drag her out of it!

CHRISTY   *[horrified]* Who – me? By God, I don't.
Who – me? Me –

JENNY *has appeared in the doorway. Although quaking inwardly,
she is neatly dressed and looks calm and fresh.*

JENNY   *[sweetly]* It's quite alright, Christy. I am here.
[she comes in, hangs her hat carefully below
RUFUS'] I came into the office early, it
occurred to me that Mr. Torrent might wish
to see me.

RUFUS   *[choking]* It occurred to you! One mistake,
Miss – !

JENNY *indicates* CHRISTY *with a discreet nod which serves to
infuriate* RUFUS *further.*

RUFUS   Get out!

CHRISTY   *[indignant]* By Grundy, that's no way to speak
to me, Mr. Torrent. By Grundy . . .

RUFUS *swings on him and* CHRISTY *retires.*

CHRISTY   No – it's no use trying to apologize! I'm not
staying here!

As CHRISTY *goes hastily,* JENNY *moves to her desk.*

RUFUS   As for you, madam – have you any explanation
for your – unwarranted – impudent,
mischievous – interference . . .

JENNY   *[cool and kind]* Are you quite well, Mr.
               Torrent . . . Your face is so flushed . . .

RUFUS, *scarlet by now, throws up a hand in despair.*

JENNY   After all – there comes a time when we all have
               to consider our health –

RUFUS   *[starting quietly]* I am not yet so old, nor so
               decrepit, Miss Milford – that I am likely to
               collapse from a – quite understandable –
               annoyance! I am perfectly at ease – *[bellow-*
               ing] PERFECTLY! *[warned by her expression*
               he drops his voice carefully] I am scarcely
               perturbed by the knowledge that my paper is
               ruined, that I am ridiculed, that my son is
               clay – wet clay, in the hands of a – a –
               [facing her straight look he drops the sentence]
               Incidentally, this morning – when I saw the
               'Argus' – I asked my son to leave my house.

JENNY   *[sincerely]* Poor Ben – I'm so sorry . . .

RUFUS *walks to desk and looks down on her.*

RUFUS   *[in a quieter voice]* I think it is only right that I
               should tell you that my son accepted full
               blame for that statement. He said he had
               done it alone. But I am not completely a
               fool, Miss Milford. I could tell from his
               bewilderment that he had not expected it to
               appear. However, he did not mean to – give
               you away.

JENNY   I did not mean to allow him to be blamed, sir.
               Surely you found my statement – and my
               resignation – on your desk?

RUFUS   *[nodding]* I found it. A typical piece of feminine
               heroics – and again disregarding the fact that
               'E I' generally follows 'C'.

JENNY *has to laugh. She realizes she has done it again. She starts
to take her belongings out of the desk drawer.* RUFUS *throws letter
in wastepaper basket. It misses.*

JENNY   I think that clears everyone of any
               responsibility – except myself. You can
               publish it as it stands. I believe it covers
               everything.

RUFUS   Except one thing. You didn't write that

editorial – and Ben did.

JENNY   And you should be proud of him! He put into
words the problem that everyone in Koolgalla
has to face – and the solution to it. He denied
them the uncertainty of the lucky strike and
he offered in its place the certainty of
planning and hard work – and a future
coming from that work that can save their
town. Though you publish fifty retractions,
Mr. Torrent, you can't wipe that article from
their thoughts.

RUFUS   I should have known, when I denied my better
judgement, and took a woman into this office
that we might expect some kind of specious
underhand, interfering feminine logic . . .!

JENNY   . . . instead of open, honest, manly illogic!

RUFUS   If you were a man, madam, I would know how
to deal with your action!

JENNY   If you were a man, Mr. Torrent, you'd stand by
it!

RUFUS *gives a fleeting thought to murder.*

CHRISTY *scuttles in.*

CHRISTY   Manson and Squires . . . *[jerks a thumb]*
downstairs. Want to see Mr. Torrent.
[delighted] And they're howling like
dingoes – the dingoes!

RUFUS   *Mister* Manson and *Mister* Dingo . . . Oh, what
the hell's the use!

He walks towards his office.

JENNY *is saying:*

JENNY   Ask them to come up, will you, Christy.

When MANSON *and* SQUIRES *come through the doorway,* MANSON
*is very angry – equally with himself for having possibly
underrated* RUFUS. RUFUS *stands at office door.*

MANSON   So you did it! I should have known when we
left yesterday afternoon and you were
standing there, raging inside! Just once or
twice I thought to myself – is he going to try
to ram this down our necks?

CHRISTY *would stay to see the fun, but a slight nod, then a more
peremptory one from* JENNY, *makes him go reluctantly.*

MANSON   Don't you know, you stupid Irish paddy, what
           directors' meetings are for? Or did you think
           we were giving you our blessings and asking
           you to sink our money – *our money!* – . . .
           My God, it's the damned insolence of it that
           sticks in my throat – the damned high-and-
           mighty, go-to-hell insolence of it!
RUFUS   *[coldly]* My secretary is present, Mr. Manson.
MANSON   Then let her go somewhere else! I want to talk
           to you! And you won't want her to hear
           some of the things I'm going to say.
JENNY *stands up to go.*
SQUIRES   I'd be discreet, Mr. Manson. Things can be
           misconstrued. I'm sure nobody thinks of
           coming to court cases, but –
MANSON   All right, Torrent, we'll go into your office.
RUFUS   Whatever you have to say, it may be said in
           front of Miss Milford. She is completely in
           my confidence.
He waves JENNY *back imperiously and she sits.*
SQUIRES   Of course, we all recognize that anything we
           say before Miss Milford is completely secret.
RUFUS   *[cutting him short]* Do you wish to add
           anything to Mr. Manson's opinions – Mr.
           Squires?
SQUIRES   Oh – no –
MANSON *glares at him.*
SQUIRES   Well, I think Mr. Manson's irritation is
           understandable, and I must say that when I
           put money into a newspaper I do expect my
           opinions to be at least considered. After all,
           we all have to look after our own –
RUFUS   I thought the devil undertook that task.
SQUIRES   *[with a pale grin]* Ah, Irish wit, sir, Irish
           wit – you can't beat it. But you must admit,
           Mr. Torrent, that we have a right to see after
           our own interests. Who's to blame us for
           that – as I said yesterday. I'm a big enough
           man to understand that it could be in your
           interest – financially or influentially – *[he
           begins to waver before* RUFUS' *look]*

MANSON   I wonder if I did misjudge you, Torrent.
            Yesterday, I said things to prickle you . . .
            [he looks at JENNY*]* but I wasn't really
            thinking about money. I wonder if you are
            getting something out of this scheme. If you
            are – so are we!

RUFUS   You accuse me of corruption?

SQUIRES   No – no. You put too harsh a word upon it . . .
            a libellous word!

MANSON   I'd put the word on it – if I knew what game
            you're playing. If it's just your bog-Irish pride
            that made you do it, then take a tip from
            me, and eat it! Retract every word of the
            damned editorial. Say it was a mistake, you
            were drunk, you were sunstruck – but deny
            every word you wrote. You did write it, I
            suppose?

RUFUS   No.

JENNY *is watching him, breathless.*

RUFUS   My son wrote it. And I may say, Mr. Manson,
(Cont'd)   I am proud of him. He took those facts that
            we refused to face and he stuck them in front
            of the eyes of the people who needed most to
            know them or under the noses, Mr. Manson,
            since you have a preference for – plain
            speaking. He did his duty as a
            journalist – with honour and skill. And if a
            few noses should turn up – well, we'll bear it.

MANSON   *We'll* bear it! By heaven, I won't!

SQUIRES   Fair is fair, Mr. Torrent. Every man must
            protect his interests. We've spent time and
            money building businesses – developing them.
            You must understand, Mr. Torrent –

MANSON   Understand, hell! I don't want him to
            understand, so long as he takes orders. And
            if he doesn't – it's retraction or ruin, Torrent.
            None of us, not even that fool Twimple, will
            follow you in this. We'll take out every
            penny we've put into the 'Argus' and I
            happen to know how much you need it for
            your grand schemes! We'll take it out!

RUFUS   *[the brogue showing]* Take it out, then – in fact,
          I'll buy you out! And be damned to you all
          for a pack of money-grabbing, small minded,
          mean-souled pedlars, and the town – and the
          paper – well rid of the lot of you.

MANSON *lowers his head like an angry bull. Then he straightens
and faces* RUFUS.

MANSON   Right, my fine gentleman. Now we know where
          we stand. Let the others do as they like. I
          know what I'll do. When I said 'ruin' I wasn't
          playing with words. You want a fight – you'll
          get it – and if it's possible to ruin you . . .
          and I've ruined men before now – I'll do it!
          I'll find some way to make you really squirm!
          I never liked you, Torrent, any more than
          you liked me. This has been coming for a
          long time, and I'm glad it's come now! By the
          time I've finished with you, you'll wish you'd
          stayed digging potatoes – you'll wish you had
          some in your stewpot. I never give quarter!

RUFUS   I never ask it.

MANSON   Good. Come on, Squires – I'm off to see
          Twimple. You coming?

SQUIRES   Yes, Mr. Manson. But there are some legal
          arrangements to be made. Mr. Torrent, since
          there are financial changes pending I think I
          may prefer another investment –

RUFUS   That will be most agreeable to me, sir.

MANSON   *[off]* Squires – where in hell are you?

SQUIRES   *[calling]* Coming, Mr. Manson. *[he lingers at
          door, comes back into room]* Er – as an old
          associate, Mr. Torrent, might I ask if there is
          something more to this scheme than might
          show to the – uninitiated, could we say?
          Some Government influence at work, some
          new discovery perhaps? Surely it would be
          friendly to tip the wink, as they say . . .

MANSON   *[off]* Squires!

RUFUS   Mr. Manson is calling for you, Mr. Squires.

SQUIRES   Coming, Mr. Manson . . .

He scurries off. RUFUS *begins to laugh. Still laughing, he walks*

*to the window, stands looking down into the street. He has
stopped laughing. He is thinking hard.* JENNY *goes to stand on
the other side of the window.*

JENNY   Can you buy them all out, Mr. Torrent?

RUFUS   *[this is what he has been considering]* No – not
all of them. *[He smiles at her]* But if I
mortgage everything I own, I can buy out
Manson and Squires, which will be good
riddance, and I can talk the others into
staying with me. I'm not an Irishman for
nothing, Miss Milford. In a year they'll be
complimenting themselves on their foresight
and public spirit – *[dryly]* – and so will I!

There is a brief tap on the head of the stairs and JOCK MacDONALD,
CHRISTY, *and a nervous but determined* BERNIE *in the rear, file
in, heavy with serious intention.*

JOCK   *[very Scots with determination]* Ye'll excuse me,
Mr. Torrent – I know you're having rather a
disturbing morning. But I thought – *[*CHRISTY
pulls his coat] All right, all right – WE
thought, but the boys asked me to do the
talking –

CHRISTY   Then get on with it!

JOCK   He's entitled to an explanation, isn't he? You do
it, then, if you think you'd do it better.

CHRISTY   Well, seeing you asked me –

BERNIE   *[in a thin, nervous squeak]* Aw no,
Christy – not you –

RUFUS   No, not you, by *God* . . . *[correctly to* JENNY*]*
Excuse me. *[to* CHRISTY*]* I want to hear what
this is about without the complication of
your life's history, Christy. Now, Jock – ?

JOCK   It's no use pretending that we don't know that
something peculiar's been going on, Mr.
Torrent. There was that editorial. We know
you never saw it –

JENNY   *[quickly]* Mr. Torrent knows that nobody was
to blame for that but me. I left him an
explanation with my resignation. You have
no need to feel concerned, Mr. MacDonald.

JOCK   *[doggedly]* We know you never saw it – we

knew it last night. But we printed it – so we're just as much to blame. You've been a fair employer and a good friend, Mr. Torrent, despite your little oddities, and we don't want to make any trouble . . . But since there's trouble already . . .

CHRISTY   We could hear Manson bellowing and Squires croaking.

RUFUS   Indeed. Right down in the composing room?

CHRISTY   I was hanging my billy on a nail I've got just above me frame –

JOCK   The point of it is, Mr. Torrent – never mind what we know – Or how we know. We're not interfering, or taking things on ourselves, Mr. Torrent – but – well, sir, if anything is going to happen to the lassie here – or to Ben – we might have to down tools. It's only right we stand by them!

RUFUS *speaks with gentle acidity.*

RUFUS   Thank you, gentlemen. I am touched by the faith in my stupidity and tyranny shown by all my staff. Had you had the opportunity to question Mr. Manson and Mr. Squires, you would have learned that I, too, am 'standing by them'. The 'Koolgalla Argus' needs no scapegoats!

General relief. CHRISTY *guffaws with satisfaction.*

CHRISTY   I could've told you – I could've told you – !

JOCK   *[who does not approve of drama in the office]* Then why didn't you, you perishing genius, and save everybody's time! Now that's settled satisfactorily, Mr. Torrent, we'll be getting back to work. *[Jerks his head toward door and they start out]*

JENNY   Wait – please.

They turn back.

JENNY   You know I can't say anything but thank you . . . and you know what this means to me. Coming here, as I did – *[She is not able to go on but she holds out her hand to them]* Thank you.

RUFUS   *[with real sincerity]* As for my son, I, too, say
        'Thank you'. He has good colleagues.

RUFUS *claps* BERNIE *on the shoulder and* BERNIE *all but collapses
under the honour and weight.* JOCK *turns very brisk and efficient.*

JOCK   We're near an hour behind.

Obediently they start out.

JOCK   You wouldn't have entered the quotes yet, Miss
        Jenny? Two jobs have come up this morning.

RUFUS   Well, we still have some business!

JENNY   I'll come down and get them, Mr. MacDonald.

She goes out with JOCK *followed by* BERNIE, CHRISTY *bringing up
the rear, but still audible as he goes downstairs.*

CHRISTY   Next time there's a piece of business like that to
        be done, Jock, you'd better leave it to me.
        You're a well meaning fellow, but you just
        haven't got the experience. I knew a feller
        once – a big fat feller – his aunt used to keep
        a pie stall in Hobart –

Alone RUFUS *stands looking after them for a moment. He glances
down at* JENNY's *desk where her handkerchief is lying beside her
typewriter. On an impulse he picks it up, raises it to his nostrils,
sniffs approvingly at the perfume, drops it back. He pulls out
his heavy watch, snaps it open, looks at the time reprovingly,
crosses and goes into his own office. He sits at his desk.*

  *The stage is empty for a minute. Then there is the sound of
someone running upstairs and* KINGSLEY MYERS, *carrying a
newspaper, comes in buoyantly.*

KINGSLEY   Ben! Ben! Where are you, Ben!

He is followed in by GWYNNE, *looking very pretty in her long
riding skirt and wide brimmed hat strapped under her chin.*

KINGSLEY   *[turning to her, disappointed]* He isn't here.
        Neither is Jenny. Where is everybody?

RUFUS   *[ill-temperedly from his office]* Here,
        endeavouring to work.

But KINGSLEY *cannot be quenched this morning. He marches to
the door of the office and hangs on it.*

KINGSLEY   Good morning, sir . . . a very good morning,
        sir, and congratulations – all the
        congratulations in the world! I've never read
        a better statement – put my own views
        exactly, but a thousand times better than I

> could do it myself . . .

RUFUS *sits at his desk with a sheaf of papers in his hand which he is tapping, to give the impression of a man held up in his work.*

KINGSLEY . . . with more breadth and clarity, if you know what I mean. Sometimes I'm not very clear –

RUFUS *[acidly]* I have noticed that tendency, Kingsley *[surprised]* You here, too, Gwynne?

GWYNNE Yes, Mr. Torrent. You see, we got the 'Argus' so much earlier and I knew that Kingsley didn't see it until later, and how much this meant to him, I got so awfully excited when I saw the paper that I – I just saddled Rainbird and rode straight over to his place to show him.

RUFUS Hmmmm. How's your mother?

GWYNNE *[knowing quite well what he means]* Not very pleased. And Father's away.

RUFUS *[non-committal]* Hmmmmm.

GWYNNE *[daring him]* Both Father and Mother are a little behind the times, Mr. Torrent. They haven't quite realized that the New Woman is so much more independent than the old!

They both look at her, KINGSLEY *admiringly,* RUFUS *amazed. Then* RUFUS *shoots a glance of cold suspicion at* JENNY's *desk.*

KINGSLEY It was wonderful of you to do it, Gwynne. And wonderful again, sir, for you to –

RUFUS *[cutting him short]* The credit's Ben's – he wrote it!

KINGSLEY But where is Ben?

JENNY *comes in looking surprised to see them.*

KINGSLEY Jenny – where's Ben?

JENNY Downstairs . . .

A great relief shows for a moment on RUFUS' *face.*

JENNY . . . seeing Mr. MacDonald about some page proofs . . .

KINGSLEY I've got to see him. We've just been telling Mr. Torrent what a wonderful thing he's done with this . . . *[waving paper]*

RUFUS And I've just been telling them – the credit belongs to Ben.

KINGSLEY *[laughing]* Come, sir – now you're being *too*

modest. Everyone knows that not a line goes
into the 'Argus' that you haven't approved.
Believe me, you'll go down in history of this
district as a man of vision. Oh, come on,
Gwynne – we must find Ben. *[taking her arm
he starts to hurry her off . . . stops for a
moment to look at* JENNY*]* And you,
Jenny – I'd risk a bet that you had a hand in
this, too. *[he practically drags* GWYNNE *out,
calling 'Ben! Ben!']*

RUFUS   Have you the grace to blush?

She sits demurely at her desk. He towers over her.

RUFUS   A man of vision! Never before has a man been
so trapped into such an undeserved
reputation!

JENNY   I don't think that matters, Mr. Torrent – so long
as you're big enough to wear it well.

KINGSLEY *comes back, arms linked with a slightly stiff backed* BEN.
GWYNNE *following, smiling.*

KINGSLEY   Hail the conquering hero! Ben, it was hair-
raising! Your father told me –

BEN   I can imagine what my father told you, King.
My father bears no responsibility. No one
bears any responsibility, except me. It was a
stroke of – of mad –

RUFUS   *[genially, yet warning* BEN *to be discreet]*
Genius, Ben – genius.

BEN   I am not worthy of your sarcasm, sir . . . *[very
stiff]* Soon I will be leaving Koolgalla, and –

RUFUS   *[cuts in]* My dear Ben, I am in earnest. Kingsley
and Gwynne have come into town especially
to congratulate you, to say what we all
feel – that with this editorial, you have made
the technical position and the future hope
clear in the mind of the common man.

BEN   *[impressed and pleased despite himself]* Did you
say that, King?

KINGSLEY   I felt it, Ben – I felt it. Of course, your father
said it . . .

BEN   *[in anguished understanding]* Ohhh! My dear
father!

KINGSLEY   *[in complete misunderstanding]* You do right to say so, Ben. He is taking no part of the credit due. He is leaving it all to you. He is proud of you, Ben. And so are we!

BEN   But I don't deserve it, King – the credit shouldn't be mine. There is someone else . . . *[he looks at* JENNY *and she shakes her head almost imperceptibly]*

KINGSLEY   I know, Ben – you don't have to tell me. But I have already told your father how I feel about his – splendid – attitude.

RUFUS *looks a little – a very little – abashed.*

BEN   *[wonderingly]* Ooh . . . my dear father!

RUFUS *stares back coolly.*

KINGSLEY   Of course, I realize that this is not the end of the battle. The 'Argus' will have to meet so many attacks. So often, you and Ben will feel that your courage has been wasted. But there are more people than you know who feel as I do – and we will be with you. And we'll take care of the soil. I tell you, there are strange new wonderful things going to happen in farming. The day will come when farming will be as exact a science as mathematics, and Koolgalla will be a great city! *[rather embarrassed by his own eloquence, he tries a laugh]* But I'm running ahead of myself – first we have to bring the torrents to this town. May they prove as fortunate for it as their namesakes!

RUFUS   *[nodding approvingly]* A very handsome toast, Kingsley. *[then seriously]* But I'm glad you realize that it won't be easy. There will be incompetence and self interest and – worst of all – indifference to fight.

GWYNNE   *[unexpectedly]* Kingsley can fight, too! So can I!

Everyone looks at her – she looks back without blushes.

RUFUS   At least, we know those who will be for or against us. We know the town. And if you have to fight, then it is common sense to choose your battleground.

He looks at JENNY *and drops his head in the faintest mocking acknowledgement.*

KINGSLEY   Well, sir, with you and Ben here –

BEN   Don't count on me, King. I may not be here.

RUFUS, *who has lost interest in the conversation and has picked up some papers from* JENNY's *table and is glancing through them, turns, surprised.* JENNY *and* GWYNNE *both look from one to the other and back at him.* KINGSLEY *is too absorbed to take it seriously.* BEN, *who has said it mainly for its effect on* JENNY, *declines to say more.*

KINGSLEY   You'll be here. You know, this feels like my
            birthday! Come, Ben – I'll buy you a
            beer . . .

BEN *shudders a little but does his best to look nonchalant under* JENNY's *eye.* More *hesitantly to* RUFUS:

KINGSLEY   I don't suppose I could persuade you, sir –

RUFUS   I never drink beer at this hour of the
        morning . . .

KINGSLEY *slightly crushed.*

RUFUS   . . . only port – as a matter of policy. And it
        might be good policy to be seen in town this
        morning. *[reaches hat from peg]*

JENNY   If you will hand me my hat, as well, Mr.
        Torrent, I will slip around the corner and see
        if Mrs. Hartman has prepared the list of her
        expected guests at her floral festival.

With a little bow, RUFUS *hands her her hat first and she pins it on.*

KINGSLEY   I can tell you who'll be there, Jenny – every
            bore in Koolgalla, and Mrs. Hartman as
            Primavera with mauve asters and her hair
            coming down. Ready, gentlemen?

They stand aside to allow JENNY *to preceed them.*

RUFUS   It's a sad pity that the ladies can't join us,
        Kingsley.

They laugh at this preposterous notion.

JENNY   *[as she goes]* Don't temp me, gentlemen – I
        might put your tolerance to the test.

They sober – she might. BEN *is about to follow them out when* GWYNNE *says:*

GWYNNE   May I speak to you alone for a moment, Ben, if
          King and your father will excuse us.

KINGSLEY *looks back wistfully.*

KINGSLEY   Thank you for coming for me, Gwynne . . .
           Ben will be seeing you home.

GWYNNE   *[with a brave effort]* I am going to my sister's
           for lunch. But afterwards – would you ride
           home with me, King?

KINGSLEY   *[delighted but puzzled]* I – I shall be only too
           happy, Gwynne . . . that is, if Ben –

GWYNNE   I have asked you, Kingsley.

KINGSLEY   *[after an embarrassed look at* BEN *and* RUFUS*]*
           Th-thank you, Gwynne . . . I shall call for
           you. *[to* RUFUS*]* Shall we go, sir?

RUFUS   *[dryly]* It may be as well.

After a shrewd glance at GWYNNE *and* BEN, RUFUS *goes out
followed by* KINGSLEY.

BEN   *[very busy sorting blocks out on the table]*
           You're very strange this morning, Gwynne.

GWYNNE   It's been a very strange morning. Is it true what
           you said, Ben, about not being here?

BEN   *[who hasn't meant it]* Now, look,
           Gwynne – just because a man says something
           vague, there's no need for you to get upset –

GWYNNE   I'm not upset, Ben.

He looks. By heaven, she isn't.

GWYNNE   It suits me very well. But I thought you might
           be going because of me, and I want you to
           know that you don't have to go – or
           stay – because of me any more. *[She takes off
           her glove and slips off her engagement ring]*
           Take it, Ben . . . *[She looks at the ring before
           she presses it into his hand]* It was your
           mother's, wasn't it? Don't give it away so
           lightly next time.

BEN   *[embarrassed – and genuinely ashamed of
           hurting her]* My dear, you mustn't do this –

GWYNNE   Do you love me, Ben?

BEN   You – you know how fond I am of you. We
           played together as kids – we've been friends
           for years. Everything has always been
           planned –

GWYNNE   *[insistently]* Do you love me, Ben?

BEN   *[meaning to reassure her]* Of course, I – *[under
       her eyes his own drop away. He is silent]*

GWYNNE I knew the answer – I've known it for a long
        time though. But it was hard to face. But this
        morning, when everything seemed to be
        changing – Are you in love with Jenny, Ben?

BEN   *[not answering that]* I could live happily with
       you, Gwynne.

GWYNNE You could fill in the hours between morning
        and night . . . This way is best. And it's not
        so bad, now that it's out and over. I expect I
        gave you up a long time ago. I imagine I'll
        always feel rather sentimental about you . . .
        I don't suppose you'll ever grow old for me,
        and I don't suppose that the woman you do
        marry will ever seem *quite* worthy of
        you – no matter how superior to you she
        may be.

BEN *is feeling the nostalgia of parting and he is nearer to being
interested in* GWYNNE *than he has been before.*

GWYNNE But now that I have faced it, I find there are
        compensations. You'll be an awful handful
        for somebody, Ben – perhaps, in a way, I feel
        rather relieved . . .

BEN's *jaw drops. Then he has the grace to laugh.*

BEN   Well – that takes the edge off my noble shame!

She picks up her gloves, starts to put them on before leaving.

BEN   Gwynne, will you give King a chance later?
       You know how much he cares.

GWYNNE I know. I expect I will – later. I like him very
        much – and next time, I think I'd be rather
        more loved than loving. And next time a
        marriage is arranged for me – I shall arrange
        it myself!

She goes over to JENNY's *piece of mirror, and begins to adjust her
hat, settling the strap under her chin.*

BEN   Did you leave Rainbird at the stables?

GWYNNE *[at mirror]* Yes . . .

BEN   I'll come down with you.

GWYNNE *[turning around]* Just as far as the door.

BEN   *[appreciating her]* Gwynne, you are so

sweet – and I do feel a cad.

GWYNNE   Ben, you are so charming – and keep away
from me in the future, please. As for being a
cad, I'm beginning to think that it's better to
be a cad than a fool. Perhaps if we had more
cads and fewer fools, we'd have fewer
tragedies, too – in the end. *[She nods
dismissal to him as* JENNY *is heard on the
stairs]*

BEN   That doesn't sound like you, Gwynne.

GWYNNE   You forget – I've known Jenny, too.

GWYNNE *smiles at the puzzled* JENNY *and goes out followed by*
BEN. *Left alone,* JENNY *shrugs her bewilderment. She goes to her
desk, shakes her head at its confusion and begins to tidy it. She
is putting some blocks back in the box when* BEN *comes back,
having run upstairs three at a time.*

BEN   *[imperiously]* Leave that alone, Jenny. I want to
talk to you.

JENNY   *[dropping blocks]* And I want to talk to you.
Ben, forgive me for putting that editorial in.
As it happens, everything has turned out
well, but still it was – well – unforgivable. It
was so *right* – and it said things so necessary
to say – Oh, Ben, I couldn't help myself!
Mind you, I'd probably do it again
tomorrow, but I do feel ashamed of myself
for having done it yesterday!

BEN   *[with a crack of laughter]* Oh, Jenny, my Jenny!

JENNY   Perhaps your father is right after all – women
are too emotional. Anyway, if you had done
the right thing and put it in yourself . . .
[laughs] But I did leave the explanation . . .
and my resignation – on your father's desk.

BEN   Protection for the weaker element.

JENNY   I didn't think you were weak Ben, – not really.

BEN   *[close to her]* Didn't you, Jenny? *[He comes
close to her. She wants to avoid what she
can see coming]*

JENNY   You're just beginning to grow up, Ben. Just
beginning to become a wonderful, strong,
fine exciting man . . . That's why . . .

BEN	*[taking her hands]* Why – what, Jenny?
JENNY	Why I think you ought to go away from here.
BEN	Well, thank you. I had no idea I was becoming such a burden to my friends.
JENNY	*[she has no time for this sort of coquetry]* Don't be silly – you know how much I'll hate to see you go. But you need to do it, Ben – you have said yourself so often that you live in your father's shadow.
BEN	*[waving it away]* Pardonable rhetoric. And don't be too bitter about the old boy – I know he hasn't been quite straight over this editorial, but –
JENNY	You do talk the most arrant nonsense, Ben. Your father is a wonderful man –
BEN	In his way –
JENNY	*[sailing on]* Where do you think you got your intelligence *[grudging]* and charm and that blind instinct for the right road to follow? He has something else, Ben – a consciousness of being alone, of pain and struggle that you haven't learned. That has given him maturity.
BEN	I can learn, Jenny.
JENNY	Not in Koolgalla where he will always lead the way.
BEN	You're right, of course, You are, always.
JENNY	Are you a good sailor?
BEN	*[grinning]* No.
JENNY	Then that's the thing for you. Ben, you have to attempt the things that don't come easily to you – the things you don't do well. Otherwise you'll always be Ben Torrent, drifting in his father's shadow, and not big enough to cast one of his own. You're like this town – this town that has to choose between digging up its good earth for the chance of gold or planting it with the certainty of fruit trees. You are like that – you – and this town – and the world beyond us, perhaps . . .

They turn. MANSON, *now calm, is standing in the doorway.*

MANSON	Interrupting something?

They look at him with hostile eyes.

MANSON I left in a hurry before – I'm a man whose
        temper bolts with him sometimes. And yet
        I'm as easy as a lamb to live with. *[to* JENNY*]*
        Would you think that?

JENNY   It isn't one of the things I'd think about at all!

MANSON You don't like me, do you? Pity – Torrent
        scored there, when he brought you here to
        work.

JENNY *goes into* RUFUS' *office – she is listening, although she closes
the door.*

BEN   Do you wish to see my father?

MANSON No. I want to see you. I've seen your father
        already. Nothing's changed there! I said I'd
        fight him to the end, and I will! And I'll
        enjoy it! When I fight I don't spare
        myself – or my money. This town won't
        die – it'll grow.

BEN   In the way Kingsley prophesied –

MANSON That's likely.

BEN   And wouldn't the joke be on you, Mr. Manson?

MANSON Don't you believe it, boy. You'll never find all
        my eggs in one basket! I've taken the bulk of
        my money out of gold years ago. It's here
        and there – some of it's in land. If Myers'
        scheme does work, I'll be one making money
        out of it! That's looking ahead, Ben. And I'm
        looking ahead too, when I say this town can
        do with another newspaper! Like to be an
        editor, Ben? I'm making you an offer.

BEN   To fight my own father!

MANSON *[shrewdly]* Wouldn't you like to? Don't be
        ashamed of it, Ben. It's the law of nature.
        The young bulls have to fight the old ones
        for their right to leadership. I'd give you a
        free hand – more or less. Think it over. If
        you make up your mind quickly, you'll find
        me in the Horseshoe Bar at the Royal. If
        Rufus Torrent's to be seen drinking in the
        morning and playing the King of Ireland – by
        heaven, so am I!

MANSON *goes out with a wave of his hand.* JENNY *comes from the inner office.* BEN, *almost duplicating* RUFUS' *earlier movement, has moved to the window and is looking down on the town.*

JENNY   *[after a pause]* Is this your chance, Ben?

BEN   You heard?

JENNY   *[nods, then says truthfully]* I was listening.

BEN   It could be – if I could give myself a good
             reason for taking it . . . if you can give it to
             me. Jenny, will you marry me?

JENNY   *[pale with emotion and responsibility]* No, Ben.

BEN   I'm sorry – I thought you cared for me.

JENNY   I do – I like you very much, Ben. But I don't
             want to spend the rest of my life looking
             after a man.

BEN   I had forgotten. The – new – woman . . .

JENNY   *[serenely – here she is untouchable now]* The
             new woman . . . who will marry and have
             children and look after them . . . not baby a
             husband, as so many have done in the past.

BEN   *[really hurt]* I thought – you said that I could be
             something better.

JENNY   *[understanding his hurt]* You will be, Ben – but
             not with me. I should simply take the place
             of your father in your life. And I should
             become a bitter, criticising, domineering
             woman, a mother to her own husband, who
             never knew the joy of being wife and friend.

BEN   *[very endearing]* It wouldn't be like that.
             [making a real and winning plea] Be a sport,
             Jenny!

JENNY   *[quietly, to combat his warmth]* You wouldn't
             wish to ruin me, Ben. And that would be real
             ruin. Not your lending library word – real
             ruin.

BEN   Oh, well – it's quite hopeless, isn't it? Sorry I
             embarrassed you . . .

BEN *starts across the room as though to go, then unable to leave it alone, comes back.*

BEN   Is that the real reason you won't marry me?

JENNY   It's enough. But apart from that . . .

BEN   Apart from that . . .?

JENNY   I think I'm going to marry your father!

BEN *is completely breathless. She walks back to her desk and he follows her.*

BEN   You did say . . .?

She nods.

BEN   But, Jenny – why?

JENNY   Because I like him. Because he's proud and stiff-necked and adult – but carries within him always a young and desperate boy from Dublin, whom no one has ever comforted. You don't know that boy, my comfortable Ben – he suffered that you should live without making his acquaintance . . . but I have been poor. I have found the world against me, and I shall find my way to his heart.

BEN   Frankly, I don't understand a word of it – except that he's old enough to be my father!

JENNY   *[tartly]* Well, he isn't mine! *[then repentant]* Oh, Ben, dear Ben, forgive me if I've hurt you. But you'll be glad – eventually.

He looks at her – he knows better. She is deeply troubled.

JENNY   Now that I've told you how I feel – what are you going to do? *[hesitantly]* Take Manson's offer?

BEN   To fight my father?

She nods, afraid of words.

BEN   No – I'm not big enough . . . yet! If someday I have to match Rufus Torrent, it will be the meeting of equals. I won't be a weapon in another man's hands.

Suddenly RUFUS *is heard on the stairs.*

RUFUS   *[off]* Right, Jock – bring them to the office in half an hour –

JENNY   *[in an urgent whisper]* No bitterness, Ben –

BEN   No bitterness, Jenny. But he must have realized how I felt about you. He might have told me that you – and he –

JENNY   He doesn't know about it – yet, Ben –

RUFUS *comes in carrying the aura of a couple of morning ports.*

RUFUS   *[affably]* What the devil are you doing.
         lounging round the office, Ben. Kingsley is
         waiting for you.

BEN   I am about to join him, sir – But I would like to
         speak to you for a moment . . .

JENNY *is in a panic.* RUFUS *stops on his way to the office.*

RUFUS   I have been trying to get into this office all the
         morning, Ben – people keep running in and
         out. *[to* JENNY*]* *I'm not in to callers for the*
         rest of the morning.

JENNY   *[her eyes on* BEN*]* No, sir.

BEN   Just one thing, Father – do you realize that we
         are both taking credit that we don't
         deserve . . . you, for publishing views you
         would never have countenanced . . .

JENNY *stops a gesture of protest half way.*

BEN   Me, for holding views I did not dare to express.
         King was right, Father, Koolgalla is ripe and
         ready for something new, and you and
         I – with Kingsley – seem to be regarded as
         architects of the change. And all the time, the
         person who dared everything – took every
         chance – sits there . . .

RUFUS *looks over his shoulder to make sure* JENNY *is sitting there.*

BEN   And the credit goes to those who least deserve
         it.

RUFUS   Of course, Ben, if you're going to spend your
         life making sure that credit for change and
         vision goes where it's due, you'll never have
         time to make the change and the vision come
         true. And that would be a pity, now,
         wouldn't it?

BEN   *[quite horrified]* But Father – you can't just
         accept Jenny's sacrifice.

RUFUS   *[swinging on* BEN*]* I accept it. This time the
         undeserved glory falls on me. I am a proud
         man, Ben – I shall be eager for the
         opportunity to repay the obligation. *[He half*
         sits, half leans on the edge of JENNY's *desk,*
         talking half to her, half to BEN*.]* But I accept
         it. For what are the saints and the heroes but

the vision and the sword of the common rest
of us. And who cares, in the long breadth of
the years who dreamed the dream, so long as
the common rest of us made it come true?

JENNY *is looking at him and* BEN, *seeing her look, catches his
breath, understanding. But* RUFUS *is looking far away.*

BEN   But Father, Jenny –

RUFUS   Jenny is more of a damned fool than I think if
she cares for anything less than the
achievement. She understands. [RUFUS *is
finished with all this talk. He makes for his
office, saying over his shoulder*] I have a
meeting I must attend after lunch, Ben, and I
want to do tomorrow's editorial before I
go – a follow up on this morning's . . . *[he
hesitates, turns]* I would like your advice,
Ben.

BEN   *[appreciating this from* RUFUS*]* Thank you,
Father. Always at your disposal. But I am
sure that you are more able than I am . . .
[his eyes are on JENNY*]* . . . in everything.

RUFUS   *[carelessly]* Probably – but no one can say that I
don't ask for advice.

*He goes into his office, slamming the door. He sits at desk, picks
up some proofs, starts to write something.*
BEN *looks at* JENNY.

BEN   I can see there is nothing for you but that.
He gets his hat from the rack.

RUFUS   *[from office]* Jenny!

*She turns to look at door with a sparkle in her face. She collects
her pad and pencil and starts for the door. Half way there, she
turns. On an impulse, but with no hint of coquetry, she kisses
her fingers to* BEN, *looking at him sorrowfully, affectionately.*

RUFUS   *[very loudly]* Jenny!!

She moves to door of the office. BEN *moves to downstairs exit.
They turn and look back at each other.* JENNY *has her hand on
the door knob.* BEN *is looking back.*
RUFUS *flings open the office door.*

RUFUS   JENNY!! I WANT YOU!!

JENNY   Yes, sir!

REFUS *turns back into office.*

BEN   *[lovingly and sadly and quizzically]* Goodbye,
      Mama –
One more smile, each to each, and JENNY *is going into the office.*
BEN *is still watching her go as . . .*

CURTAIN

Antigone Kefala, 1935–

Born in Roumania, of Greek parents, she lived in
Greece after World War II and in 1951, migrated to
New Zealand where she studied at Victoria
University, Wellington. She moved to Australia in
the 1960s and has published a steady stream of work
in magazines and anthologies as well as being
broadcast on radio.

Among her poetry publications are *The Alien*
(1973), *Thirsty Weather* (1978) while her fiction
includes *The First Journey* (1975, Wild and Woolley,
Sydney), *The Island* (1984, Hale & Iremonger,
Sydney), and *Alexia* (1984, John Ferguson, Sydney).

The following short story has been taken from
Aspect, Vol. 2/3, March 1977.

SUNDAY LUNCH

The train was half empty. Carefully dressed ladies carrying
flowers. Children returning from church, bored. The spring wind
moved the grass along the tracks. The sun was shining on
corrugated iron roofs, back yards, lime factories. The waiting
room smelt of disinfectant.

Another block of flats had been built next door and all along
the fence the peach trees were in bloom. I was ready to knock
when the door opened from inside. He had shrunk slightly and
his eyes were dimmer, but he held himself erect. He embraced
me with something of his old warmth and gallantry. The flat was
as usual impeccably arranged and silent. Cheri was in the kitchen
with the sister.

They moved like round, heavy seals, setting the table, bringing the meat, the horse radish, the glazed potatoes. Dishes were passed with appropriate remarks, he with trembling hands, enormous silences waiting suspended from the still air between words. The crockery, the cutlery making cracking noises like the sound of dentures. I smiled a lot, laughed a lot, tried to warm the air, we all tried, but the air moved slowly, unwillingly, watched us with dim tired eyes.

The sister had surprising blue forget-me-not eyes, a tortured face, a small thin mouth. She spoke in a high pitched matter of fact voice, of illness, operations, death, cremation, the cost of funerals, the voice of Christ which scientists had now reconstituted electronically. 'What language does he speak?' I asked laughingly. 'Hebrew, I presume. If he speaks Latin, he must be a fake. If he speaks Greek, one could make some concessions.'

He waited, slower than I remembered, disconnected from us, as if trapped at the dead centre of a field, space growing out of him in every direction, grey, misty space. He was already turning to stone and he stretched towards us the familiar gestures, shadows of his old affections.

There was a new painting in the lounge room. Sue had done it. The white lilies sitting naive and awkward in the golden vase against the deep red background. The white had a lot of innocence in it, and a spring exuberance. It was difficult to imagine that Sue's heart was like this. We listened to Schubert – who had died so young. Outside, the spring wind moved the trees. Unsettled wind, blowing the hair of the girl next door sitting under the trees. Through the glass doors they seemed to move in an aquarium of light, the child and later the man. Their gestures arrested in the sun, altered by the wind.

Over the coffee the spoons began the discussion. A present in 1935 from Uncle Jules. A whole silver service, only the spoons left. And poor Aunt Clara, unhinged by the great fire. Rock melons one remembered most in the country, and the spring water. The rock of horses, sleeping under a straw hat, reading *Nana*, the walnut trees at the back of the river. The smell of things in those days. The barrels of kippers being opened.

I had met the sister in the street. Her face more tortured than usual, as if washed over by great waves, her eyes desperate. 'A stroke,' she said. 'He moved about lost, could not speak, the doctors did not say much.' I rang Cheri. The telephone kept ringing. Then someone picked up the receiver. There was a groan at the other end. I said 'Cheri is that you?' There was no answer. The great waves of space sounded on the line. I was silent. I thought that he had just died, that she had been struck dumb, that she could not articulate, gather her thoughts.

I cried out – 'Cheri . . . Cheri . . . speak to me. What is the matter?' The voice at the other end struggled as if through interminable corridors of silence to say something, one could feel the strain coming over in waves, more and more agonising.

I tried to sound calm, to coax it. 'Are you all right Cheri? Is everything all right? Just say yes only, nothing more. I just want to hear your voice.' I wanted to say, has he died my God? Has he died? But did not dare. To say it was to make it an accomplished thing, but went on cajoling the silence at the other end.

And suddenly the voice, somehow altered beyond recognition, rising from dark depths, said slowly, as if each letter had to be formed with an almost inhuman effort, as if each syllable meant a victory, as if the word was a triumph . . . 'Cheri . . .' I helped it along, '. . . is . . . out . . .' 'Oh,' I said, my voice ringing with joy and fear, 'is it you, is it you Bubo? I am so glad you answered the phone . . .'

I went on, my voice jumping over stones in the sun, riding in the wind . . .

GERMAINE GREER, 1939–

Writer, journalist, broadcaster and fervent feminist,
she was born in Melbourne and was educated at the
Universities of Melbourne, Sydney and Cambridge.
Best known for her feminist treatise, *The Female
Eunuch* (1970), the book was and still is hugely
successful, having been reprinted more than fifteen
times and translated into more than ten languages. It
stands as one of the classic coverages of women's
position in the western world and has been highly
influential in setting some of the parameters of
women's liberation demands and debates.

The author of a wide range of popular articles,
many of which are audacious and irreverent,
Germaine Greer has also undertaken serious and
systematic research on the constraints imposed on
women artists (*The Obstacle Race*, 1979) and on the
conditions that govern women's reproduction (*Sex
and Destiny; The Politics of Human Fertility*, 1984).
Her other works include *The Madwoman's
Underclothes, Essays and Occasional Writings
1968–1985* (1986) and a forthcoming anthology of
women's poetry.

The following extract has been taken from *The
Female Eunuch* (1987 edition, Paladin, London) and
gives some indication of the author's policy and
passion.

THE FEMALE EUNUCH

Summary

'The World has lost its soul, and I my sex' (Toller, *Hinkemann*)

This book is a part of the second feminist wave. The old suffragettes, who served their prison term and lived on through the years of gradual admission of women into professions which they declined to follow, into parliamentary freedoms which they declined to exercise, into academies which they used more and more as shops where they could take out degrees while waiting to get married, have seen their spirit revive in younger women with a new and vital cast. Mrs Hazel Hunkins-Hallinan, leader of the Six Point Group, welcomed the younger militants and even welcomed their sexual frankness. 'They're young,' she said to Irma Kurtz, 'and utterly unsophisticated politically, but they're full of beans. The membership of our group until recently has been far too old for my liking.'[1] After the ecstasy of direct action, the militant ladies of two generations ago settled down to work of consolidation in hosts of small organizations, while the main force of their energy filtered away in post-war retrenchments and the revival of frills, corsets and femininity after the permissive twenties, through the sexual sell of the fifties, ever dwindling, ever more respectable. Evangelism withered into eccentricity.

The new emphasis is different. Then genteel middle-class ladies clamoured for reform, now ungenteel middle-class women are calling for revolution. For many of them the call for revolution came before the call for the liberation of women. The New Left has been the forcing house for most movements, and for many of them liberation is dependent upon the coming of the classless society and the withering away of the state. The difference is radical, for the faith that the suffragettes had in the existing political systems and their deep desire to participate in them have perished. In the old days ladies were anxious to point out that they did not seek to disrupt society or to unseat God. Marriage, the family, private property and the state were threatened by their actions, but they were anxious to allay the fears of conservatives, and in doing so the suffragettes betrayed their own cause and prepared the way for the failure of emancipation. Five years ago

---

[1] 'Boadicea Rides Again', *Sunday Times Magazine*, 21 September 1969.

it seemed clear that emancipation had failed: the number of women in Parliament had settled at a low level; the number of professional women had stabilized as a tiny minority; the pattern of female employment had emerged as underpaid, menial and supportive. The cage door had been opened but the canary had refused to fly out. The conclusion was that the cage door ought never to have been opened because canaries are made for captivity; the suggestion of an alternative had only confused and saddened them.

There are feminist organizations still in existence which follow the reforming tracks laid down by the suffragettes. Betty Friedan's National Organization for Women is represented in congressional committees, especially the ones considered to be of special relevance to women. Women politicians still represent female interests, but they are most often the interests of women as dependants, to be protected from easy divorce and all sorts of Casanova's charters. Mrs Hunkins-Hallinan's Six Point Group is a respected political entity. What is new about the situation is that such groups are enjoying new limelight. The media insist upon exposing women's liberation weekly, even daily. The change is that suddenly everyone is interested in the subject of women. They may not be in favour of the movements that exist, but they are concerned about the issues. Among young women in universities the movement might be expected to find strong support. It is not surprising that exploited women workers might decide to hold the Government to ransom at last. It is surprising that women who seem to have nothing to complain about have begun to murmur. Speaking to quiet audiences of provincial women decently hatted and dressed, I have been surprised to find that the most radical ideas are gladly entertained, and the most telling criticisms and sharpest protests are uttered. Even the suffragettes could not claim the grass-roots support that the new feminism gains day by day.

We can only speculate about the causes of this new activity. Perhaps the sexual sell was oversell. Perhaps women have never really believed the account of themselves which they were forced to accept from psychologists, religious leaders, women's magazines and men. Perhaps the reforms which did happen eventually led them to the position from which they could at last see the whole perspective and begin to understand the rationale of their situation. Perhaps because they are not enmeshed in unwilling child-

birth and heavy menial labour in the home, they have had time
to think. Perhaps the plight of our society has become so desperate
and so apparent that women can no longer be content to leave
it to other people. The enemies of women have blamed such circumstances for female discontent. Women must prize this discontent as the first stirring of the demand for life; they have begun
to speak out and to speak to each other. The sight of women
talking together has always made men uneasy; nowadays it means
rank subversion. 'Right on!'

The organized liberationists are a well-publicized minority; the
same faces appear every time a feminist issue is discussed. Inevitably they are presented as the leaders of a movement which is
essentially leaderless. They are not much nearer to providing a
revolutionary strategy than they ever were; demonstrating, compiling reading lists and sitting on committees are not themselves
liberated behaviour, especially when they are still embedded in
a context of housework and feminine wiles. As means of educating
the people who must take action to liberate themselves, their
effectiveness is limited. The concept of liberty implied by such
liberation is vacuous; at worst it is defined by the condition of
men, themselves unfree, and at best it is left undefined in a world
of very limited possibilities. On the one hand, feminists can be
found who serve the notion of equality 'social, legal, occupational,
economic, political and moral', whose enemy is discrimination,
whose means are competition and demand. On the other hand
there are those who cherish an ideal of a better life, which will
follow when a better life is assured for all by the correct political
means. To women disgusted with conventional political methods,
whether constitutional or totalitarian or revolutionary, neither
alternative can make much appeal. The housewife who must wait
for the success of world revolution for her liberty might be excused
for losing hope, while conservative political methods can invent
no way in which the economically necessary unit of the one-man
family could be diversified. But there is another dimension in
which she can find motive and cause for action, although she
might not find a blue-print for Utopia. She could begin not by
changing the world, but by re-assessing herself.

It is impossible to argue a case for female liberation if there
is no certainty about the degree of inferiority or natural
dependence which is unalterably female. That is why this book
begins with the *Body*. We know what we are, but know not what

we may be, or what we might have been. The dogmatism of science expresses the status quo as the ineluctable result of law: women must learn how to question the most basic assumptions about feminine normality in order to reopen the possibilities for development which have been successively locked off by conditioning. So, we begin at the beginning, with the sex of cells. Nothing much can be made of chromosomal difference until it is manifested in development, and development cannot take place in a vacuum: from the outset our observation of the female is consciously and unconsciously biassed by assumptions that we cannot help making and cannot always identify when they have been made. The new assumption behind the discussion of the body is that everything that we may observe *could be otherwise*. In order to demonstrate some of the aspects of conditioning a discussion follows of the effects of behaviour upon the skeleton. From *Bones* we move to *Curves*, which is still essential to assumptions about the female sex, and then to *Hair*, for a long time considered a basic secondary sexual characteristic.

Female sexuality has always been a fascinating topic; this discussion of it attempts to show how female sexuality has been masked and deformed by most observers, and never more so than in our own time. The conformation of the female has already been described in terms of a particular type of conditioning, and now the specific character of that conditioning begins to emerge. What happens is that the female is considered as a sexual object for the use and appreciation of other sexual beings, men. Her sexuality is both denied and misrepresented by being identified as passivity. The vagina is obliterated from the imagery of femininity in the same way that the signs of independence and vigour in the rest of her body are suppressed. The characteristics that are praised and rewarded are those of the castrate – timidity, plumpness, languor, delicacy and preciosity. *Body* ends with a look at the way in which female reproduction is thought to influence the whole organism in the operations of the *Wicked Womb*, source of hysteria, menstrual depression, weakness, and unfitness for any sustained enterprise.

The compound of induced characteristics of soul and body is the myth of the Eternal Feminine, nowadays called the *Stereotype*. This is the dominant image of femininity which rules our culture and to which all women aspire. Assuming that the goddess of consumer culture is an artifact, we embark on an examination of how she comes to be made, the manufacture of the *Soul*. The chief element in this process is like the castration that we saw practised upon the body, the suppression and deflection of *Energy*. Following the same simple pattern, we begin at the beginning with *Baby*, showing how of the greater the less is made. The *Girl* struggles to reconcile her schooling along masculine lines with her feminine conditioning until *Puberty* resolves the ambiguity and anchors her safely in the feminine posture, if it works. When it doesn't she is given further conditioning as a corrective, especially by psychologists, whose assumptions and prescriptions are described as the *Psychological Sell*.

Because so many assumptions about the sex of mind cloud the issue of female mental ability, there follows a brief account of the failure of fifty years of thorough and diversified testing to discover any pattern of differentiation in male and female intellectual powers, called *The Raw Material*. Because the tests have been irrelevant to the continuing conviction that women are illogical, subjective and generally silly, *Womanpower* takes a coherent expression of all such prejudice, Otto Weininger's *Sex and Character*, and turns all the defects which it defines into advantages, by rejecting Weininger's concepts of virtue and intelligence and espousing those of Whitehead and others. As a corrective to such a theoretical view of how valuable such female minds might be, *Work* provides a factual account of the patterns that the female contribution actually takes and how it is valued.

The castration of women has been carried out in terms of a masculine-feminine polarity, in which men have commandeered all the energy and streamlined it into an aggressive conquistatorial power, reducing all heterosexual contact to a sadomasochistic pattern. This has meant the distortion of our concepts of *Love*. Beginning with a celebration of an *Ideal, Love* proceeds to describe some of the chief perversions, *Altruism, Egotism*, and *Obsession*. These distortions masquerade under various mythic guises, of which two follow – *Romance*, an account of the fantasies on which the appetent and the disappointed woman is nourished, and *The Object of Male Fantasy*, which deals with the favourite ways in which women are presented in specifically male literature. *The Middle-Class Myth of Love and Marriage* records the rise of the most commonly accepted mutual fantasy of heterosexual love in our society, as a prelude to a discussion of the normal form of life as we understand it, the *Family*. The nuclear family of our time is severely criticized, and some vague alternatives are suggested, but the chief function of this part, as of the whole book, is mostly to suggest the possibility and the desirability of an alternative. The chief bogy of those who fear freedom is insecurity, and so *Love* ends with an animadversion on the illusoriness of *Security*, the ruling deity of the welfare state, never more insubstantial than it is in the age of total warfare, global pollution and population explosion.

Because love has been so perverted, it has in many cases come to involve a measure of hatred. In extreme cases it takes the form of *Loathing and Disgust* occasioned by sadism, fastidiousness and guilt, and inspires hideous crimes on the bodies of women, but more often it is limited to *Abuse* and ridicule, expressed by casual insult and facetiousness. Rather than dwell upon the injustices suffered by women in their individual domestic circumstances, these parts deal with more or less public occasions in which the complicated patterns of mutual exploitation do not supply any ambiguous context. There are many subjective accounts of suffering to be found in feminist literature, so *Misery* deals with the problem on a broader scale, showing how much objective evidence there is that women are not happy even when they do follow the blueprint set out by sentimental and marriage guidance counsellors and the system that they represent. Although there is no pattern of female assault on men to parallel their violence to women, there is plenty of evidence of the operation of *Resentment* in bitter, non-physical sexual conflict, usually enacted as a kind of game, a ritualized situation in which the real issues never emerge. This unconscious vindictiveness has its parallels in more organized and articulate female *Rebellion*, in that it seeks to characterize men as the enemy and either to compete with or confront or attack them. Insofar as such movements *demand* of men, or *force* men to grant their liberty, they perpetuate the estrangement of the sexes and their own dependency.

Revolution ought to entail the correction of some of the false perspectives which our assumptions about womanhood, sex, love and society have combined to create. Tentatively it gestures towards the re-deployment of energy, no longer to be used in repression, but in desire, movement and creation. Sex must be rescued from the traffic between powerful and powerless, masterful and mastered, sexual and neutral, to become a form of communication between potent, gentle, tender people, which cannot be accomplished by denial of heterosexual contact. The Ultra-feminine must refuse any longer to countenance the self-deception of the Omnipotent Administrator, not so much by assailing him as freeing herself from the desire to fulfil his expectations. It might be expected that men would resist female liberation because it threatens the foundations of phallic narcissism, but there are indications that men themselves are seeking a more satisfying role. If women liberate themselves, they will perforce liberate their oppressors: men might well feel that as sole custodians of sexual energy and universal protectors of women and children they have undertaken the impossible, especially now that their misdirected energies have produced the ultimate weapon. In admitting women to male-dominated areas of life, men have already shown a willingness to share responsibility, even if the invitation has not been taken up. Now that it might be construed that women are to help carry the can full of the mess that men have made, it need not be surprising that women have not leapt at the chance. If women could think that civilization would come to maturity only when they were involved in it wholly, they might feel more optimism in the possibilities of change and new development. The spiritual crisis we are at present traversing might be just another growing pain.

Revolution does little more than 'peep to what it would'. It hints that women ought not to enter into socially sanctioned relationships, like marriage, and that once unhappily in they ought not to scruple to run away. It might even be thought to suggest that women should be deliberately promiscuous. It certainly maintains that they should be self-sufficient and consciously refrain from establishing exclusive dependencies and other kinds of neurotic symbioses. Much of what it points to is sheer irresponsibility, but when the stake is life and freedom, and the necessary condition is the recovery of a will to live, irresponsibility might be thought a small risk. It is almost a hundred years since Nora asked Helmer 'What do you consider is my most sacred duty?' and when he answered 'Your duty to your husband and children', she demurred.

I have another duty, just as sacred. . . . My duty to myself. . . . I believe that before everything else I'm a human being – just as much as you are . . . or at any rate I shall try to become one. I know quite well that most people would agree with you, Torvald, and that you have a warrant for it in books;

but I can't be satisfied any longer with what most people say, and with what's in books. I must think things out for myself and try to understand them.[2]

The relationships recognized by our society, and dignified with full privileges, are only those which are binding, symbiotic, economically determined. The most generous, tender, spontaneous relationship deliquesces into the approved mould when it avails itself of the approved buttresses, legality, security, permanence. Marriage cannot be a *job* as it has become. Status ought not to be measured for women in terms of attracting and snaring a man. The woman who realizes that she is bound by a million Lilliputian threads in an attitude of impotence and hatred masquerading as tranquillity and love has no option but to run away, if she is not to be corrupted and extinguished utterly. Liberty is terrifying but it is also exhilarating. Life is not easier or more pleasant for the Noras who have set off on their journey to awareness, but it is more interesting, nobler even. Such counsel will be called encouragement of irresponsibility, but the woman who accepts a way of life which she has not knowingly chosen, acting out a series of contingencies falsely presented as destiny, is truly irresponsible. To abdicate one's own moral understanding, to tolerate crimes against humanity, to leave everything to someone else, the father-ruler-king-computer, is the only irresponsibility. To deny that a mistake has been made when its results are chaos visible and tangible on all sides, *that* is irresponsibility. What oppression lays upon us is not responsibility but guilt.

The revolutionary woman must know her enemies, the doctors, psychiatrists, health visitors, priests, marriage counsellors, policemen, magistrates and genteel reformers, all the authoritarians and dogmatists who flock about her with warnings and advice. She must know her friends, her sisters, and seek in their lineaments her own. With them she can discover co-operation, sympathy and love. The end cannot justify the means: if she finds that her revolutionary way leads only to further discipline and continuing incomprehension, with their corollaries of bitterness and diminution, no matter how glittering the objective which would justify it, she must understand that it is a wrong way and an illusory end. The struggle which is not joyous is the wrong struggle. The joy of the struggle is not hedonism and hilarity, but the sense of purpose, achievement and dignity which is the

[2] Henrik Ibsen, *A Doll's House*, Act III.

reflowering of etiolated energy. Only these can sustain her and keep the flow of energy coming. The problems are only equalled by the possibilities: every mistake made is redeemed when it is understood. The only ways in which she can feel such joy are radical ones: the more derided and maligned the action that she undertakes, the more radical.

The way is unknown, just as the sex of the uncastrated female is unknown. However far we can see it is not far enough to discern the contours of what is ultimately desirable. And so no ultimate strategy can be designed. To be free to start out, and to find companions for the journey is as far as we need to see from where we stand. The first exercise of the free woman is to devise her own mode of revolt, a mode which will reflect her own independence and originality. The more clearly the forms of oppression emerge in her understanding, the more clearly she can see the shape of future action. In the search for political awareness there is no substitute for confrontation. It would be too easy to present women with yet another form of self-abnegation, more opportunities for appetence and forlorn hope, but women have had enough bullying. They have been led by the nose and every other way until they have to acknowledge that, like everyone else, they are lost. A feminist elite might seek to lead uncomprehending women in another arbitrary direction, training them as a task force in a battle that might, that ought never to eventuate. If there is a pitched battle women will lose, because the best man never wins; the consequences of militancy do not disappear when the need for militancy is over. Freedom is fragile and must be protected. To sacrifice it, even as a temporary measure, is to betray it. It is not a question of telling women what to do next, or even what to want to do next. The hope in which this book was written is that women will discover that they have a will; once that happens they will be able to tell us how and what they want.

The fear of freedom is strong in us. We call it chaos or anarchy, and the words are threatening. We live in a true chaos of contradicting authorities, an age of conformism without community, of proximity without communication. We could only fear chaos if we imagined that it was unknown to us, but in fact we know it very well. It is unlikely that the techniques of liberation spontaneously adopted by women will be in such fierce conflict as exists between warring self-interests and conflicting dogmas, for they will not seek to eliminate all systems but their own. However diverse they may be, they need not be utterly irreconcilable, because they will not be conquistatorial.

Hopefully, this book is subversive. Hopefully, it will draw fire from all the articulate sections of the community. The conventional moralist will find much that is reprehensible in the denial of the Holy Family, in the denigration of sacred motherhood, and the inference that women are not by nature monogamous. The political conservatives ought to object that by advocating the destruction of the patterns of consumption carried out by the chief spenders, the housewives, the book invites depression and hardship. This is tantamount to admitting that the oppression of women is necessary to the maintenance of the economy, and simply ratifies the point. If the present economic structure can change only by collapsing, then it had better collapse as soon as possible. The nation that acknowledges that all labourers are worthy of their hire and then withholds payment from 19,500,000 workers cannot continue. Freudians will object that by setting aside the conventional account of the female psyche, and relying upon a concept of woman which cannot be found to exist, the book is mere metaphysics, forgetting the metaphysical basis of their own doctrine. The reformers will lament that the image of womanhood is cheapened by the advocacy of delinquency, so that women are being drawn further and further away from the real centres of power. In the computer kingdom the centres of political power have become centres of impotence, but even so, nothing in the book precludes the use of the political machine, although reliance on it may be contra-indicated. The most telling criticisms will come from my sisters of the left, the Maoists, the Trots, the I.S., the S.D.S., because of my fantasy that it might be possible to leap the steps of revolution and arrive somehow at liberty and communism without strategy or revolutionary discipline. But if women are the true proletariat, the truly oppressed majority, the revolution can only be drawn nearer by their withdrawal of support for the capitalist system. The weapon that I suggest is that most honoured of the proletariat, withdrawal of labour. Nevertheless it is clear that I do not find the factory the real heart of civilization or the re-entry of women into industry as the necessary condition of liberation. Unless the concepts of work and play and reward for work change absolutely, women must continue to provide cheap labour, and even more, free labour exacted of right by an employer possessed of a contract for life, made out in his favour.

This book represents only another contribution to a continuing dialogue between the wondering woman and the world. No questions have been answered but perhaps some have been asked in a more proper way than heretofore. If it is not ridiculed or reviled, it will have failed of its intention. If the most successful feminine parasites do not find it offensive, than it is innocuous. What they can tolerate is intolerable for a woman with any pride. The opponents of female suffrage lamented that woman's emancipation would mean the end of marriage, morality and the state; their extremism was more clear-sighted than the woolly benevolence of liberals and humanists, who thought that giving women a measure of freedom would not upset anything. When we reap the harvest which the unwitting suffragettes sowed we shall see that the anti-feminists were after all right . . .

References and Further Reading

ADELAIDE, Debra (ed), 1988
Australian Women Writers: A Bibliographic Guide
Pandora Press, London
BANDLER, Faith, 1977
Wacvie
Rigby, Adelaide
BARKER, Lady Mary Anne ('Lady Broome') (1870) 1984
Station Life in New Zealand
Virago, London
BARNARD, Marjorie, (1943), 1985
The Persimmon Tree and Other Stories
Virago, London
BAXTER, Annie, 1873
Memories of the Past by a Lady in Australia
W. H. Williams, Melbourne
BAYNTON, Barbara, (1980) 1988
The Portable Barbara Baynton
(Sally Krimmer, Alan Lawson, eds), UQP Australian Authors, University of Queensland Press, St Lucia
BOSWELL, Annabella (1965) 1981
Journal
Introduced by Morton Herman
Angus & Robertson, Sydney
BRISBANE, K. (ed), 1974
Katharine Susannah Prichard, *Brumby Innes and Bid Me to Love*
Currency Press, Sydney
BUNN, Anna Maria, 1838
The Guardian
J. Spilsbury, Sydney
BURNEY, Fanny, (1778) 1982
Evelina
Oxford University Press, London

CAMBRIDGE, Ada, 1903
  Thirty Years in Australia
  Methuen, London
CAMBRIDGE, Ada (1904) (forthcoming)
  Sisters
  Penguin Australian Women's Library
  Penguin, Melbourne
CLACY, Ellen, (1853) 1963
  A Lady's Visit to the Gold Diggings of Australia in 1852–1853
  (Patricia Thompson, ed.)
  Lansdowne Press, Melbourne
DEVANNY, Jean, 1986
  Point of Departure
  (Carole Ferrier, ed.)
  University of Queensland Press, St Lucia
DRAKE-BROCKMAN, Henrietta (ed.) 1954
  Australian Legendary Tales by
  Catherine Langloh Parker, illustrated by Elizabeth Durack
  Angus & Robertson, Sydney
DRAKE-BROCKMAN, Henrietta (ed.) 1959
  West Coast Stories: An anthology
  edited for the Western Australian Section of the Fellowship of
  Australian Writers
  Angus & Robertson, Sydney
FRANKLIN, Miles (1901) 1980
  My Brilliant Career
  Angus & Robertson, Sydney
GARE, Nene, 1978
  Bend to the Wind
  Macmillan, Melbourne
GAUNT, Mary, (1897) 1988
  Kirkham's Find
  (introduced by Kylie Tennant)
  Penguin, Melbourne
GREEN, Dorothy 1986
  Henry Handel Richardson and Her Fiction
  Allen & Unwin, Sydney
GREER, Germaine, 1987
  The Female Eunuch
  Paladin, London
GUNN, Jeannie, (1908) 1983
  We of the Never-Never
  Hutchinson, Melbourne

HAMPTON, Susan and Kate LLEWELLYN (eds) 1986
Penguin Book of Australian Women Poets
Penguin, Melbourne
HASLUCK, Alexandra, 1955
Portrait with Background: A Life of Georgiana Molloy
Oxford University Press, London
HENEY, Helen (ed.) 1985
Dear Fanny
Australian National University/Pergamon Press, Sydney
HENNING, Rachel, 1952
The Letters of Rachel Henning
(David Armstrong, ed.)
Bulletin, Sydney
LANGLEY, Eve (1942) 1976
The Pea Pickers
Angus & Robertson, Sydney
LANGLEY, Eve, 1954
White Topee
Angus & Robertson, Sydney
LEAKEY, Caroline ('Oline Keese') 1859
The Broad Arrow: Being Passages from the History of Maida Gwynnham, a Lifer
Bentley, London
MACARTHUR, Elizabeth
The Journal and Letters of Elizabeth Macarthur, 1789-1791
(Joy N. Hughes, ed.)
Elizabeth Farm Occasional Papers
McCRAE, Georgiana, (1934/1966) 1983
Georgiana's Journal, Melbourne, 1841–1865
(Hugh McCrae, ed.)
William Brooks, Sydney
McKAY, Prue (ed.) 1986
The Peculiar Honeymoon and Other Writings by Mary Grant Bruce
McPhee Gribble, Melbourne
MARTIN, Catherine (1890) 1988
An Australian Girl
Pandora Press, London
MARTIN, Catherine (1923) 1987
The Incredible Journey
Pandora Press, London
MARTIN, Mrs Patchett (ed.) 1891
Coo-ee: Tales of Australian Life by Australian Ladies
Richard Edward King, London

MASTERS, Olga, 1984
  The Home Girls
  University of Queensland Press, St Lucia
MORGAN, Sally 1987
  My Place
  Fremantle Arts Press, Fremantle
MURRAY, Elizabeth A. (1864) 1985
  Ella Norman: A Woman's Perils
  Hill of Content, Melbourne
PALMER, Nettie, 1950
  Henry Handel Richardson: A Study
  Angus and Robertson, Sydney
PALMER, Nettie (1948) 1988
  Fourteen Years: Extracts from a Private Journal 1925–1939
  (Vivian Smith, ed.)
  UQP Authors, University of Queensland Press, St Lucia
POOLE, Phillipa (ed.) 1979
  The Diaries of Ethel Turner
  Ure Smith, Sydney
PRAED, Rosa, (1880) forthcoming
  An Australian Heroine
  (introduced by Kate Grenville)
  Penguin, Melbourne
PRAED, Rosa (1887) (1987)
  The Bond of Wedlock
  (introduced by Lynne Spender)
  Pandora Press, London
PRAED, Rosa, (1893) 1988
  Outlaw and Lawmaker
  (introduced by Dale Spender)
  Pandora Press, London
PRAED, Rosa (1881), 1988
  Policy and Passion
  Virago, London
SIMPSON, Helen, 1932
  Boomerang
  Heinemann, London
SIMPSON, Helen (1937) 1983
  Under Capricorn
  Angus & Robertson, Sydney
SPENCE, Catherine Helen, 1984
  Handfasted
  Penguin, Melbourne

SPENDER, Dale, 1982
Women of Ideas–And What Men Have Done to Them
Routledge & Kegan Paul, London
SPENDER, Dale, 1987
Mothers of the Novel: 100 Good Women Writers Before Jane Austen
Pandora Press, London
SPENDER, Dale, 1988
Writing a New World: Two Centuries of Australian Women Writers
Pandora Press, London
SPENDER, Lynne, 1983
Intruders on the Rights of Men: Women's Unpublished Heritage
Pandora Press, London
STEAD, Christina, 1986
Ocean of Story; The Uncollected Stories of Christina Stead
Penguin, Melbourne
'TASMA' (Jessie Couvreur), 1889
A Sydney Sovereign and Other Tales
Frank Lovell, New York
TENNANT, Kylie, 1959
Speak You So Gently
Gollancz, London
THOMSON, Helen, 1984
'Preface and Afterword in Catherine Helen Spence, *Handfasted*
Penguin, Melbourne
THOMSON, Helen (ed.) forthcoming
The Mad Woman in the Bush
Penguin, Melbourne
THROSSELL, Ric, (ed.) 1982
Katharine Susannah Prichard,
Straight Left
Wild & Woolley, Sydney
WEBBY, Elizabeth and Lydia WEVERS (eds) 1987
*Happy Endings: Stories by Australian and New Zealand Women,
1850s–1930s*
Allen & Unwin, New Zealand
WILDE, W. H. and T. Inglis MOORE, (eds) 1980
Letters of Mary Gilmore
Melbourne University Press, Melbourne

SOURCES

Margaret Catchpole
Extracts from Sydney. Source Mitchell Library, A1508; quoted in Helen Heney, pp23-25. Mitchell Library, typescript copies A3D59.

Elizabeth Macarthur
To Mitchell Library and Joy N. Hughes (ed), The Journal and Letters of Elizabeth Macarthur 1789-1791, Elizabeth Farm Occasional Papers.

Georgiana McCrae
Georgiana's Journal, edited by Hugh McCrae, 1983, Melbourne 1841-65, William Brooks, Sydney.

Louisa Anne Meredith
My Home in Tasmania During a Residence of Nine Years, 1852 (courtesy of Fisher Library/Sydney University).

Catherine Helen Spence
'Afloat or Ashore', *Australasian*, 1878.

Ellen Clacy
A Lady's Visit to the Gold Diggings of Australia in 1852-1853, (1853), reprint edited by Patricia Thompson, 1963, Lansdowne Press, Melbourne.

Mary Fortune ('Waif Wander')
'Kirsty Oglevie', *Australian Journal*, 1866.

Ada Cambridge
'A Girl's Ideal', *Age*, 1881.

Louisa Lawson
Dawn, 1 April 1904, 1 October 1904.

Jessie Couvreur ('Tasma')
'An Old Time Episode in Tasmania', *Coo-ee; Tales of Australian Life by Australian Ladies*, 1891, edited by Mrs Patchett Martin.

Rosa Praed
My Australian Girlhood, Fisher Unwin, 1904, London.

Catherine Langloh Parker (1855–1940)
Australian Legendary Tales, edited by Henrietta Drake-Brockman (1902–1968), 1954, Angus & Robertson.

Barbara Baynton
'Squeaker's Mate', *The Portable Barbara Baynton*, edited by Sally Krimmer & Alan Lawson, UQP Australian Authors Series, St. Lucia, University of Queensland Press, 1980, revised ed. 1988.

Mary Gaunt
'Dick Stanesby's Hutkeeper', *The Moving Finger*, Methuen, 1895.

Mary Gilmore
Letters of Mary Gilmore, edited by W. H. Wilde & T. Inglis Moore, Melbourne University Press, 1980.

'Henry Handel Richardson'
'The Bathe: a Grotesque' *The End of a Childhood and Other Stories*, Heinemann, London, 1934.

Ethel Turner
The Diaries of Ethel Turner, compiled by Phillipa Poole, Ure Smith, 1979, Sydney.

'G. B. Lancaster'
'Why Mollie Wouldn't', Margaret Garrett – literary executor.

Mollie Skinner
'The Witch of Wellaway', *West Coast Stories*, edited by Henrietta Drake-Brockman, 1959, Angus & Robertson.

Mary Grant Bruce
From *The Peculiar Honeymoon & Other Writings* edited by Prue McKay, 1986, McPhee Gribble, Melbourne.

Miles Franklin & Dymphna Cusack
'Call Up Your Ghosts'. Manuscript – Mitchell Library. Dymphna Cusack

courtesy of Tim Curnow, Curtis Brown; Miles Franklin courtesy of
Permanent Trustee Company.

Katharine Susannah Prichard
Brumby Innes and Bid Me to Love, edited by Katharine Brisbane, The
Currency Press, Sydney, 1974. 'Brumby Innes' courtesy of Ric Throssell.

Nettie Palmer
Fourteen Years: Extracts from a Private Journal, 1925–1939 – being
reprinted by University of Queensland Press.
Nettie Palmer, edited by Vivian Smith, UQP Australian Authors, St.
Lucia, University of Queensland Press, 1988.
Estate of E. V. & J. G. Palmer – controlled by The Equity Trustees,
Executors & Agency Co. Ltd., 472 Bourke Street, Melbourne 3000.

Marjorie Barnard
'Habit', *The Persimmon Tree and Other Stories*, Virago, 1985, London.

Eleanor Dark
'Sweet and Low' *Lantana Lane*, Virago, 1986, London.

Dorothy Cottrell
'Cabbage Roses', courtesy of Barbara Ross, literary executor.

Christina Stead
'A Writer's Friends', *Ocean of Story*, Penguin, 1986.

Sarah Campion
Mo Burdekin, Peter Davies, 1941, London.

Kylie Tennant
Speak You So Gently, Gollancz, 1959.

Nancy Cato
'The Olive Stealers', *Quadrant*, 1970.

Faith Bandler
Wacvie, Rigby, Adelaide, 1977.

Nene Gare
'A Good Job', *Bend to the Wind*, Macmillan, 1978.

Olga Masters
'The Home Girls' from *The Home Girls*, University of Queensland Press,
1987.

Oriel Gray
'The Torrents' to the author.

Antigone Kefala
Aspect Vol. 2/3, March 1977.

Germaine Greer
The Female Eunuch, Paladin, London, 1970.

FOR THE BEST IN PAPERBACKS, LOOK FOR THE

PENGUIN

Mr Hogarth's Will   by Catherine Helen Spence

Jane and Alice Melville have been disinherited by their uncle, who believes that a 'boys' education will serve them better than an inheritance.

The sisters' struggle for independence and fulfilment takes them from Scotland to Australia and a new vision of their lives.

First published in 1867.

Kirkham's Find   by Mary Gaunt

Phoebe Marsden wants a place of her own. At twenty-four she refuses to compromise her ideals and marry for expediency. Her younger sister Nancy does not share her ideals. Against everyone's advice Phoebe decides to set up on her own and keep bees.

Phoebe is one of the first Australian heroines to choose between marriage and a career. Her choice has unexpected ramifications for another sister, Lydia.

First published in 1897.

FOR THE BEST IN PAPERBACKS, LOOK FOR THE

PENGUIN

The Peaceful Army   edited by Flora Eldershaw

In 1938, at the time of Australia's 150th Anniversary, this collection was published in honour of women's contribution. The list of contributors is a veritable 'who's who' of women in Australian cultural life. They include: Margaret Preston, Marjorie Barnard, Miles Franklin, Dymphna Cusack and a young Kylie Tennant. They write about Elizabeth Macarthur, Caroline Chisholm, Rose Scott and early women writers and artists.

In 1938 Kylie Tennant concludes the volume. Just before her death in 1988 she reflected on the intervening fifty years.

Her Selection:
Writings by Nineteenth-Century Australian Women edited by Lynne Spender

Nineteenth-century Australian women writers were published widely in magazines, newspapers and books in Australia and abroad. Their writings provide an insight into the lives of women, the opportunities and obstacles, the hardships and the successes. This lively collection brings together works that have been unavailable for many years.

Included are works by: Georgiana Molloy, Louisa Lawson, Annabella Boswell, Mary Fortune and 'Tasma'.

A Bright and Fiery Troop:
Australian Women Writers of the Nineteenth Century   edited by Debra Adelaide

Who was the most popular detective story writer of the nineteenth century? A woman, Mary Fortune.
Who was the internationally famous botanist and artist who also wrote novels? A woman, Louisa Atkinson.
Who wrote the first convict novel? A woman, Caroline Leakey.
Who wrote the first novel with an Aboriginal protagonist? A woman, Catherine Martin.

This book opens up the hidden history of Australian literature and is the first critical appraisal of the major Australian women writers of the nineteenth century.

The book includes photographs.

FOR THE BEST IN PAPERBACKS, LOOK FOR THE

PENGUIN

BOOKS BY JESSICA ANDERSON IN PENGUIN

Tirra Lirra by the River

A beautifully written novel of a woman's seventy-year search to find a place where she truly belongs.

For Nora Porteous, life is a series of escapes. To escape her tightly knit small-town family, she marries, only to find herself confined again, this time in a stifling Sydney suburb with a selfish, sanctimonious husband. With a courage born of desperation and sustained by a spirited sense of humor, Nora travels to London, and it is there that she becomes the woman she wants to be. Or does she? Winner of the Miles Franklin Award.

Stories From the Warm Zone and Sydney Stories

Jessica Anderson's evocative stories recreate, through the eyes of a child, the atmosphere of Australia between the wars. A stammer becomes a blessing in disguise; the prospect of a middle name converts a reluctant child to baptism. These autobiographical stories of a Brisbane childhood glow with the warmth of memory.

The formless sprawl of Sydney in the 1980s is a very different world. Here the lives of other characters are changed by the uncertainties of divorce, chance meetings and the disintegration and generation of relationships.

Winner of The Age Book of the Year Award

Last Man's Head

Detective Alec Probyn has his enemies too. His recent stand on police violence has led to his being suspended from duty. He has a growing suspicion that a vicious crime is about to be committed. All the more disturbing as the suspect and the victim are both members of his own family.

How can Probyn prevent this crime and its shattering consequences? In the savage resolution he discovers that his anti-violent stand has not magically cancelled out the violence in himself.